THE

Created by
KURT BUSIEK & JAMES W. FRY
Writer   **Penciller**

Additional pencils: Richard Howell
Inks: Doug Hazlewood
Additional inks: Richard Howell, Sam De La Rosa, Art Nichols, Rus Sever
Lettering: Mindy Eisman
Cover by James W. Fry, Andrew Pepoy, and Tom Luth

About Comics
Thousand Oaks, California, USA
www.aboutcomics.com

This material originally serialized in *The Liberty Project* issues 1 through 8 and *Total Eclipse: The Seraphim Objective*, edited by Fred Burke, colored by Adam Philips and Marcus David, and published by Eclipse Comics.

Story copyright 1987, 1988, 2003 Kurt Busiek. Art copyright 1987, 1988, 2003 James W. Fry, Doug Hazlewood, Richard Howell, and Sam De La Rosa.

"The Liberty Project" and all characters are TM Busiek & Fry.

Zzed, Valkyrie, Misery, Heap, Airboy, Skywolf and Total Eclipse are © and TM Todd McFarlane Productions, Inc. 1987, 1988, and 2003. Used with permission.

HE'S A REBEL, by Gene Pitney
© 1962 Six Continents Music Publishing
© Renewed and Assigned to Unichappell Music, Inc.
All Rights Reserved   Used by Permission
WARNER BROS. PUBLICATIONS U.S. INC., Miami, FL. 33014

First printing: July 2003

Printed in Canada

For more information on About Comics, go to www.aboutcomics.com

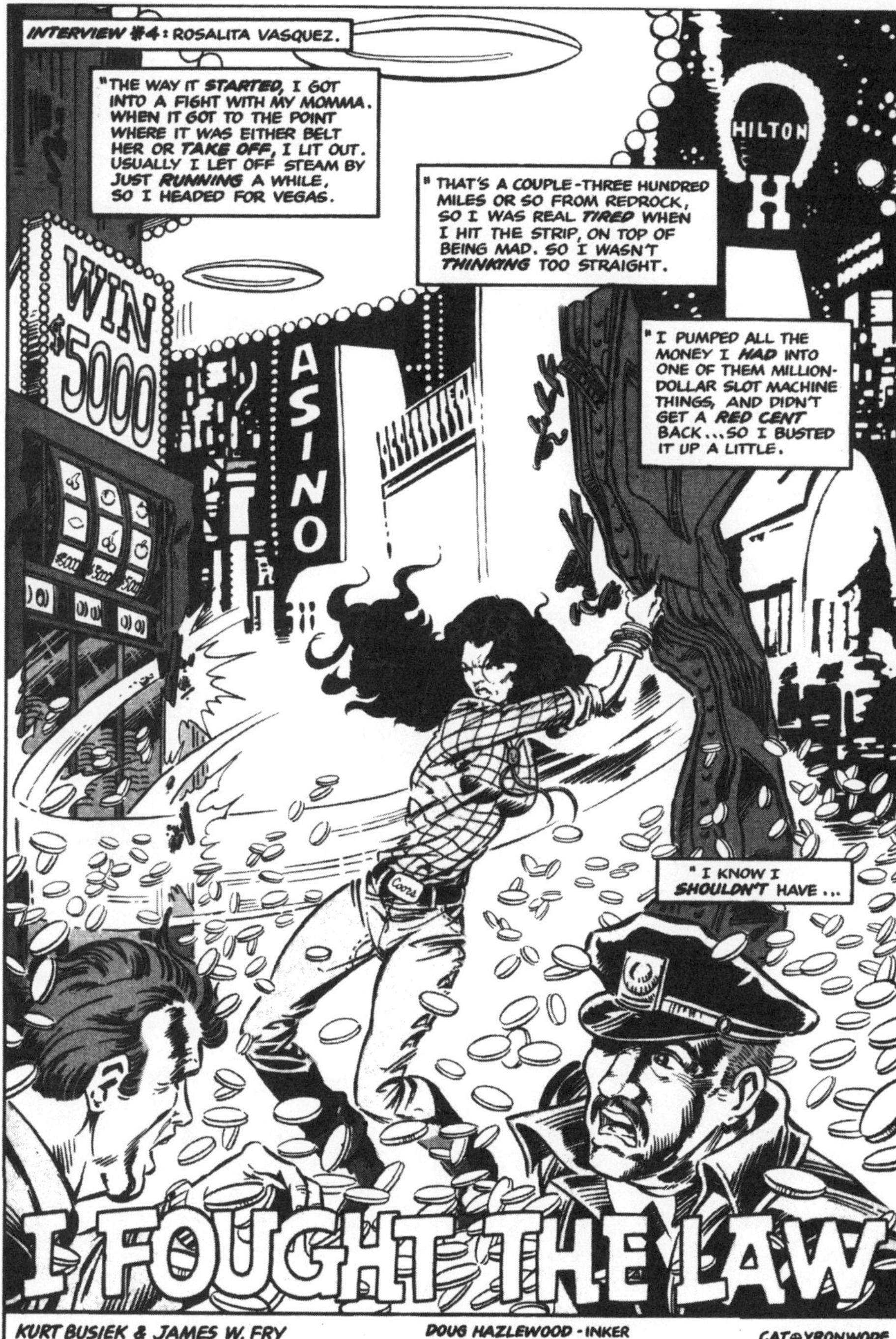
INTERVIEW #4: ROSALITA VASQUEZ.
"THE WAY IT STARTED, I GOT INTO A FIGHT WITH MY MOMMA. WHEN IT GOT TO THE POINT WHERE IT WAS EITHER BELT HER OR TAKE OFF, I LIT OUT. USUALLY I LET OFF STEAM BY JUST RUNNING A WHILE, SO I HEADED FOR VEGAS.
"THAT'S A COUPLE-THREE HUNDRED MILES OR SO FROM REDROCK, SO I WAS REAL TIRED WHEN I HIT THE STRIP, ON TOP OF BEING MAD. SO I WASN'T THINKING TOO STRAIGHT.
"I PUMPED ALL THE MONEY I HAD INTO ONE OF THEM MILLION-DOLLAR SLOT MACHINE THINGS, AND DIDN'T GET A RED CENT BACK...SO I BUSTED IT UP A LITTLE.
"I KNOW I SHOULDN'T HAVE...
HILTON
WIN $5000
ASINO
I FOUGHT THE LAW
KURT BUSIEK & JAMES W. FRY
WRITER · CO-CREATORS · PENCILER
DOUG HAZLEWOOD - INKER
MINDY EISMAN - LETTERER
FRED BURKE - EDITOR
CAT YRONWODE
CHIEF

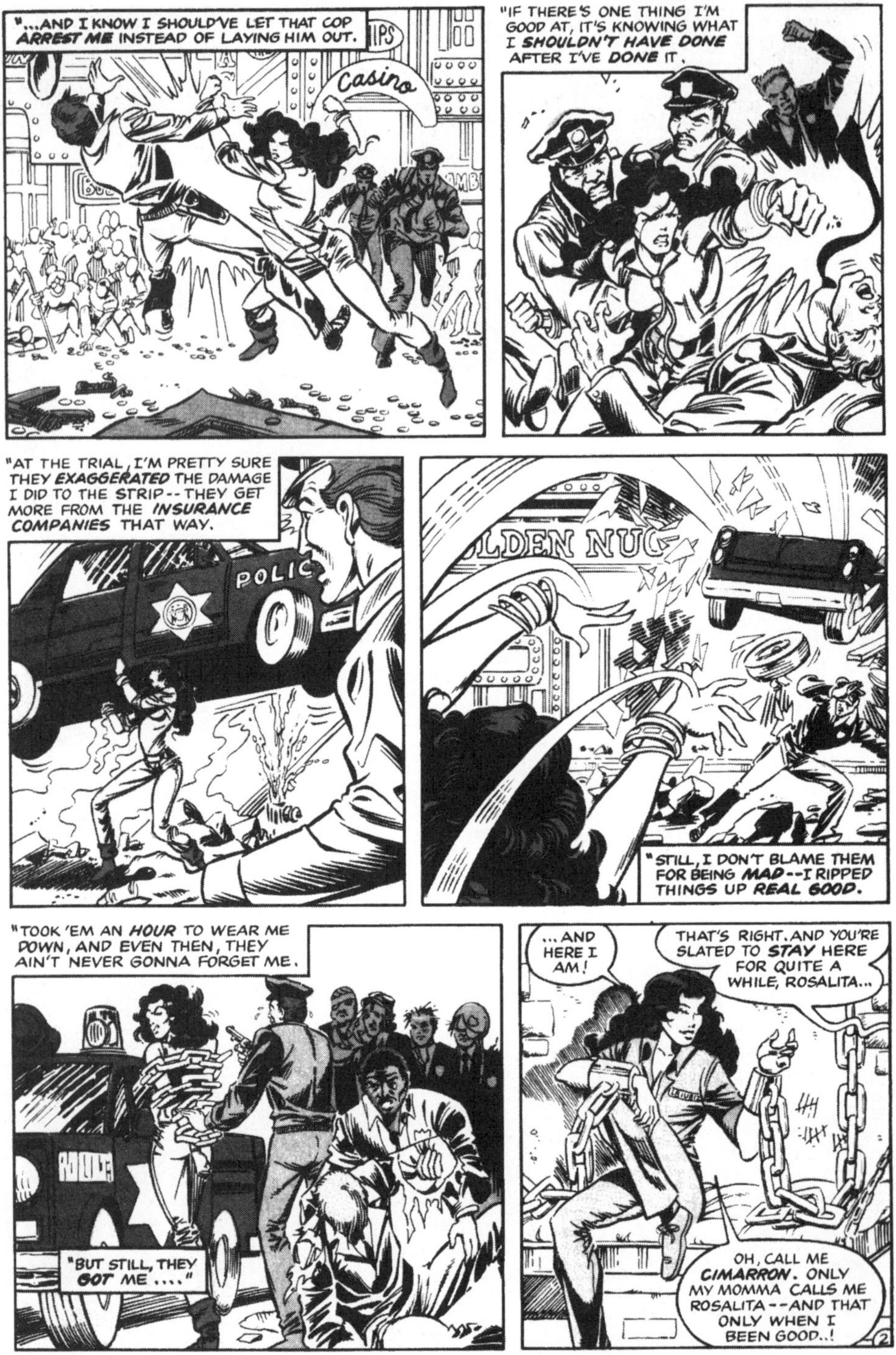
"...AND I KNOW I SHOULD'VE LET THAT COP ARREST ME INSTEAD OF LAYING HIM OUT.
Casino
"IF THERE'S ONE THING I'M GOOD AT, IT'S KNOWING WHAT I SHOULDN'T HAVE DONE AFTER I'VE DONE IT.
"AT THE TRIAL, I'M PRETTY SURE THEY EXAGGERATED THE DAMAGE I DID TO THE STRIP--THEY GET MORE FROM THE INSURANCE COMPANIES THAT WAY.
POLIC
OLDEN NUG
"STILL, I DON'T BLAME THEM FOR BEING MAD--I RIPPED THINGS UP REAL GOOD.
"TOOK 'EM AN HOUR TO WEAR ME DOWN, AND EVEN THEN, THEY AIN'T NEVER GONNA FORGET ME.
"BUT STILL, THEY GOT ME ...."
...AND HERE I AM!
THAT'S RIGHT. AND YOU'RE SLATED TO STAY HERE FOR QUITE A WHILE, ROSALITA...
OH, CALL ME CIMARRON. ONLY MY MOMMA CALLS ME ROSALITA--AND THAT ONLY WHEN I BEEN GOOD..!
2

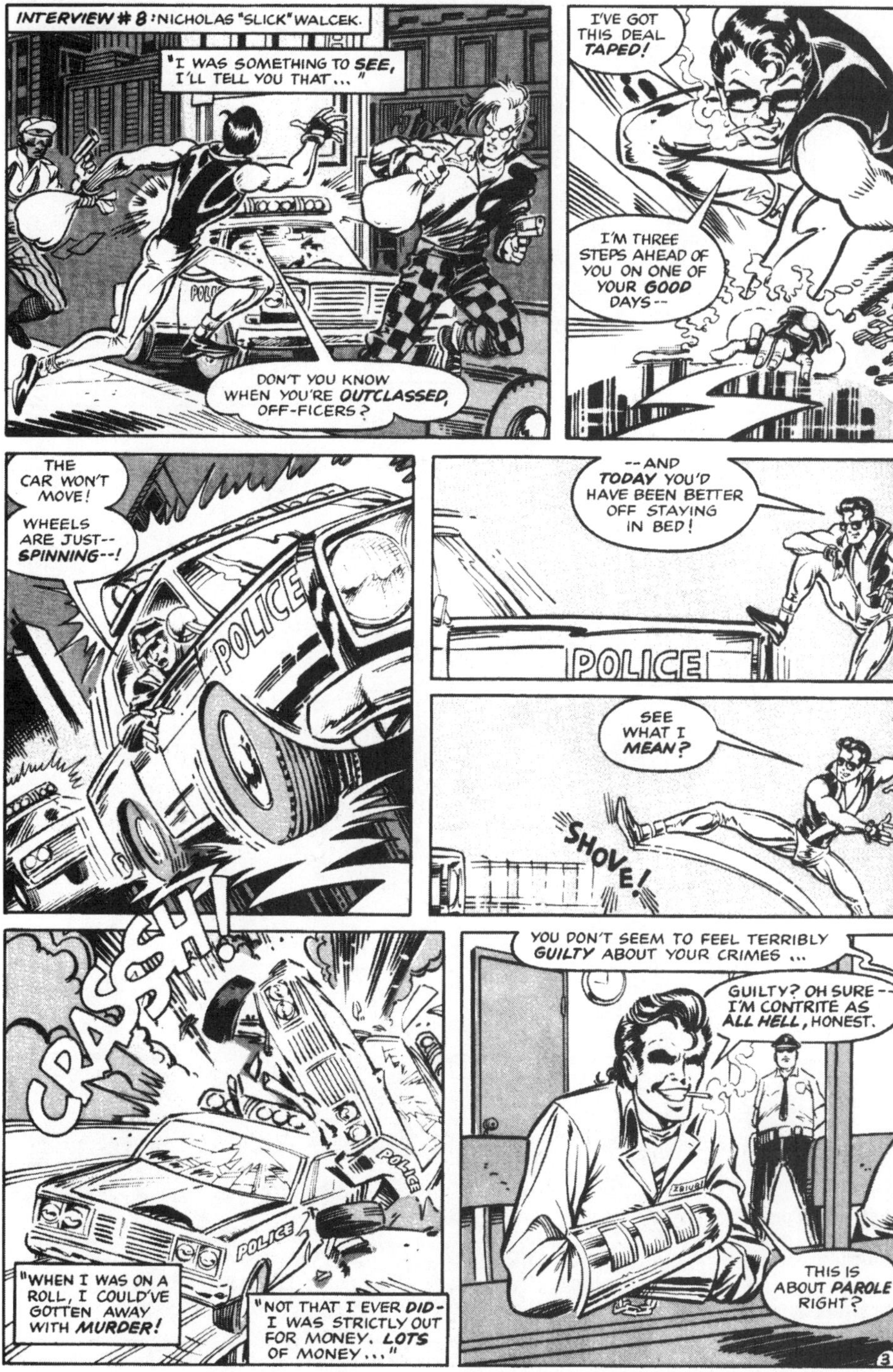

INTERVIEW #8: NICHOLAS "SLICK" WALCEK.
"I WAS SOMETHING TO SEE, I'LL TELL YOU THAT..."
DON'T YOU KNOW WHEN YOU'RE OUTCLASSED, OFF-FICERS?
I'VE GOT THIS DEAL TAPED!
I'M THREE STEPS AHEAD OF YOU ON ONE OF YOUR GOOD DAYS--
THE CAR WON'T MOVE!
WHEELS ARE JUST-- SPINNING--!
POLICE
--AND TODAY YOU'D HAVE BEEN BETTER OFF STAYING IN BED!
POLICE
SEE WHAT I MEAN?
SHOVE!
CRASH!
POLICE
POLICE
"WHEN I WAS ON A ROLL, I COULD'VE GOTTEN AWAY WITH MURDER!
"NOT THAT I EVER DID- I WAS STRICTLY OUT FOR MONEY. LOTS OF MONEY..."
YOU DON'T SEEM TO FEEL TERRIBLY GUILTY ABOUT YOUR CRIMES...
GUILTY? OH SURE-- I'M CONTRITE AS ALL HELL, HONEST.
THIS IS ABOUT PAROLE RIGHT?
3

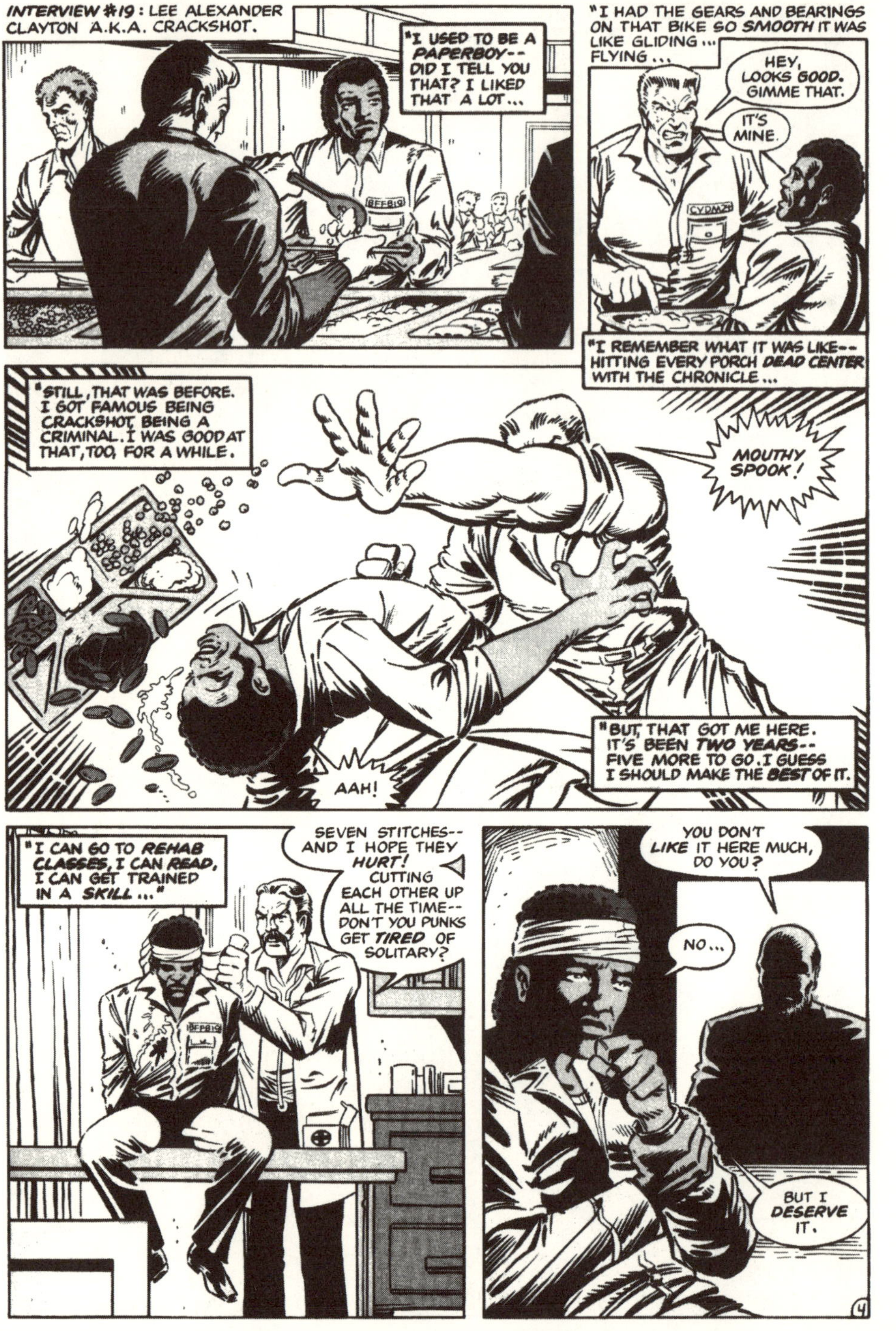
INTERVIEW #19: LEE ALEXANDER CLAYTON A.K.A. CRACKSHOT.
"I USED TO BE A PAPERBOY--DID I TELL YOU THAT? I LIKED THAT A LOT...
BFF819
"I HAD THE GEARS AND BEARINGS ON THAT BIKE SO SMOOTH IT WAS LIKE GLIDING... FLYING...
HEY, LOOKS GOOD. GIMME THAT.
IT'S MINE.
CYDM24
"I REMEMBER WHAT IT WAS LIKE--HITTING EVERY PORCH DEAD CENTER WITH THE CHRONICLE...
"STILL, THAT WAS BEFORE. I GOT FAMOUS BEING CRACKSHOT, BEING A CRIMINAL. I WAS GOOD AT THAT, TOO, FOR A WHILE.
MOUTHY SPOOK!
"BUT, THAT GOT ME HERE. IT'S BEEN TWO YEARS--FIVE MORE TO GO. I GUESS I SHOULD MAKE THE BEST OF IT.
AAH!
"I CAN GO TO REHAB CLASSES, I CAN READ, I CAN GET TRAINED IN A SKILL..."
SEVEN STITCHES--AND I HOPE THEY HURT! CUTTING EACH OTHER UP ALL THE TIME--DON'T YOU PUNKS GET TIRED OF SOLITARY?
BFF819
YOU DON'T LIKE IT HERE MUCH, DO YOU?
NO...
BUT I DESERVE IT.
4

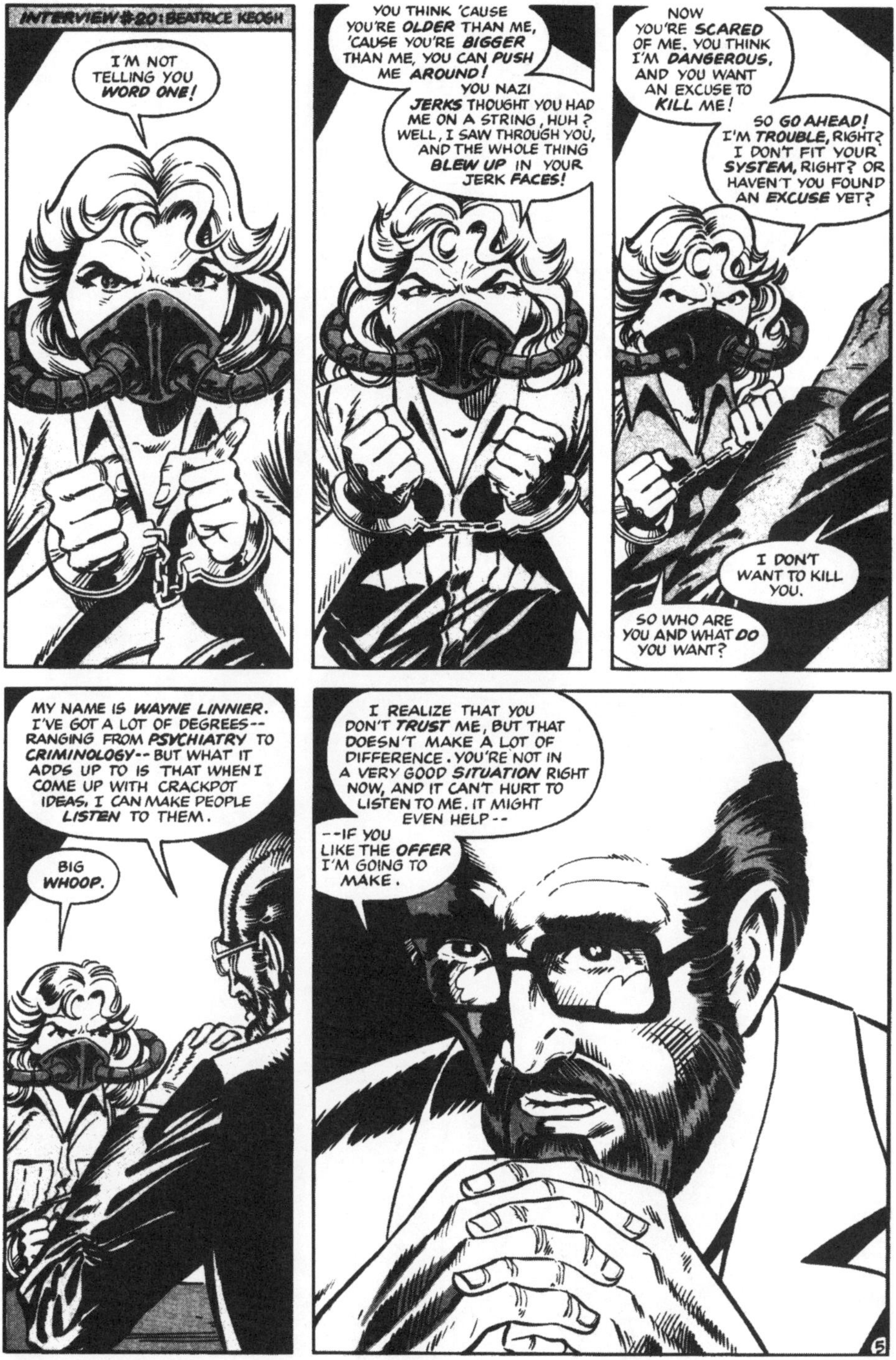

INTERVIEW #20: BEATRICE KEOGH
I'M NOT TELLING YOU WORD ONE!
YOU THINK 'CAUSE YOU'RE OLDER THAN ME, 'CAUSE YOU'RE BIGGER THAN ME, YOU CAN PUSH ME AROUND!
YOU NAZI JERKS THOUGHT YOU HAD ME ON A STRING, HUH? WELL, I SAW THROUGH YOU, AND THE WHOLE THING BLEW UP IN YOUR JERK FACES!
NOW YOU'RE SCARED OF ME. YOU THINK I'M DANGEROUS, AND YOU WANT AN EXCUSE TO KILL ME!
SO GO AHEAD! I'M TROUBLE, RIGHT? I DON'T FIT YOUR SYSTEM, RIGHT? OR HAVEN'T YOU FOUND AN EXCUSE YET?
I DON'T WANT TO KILL YOU.
SO WHO ARE YOU AND WHAT DO YOU WANT?
MY NAME IS WAYNE LINNIER. I'VE GOT A LOT OF DEGREES-- RANGING FROM PSYCHIATRY TO CRIMINOLOGY-- BUT WHAT IT ADDS UP TO IS THAT WHEN I COME UP WITH CRACKPOT IDEAS, I CAN MAKE PEOPLE LISTEN TO THEM.
BIG WHOOP.
I REALIZE THAT YOU DON'T TRUST ME, BUT THAT DOESN'T MAKE A LOT OF DIFFERENCE. YOU'RE NOT IN A VERY GOOD SITUATION RIGHT NOW, AND IT CAN'T HURT TO LISTEN TO ME. IT MIGHT EVEN HELP--
--IF YOU LIKE THE OFFER I'M GOING TO MAKE.
5

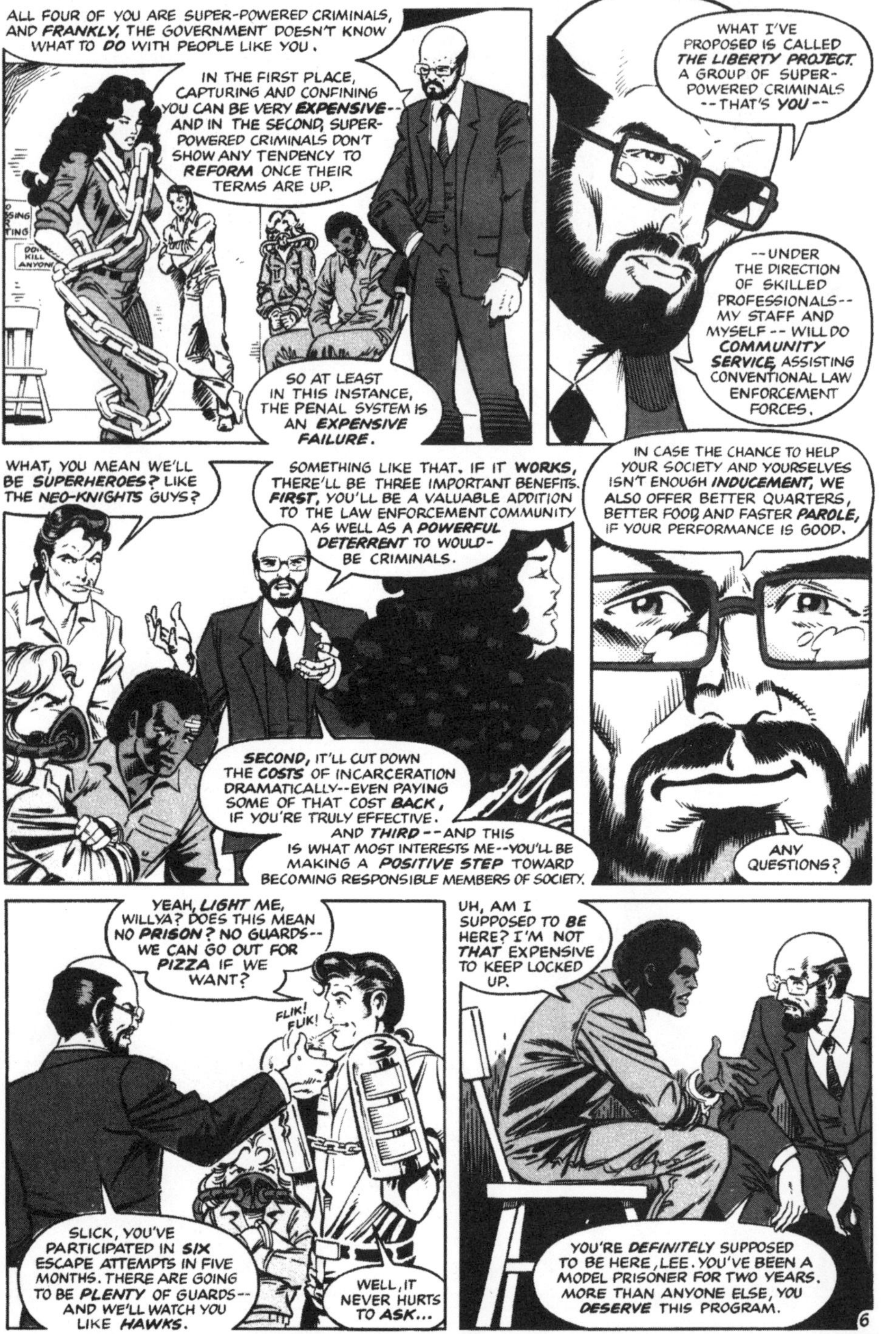
ALL FOUR OF YOU ARE SUPER-POWERED CRIMINALS, AND FRANKLY, THE GOVERNMENT DOESN'T KNOW WHAT TO DO WITH PEOPLE LIKE YOU.
IN THE FIRST PLACE, CAPTURING AND CONFINING YOU CAN BE VERY EXPENSIVE-- AND IN THE SECOND, SUPER-POWERED CRIMINALS DON'T SHOW ANY TENDENCY TO REFORM ONCE THEIR TERMS ARE UP.
SO AT LEAST IN THIS INSTANCE, THE PENAL SYSTEM IS AN EXPENSIVE FAILURE.
WHAT I'VE PROPOSED IS CALLED THE LIBERTY PROJECT. A GROUP OF SUPER-POWERED CRIMINALS --THAT'S YOU--
--UNDER THE DIRECTION OF SKILLED PROFESSIONALS-- MY STAFF AND MYSELF -- WILL DO COMMUNITY SERVICE, ASSISTING CONVENTIONAL LAW ENFORCEMENT FORCES.
WHAT, YOU MEAN WE'LL BE SUPERHEROES? LIKE THE NEO-KNIGHTS GUYS?
SOMETHING LIKE THAT. IF IT WORKS, THERE'LL BE THREE IMPORTANT BENEFITS. FIRST, YOU'LL BE A VALUABLE ADDITION TO THE LAW ENFORCEMENT COMMUNITY AS WELL AS A POWERFUL DETERRENT TO WOULD-BE CRIMINALS.
SECOND, IT'LL CUT DOWN THE COSTS OF INCARCERATION DRAMATICALLY--EVEN PAYING SOME OF THAT COST BACK, IF YOU'RE TRULY EFFECTIVE.
AND THIRD--AND THIS IS WHAT MOST INTERESTS ME--YOU'LL BE MAKING A POSITIVE STEP TOWARD BECOMING RESPONSIBLE MEMBERS OF SOCIETY.
IN CASE THE CHANCE TO HELP YOUR SOCIETY AND YOURSELVES ISN'T ENOUGH INDUCEMENT, WE ALSO OFFER BETTER QUARTERS, BETTER FOOD, AND FASTER PAROLE, IF YOUR PERFORMANCE IS GOOD.
ANY QUESTIONS?
YEAH, LIGHT ME, WILLYA? DOES THIS MEAN NO PRISON? NO GUARDS-- WE CAN GO OUT FOR PIZZA IF WE WANT?
FLIK! FLIK!
SLICK, YOU'VE PARTICIPATED IN SIX ESCAPE ATTEMPTS IN FIVE MONTHS. THERE ARE GOING TO BE PLENTY OF GUARDS-- AND WE'LL WATCH YOU LIKE HAWKS.
WELL, IT NEVER HURTS TO ASK...
UH, AM I SUPPOSED TO BE HERE? I'M NOT THAT EXPENSIVE TO KEEP LOCKED UP.
YOU'RE DEFINITELY SUPPOSED TO BE HERE, LEE. YOU'VE BEEN A MODEL PRISONER FOR TWO YEARS. MORE THAN ANYONE ELSE, YOU DESERVE THIS PROGRAM.
6

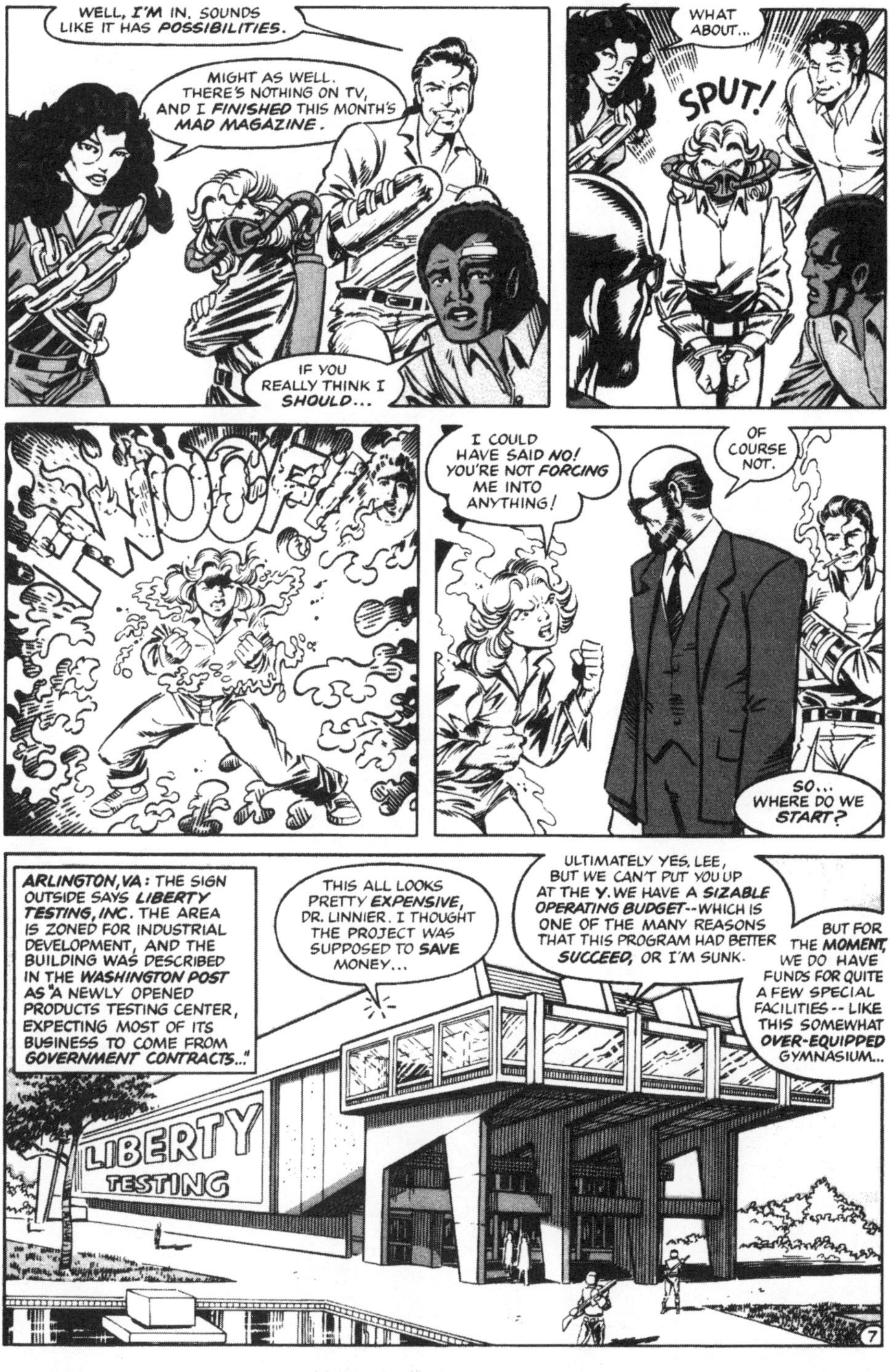
WELL, I'M IN. SOUNDS LIKE IT HAS POSSIBILITIES.
MIGHT AS WELL. THERE'S NOTHING ON TV, AND I FINISHED THIS MONTH'S MAD MAGAZINE.
IF YOU REALLY THINK I SHOULD...
WHAT ABOUT...
SPUT!
WOOF!!
I COULD HAVE SAID NO! YOU'RE NOT FORCING ME INTO ANYTHING!
OF COURSE NOT.
SO... WHERE DO WE START?
ARLINGTON, VA: THE SIGN OUTSIDE SAYS LIBERTY TESTING, INC. THE AREA IS ZONED FOR INDUSTRIAL DEVELOPMENT, AND THE BUILDING WAS DESCRIBED IN THE WASHINGTON POST AS "A NEWLY OPENED PRODUCTS TESTING CENTER, EXPECTING MOST OF ITS BUSINESS TO COME FROM GOVERNMENT CONTRACTS..."
THIS ALL LOOKS PRETTY EXPENSIVE, DR. LINNIER. I THOUGHT THE PROJECT WAS SUPPOSED TO SAVE MONEY...
ULTIMATELY YES, LEE, BUT WE CAN'T PUT YOU UP AT THE Y. WE HAVE A SIZABLE OPERATING BUDGET--WHICH IS ONE OF THE MANY REASONS THAT THIS PROGRAM HAD BETTER SUCCEED, OR I'M SUNK.
BUT FOR THE MOMENT, WE DO HAVE FUNDS FOR QUITE A FEW SPECIAL FACILITIES -- LIKE THIS SOMEWHAT OVER-EQUIPPED GYMNASIUM...
LIBERTY TESTING
7

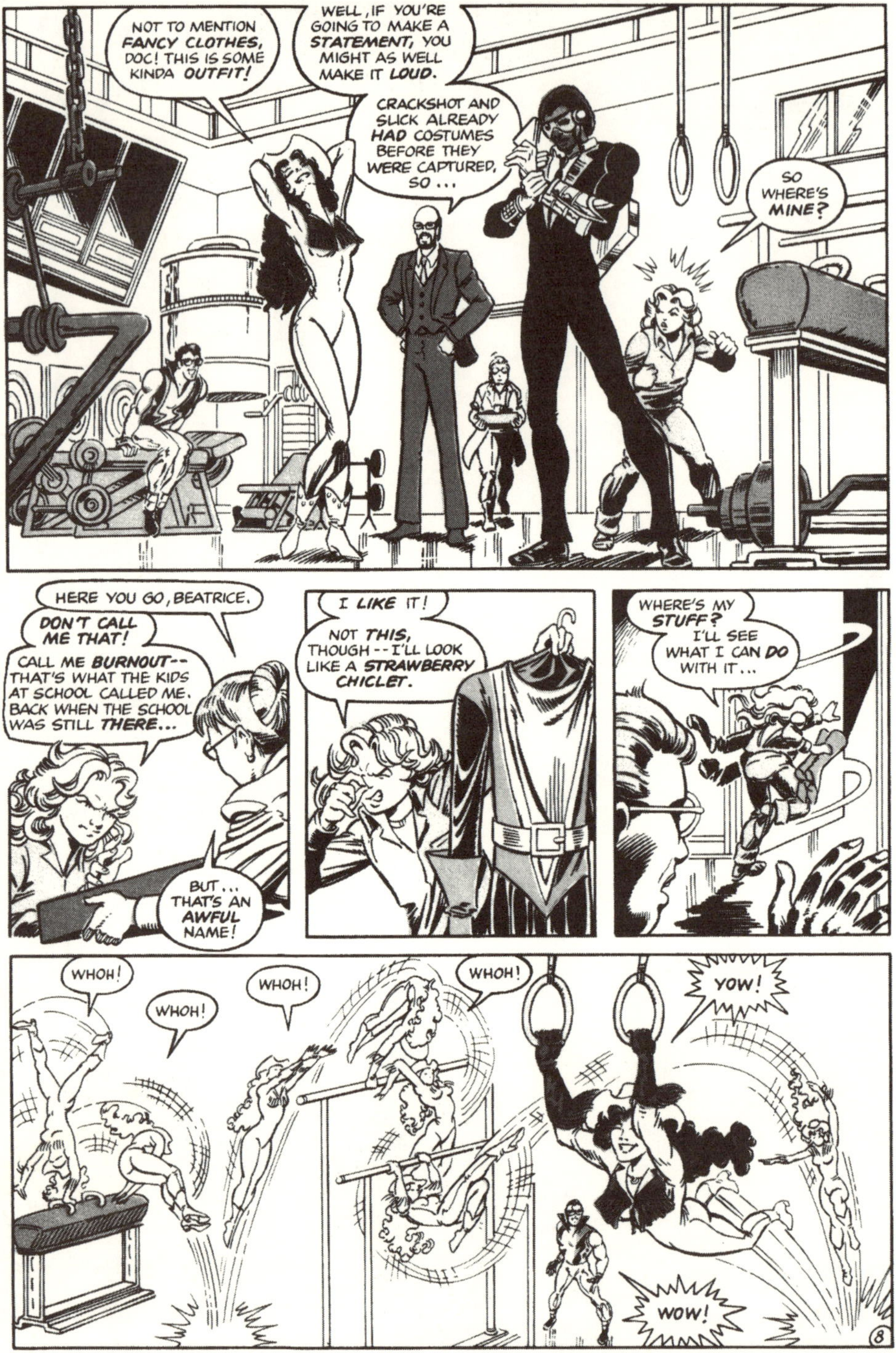

NOT TO MENTION FANCY CLOTHES, DOC! THIS IS SOME KINDA OUTFIT!
WELL, IF YOU'RE GOING TO MAKE A STATEMENT, YOU MIGHT AS WELL MAKE IT LOUD.
CRACKSHOT AND SLICK ALREADY HAD COSTUMES BEFORE THEY WERE CAPTURED, SO ...
SO WHERE'S MINE?
HERE YOU GO, BEATRICE.
DON'T CALL ME THAT!
CALL ME BURNOUT-- THAT'S WHAT THE KIDS AT SCHOOL CALLED ME. BACK WHEN THE SCHOOL WAS STILL THERE...
BUT... THAT'S AN AWFUL NAME!
I LIKE IT!
NOT THIS, THOUGH--I'LL LOOK LIKE A STRAWBERRY CHICLET.
WHERE'S MY STUFF?
I'LL SEE WHAT I CAN DO WITH IT...
WHOH!
WHOH!
WHOH!
WHOH!
YOW!
WOW!
8

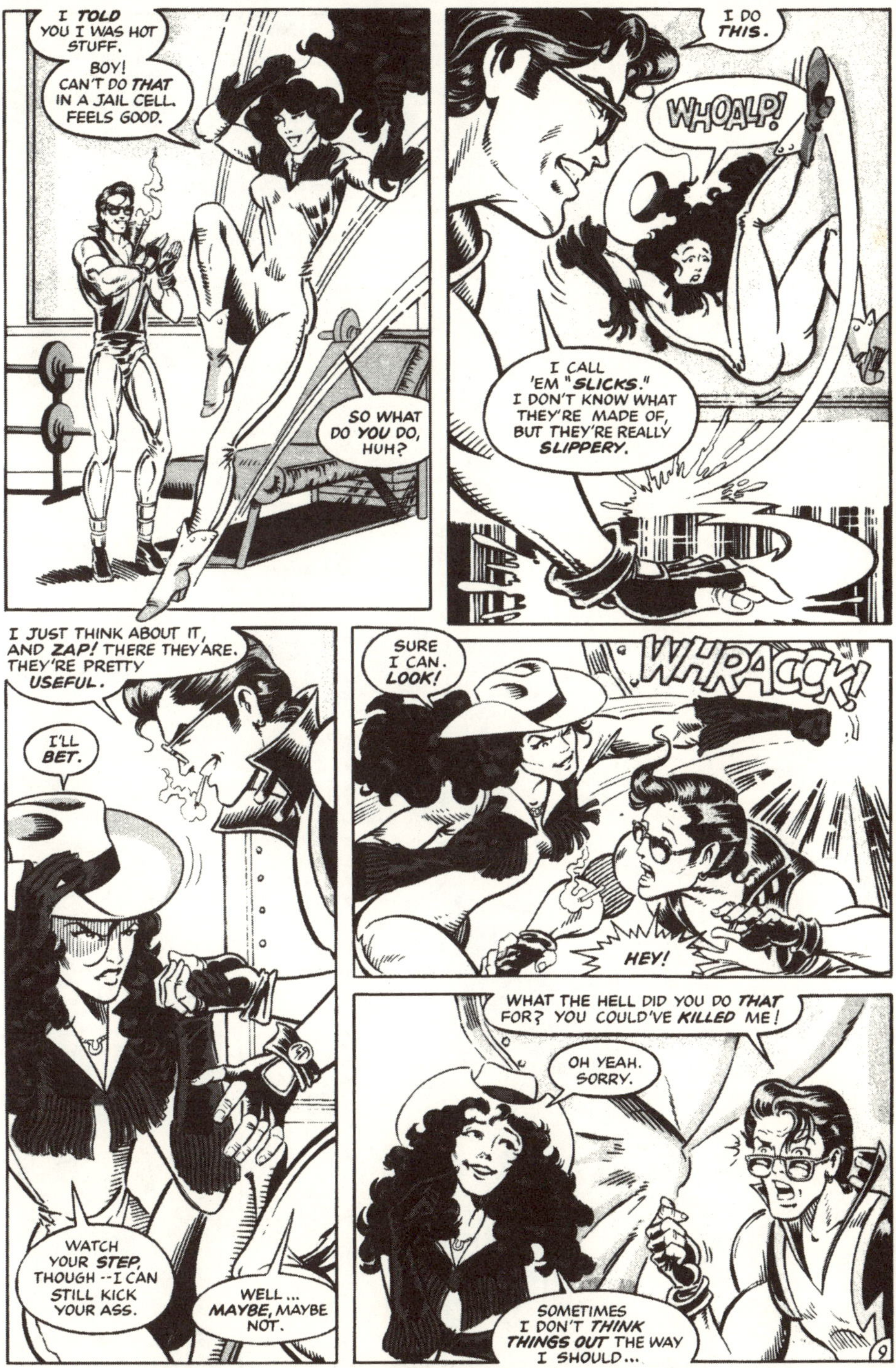

I TOLD YOU I WAS HOT STUFF.
BOY! CAN'T DO THAT IN A JAIL CELL. FEELS GOOD.
SO WHAT DO YOU DO, HUH?
I DO THIS.
WHOALP!
I CALL 'EM "SLICKS." I DON'T KNOW WHAT THEY'RE MADE OF, BUT THEY'RE REALLY SLIPPERY.
I JUST THINK ABOUT IT, AND ZAP! THERE THEY ARE. THEY'RE PRETTY USEFUL.
I'LL BET.
WATCH YOUR STEP, THOUGH --I CAN STILL KICK YOUR ASS.
WELL ... MAYBE, MAYBE NOT.
SURE I CAN. LOOK!
WHRACCK!
HEY!
WHAT THE HELL DID YOU DO THAT FOR? YOU COULD'VE KILLED ME!
OH YEAH. SORRY.
SOMETIMES I DON'T THINK THINGS OUT THE WAY I SHOULD...
9

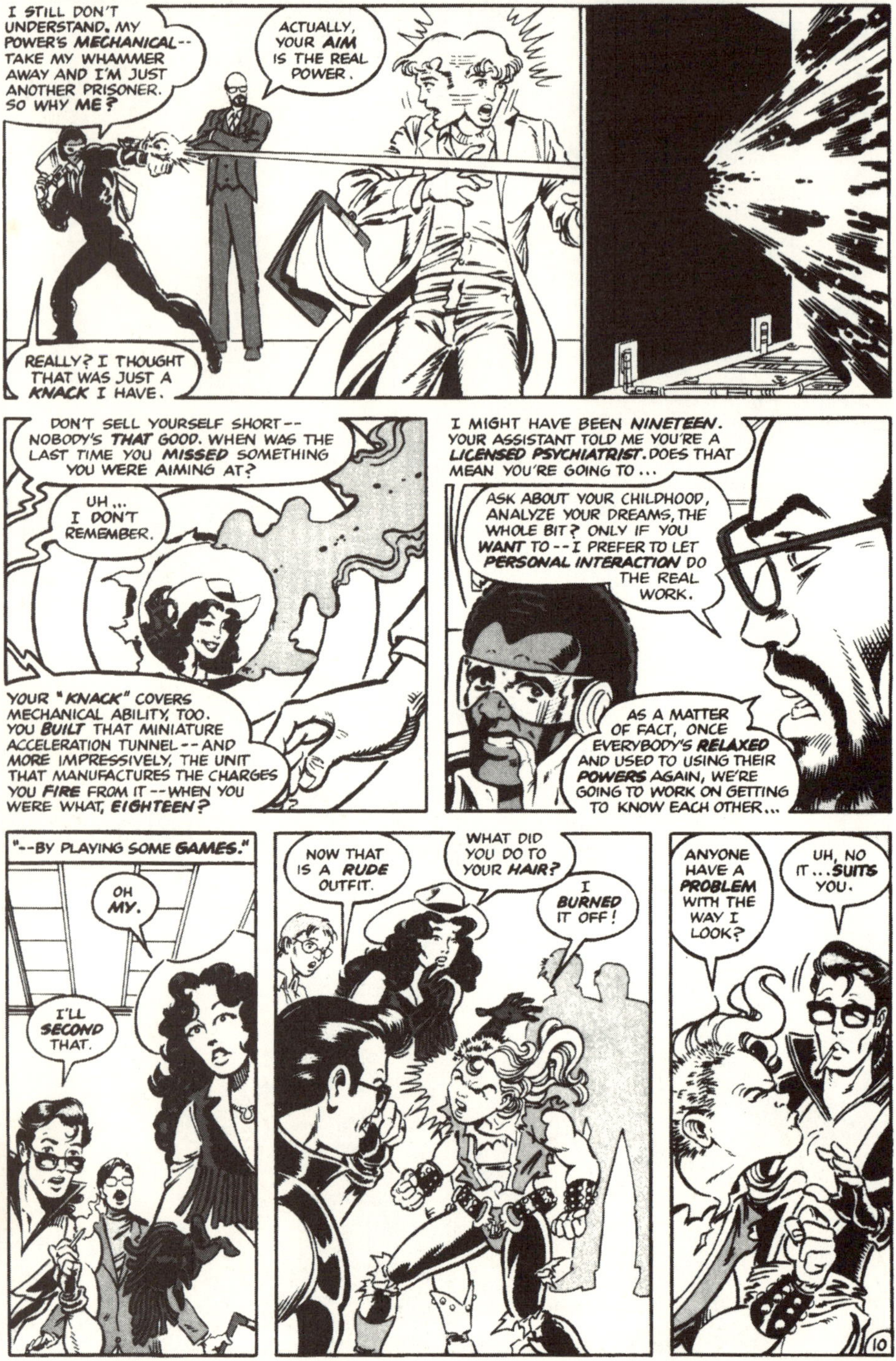
I STILL DON'T UNDERSTAND. MY POWER'S MECHANICAL-- TAKE MY WHAMMER AWAY AND I'M JUST ANOTHER PRISONER. SO WHY ME?
ACTUALLY, YOUR AIM IS THE REAL POWER.
REALLY? I THOUGHT THAT WAS JUST A KNACK I HAVE.
DON'T SELL YOURSELF SHORT-- NOBODY'S THAT GOOD. WHEN WAS THE LAST TIME YOU MISSED SOMETHING YOU WERE AIMING AT?
UH... I DON'T REMEMBER.
YOUR "KNACK" COVERS MECHANICAL ABILITY, TOO. YOU BUILT THAT MINIATURE ACCELERATION TUNNEL--AND MORE IMPRESSIVELY, THE UNIT THAT MANUFACTURES THE CHARGES YOU FIRE FROM IT--WHEN YOU WERE WHAT, EIGHTEEN?
I MIGHT HAVE BEEN NINETEEN. YOUR ASSISTANT TOLD ME YOU'RE A LICENSED PSYCHIATRIST. DOES THAT MEAN YOU'RE GOING TO...
ASK ABOUT YOUR CHILDHOOD, ANALYZE YOUR DREAMS, THE WHOLE BIT? ONLY IF YOU WANT TO--I PREFER TO LET PERSONAL INTERACTION DO THE REAL WORK.
AS A MATTER OF FACT, ONCE EVERYBODY'S RELAXED AND USED TO USING THEIR POWERS AGAIN, WE'RE GOING TO WORK ON GETTING TO KNOW EACH OTHER...
"--BY PLAYING SOME GAMES."
OH MY.
I'LL SECOND THAT.
NOW THAT IS A RUDE OUTFIT.
WHAT DID YOU DO TO YOUR HAIR?
I BURNED IT OFF!
ANYONE HAVE A PROBLEM WITH THE WAY I LOOK?
UH, NO IT...SUITS YOU.
10

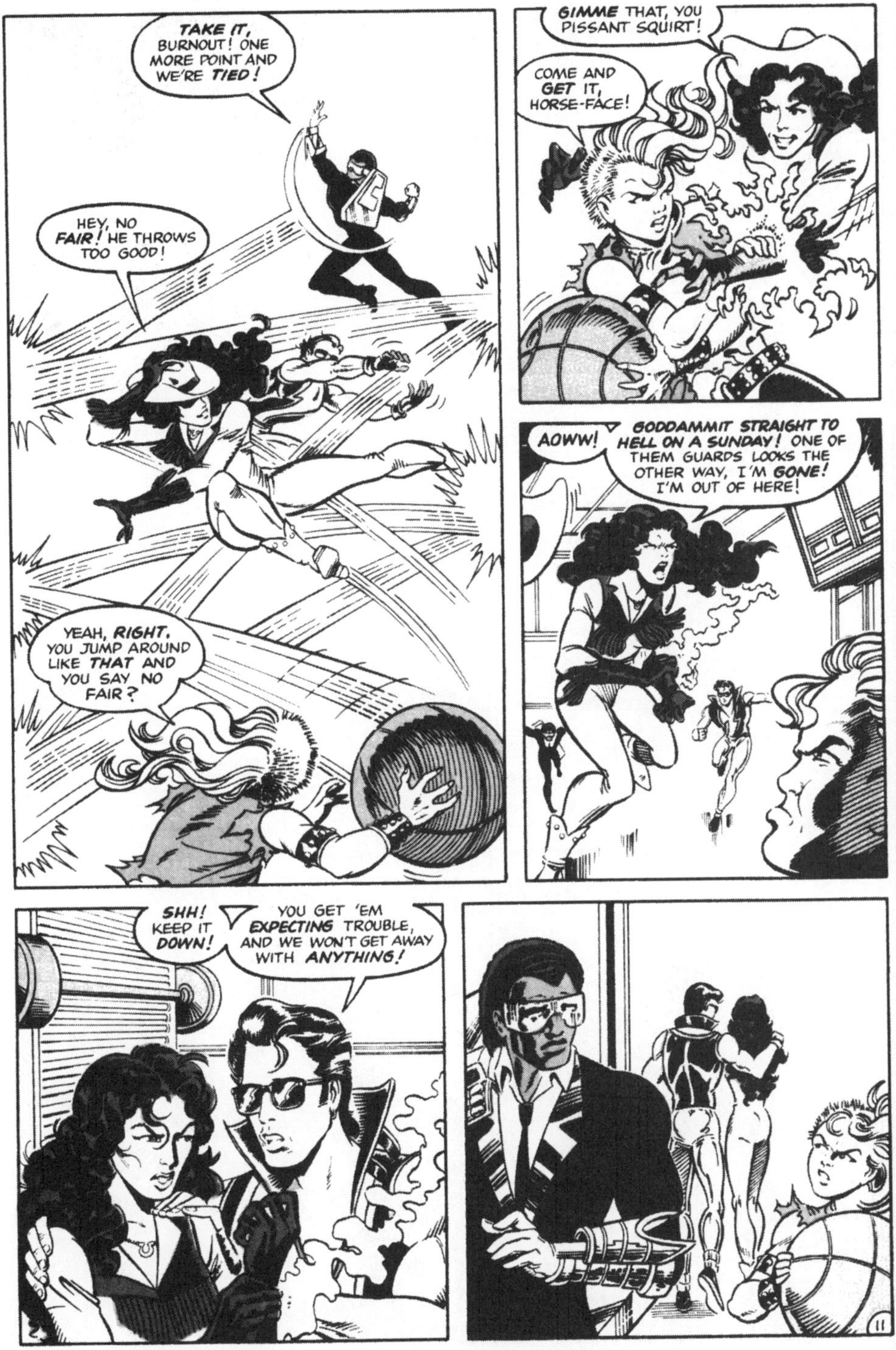
TAKE IT, BURNOUT! ONE MORE POINT AND WE'RE TIED!
HEY, NO FAIR! HE THROWS TOO GOOD!
YEAH, RIGHT. YOU JUMP AROUND LIKE THAT AND YOU SAY NO FAIR?
GIMME THAT, YOU PISSANT SQUIRT!
COME AND GET IT, HORSE-FACE!
AOWW!
GODDAMMIT STRAIGHT TO HELL ON A SUNDAY! ONE OF THEM GUARDS LOOKS THE OTHER WAY, I'M GONE! I'M OUT OF HERE!
SHH! KEEP IT DOWN!
YOU GET 'EM EXPECTING TROUBLE, AND WE WON'T GET AWAY WITH ANYTHING!

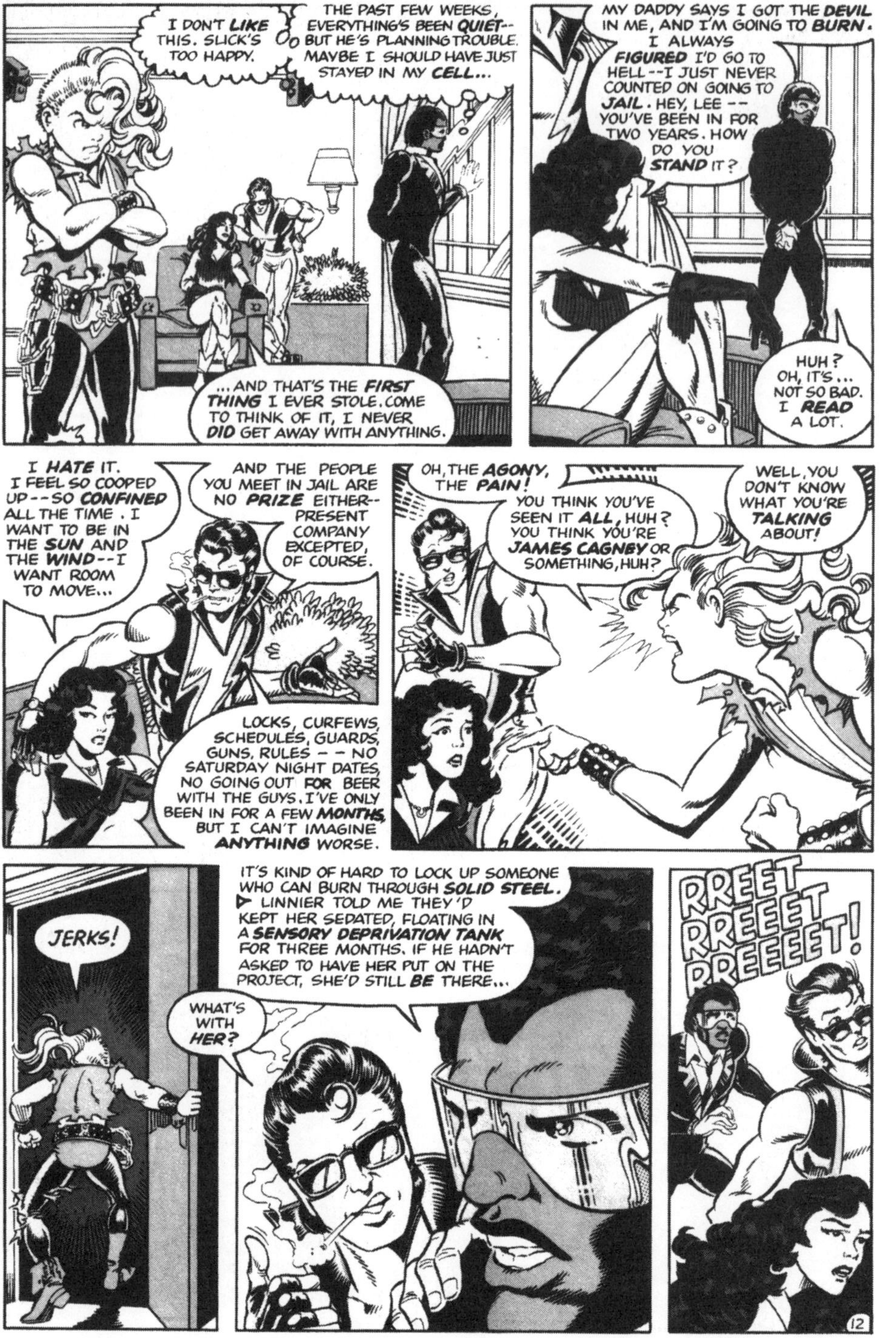
I DON'T LIKE THIS. SLICK'S TOO HAPPY.
THE PAST FEW WEEKS, EVERYTHING'S BEEN QUIET-- BUT HE'S PLANNING TROUBLE. MAYBE I SHOULD HAVE JUST STAYED IN MY CELL...
...AND THAT'S THE FIRST THING I EVER STOLE. COME TO THINK OF IT, I NEVER DID GET AWAY WITH ANYTHING.
MY DADDY SAYS I GOT THE DEVIL IN ME, AND I'M GOING TO BURN. I ALWAYS FIGURED I'D GO TO HELL--I JUST NEVER COUNTED ON GOING TO JAIL. HEY, LEE -- YOU'VE BEEN IN FOR TWO YEARS. HOW DO YOU STAND IT?
HUH? OH, IT'S... NOT SO BAD. I READ A LOT.
I HATE IT. I FEEL SO COOPED UP--SO CONFINED ALL THE TIME. I WANT TO BE IN THE SUN AND THE WIND--I WANT ROOM TO MOVE...
AND THE PEOPLE YOU MEET IN JAIL ARE NO PRIZE EITHER-- PRESENT COMPANY EXCEPTED, OF COURSE.
LOCKS, CURFEWS, SCHEDULES, GUARDS, GUNS, RULES -- NO SATURDAY NIGHT DATES, NO GOING OUT FOR BEER WITH THE GUYS. I'VE ONLY BEEN IN FOR A FEW MONTHS, BUT I CAN'T IMAGINE ANYTHING WORSE.
OH, THE AGONY, THE PAIN!
YOU THINK YOU'VE SEEN IT ALL, HUH? YOU THINK YOU'RE JAMES CAGNBY OR SOMETHING, HUH?
WELL, YOU DON'T KNOW WHAT YOU'RE TALKING ABOUT!
JERKS!
IT'S KIND OF HARD TO LOCK UP SOMEONE WHO CAN BURN THROUGH SOLID STEEL. LINNIER TOLD ME THEY'D KEPT HER SEDATED, FLOATING IN A SENSORY DEPRIVATION TANK FOR THREE MONTHS. IF HE HADN'T ASKED TO HAVE HER PUT ON THE PROJECT, SHE'D STILL BE THERE...
WHAT'S WITH HER?
RREET RREEET RREEEET!
12

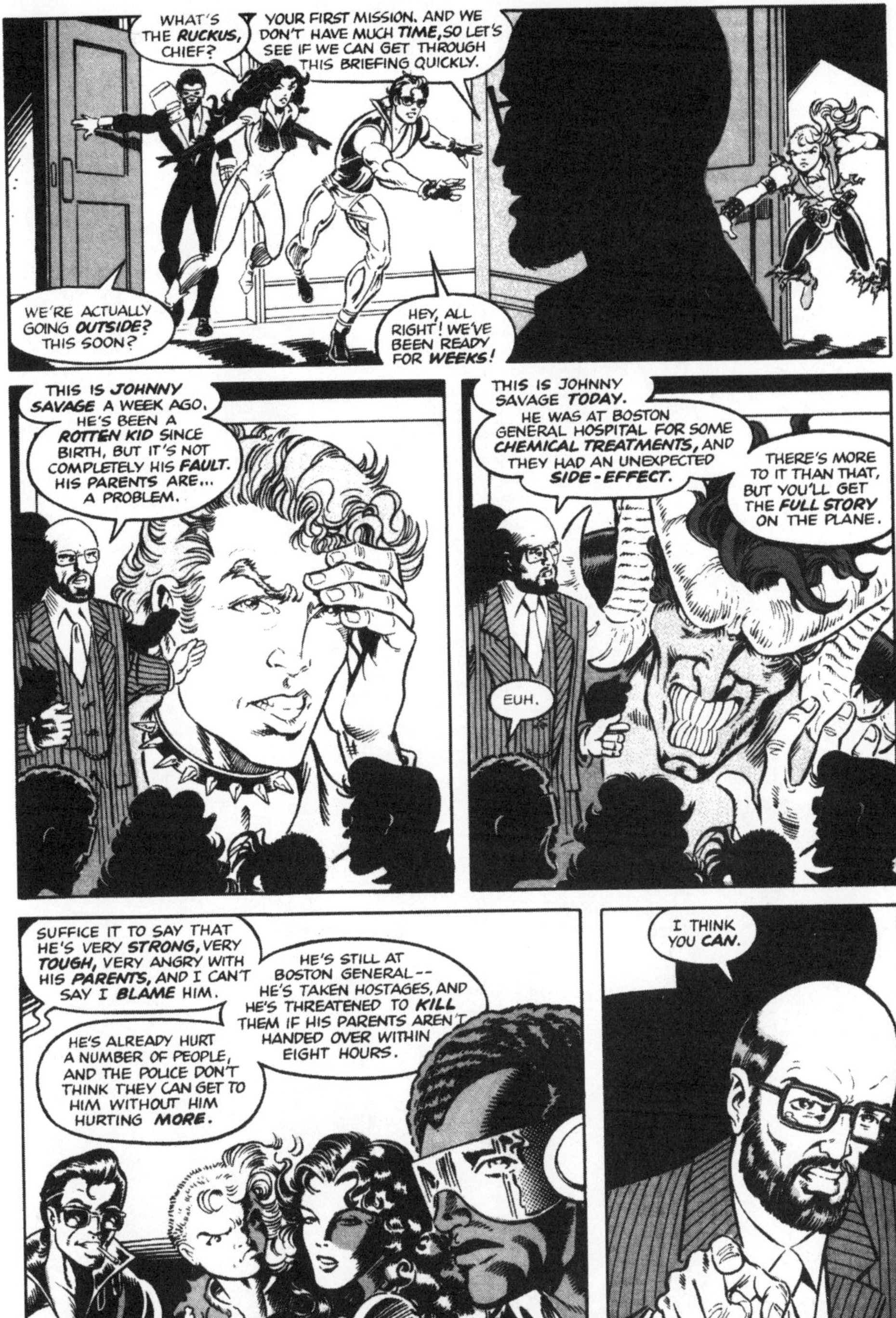
WHAT'S THE RUCKUS, CHIEF?
YOUR FIRST MISSION. AND WE DON'T HAVE MUCH TIME, SO LET'S SEE IF WE CAN GET THROUGH THIS BRIEFING QUICKLY.
WE'RE ACTUALLY GOING OUTSIDE? THIS SOON?
HEY, ALL RIGHT! WE'VE BEEN READY FOR WEEKS!
THIS IS JOHNNY SAVAGE A WEEK AGO. HE'S BEEN A ROTTEN KID SINCE BIRTH, BUT IT'S NOT COMPLETELY HIS FAULT. HIS PARENTS ARE... A PROBLEM.
THIS IS JOHNNY SAVAGE TODAY. HE WAS AT BOSTON GENERAL HOSPITAL FOR SOME CHEMICAL TREATMENTS, AND THEY HAD AN UNEXPECTED SIDE-EFFECT.
THERE'S MORE TO IT THAN THAT, BUT YOU'LL GET THE FULL STORY ON THE PLANE.
EUH.
SUFFICE IT TO SAY THAT HE'S VERY STRONG, VERY TOUGH, VERY ANGRY WITH HIS PARENTS, AND I CAN'T SAY I BLAME HIM.
HE'S ALREADY HURT A NUMBER OF PEOPLE, AND THE POLICE DON'T THINK THEY CAN GET TO HIM WITHOUT HIM HURTING MORE.
HE'S STILL AT BOSTON GENERAL-- HE'S TAKEN HOSTAGES, AND HE'S THREATENED TO KILL THEM IF HIS PARENTS AREN'T HANDED OVER WITHIN EIGHT HOURS.
I THINK YOU CAN.
13

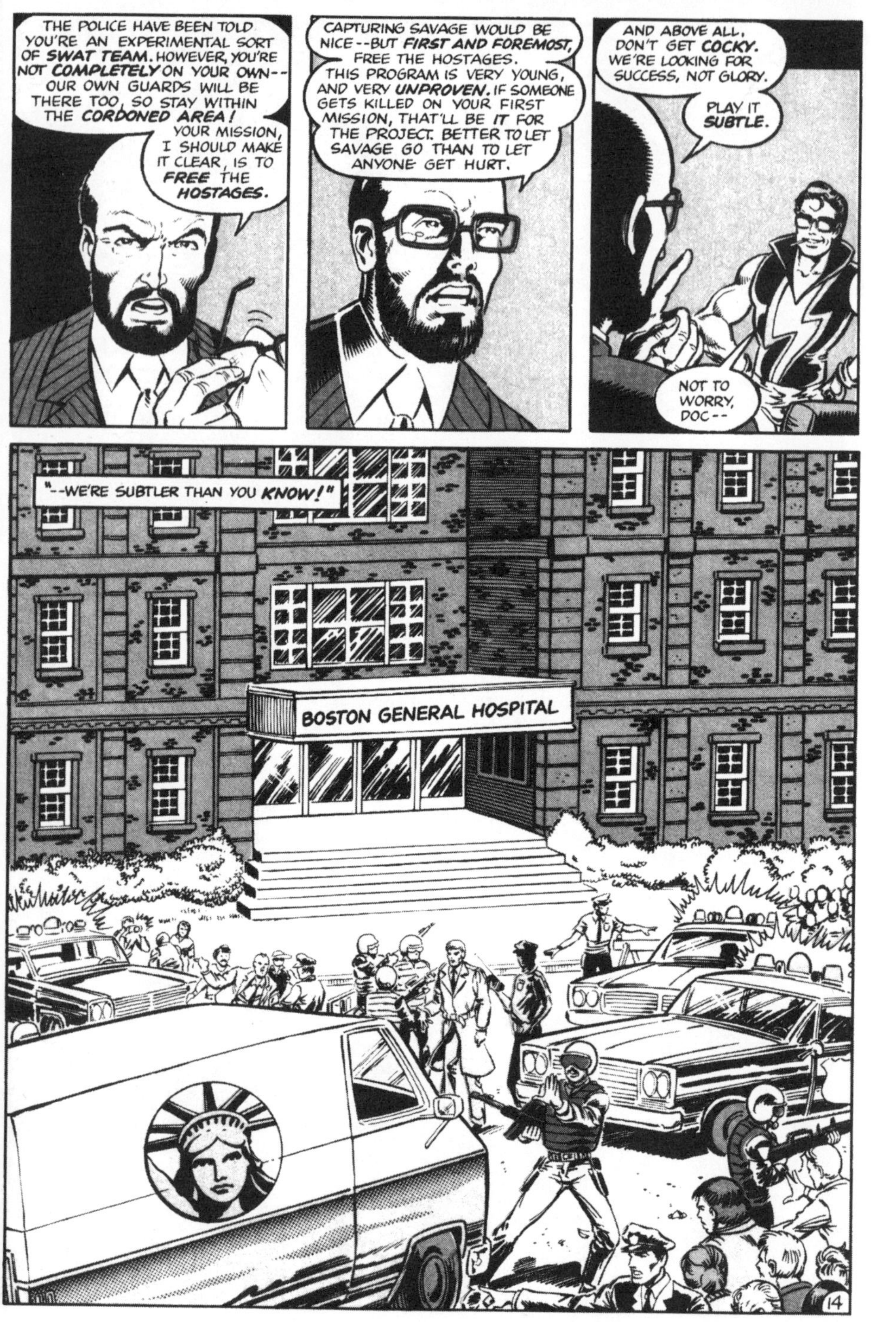
THE POLICE HAVE BEEN TOLD YOU'RE AN EXPERIMENTAL SORT OF SWAT TEAM. HOWEVER, YOU'RE NOT COMPLETELY ON YOUR OWN-- OUR OWN GUARDS WILL BE THERE TOO, SO STAY WITHIN THE CORDONED AREA!
YOUR MISSION, I SHOULD MAKE IT CLEAR, IS TO FREE THE HOSTAGES.
CAPTURING SAVAGE WOULD BE NICE--BUT FIRST AND FOREMOST, FREE THE HOSTAGES. THIS PROGRAM IS VERY YOUNG, AND VERY UNPROVEN. IF SOMEONE GETS KILLED ON YOUR FIRST MISSION, THAT'LL BE IT FOR THE PROJECT. BETTER TO LET SAVAGE GO THAN TO LET ANYONE GET HURT.
AND ABOVE ALL, DON'T GET COCKY. WE'RE LOOKING FOR SUCCESS, NOT GLORY.
PLAY IT SUBTLE.
NOT TO WORRY, DOC--
"--WE'RE SUBTLER THAN YOU KNOW!"
BOSTON GENERAL HOSPITAL
14

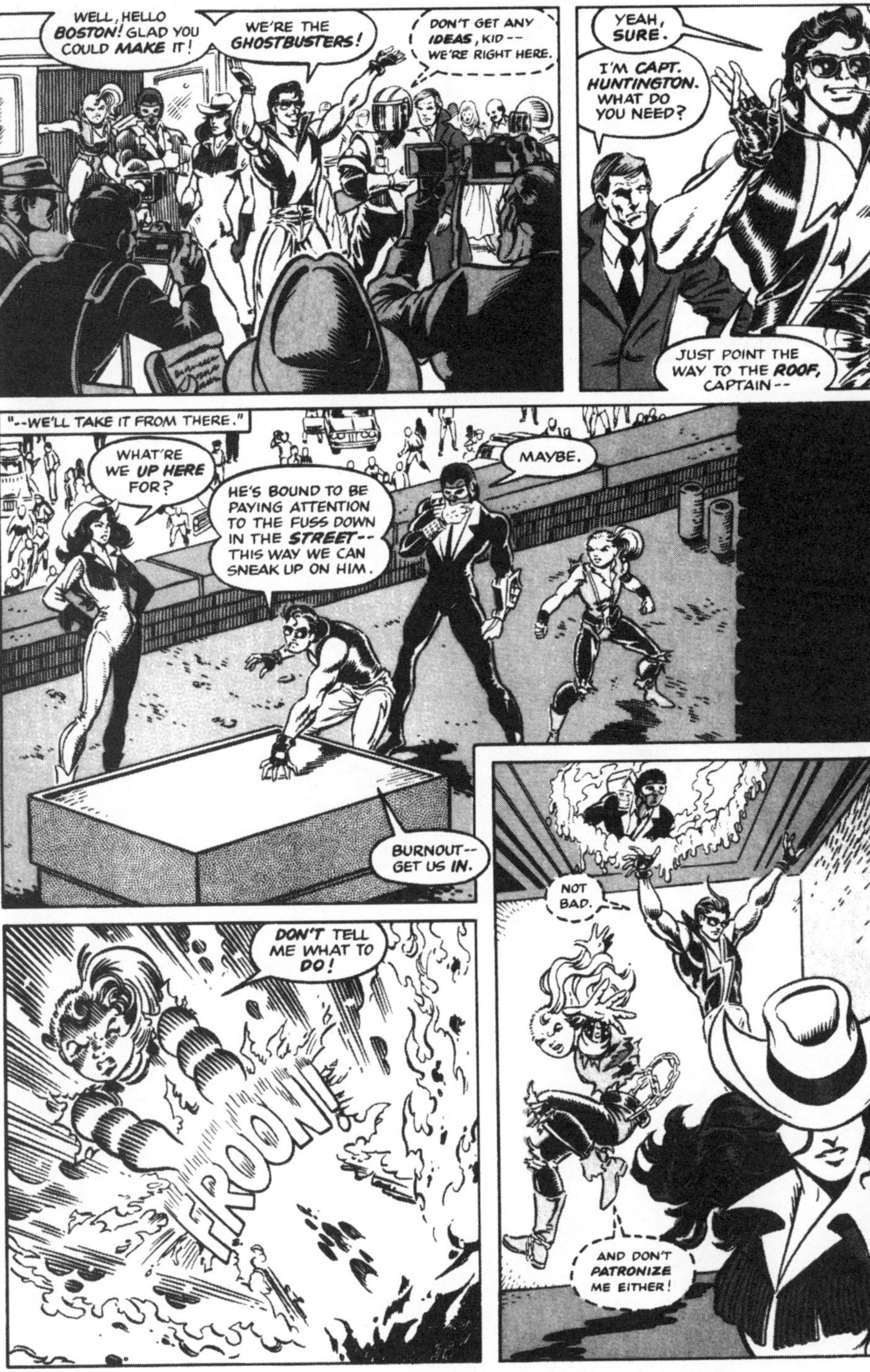
WELL, HELLO BOSTON! GLAD YOU COULD MAKE IT!
WE'RE THE GHOSTBUSTERS!
DON'T GET ANY IDEAS, KID -- WE'RE RIGHT HERE.
YEAH, SURE.
I'M CAPT. HUNTINGTON. WHAT DO YOU NEED?
JUST POINT THE WAY TO THE ROOF, CAPTAIN --
"--WE'LL TAKE IT FROM THERE."
WHAT'RE WE UP HERE FOR?
HE'S BOUND TO BE PAYING ATTENTION TO THE FUSS DOWN IN THE STREET-- THIS WAY WE CAN SNEAK UP ON HIM.
MAYBE.
BURNOUT-- GET US IN.
DON'T TELL ME WHAT TO DO!
KROOM!
NOT BAD.
AND DON'T PATRONIZE ME EITHER!
15

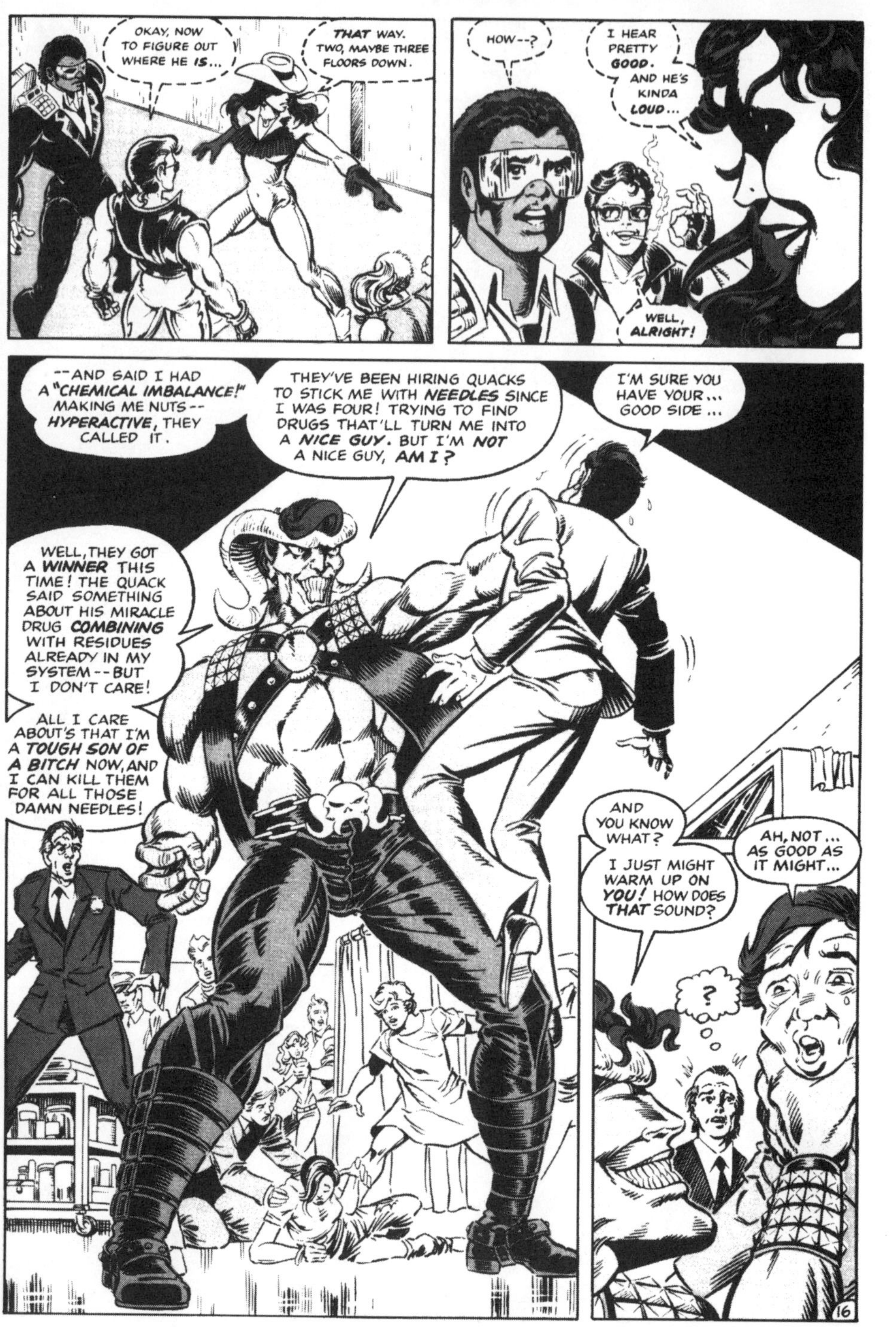
OKAY, NOW TO FIGURE OUT WHERE HE IS...
THAT WAY. TWO, MAYBE THREE FLOORS DOWN.
HOW--?
I HEAR PRETTY GOOD. AND HE'S KINDA LOUD...
WELL, ALRIGHT!
--AND SAID I HAD A "CHEMICAL IMBALANCE!" MAKING ME NUTS--HYPERACTIVE, THEY CALLED IT.
THEY'VE BEEN HIRING QUACKS TO STICK ME WITH NEEDLES SINCE I WAS FOUR! TRYING TO FIND DRUGS THAT'LL TURN ME INTO A NICE GUY. BUT I'M NOT A NICE GUY, AM I?
I'M SURE YOU HAVE YOUR... GOOD SIDE...
WELL, THEY GOT A WINNER THIS TIME! THE QUACK SAID SOMETHING ABOUT HIS MIRACLE DRUG COMBINING WITH RESIDUES ALREADY IN MY SYSTEM--BUT I DON'T CARE!
ALL I CARE ABOUT'S THAT I'M A TOUGH SON OF A BITCH NOW, AND I CAN KILL THEM FOR ALL THOSE DAMN NEEDLES!
AND YOU KNOW WHAT?
I JUST MIGHT WARM UP ON YOU! HOW DOES THAT SOUND?
AH, NOT... AS GOOD AS IT MIGHT...
?
16

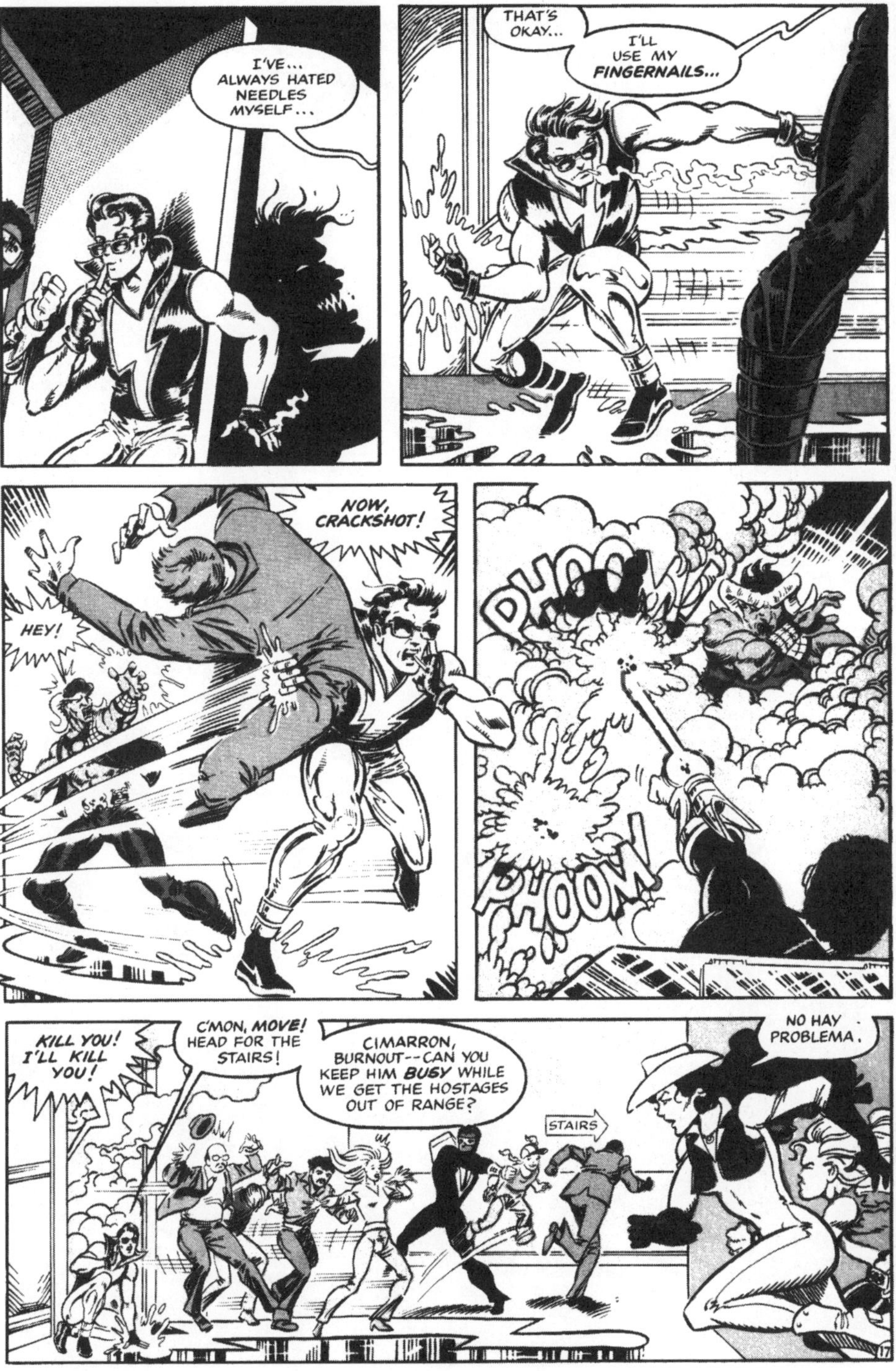
I'VE... ALWAYS HATED NEEDLES MYSELF...
THAT'S OKAY...
I'LL USE MY **FINGERNAILS...**
NOW, CRACKSHOT!
HEY!
PHOOM
PHOOM!
KILL YOU! I'LL KILL YOU!
C'MON, **MOVE!** HEAD FOR THE STAIRS!
CIMARRON, BURNOUT--CAN YOU KEEP HIM **BUSY** WHILE WE GET THE HOSTAGES OUT OF RANGE?
STAIRS
NO HAY PROBLEMA.
17

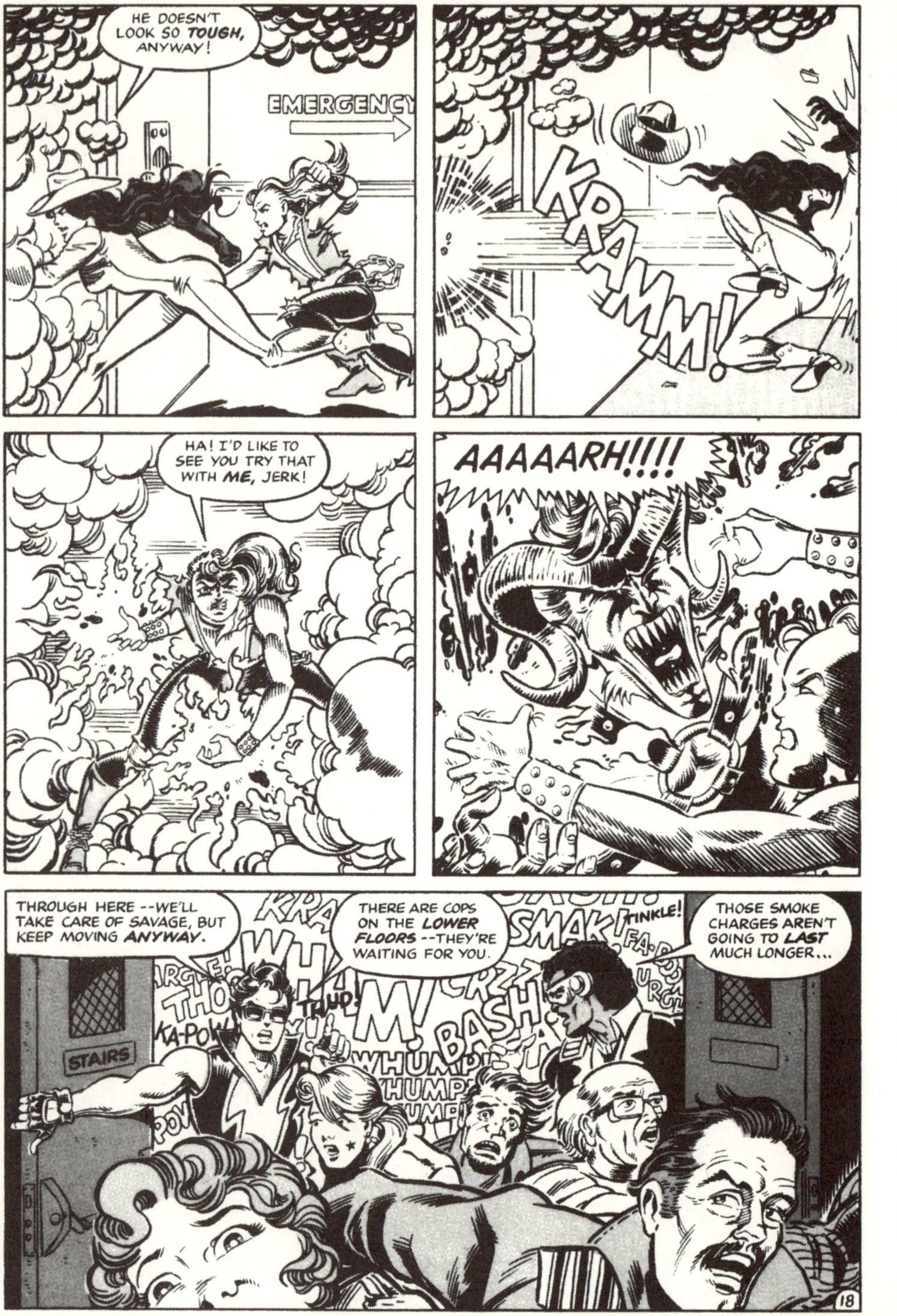
HE DOESN'T LOOK SO TOUGH, ANYWAY!
EMERGENCY
KRAMMM!
HA! I'D LIKE TO SEE YOU TRY THAT WITH ME, JERK!
AAAAARH!!!!!
THROUGH HERE --WE'LL TAKE CARE OF SAVAGE, BUT KEEP MOVING ANYWAY.
THERE ARE COPS ON THE LOWER FLOORS --THEY'RE WAITING FOR YOU.
THOSE SMOKE CHARGES AREN'T GOING TO LAST MUCH LONGER...
SMAK!
TINKLE!
KA-POW
THUD!
BASH
WHUMP
STAIRS
18

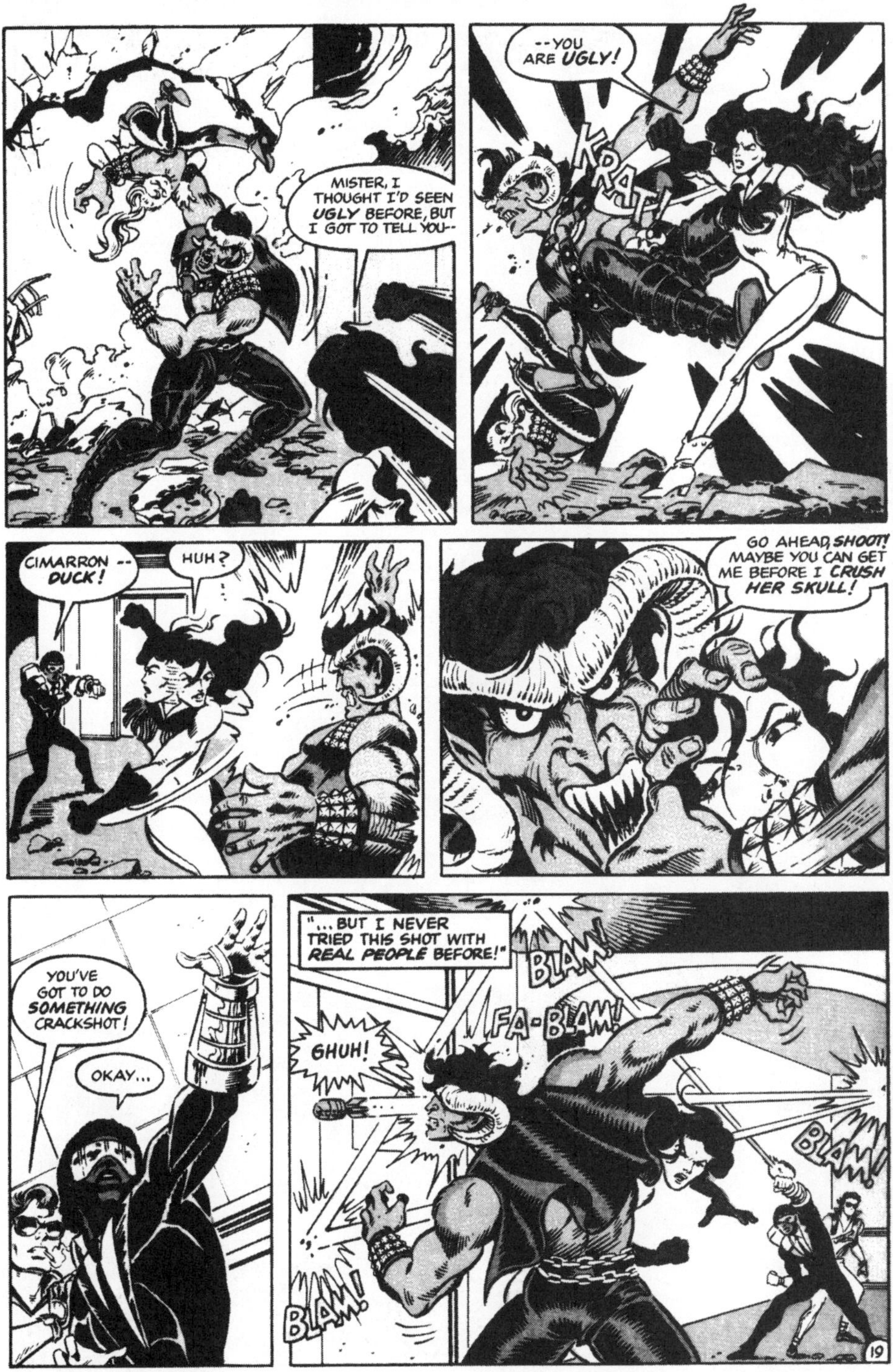
MISTER, I THOUGHT I'D SEEN UGLY BEFORE, BUT I GOT TO TELL YOU--
--YOU ARE UGLY!
KRAT!
CIMARRON -- DUCK!
HUH?
GO AHEAD, SHOOT! MAYBE YOU CAN GET ME BEFORE I CRUSH HER SKULL!
YOU'VE GOT TO DO SOMETHING CRACKSHOT!
OKAY...
"...BUT I NEVER TRIED THIS SHOT WITH REAL PEOPLE BEFORE!"
BLAM!
FA-BLAM!
GHUH!
BLAM!
BLAM!
19

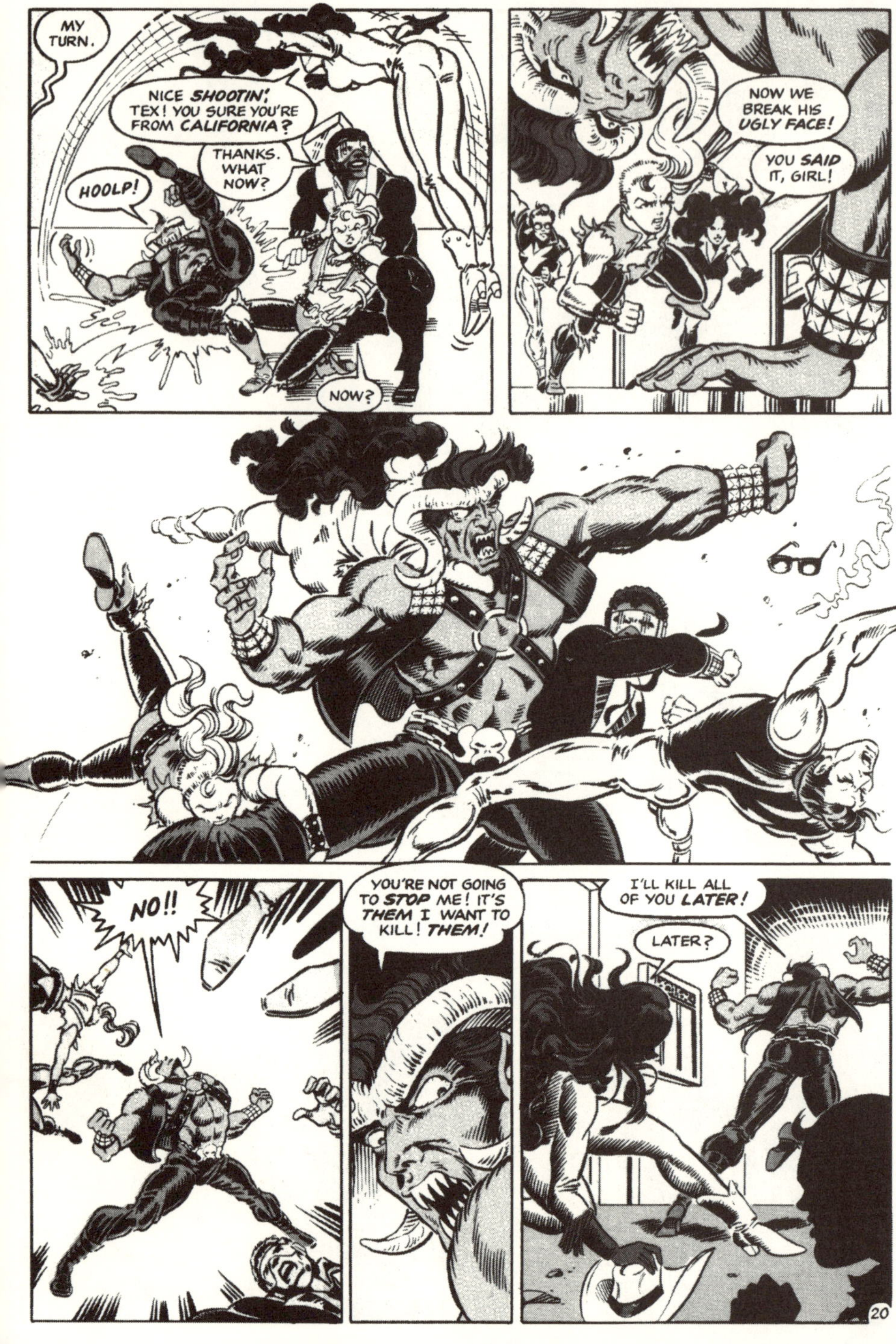
MY TURN.
NICE SHOOTIN', TEX! YOU SURE YOU'RE FROM CALIFORNIA?
THANKS. WHAT NOW?
HOOLP!
NOW?
NOW WE BREAK HIS UGLY FACE!
YOU SAID IT, GIRL!
NO!!
YOU'RE NOT GOING TO STOP ME! IT'S THEM I WANT TO KILL! THEM!
I'LL KILL ALL OF YOU LATER!
LATER?
20

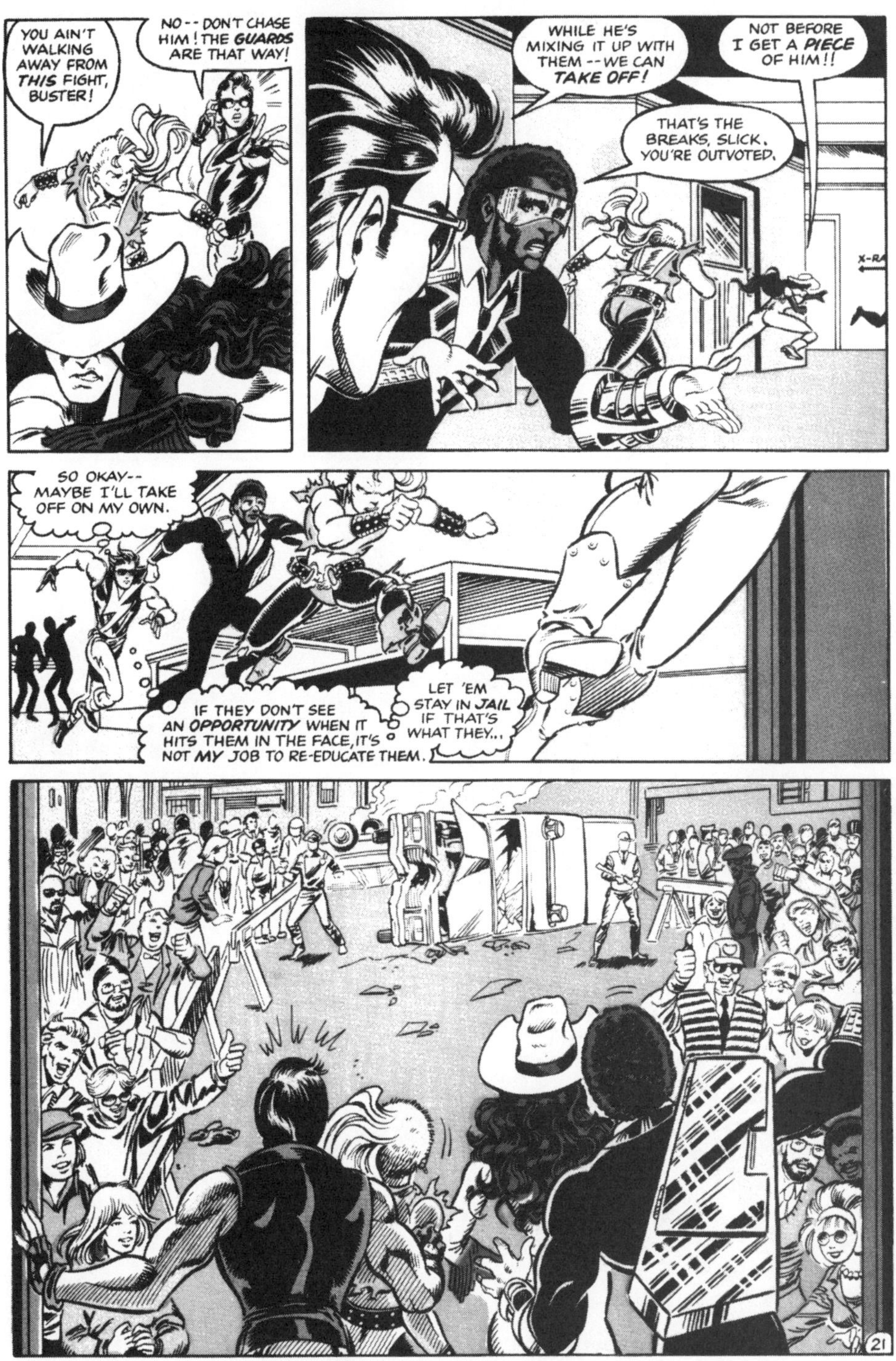
YOU AIN'T WALKING AWAY FROM THIS FIGHT, BUSTER!
NO -- DON'T CHASE HIM! THE GUARDS ARE THAT WAY!
WHILE HE'S MIXING IT UP WITH THEM -- WE CAN TAKE OFF!
NOT BEFORE I GET A PIECE OF HIM!!
THAT'S THE BREAKS, SLICK. YOU'RE OUTVOTED.
SO OKAY-- MAYBE I'LL TAKE OFF ON MY OWN.
IF THEY DON'T SEE AN OPPORTUNITY WHEN IT HITS THEM IN THE FACE, IT'S NOT MY JOB TO RE-EDUCATE THEM.
LET 'EM STAY IN JAIL IF THAT'S WHAT THEY...
21

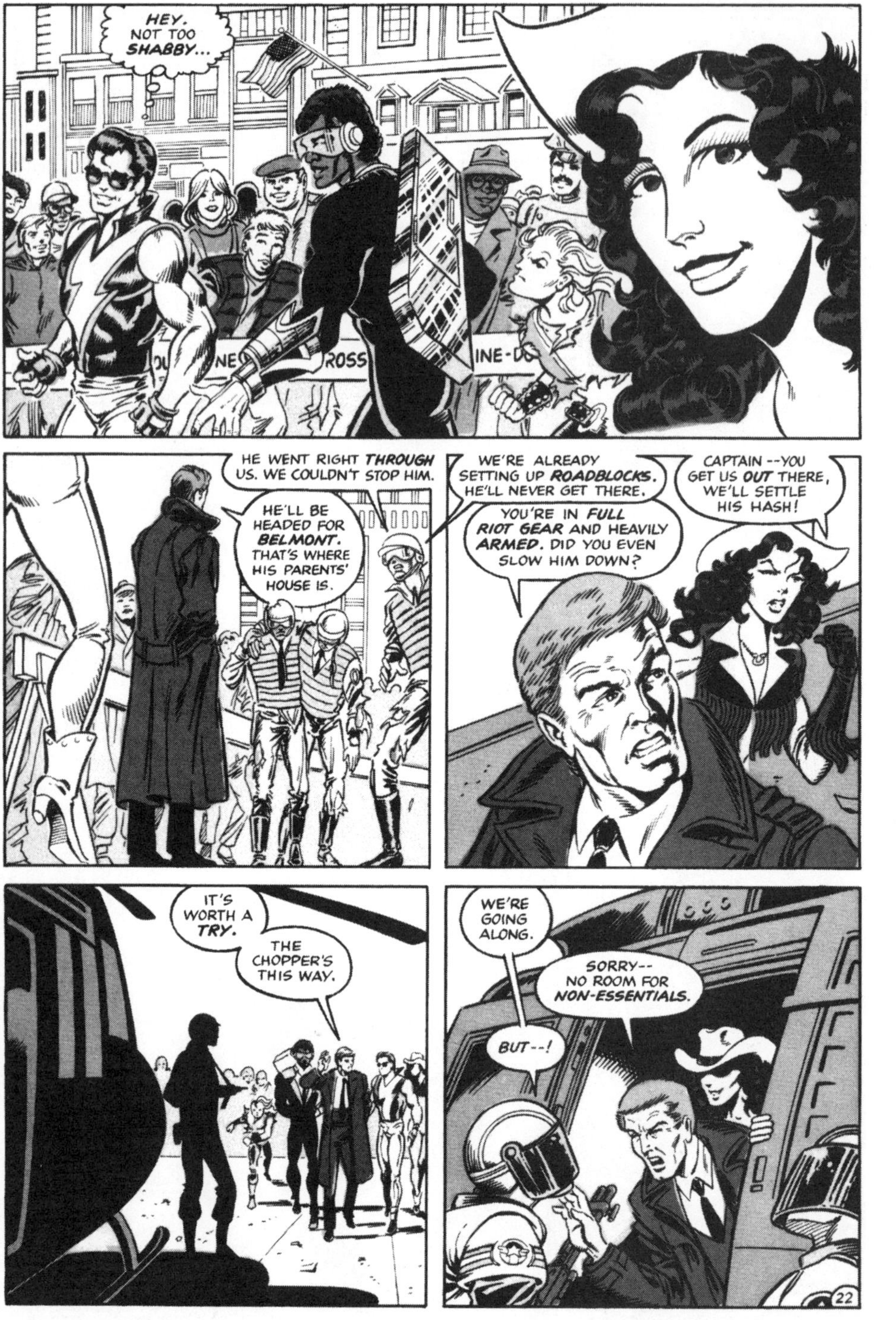
HEY. NOT TOO SHABBY...
HE WENT RIGHT THROUGH US. WE COULDN'T STOP HIM.
HE'LL BE HEADED FOR BELMONT. THAT'S WHERE HIS PARENTS' HOUSE IS.
WE'RE ALREADY SETTING UP ROADBLOCKS. HE'LL NEVER GET THERE.
YOU'RE IN FULL RIOT GEAR AND HEAVILY ARMED. DID YOU EVEN SLOW HIM DOWN?
CAPTAIN --YOU GET US OUT THERE, WE'LL SETTLE HIS HASH!
IT'S WORTH A TRY.
THE CHOPPER'S THIS WAY.
WE'RE GOING ALONG.
SORRY-- NO ROOM FOR NON-ESSENTIALS.
BUT--!
22

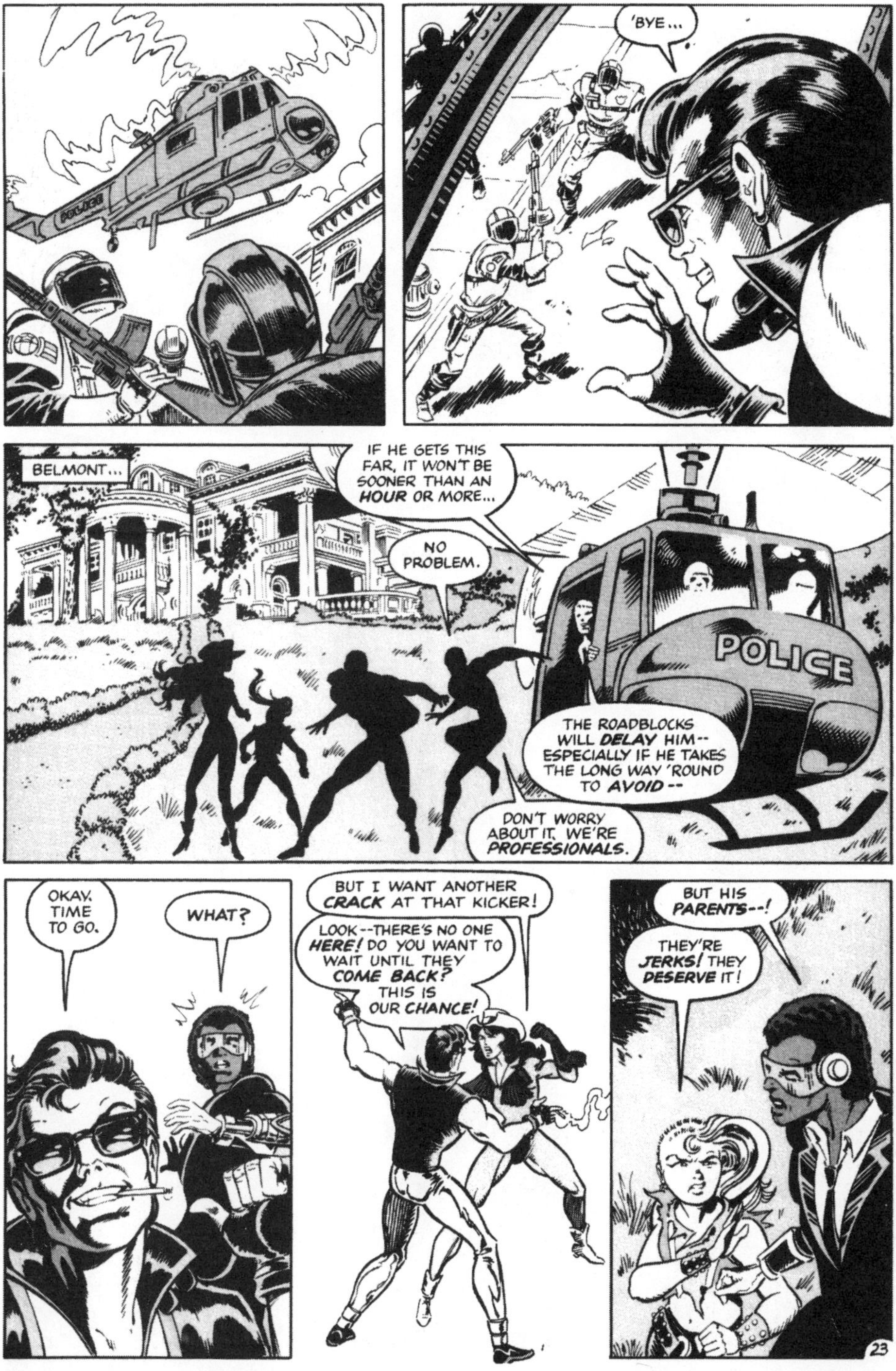
'BYE...
BELMONT...
IF HE GETS THIS FAR, IT WON'T BE SOONER THAN AN HOUR OR MORE...
NO PROBLEM.
THE ROADBLOCKS WILL DELAY HIM-- ESPECIALLY IF HE TAKES THE LONG WAY 'ROUND TO AVOID--
DON'T WORRY ABOUT IT. WE'RE PROFESSIONALS.
POLICE
OKAY. TIME TO GO.
WHAT?
BUT I WANT ANOTHER CRACK AT THAT KICKER!
LOOK--THERE'S NO ONE HERE! DO YOU WANT TO WAIT UNTIL THEY COME BACK? THIS IS OUR CHANCE!
BUT HIS PARENTS--!
THEY'RE JERKS! THEY DESERVE IT!
23

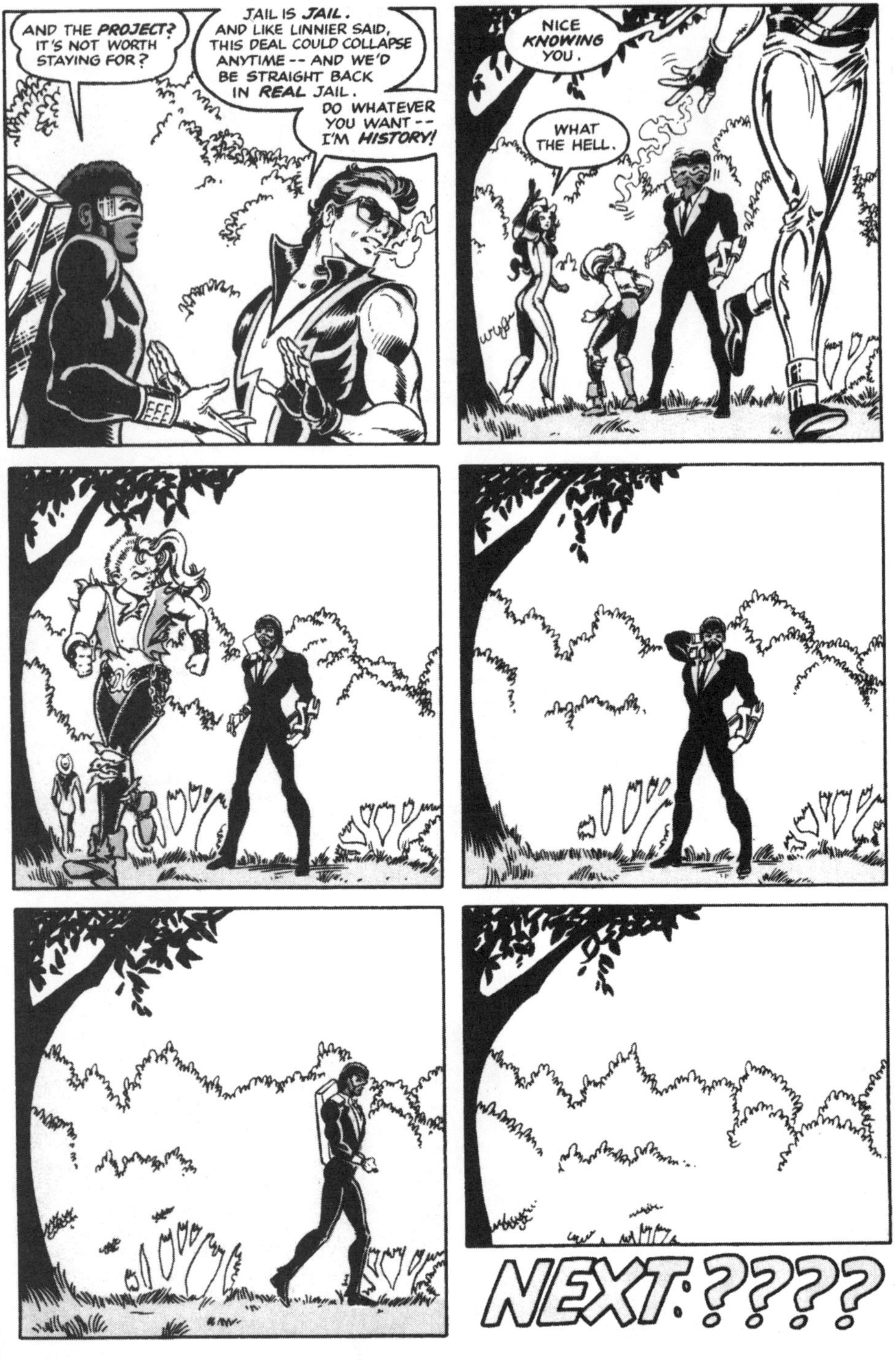

AND THE PROJECT? IT'S NOT WORTH STAYING FOR?
JAIL IS JAIL. AND LIKE LINNIER SAID, THIS DEAL COULD COLLAPSE ANYTIME -- AND WE'D BE STRAIGHT BACK IN REAL JAIL.
DO WHATEVER YOU WANT -- I'M HISTORY!
NICE KNOWING YOU.
WHAT THE HELL.
NEXT: ????

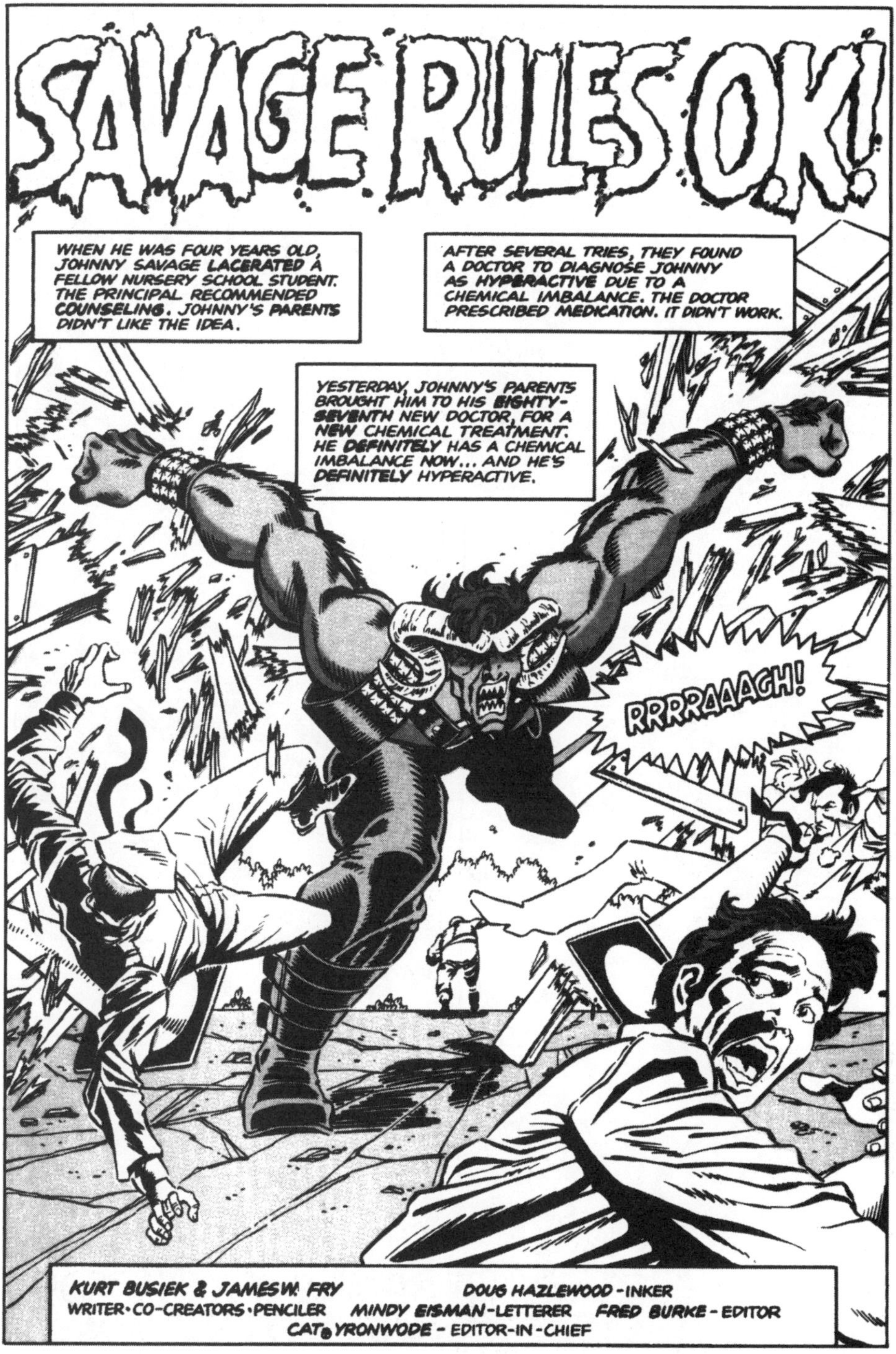
SAVAGE RULES O.K.!
WHEN HE WAS FOUR YEARS OLD, JOHNNY SAVAGE LACERATED A FELLOW NURSERY SCHOOL STUDENT. THE PRINCIPAL RECOMMENDED COUNSELING. JOHNNY'S PARENTS DIDN'T LIKE THE IDEA.
AFTER SEVERAL TRIES, THEY FOUND A DOCTOR TO DIAGNOSE JOHNNY AS HYPERACTIVE DUE TO A CHEMICAL IMBALANCE. THE DOCTOR PRESCRIBED MEDICATION. IT DIDN'T WORK.
YESTERDAY, JOHNNY'S PARENTS BROUGHT HIM TO HIS EIGHTY-SEVENTH NEW DOCTOR, FOR A NEW CHEMICAL TREATMENT. HE DEFINITELY HAS A CHEMICAL IMBALANCE NOW... AND HE'S DEFINITELY HYPERACTIVE.
RRRRAAAGH!
KURT BUSIEK & JAMES W. FRY WRITER·CO-CREATORS·PENCILER
DOUG HAZLEWOOD-INKER
MINDY EISMAN-LETTERER
FRED BURKE-EDITOR
CAT YRONWODE-EDITOR-IN-CHIEF

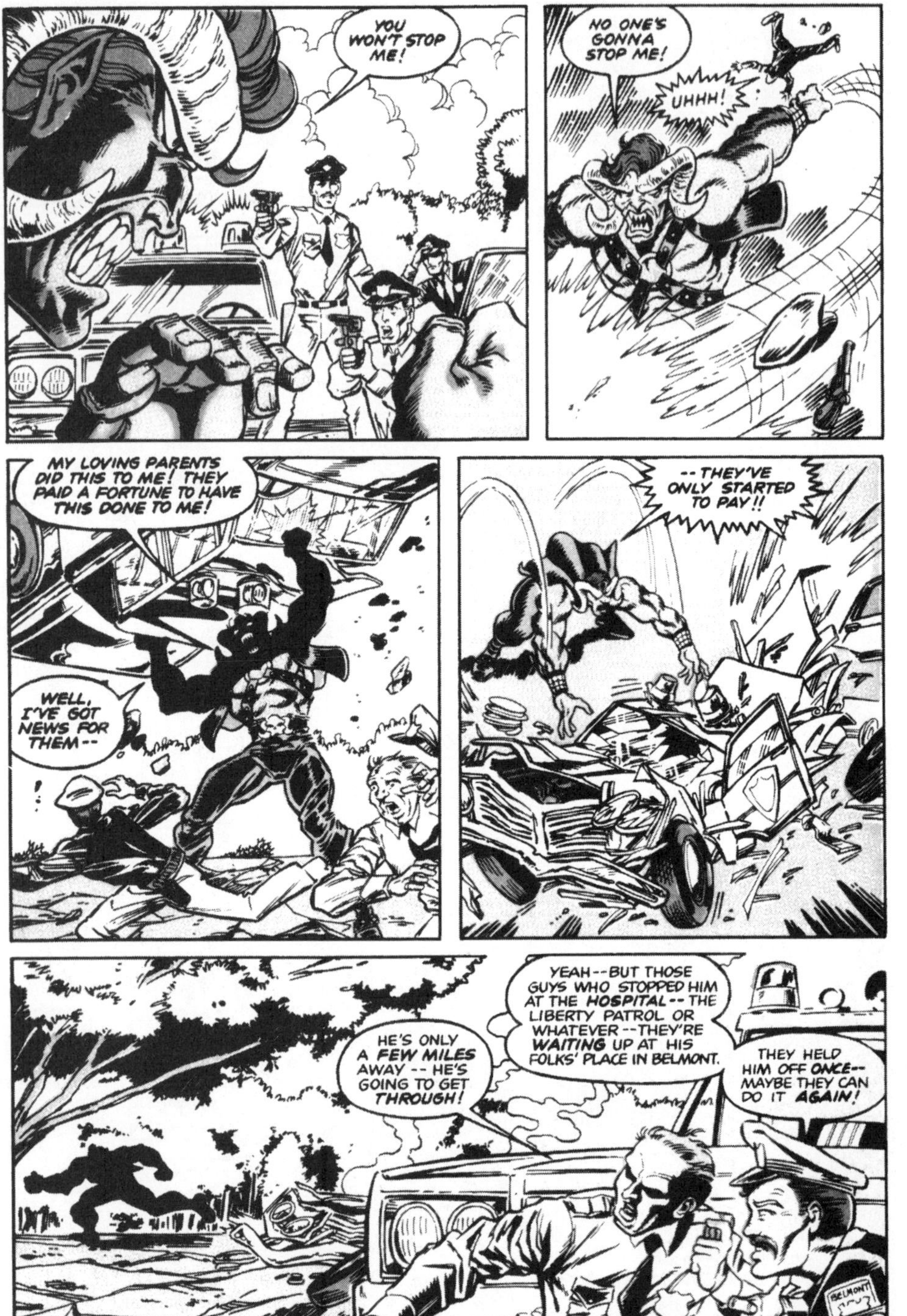
YOU WON'T STOP ME!
NO ONE'S GONNA STOP ME!
UHHH!
MY LOVING PARENTS DID THIS TO ME! THEY PAID A FORTUNE TO HAVE THIS DONE TO ME!
WELL, I'VE GOT NEWS FOR THEM--
--THEY'VE ONLY STARTED TO PAY!!
HE'S ONLY A FEW MILES AWAY -- HE'S GOING TO GET THROUGH!
YEAH--BUT THOSE GUYS WHO STOPPED HIM AT THE HOSPITAL--THE LIBERTY PATROL OR WHATEVER--THEY'RE WAITING UP AT HIS FOLKS' PLACE IN BELMONT.
THEY HELD HIM OFF ONCE-- MAYBE THEY CAN DO IT AGAIN!
BELMONT

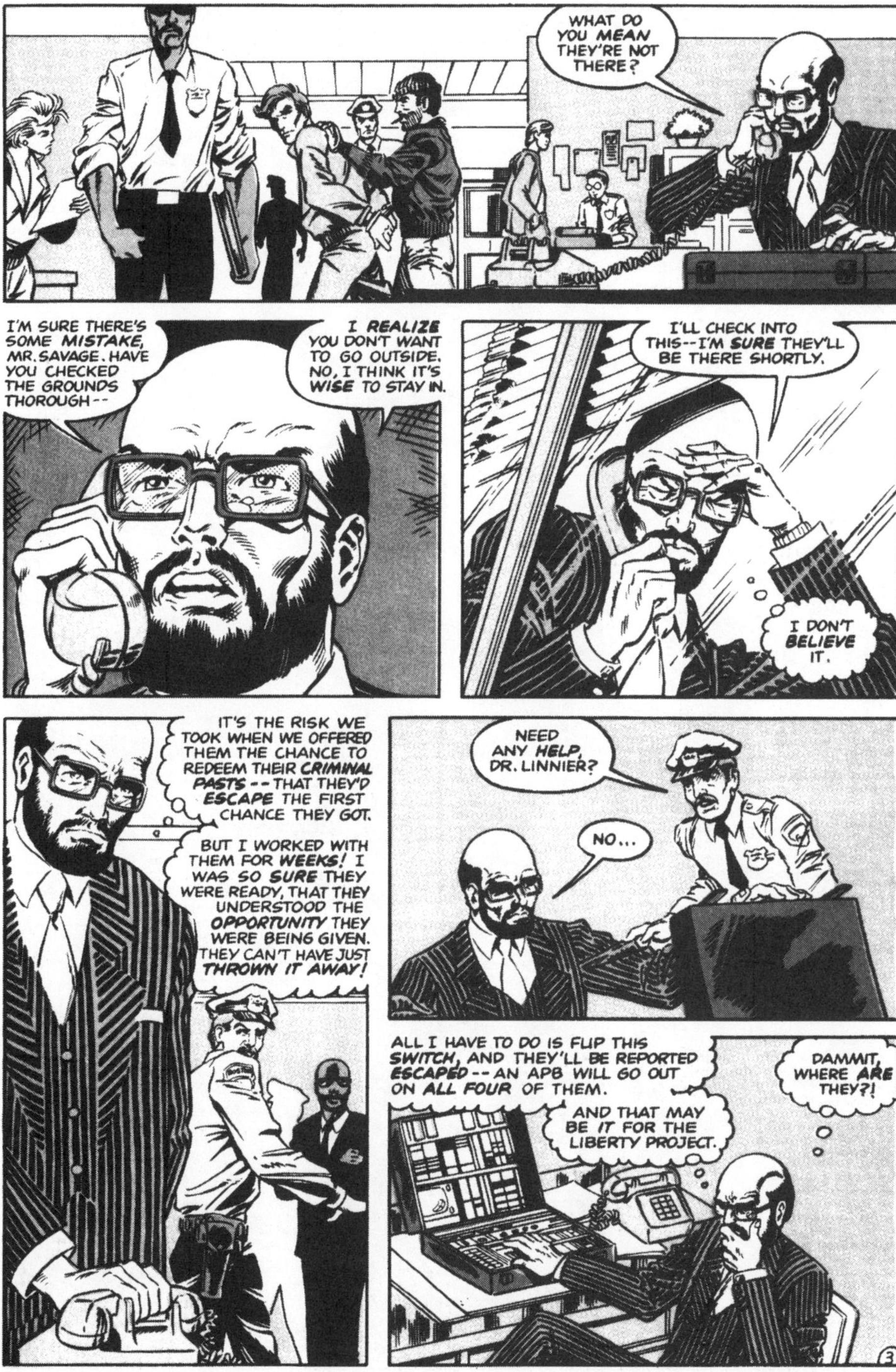
WHAT DO YOU MEAN THEY'RE NOT THERE?
I'M SURE THERE'S SOME MISTAKE, MR. SAVAGE. HAVE YOU CHECKED THE GROUNDS THOROUGH--
I REALIZE YOU DON'T WANT TO GO OUTSIDE. NO, I THINK IT'S WISE TO STAY IN.
I'LL CHECK INTO THIS--I'M SURE THEY'LL BE THERE SHORTLY.
I DON'T BELIEVE IT.
IT'S THE RISK WE TOOK WHEN WE OFFERED THEM THE CHANCE TO REDEEM THEIR CRIMINAL PASTS--THAT THEY'D ESCAPE THE FIRST CHANCE THEY GOT.
BUT I WORKED WITH THEM FOR WEEKS! I WAS SO SURE THEY WERE READY, THAT THEY UNDERSTOOD THE OPPORTUNITY THEY WERE BEING GIVEN. THEY CAN'T HAVE JUST THROWN IT AWAY!
NEED ANY HELP, DR. LINNIER?
NO...
ALL I HAVE TO DO IS FLIP THIS SWITCH, AND THEY'LL BE REPORTED ESCAPED--AN APB WILL GO OUT ON ALL FOUR OF THEM.
AND THAT MAY BE IT FOR THE LIBERTY PROJECT.
DAMMIT, WHERE ARE THEY?!
3

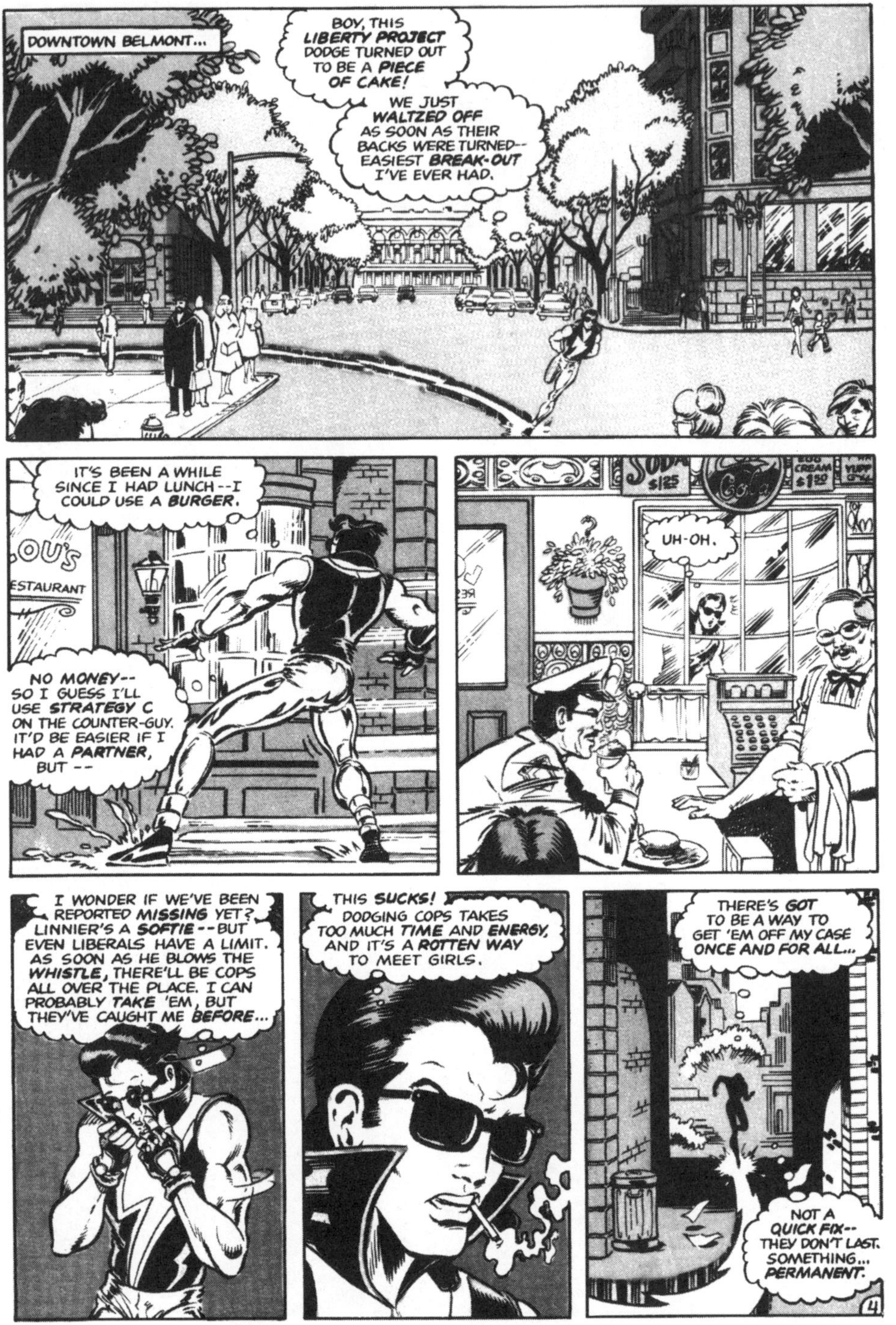
DOWNTOWN BELMONT...
BOY, THIS LIBERTY PROJECT DODGE TURNED OUT TO BE A PIECE OF CAKE!
WE JUST WALTZED OFF AS SOON AS THEIR BACKS WERE TURNED-- EASIEST BREAK-OUT I'VE EVER HAD.
IT'S BEEN A WHILE SINCE I HAD LUNCH --I COULD USE A BURGER.
LOU'S
RESTAURANT
NO MONEY-- SO I GUESS I'LL USE STRATEGY C ON THE COUNTER-GUY. IT'D BE EASIER IF I HAD A PARTNER, BUT --
SODA $1.25
ICE CREAM $1.50
UH-OH.
I WONDER IF WE'VE BEEN REPORTED MISSING YET? LINNIER'S A SOFTIE --BUT EVEN LIBERALS HAVE A LIMIT. AS SOON AS HE BLOWS THE WHISTLE, THERE'LL BE COPS ALL OVER THE PLACE. I CAN PROBABLY TAKE 'EM, BUT THEY'VE CAUGHT ME BEFORE...
THIS SUCKS! DODGING COPS TAKES TOO MUCH TIME AND ENERGY, AND IT'S A ROTTEN WAY TO MEET GIRLS.
THERE'S GOT TO BE A WAY TO GET 'EM OFF MY CASE ONCE AND FOR ALL...
NOT A QUICK FIX-- THEY DON'T LAST. SOMETHING... PERMANENT.
4

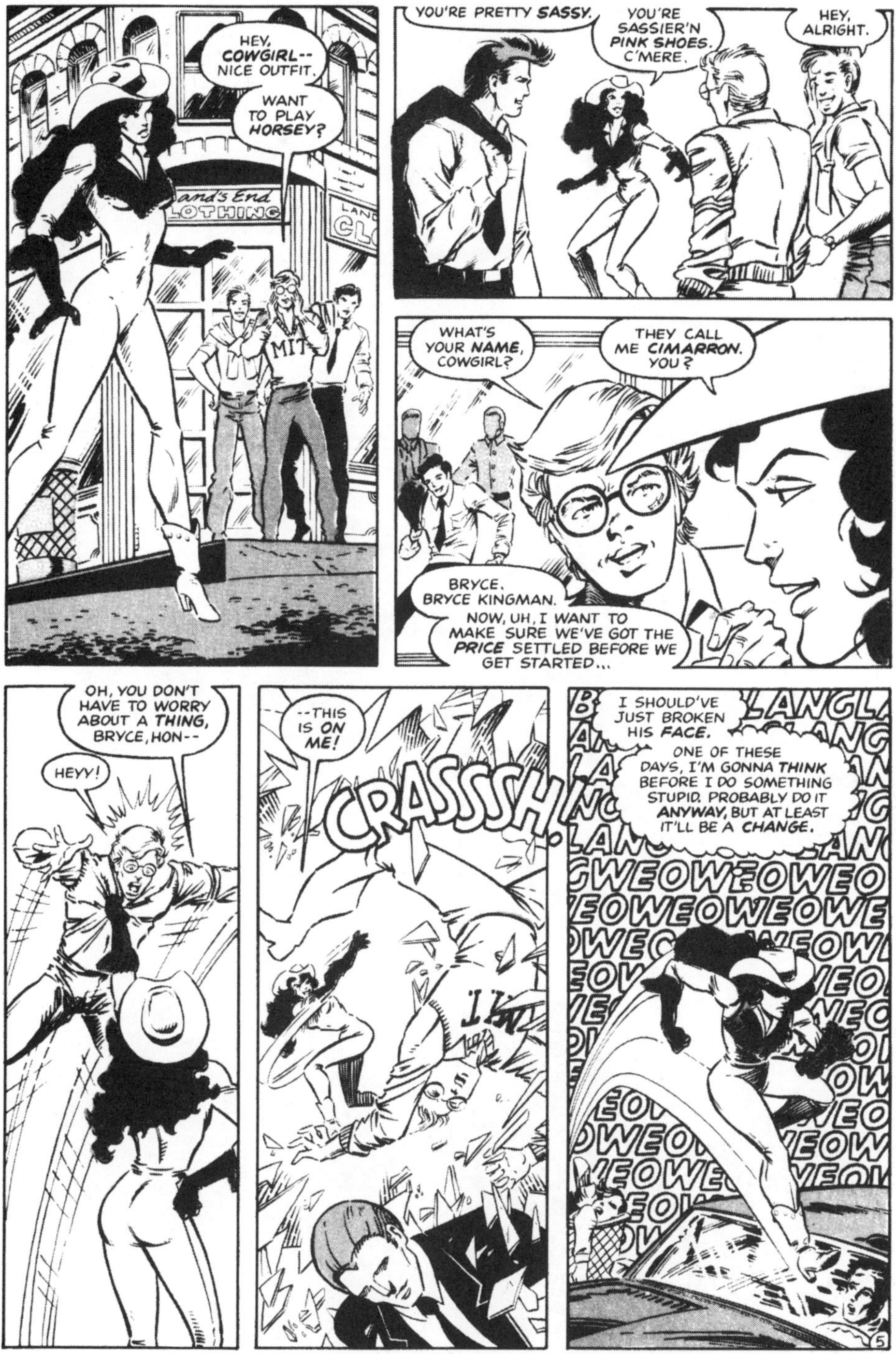
HEY, COWGIRL-- NICE OUTFIT.
WANT TO PLAY HORSEY?
Land's End CLOTHING
MIT
YOU'RE PRETTY SASSY.
YOU'RE SASSIER'N PINK SHOES. C'MERE.
HEY, ALRIGHT.
WHAT'S YOUR NAME, COWGIRL?
THEY CALL ME CIMARRON. YOU?
BRYCE. BRYCE KINGMAN.
NOW, UH, I WANT TO MAKE SURE WE'VE GOT THE PRICE SETTLED BEFORE WE GET STARTED...
OH, YOU DON'T HAVE TO WORRY ABOUT A THING, BRYCE, HON--
HEYY!
--THIS IS ON ME!
CRASSSH!
I SHOULD'VE JUST BROKEN HIS FACE.
ONE OF THESE DAYS, I'M GONNA THINK BEFORE I DO SOMETHING STUPID. PROBABLY DO IT ANYWAY, BUT AT LEAST IT'LL BE A CHANGE.
5

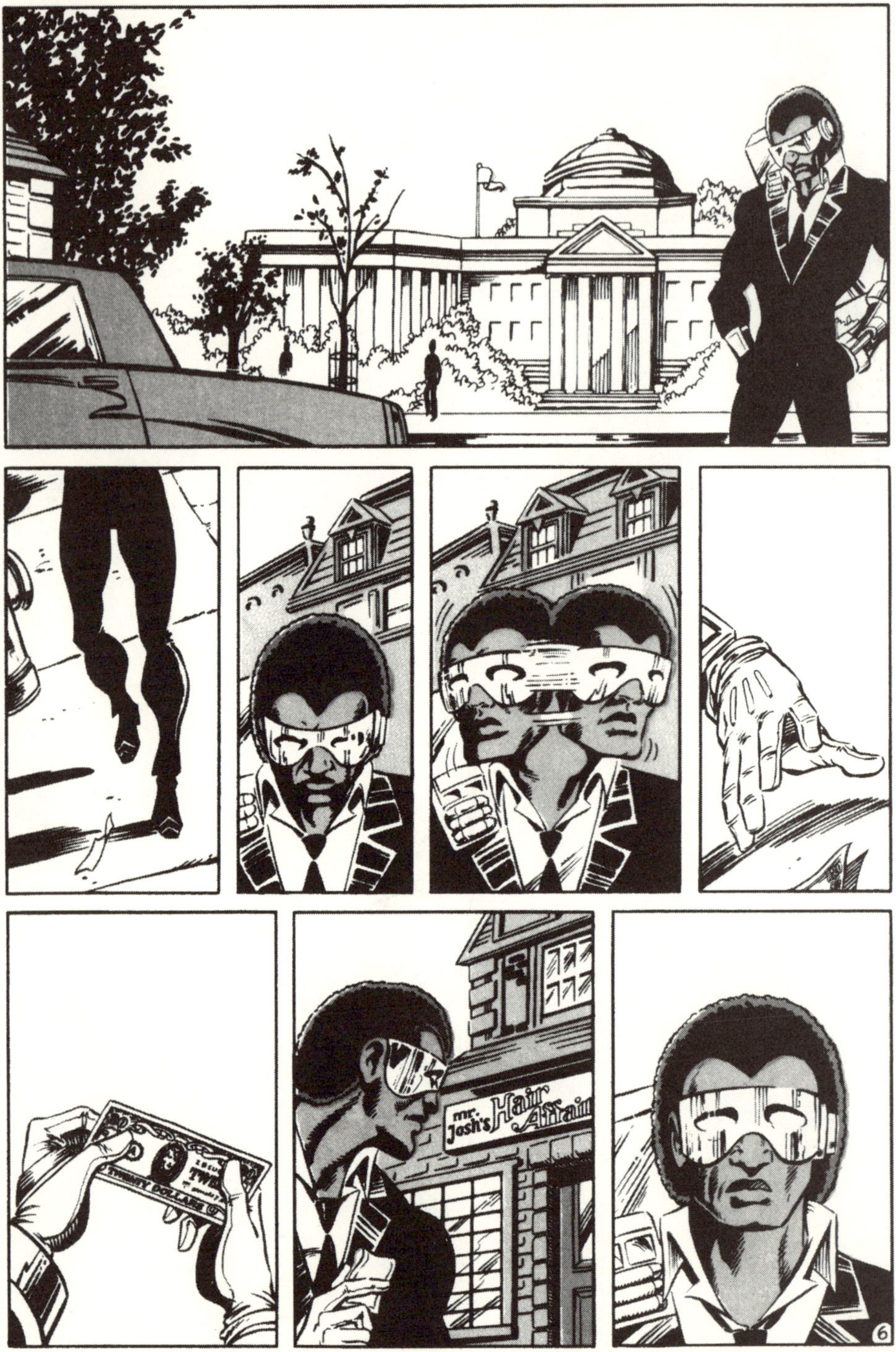
mr. Josh's
Hair

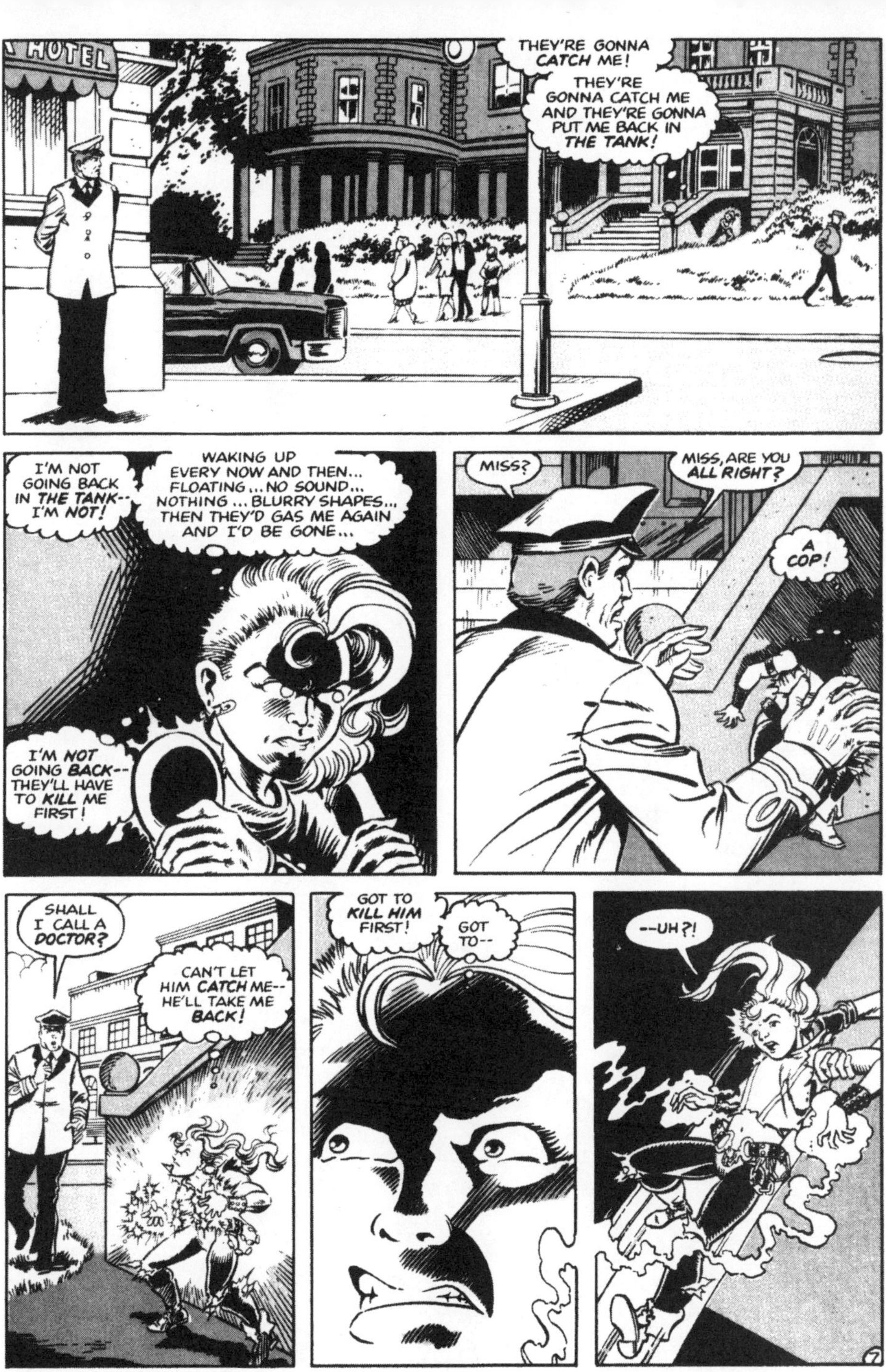
HOTEL
THEY'RE GONNA CATCH ME!
THEY'RE GONNA CATCH ME AND THEY'RE GONNA PUT ME BACK IN THE TANK!
I'M NOT GOING BACK IN THE TANK-- I'M NOT!
WAKING UP EVERY NOW AND THEN... FLOATING... NO SOUND... NOTHING... BLURRY SHAPES... THEN THEY'D GAS ME AGAIN AND I'D BE GONE...
I'M NOT GOING BACK-- THEY'LL HAVE TO KILL ME FIRST!
MISS?
MISS, ARE YOU ALL RIGHT?
A COP!
SHALL I CALL A DOCTOR?
CAN'T LET HIM CATCH ME-- HE'LL TAKE ME BACK!
GOT TO KILL HIM FIRST!
GOT TO--
--UH?!
7

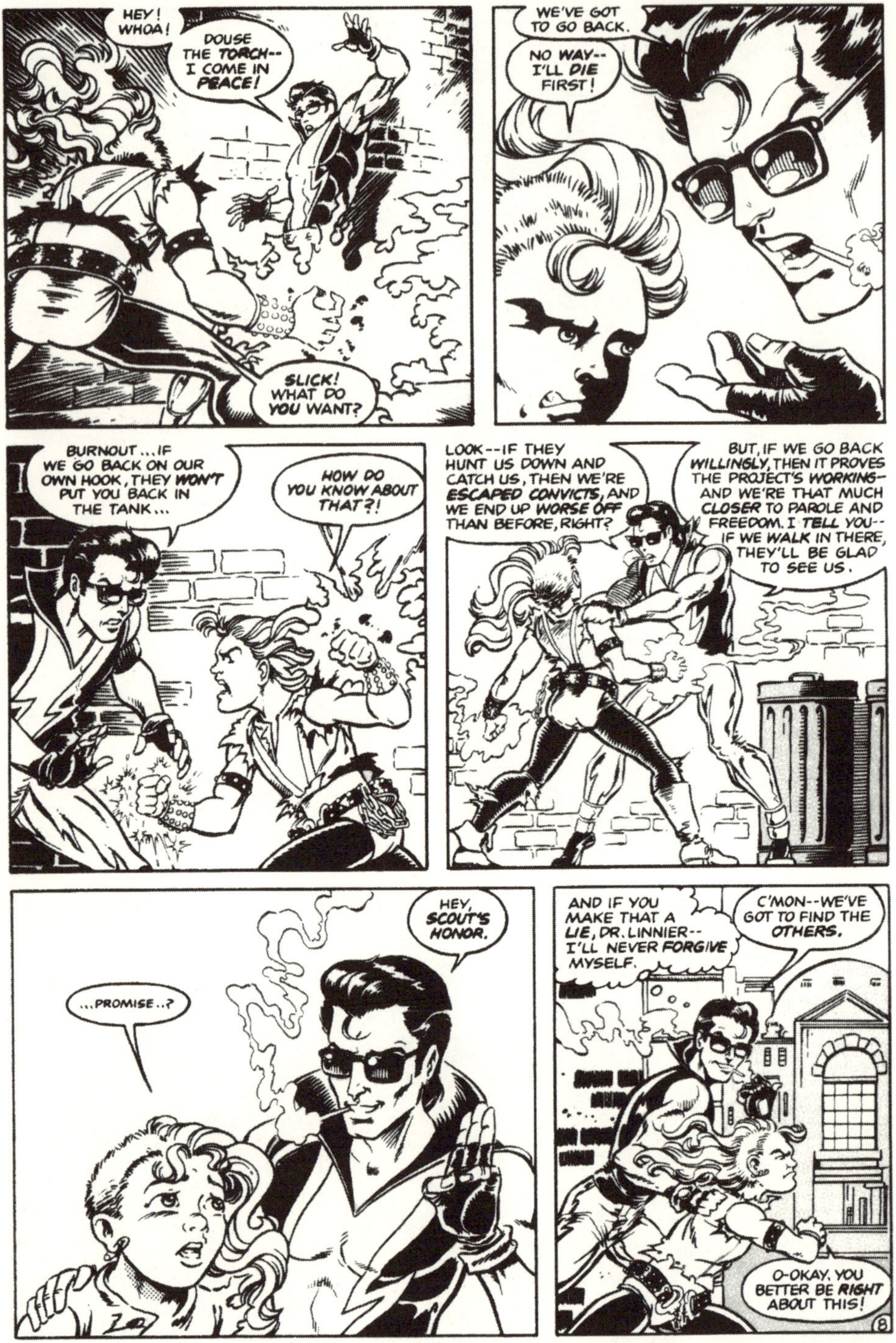
HEY! WHOA!
DOUSE THE TORCH-- I COME IN PEACE!
SLICK! WHAT DO YOU WANT?
WE'VE GOT TO GO BACK.
NO WAY-- I'LL DIE FIRST!
BURNOUT...IF WE GO BACK ON OUR OWN HOOK, THEY WON'T PUT YOU BACK IN THE TANK...
HOW DO YOU KNOW ABOUT THAT?!
LOOK--IF THEY HUNT US DOWN AND CATCH US, THEN WE'RE ESCAPED CONVICTS, AND WE END UP WORSE OFF THAN BEFORE, RIGHT?
BUT, IF WE GO BACK WILLINGLY, THEN IT PROVES THE PROJECT'S WORKING-- AND WE'RE THAT MUCH CLOSER TO PAROLE AND FREEDOM. I TELL YOU-- IF WE WALK IN THERE, THEY'LL BE GLAD TO SEE US.
...PROMISE..?
HEY, SCOUT'S HONOR.
AND IF YOU MAKE THAT A LIE, DR. LINNIER-- I'LL NEVER FORGIVE MYSELF.
C'MON--WE'VE GOT TO FIND THE OTHERS.
O-OKAY. YOU BETTER BE RIGHT ABOUT THIS!
8

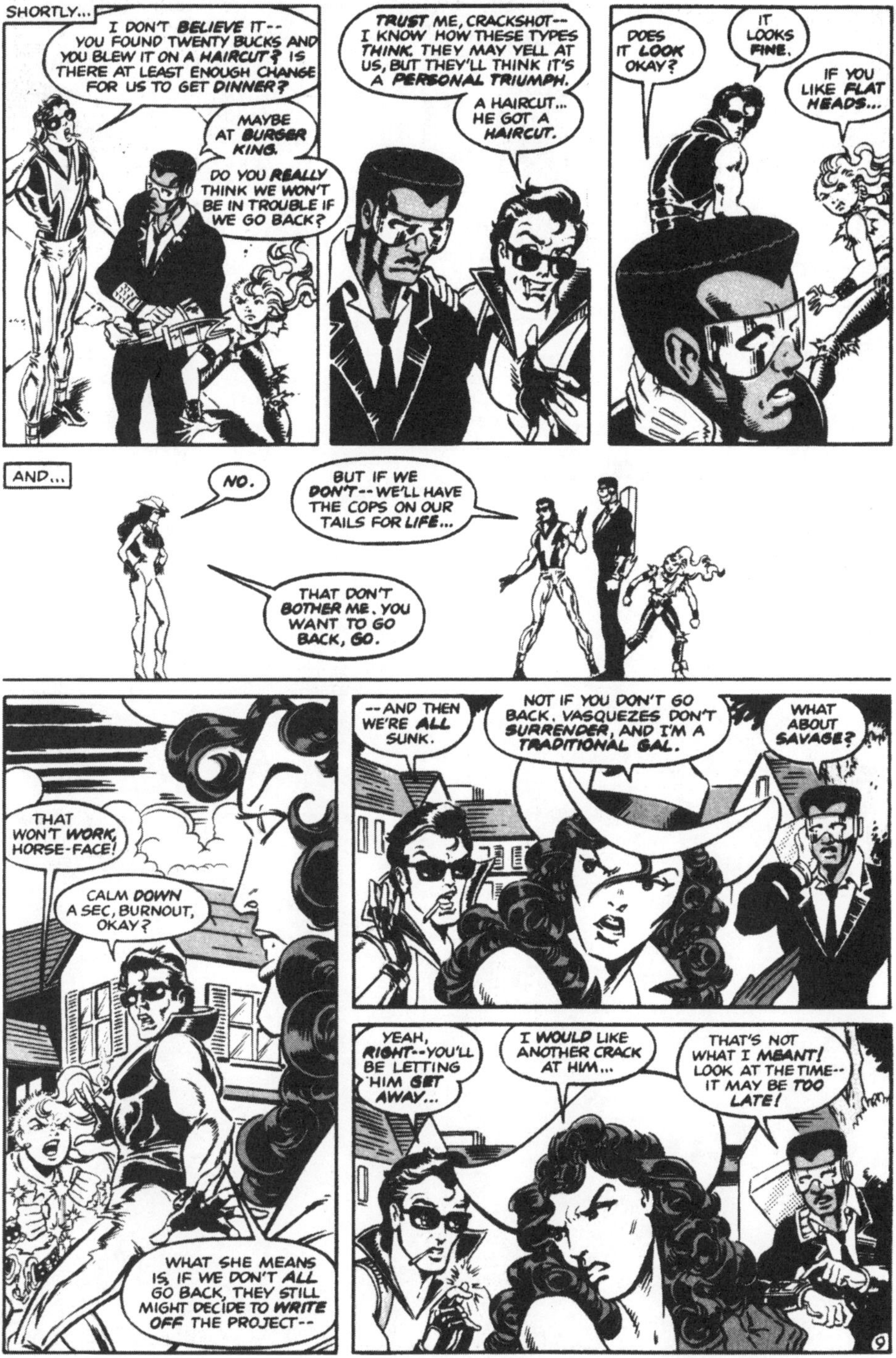
SHORTLY...
I DON'T BELIEVE IT-- YOU FOUND TWENTY BUCKS AND YOU BLEW IT ON A HAIRCUT? IS THERE AT LEAST ENOUGH CHANGE FOR US TO GET DINNER?
MAYBE AT BURGER KING.
DO YOU REALLY THINK WE WON'T BE IN TROUBLE IF WE GO BACK?
TRUST ME, CRACKSHOT-- I KNOW HOW THESE TYPES THINK. THEY MAY YELL AT US, BUT THEY'LL THINK IT'S A PERSONAL TRIUMPH.
A HAIRCUT... HE GOT A HAIRCUT.
DOES IT LOOK OKAY?
IT LOOKS FINE.
IF YOU LIKE FLAT HEADS...
AND...
NO.
BUT IF WE DON'T-- WE'LL HAVE THE COPS ON OUR TAILS FOR LIFE...
THAT DON'T BOTHER ME. YOU WANT TO GO BACK, GO.
THAT WON'T WORK, HORSE-FACE!
CALM DOWN A SEC, BURNOUT, OKAY?
WHAT SHE MEANS IS, IF WE DON'T ALL GO BACK, THEY STILL MIGHT DECIDE TO WRITE OFF THE PROJECT--
--AND THEN WE'RE ALL SUNK.
NOT IF YOU DON'T GO BACK. VASQUEZES DON'T SURRENDER, AND I'M A TRADITIONAL GAL.
WHAT ABOUT SAVAGE?
YEAH, RIGHT--YOU'LL BE LETTING HIM GET AWAY...
I WOULD LIKE ANOTHER CRACK AT HIM...
THAT'S NOT WHAT I MEANT! LOOK AT THE TIME-- IT MAY BE TOO LATE!
9

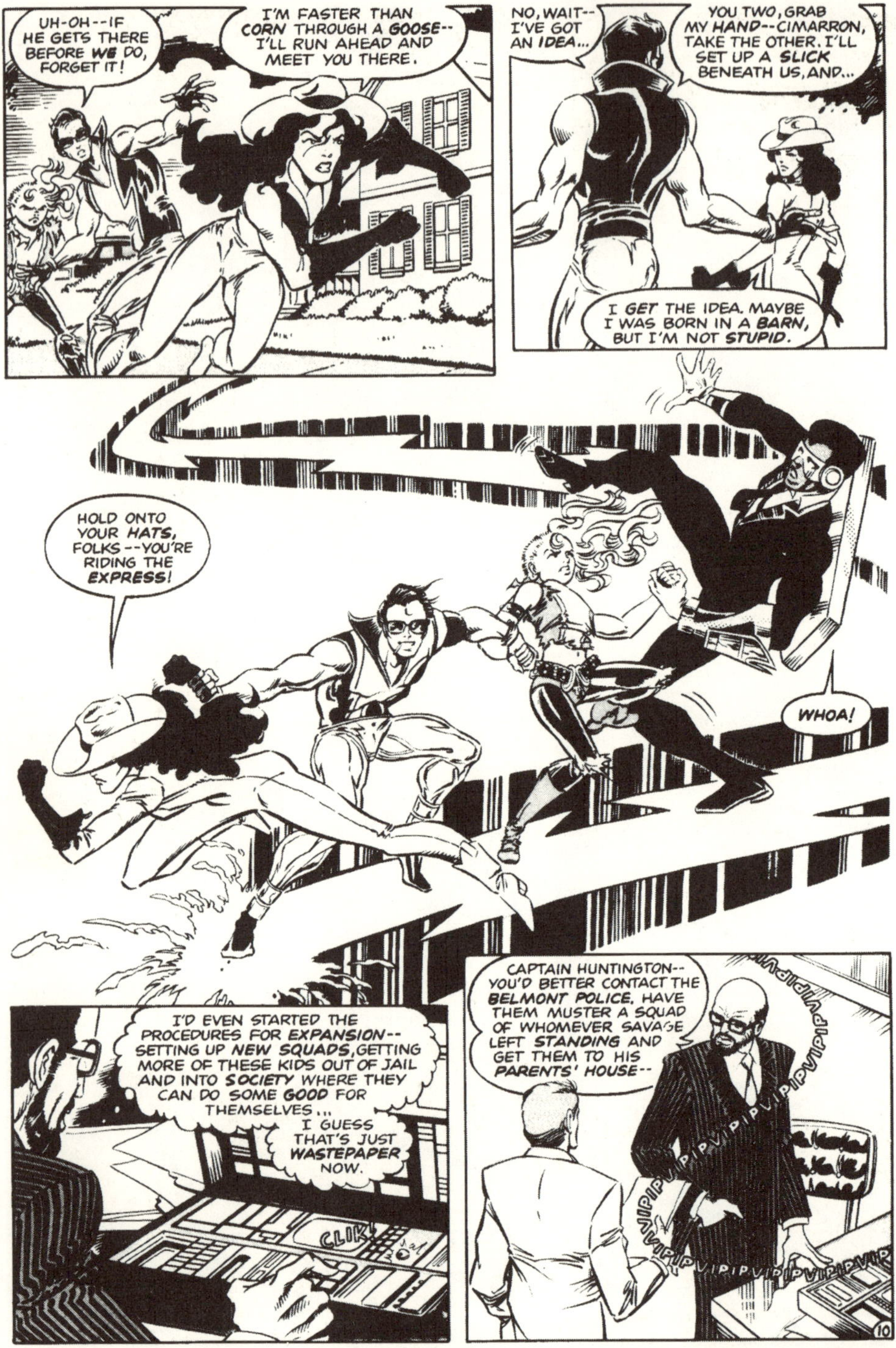

UH-OH--IF HE GETS THERE BEFORE WE DO, FORGET IT!
I'M FASTER THAN CORN THROUGH A GOOSE-- I'LL RUN AHEAD AND MEET YOU THERE.
NO, WAIT-- I'VE GOT AN IDEA...
YOU TWO, GRAB MY HAND--CIMARRON, TAKE THE OTHER. I'LL SET UP A SLICK BENEATH US, AND...
I GET THE IDEA. MAYBE I WAS BORN IN A BARN, BUT I'M NOT STUPID.
HOLD ONTO YOUR HATS, FOLKS--YOU'RE RIDING THE EXPRESS!
WHOA!
I'D EVEN STARTED THE PROCEDURES FOR EXPANSION-- SETTING UP NEW SQUADS, GETTING MORE OF THESE KIDS OUT OF JAIL AND INTO SOCIETY WHERE THEY CAN DO SOME GOOD FOR THEMSELVES...
I GUESS THAT'S JUST WASTEPAPER NOW.
CLIK!
CAPTAIN HUNTINGTON-- YOU'D BETTER CONTACT THE BELMONT POLICE. HAVE THEM MUSTER A SQUAD OF WHOMEVER SAVAGE LEFT STANDING AND GET THEM TO HIS PARENTS' HOUSE--
VIPIPVIPIPVIPIPVIPIPVIPIPVIP
10

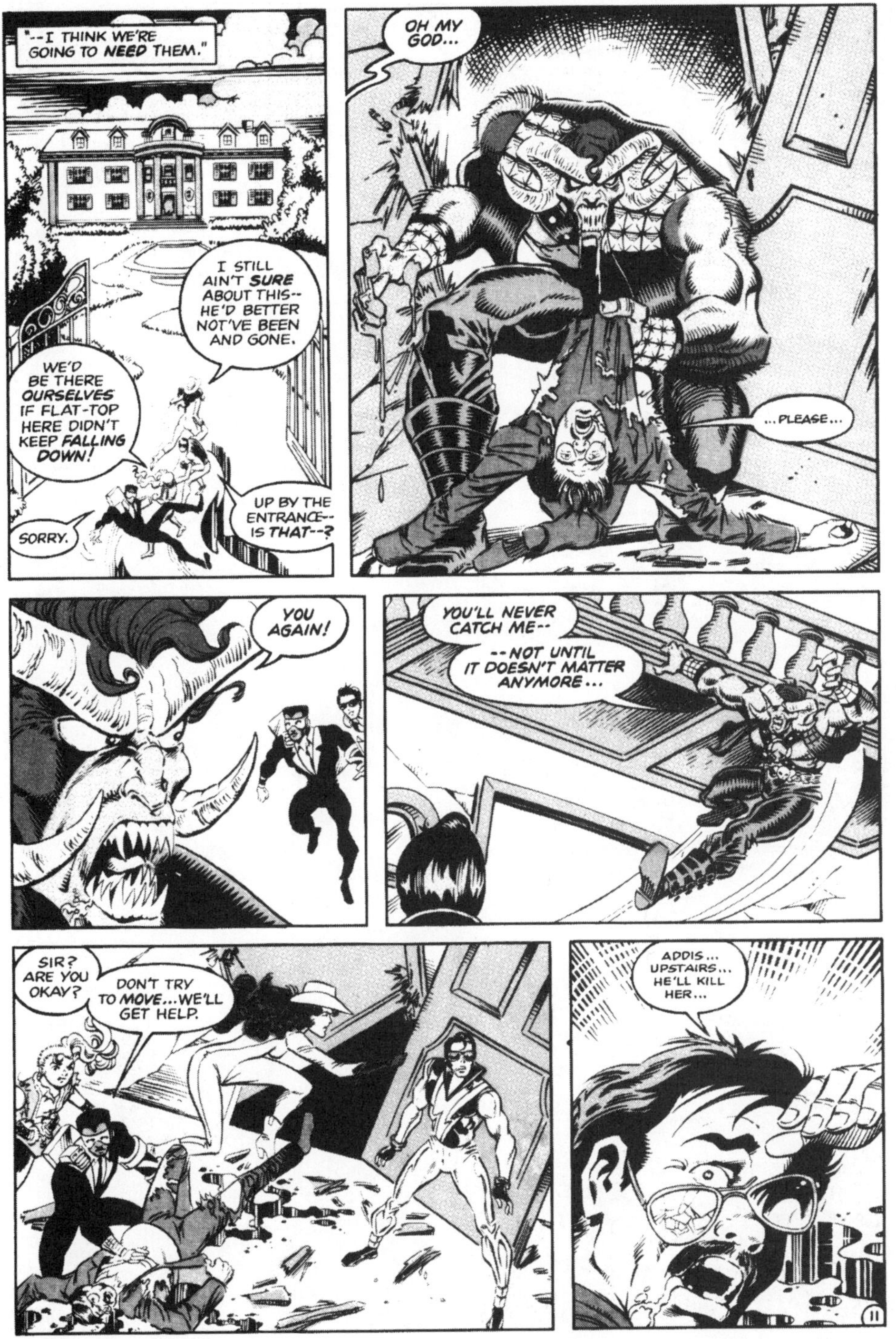
"--I THINK WE'RE GOING TO NEED THEM."
I STILL AIN'T SURE ABOUT THIS-- HE'D BETTER NOT'VE BEEN AND GONE.
WE'D BE THERE OURSELVES IF FLAT-TOP HERE DIDN'T KEEP FALLING DOWN!
SORRY.
UP BY THE ENTRANCE-- IS THAT--?
OH MY GOD...
...PLEASE...
YOU AGAIN!
YOU'LL NEVER CATCH ME--
--NOT UNTIL IT DOESN'T MATTER ANYMORE...
SIR? ARE YOU OKAY?
DON'T TRY TO MOVE...WE'LL GET HELP.
ADDIS... UPSTAIRS... HE'LL KILL HER...
11

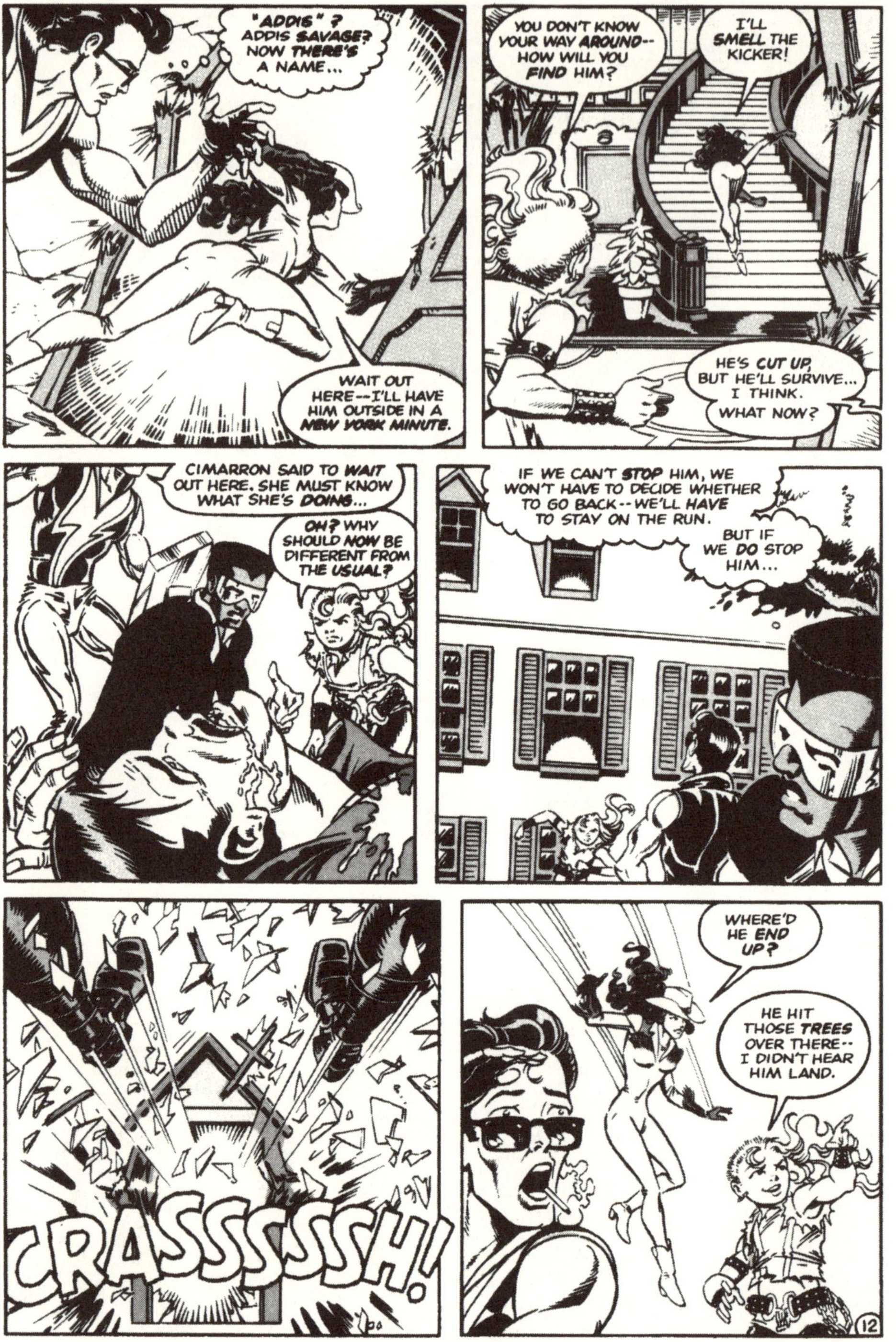
"ADDIS"? ADDIS SAVAGE? NOW THERE'S A NAME...
WAIT OUT HERE--I'LL HAVE HIM OUTSIDE IN A NEW YORK MINUTE.
YOU DON'T KNOW YOUR WAY AROUND--HOW WILL YOU FIND HIM?
I'LL SMELL THE KICKER!
HE'S CUT UP, BUT HE'LL SURVIVE... I THINK.
WHAT NOW?
CIMARRON SAID TO WAIT OUT HERE. SHE MUST KNOW WHAT SHE'S DOING...
OH? WHY SHOULD NOW BE DIFFERENT FROM THE USUAL?
IF WE CAN'T STOP HIM, WE WON'T HAVE TO DECIDE WHETHER TO GO BACK--WE'LL HAVE TO STAY ON THE RUN.
BUT IF WE DO STOP HIM...
CRASSSSSH!
WHERE'D HE END UP?
HE HIT THOSE TREES OVER THERE--I DIDN'T HEAR HIM LAND.
12

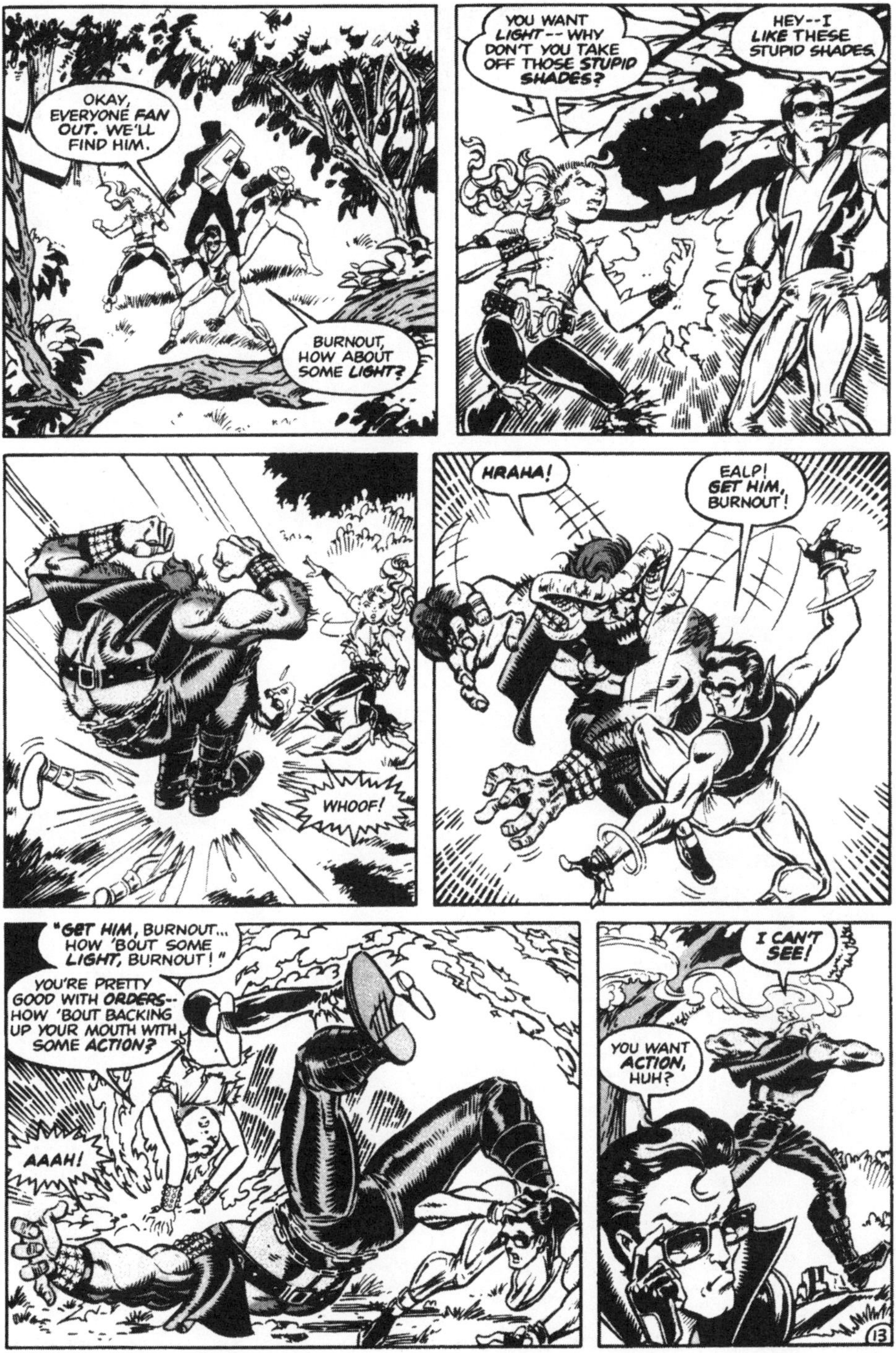
OKAY, EVERYONE FAN OUT. WE'LL FIND HIM.
BURNOUT, HOW ABOUT SOME LIGHT?
YOU WANT LIGHT-- WHY DON'T YOU TAKE OFF THOSE STUPID SHADES?
HEY--I LIKE THESE STUPID SHADES.
WHOOF!
HRAHA!
EALP! GET HIM, BURNOUT!
"GET HIM, BURNOUT... HOW 'BOUT SOME LIGHT, BURNOUT!"
YOU'RE PRETTY GOOD WITH ORDERS-- HOW 'BOUT BACKING UP YOUR MOUTH WITH SOME ACTION?
AAAH!
I CAN'T SEE!
YOU WANT ACTION, HUH?
13

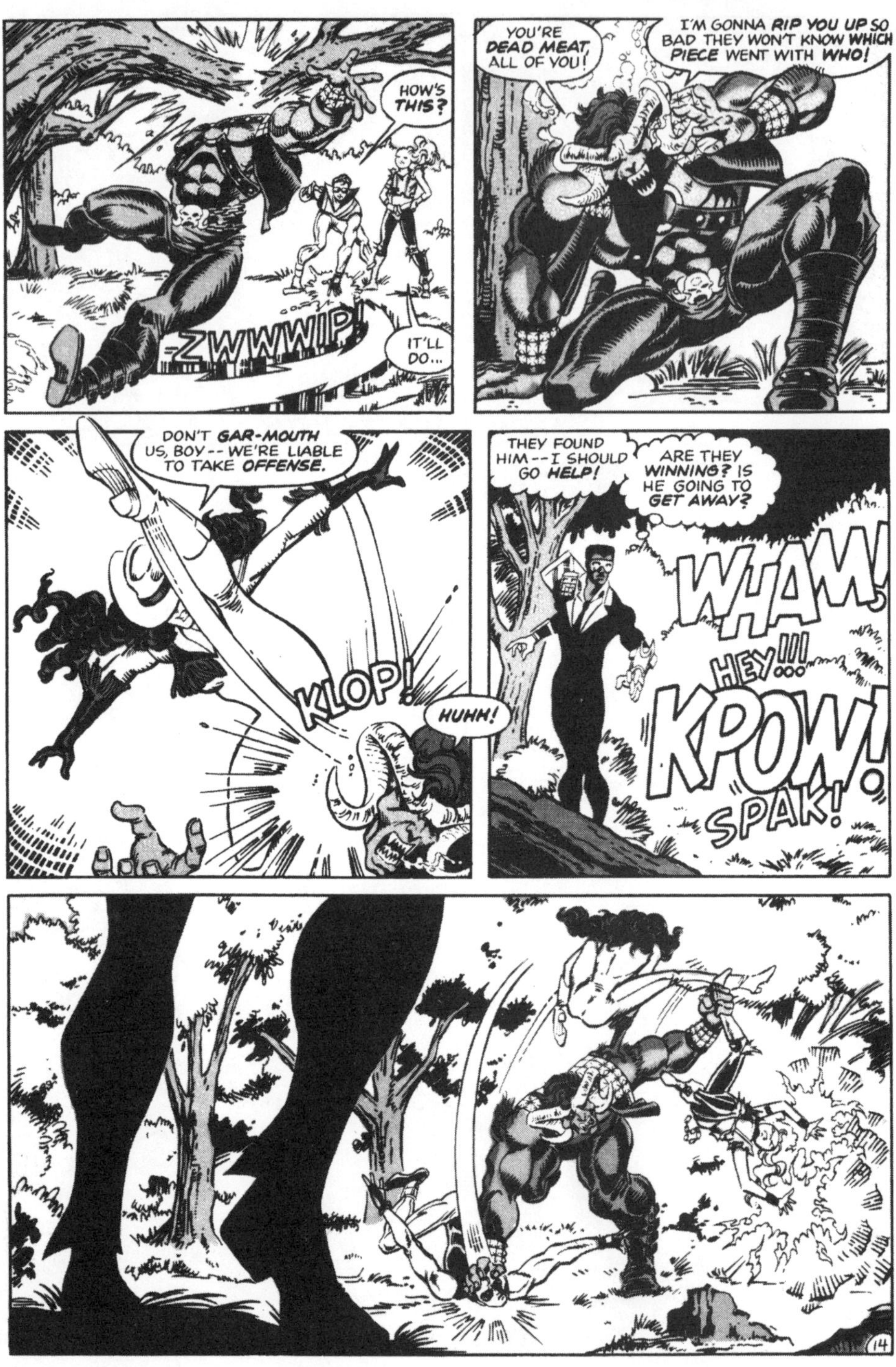
HOW'S THIS?
ZWWWIP!
IT'LL DO...
YOU'RE DEAD MEAT, ALL OF YOU!
I'M GONNA RIP YOU UP SO BAD THEY WON'T KNOW WHICH PIECE WENT WITH WHO!
DON'T GAR-MOUTH US, BOY-- WE'RE LIABLE TO TAKE OFFENSE.
KLOP!
HUHH!
THEY FOUND HIM--I SHOULD GO HELP!
ARE THEY WINNING? IS HE GOING TO GET AWAY?
WHAM!
HEY!!!...
KPOW!
SPAK!
14

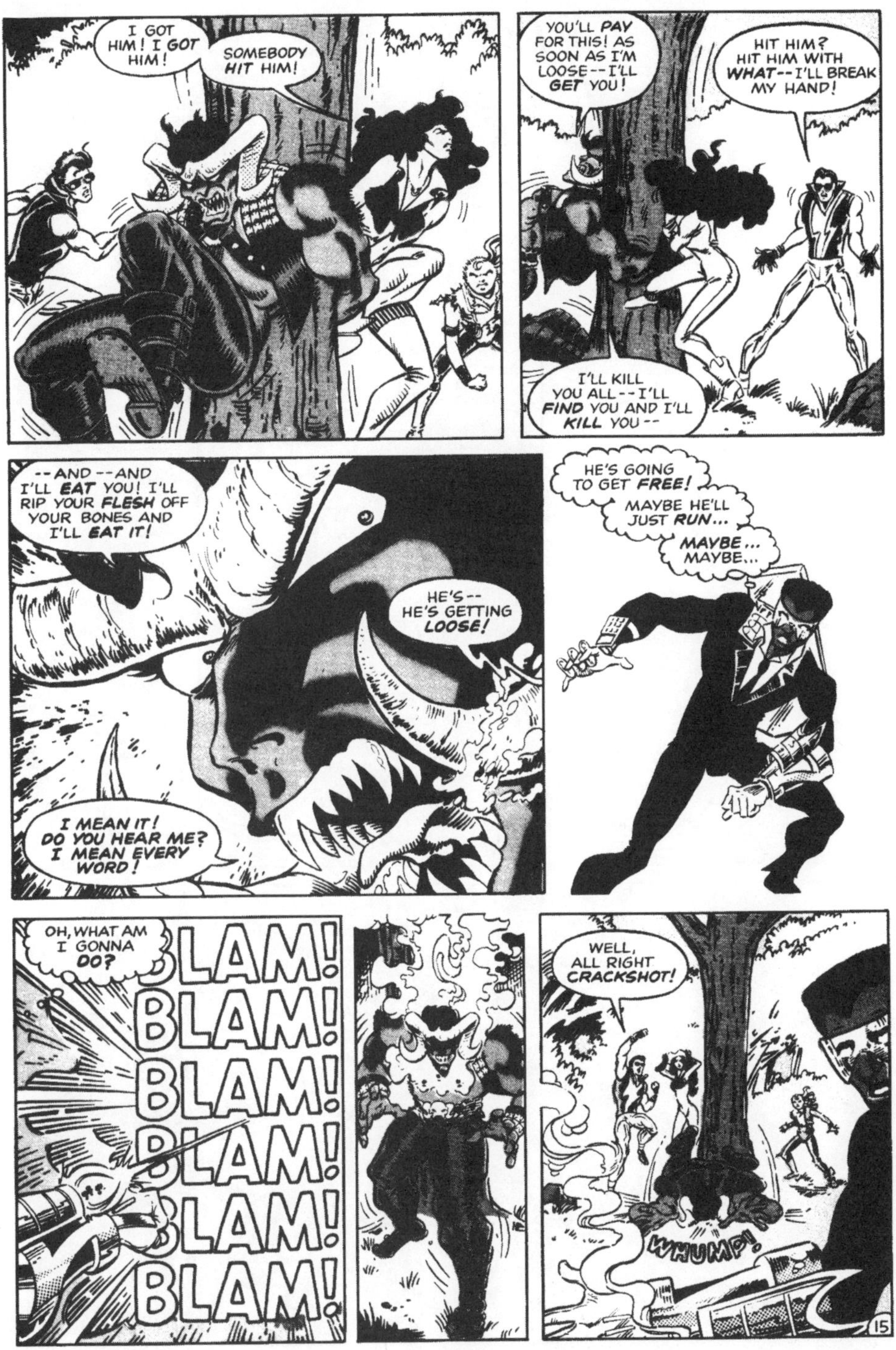
I GOT HIM! I GOT HIM!
SOMEBODY HIT HIM!
YOU'LL PAY FOR THIS! AS SOON AS I'M LOOSE--I'LL GET YOU!
HIT HIM? HIT HIM WITH WHAT--I'LL BREAK MY HAND!
I'LL KILL YOU ALL--I'LL FIND YOU AND I'LL KILL YOU--
--AND--AND I'LL EAT YOU! I'LL RIP YOUR FLESH OFF YOUR BONES AND I'LL EAT IT!
HE'S-- HE'S GETTING LOOSE!
I MEAN IT! DO YOU HEAR ME? I MEAN EVERY WORD!
HE'S GOING TO GET FREE!
MAYBE HE'LL JUST RUN...
MAYBE... MAYBE...
OH, WHAT AM I GONNA DO?
BLAM! BLAM! BLAM! BLAM! BLAM! BLAM!
WELL, ALL RIGHT CRACKSHOT!
WHUMP!
15

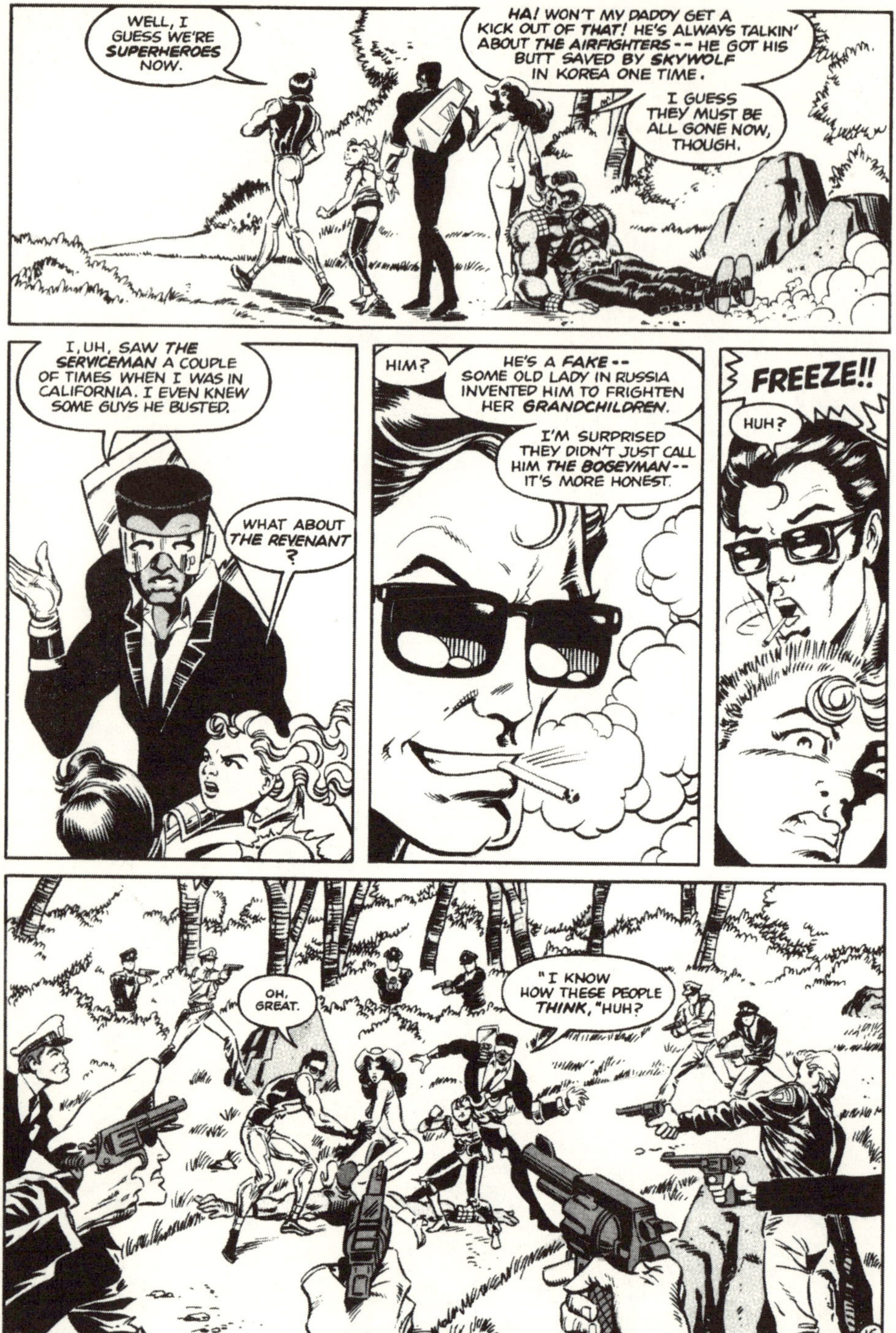
WELL, I GUESS WE'RE SUPERHEROES NOW.
HA! WON'T MY DADDY GET A KICK OUT OF THAT! HE'S ALWAYS TALKIN' ABOUT THE AIRFIGHTERS -- HE GOT HIS BUTT SAVED BY SKYWOLF IN KOREA ONE TIME.
I GUESS THEY MUST BE ALL GONE NOW, THOUGH.
I, UH, SAW THE SERVICEMAN A COUPLE OF TIMES WHEN I WAS IN CALIFORNIA. I EVEN KNEW SOME GUYS HE BUSTED.
WHAT ABOUT THE REVENANT ?
HIM?
HE'S A FAKE -- SOME OLD LADY IN RUSSIA INVENTED HIM TO FRIGHTEN HER GRANDCHILDREN.
I'M SURPRISED THEY DIDN'T JUST CALL HIM THE BOGEYMAN -- IT'S MORE HONEST.
FREEZE!!
HUH?
OH, GREAT.
"I KNOW HOW THESE PEOPLE THINK," HUH?
16

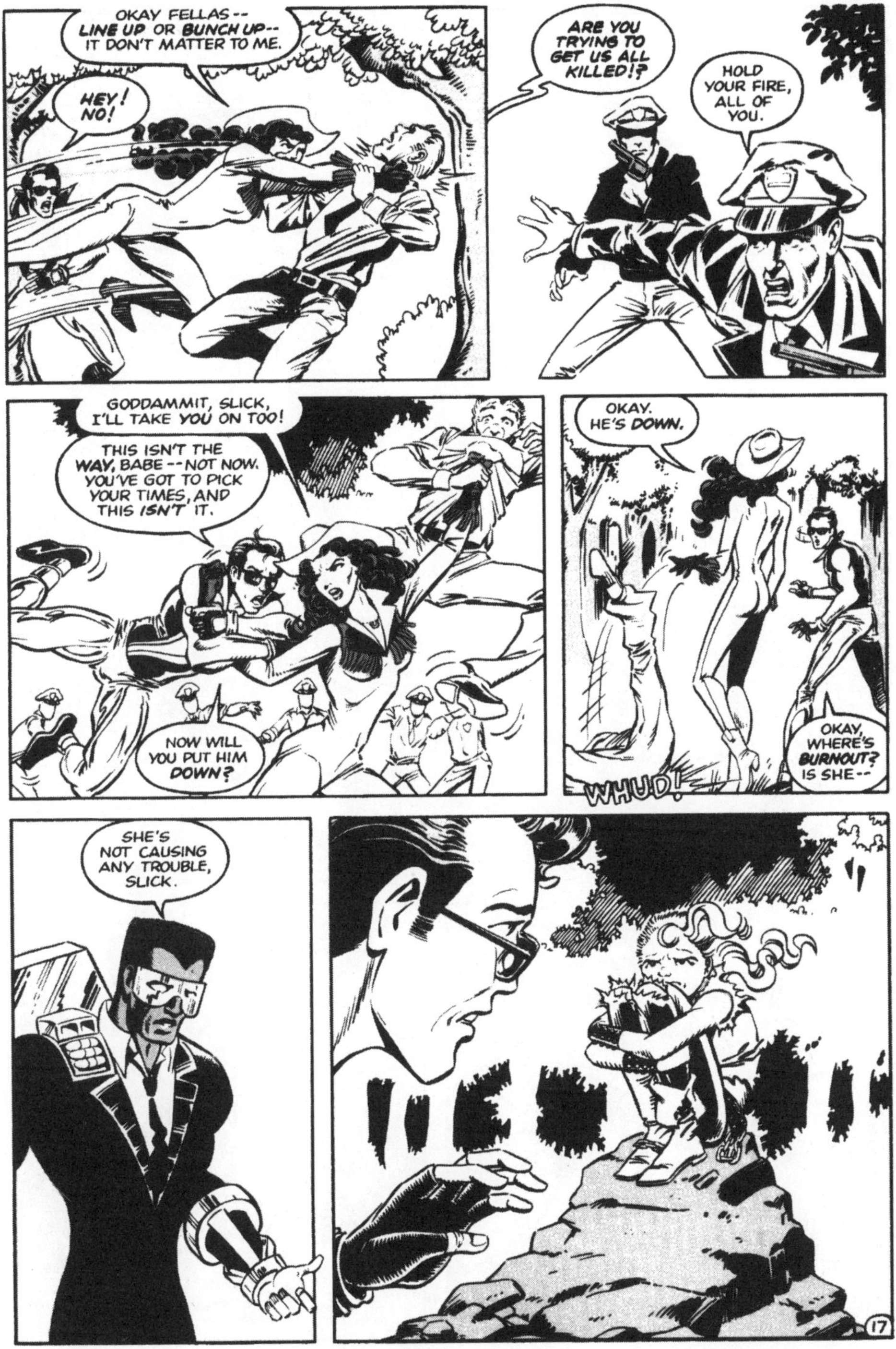
OKAY FELLAS-- LINE UP OR BUNCH UP-- IT DON'T MATTER TO ME.
HEY! NO!
ARE YOU TRYING TO GET US ALL KILLED!?
HOLD YOUR FIRE, ALL OF YOU.
GODDAMMIT, SLICK, I'LL TAKE YOU ON TOO!
THIS ISN'T THE WAY, BABE--NOT NOW. YOU'VE GOT TO PICK YOUR TIMES, AND THIS ISN'T IT.
NOW WILL YOU PUT HIM DOWN?
OKAY. HE'S DOWN.
WHUD!
OKAY, WHERE'S BURNOUT? IS SHE--
SHE'S NOT CAUSING ANY TROUBLE, SLICK.
17

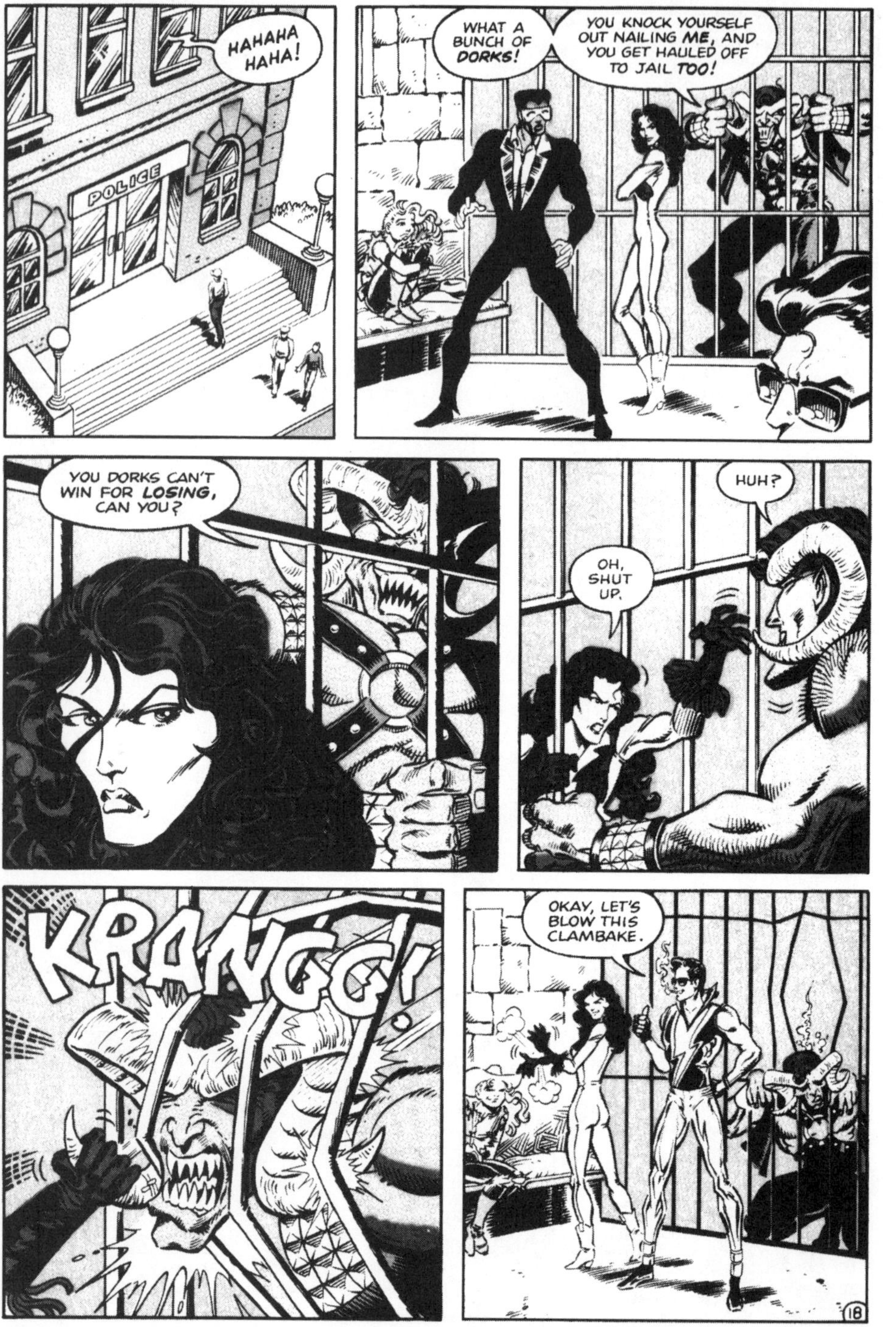
HAHAHA HAHA!
POLICE
WHAT A BUNCH OF DORKS!
YOU KNOCK YOURSELF OUT NAILING ME, AND YOU GET HAULED OFF TO JAIL TOO!
YOU DORKS CAN'T WIN FOR LOSING, CAN YOU?
HUH?
OH, SHUT UP.
KRANGG!
OKAY, LET'S BLOW THIS CLAMBAKE.
18

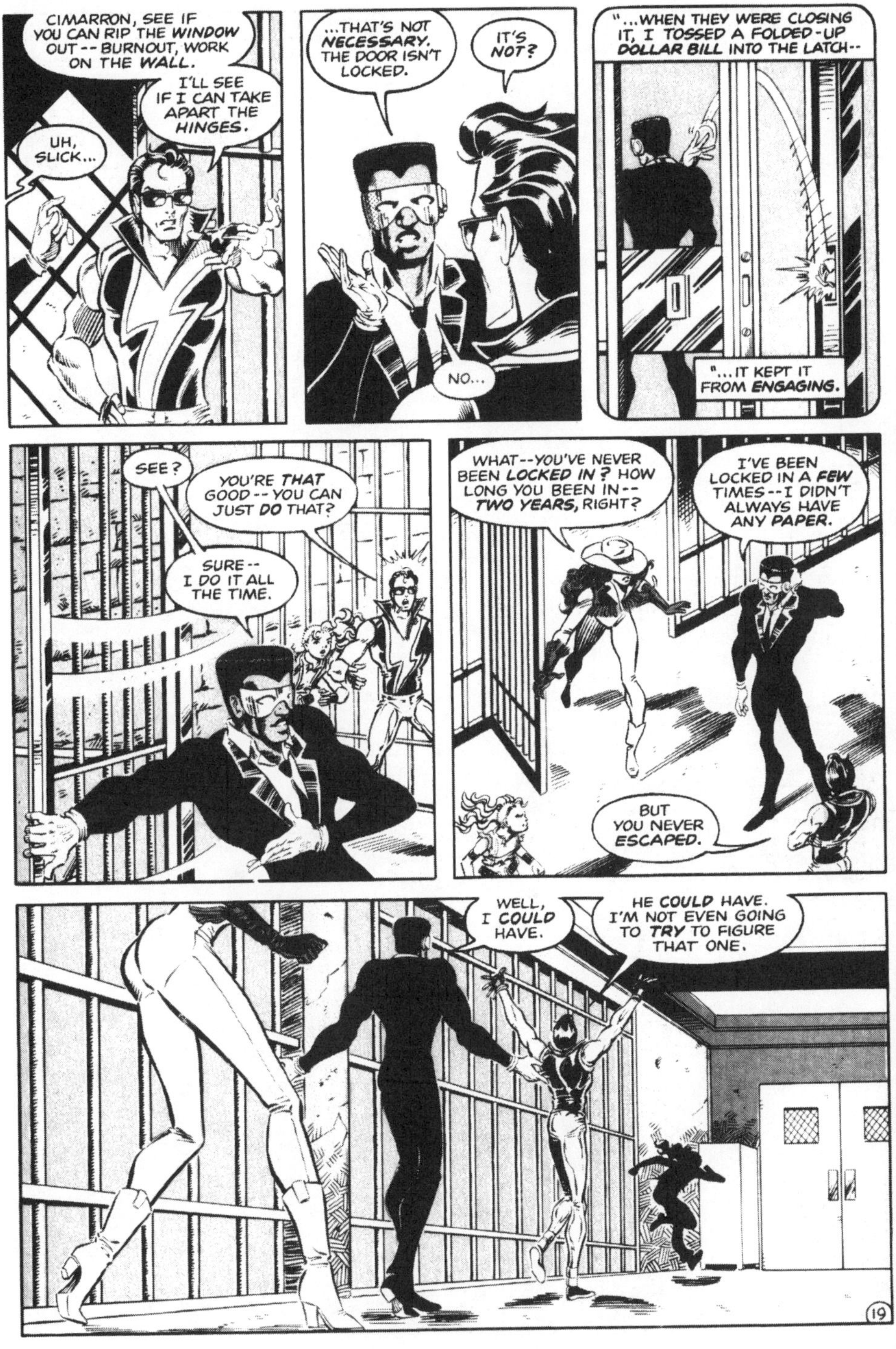

CIMARRON, SEE IF YOU CAN RIP THE WINDOW OUT -- BURNOUT, WORK ON THE WALL.
I'LL SEE IF I CAN TAKE APART THE HINGES.
UH, SLICK...
...THAT'S NOT NECESSARY. THE DOOR ISN'T LOCKED.
IT'S NOT?
NO...
"...WHEN THEY WERE CLOSING IT, I TOSSED A FOLDED-UP DOLLAR BILL INTO THE LATCH--
"...IT KEPT IT FROM ENGAGING.
SEE?
YOU'RE THAT GOOD -- YOU CAN JUST DO THAT?
SURE -- I DO IT ALL THE TIME.
WHAT--YOU'VE NEVER BEEN LOCKED IN? HOW LONG YOU BEEN IN -- TWO YEARS, RIGHT?
I'VE BEEN LOCKED IN A FEW TIMES -- I DIDN'T ALWAYS HAVE ANY PAPER.
BUT YOU NEVER ESCAPED.
WELL, I COULD HAVE.
HE COULD HAVE. I'M NOT EVEN GOING TO TRY TO FIGURE THAT ONE.
19

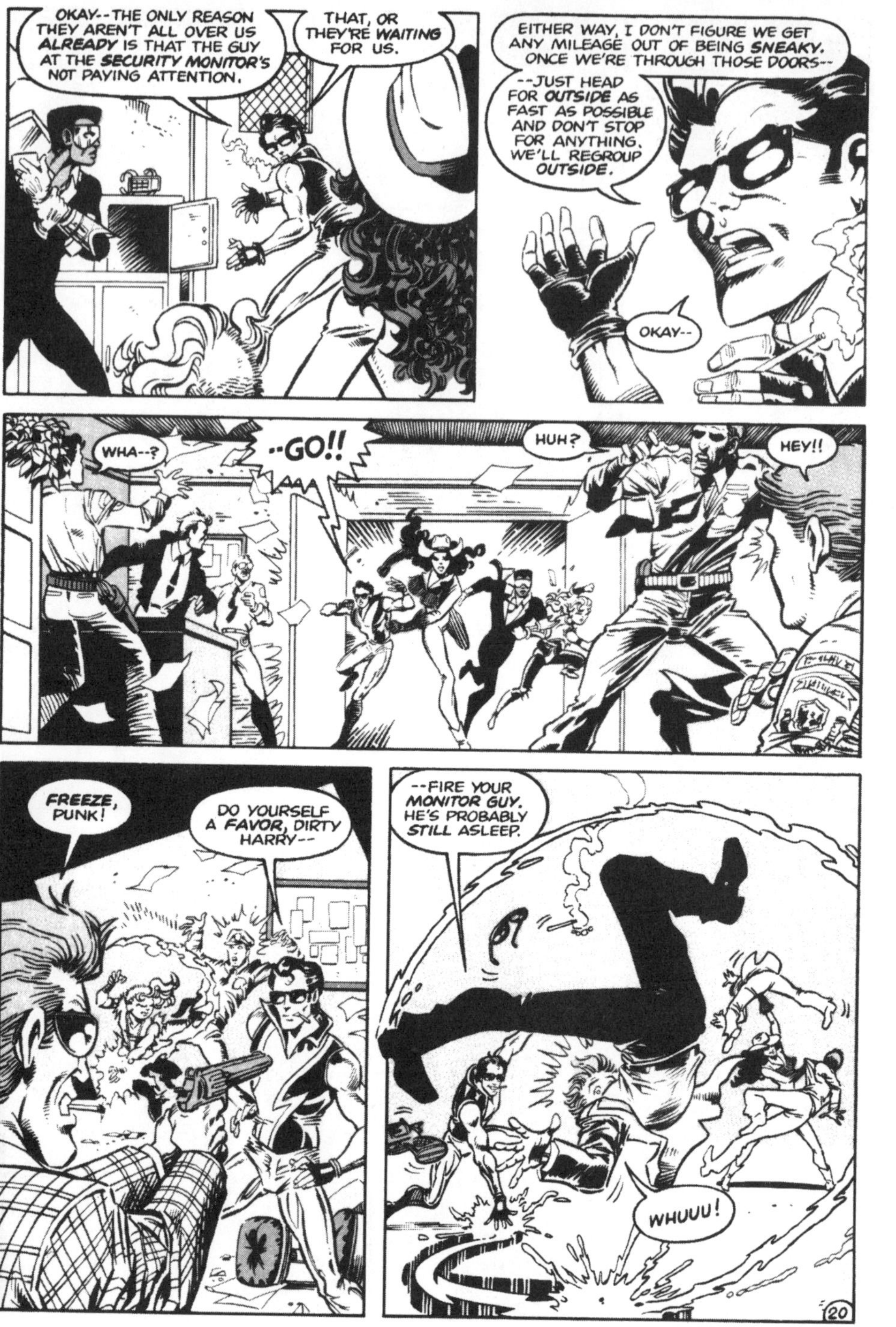

OKAY--THE ONLY REASON THEY AREN'T ALL OVER US ALREADY IS THAT THE GUY AT THE SECURITY MONITOR'S NOT PAYING ATTENTION.
THAT, OR THEY'RE WAITING FOR US.
EITHER WAY, I DON'T FIGURE WE GET ANY MILEAGE OUT OF BEING SNEAKY. ONCE WE'RE THROUGH THOSE DOORS--
--JUST HEAD FOR OUTSIDE AS FAST AS POSSIBLE AND DON'T STOP FOR ANYTHING. WE'LL REGROUP OUTSIDE.
OKAY--
WHA--?
--GO!!
HUH?
HEY!!
FREEZE, PUNK!
DO YOURSELF A FAVOR, DIRTY HARRY--
--FIRE YOUR MONITOR GUY. HE'S PROBABLY STILL ASLEEP.
WHUUU!
20

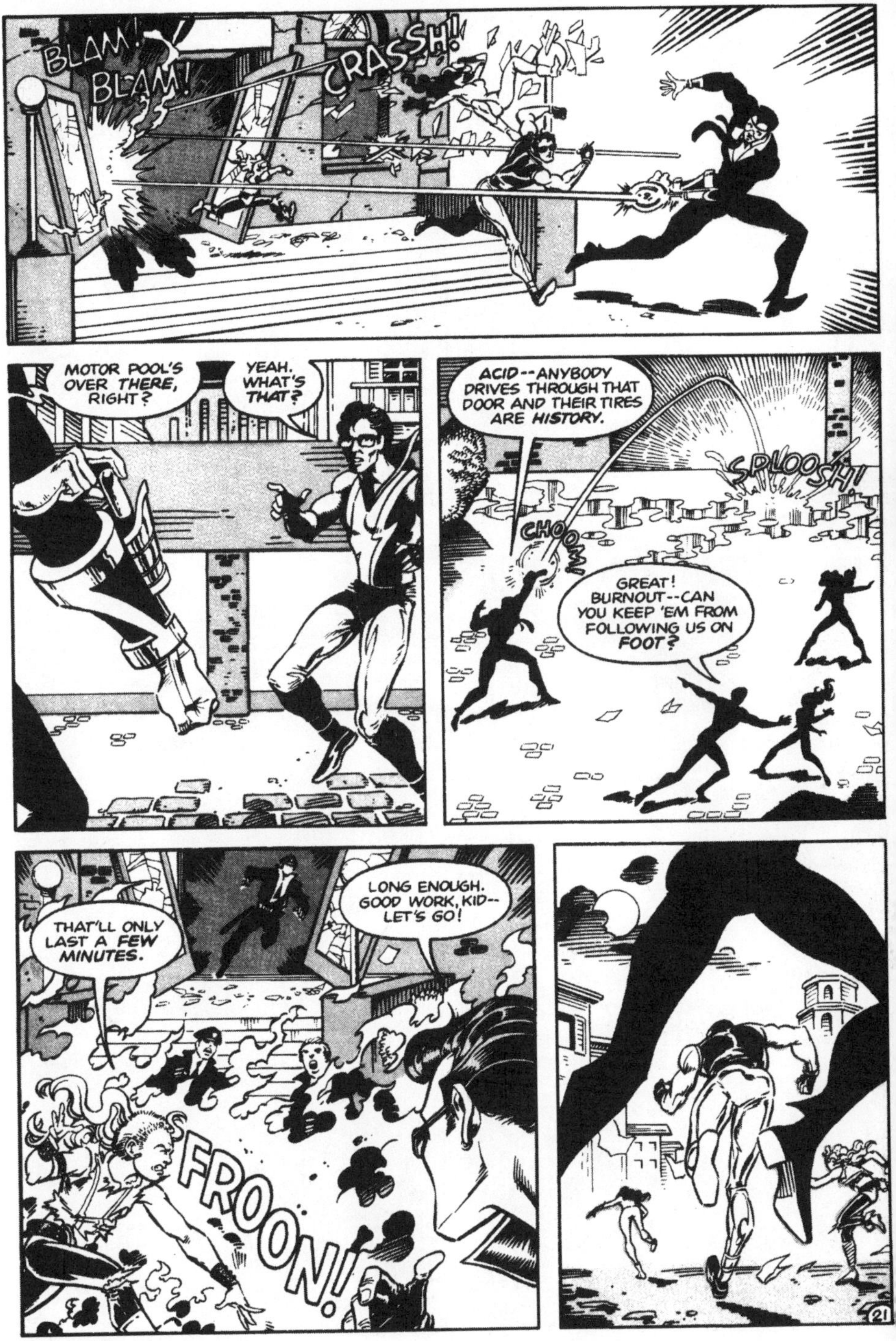

BLAM! BLAM!
CRASSH!
MOTOR POOL'S OVER THERE, RIGHT?
YEAH. WHAT'S THAT?
ACID--ANYBODY DRIVES THROUGH THAT DOOR AND THEIR TIRES ARE HISTORY.
SPLOOSH!
CHOOM!
GREAT! BURNOUT--CAN YOU KEEP 'EM FROM FOLLOWING US ON FOOT?
THAT'LL ONLY LAST A FEW MINUTES.
LONG ENOUGH. GOOD WORK, KID-- LET'S GO!
FROOON!
21

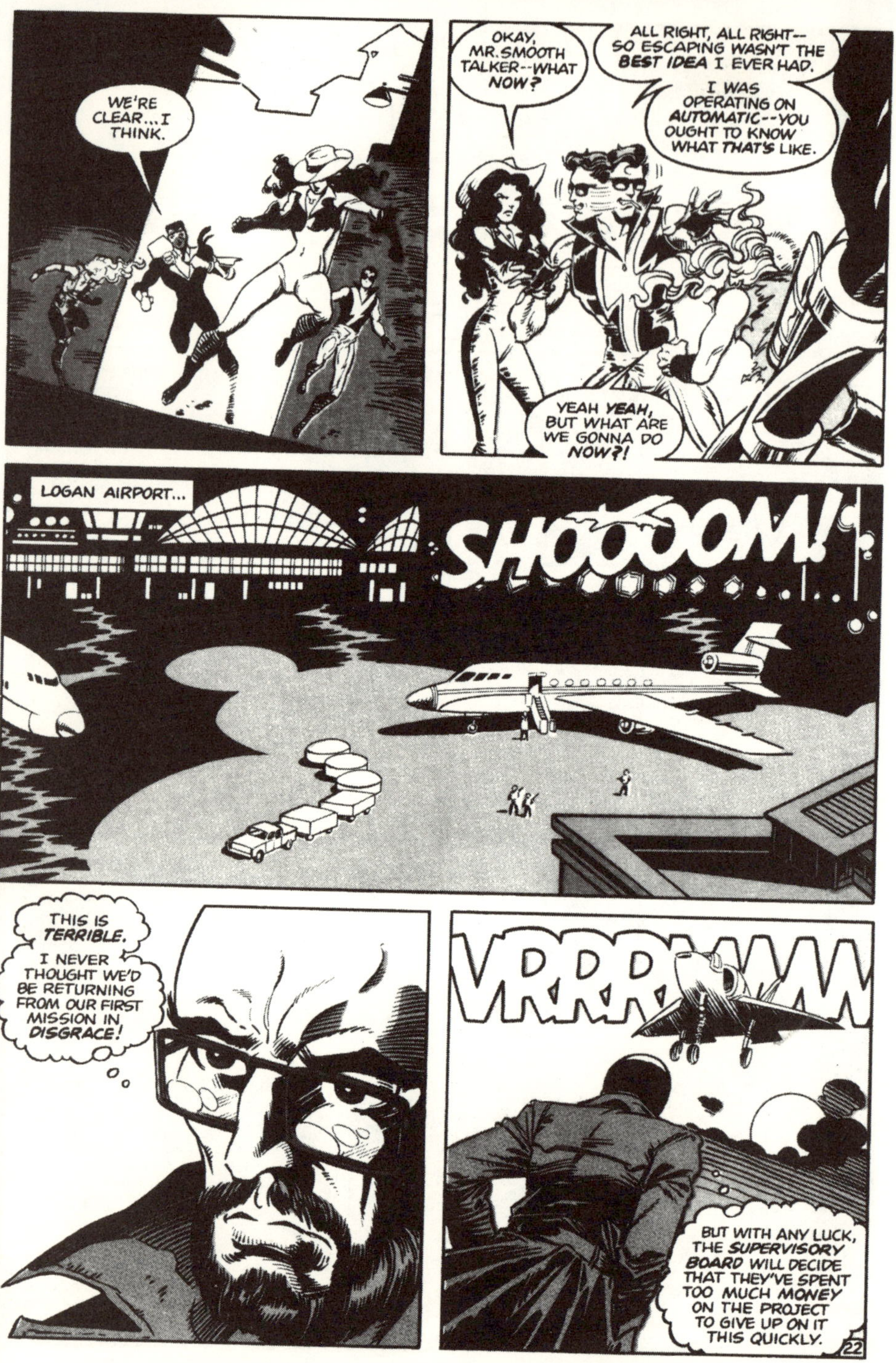
WE'RE CLEAR... I THINK.
OKAY, MR. SMOOTH TALKER--WHAT NOW?
ALL RIGHT, ALL RIGHT-- SO ESCAPING WASN'T THE BEST IDEA I EVER HAD.
I WAS OPERATING ON AUTOMATIC--YOU OUGHT TO KNOW WHAT THAT'S LIKE.
YEAH YEAH, BUT WHAT ARE WE GONNA DO NOW?!
LOGAN AIRPORT...
SHOOOOM!
THIS IS TERRIBLE.
I NEVER THOUGHT WE'D BE RETURNING FROM OUR FIRST MISSION IN DISGRACE!
VRRRMMM
BUT WITH ANY LUCK, THE SUPERVISORY BOARD WILL DECIDE THAT THEY'VE SPENT TOO MUCH MONEY ON THE PROJECT TO GIVE UP ON IT THIS QUICKLY.
22

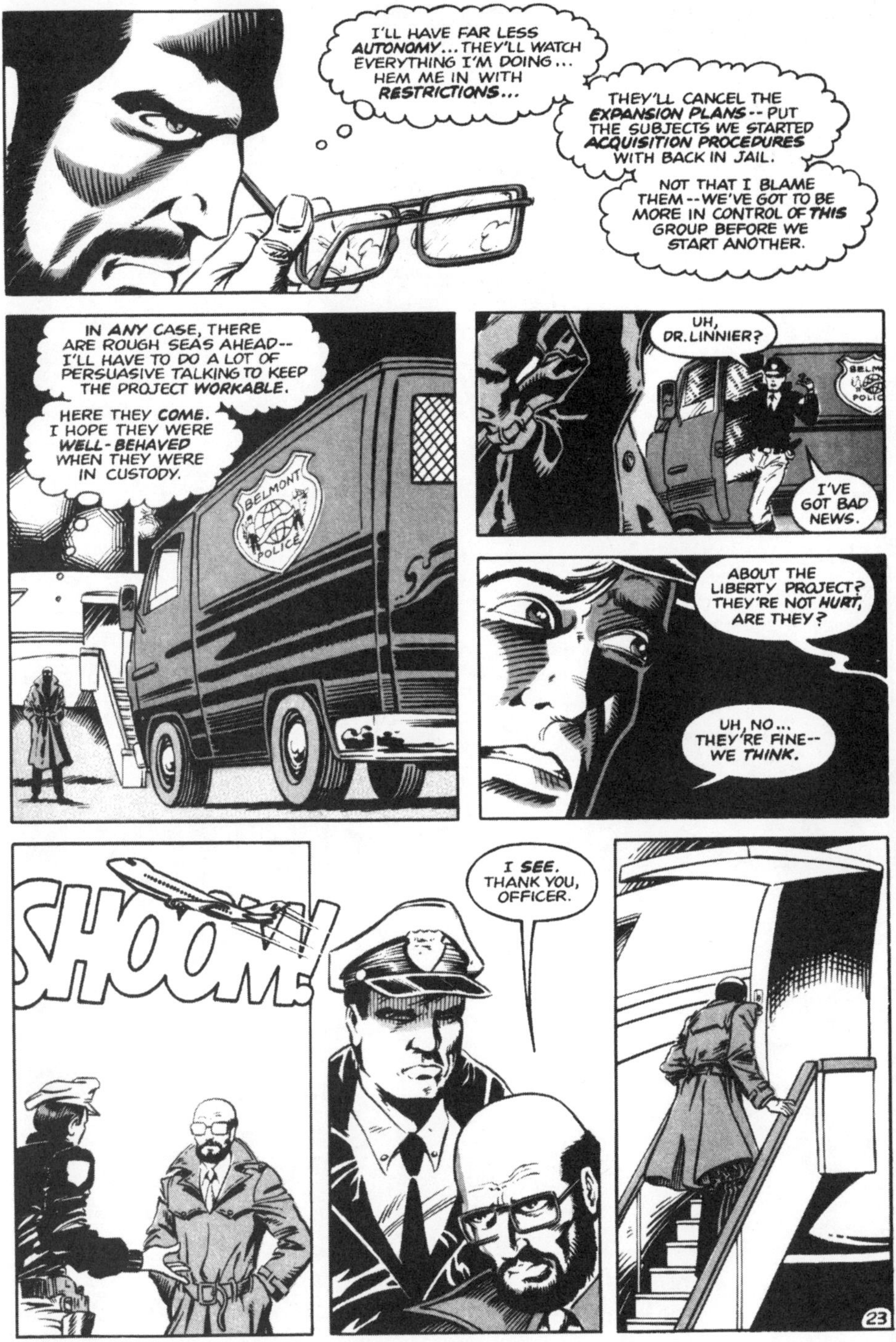
I'LL HAVE FAR LESS AUTONOMY... THEY'LL WATCH EVERYTHING I'M DOING... HEM ME IN WITH RESTRICTIONS...
THEY'LL CANCEL THE EXPANSION PLANS-- PUT THE SUBJECTS WE STARTED ACQUISITION PROCEDURES WITH BACK IN JAIL.
NOT THAT I BLAME THEM--WE'VE GOT TO BE MORE IN CONTROL OF THIS GROUP BEFORE WE START ANOTHER.
IN ANY CASE, THERE ARE ROUGH SEAS AHEAD-- I'LL HAVE TO DO A LOT OF PERSUASIVE TALKING TO KEEP THE PROJECT WORKABLE.
HERE THEY COME. I HOPE THEY WERE WELL-BEHAVED WHEN THEY WERE IN CUSTODY.
BELMONT POLICE
UH, DR. LINNIER?
I'VE GOT BAD NEWS.
ABOUT THE LIBERTY PROJECT? THEY'RE NOT HURT, ARE THEY?
UH, NO... THEY'RE FINE-- WE THINK.
SHOOM!
I SEE. THANK YOU, OFFICER.
23

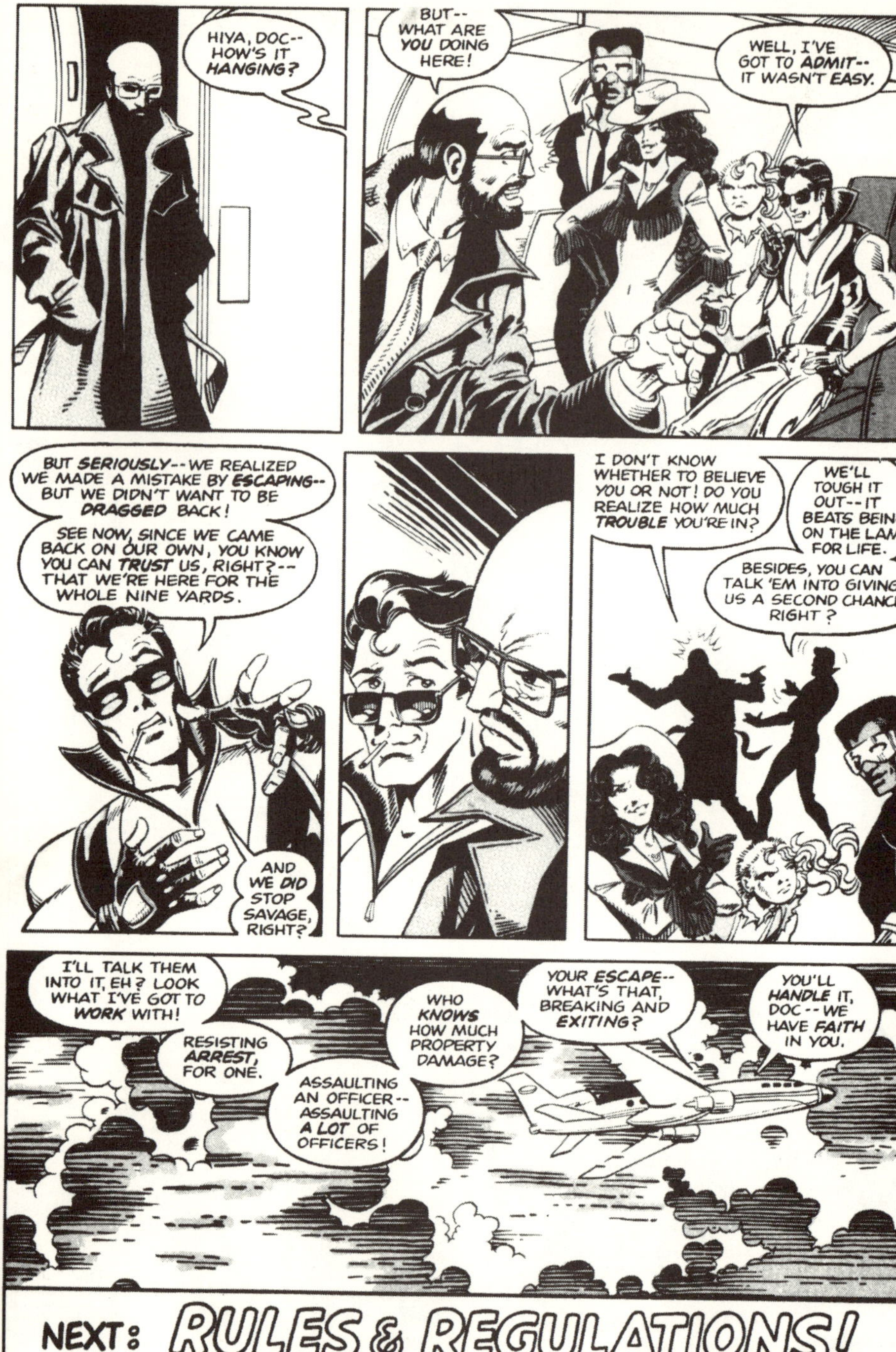
HIYA, DOC-- HOW'S IT HANGING?
BUT-- WHAT ARE YOU DOING HERE!
WELL, I'VE GOT TO ADMIT-- IT WASN'T EASY.
BUT SERIOUSLY--WE REALIZED WE MADE A MISTAKE BY ESCAPING-- BUT WE DIDN'T WANT TO BE DRAGGED BACK!
SEE NOW, SINCE WE CAME BACK ON OUR OWN, YOU KNOW YOU CAN TRUST US, RIGHT?-- THAT WE'RE HERE FOR THE WHOLE NINE YARDS.
AND WE DID STOP SAVAGE, RIGHT?
I DON'T KNOW WHETHER TO BELIEVE YOU OR NOT! DO YOU REALIZE HOW MUCH TROUBLE YOU'RE IN?
WE'LL TOUGH IT OUT-- IT BEATS BEING ON THE LAM FOR LIFE.
BESIDES, YOU CAN TALK 'EM INTO GIVING US A SECOND CHANCE, RIGHT?
I'LL TALK THEM INTO IT, EH? LOOK WHAT I'VE GOT TO WORK WITH!
RESISTING ARREST, FOR ONE.
WHO KNOWS HOW MUCH PROPERTY DAMAGE?
ASSAULTING AN OFFICER-- ASSAULTING A LOT OF OFFICERS!
YOUR ESCAPE-- WHAT'S THAT, BREAKING AND EXITING?
YOU'LL HANDLE IT, DOC--WE HAVE FAITH IN YOU.
NEXT: RULES & REGULATIONS!

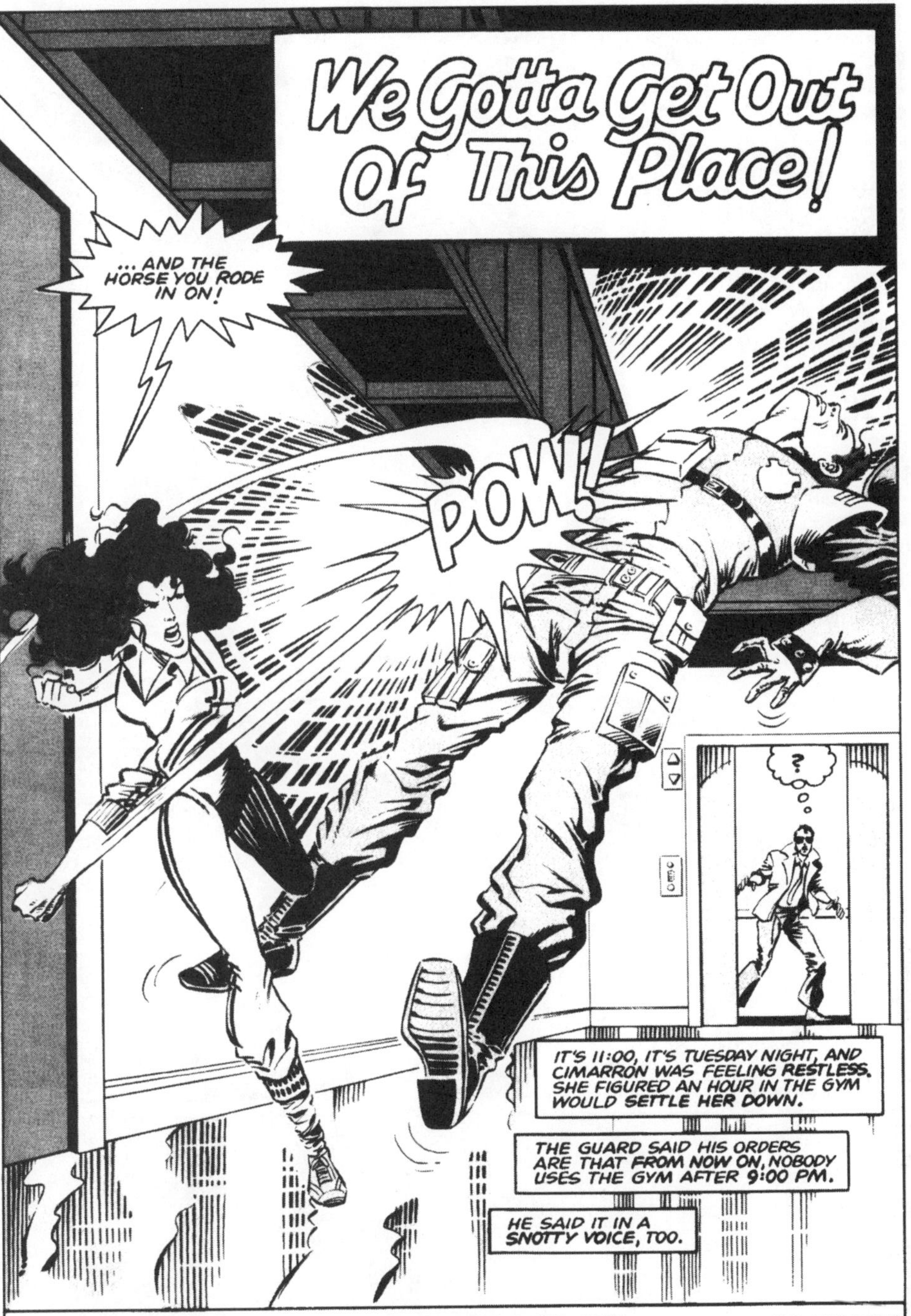
We Gotta Get Out Of This Place!
... AND THE HORSE YOU RODE IN ON!
POW!
?
IT'S 11:00, IT'S TUESDAY NIGHT, AND CIMARRON WAS FEELING RESTLESS. SHE FIGURED AN HOUR IN THE GYM WOULD SETTLE HER DOWN.
THE GUARD SAID HIS ORDERS ARE THAT FROM NOW ON, NOBODY USES THE GYM AFTER 9:00 PM.
HE SAID IT IN A SNOTTY VOICE, TOO.

KURT BUSIEK & JAMES W. FRY
WRITER · CO-CREATORS · PENCILER
DOUG HAZLEWOOD - INKER
MINDY EISMAN - LETTERER
FRED BURKE - EDITOR
CAT YRONWODE
CHIEF

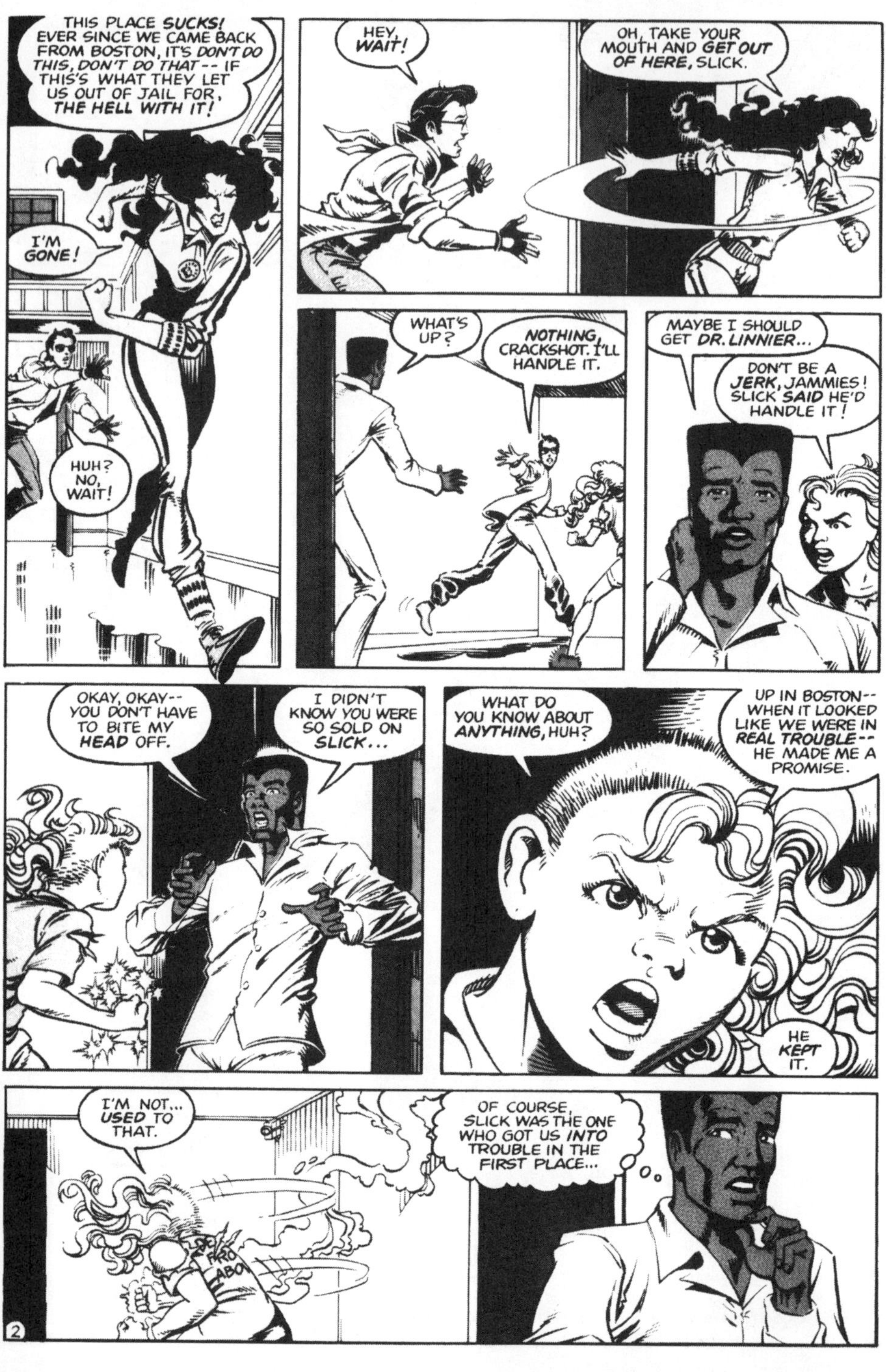
THIS PLACE SUCKS! EVER SINCE WE CAME BACK FROM BOSTON, IT'S DON'T DO THIS, DON'T DO THAT -- IF THIS'S WHAT THEY LET US OUT OF JAIL FOR, THE HELL WITH IT!
I'M GONE!
HUH? NO, WAIT!
HEY, WAIT!
OH, TAKE YOUR MOUTH AND GET OUT OF HERE, SLICK.
WHAT'S UP?
NOTHING, CRACKSHOT. I'LL HANDLE IT.
MAYBE I SHOULD GET DR. LINNIER...
DON'T BE A JERK, JAMMIES! SLICK SAID HE'D HANDLE IT!
OKAY, OKAY-- YOU DON'T HAVE TO BITE MY HEAD OFF.
I DIDN'T KNOW YOU WERE SO SOLD ON SLICK...
WHAT DO YOU KNOW ABOUT ANYTHING, HUH?
UP IN BOSTON-- WHEN IT LOOKED LIKE WE WERE IN REAL TROUBLE-- HE MADE ME A PROMISE.
HE KEPT IT.
I'M NOT... USED TO THAT.
OF COURSE, SLICK WAS THE ONE WHO GOT US INTO TROUBLE IN THE FIRST PLACE...
2

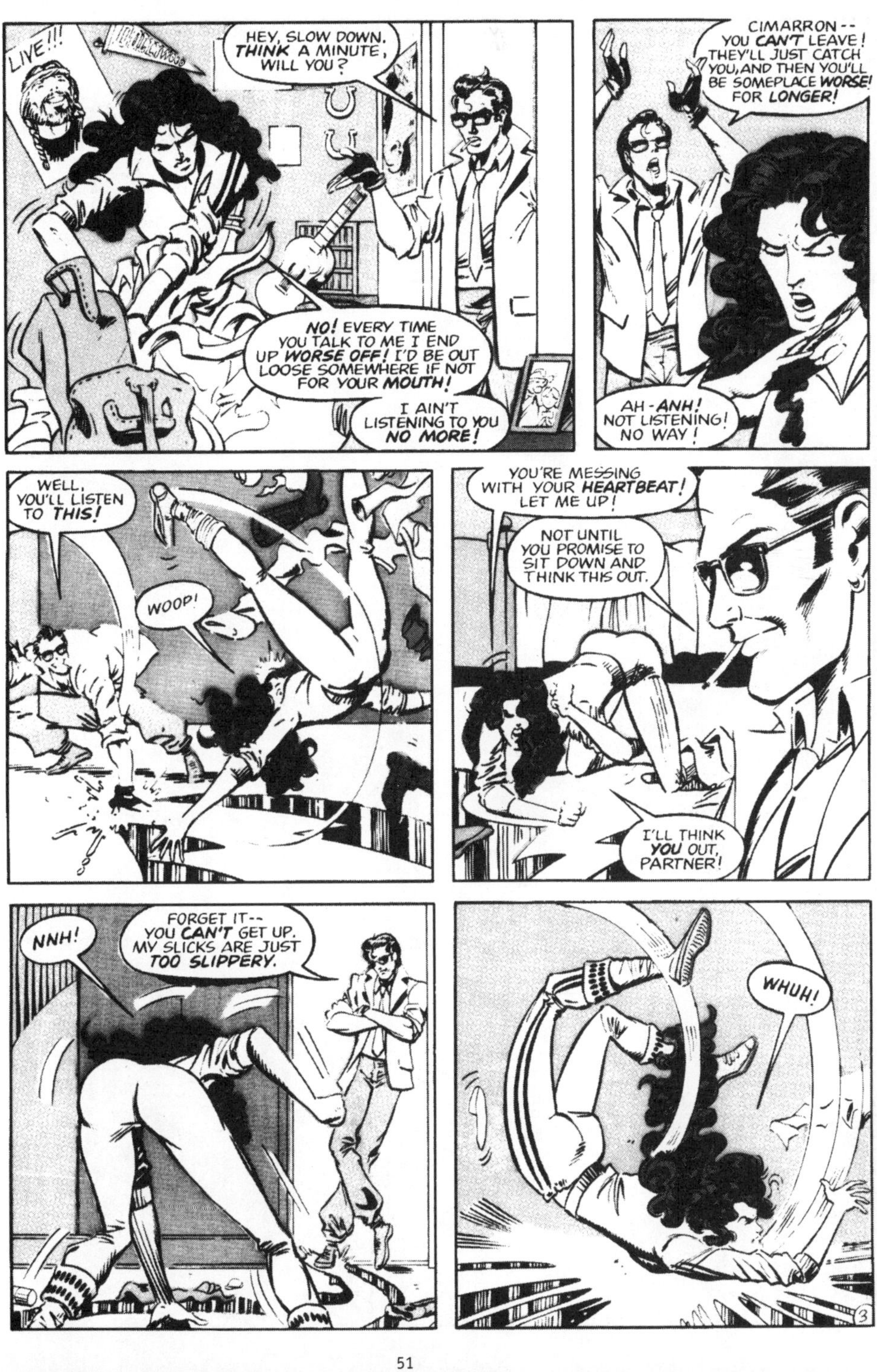
LIVE!!!
HEY, SLOW DOWN. THINK A MINUTE, WILL YOU?
NO! EVERY TIME YOU TALK TO ME I END UP WORSE OFF! I'D BE OUT LOOSE SOMEWHERE IF NOT FOR YOUR MOUTH!
I AIN'T LISTENING TO YOU NO MORE!
CIMARRON -- YOU CAN'T LEAVE! THEY'LL JUST CATCH YOU, AND THEN YOU'LL BE SOMEPLACE WORSE! FOR LONGER!
AH-ANH! NOT LISTENING! NO WAY!
WELL, YOU'LL LISTEN TO THIS!
WOOP!
YOU'RE MESSING WITH YOUR HEARTBEAT! LET ME UP!
NOT UNTIL YOU PROMISE TO SIT DOWN AND THINK THIS OUT.
I'LL THINK YOU OUT, PARTNER!
NNH!
FORGET IT-- YOU CAN'T GET UP. MY SLICKS ARE JUST TOO SLIPPERY.
WHUH!
3

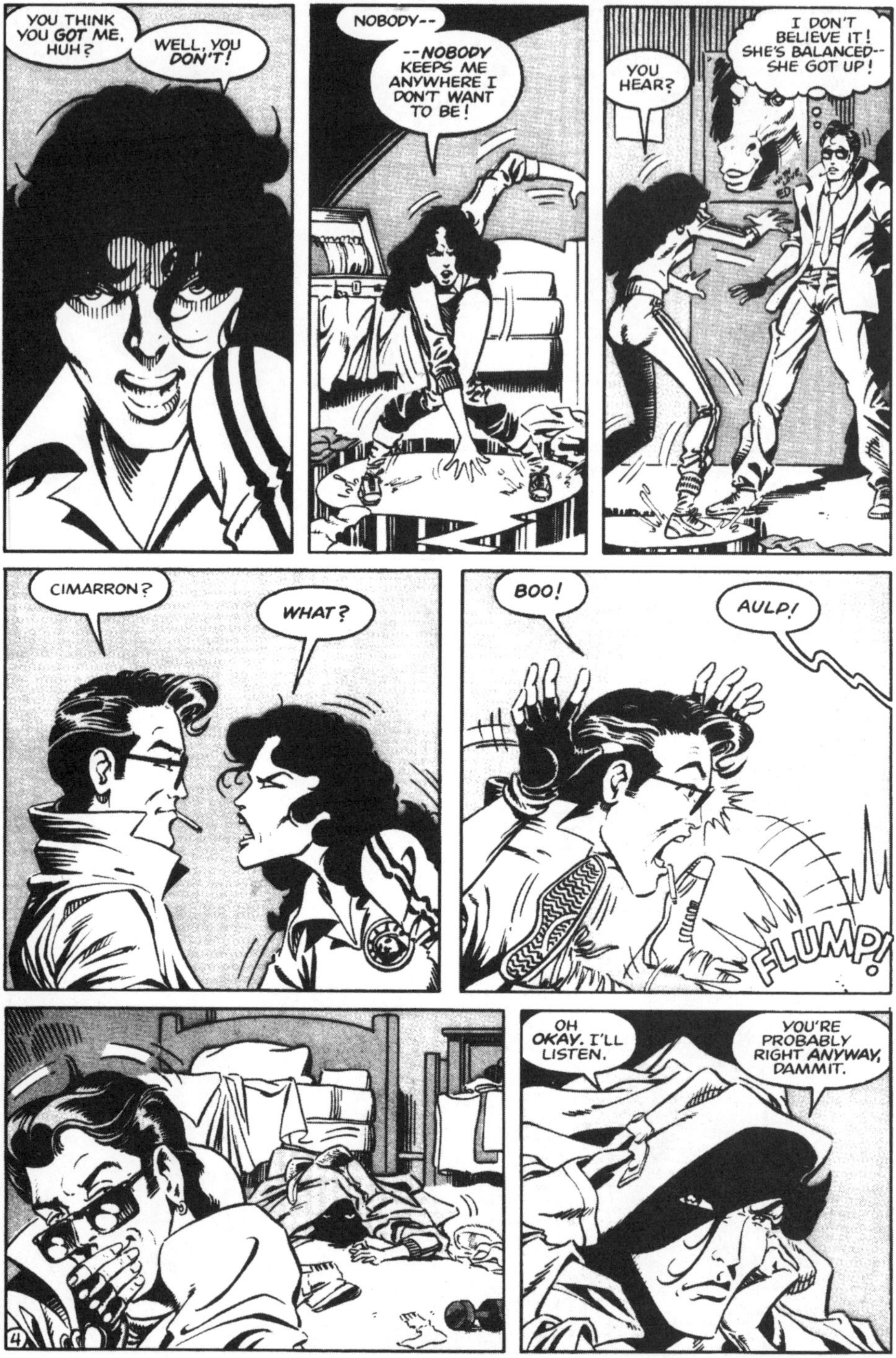
YOU THINK YOU GOT ME, HUH?
WELL, YOU DON'T!
NOBODY--
--NOBODY KEEPS ME ANYWHERE I DON'T WANT TO BE!
YOU HEAR?
I DON'T BELIEVE IT! SHE'S BALANCED-- SHE GOT UP!
CIMARRON?
WHAT?
BOO!
AULP!
FLUMP!
OH OKAY. I'LL LISTEN.
YOU'RE PROBABLY RIGHT ANYWAY, DAMMIT.

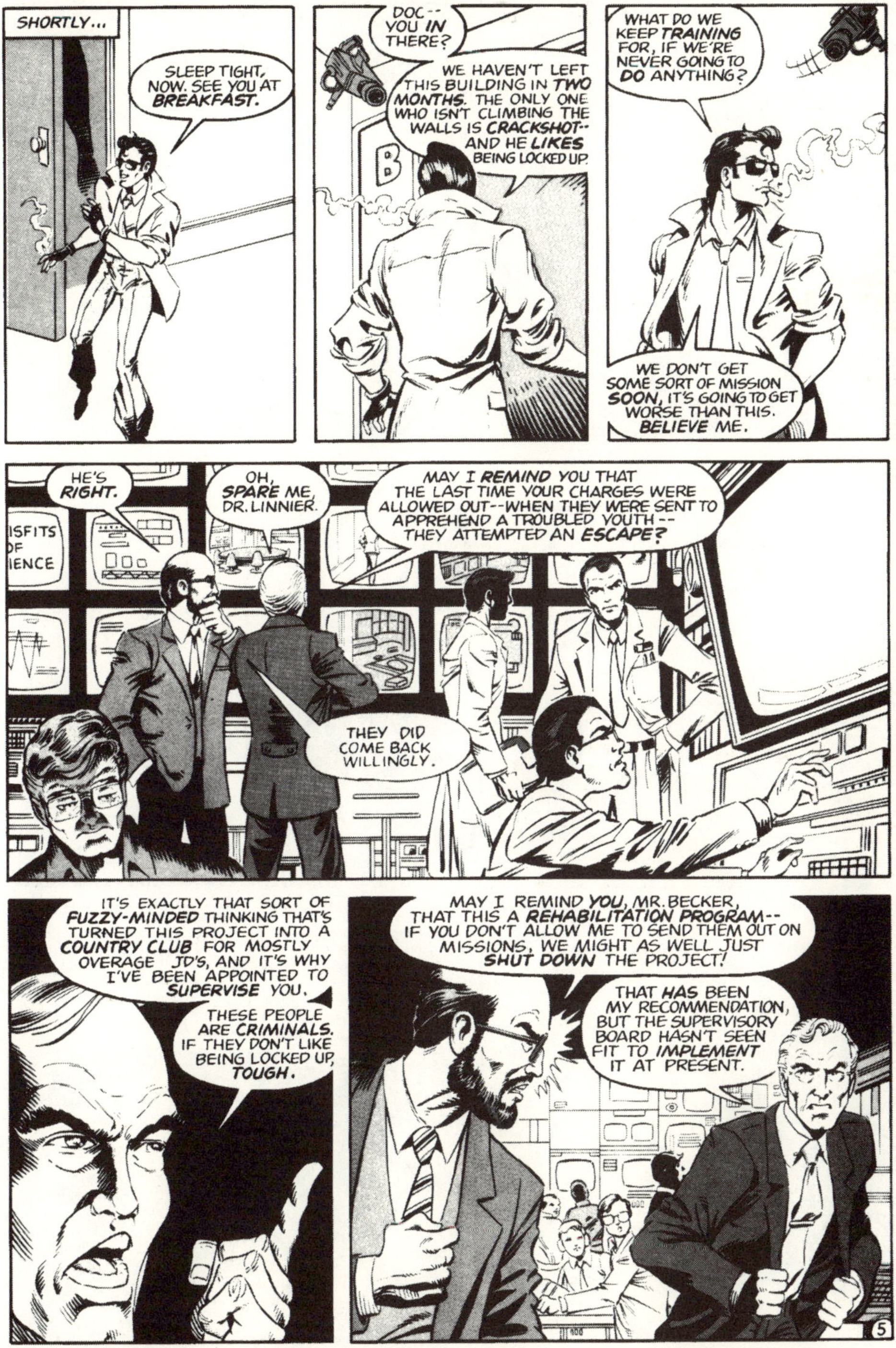
SHORTLY...
SLEEP TIGHT, NOW. SEE YOU AT BREAKFAST.
DOC-- YOU IN THERE?
WE HAVEN'T LEFT THIS BUILDING IN TWO MONTHS. THE ONLY ONE WHO ISN'T CLIMBING THE WALLS IS CRACKSHOT-- AND HE LIKES BEING LOCKED UP.
WHAT DO WE KEEP TRAINING FOR, IF WE'RE NEVER GOING TO DO ANYTHING?
WE DON'T GET SOME SORT OF MISSION SOON, IT'S GOING TO GET WORSE THAN THIS. BELIEVE ME.
HE'S RIGHT.
OH, SPARE ME, DR. LINNIER.
MAY I REMIND YOU THAT THE LAST TIME YOUR CHARGES WERE ALLOWED OUT--WHEN THEY WERE SENT TO APPREHEND A TROUBLED YOUTH-- THEY ATTEMPTED AN ESCAPE?
THEY DID COME BACK WILLINGLY.
IT'S EXACTLY THAT SORT OF FUZZY-MINDED THINKING THAT'S TURNED THIS PROJECT INTO A COUNTRY CLUB FOR MOSTLY OVERAGE JD'S, AND IT'S WHY I'VE BEEN APPOINTED TO SUPERVISE YOU.
THESE PEOPLE ARE CRIMINALS. IF THEY DON'T LIKE BEING LOCKED UP, TOUGH.
MAY I REMIND YOU, MR. BECKER, THAT THIS A REHABILITATION PROGRAM-- IF YOU DON'T ALLOW ME TO SEND THEM OUT ON MISSIONS, WE MIGHT AS WELL JUST SHUT DOWN THE PROJECT!
THAT HAS BEEN MY RECOMMENDATION, BUT THE SUPERVISORY BOARD HASN'T SEEN FIT TO IMPLEMENT IT AT PRESENT.
5

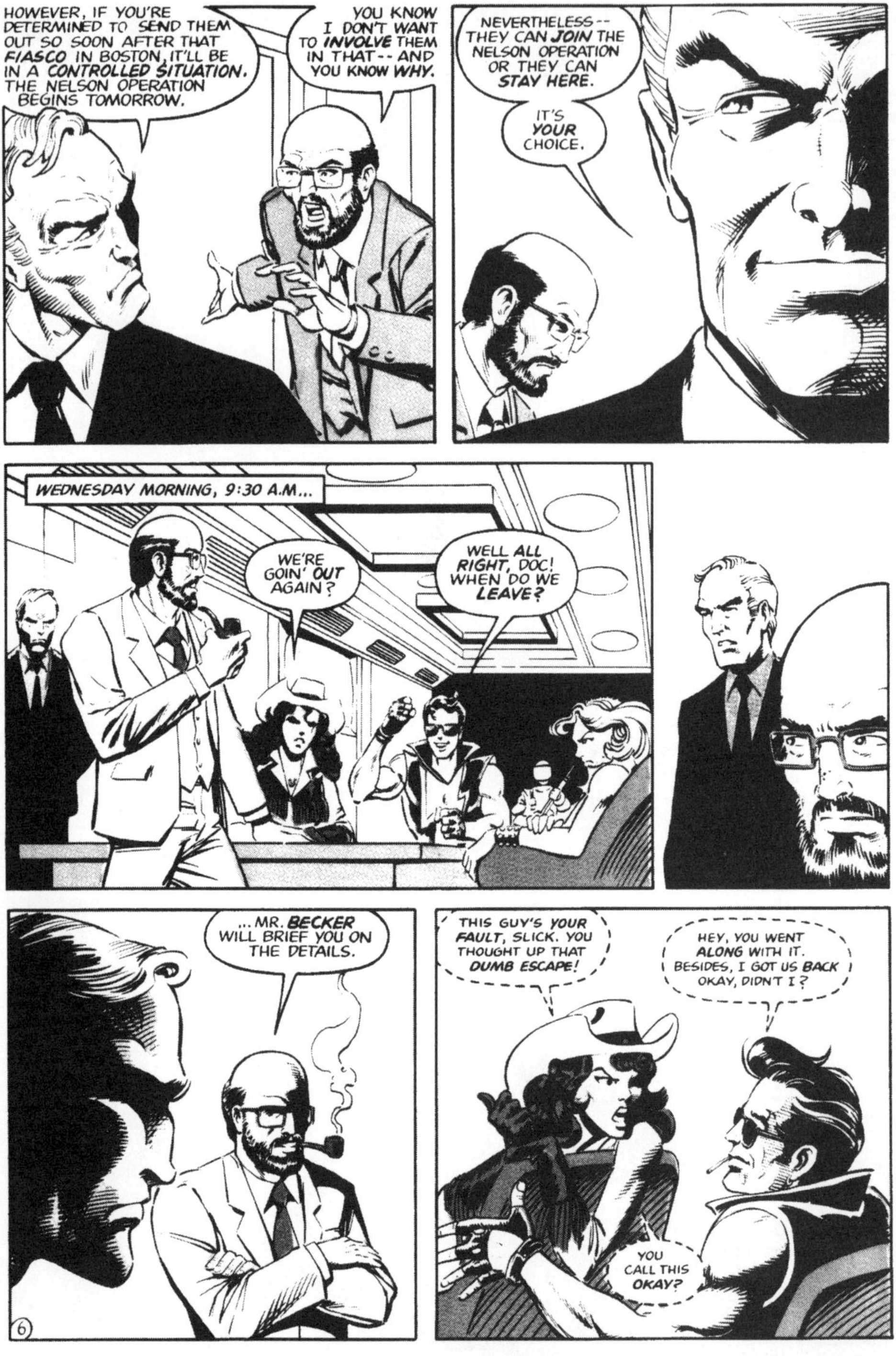
HOWEVER, IF YOU'RE DETERMINED TO SEND THEM OUT SO SOON AFTER THAT FIASCO IN BOSTON, IT'LL BE IN A CONTROLLED SITUATION. THE NELSON OPERATION BEGINS TOMORROW.
YOU KNOW I DON'T WANT TO INVOLVE THEM IN THAT-- AND YOU KNOW WHY.
NEVERTHELESS-- THEY CAN JOIN THE NELSON OPERATION OR THEY CAN STAY HERE.
IT'S YOUR CHOICE.
WEDNESDAY MORNING, 9:30 A.M...
WE'RE GOIN' OUT AGAIN?
WELL ALL RIGHT, DOC! WHEN DO WE LEAVE?
...MR. BECKER WILL BRIEF YOU ON THE DETAILS.
6
THIS GUY'S YOUR FAULT, SLICK. YOU THOUGHT UP THAT DUMB ESCAPE!
HEY, YOU WENT ALONG WITH IT. BESIDES, I GOT US BACK OKAY, DIDN'T I?
YOU CALL THIS OKAY?

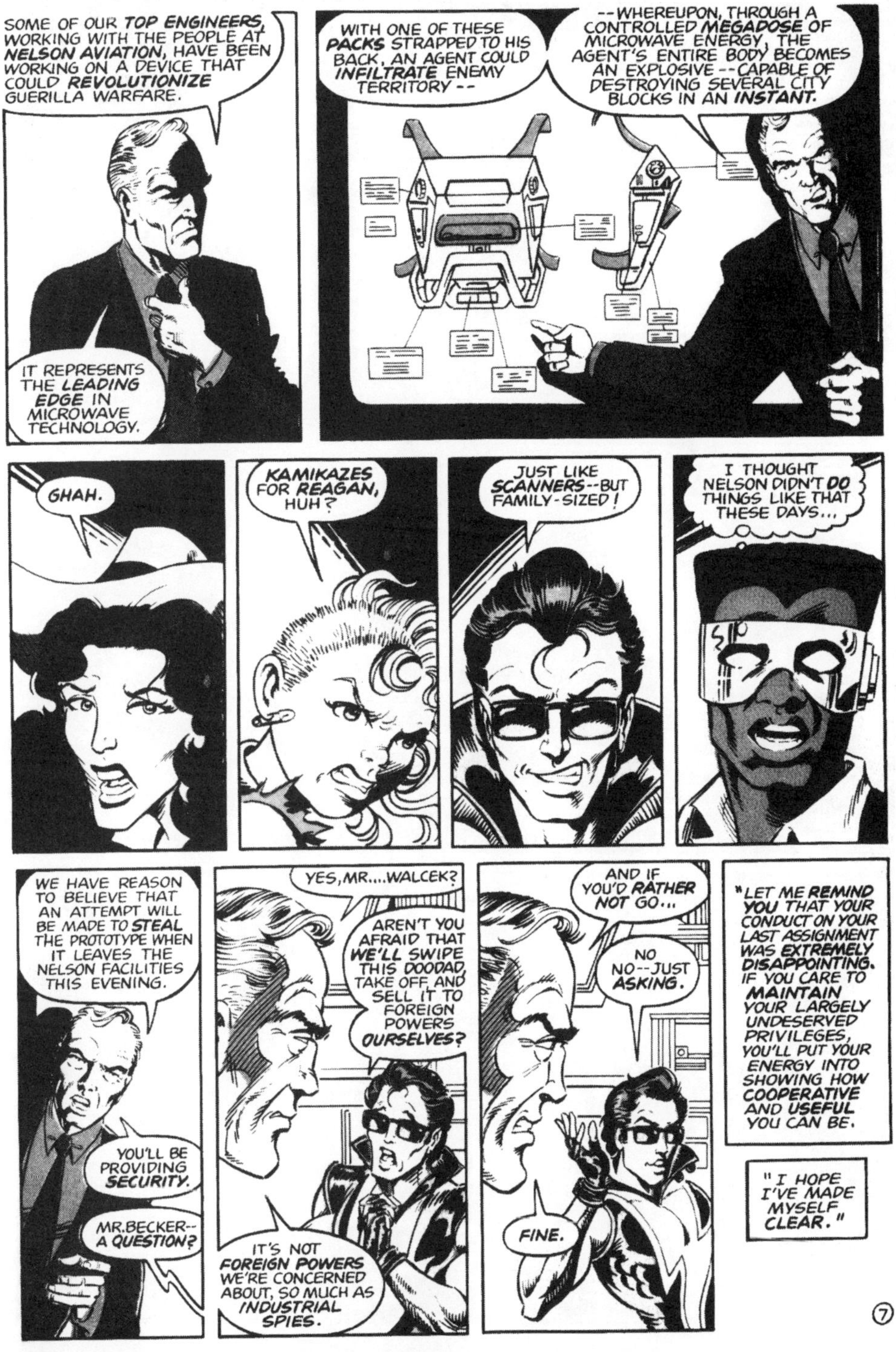
SOME OF OUR TOP ENGINEERS, WORKING WITH THE PEOPLE AT NELSON AVIATION, HAVE BEEN WORKING ON A DEVICE THAT COULD REVOLUTIONIZE GUERILLA WARFARE.
IT REPRESENTS THE LEADING EDGE IN MICROWAVE TECHNOLOGY.
WITH ONE OF THESE PACKS STRAPPED TO HIS BACK, AN AGENT COULD INFILTRATE ENEMY TERRITORY --
--WHEREUPON, THROUGH A CONTROLLED MEGADOSE OF MICROWAVE ENERGY, THE AGENT'S ENTIRE BODY BECOMES AN EXPLOSIVE --CAPABLE OF DESTROYING SEVERAL CITY BLOCKS IN AN INSTANT.
GHAH.
KAMIKAZES FOR REAGAN, HUH?
JUST LIKE SCANNERS--BUT FAMILY-SIZED!
I THOUGHT NELSON DIDN'T DO THINGS LIKE THAT THESE DAYS...
WE HAVE REASON TO BELIEVE THAT AN ATTEMPT WILL BE MADE TO STEAL THE PROTOTYPE WHEN IT LEAVES THE NELSON FACILITIES THIS EVENING.
YOU'LL BE PROVIDING SECURITY.
MR.BECKER-- A QUESTION?
YES, MR....WALCEK?
AREN'T YOU AFRAID THAT WE'LL SWIPE THIS DOODAD, TAKE OFF, AND SELL IT TO FOREIGN POWERS OURSELVES?
IT'S NOT FOREIGN POWERS WE'RE CONCERNED ABOUT, SO MUCH AS INDUSTRIAL SPIES.
AND IF YOU'D RATHER NOT GO...
NO NO--JUST ASKING.
FINE.
"LET ME REMIND YOU THAT YOUR CONDUCT ON YOUR LAST ASSIGNMENT WAS EXTREMELY DISAPPOINTING. IF YOU CARE TO MAINTAIN YOUR LARGELY UNDESERVED PRIVILEGES, YOU'LL PUT YOUR ENERGY INTO SHOWING HOW COOPERATIVE AND USEFUL YOU CAN BE.
"I HOPE I'VE MADE MYSELF CLEAR."
7

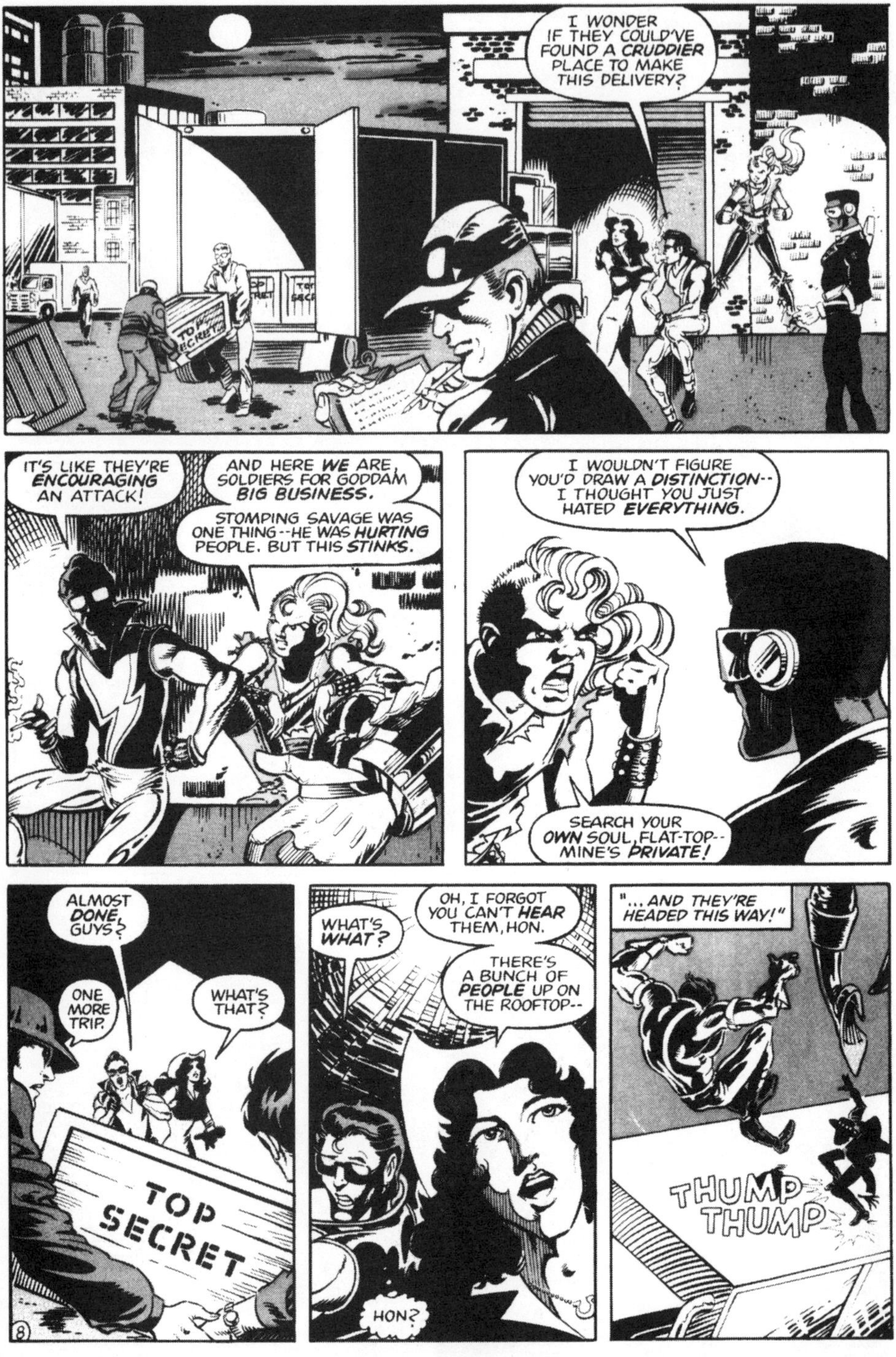
I WONDER IF THEY COULD'VE FOUND A CRUDDIER PLACE TO MAKE THIS DELIVERY?
TOP SECRET
IT'S LIKE THEY'RE ENCOURAGING AN ATTACK!
AND HERE WE ARE, SOLDIERS FOR GODDAM BIG BUSINESS.
STOMPING SAVAGE WAS ONE THING--HE WAS HURTING PEOPLE. BUT THIS STINKS.
I WOULDN'T FIGURE YOU'D DRAW A DISTINCTION--I THOUGHT YOU JUST HATED EVERYTHING.
SEARCH YOUR OWN SOUL, FLAT-TOP--MINE'S PRIVATE!
ALMOST DONE, GUYS?
ONE MORE TRIP.
WHAT'S THAT?
TOP SECRET
8
WHAT'S WHAT?
OH, I FORGOT YOU CAN'T HEAR THEM, HON.
THERE'S A BUNCH OF PEOPLE UP ON THE ROOFTOP--
HON?
"... AND THEY'RE HEADED THIS WAY!"
THUMP
THUMP

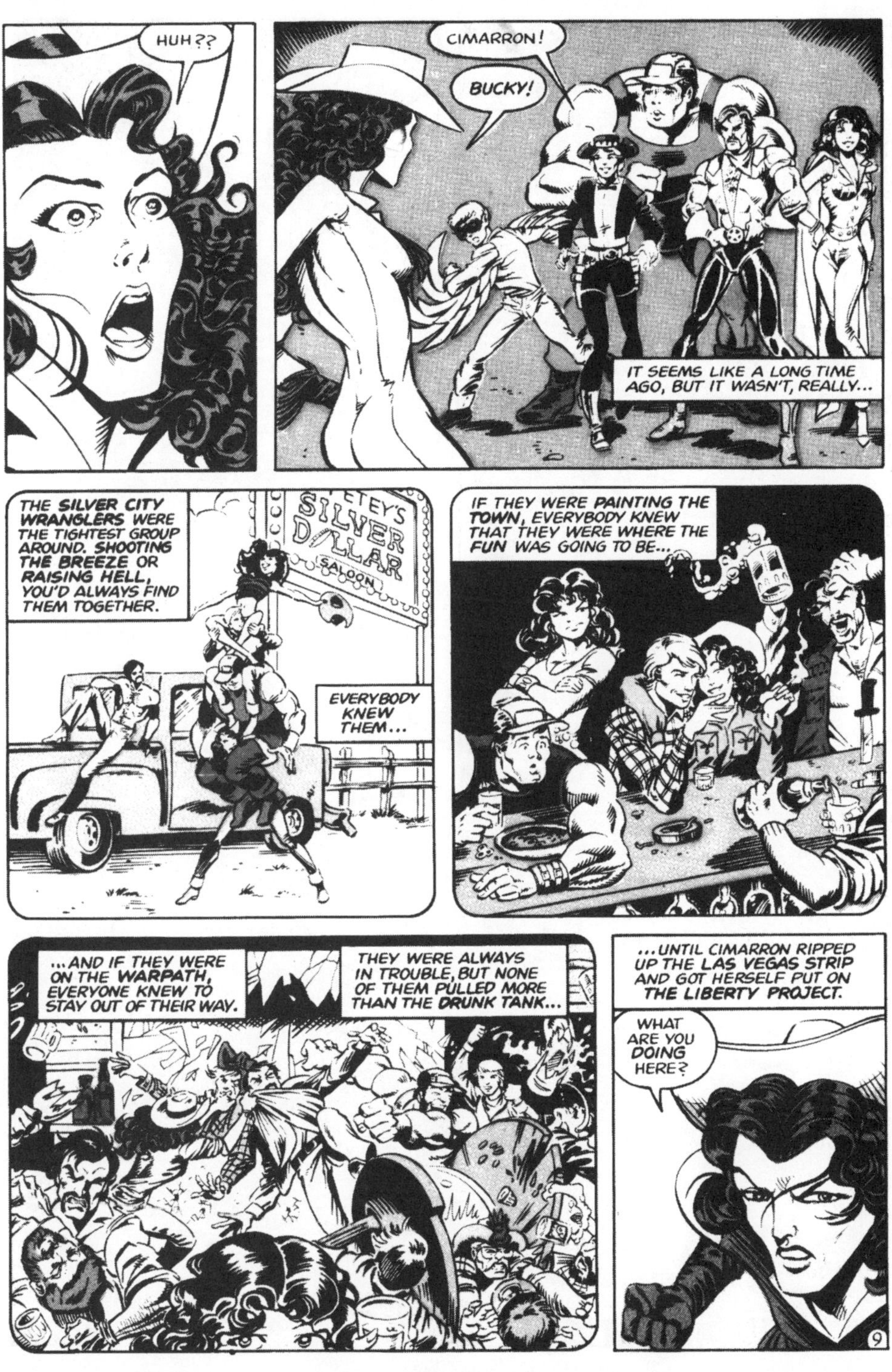
HUH??
CIMARRON!
BUCKY!
IT SEEMS LIKE A LONG TIME AGO, BUT IT WASN'T, REALLY...
THE SILVER CITY WRANGLERS WERE THE TIGHTEST GROUP AROUND. SHOOTING THE BREEZE OR RAISING HELL, YOU'D ALWAYS FIND THEM TOGETHER.
PETEY'S SILVER DOLLAR SALOON
EVERYBODY KNEW THEM...
IF THEY WERE PAINTING THE TOWN, EVERYBODY KNEW THAT THEY WERE WHERE THE FUN WAS GOING TO BE...
...AND IF THEY WERE ON THE WARPATH, EVERYONE KNEW TO STAY OUT OF THEIR WAY.
THEY WERE ALWAYS IN TROUBLE, BUT NONE OF THEM PULLED MORE THAN THE DRUNK TANK...
...UNTIL CIMARRON RIPPED UP THE LAS VEGAS STRIP AND GOT HERSELF PUT ON THE LIBERTY PROJECT.
WHAT ARE YOU DOING HERE?
9

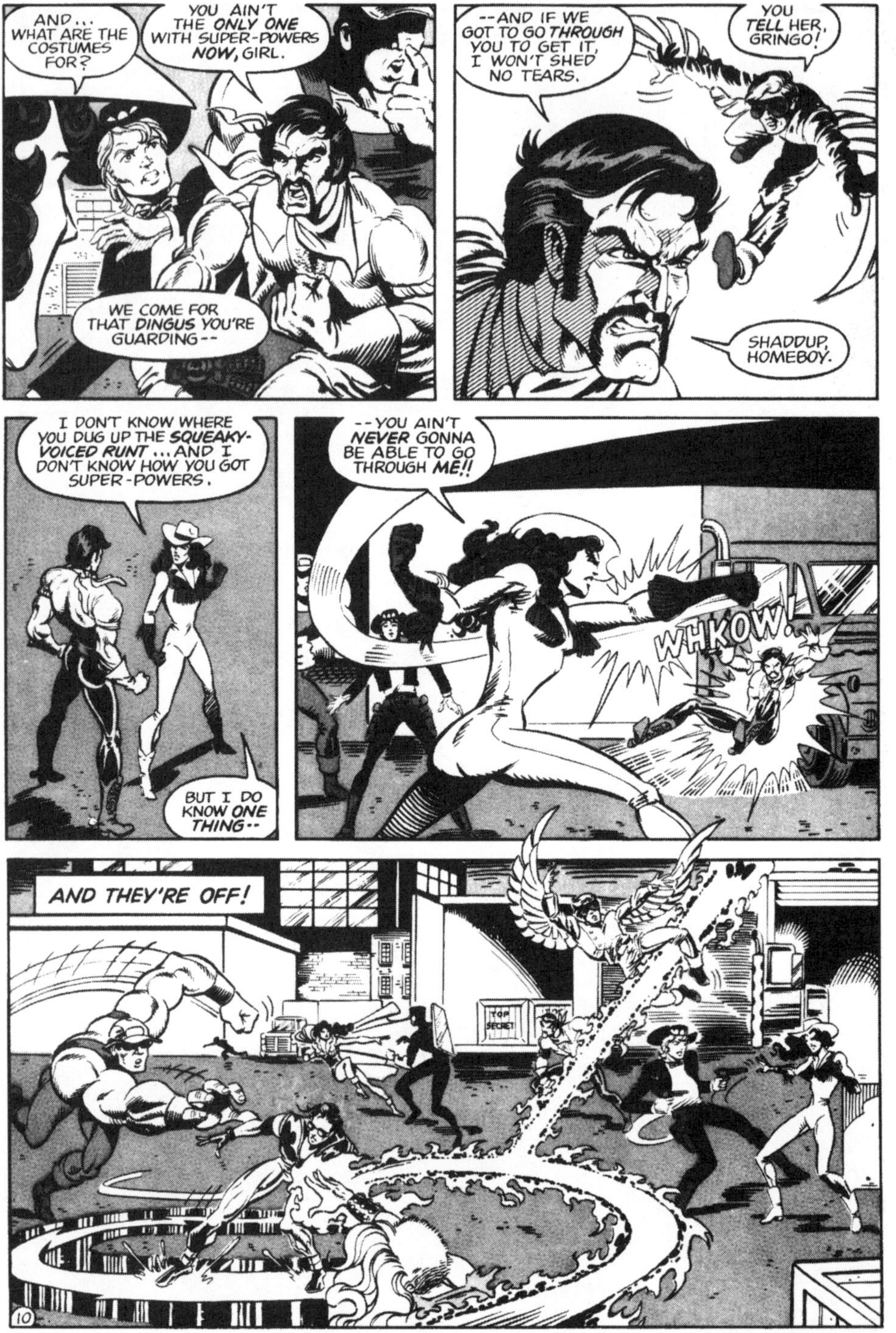
AND... WHAT ARE THE COSTUMES FOR?
YOU AIN'T THE ONLY ONE WITH SUPER-POWERS NOW, GIRL.
WE COME FOR THAT DINGUS YOU'RE GUARDING--
--AND IF WE GOT TO GO THROUGH YOU TO GET IT, I WON'T SHED NO TEARS.
YOU TELL HER, GRINGO!
SHADDUP, HOMEBOY.
I DON'T KNOW WHERE YOU DUG UP THE SQUEAKY-VOICED RUNT...AND I DON'T KNOW HOW YOU GOT SUPER-POWERS.
BUT I DO KNOW ONE THING--
--YOU AIN'T NEVER GONNA BE ABLE TO GO THROUGH ME!!
WHKOW!
AND THEY'RE OFF!
TOP SECRET
10

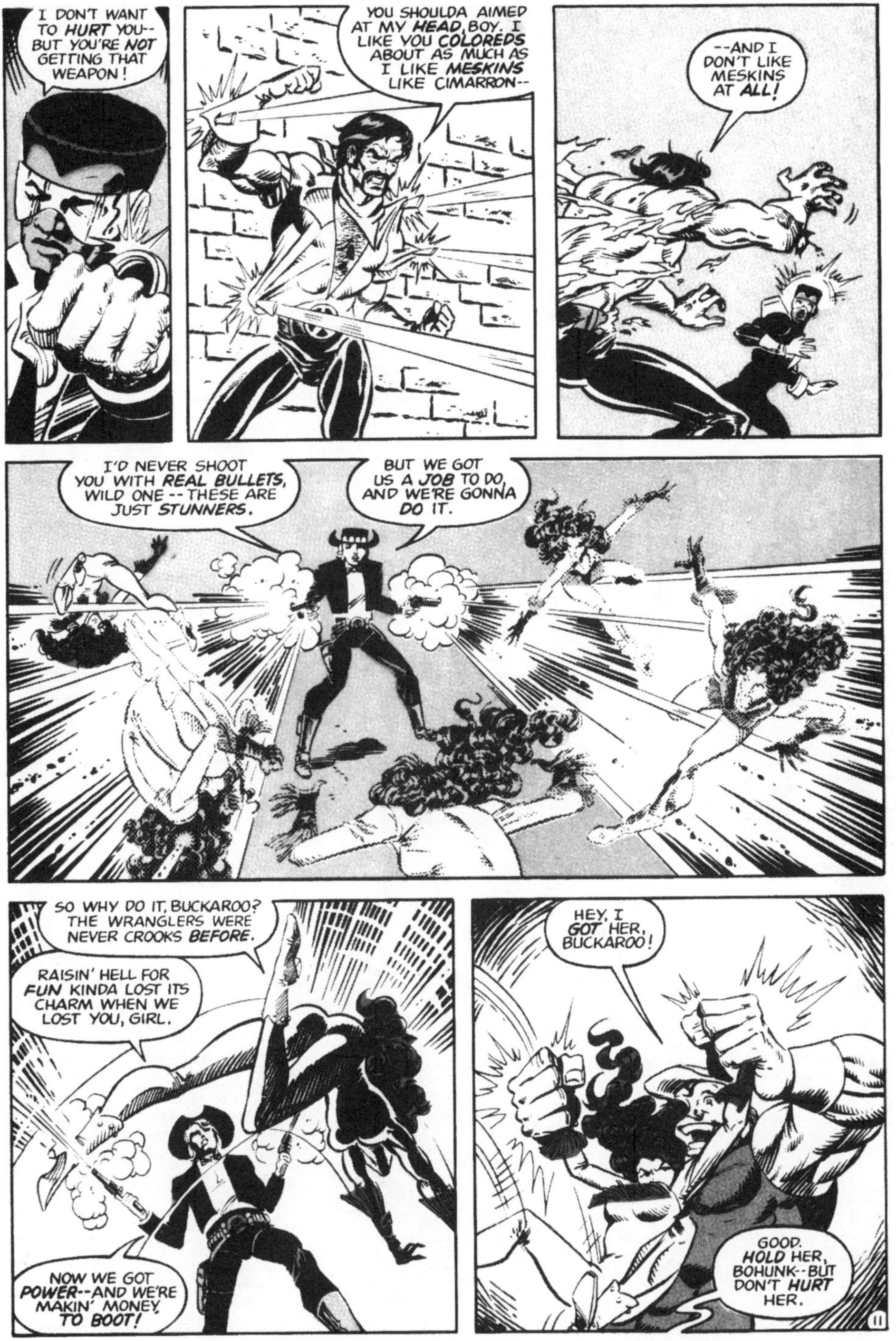
I DON'T WANT TO HURT YOU-- BUT YOU'RE NOT GETTING THAT WEAPON!
YOU SHOULDA AIMED AT MY HEAD, BOY. I LIKE YOU COLOREDS ABOUT AS MUCH AS I LIKE MESKINS LIKE CIMARRON--
--AND I DON'T LIKE MESKINS AT ALL!
I'D NEVER SHOOT YOU WITH REAL BULLETS, WILD ONE--THESE ARE JUST STUNNERS.
BUT WE GOT US A JOB TO DO, AND WE'RE GONNA DO IT.
SO WHY DO IT, BUCKAROO? THE WRANGLERS WERE NEVER CROOKS BEFORE.
RAISIN' HELL FOR FUN KINDA LOST ITS CHARM WHEN WE LOST YOU, GIRL.
NOW WE GOT POWER--AND WE'RE MAKIN' MONEY TO BOOT!
HEY, I GOT HER, BUCKAROO!
GOOD. HOLD HER, BOHUNK--BUT DON'T HURT HER.
11

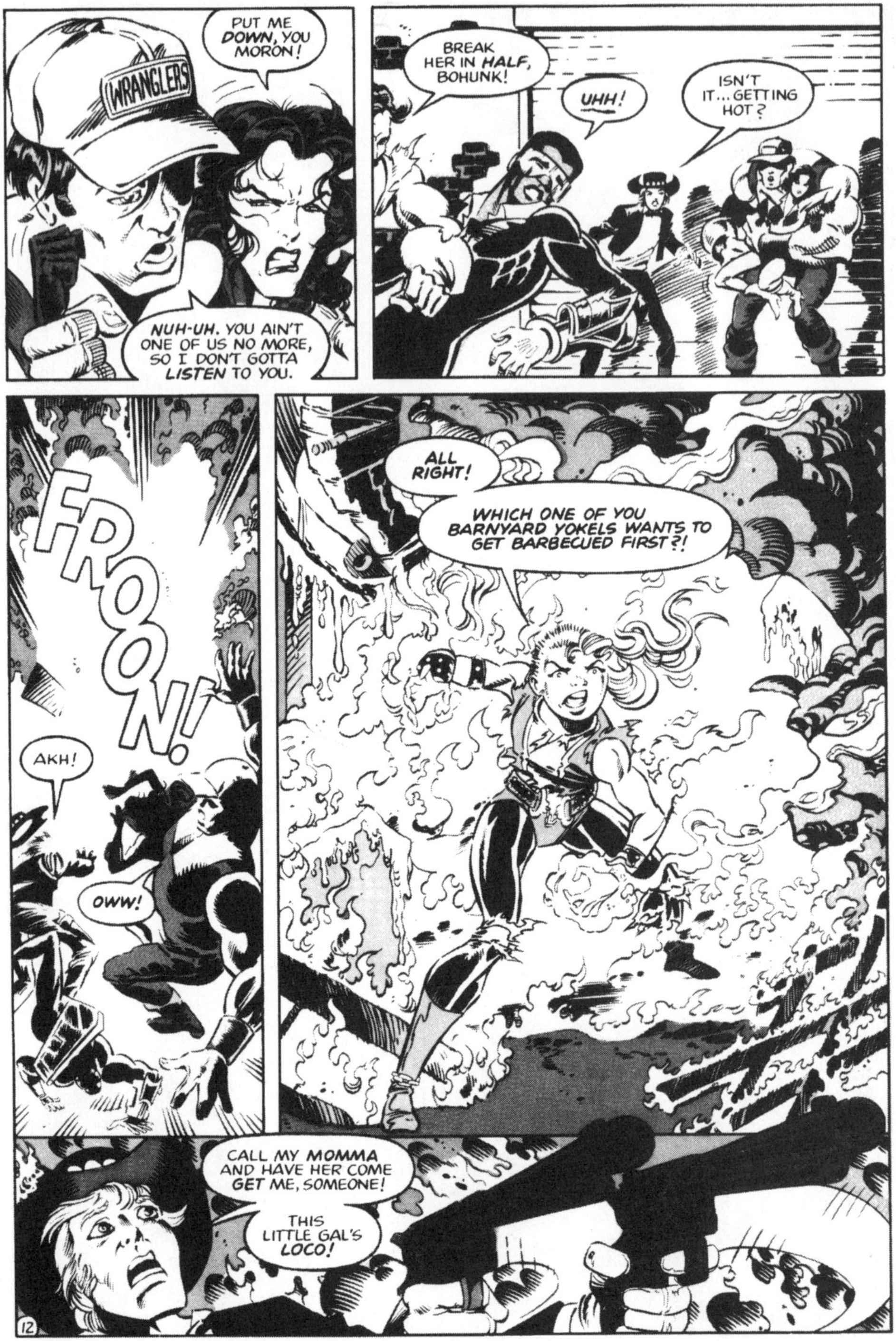
PUT ME DOWN, YOU MORON!
WRANGLERS
NUH-UH. YOU AIN'T ONE OF US NO MORE, SO I DON'T GOTTA LISTEN TO YOU.
BREAK HER IN HALF, BOHUNK!
UHH!
ISN'T IT... GETTING HOT?
FROON!
AKH!
OWW!
ALL RIGHT!
WHICH ONE OF YOU BARNYARD YOKELS WANTS TO GET BARBECUED FIRST?!
CALL MY MOMMA AND HAVE HER COME GET ME, SOMEONE!
THIS LITTLE GAL'S LOCO!
12

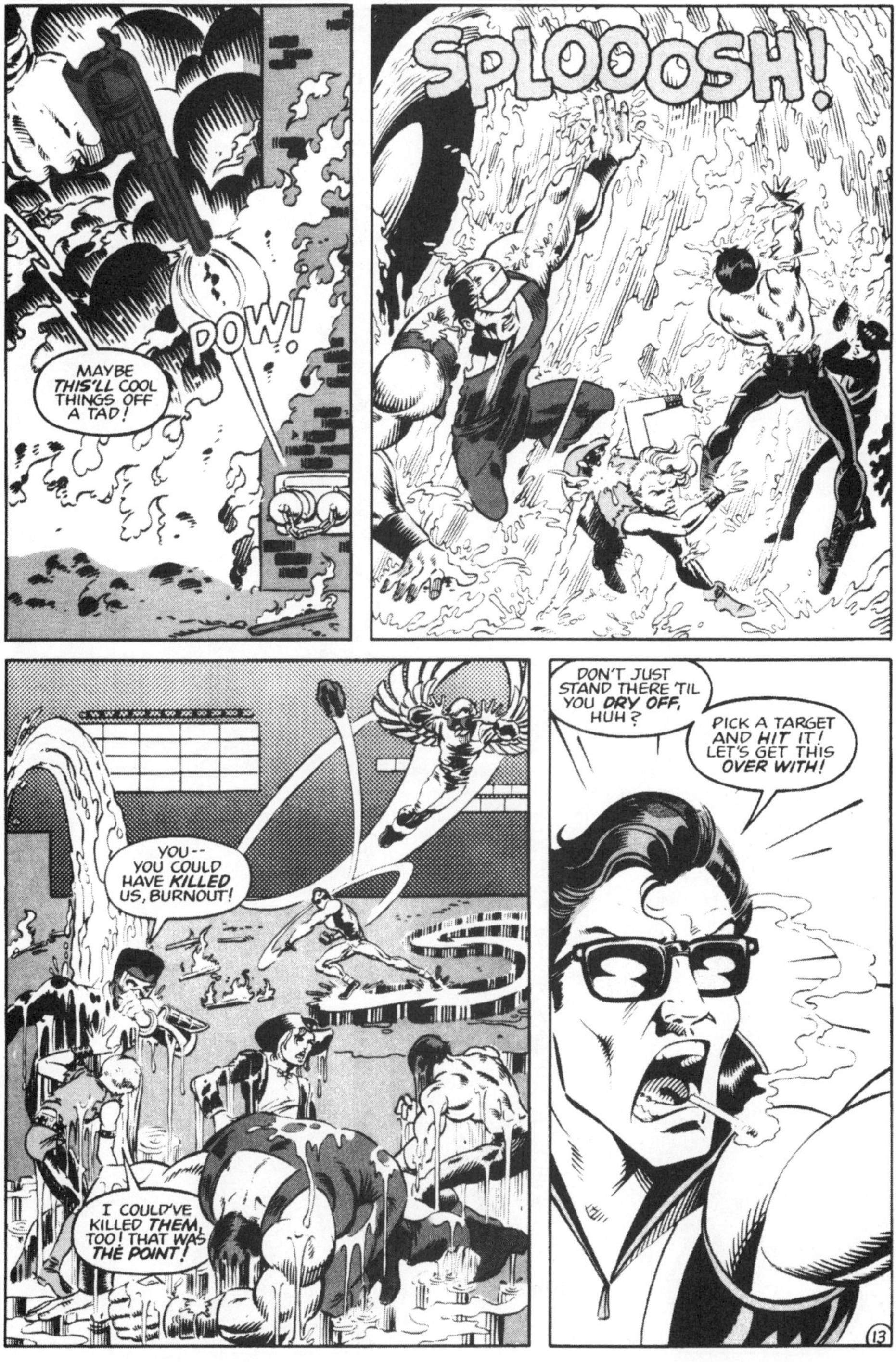
POW!
MAYBE THIS'LL COOL THINGS OFF A TAD!
SPLOOOSH!
YOU-- YOU COULD HAVE KILLED US, BURNOUT!
I COULD'VE KILLED THEM, TOO! THAT WAS THE POINT!
DON'T JUST STAND THERE 'TIL YOU DRY OFF, HUH?
PICK A TARGET AND HIT IT! LET'S GET THIS OVER WITH!
13

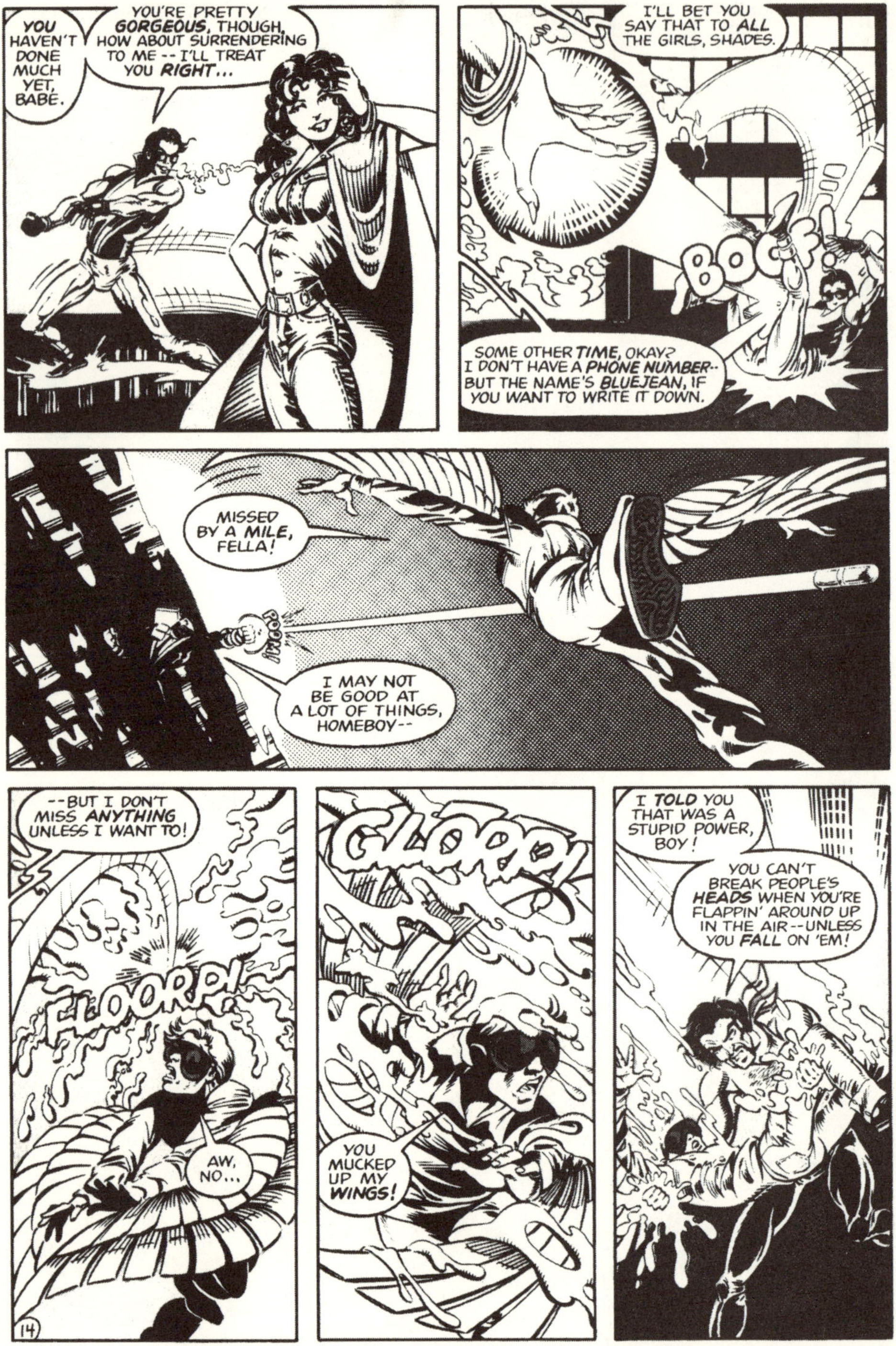
YOU HAVEN'T DONE MUCH YET, BABE.
YOU'RE PRETTY GORGEOUS, THOUGH. HOW ABOUT SURRENDERING TO ME -- I'LL TREAT YOU RIGHT...
I'LL BET YOU SAY THAT TO ALL THE GIRLS, SHADES.
BOOF!
SOME OTHER TIME, OKAY? I DON'T HAVE A PHONE NUMBER-- BUT THE NAME'S BLUEJEAN, IF YOU WANT TO WRITE IT DOWN.
MISSED BY A MILE, FELLA!
POOM!
I MAY NOT BE GOOD AT A LOT OF THINGS, HOMEBOY--
--BUT I DON'T MISS ANYTHING UNLESS I WANT TO!
FLOORP!
AW, NO...
14
GLORP!
YOU MUCKED UP MY WINGS!
I TOLD YOU THAT WAS A STUPID POWER, BOY!
YOU CAN'T BREAK PEOPLE'S HEADS WHEN YOU'RE FLAPPIN' AROUND UP IN THE AIR--UNLESS YOU FALL ON 'EM!

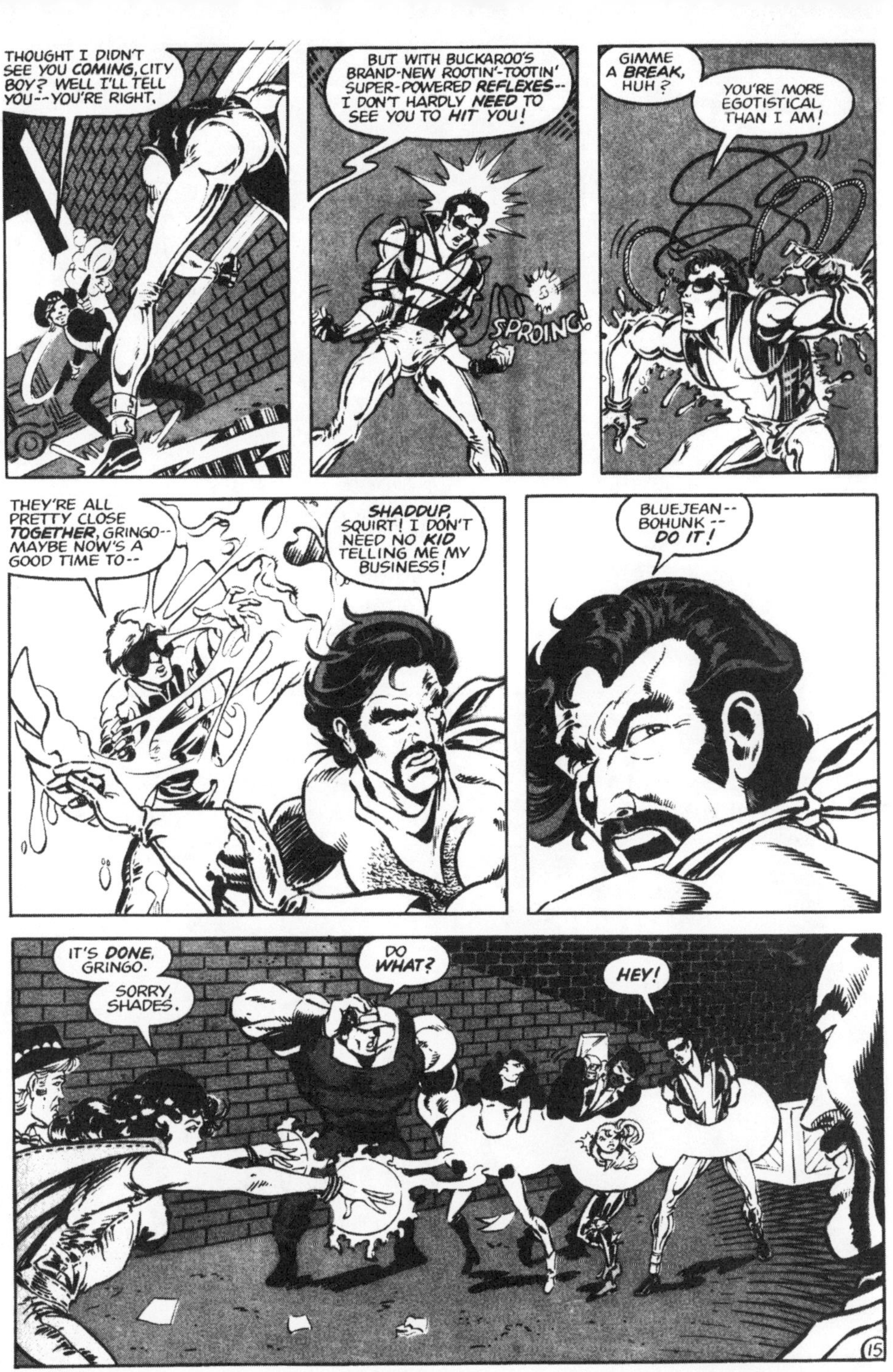
THOUGHT I DIDN'T SEE YOU COMING, CITY BOY? WELL I'LL TELL YOU--YOU'RE RIGHT.
BUT WITH BUCKAROO'S BRAND-NEW ROOTIN'-TOOTIN' SUPER-POWERED REFLEXES--I DON'T HARDLY NEED TO SEE YOU TO HIT YOU!
SPROING!
GIMME A BREAK, HUH?
YOU'RE MORE EGOTISTICAL THAN I AM!
THEY'RE ALL PRETTY CLOSE TOGETHER, GRINGO--MAYBE NOW'S A GOOD TIME TO--
SHADDUP, SQUIRT! I DON'T NEED NO KID TELLING ME MY BUSINESS!
BLUEJEAN--BOHUNK--DO IT!
IT'S DONE, GRINGO.
SORRY, SHADES.
DO WHAT?
HEY!
15

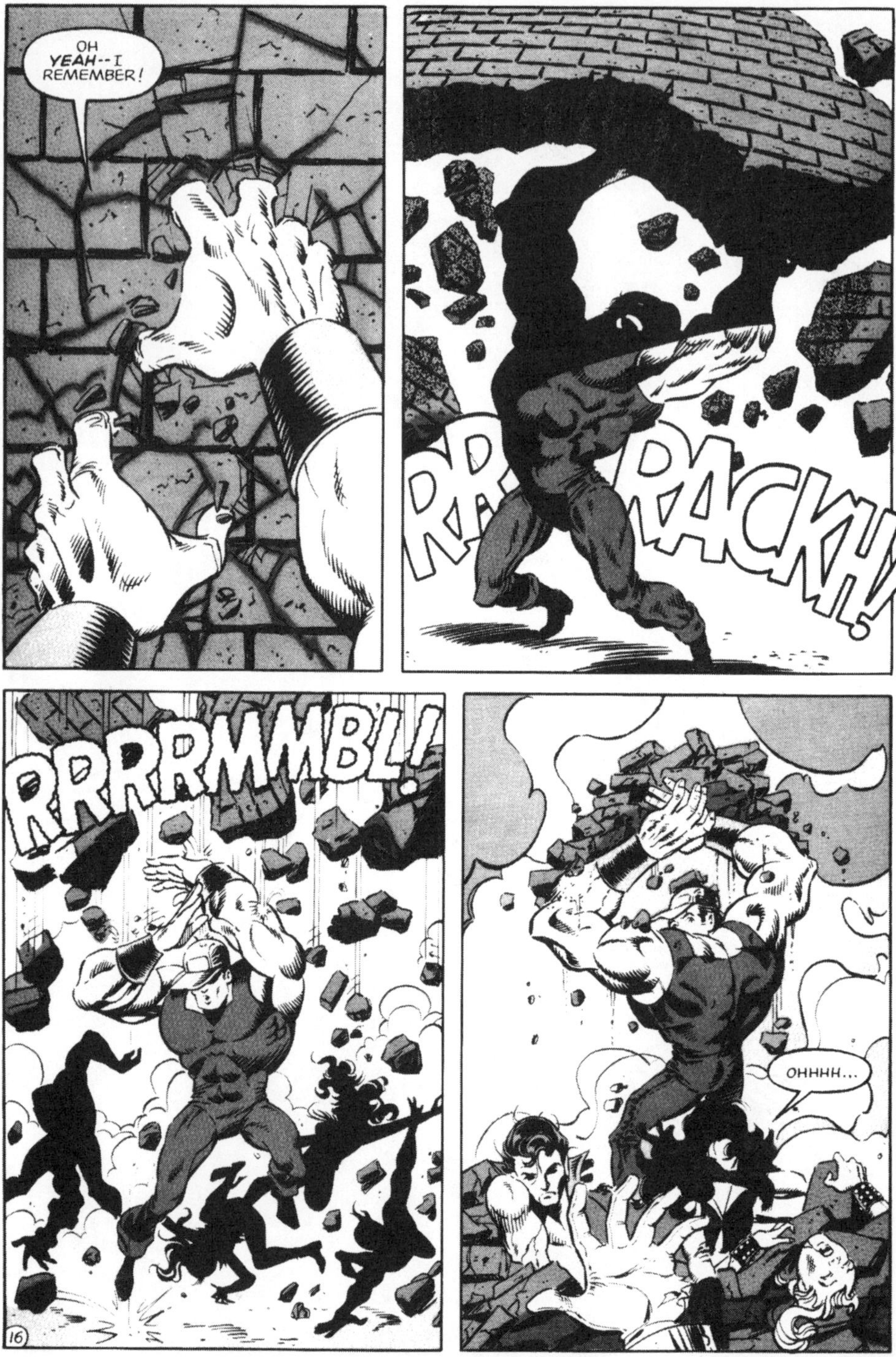
OH YEAH--I REMEMBER!
RACKH!
RRRRMMBL!
16
OHHHH...

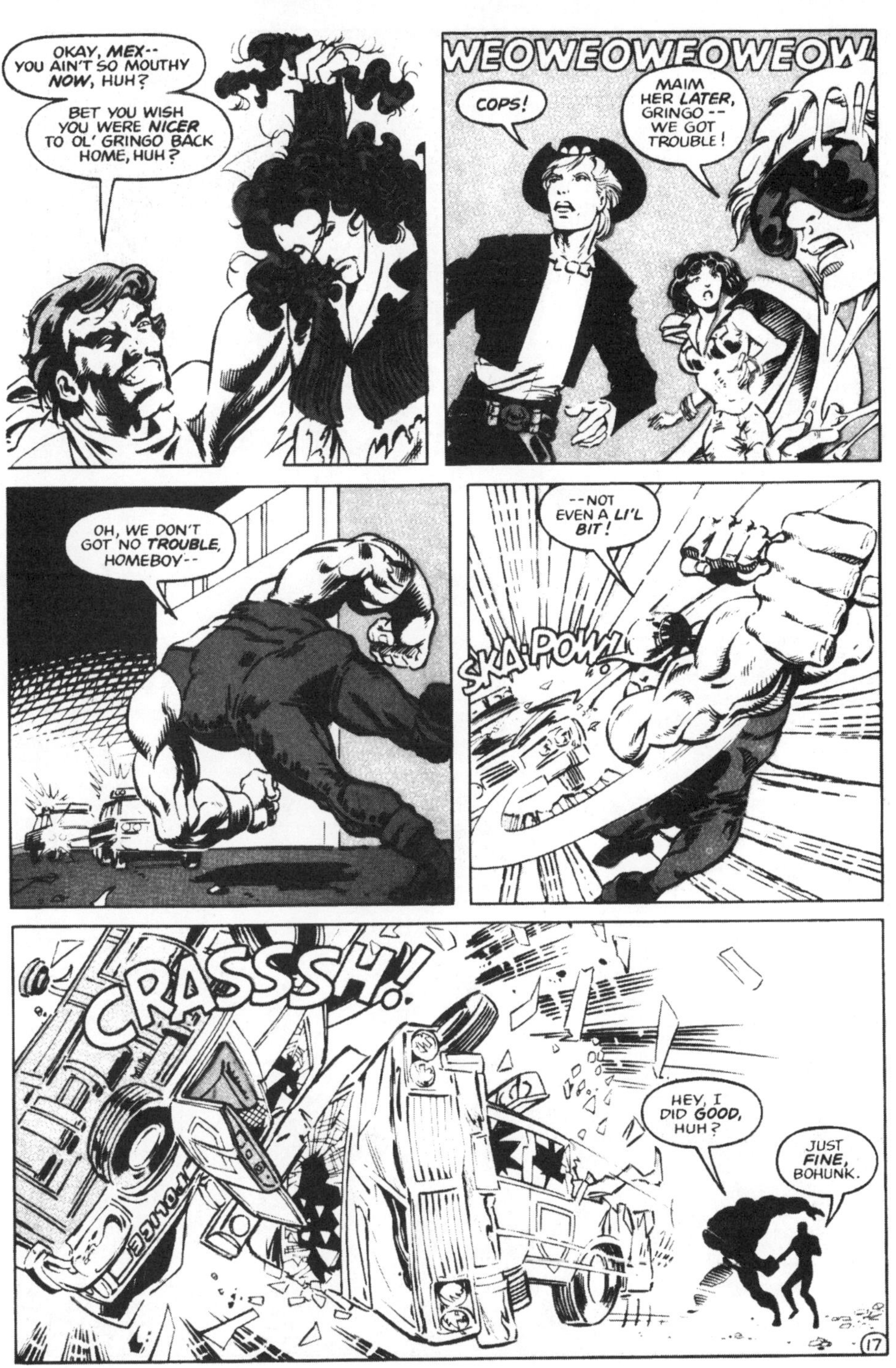
OKAY, MEX-- YOU AIN'T SO MOUTHY NOW, HUH?
BET YOU WISH YOU WERE NICER TO OL' GRINGO BACK HOME, HUH?
WEOWWEOWWEOWWEOW
COPS!
MAIM HER LATER, GRINGO -- WE GOT TROUBLE!
OH, WE DON'T GOT NO TROUBLE, HOMEBOY--
--NOT EVEN A LI'L BIT!
SKA-POW!
CRASSSH!
HEY, I DID GOOD, HUH?
JUST FINE, BOHUNK.
17

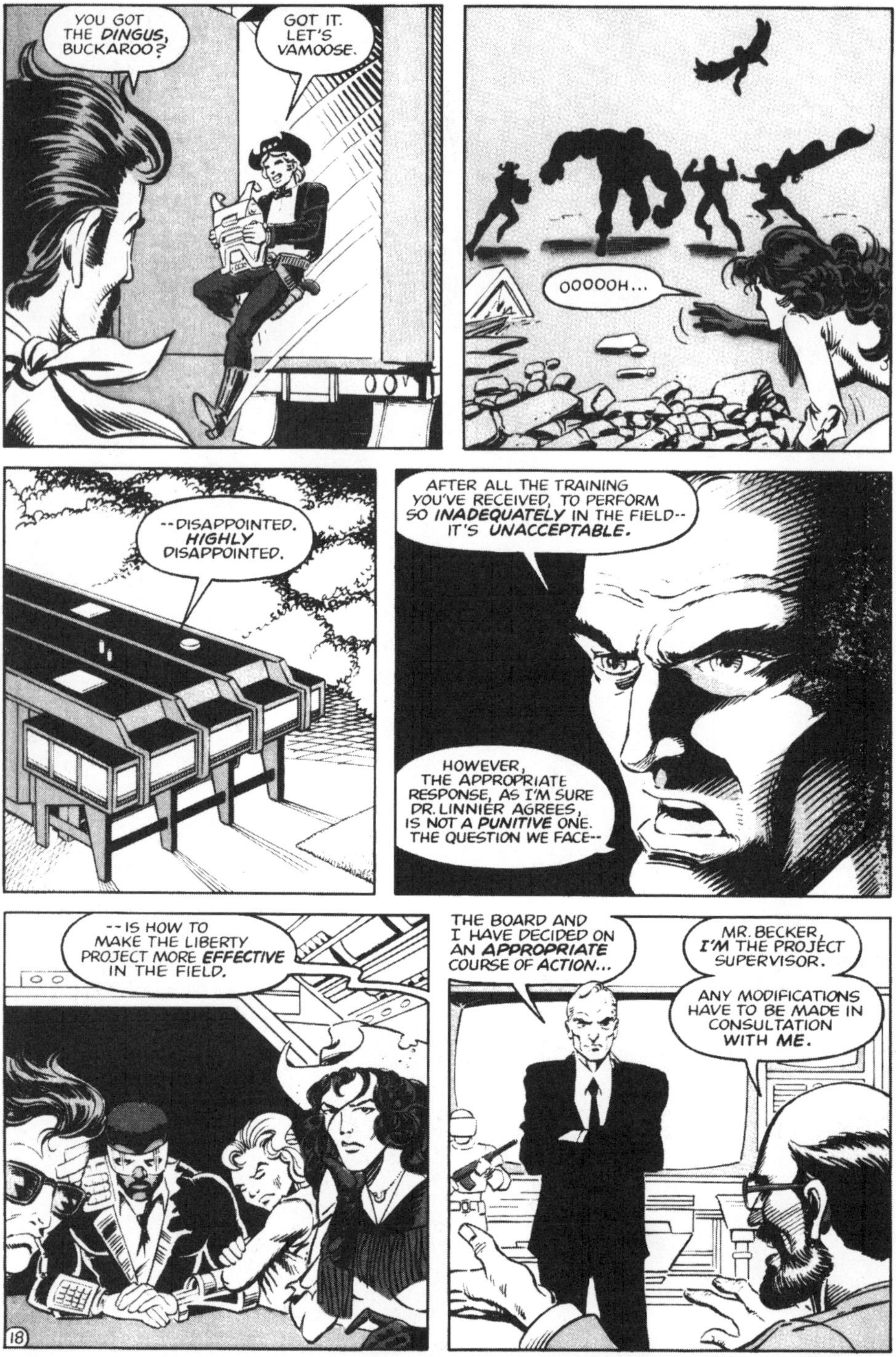
YOU GOT THE DINGUS, BUCKAROO?
GOT IT. LET'S VAMOOSE.
OOOOOH...
--DISAPPOINTED. HIGHLY DISAPPOINTED.
AFTER ALL THE TRAINING YOU'VE RECEIVED, TO PERFORM SO INADEQUATELY IN THE FIELD-- IT'S UNACCEPTABLE.
HOWEVER, THE APPROPRIATE RESPONSE, AS I'M SURE DR. LINNIER AGREES, IS NOT A PUNITIVE ONE. THE QUESTION WE FACE--
--IS HOW TO MAKE THE LIBERTY PROJECT MORE EFFECTIVE IN THE FIELD.
18
THE BOARD AND I HAVE DECIDED ON AN APPROPRIATE COURSE OF ACTION...
MR. BECKER, I'M THE PROJECT SUPERVISOR.
ANY MODIFICATIONS HAVE TO BE MADE IN CONSULTATION WITH ME.

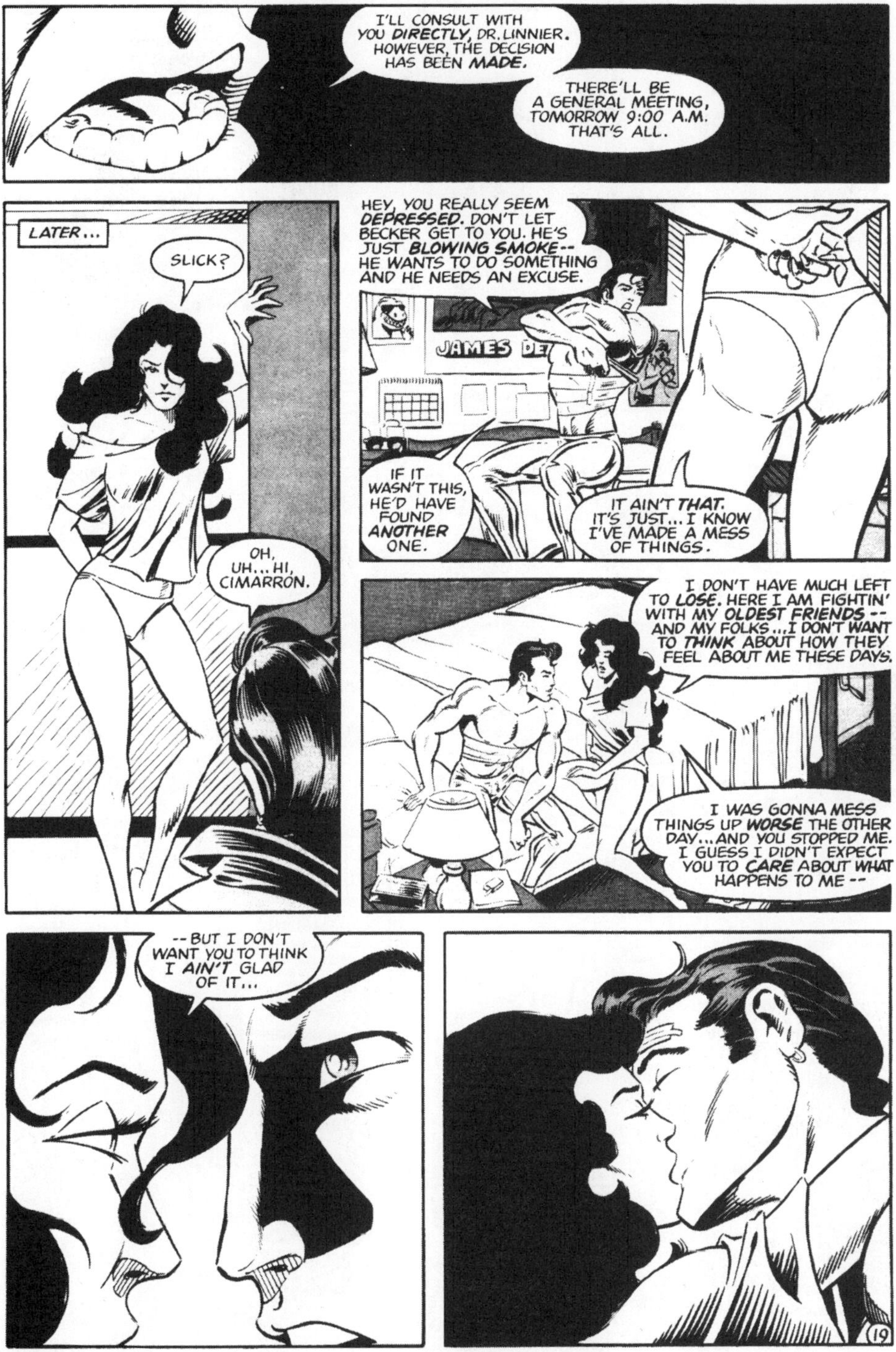
I'LL CONSULT WITH YOU DIRECTLY, DR. LINNIER. HOWEVER, THE DECISION HAS BEEN MADE.
THERE'LL BE A GENERAL MEETING, TOMORROW 9:00 A.M. THAT'S ALL.
LATER...
SLICK?
OH, UH... HI, CIMARRON.
HEY, YOU REALLY SEEM DEPRESSED. DON'T LET BECKER GET TO YOU. HE'S JUST BLOWING SMOKE-- HE WANTS TO DO SOMETHING AND HE NEEDS AN EXCUSE.
JAMES DE
IF IT WASN'T THIS, HE'D HAVE FOUND ANOTHER ONE.
IT AIN'T THAT. IT'S JUST... I KNOW I'VE MADE A MESS OF THINGS.
I DON'T HAVE MUCH LEFT TO LOSE. HERE I AM FIGHTIN' WITH MY OLDEST FRIENDS -- AND MY FOLKS... I DON'T WANT TO THINK ABOUT HOW THEY FEEL ABOUT ME THESE DAYS.
I WAS GONNA MESS THINGS UP WORSE THE OTHER DAY... AND YOU STOPPED ME. I GUESS I DIDN'T EXPECT YOU TO CARE ABOUT WHAT HAPPENS TO ME --
-- BUT I DON'T WANT YOU TO THINK I AIN'T GLAD OF IT...
19

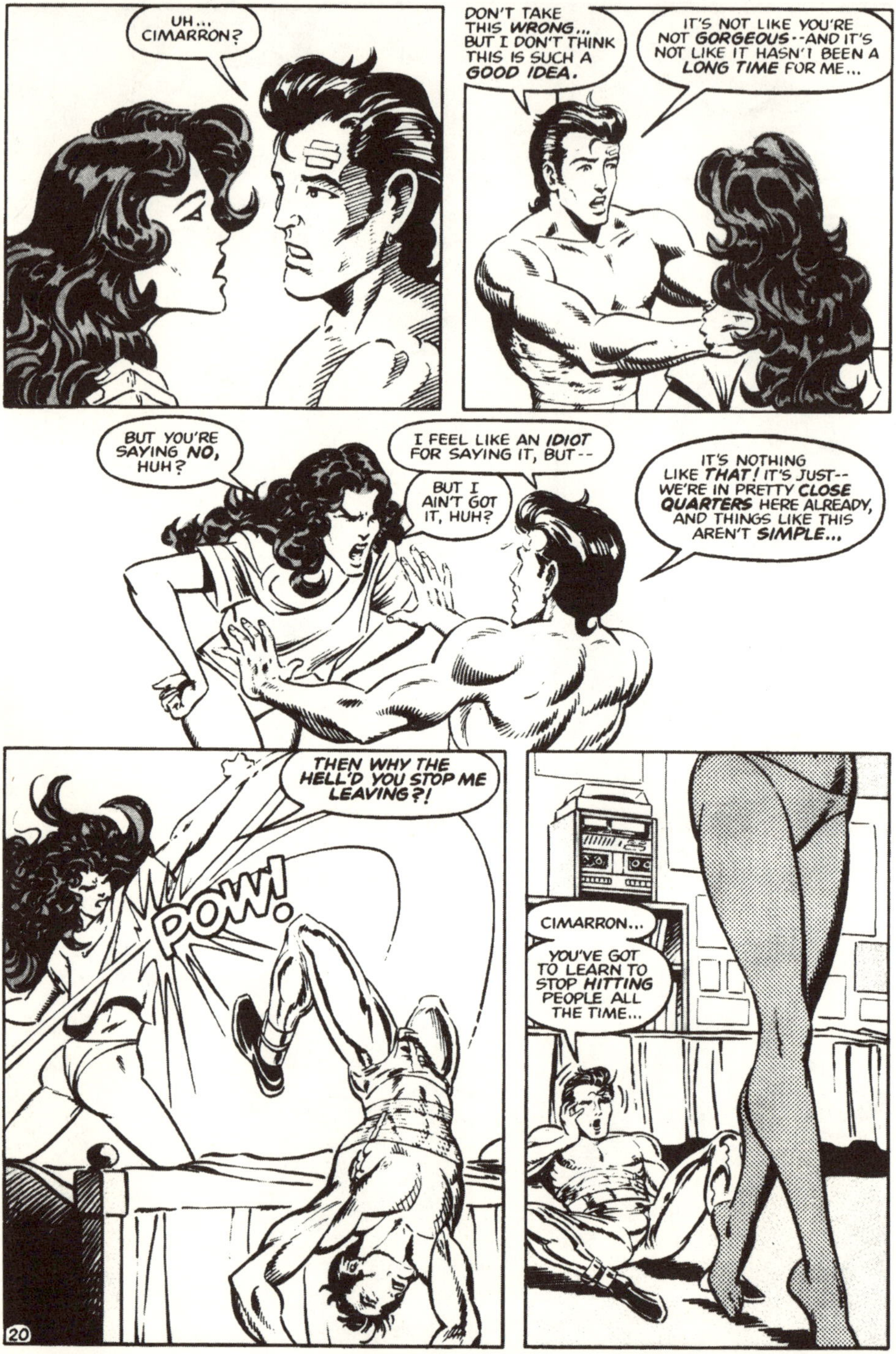
UH... CIMARRON?
DON'T TAKE THIS WRONG... BUT I DON'T THINK THIS IS SUCH A GOOD IDEA.
IT'S NOT LIKE YOU'RE NOT GORGEOUS--AND IT'S NOT LIKE IT HASN'T BEEN A LONG TIME FOR ME...
BUT YOU'RE SAYING NO, HUH?
I FEEL LIKE AN IDIOT FOR SAYING IT, BUT--
BUT I AIN'T GOT IT, HUH?
IT'S NOTHING LIKE THAT! IT'S JUST-- WE'RE IN PRETTY CLOSE QUARTERS HERE ALREADY, AND THINGS LIKE THIS AREN'T SIMPLE...
THEN WHY THE HELL'D YOU STOP ME LEAVING?!
POW!
CIMARRON...
YOU'VE GOT TO LEARN TO STOP HITTING PEOPLE ALL THE TIME...
20

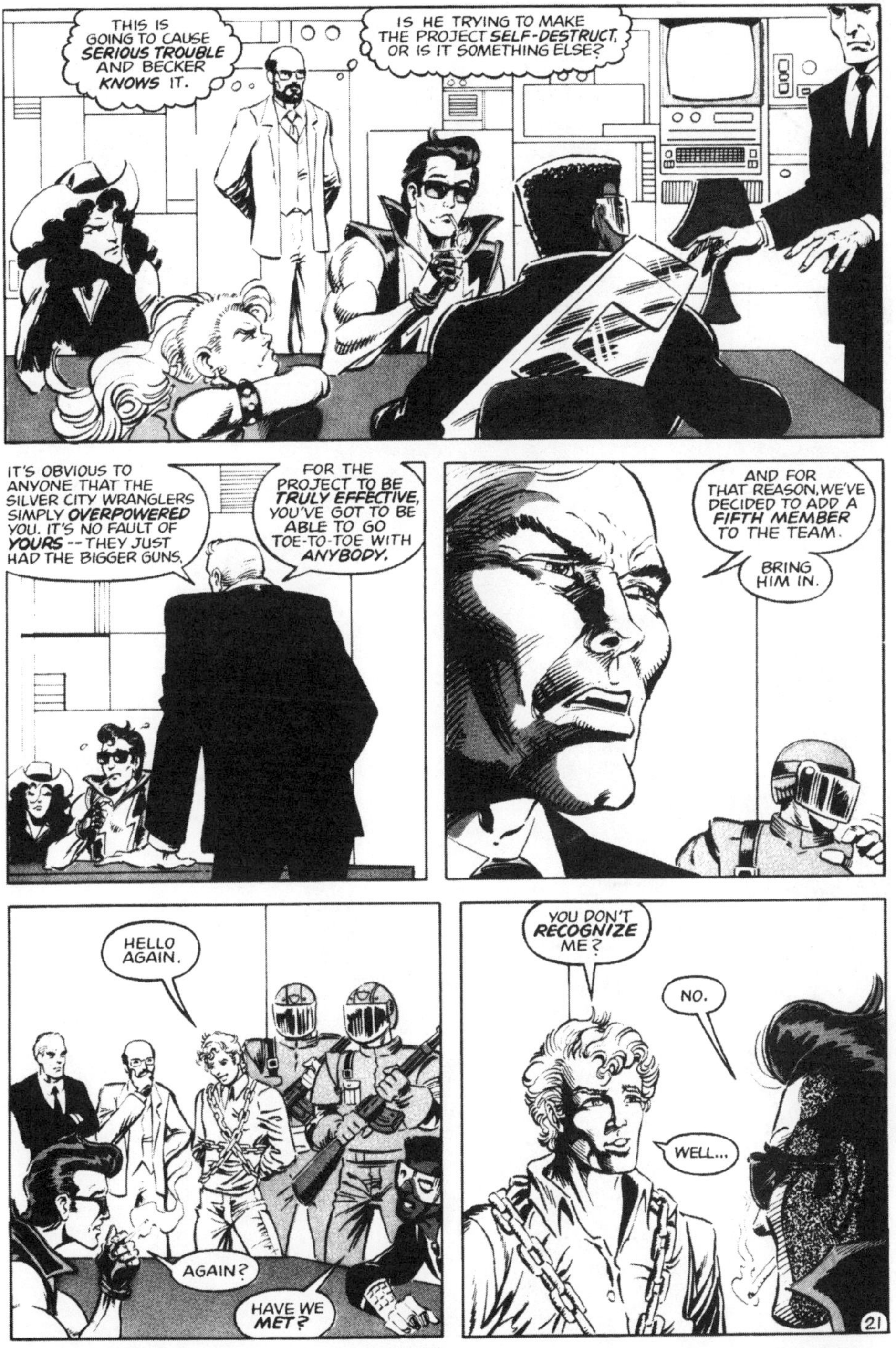
THIS IS GOING TO CAUSE SERIOUS TROUBLE AND BECKER KNOWS IT.
IS HE TRYING TO MAKE THE PROJECT SELF-DESTRUCT, OR IS IT SOMETHING ELSE?
IT'S OBVIOUS TO ANYONE THAT THE SILVER CITY WRANGLERS SIMPLY OVERPOWERED YOU. IT'S NO FAULT OF YOURS -- THEY JUST HAD THE BIGGER GUNS.
FOR THE PROJECT TO BE TRULY EFFECTIVE, YOU'VE GOT TO BE ABLE TO GO TOE-TO-TOE WITH ANYBODY.
AND FOR THAT REASON, WE'VE DECIDED TO ADD A FIFTH MEMBER TO THE TEAM.
BRING HIM IN.
HELLO AGAIN.
AGAIN?
HAVE WE MET?
YOU DON'T RECOGNIZE ME?
NO.
WELL...
21

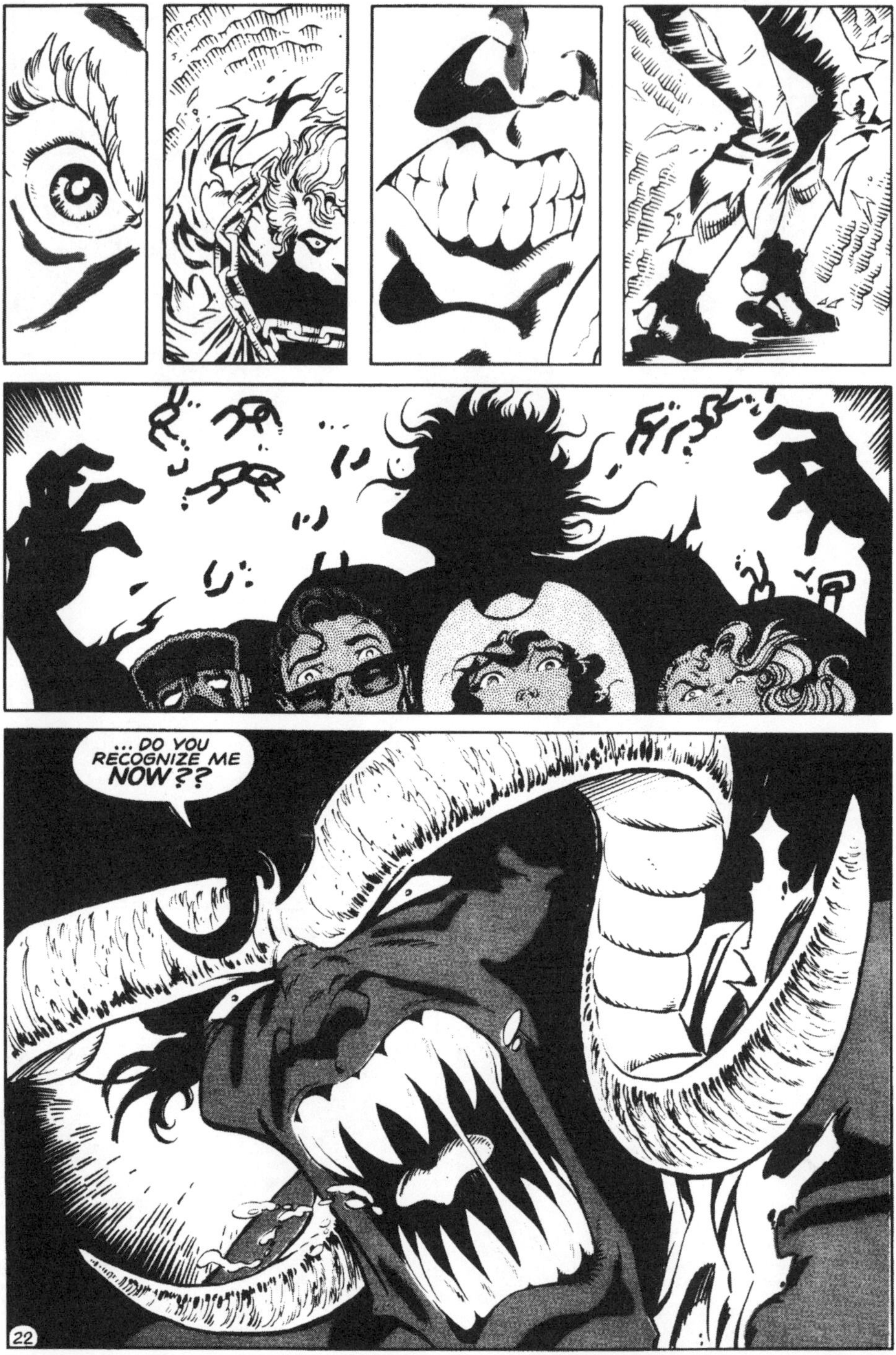
...DO YOU RECOGNIZE ME NOW??
22

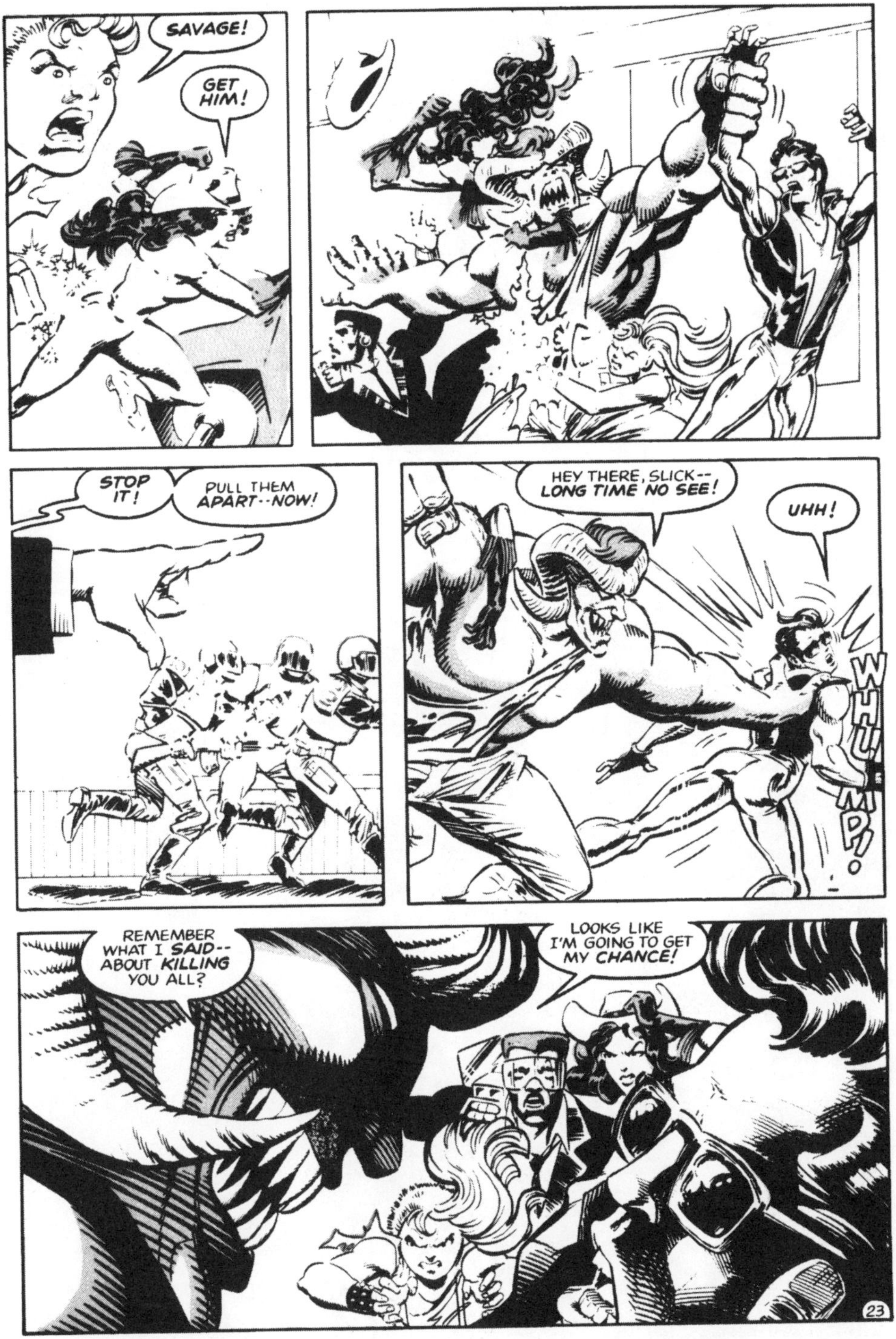
SAVAGE!
GET HIM!
STOP IT!
PULL THEM APART--NOW!
HEY THERE, SLICK--LONG TIME NO SEE!
UHH!
WHUMP!
REMEMBER WHAT I SAID--ABOUT KILLING YOU ALL?
LOOKS LIKE I'M GOING TO GET MY CHANCE!
23

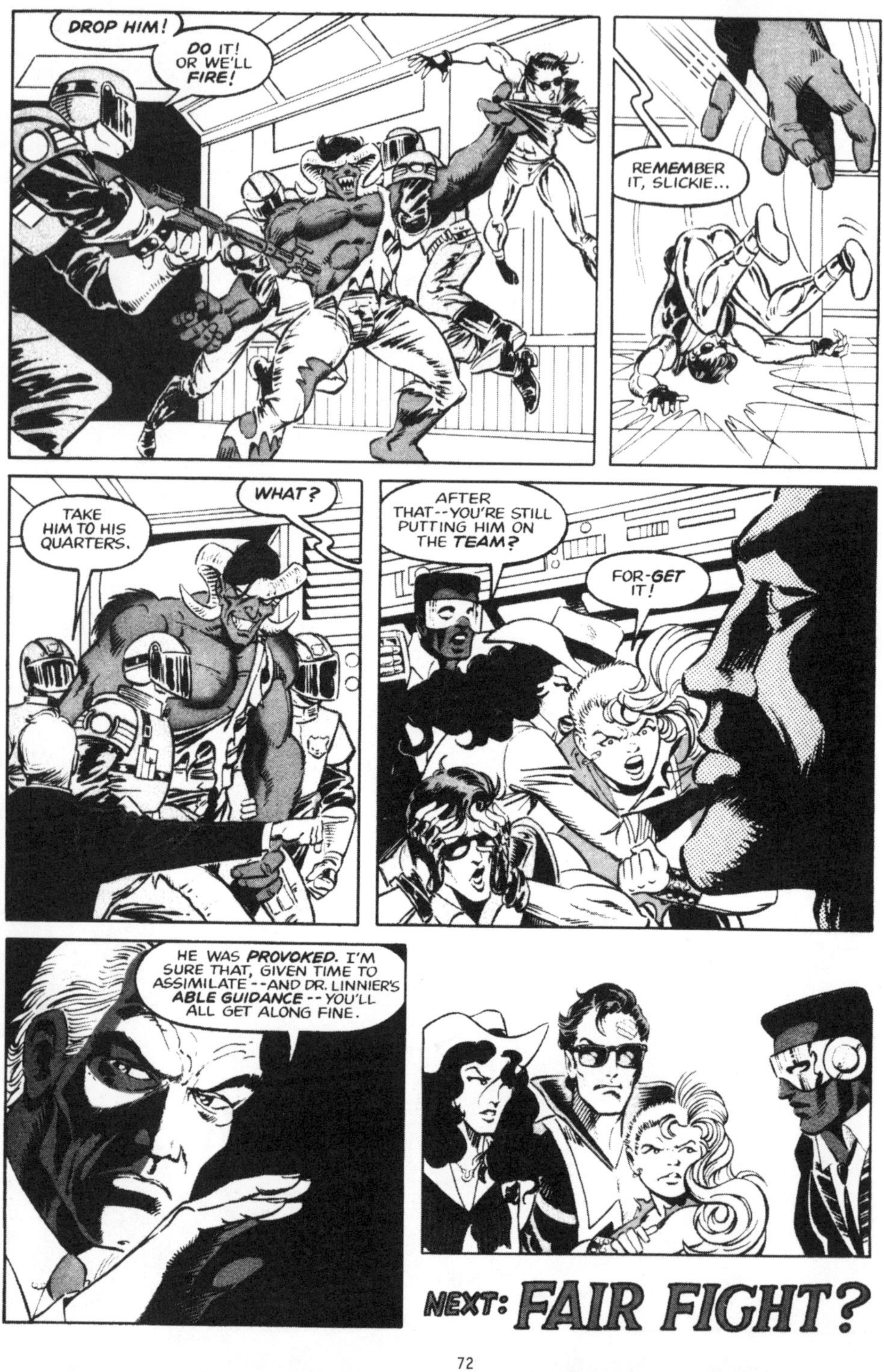

DROP HIM!
DO IT! OR WE'LL FIRE!
REMEMBER IT, SLICKIE...
TAKE HIM TO HIS QUARTERS.
WHAT?
AFTER THAT--YOU'RE STILL PUTTING HIM ON THE TEAM?
FOR-GET IT!
HE WAS PROVOKED. I'M SURE THAT, GIVEN TIME TO ASSIMILATE--AND DR. LINNIER'S ABLE GUIDANCE--YOU'LL ALL GET ALONG FINE.
NEXT: FAIR FIGHT?

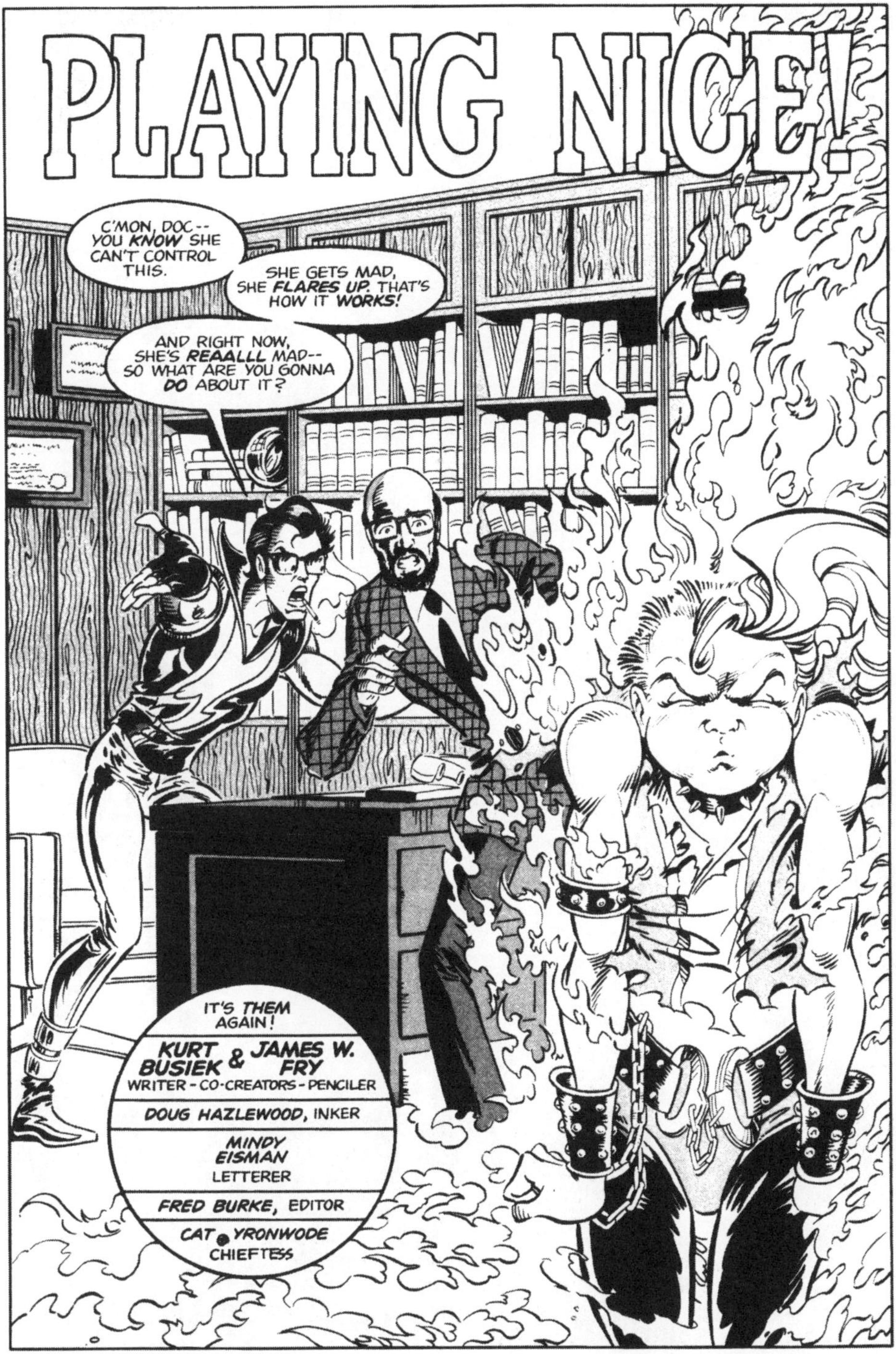
PLAYING NICE!
C'MON, DOC-- YOU KNOW SHE CAN'T CONTROL THIS.
SHE GETS MAD, SHE FLARES UP. THAT'S HOW IT WORKS!
AND RIGHT NOW, SHE'S REAALLL MAD-- SO WHAT ARE YOU GONNA DO ABOUT IT?
IT'S THEM AGAIN!
KURT BUSIEK & JAMES W. FRY
WRITER - CO-CREATORS - PENCILER
DOUG HAZLEWOOD, INKER
MINDY EISMAN
LETTERER
FRED BURKE, EDITOR
CAT YRONWODE
CHIEFTESS

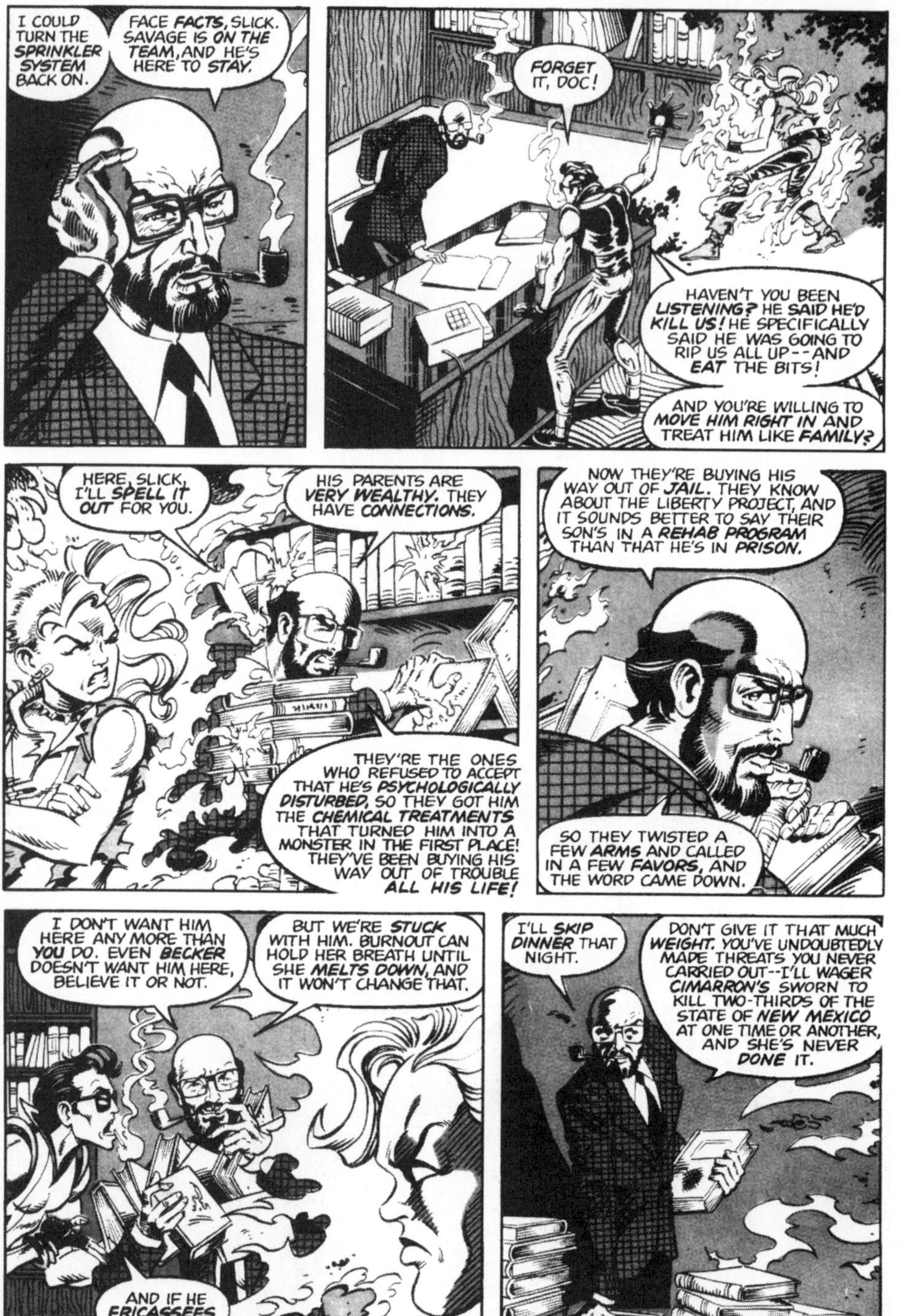
I COULD TURN THE SPRINKLER SYSTEM BACK ON.
FACE FACTS, SLICK. SAVAGE IS ON THE TEAM, AND HE'S HERE TO STAY.
FORGET IT, DOC!
HAVEN'T YOU BEEN LISTENING? HE SAID HE'D KILL US! HE SPECIFICALLY SAID HE WAS GOING TO RIP US ALL UP--AND EAT THE BITS!
AND YOU'RE WILLING TO MOVE HIM RIGHT IN AND TREAT HIM LIKE FAMILY?
HERE, SLICK, I'LL SPELL IT OUT FOR YOU.
HIS PARENTS ARE VERY WEALTHY. THEY HAVE CONNECTIONS.
THEY'RE THE ONES WHO REFUSED TO ACCEPT THAT HE'S PSYCHOLOGICALLY DISTURBED, SO THEY GOT HIM THE CHEMICAL TREATMENTS THAT TURNED HIM INTO A MONSTER IN THE FIRST PLACE! THEY'VE BEEN BUYING HIS WAY OUT OF TROUBLE ALL HIS LIFE!
NOW THEY'RE BUYING HIS WAY OUT OF JAIL. THEY KNOW ABOUT THE LIBERTY PROJECT, AND IT SOUNDS BETTER TO SAY THEIR SON'S IN A REHAB PROGRAM THAN THAT HE'S IN PRISON.
SO THEY TWISTED A FEW ARMS AND CALLED IN A FEW FAVORS, AND THE WORD CAME DOWN.
I DON'T WANT HIM HERE ANY MORE THAN YOU DO. EVEN BECKER DOESN'T WANT HIM HERE, BELIEVE IT OR NOT.
BUT WE'RE STUCK WITH HIM. BURNOUT CAN HOLD HER BREATH UNTIL SHE MELTS DOWN, AND IT WON'T CHANGE THAT.
AND IF HE FRICASSEES US?
2
I'LL SKIP DINNER THAT NIGHT.
DON'T GIVE IT THAT MUCH WEIGHT. YOU'VE UNDOUBTEDLY MADE THREATS YOU NEVER CARRIED OUT--I'LL WAGER CIMARRON'S SWORN TO KILL TWO-THIRDS OF THE STATE OF NEW MEXICO AT ONE TIME OR ANOTHER, AND SHE'S NEVER DONE IT.

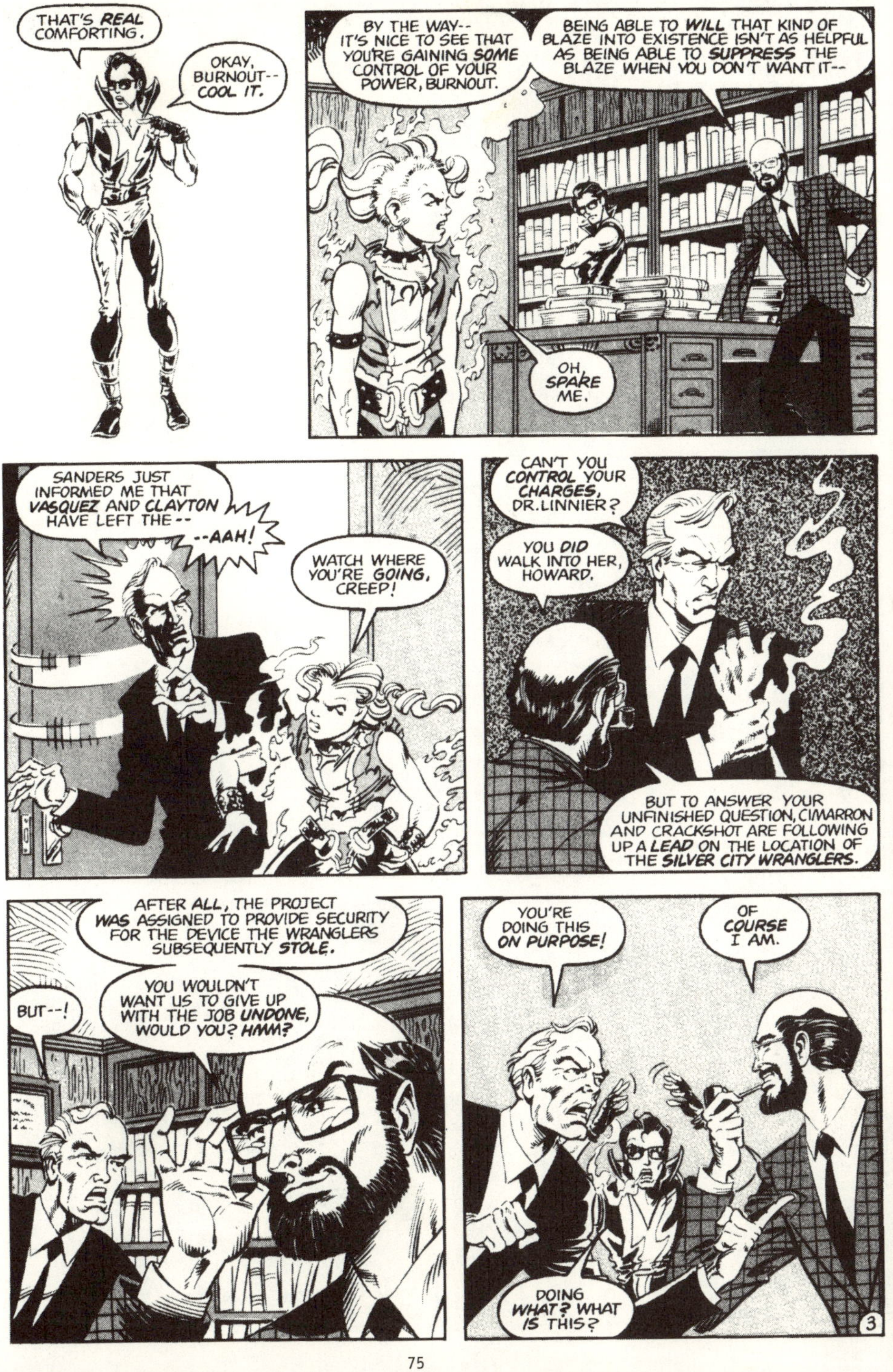
THAT'S REAL COMFORTING.
OKAY, BURNOUT-- COOL IT.
BY THE WAY-- IT'S NICE TO SEE THAT YOU'RE GAINING SOME CONTROL OF YOUR POWER, BURNOUT.
BEING ABLE TO WILL THAT KIND OF BLAZE INTO EXISTENCE ISN'T AS HELPFUL AS BEING ABLE TO SUPPRESS THE BLAZE WHEN YOU DON'T WANT IT--
OH, SPARE ME.
SANDERS JUST INFORMED ME THAT VASQUEZ AND CLAYTON HAVE LEFT THE--
--AAH!
WATCH WHERE YOU'RE GOING, CREEP!
CAN'T YOU CONTROL YOUR CHARGES, DR. LINNIER?
YOU DID WALK INTO HER, HOWARD.
BUT TO ANSWER YOUR UNFINISHED QUESTION, CIMARRON AND CRACKSHOT ARE FOLLOWING UP A LEAD ON THE LOCATION OF THE SILVER CITY WRANGLERS.
AFTER ALL, THE PROJECT WAS ASSIGNED TO PROVIDE SECURITY FOR THE DEVICE THE WRANGLERS SUBSEQUENTLY STOLE.
BUT--!
YOU WOULDN'T WANT US TO GIVE UP WITH THE JOB UNDONE, WOULD YOU? HMM?
YOU'RE DOING THIS ON PURPOSE!
OF COURSE I AM.
DOING WHAT? WHAT IS THIS?
3

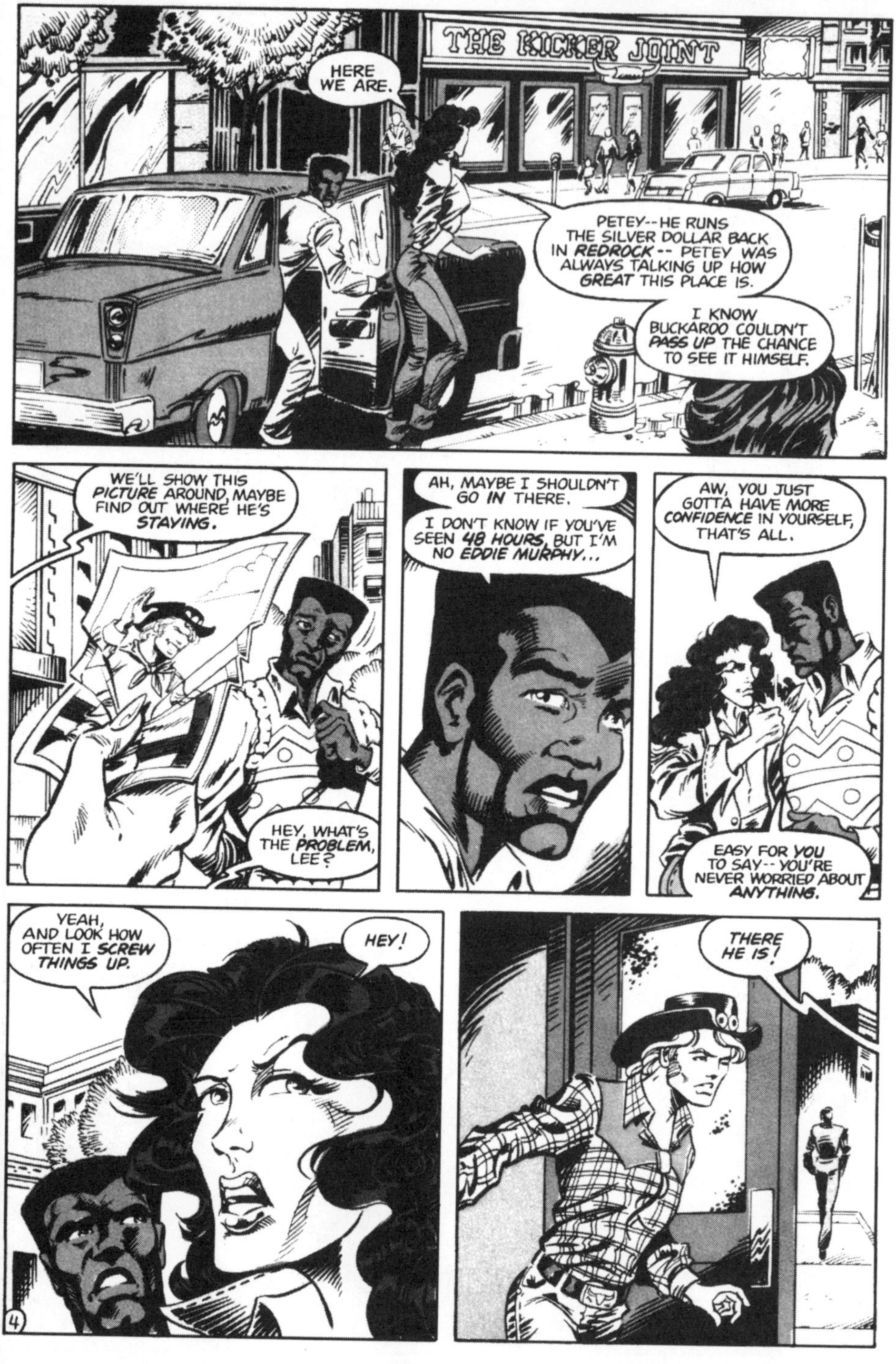
THE KICKER JOINT
HERE WE ARE.
PETEY--HE RUNS THE SILVER DOLLAR BACK IN REDROCK-- PETEY WAS ALWAYS TALKING UP HOW GREAT THIS PLACE IS.
I KNOW BUCKAROO COULDN'T PASS UP THE CHANCE TO SEE IT HIMSELF.
WE'LL SHOW THIS PICTURE AROUND, MAYBE FIND OUT WHERE HE'S STAYING.
HEY, WHAT'S THE PROBLEM, LEE?
AH, MAYBE I SHOULDN'T GO IN THERE.
I DON'T KNOW IF YOU'VE SEEN 48 HOURS, BUT I'M NO EDDIE MURPHY...
AW, YOU JUST GOTTA HAVE MORE CONFIDENCE IN YOURSELF, THAT'S ALL.
EASY FOR YOU TO SAY-- YOU'RE NEVER WORRIED ABOUT ANYTHING.
YEAH, AND LOOK HOW OFTEN I SCREW THINGS UP.
HEY!
THERE HE IS!
4

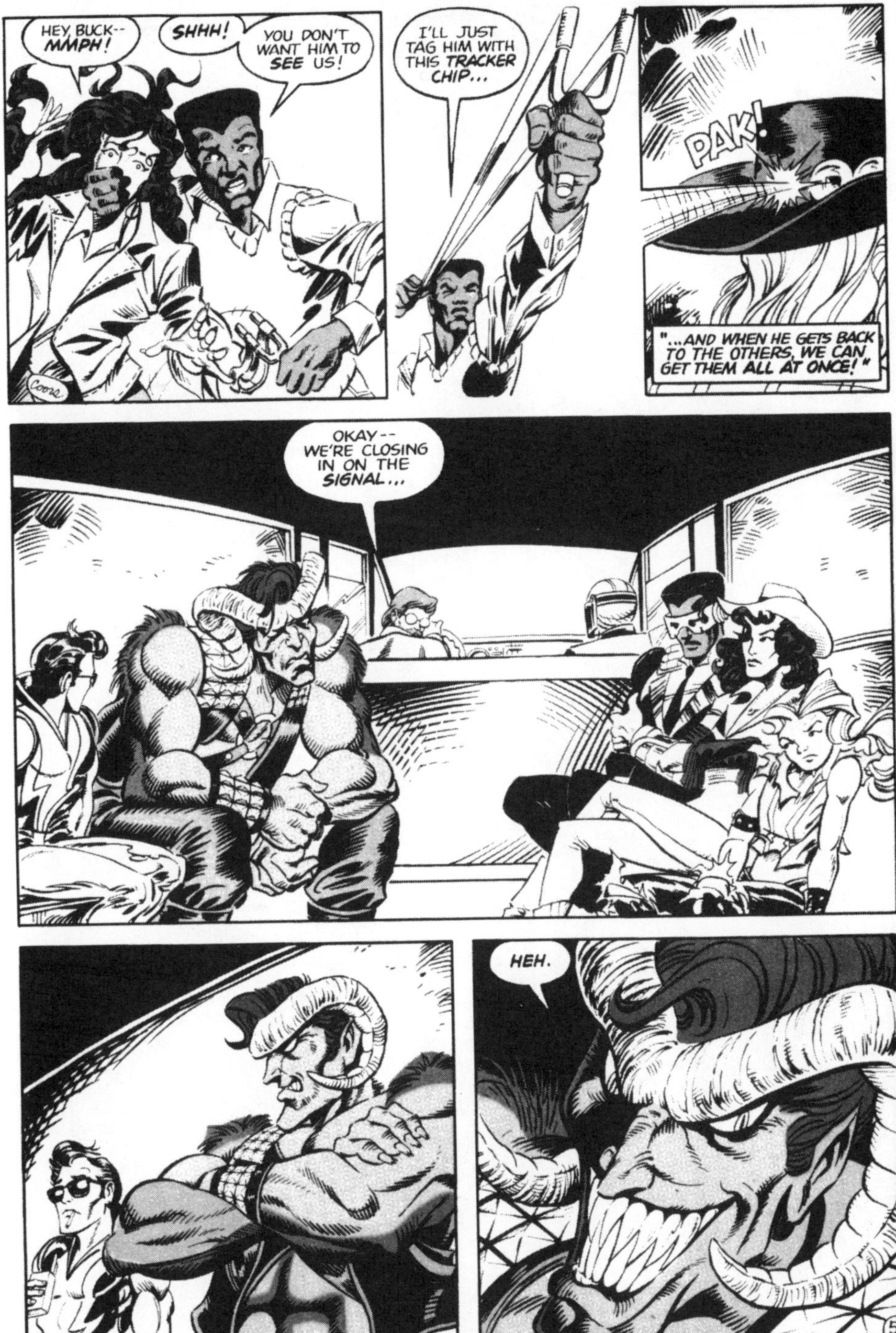
HEY, BUCK-- MMPH!
SHHH!
YOU DON'T WANT HIM TO SEE US!
I'LL JUST TAG HIM WITH THIS TRACKER CHIP...
PAK!
"...AND WHEN HE GETS BACK TO THE OTHERS, WE CAN GET THEM ALL AT ONCE!"
OKAY-- WE'RE CLOSING IN ON THE SIGNAL...
HEH.
5

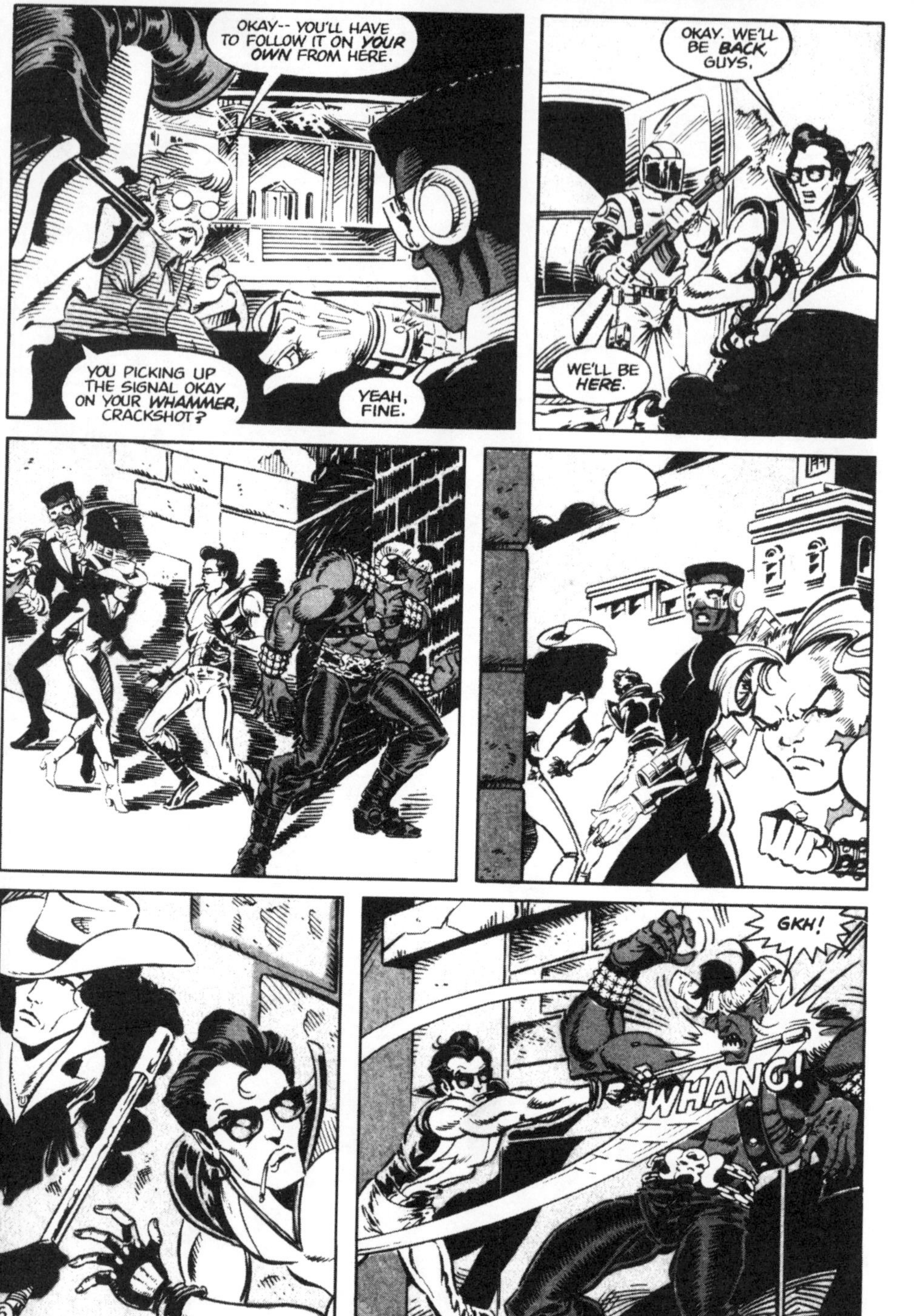
OKAY-- YOU'LL HAVE TO FOLLOW IT ON YOUR OWN FROM HERE.
YOU PICKING UP THE SIGNAL OKAY ON YOUR WHAMMER, CRACKSHOT?
YEAH, FINE.
OKAY. WE'LL BE BACK, GUYS.
WE'LL BE HERE.
GKH!
WHANG!

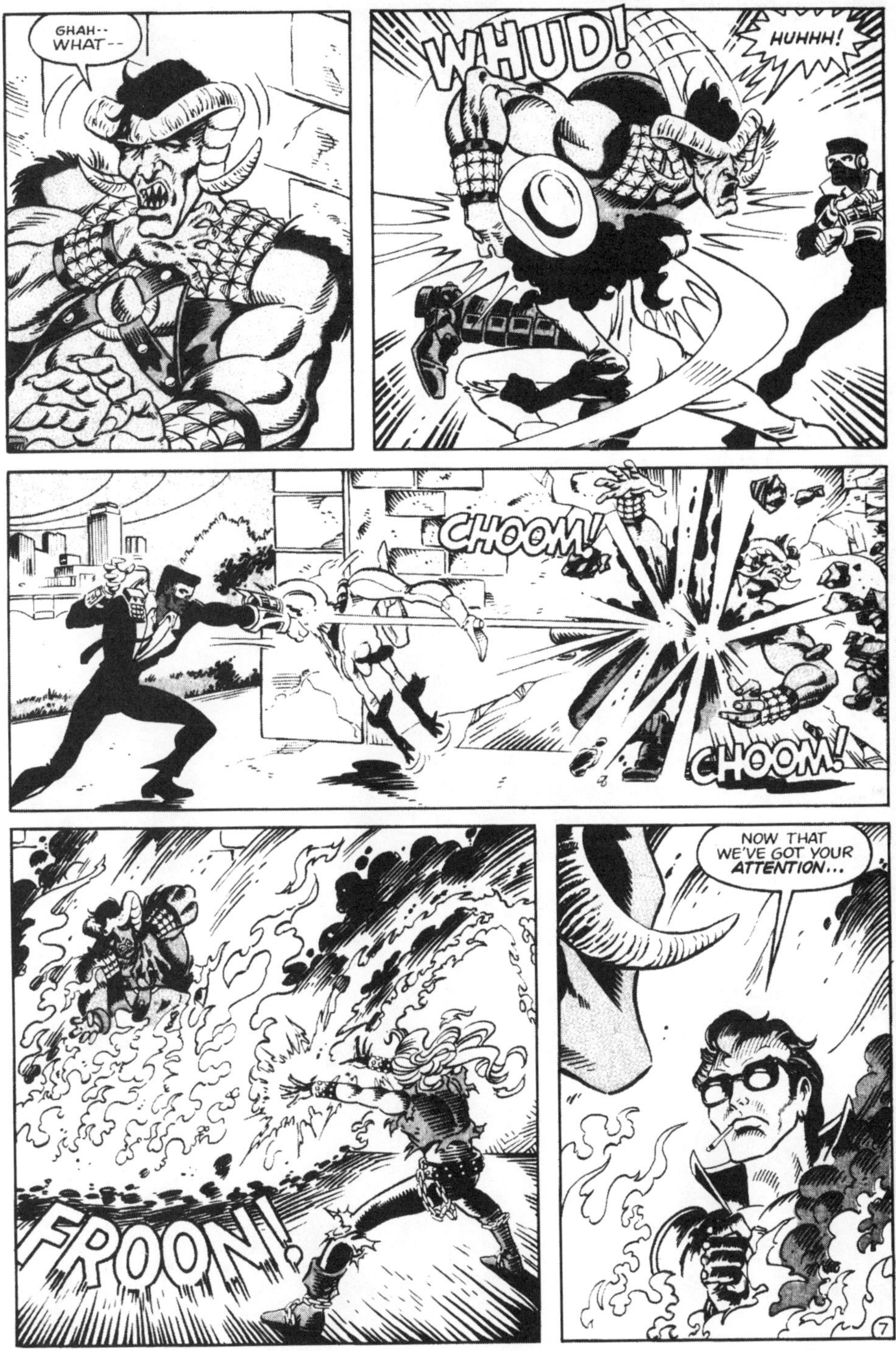
GHAH--
WHAT--
WHUD!
HUHHH!
CHOOM!
CHOOM!
FROON!
NOW THAT WE'VE GOT YOUR ATTENTION...
7

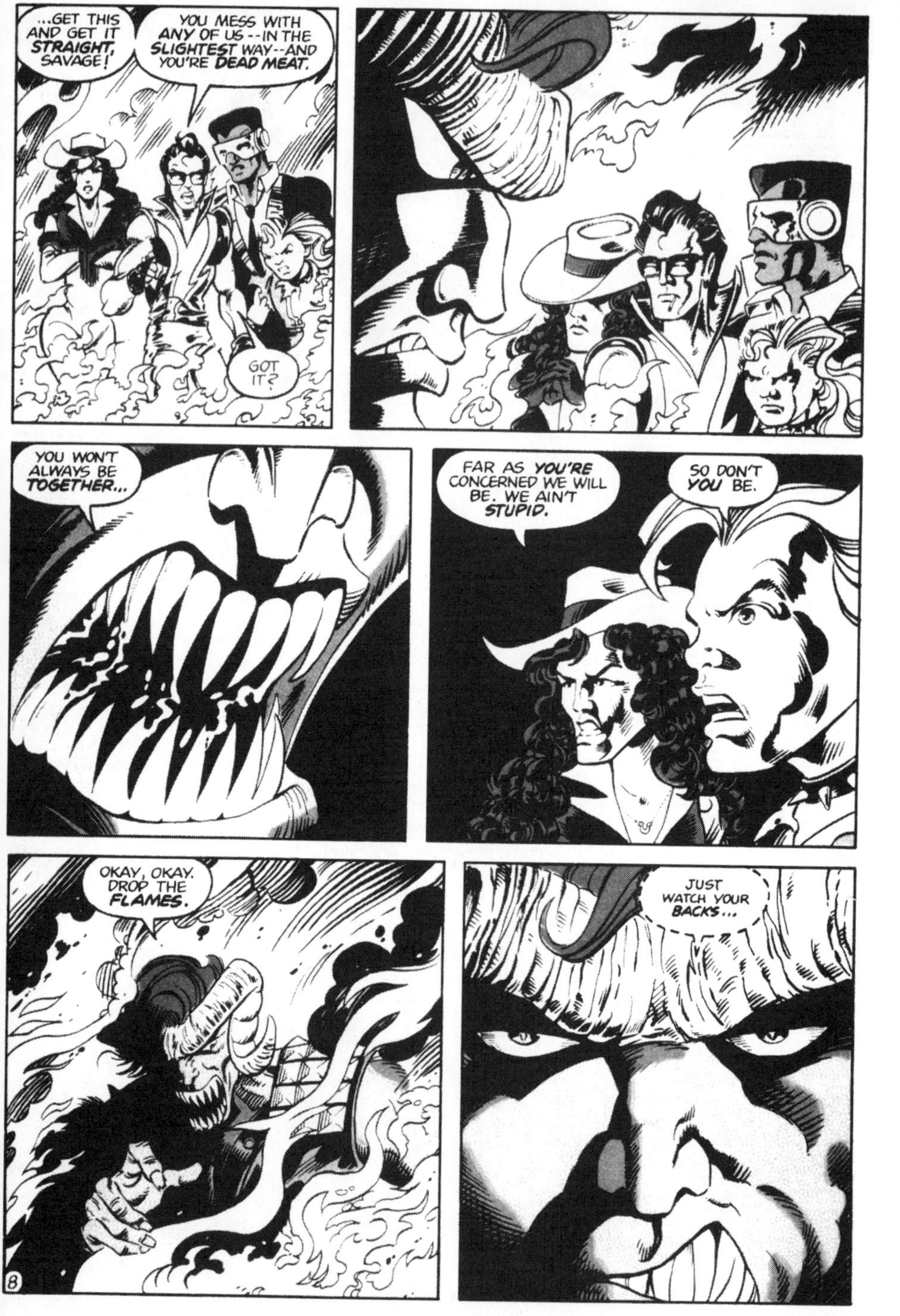

...GET THIS AND GET IT STRAIGHT, SAVAGE!
YOU MESS WITH ANY OF US--IN THE SLIGHTEST WAY--AND YOU'RE DEAD MEAT.
GOT IT?
YOU WON'T ALWAYS BE TOGETHER...
FAR AS YOU'RE CONCERNED WE WILL BE. WE AIN'T STUPID.
SO DON'T YOU BE.
OKAY, OKAY. DROP THE FLAMES.
JUST WATCH YOUR BACKS...
8

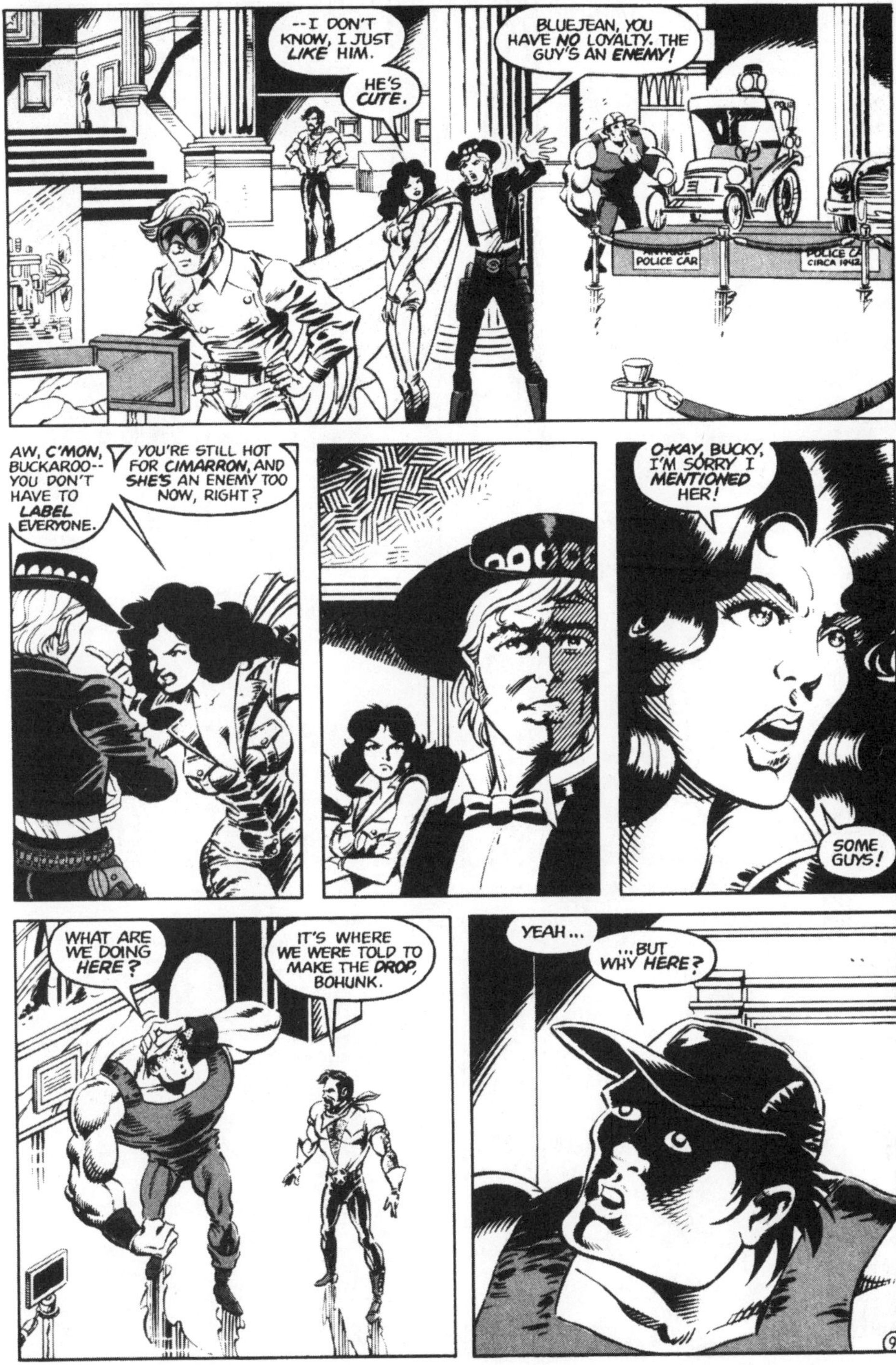

--I DON'T KNOW, I JUST LIKE HIM.
HE'S CUTE.
BLUEJEAN, YOU HAVE NO LOYALTY. THE GUY'S AN ENEMY!
POLICE CAR
POLICE CA
CIRCA 1942
AW, C'MON, BUCKAROO-- YOU DON'T HAVE TO LABEL EVERYONE.
YOU'RE STILL HOT FOR CIMARRON, AND SHE'S AN ENEMY TOO NOW, RIGHT?
O-KAY, BUCKY, I'M SORRY I MENTIONED HER!
SOME GUYS!
WHAT ARE WE DOING HERE?
IT'S WHERE WE WERE TOLD TO MAKE THE DROP, BOHUNK.
YEAH...
...BUT WHY HERE?
9

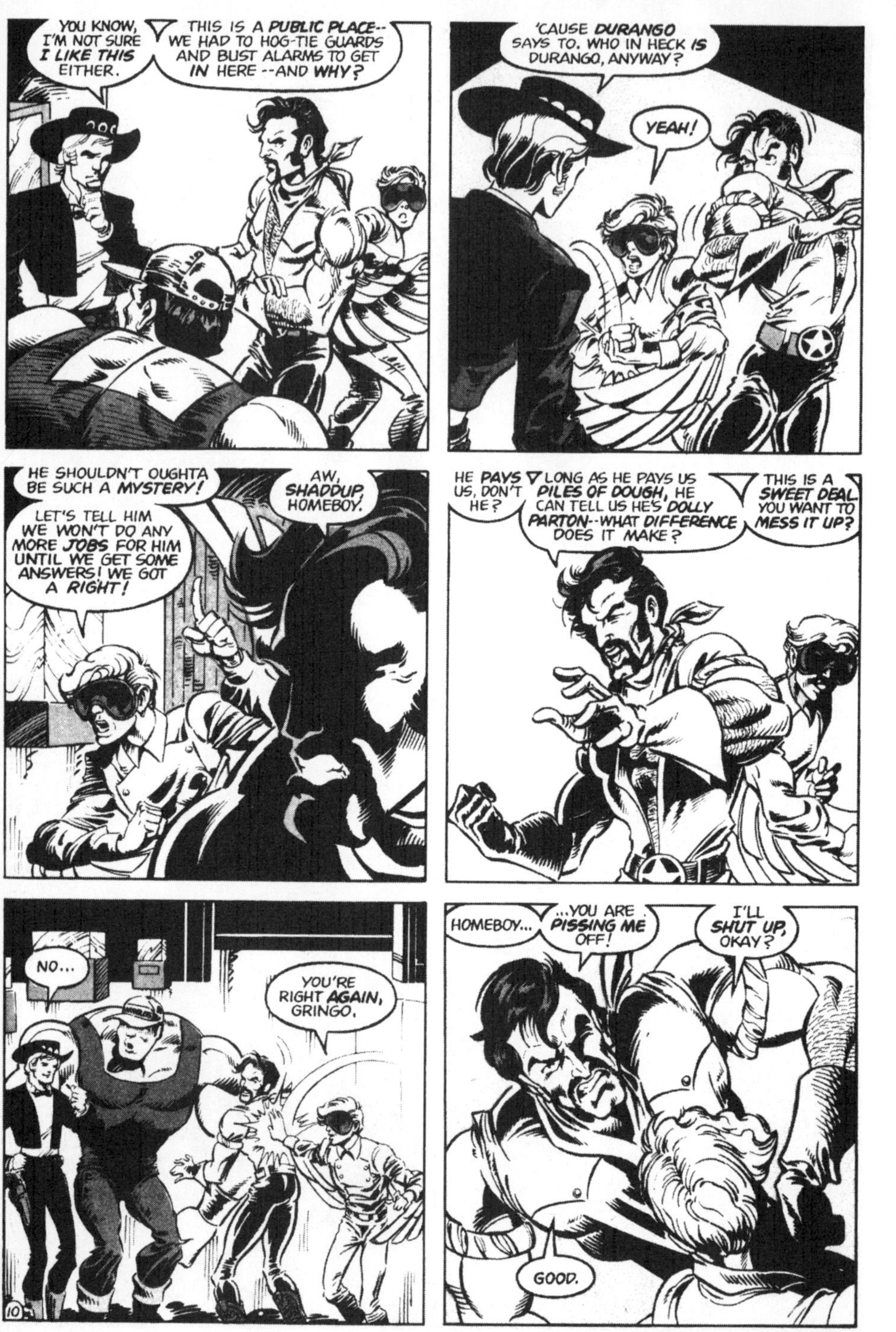
YOU KNOW, I'M NOT SURE I LIKE THIS EITHER.
THIS IS A PUBLIC PLACE-- WE HAD TO HOG-TIE GUARDS AND BUST ALARMS TO GET IN HERE --AND WHY?
'CAUSE DURANGO SAYS TO. WHO IN HECK IS DURANGO, ANYWAY?
YEAH!
HE SHOULDN'T OUGHTA BE SUCH A MYSTERY!
LET'S TELL HIM WE WON'T DO ANY MORE JOBS FOR HIM UNTIL WE GET SOME ANSWERS! WE GOT A RIGHT!
AW, SHADDUP, HOMEBOY.
HE PAYS US, DON'T HE?
LONG AS HE PAYS US PILES OF DOUGH, HE CAN TELL US HE'S DOLLY PARTON--WHAT DIFFERENCE DOES IT MAKE?
THIS IS A SWEET DEAL. YOU WANT TO MESS IT UP?
NO...
YOU'RE RIGHT AGAIN, GRINGO.
10
HOMEBOY...
...YOU ARE PISSING ME OFF!
I'LL SHUT UP, OKAY?
GOOD.

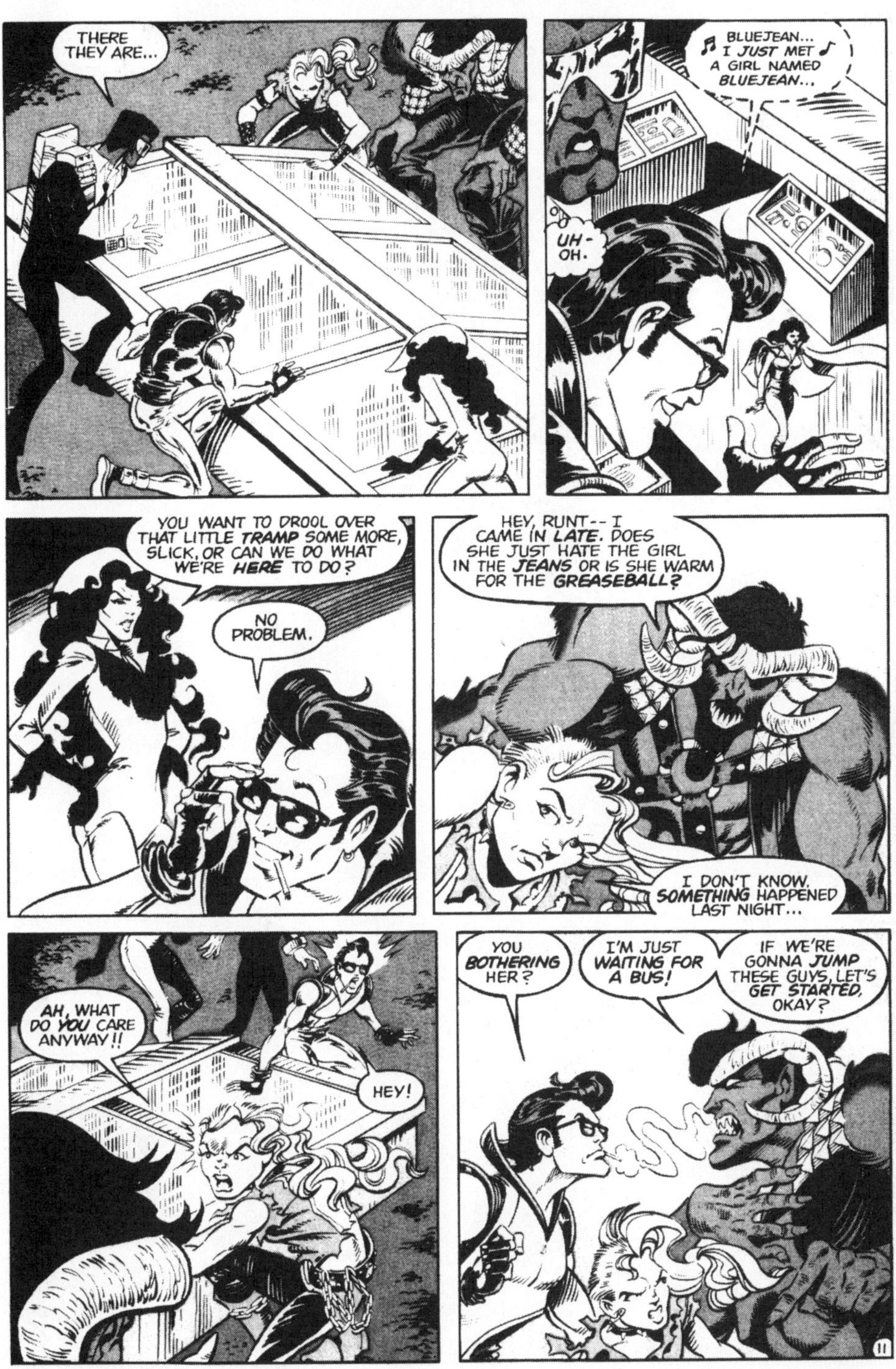
THERE THEY ARE...
♫ BLUEJEAN... I JUST MET A GIRL NAMED BLUEJEAN... ♪
UH-OH.
YOU WANT TO DROOL OVER THAT LITTLE TRAMP SOME MORE, SLICK, OR CAN WE DO WHAT WE'RE HERE TO DO?
NO PROBLEM.
HEY, RUNT-- I CAME IN LATE. DOES SHE JUST HATE THE GIRL IN THE JEANS OR IS SHE WARM FOR THE GREASEBALL?
I DON'T KNOW. SOMETHING HAPPENED LAST NIGHT...
AH, WHAT DO YOU CARE ANYWAY!!
HEY!
YOU BOTHERING HER?
I'M JUST WAITING FOR A BUS!
IF WE'RE GONNA JUMP THESE GUYS, LET'S GET STARTED, OKAY?
11

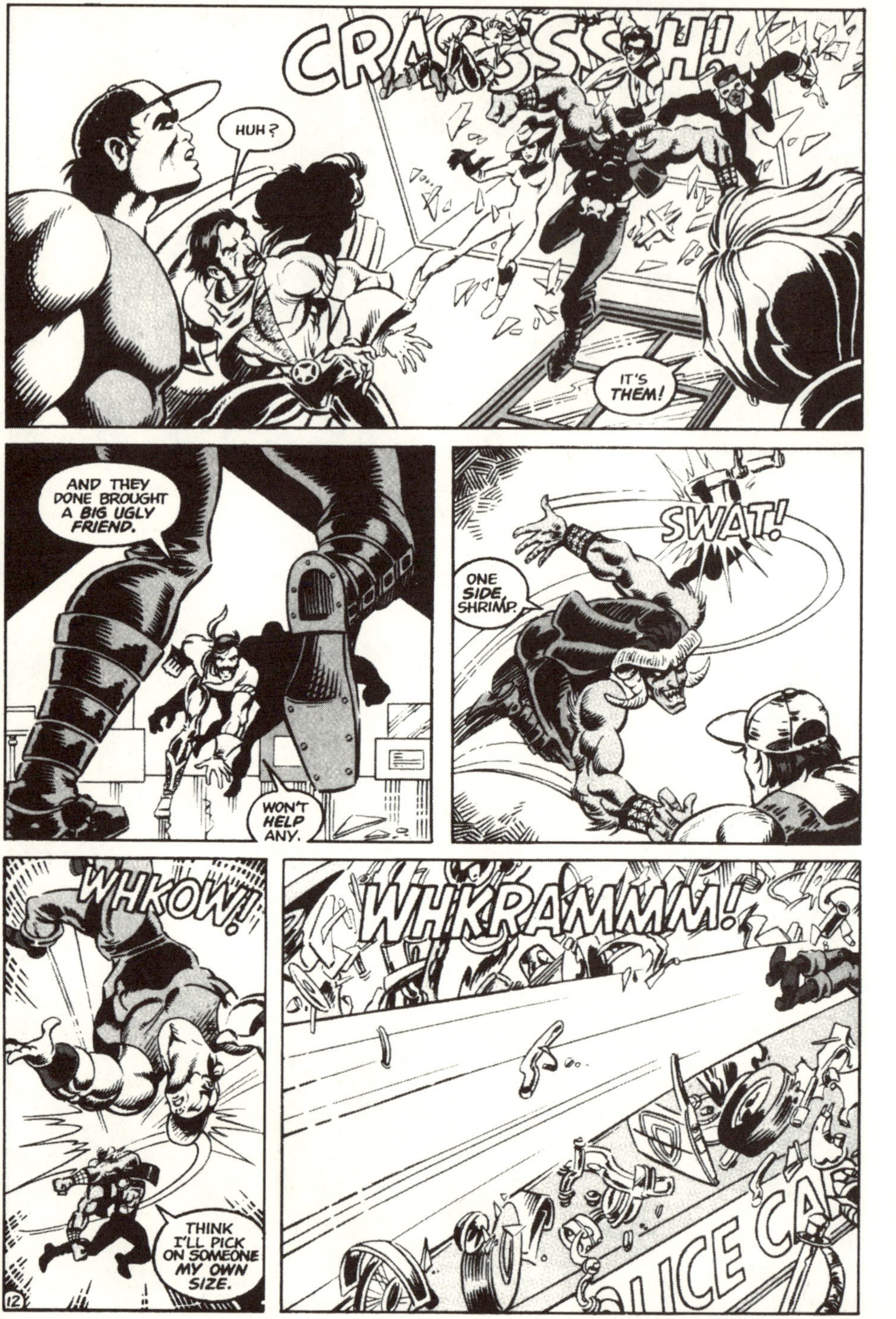
CRASSSSH!
HUH?
IT'S THEM!
AND THEY DONE BROUGHT A BIG UGLY FRIEND.
WON'T HELP ANY.
SWAT!
ONE SIDE, SHRIMP.
WHKOW!
THINK I'LL PICK ON SOMEONE MY OWN SIZE.
12
WHKRAMMMM!
LICE CA

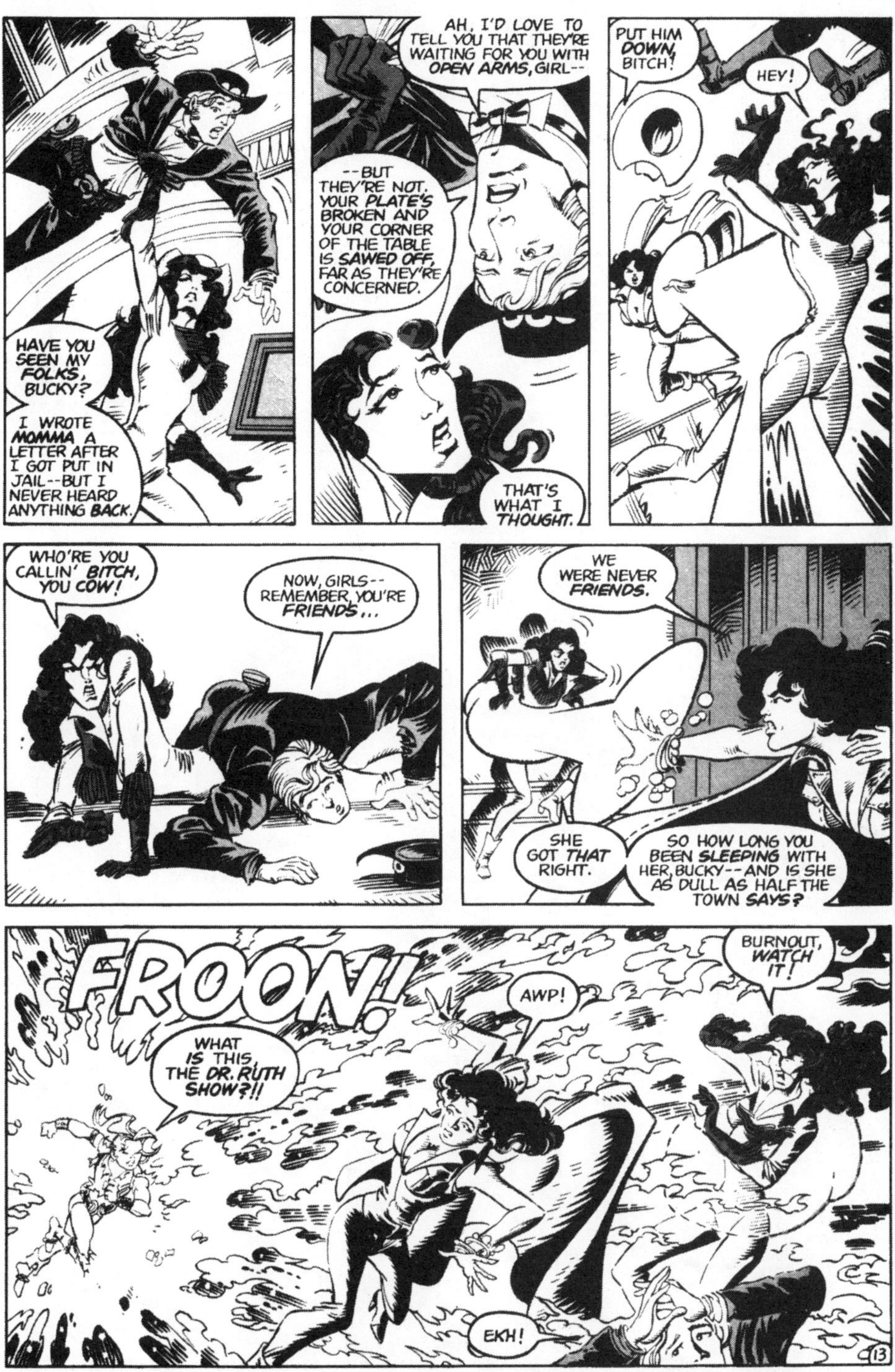
HAVE YOU SEEN MY FOLKS, BUCKY?
I WROTE MOMMA A LETTER AFTER I GOT PUT IN JAIL--BUT I NEVER HEARD ANYTHING BACK.
AH, I'D LOVE TO TELL YOU THAT THEY'RE WAITING FOR YOU WITH OPEN ARMS, GIRL--
--BUT THEY'RE NOT. YOUR PLATE'S BROKEN AND YOUR CORNER OF THE TABLE IS SAWED OFF, FAR AS THEY'RE CONCERNED.
THAT'S WHAT I THOUGHT.
PUT HIM DOWN, BITCH!
HEY!
WHO'RE YOU CALLIN' BITCH, YOU COW!
NOW, GIRLS-- REMEMBER, YOU'RE FRIENDS...
WE WERE NEVER FRIENDS.
SHE GOT THAT RIGHT.
SO HOW LONG YOU BEEN SLEEPING WITH HER, BUCKY--AND IS SHE AS DULL AS HALF THE TOWN SAYS?
FROON!
WHAT IS THIS, THE DR. RUTH SHOW?!!
AWP!
BURNOUT, WATCH IT!
EKH!
13

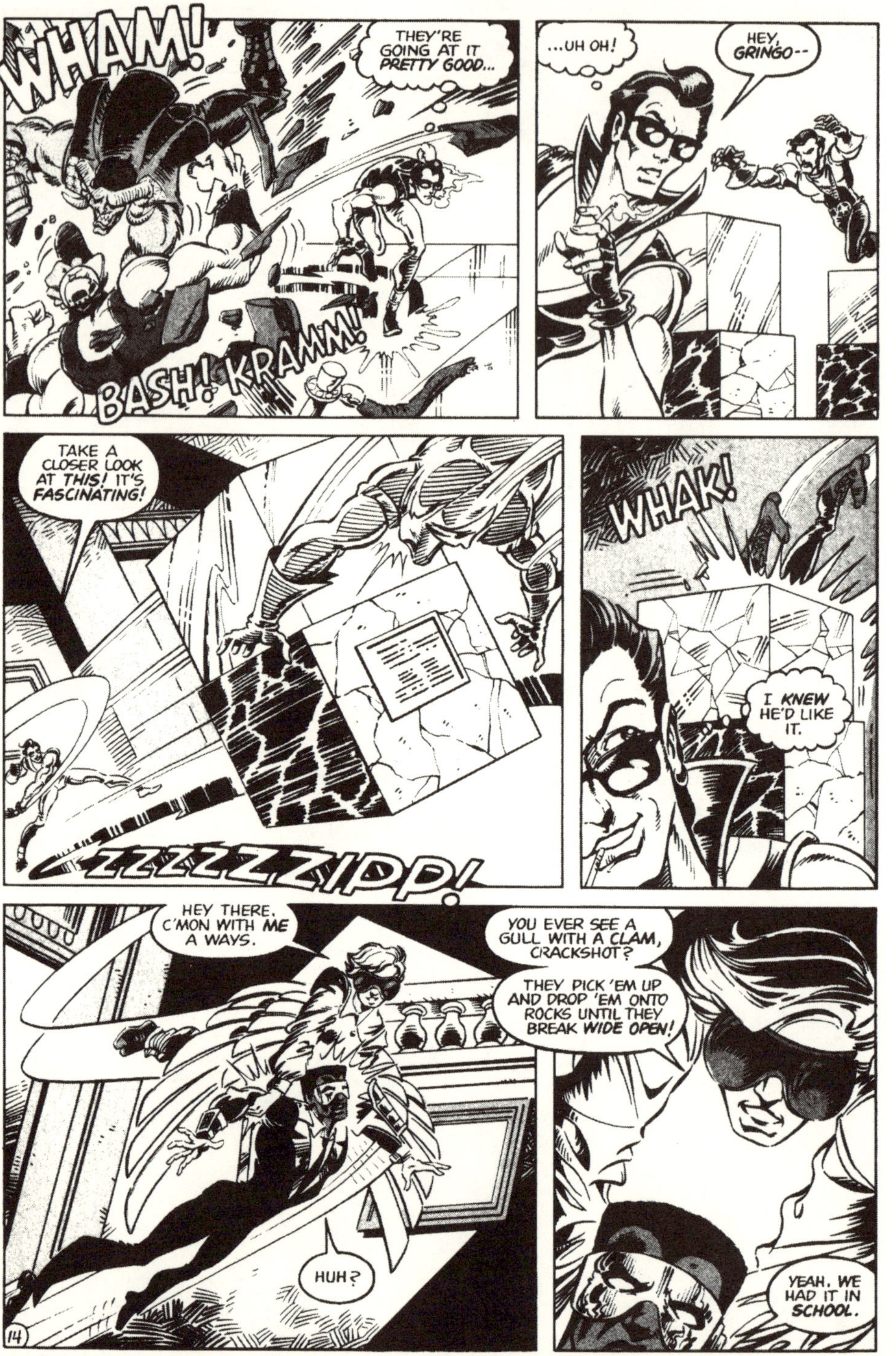
WHAM!
THEY'RE GOING AT IT PRETTY GOOD...
BASH! KRAMM!
...UH OH!
HEY, GRINGO--
TAKE A CLOSER LOOK AT THIS! IT'S FASCINATING!
ZZZZZZIPP!
WHAK!
I KNEW HE'D LIKE IT.
HEY THERE. C'MON WITH ME A WAYS.
HUH?
YOU EVER SEE A GULL WITH A CLAM, CRACKSHOT?
THEY PICK 'EM UP AND DROP 'EM ONTO ROCKS UNTIL THEY BREAK WIDE OPEN!
YEAH. WE HAD IT IN SCHOOL.
14

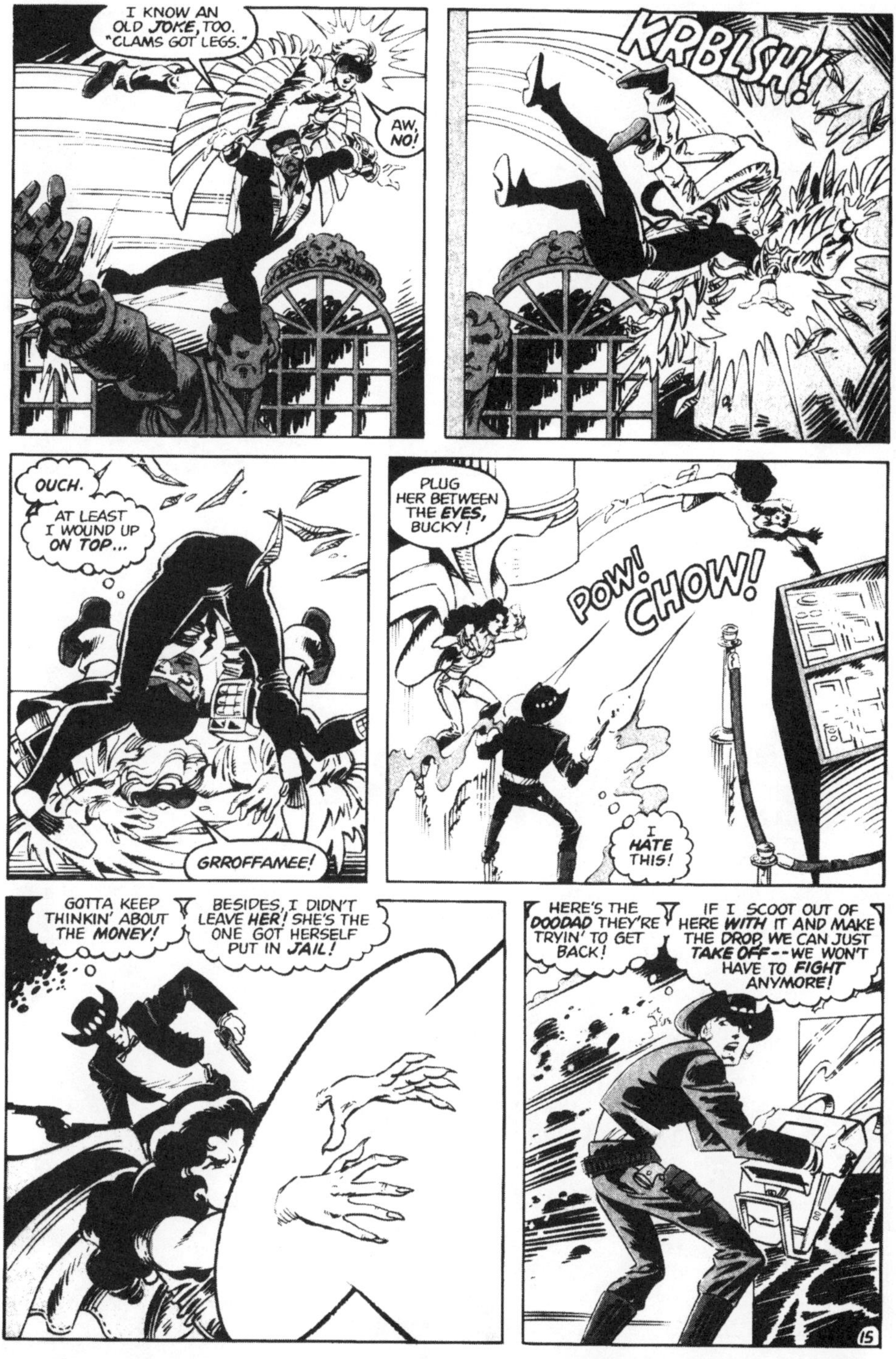

I KNOW AN OLD JOKE, TOO. "CLAMS GOT LEGS."
AW, NO!
KRBLSH!
OUCH.
AT LEAST I WOUND UP ON TOP...
GRROFFAMEE!
PLUG HER BETWEEN THE EYES, BUCKY!
POW! CHOW!
I HATE THIS!
GOTTA KEEP THINKIN' ABOUT THE MONEY!
BESIDES, I DIDN'T LEAVE HER! SHE'S THE ONE GOT HERSELF PUT IN JAIL!
HERE'S THE DOODAD THEY'RE TRYIN' TO GET BACK!
IF I SCOOT OUT OF HERE WITH IT AND MAKE THE DROP, WE CAN JUST TAKE OFF--WE WON'T HAVE TO FIGHT ANYMORE!
15

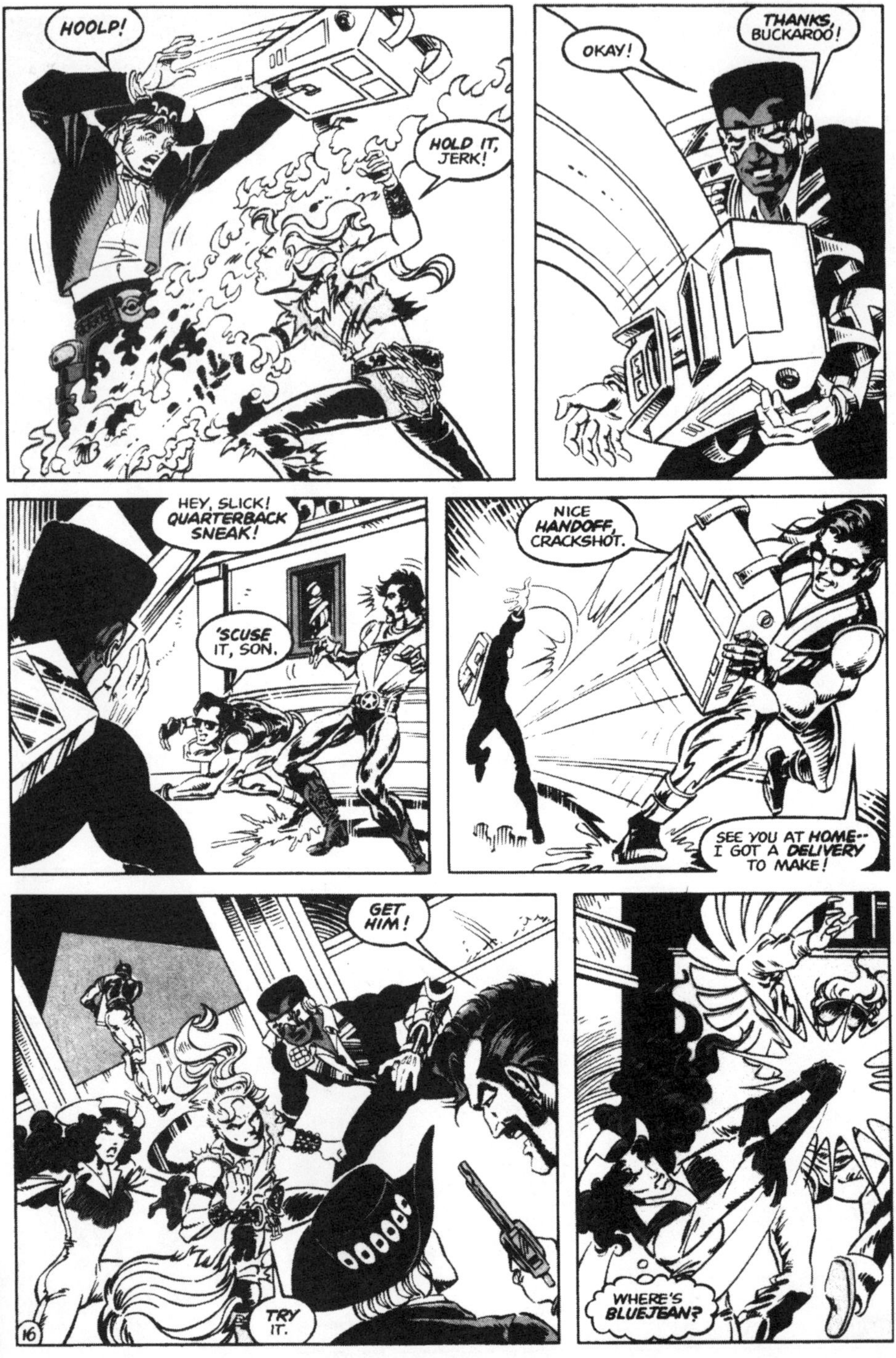
HOOLP!
HOLD IT, JERK!
OKAY!
THANKS, BUCKAROO!
HEY, SLICK! QUARTERBACK SNEAK!
'SCUSE IT, SON.
NICE HANDOFF, CRACKSHOT.
SEE YOU AT HOME-- I GOT A DELIVERY TO MAKE!
GET HIM!
TRY IT.
16
WHERE'S BLUEJEAN?

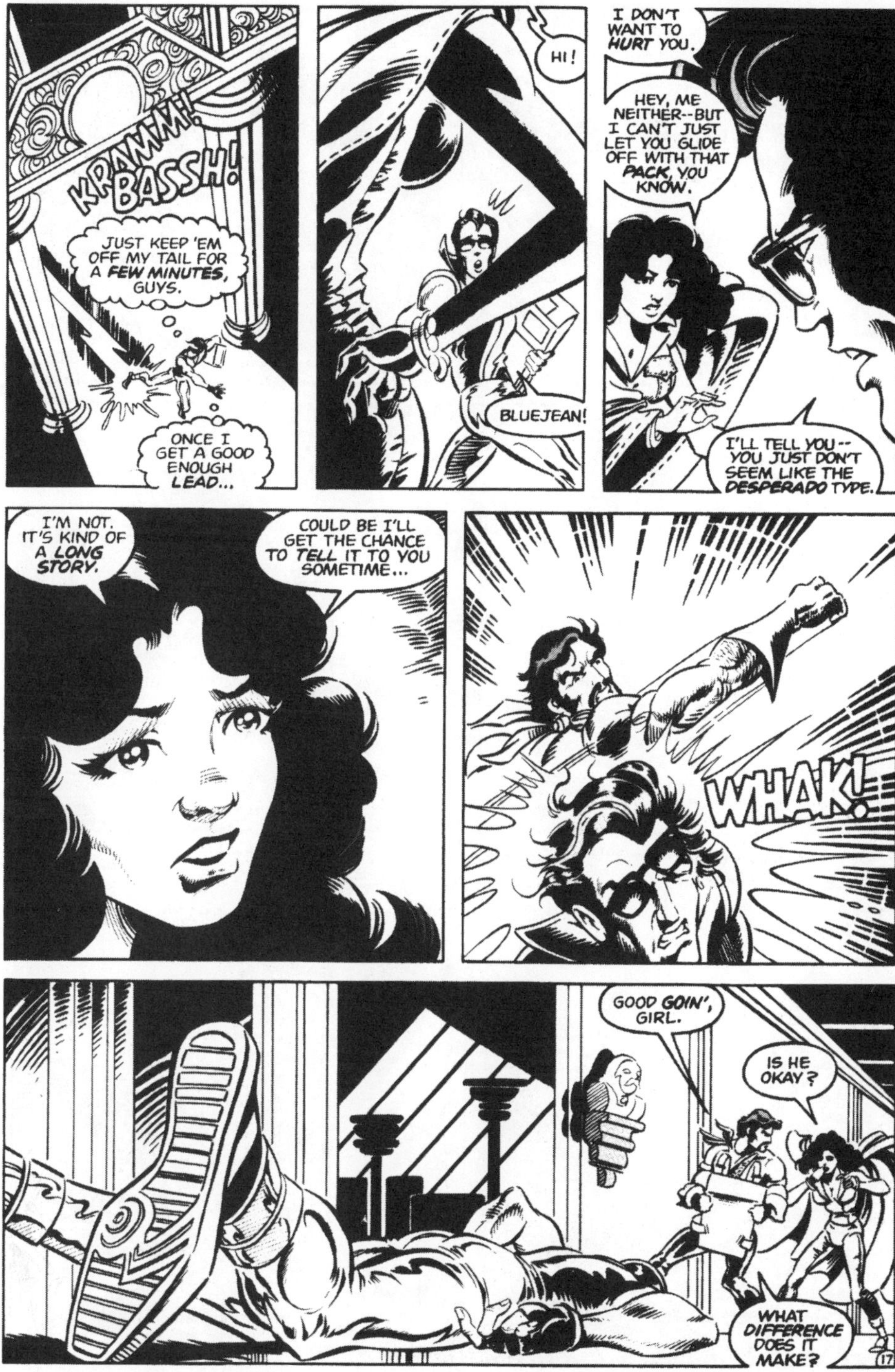
KRAMM! BASSH!
JUST KEEP 'EM OFF MY TAIL FOR A FEW MINUTES, GUYS.
ONCE I GET A GOOD ENOUGH LEAD...
HI!
BLUEJEAN!
I DON'T WANT TO HURT YOU.
HEY, ME NEITHER--BUT I CAN'T JUST LET YOU GLIDE OFF WITH THAT PACK, YOU KNOW.
I'LL TELL YOU-- YOU JUST DON'T SEEM LIKE THE DESPERADO TYPE.
I'M NOT. IT'S KIND OF A LONG STORY.
COULD BE I'LL GET THE CHANCE TO TELL IT TO YOU SOMETIME...
WHAK!
GOOD GOIN', GIRL.
IS HE OKAY?
WHAT DIFFERENCE DOES IT MAKE?
17

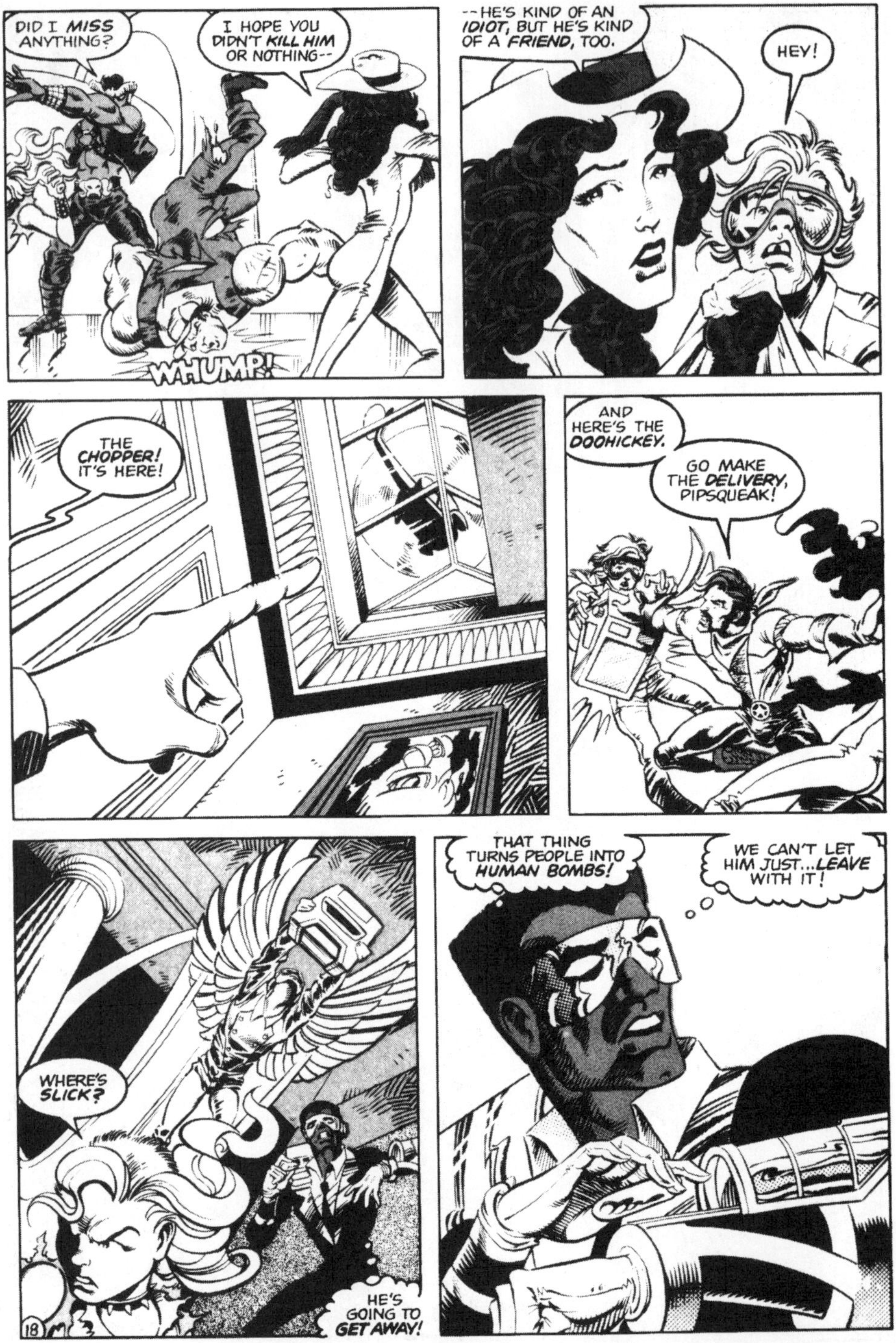
DID I MISS ANYTHING?
I HOPE YOU DIDN'T KILL HIM OR NOTHING--
WHUMP!
--HE'S KIND OF AN IDIOT, BUT HE'S KIND OF A FRIEND, TOO.
HEY!
THE CHOPPER! IT'S HERE!
AND HERE'S THE DOOHICKEY.
GO MAKE THE DELIVERY, PIPSQUEAK!
WHERE'S SLICK?
HE'S GOING TO GET AWAY!
18
THAT THING TURNS PEOPLE INTO HUMAN BOMBS!
WE CAN'T LET HIM JUST...LEAVE WITH IT!

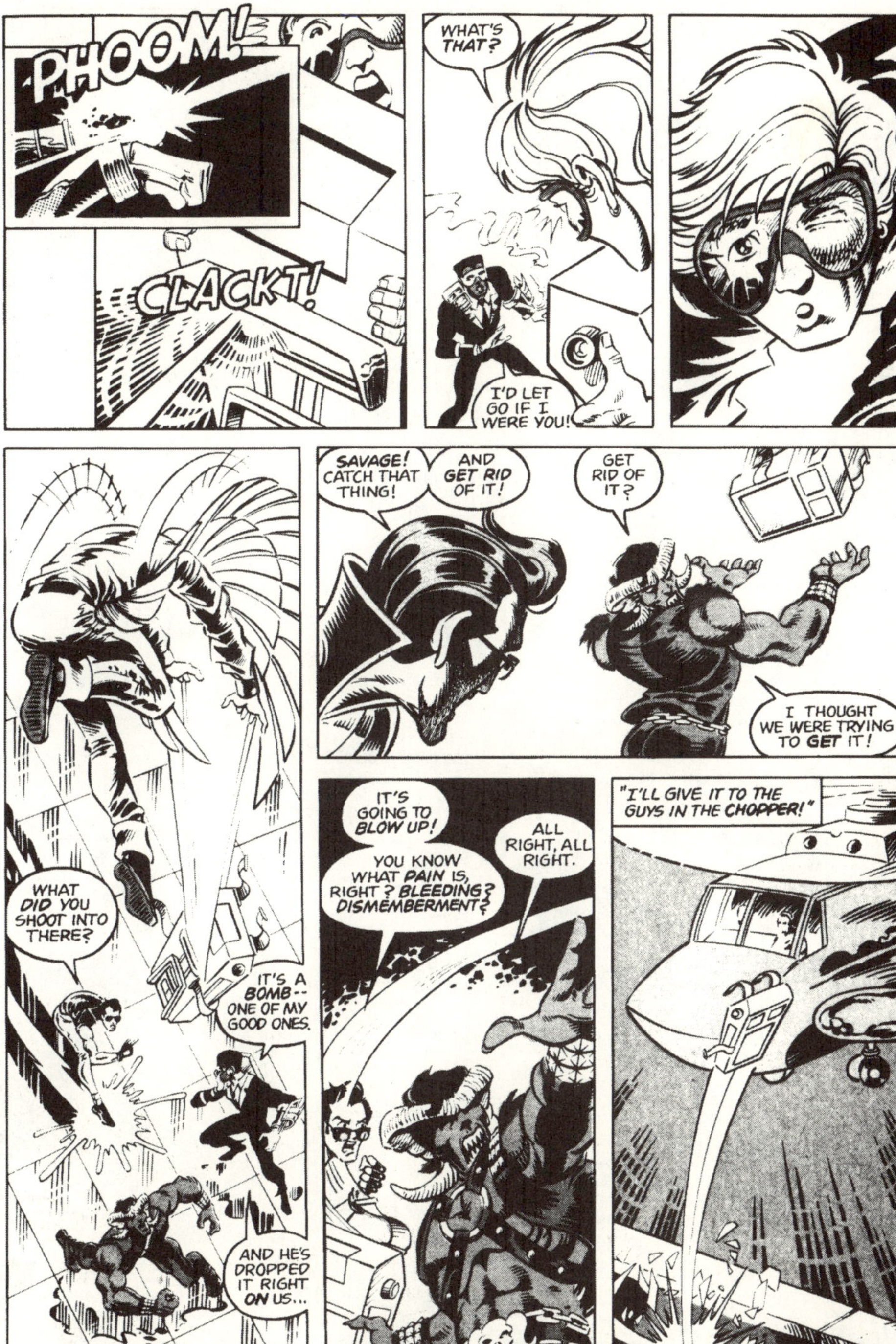
PHOOM!
CLACKT!
WHAT'S THAT?
I'D LET GO IF I WERE YOU!
SAVAGE! CATCH THAT THING!
AND GET RID OF IT!
GET RID OF IT?
I THOUGHT WE WERE TRYING TO GET IT!
WHAT DID YOU SHOOT INTO THERE?
IT'S A BOMB-- ONE OF MY GOOD ONES.
AND HE'S DROPPED IT RIGHT ON US...
IT'S GOING TO BLOW UP!
YOU KNOW WHAT PAIN IS, RIGHT? BLEEDING? DISMEMBERMENT?
ALL RIGHT, ALL RIGHT.
"I'LL GIVE IT TO THE GUYS IN THE CHOPPER!"
19

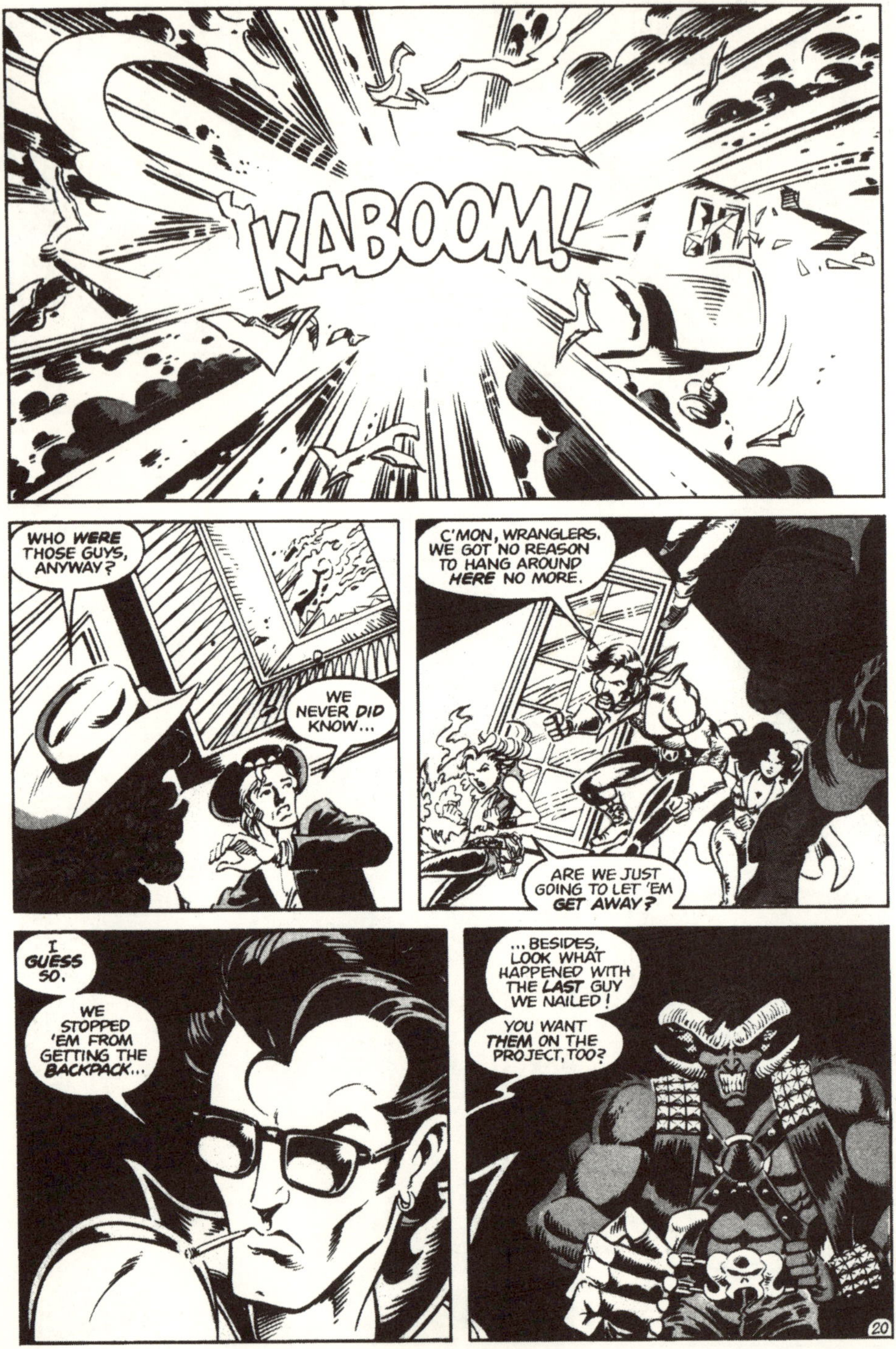
KABOOM!
WHO WERE THOSE GUYS, ANYWAY?
WE NEVER DID KNOW...
C'MON, WRANGLERS. WE GOT NO REASON TO HANG AROUND HERE NO MORE.
ARE WE JUST GOING TO LET 'EM GET AWAY?
I GUESS SO.
WE STOPPED 'EM FROM GETTING THE BACKPACK...
...BESIDES, LOOK WHAT HAPPENED WITH THE LAST GUY WE NAILED!
YOU WANT THEM ON THE PROJECT, TOO?
20

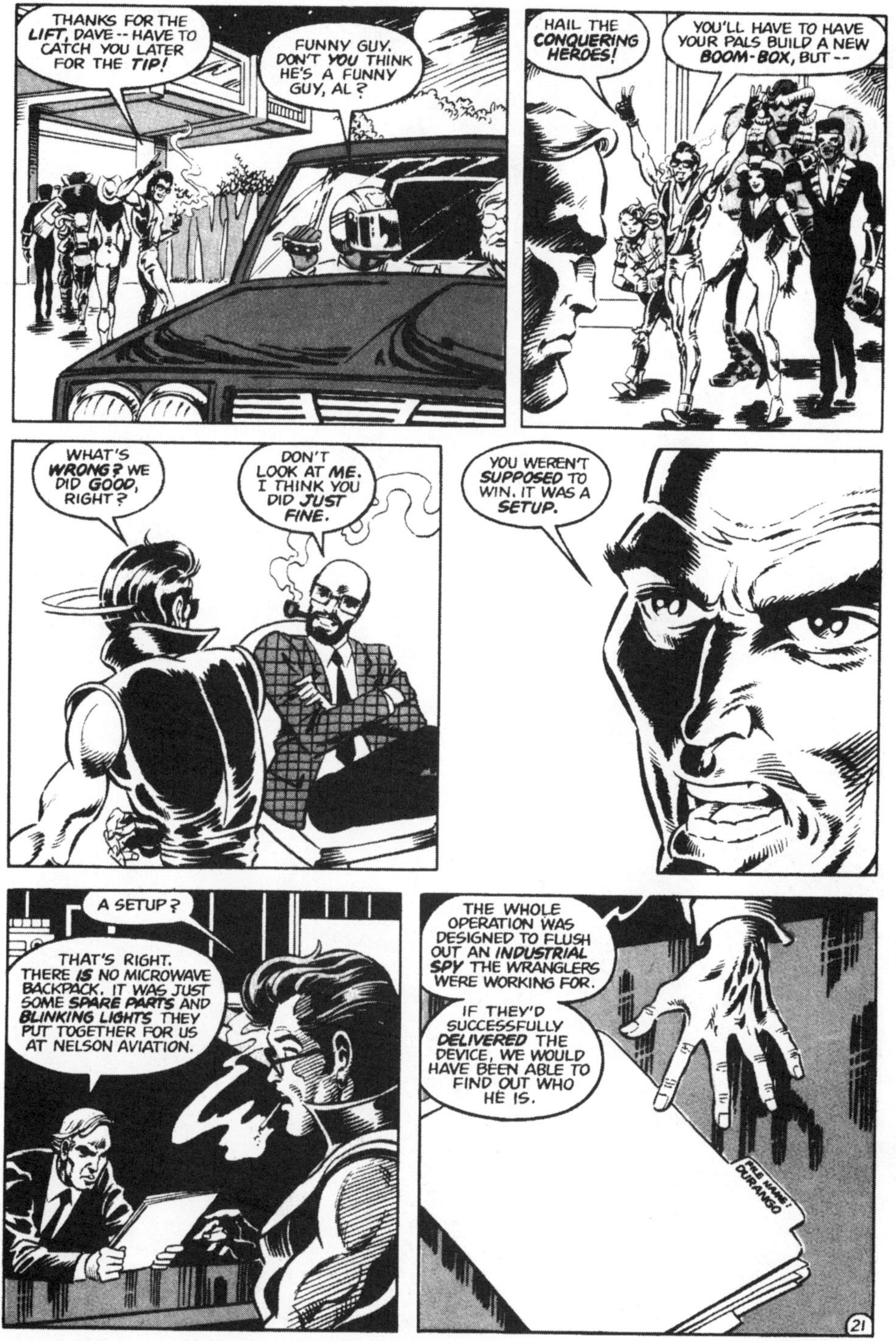
THANKS FOR THE LIFT, DAVE -- HAVE TO CATCH YOU LATER FOR THE TIP!
FUNNY GUY. DON'T YOU THINK HE'S A FUNNY GUY, AL?
HAIL THE CONQUERING HEROES!
YOU'LL HAVE TO HAVE YOUR PALS BUILD A NEW BOOM-BOX, BUT --
WHAT'S WRONG? WE DID GOOD, RIGHT?
DON'T LOOK AT ME. I THINK YOU DID JUST FINE.
YOU WEREN'T SUPPOSED TO WIN. IT WAS A SETUP.
A SETUP?
THAT'S RIGHT. THERE IS NO MICROWAVE BACKPACK. IT WAS JUST SOME SPARE PARTS AND BLINKING LIGHTS THEY PUT TOGETHER FOR US AT NELSON AVIATION.
THE WHOLE OPERATION WAS DESIGNED TO FLUSH OUT AN INDUSTRIAL SPY THE WRANGLERS WERE WORKING FOR.
IF THEY'D SUCCESSFULLY DELIVERED THE DEVICE, WE WOULD HAVE BEEN ABLE TO FIND OUT WHO HE IS.
FILE NAME: DURANGO
21

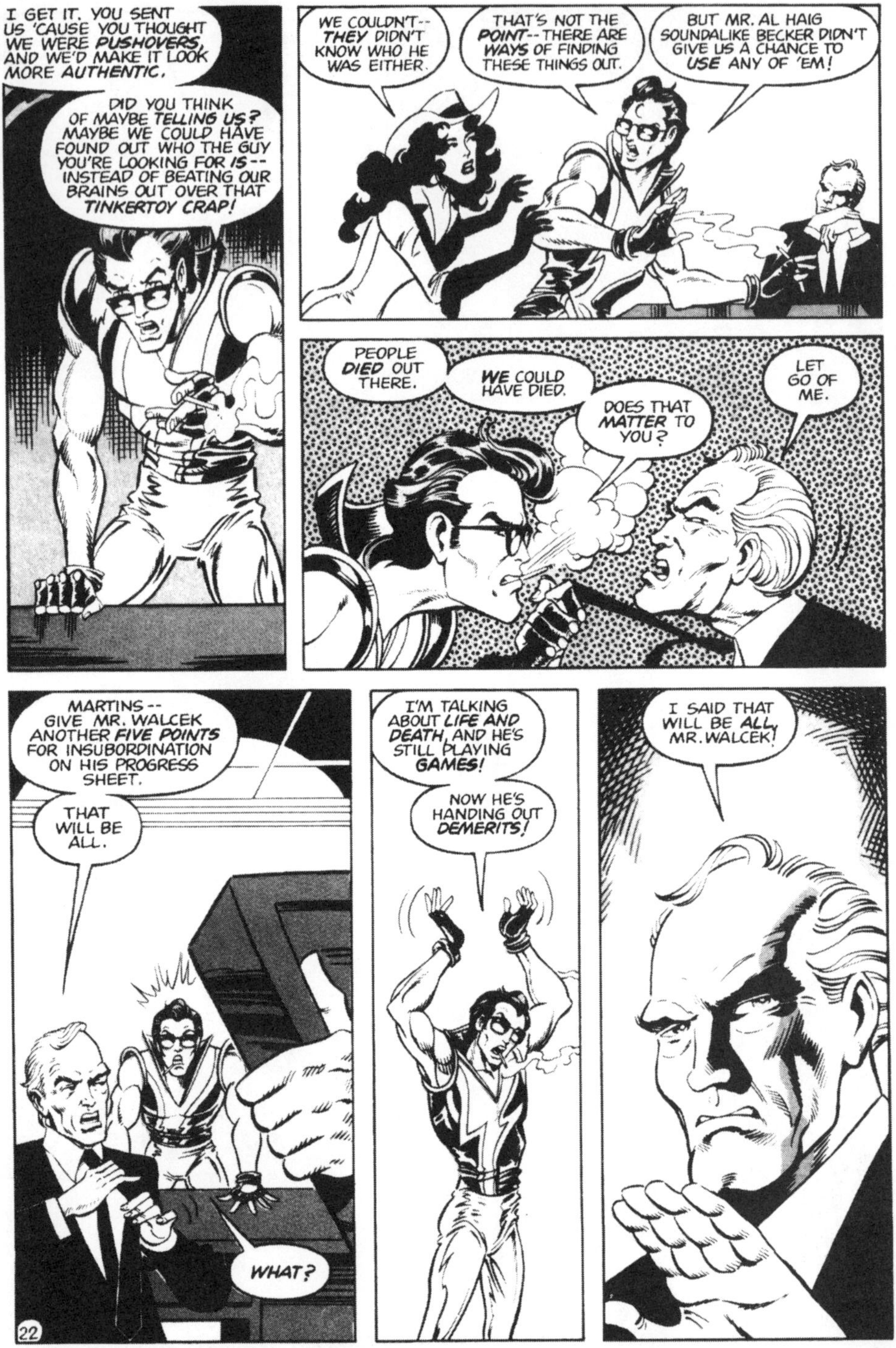
I GET IT. YOU SENT US 'CAUSE YOU THOUGHT WE WERE PUSHOVERS, AND WE'D MAKE IT LOOK MORE AUTHENTIC.
DID YOU THINK OF MAYBE TELLING US? MAYBE WE COULD HAVE FOUND OUT WHO THE GUY YOU'RE LOOKING FOR IS-- INSTEAD OF BEATING OUR BRAINS OUT OVER THAT TINKERTOY CRAP!
WE COULDN'T-- THEY DIDN'T KNOW WHO HE WAS EITHER.
THAT'S NOT THE POINT--THERE ARE WAYS OF FINDING THESE THINGS OUT.
BUT MR. AL HAIG SOUNDALIKE BECKER DIDN'T GIVE US A CHANCE TO USE ANY OF 'EM!
PEOPLE DIED OUT THERE.
WE COULD HAVE DIED.
DOES THAT MATTER TO YOU?
LET GO OF ME.
MARTINS-- GIVE MR. WALCEK ANOTHER FIVE POINTS FOR INSUBORDINATION ON HIS PROGRESS SHEET.
THAT WILL BE ALL.
WHAT?
I'M TALKING ABOUT LIFE AND DEATH, AND HE'S STILL PLAYING GAMES!
NOW HE'S HANDING OUT DEMERITS!
I SAID THAT WILL BE ALL, MR. WALCEK!
22

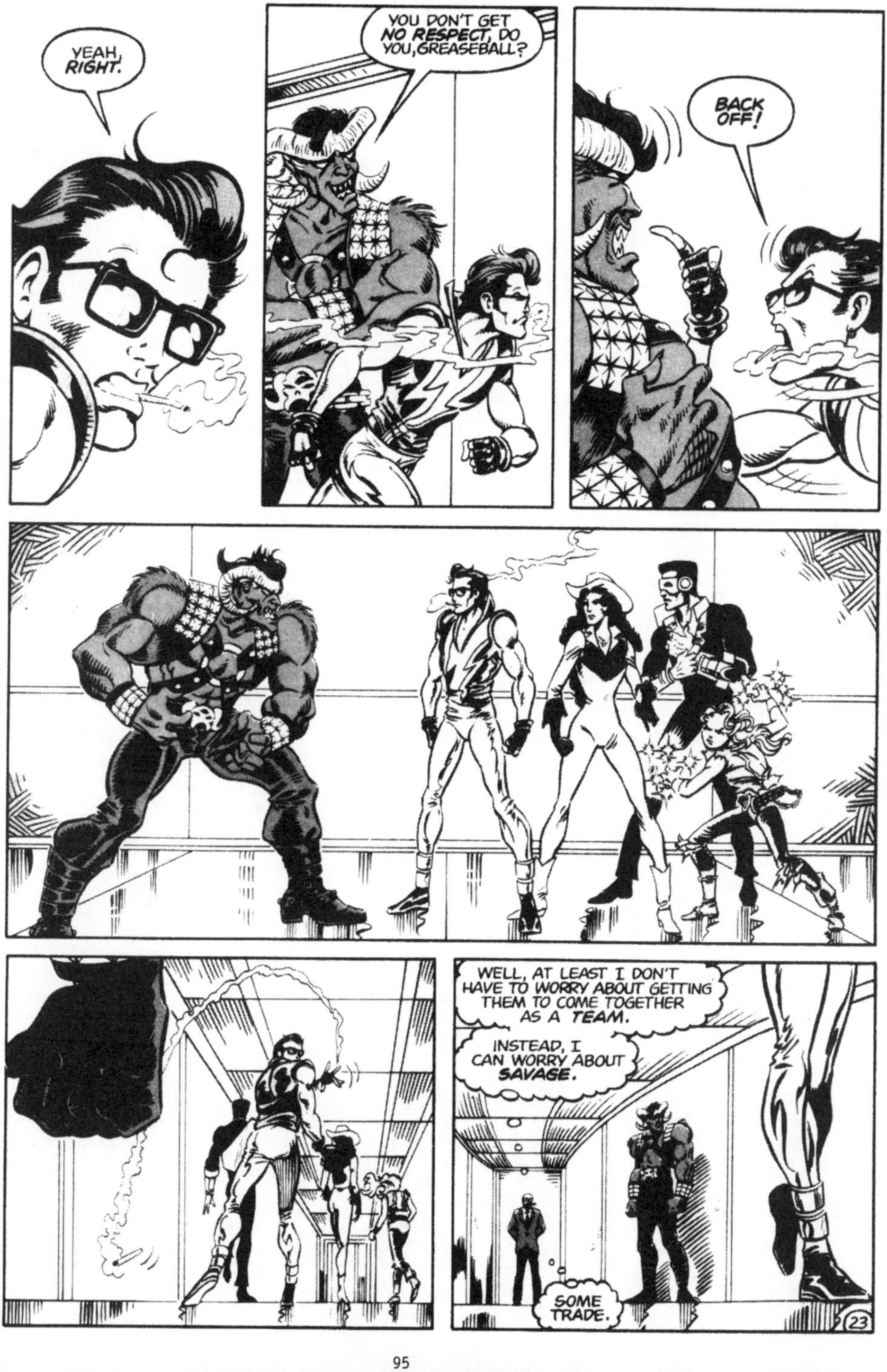
YEAH, RIGHT.
YOU DON'T GET NO RESPECT, DO YOU, GREASEBALL?
BACK OFF!
WELL, AT LEAST I DON'T HAVE TO WORRY ABOUT GETTING THEM TO COME TOGETHER AS A TEAM.
INSTEAD, I CAN WORRY ABOUT SAVAGE.
SOME TRADE.
23

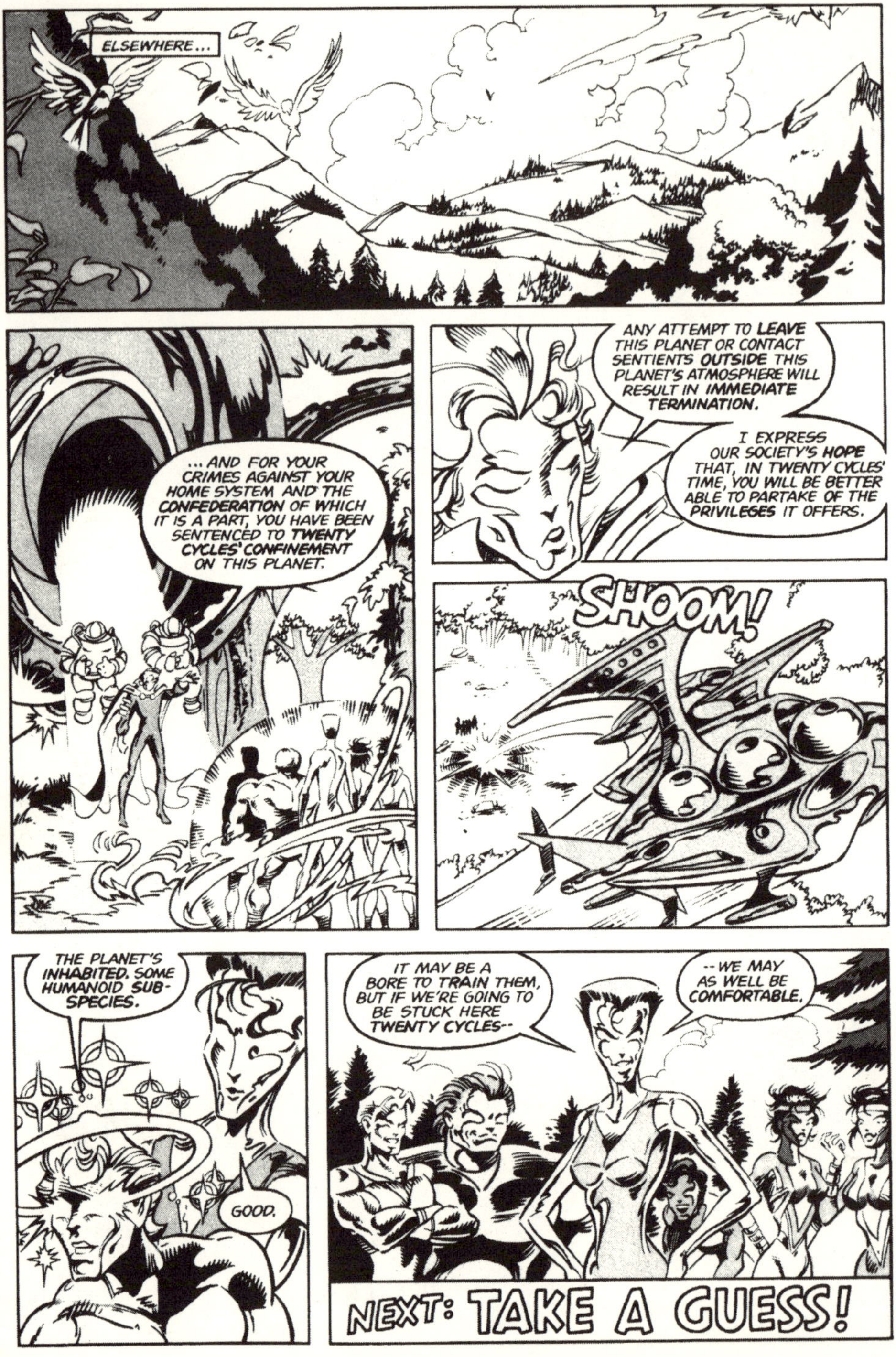
ELSEWHERE...
...AND FOR YOUR CRIMES AGAINST YOUR HOME SYSTEM AND THE CONFEDERATION OF WHICH IT IS A PART, YOU HAVE BEEN SENTENCED TO TWENTY CYCLES' CONFINEMENT ON THIS PLANET.
ANY ATTEMPT TO LEAVE THIS PLANET OR CONTACT SENTIENTS OUTSIDE THIS PLANET'S ATMOSPHERE WILL RESULT IN IMMEDIATE TERMINATION.
I EXPRESS OUR SOCIETY'S HOPE THAT, IN TWENTY CYCLES' TIME, YOU WILL BE BETTER ABLE TO PARTAKE OF THE PRIVILEGES IT OFFERS.
SHOOM!
THE PLANET'S INHABITED. SOME HUMANOID SUB-SPECIES.
GOOD.
IT MAY BE A BORE TO TRAIN THEM, BUT IF WE'RE GOING TO BE STUCK HERE TWENTY CYCLES--
--WE MAY AS WELL BE COMFORTABLE.
NEXT: TAKE A GUESS!

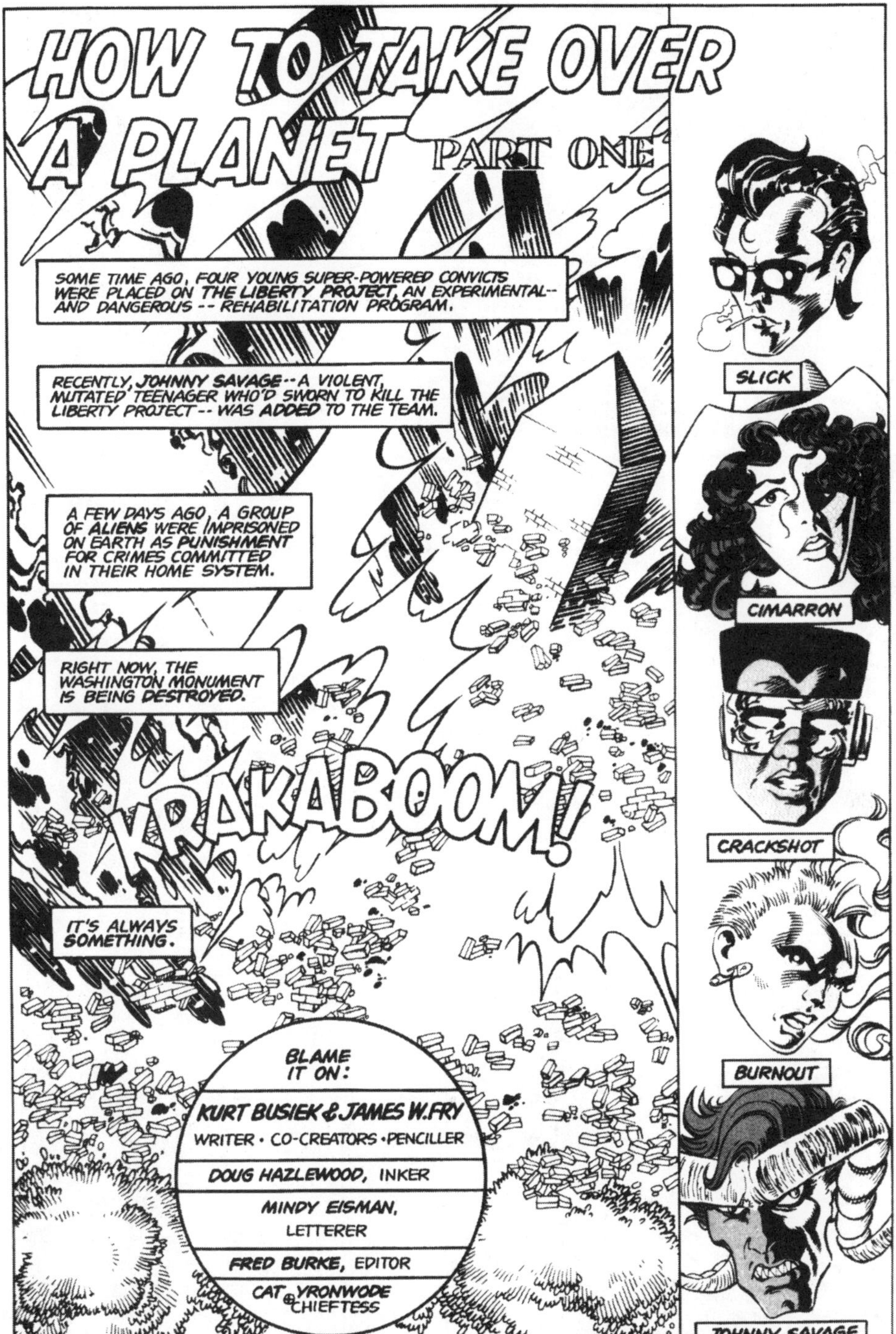
HOW TO TAKE OVER A PLANET PART ONE
SOME TIME AGO, FOUR YOUNG SUPER-POWERED CONVICTS WERE PLACED ON THE LIBERTY PROJECT, AN EXPERIMENTAL-- AND DANGEROUS -- REHABILITATION PROGRAM.
RECENTLY, JOHNNY SAVAGE-- A VIOLENT, MUTATED TEENAGER WHO'D SWORN TO KILL THE LIBERTY PROJECT -- WAS ADDED TO THE TEAM.
A FEW DAYS AGO, A GROUP OF ALIENS WERE IMPRISONED ON EARTH AS PUNISHMENT FOR CRIMES COMMITTED IN THEIR HOME SYSTEM.
RIGHT NOW, THE WASHINGTON MONUMENT IS BEING DESTROYED.
KRAKABOOM!
IT'S ALWAYS SOMETHING.
BLAME IT ON:
KURT BUSIEK & JAMES W. FRY
WRITER · CO-CREATORS · PENCILLER
DOUG HAZLEWOOD, INKER
MINDY EISMAN, LETTERER
FRED BURKE, EDITOR
CAT YRONWODE CHIEFTESS
SLICK
CIMARRON
CRACKSHOT
BURNOUT
JOHNNY SAVAGE

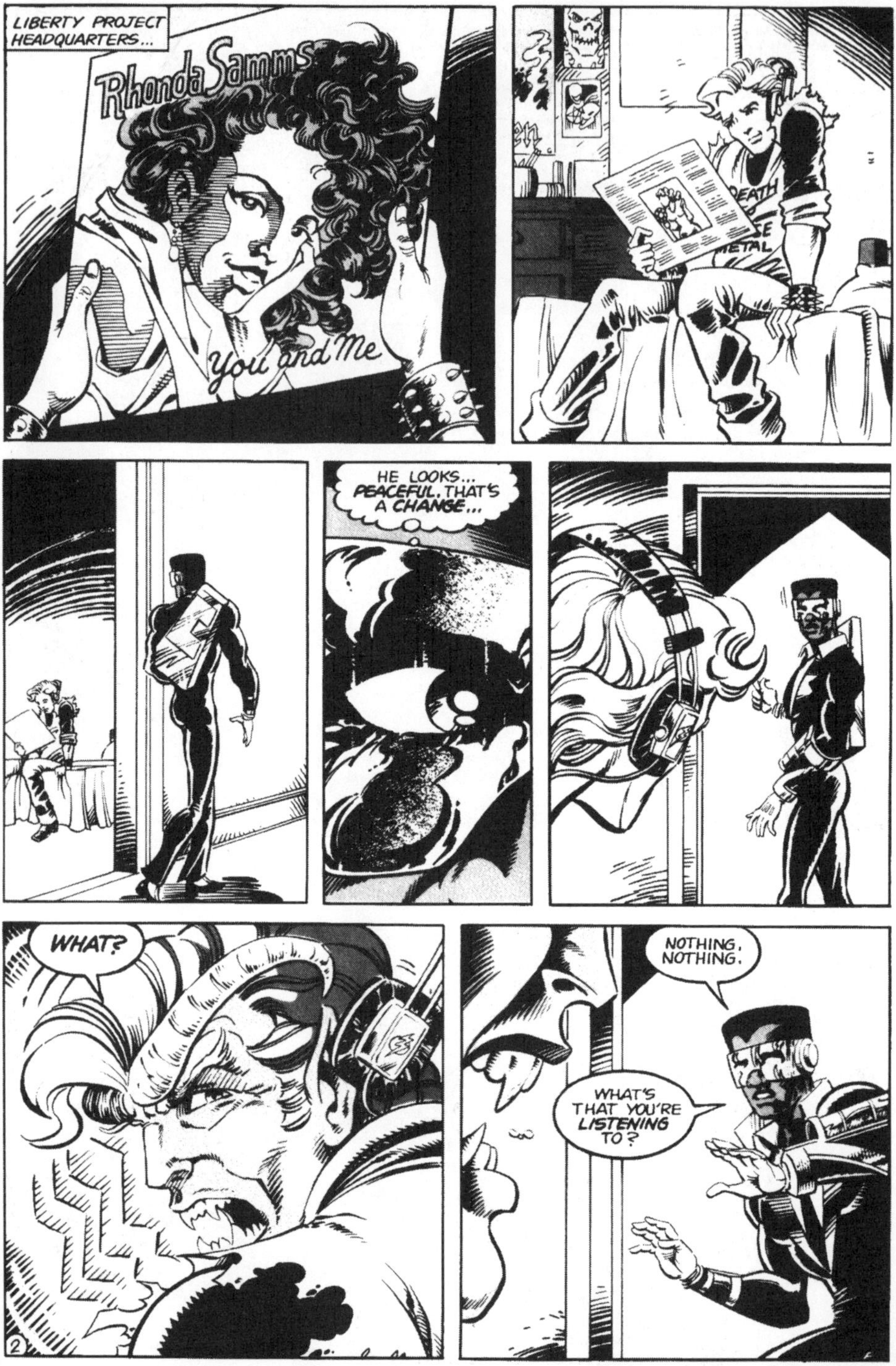
LIBERTY PROJECT HEADQUARTERS...
Rhonda Samms
You and Me
HE LOOKS... PEACEFUL, THAT'S A CHANGE...
WHAT?
NOTHING, NOTHING.
WHAT'S THAT YOU'RE LISTENING TO?

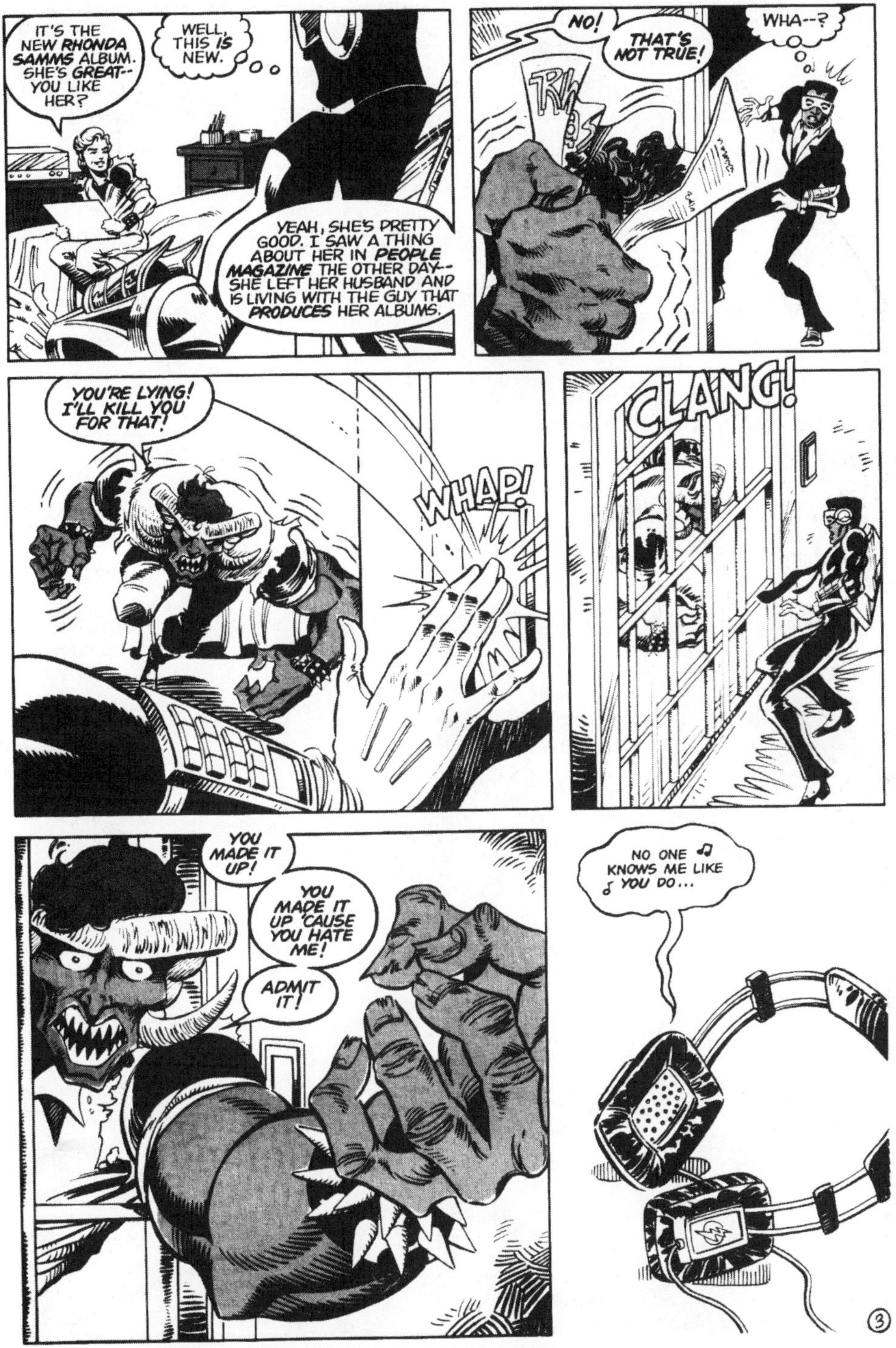
IT'S THE NEW RHONDA SAMMS ALBUM. SHE'S GREAT-- YOU LIKE HER?
WELL, THIS IS NEW.
YEAH, SHE'S PRETTY GOOD. I SAW A THING ABOUT HER IN PEOPLE MAGAZINE THE OTHER DAY-- SHE LEFT HER HUSBAND AND IS LIVING WITH THE GUY THAT PRODUCES HER ALBUMS.
NO!
THAT'S NOT TRUE!
WHA--?
YOU'RE LYING! I'LL KILL YOU FOR THAT!
WHAP!
CLANG!
YOU MADE IT UP!
YOU MADE IT UP 'CAUSE YOU HATE ME!
ADMIT IT!
NO ONE KNOWS ME LIKE YOU DO...
3

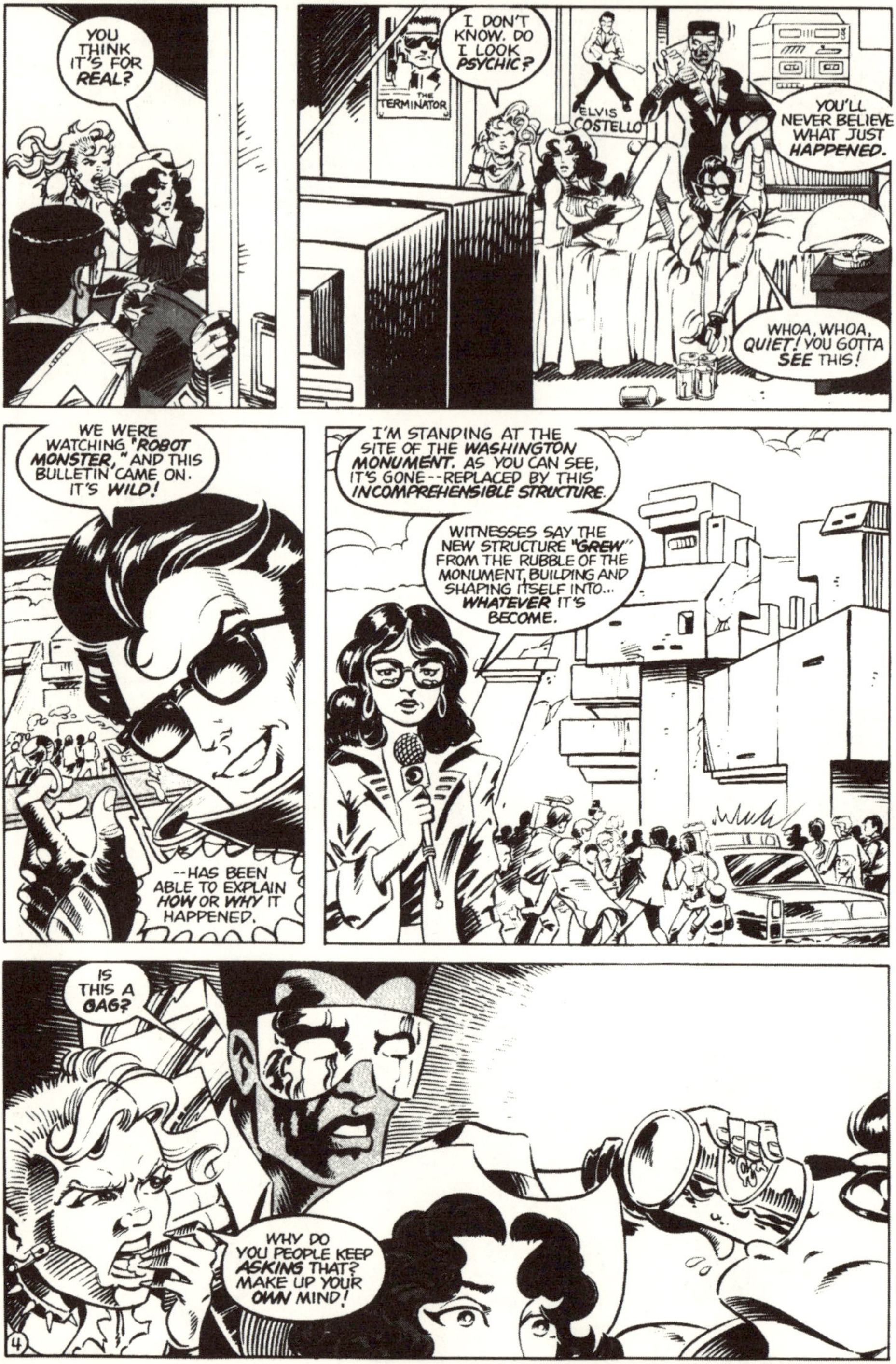

YOU THINK IT'S FOR REAL?
THE TERMINATOR
I DON'T KNOW. DO I LOOK PSYCHIC?
ELVIS COSTELLO
YOU'LL NEVER BELIEVE WHAT JUST HAPPENED.
WHOA, WHOA, QUIET! YOU GOTTA SEE THIS!
WE WERE WATCHING "ROBOT MONSTER," AND THIS BULLETIN CAME ON. IT'S WILD!
--HAS BEEN ABLE TO EXPLAIN HOW OR WHY IT HAPPENED.
I'M STANDING AT THE SITE OF THE WASHINGTON MONUMENT. AS YOU CAN SEE, IT'S GONE--REPLACED BY THIS INCOMPREHENSIBLE STRUCTURE.
WITNESSES SAY THE NEW STRUCTURE "GREW" FROM THE RUBBLE OF THE MONUMENT, BUILDING AND SHAPING ITSELF INTO... WHATEVER IT'S BECOME.
IS THIS A GAG?
WHY DO YOU PEOPLE KEEP ASKING THAT? MAKE UP YOUR OWN MIND!
4

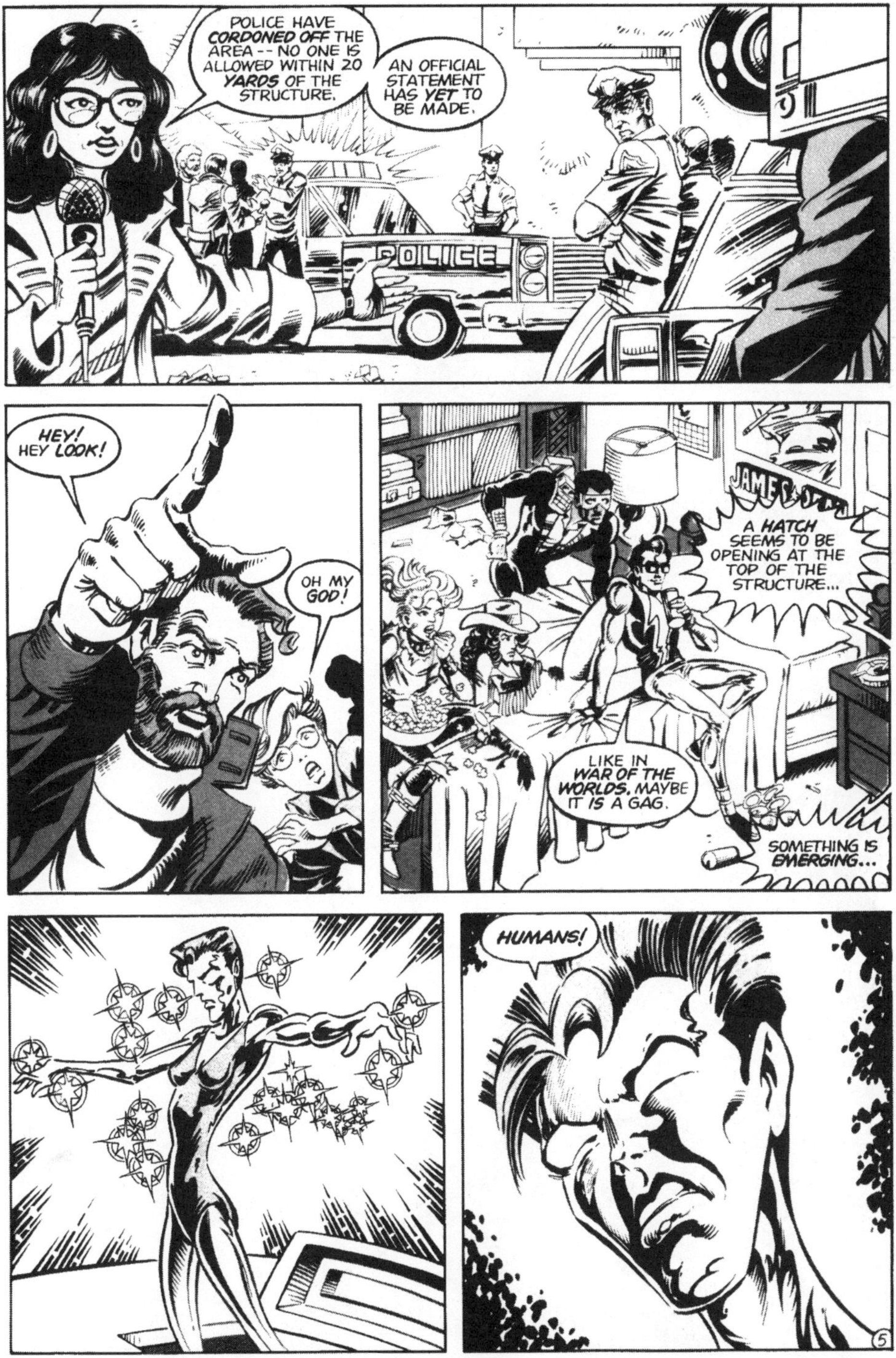
POLICE HAVE CORDONED OFF THE AREA -- NO ONE IS ALLOWED WITHIN 20 YARDS OF THE STRUCTURE.
AN OFFICIAL STATEMENT HAS YET TO BE MADE.
POLICE
HEY! HEY LOOK!
OH MY GOD!
A HATCH SEEMS TO BE OPENING AT THE TOP OF THE STRUCTURE...
LIKE IN WAR OF THE WORLDS. MAYBE IT IS A GAG.
SOMETHING IS EMERGING...
HUMANS!
5

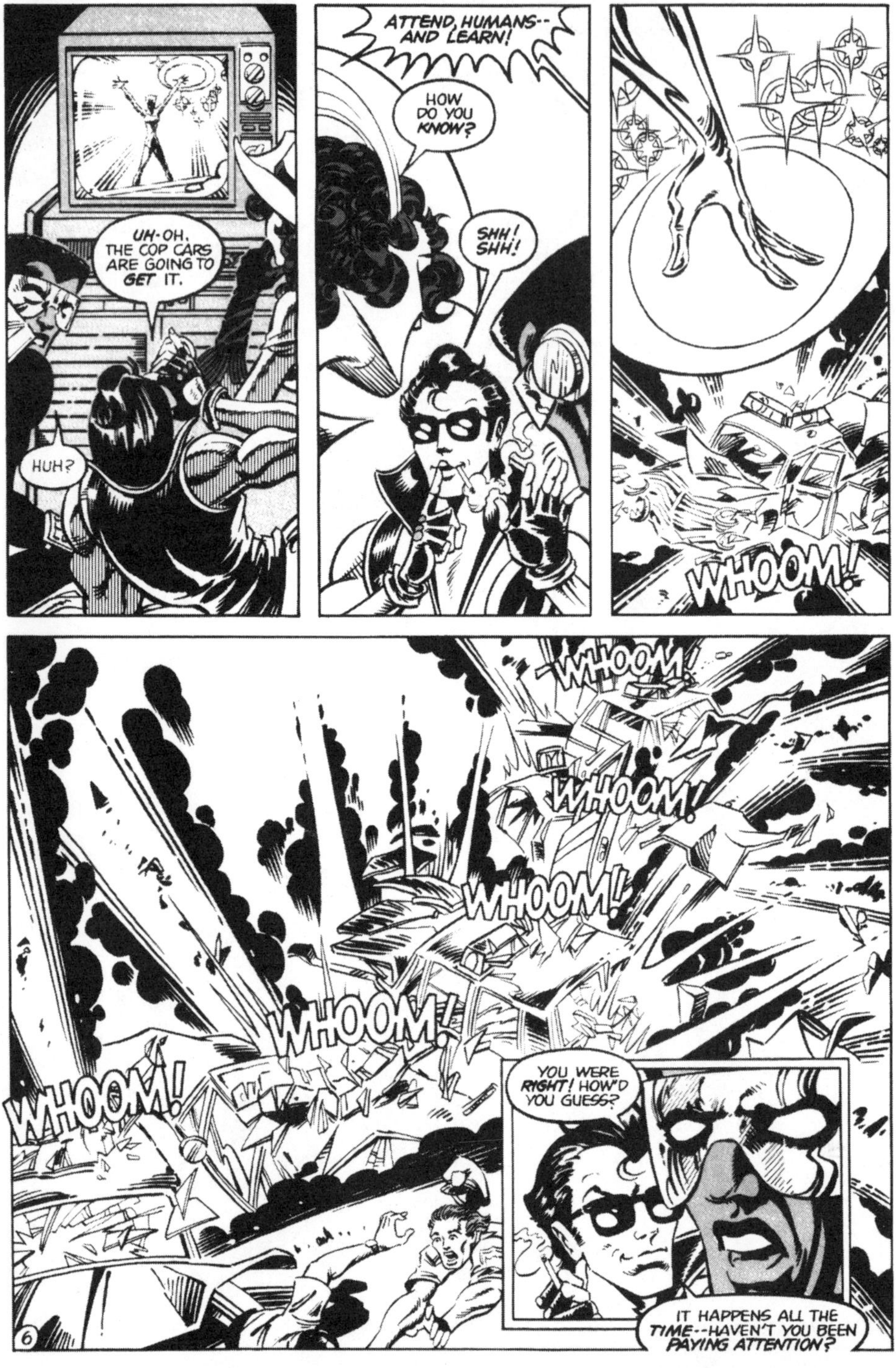
UH-OH, THE COP CARS ARE GOING TO GET IT.
HUH?
ATTEND, HUMANS-- AND LEARN!
HOW DO YOU KNOW?
SHH! SHH!
WHOOM!
WHOOM!
WHOOM!
WHOOM!
WHOOM!
WHOOM!
YOU WERE RIGHT! HOW'D YOU GUESS?
IT HAPPENS ALL THE TIME--HAVEN'T YOU BEEN PAYING ATTENTION?
6

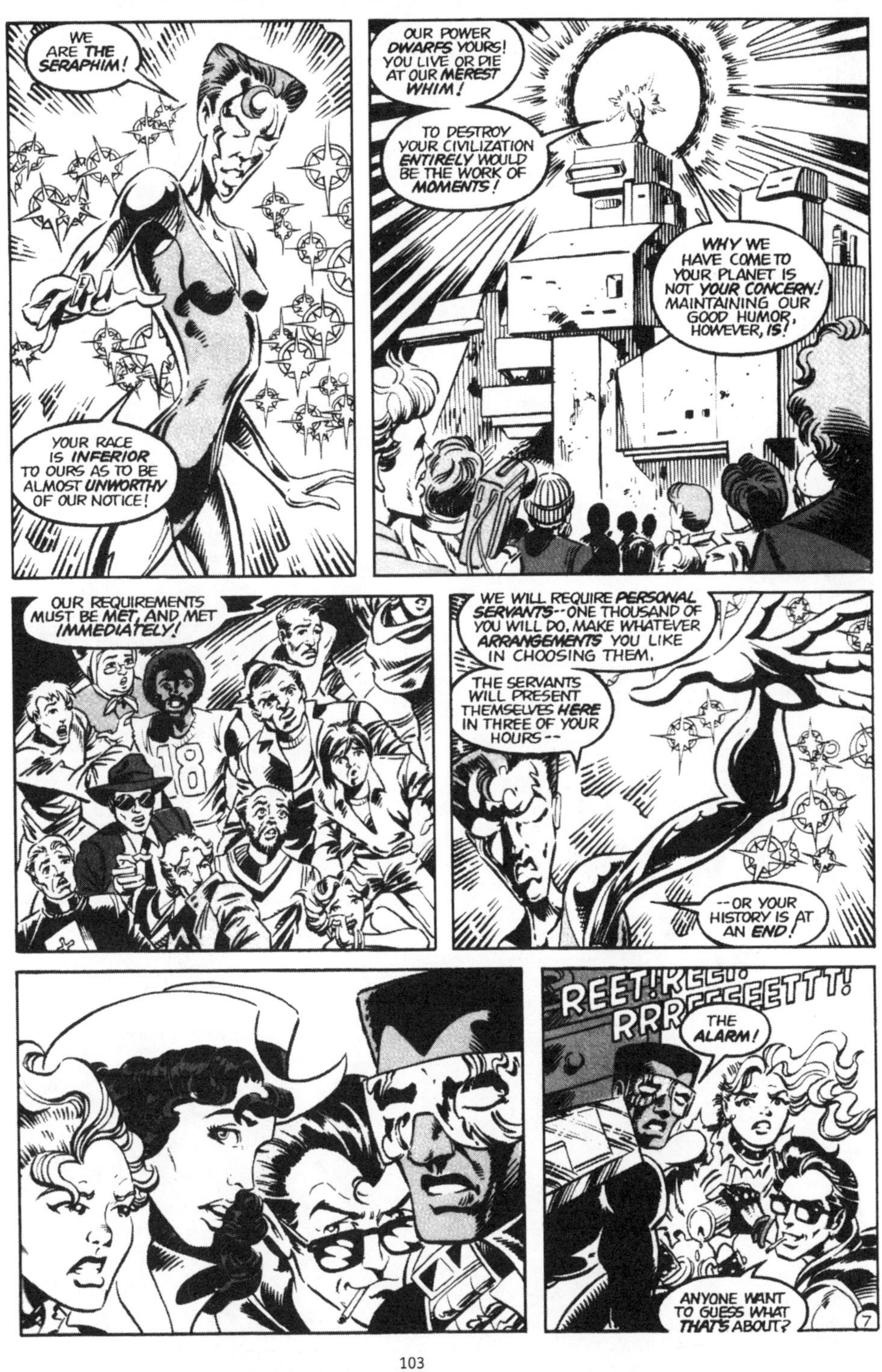

WE ARE THE SERAPHIM!
YOUR RACE IS INFERIOR TO OURS AS TO BE ALMOST UNWORTHY OF OUR NOTICE!
OUR POWER DWARFS YOURS! YOU LIVE OR DIE AT OUR MEREST WHIM!
TO DESTROY YOUR CIVILIZATION ENTIRELY WOULD BE THE WORK OF MOMENTS!
WHY WE HAVE COME TO YOUR PLANET IS NOT YOUR CONCERN! MAINTAINING OUR GOOD HUMOR, HOWEVER, IS!
OUR REQUIREMENTS MUST BE MET, AND MET IMMEDIATELY!
18
WE WILL REQUIRE PERSONAL SERVANTS--ONE THOUSAND OF YOU WILL DO. MAKE WHATEVER ARRANGEMENTS YOU LIKE IN CHOOSING THEM.
THE SERVANTS WILL PRESENT THEMSELVES HERE IN THREE OF YOUR HOURS--
--OR YOUR HISTORY IS AT AN END!
REET! REET! RRREEEEETTT!
THE ALARM!
ANYONE WANT TO GUESS WHAT THAT'S ABOUT?
7

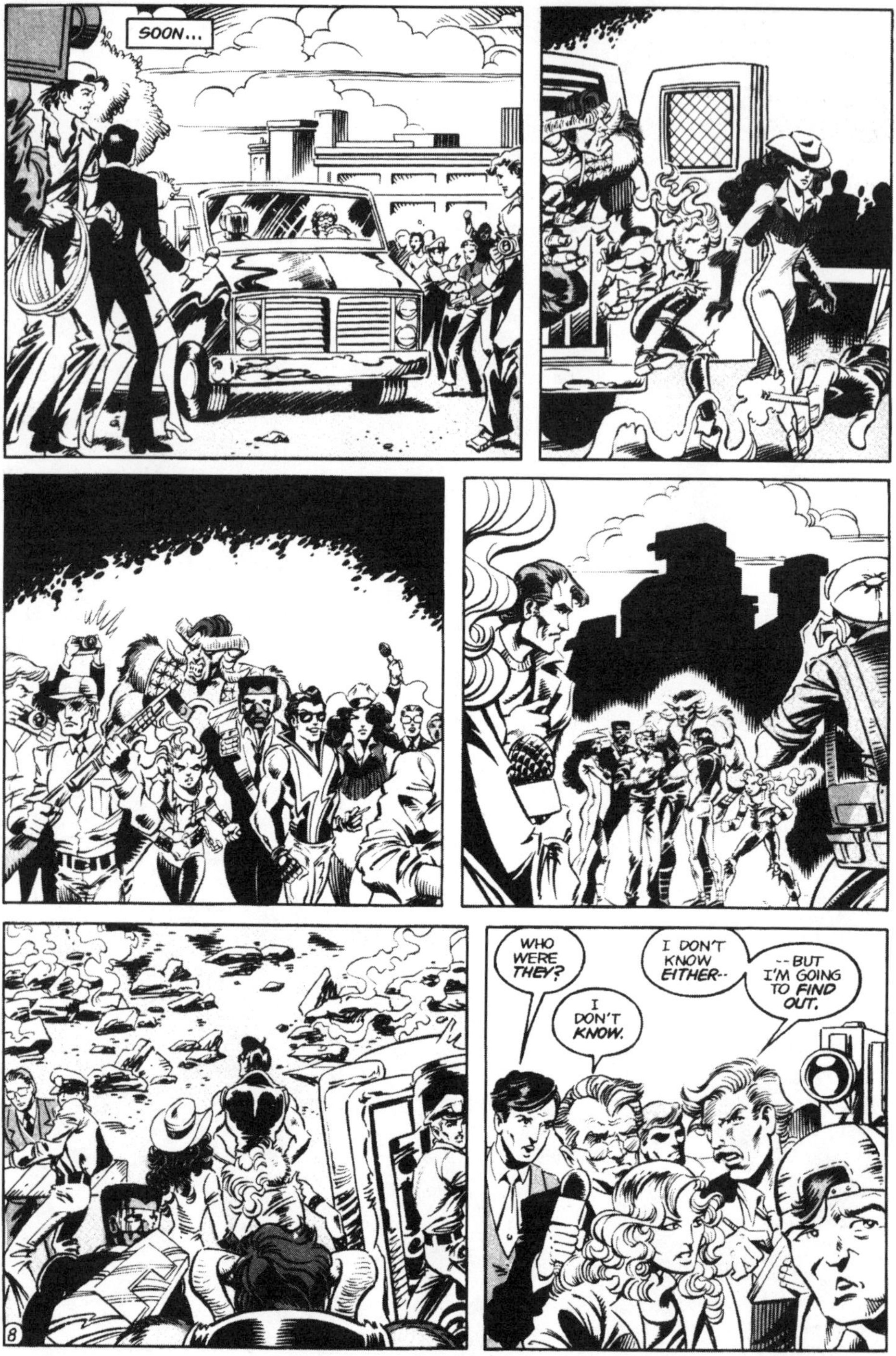
SOON...
WHO WERE *THEY?*
I DON'T *KNOW.*
I DON'T KNOW *EITHER*--
--BUT I'M GOING TO *FIND OUT.*
8

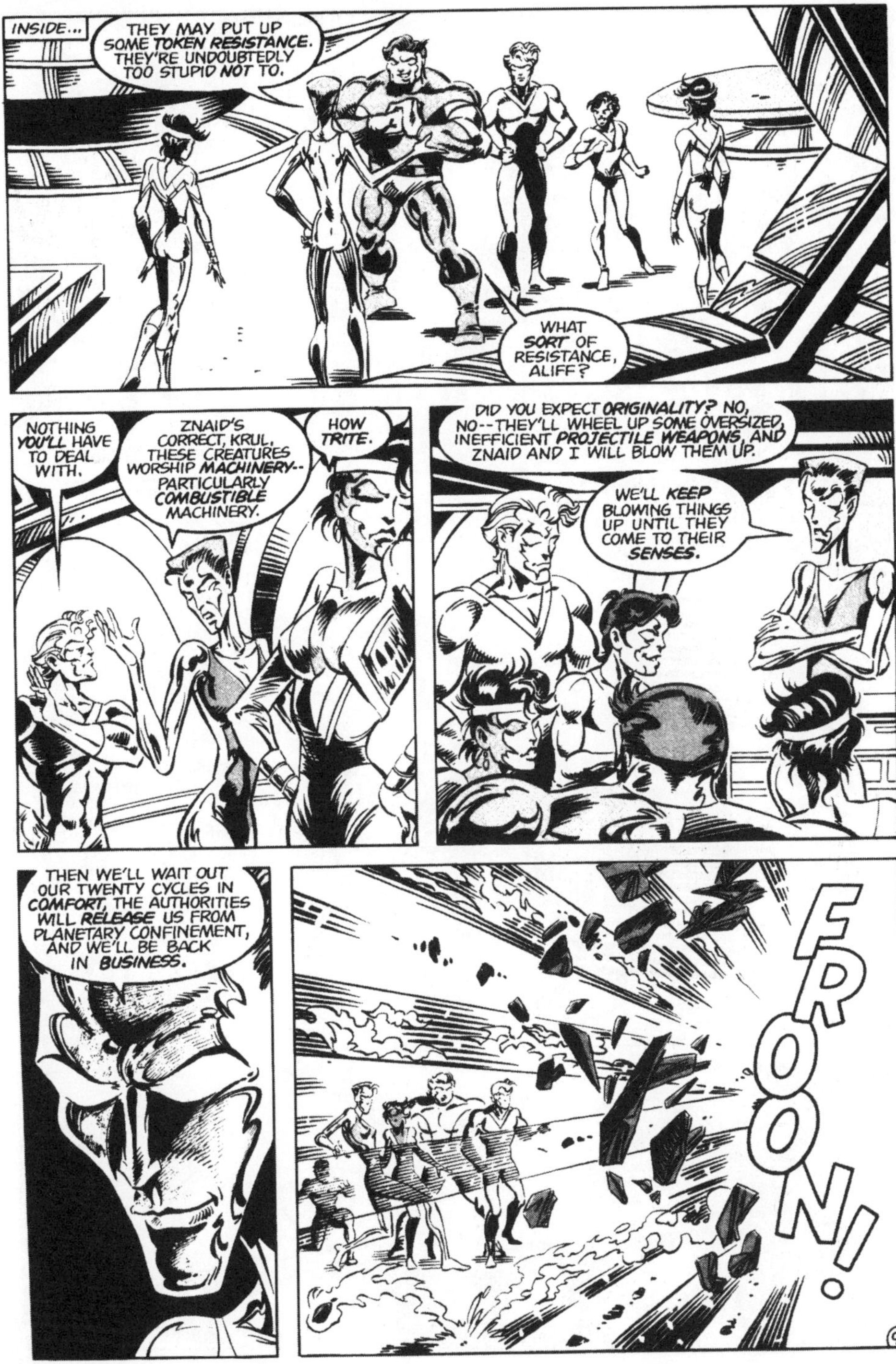

INSIDE...
THEY MAY PUT UP SOME TOKEN RESISTANCE. THEY'RE UNDOUBTEDLY TOO STUPID NOT TO.
WHAT SORT OF RESISTANCE, ALIFF?
NOTHING YOU'LL HAVE TO DEAL WITH.
ZNAID'S CORRECT, KRUL, THESE CREATURES WORSHIP MACHINERY-- PARTICULARLY COMBUSTIBLE MACHINERY.
HOW TRITE.
DID YOU EXPECT ORIGINALITY? NO, NO--THEY'LL WHEEL UP SOME OVERSIZED, INEFFICIENT PROJECTILE WEAPONS, AND ZNAID AND I WILL BLOW THEM UP.
WE'LL KEEP BLOWING THINGS UP UNTIL THEY COME TO THEIR SENSES.
THEN WE'LL WAIT OUT OUR TWENTY CYCLES IN COMFORT, THE AUTHORITIES WILL RELEASE US FROM PLANETARY CONFINEMENT, AND WE'LL BE BACK IN BUSINESS.
FROOON!
9

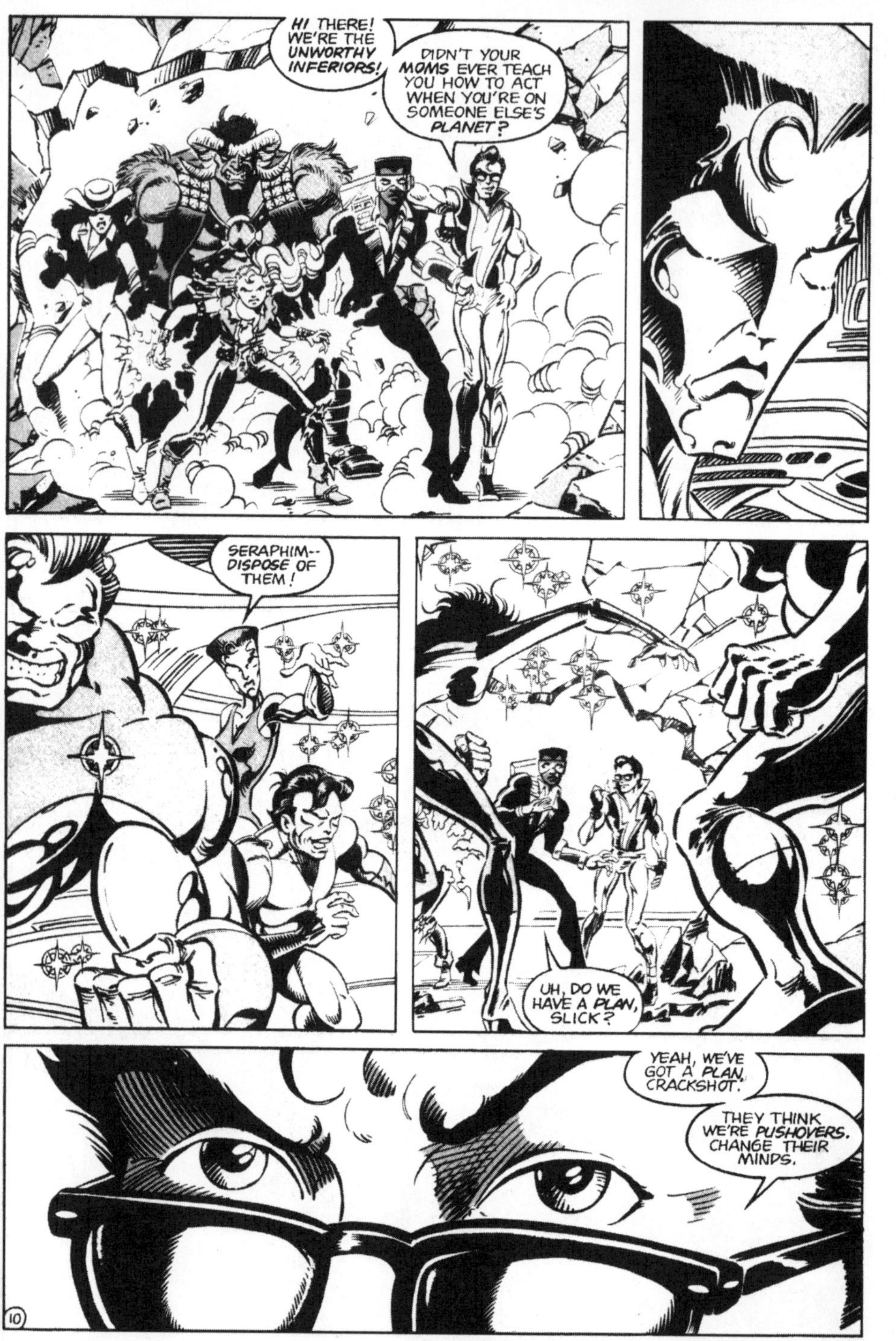
HI THERE! WE'RE THE UNWORTHY INFERIORS!
DIDN'T YOUR MOMS EVER TEACH YOU HOW TO ACT WHEN YOU'RE ON SOMEONE ELSE'S PLANET?
SERAPHIM-- DISPOSE OF THEM!
UH, DO WE HAVE A PLAN, SLICK?
YEAH, WE'VE GOT A PLAN, CRACKSHOT.
THEY THINK WE'RE PUSHOVERS. CHANGE THEIR MINDS.
10

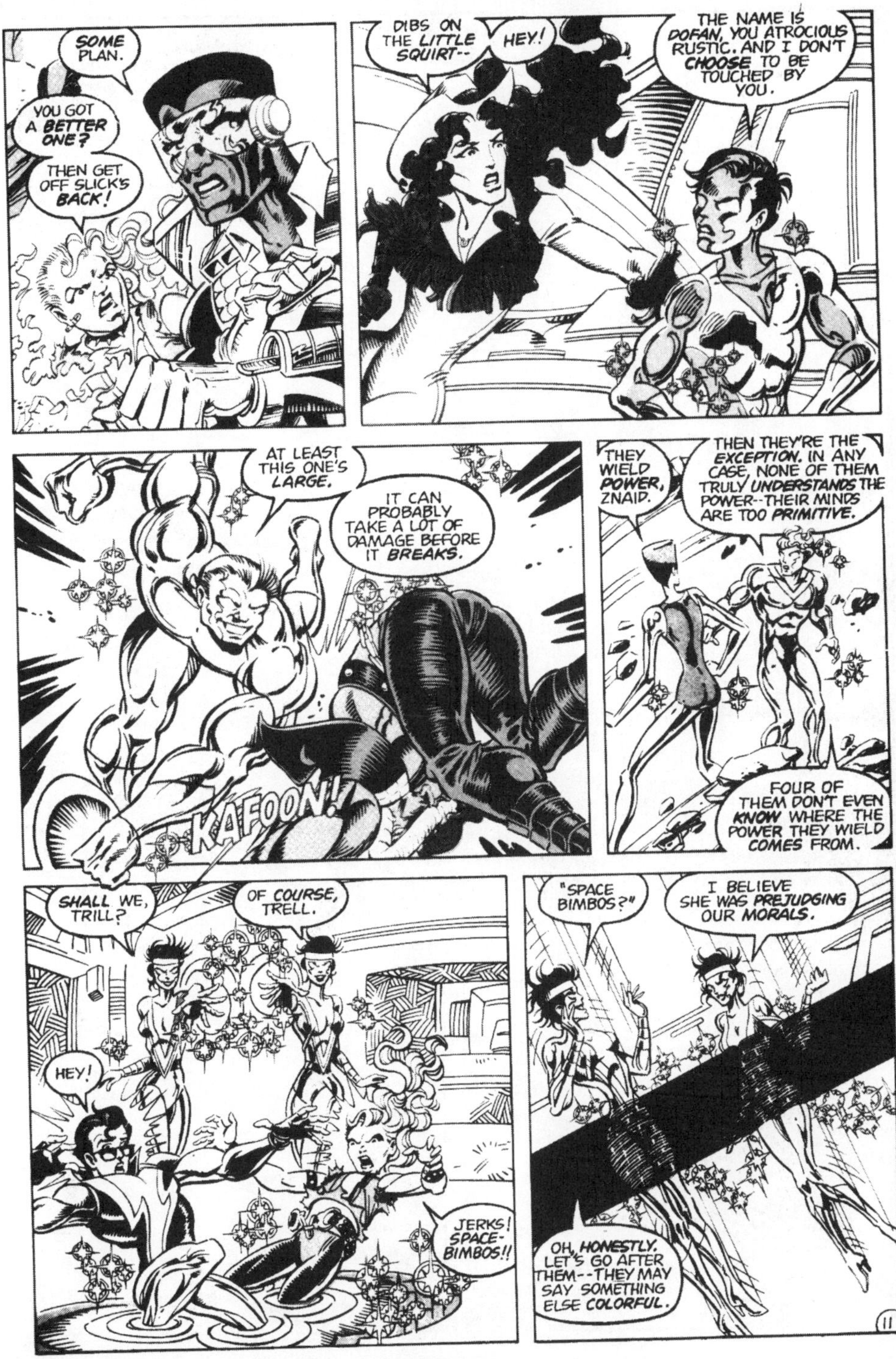
SOME PLAN.
YOU GOT A BETTER ONE?
THEN GET OFF SLICK'S BACK!
DIBS ON THE LITTLE SQUIRT--
HEY!
THE NAME IS DOFAN, YOU ATROCIOUS RUSTIC. AND I DON'T CHOOSE TO BE TOUCHED BY YOU.
AT LEAST THIS ONE'S LARGE.
IT CAN PROBABLY TAKE A LOT OF DAMAGE BEFORE IT BREAKS.
KAFOON!!
THEY WIELD POWER, ZNAID.
THEN THEY'RE THE EXCEPTION. IN ANY CASE, NONE OF THEM TRULY UNDERSTANDS THE POWER--THEIR MINDS ARE TOO PRIMITIVE.
FOUR OF THEM DON'T EVEN KNOW WHERE THE POWER THEY WIELD COMES FROM.
SHALL WE, TRILL?
OF COURSE, TRELL.
HEY!
JERKS! SPACE-BIMBOS!!
"SPACE BIMBOS?"
I BELIEVE SHE WAS PREJUDGING OUR MORALS.
OH, HONESTLY. LET'S GO AFTER THEM--THEY MAY SAY SOMETHING ELSE COLORFUL.
11

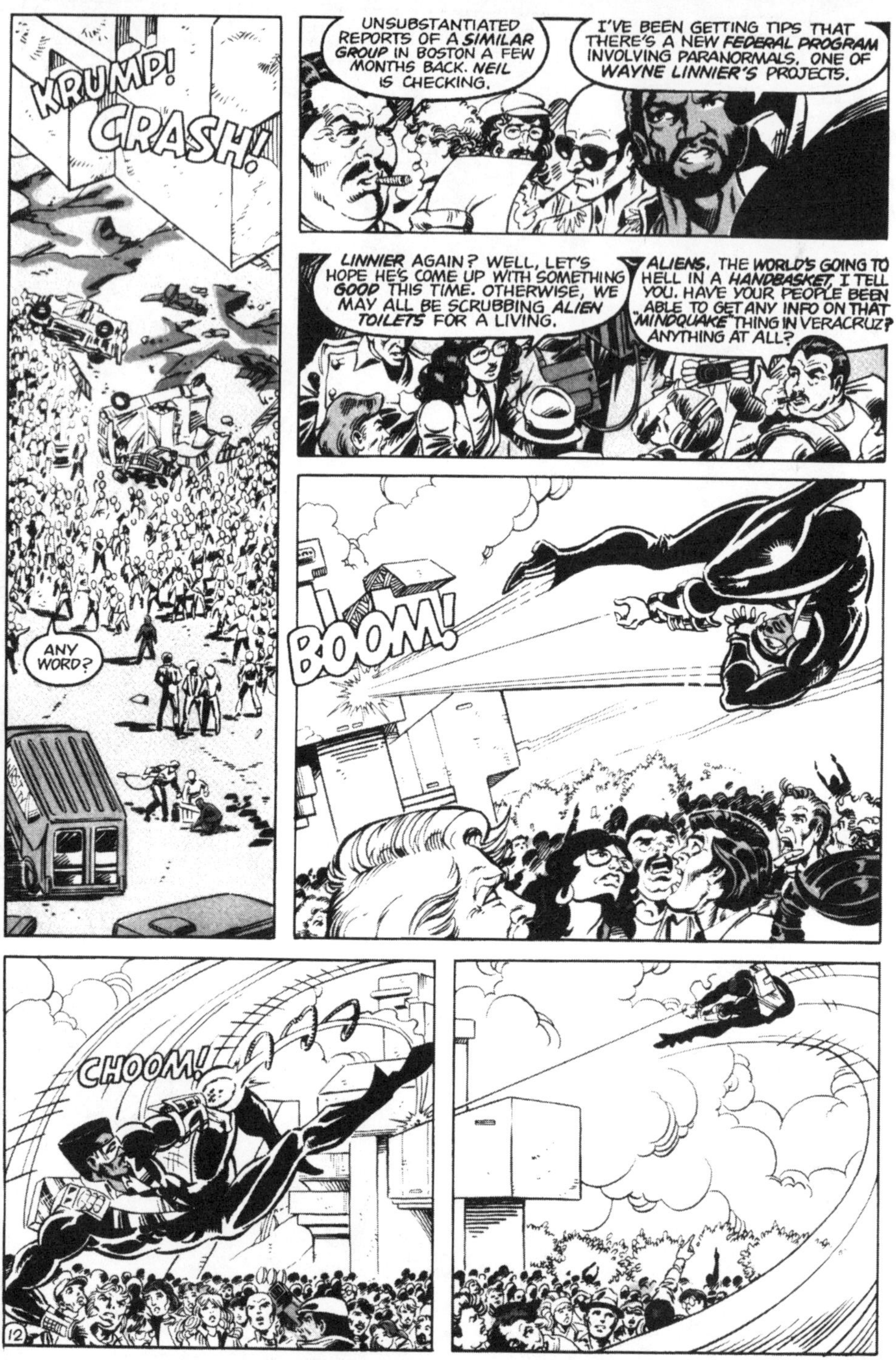
KRUMP!
CRASH!
UNSUBSTANTIATED REPORTS OF A SIMILAR GROUP IN BOSTON A FEW MONTHS BACK. NEIL IS CHECKING.
I'VE BEEN GETTING TIPS THAT THERE'S A NEW FEDERAL PROGRAM INVOLVING PARANORMALS. ONE OF WAYNE LINNIER'S PROJECTS.
LINNIER AGAIN? WELL, LET'S HOPE HE'S COME UP WITH SOMETHING GOOD THIS TIME. OTHERWISE, WE MAY ALL BE SCRUBBING ALIEN TOILETS FOR A LIVING.
ALIENS. THE WORLD'S GOING TO HELL IN A HANDBASKET, I TELL YOU. HAVE YOUR PEOPLE BEEN ABLE TO GET ANY INFO ON THAT "MINDQUAKE" THING IN VERACRUZ? ANYTHING AT ALL?
ANY WORD?
BOOM!
CHOOM!
12

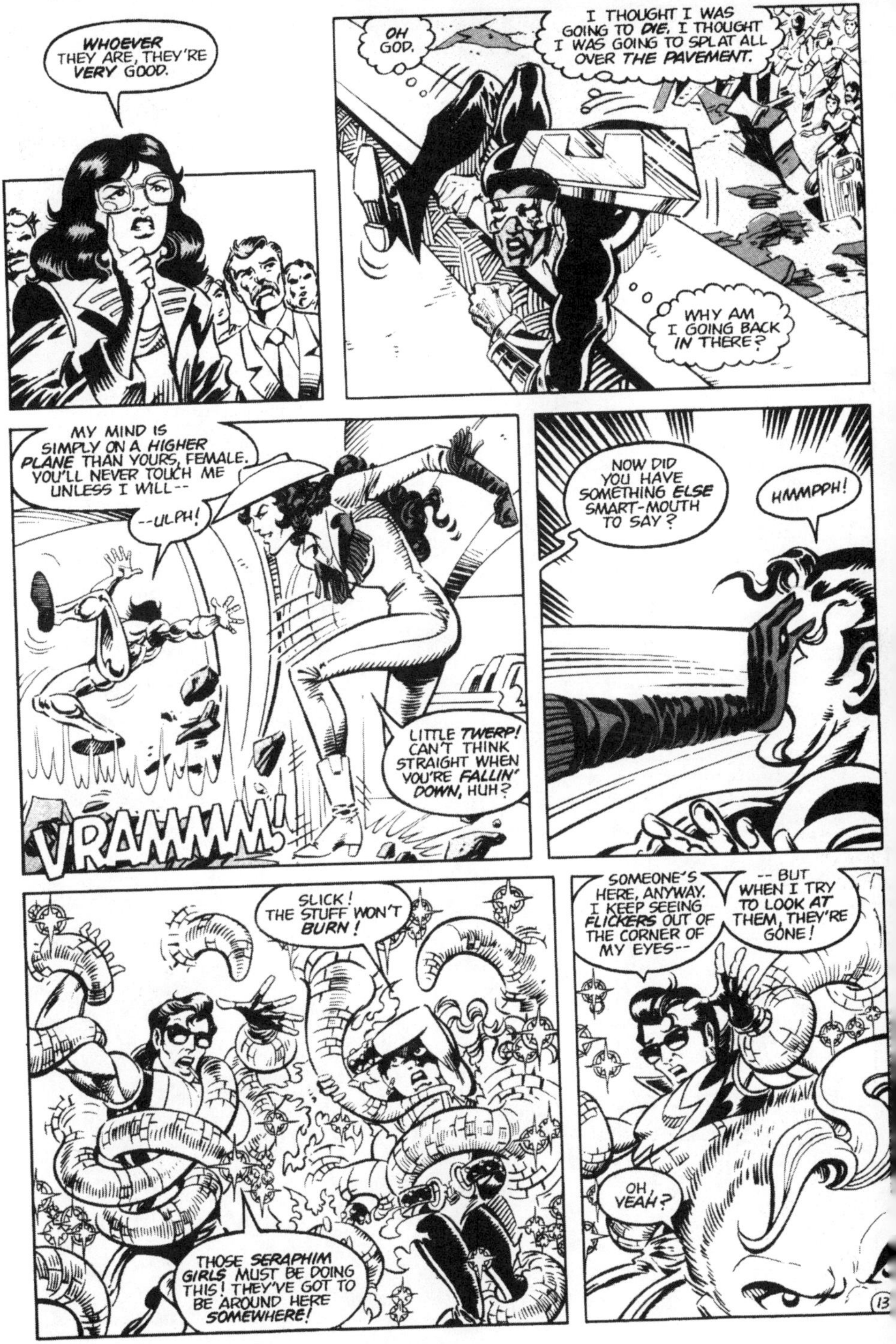

WHOEVER THEY ARE, THEY'RE VERY GOOD.
OH GOD.
I THOUGHT I WAS GOING TO DIE. I THOUGHT I WAS GOING TO SPLAT ALL OVER THE PAVEMENT.
WHY AM I GOING BACK IN THERE?
MY MIND IS SIMPLY ON A HIGHER PLANE THAN YOURS, FEMALE. YOU'LL NEVER TOUCH ME UNLESS I WILL--
--ULPH!
LITTLE TWERP! CAN'T THINK STRAIGHT WHEN YOU'RE FALLIN' DOWN, HUH?
VRAMMMM!
NOW DID YOU HAVE SOMETHING ELSE SMART-MOUTH TO SAY?
HMMPPH!
SLICK! THE STUFF WON'T BURN!
THOSE SERAPHIM GIRLS MUST BE DOING THIS! THEY'VE GOT TO BE AROUND HERE SOMEWHERE!
SOMEONE'S HERE, ANYWAY. I KEEP SEEING FLICKERS OUT OF THE CORNER OF MY EYES--
-- BUT WHEN I TRY TO LOOK AT THEM, THEY'RE GONE!
OH, YEAH?
13

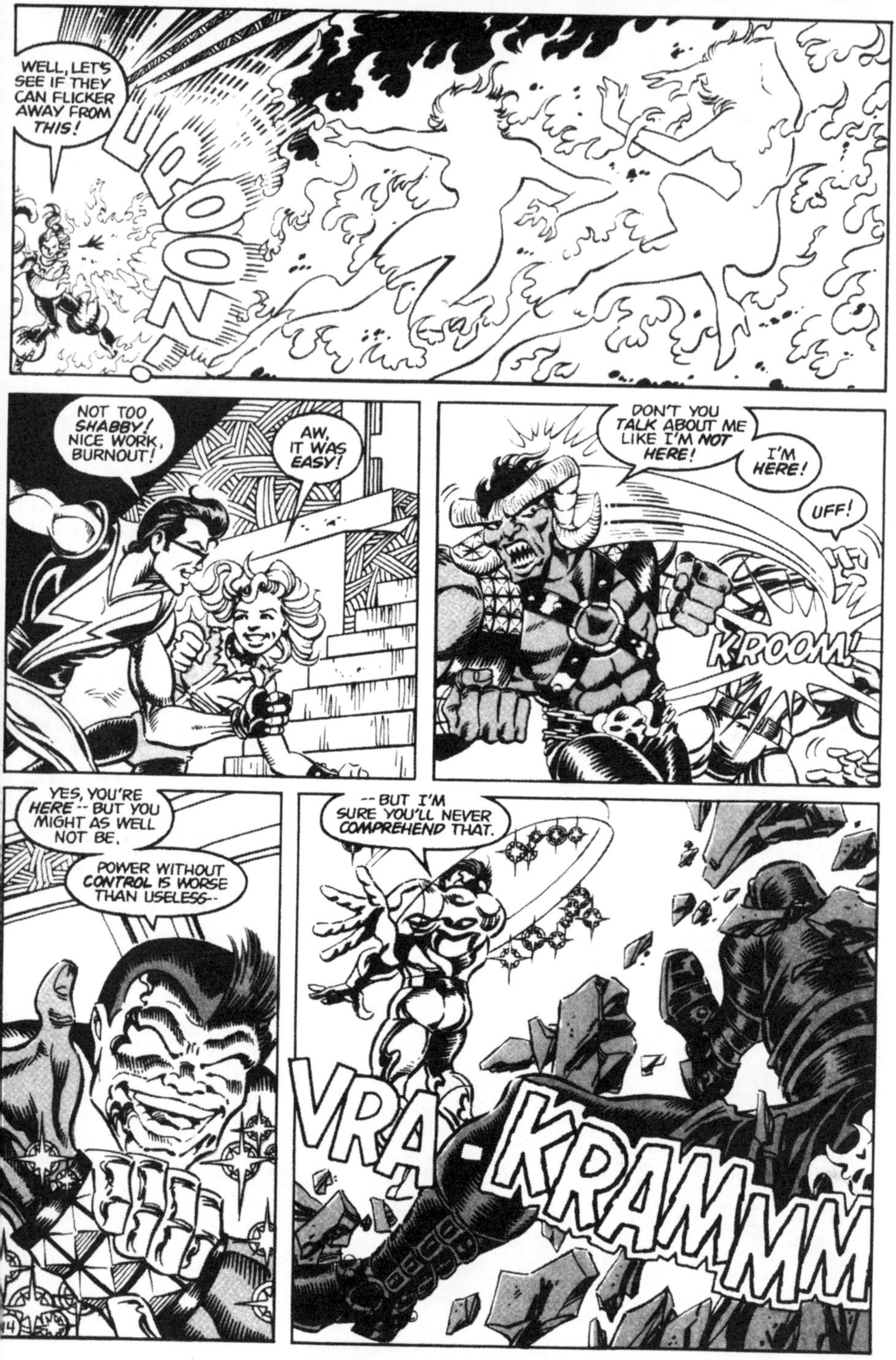

WELL, LET'S SEE IF THEY CAN FLICKER AWAY FROM THIS!
VROOOON!
NOT TOO SHABBY! NICE WORK, BURNOUT!
AW, IT WAS EASY!
DON'T YOU TALK ABOUT ME LIKE I'M NOT HERE!
I'M HERE!
UFF!
KROOM!
YES, YOU'RE HERE -- BUT YOU MIGHT AS WELL NOT BE.
POWER WITHOUT CONTROL IS WORSE THAN USELESS--
-- BUT I'M SURE YOU'LL NEVER COMPREHEND THAT.
VRA-KRAMMMM

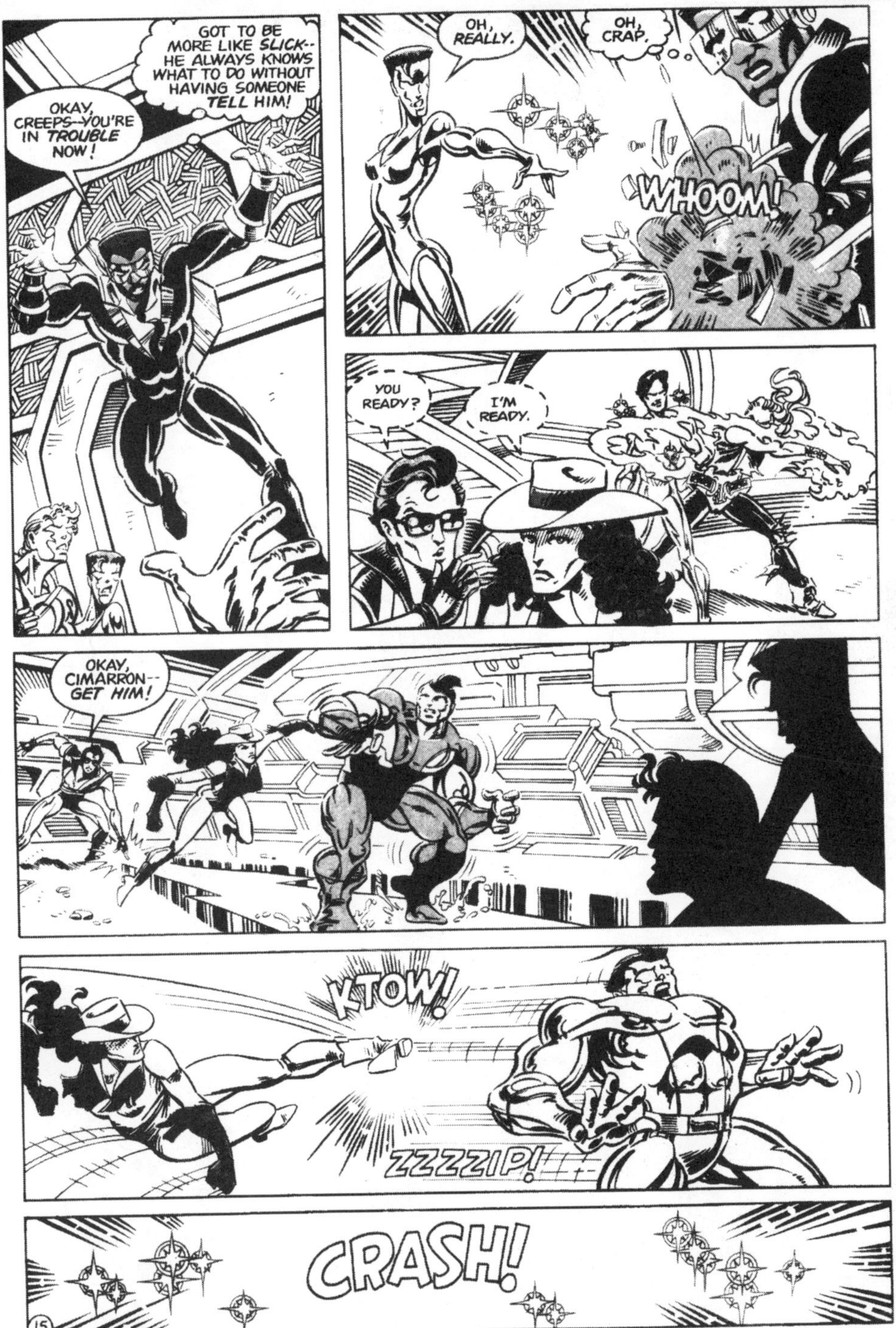
GOT TO BE MORE LIKE SLICK-- HE ALWAYS KNOWS WHAT TO DO WITHOUT HAVING SOMEONE TELL HIM!
OKAY, CREEPS--YOU'RE IN TROUBLE NOW!
OH, REALLY.
OH, CRAP.
WHOOM!
YOU READY?
I'M READY.
OKAY, CIMARRON-- GET HIM!
KTOW!
ZZZZIP!
CRASH!
15

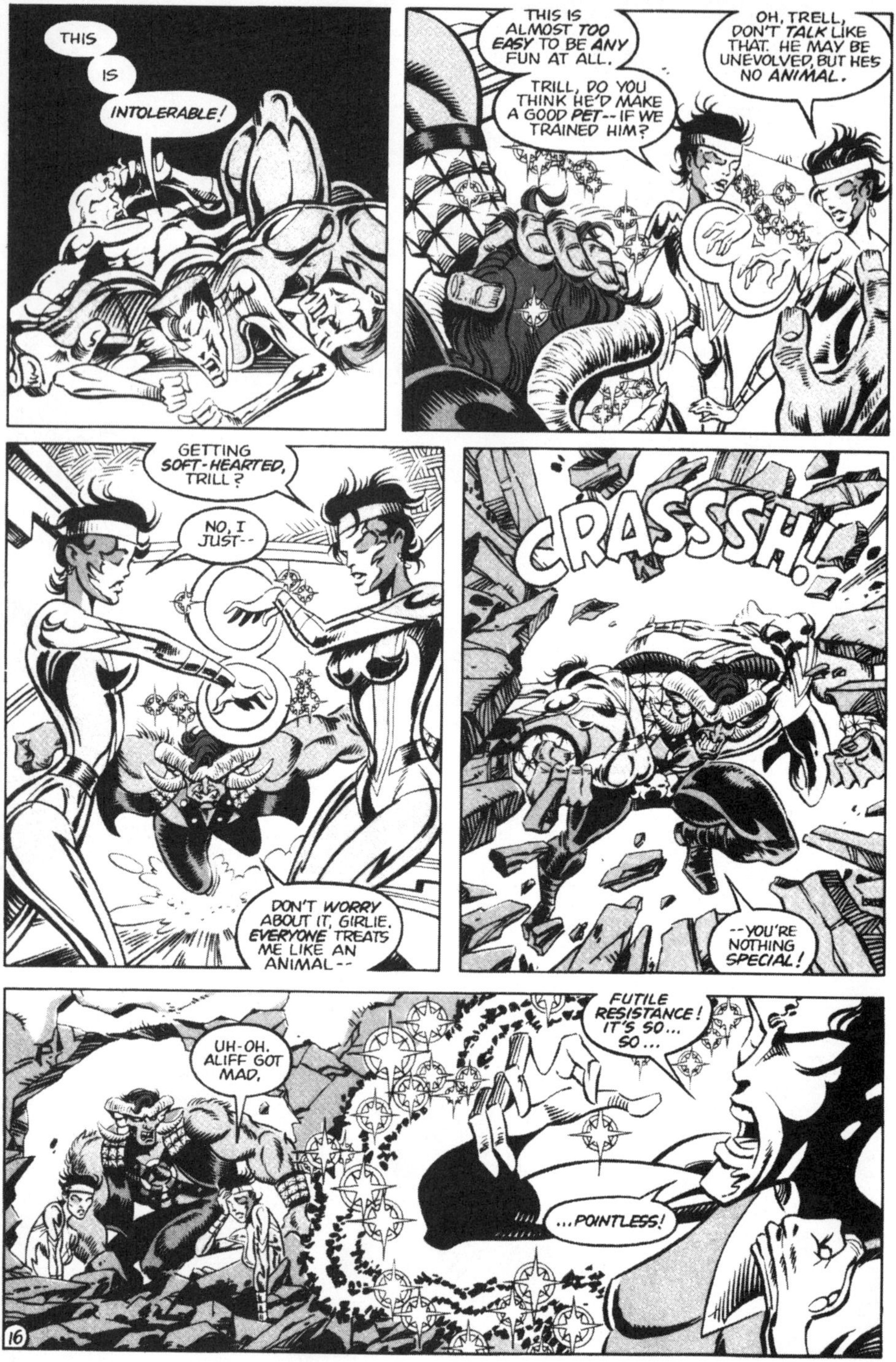
THIS
IS
INTOLERABLE!
THIS IS ALMOST TOO EASY TO BE ANY FUN AT ALL.
TRILL, DO YOU THINK HE'D MAKE A GOOD PET-- IF WE TRAINED HIM?
OH, TRELL, DON'T TALK LIKE THAT. HE MAY BE UNEVOLVED, BUT HE'S NO ANIMAL.
GETTING SOFT-HEARTED, TRILL?
NO, I JUST--
DON'T WORRY ABOUT IT, GIRLIE. EVERYONE TREATS ME LIKE AN ANIMAL--
CRASSSH!
--YOU'RE NOTHING SPECIAL!
UH-OH. ALIFF GOT MAD.
FUTILE RESISTANCE! IT'S SO... SO...
...POINTLESS!
16

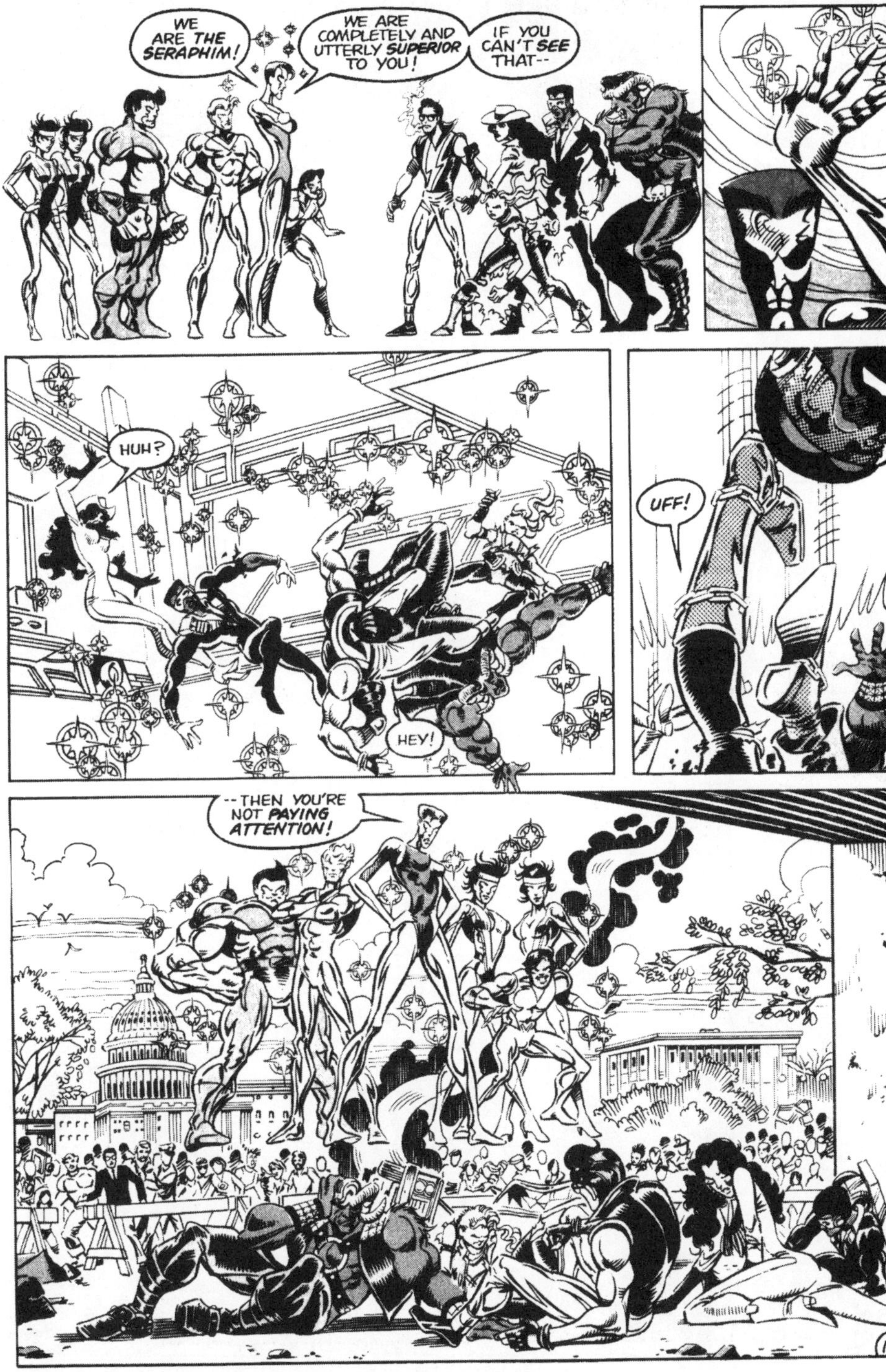
WE ARE THE SERAPHIM!
WE ARE COMPLETELY AND UTTERLY SUPERIOR TO YOU!
IF YOU CAN'T SEE THAT--
HUH?
HEY!
UFF!
--THEN YOU'RE NOT PAYING ATTENTION!
17

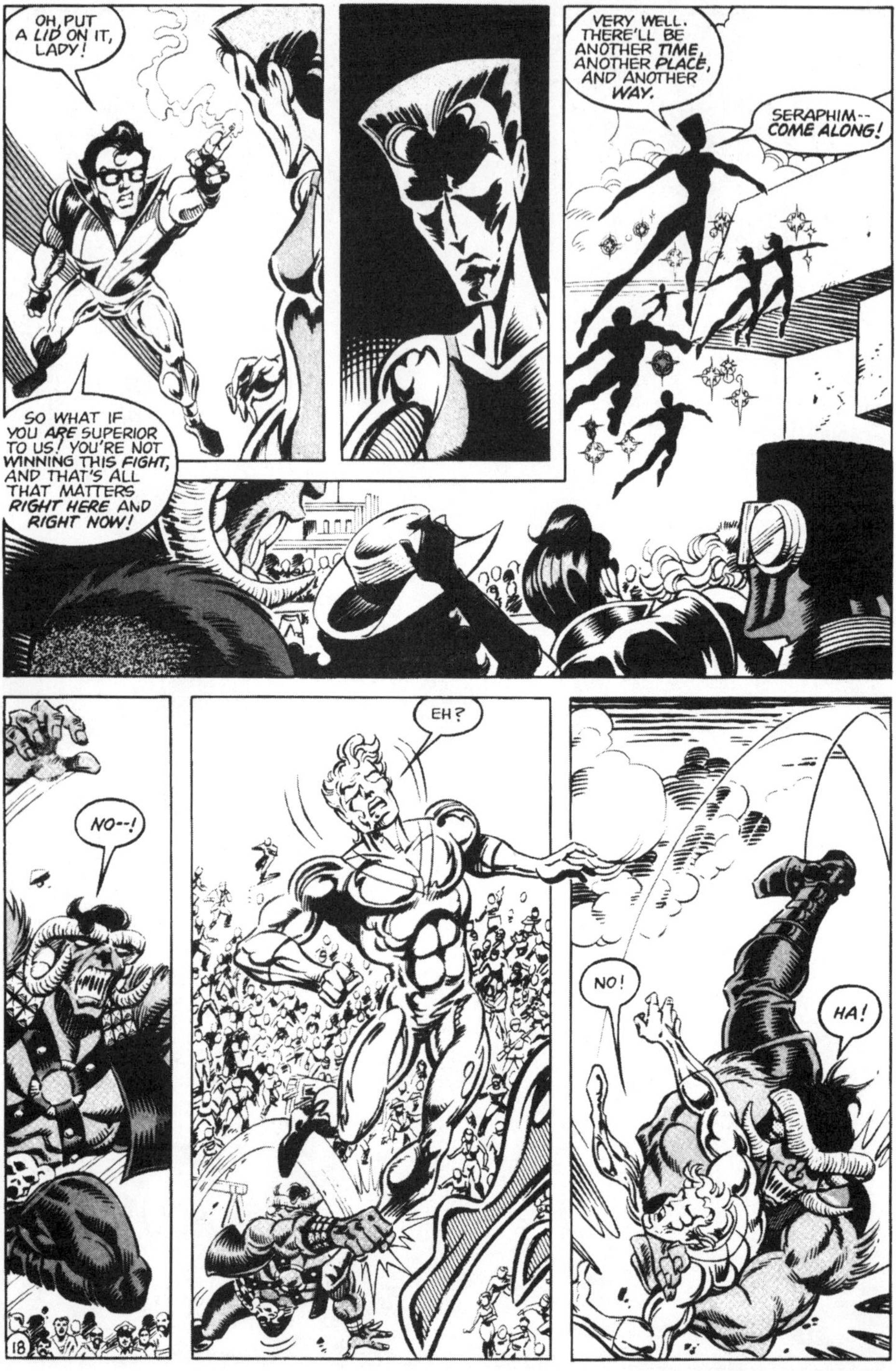
OH, PUT A LID ON IT, LADY!
SO WHAT IF YOU ARE SUPERIOR TO US! YOU'RE NOT WINNING THIS FIGHT, AND THAT'S ALL THAT MATTERS RIGHT HERE AND RIGHT NOW!
VERY WELL. THERE'LL BE ANOTHER TIME, ANOTHER PLACE, AND ANOTHER WAY.
SERAPHIM-- COME ALONG!
NO--!
EH?
NO!
HA!
18

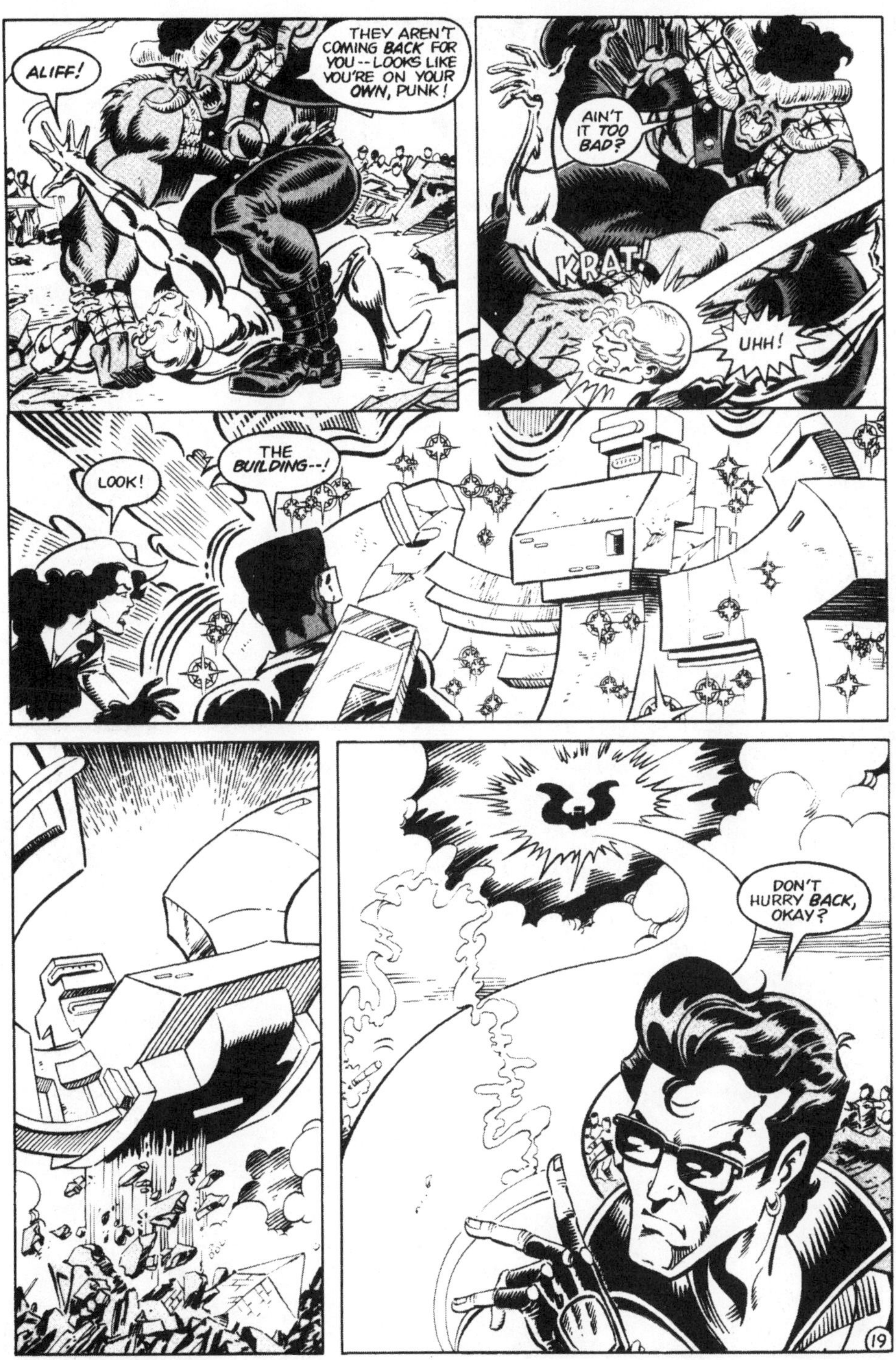
ALIFF!
THEY AREN'T COMING BACK FOR YOU--LOOKS LIKE YOU'RE ON YOUR OWN, PUNK!
AIN'T IT TOO BAD?
KRAT!
UHH!
LOOK!
THE BUILDING--!
DON'T HURRY BACK, OKAY?
19

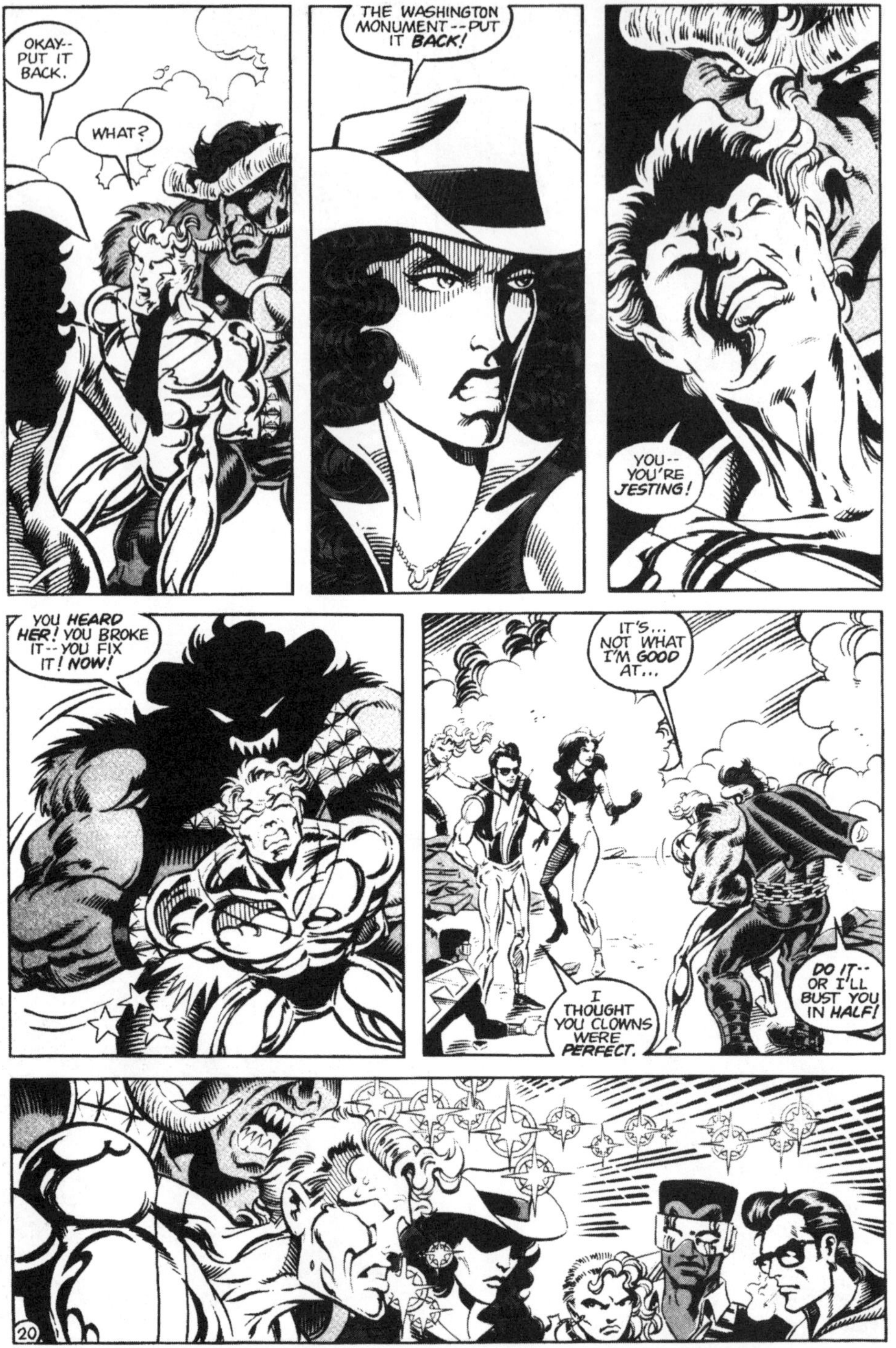
OKAY-- PUT IT BACK.
WHAT?
THE WASHINGTON MONUMENT--PUT IT BACK!
YOU-- YOU'RE JESTING!
YOU HEARD HER! YOU BROKE IT--YOU FIX IT! NOW!
IT'S... NOT WHAT I'M GOOD AT...
I THOUGHT YOU CLOWNS WERE PERFECT.
DO IT-- OR I'LL BUST YOU IN HALF!
20

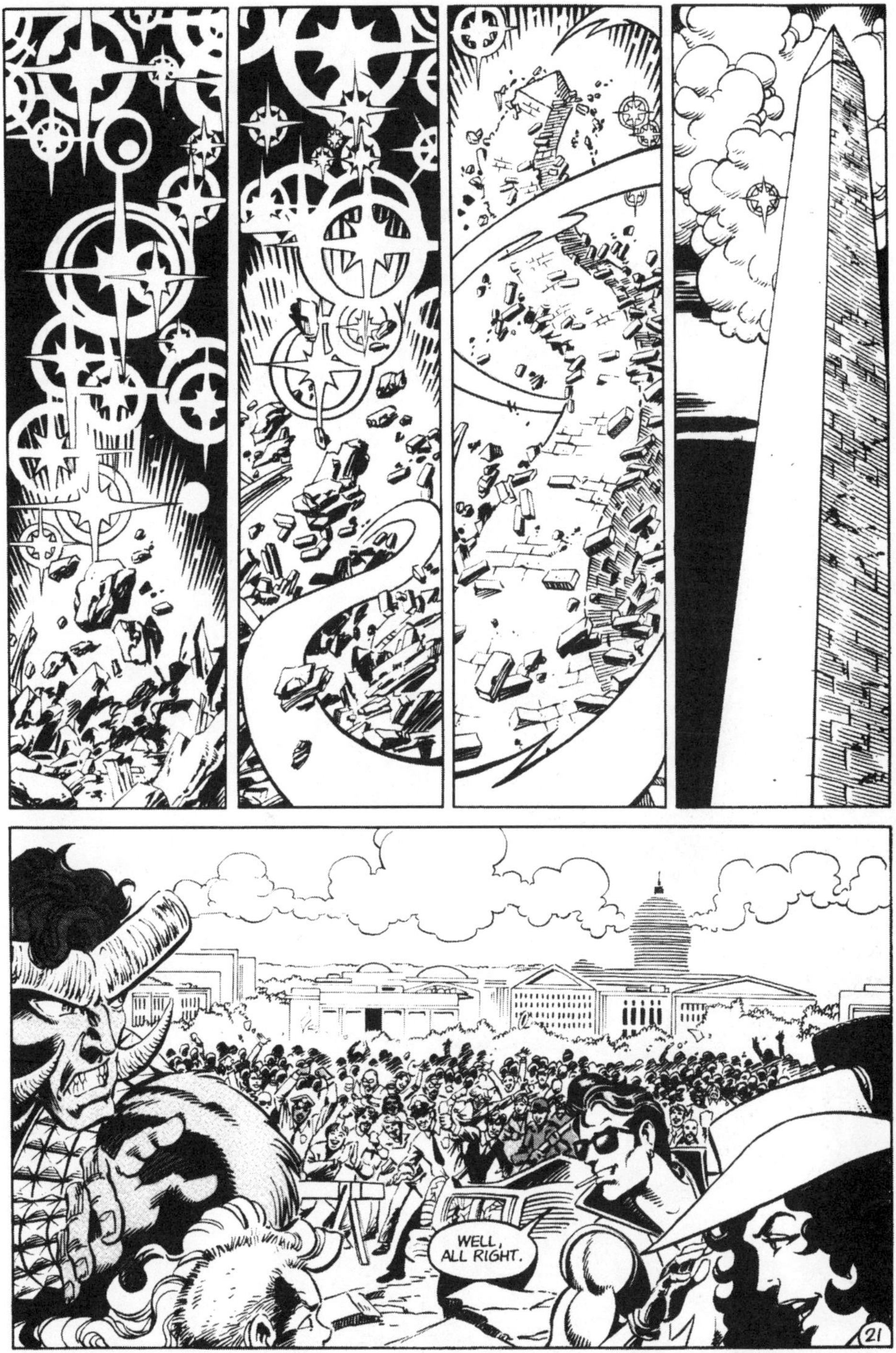
WELL, ALL RIGHT.
21

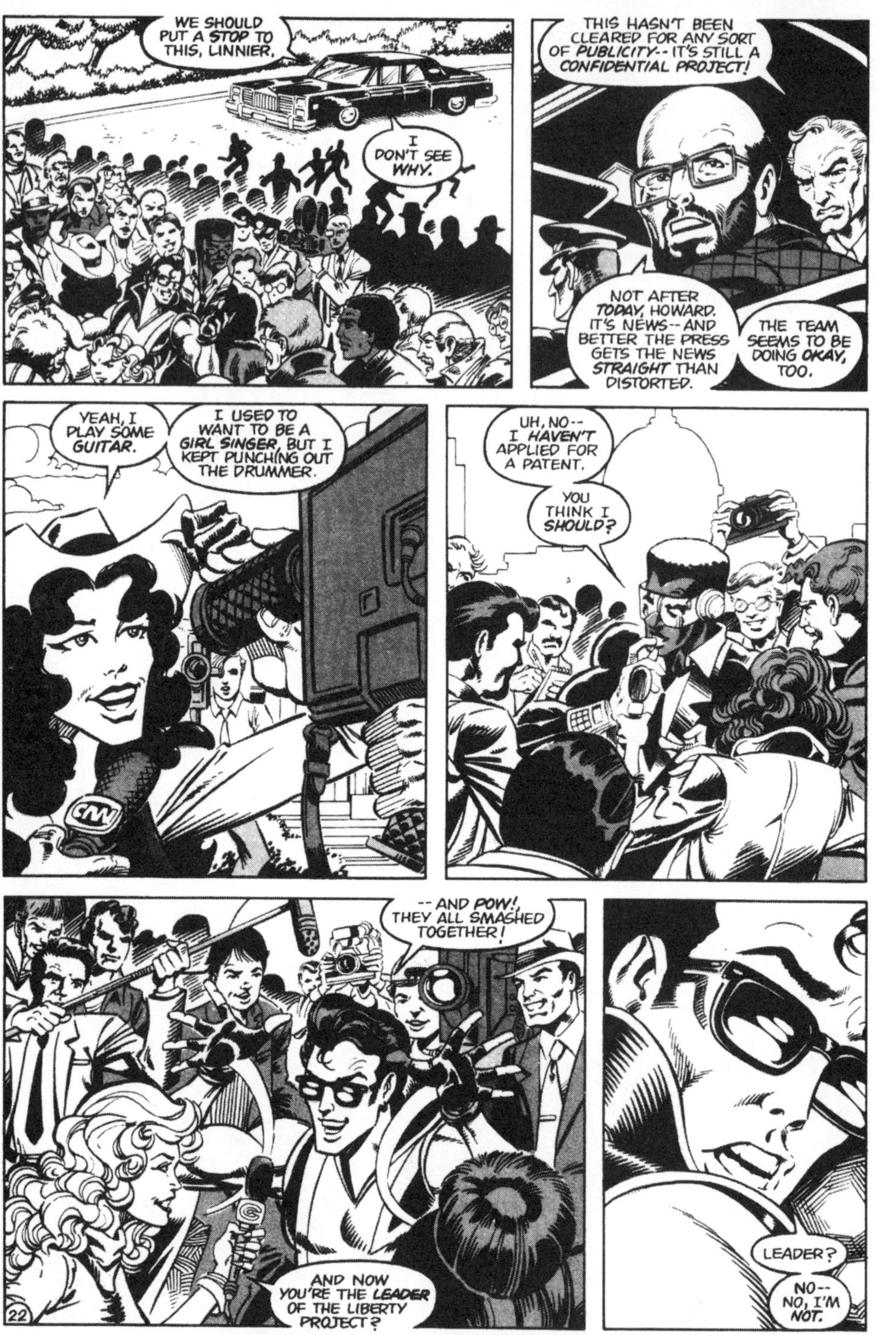
WE SHOULD PUT A STOP TO THIS, LINNIER.
I DON'T SEE WHY.
THIS HASN'T BEEN CLEARED FOR ANY SORT OF PUBLICITY-- IT'S STILL A CONFIDENTIAL PROJECT!
NOT AFTER TODAY, HOWARD. IT'S NEWS-- AND BETTER THE PRESS GETS THE NEWS STRAIGHT THAN DISTORTED.
THE TEAM SEEMS TO BE DOING OKAY, TOO.
YEAH, I PLAY SOME GUITAR.
I USED TO WANT TO BE A GIRL SINGER, BUT I KEPT PUNCHING OUT THE DRUMMER.
CNN
UH, NO-- I HAVEN'T APPLIED FOR A PATENT.
YOU THINK I SHOULD?
-- AND POW!, THEY ALL SMASHED TOGETHER!
AND NOW YOU'RE THE LEADER OF THE LIBERTY PROJECT?
22
LEADER?
NO-- NO, I'M NOT.

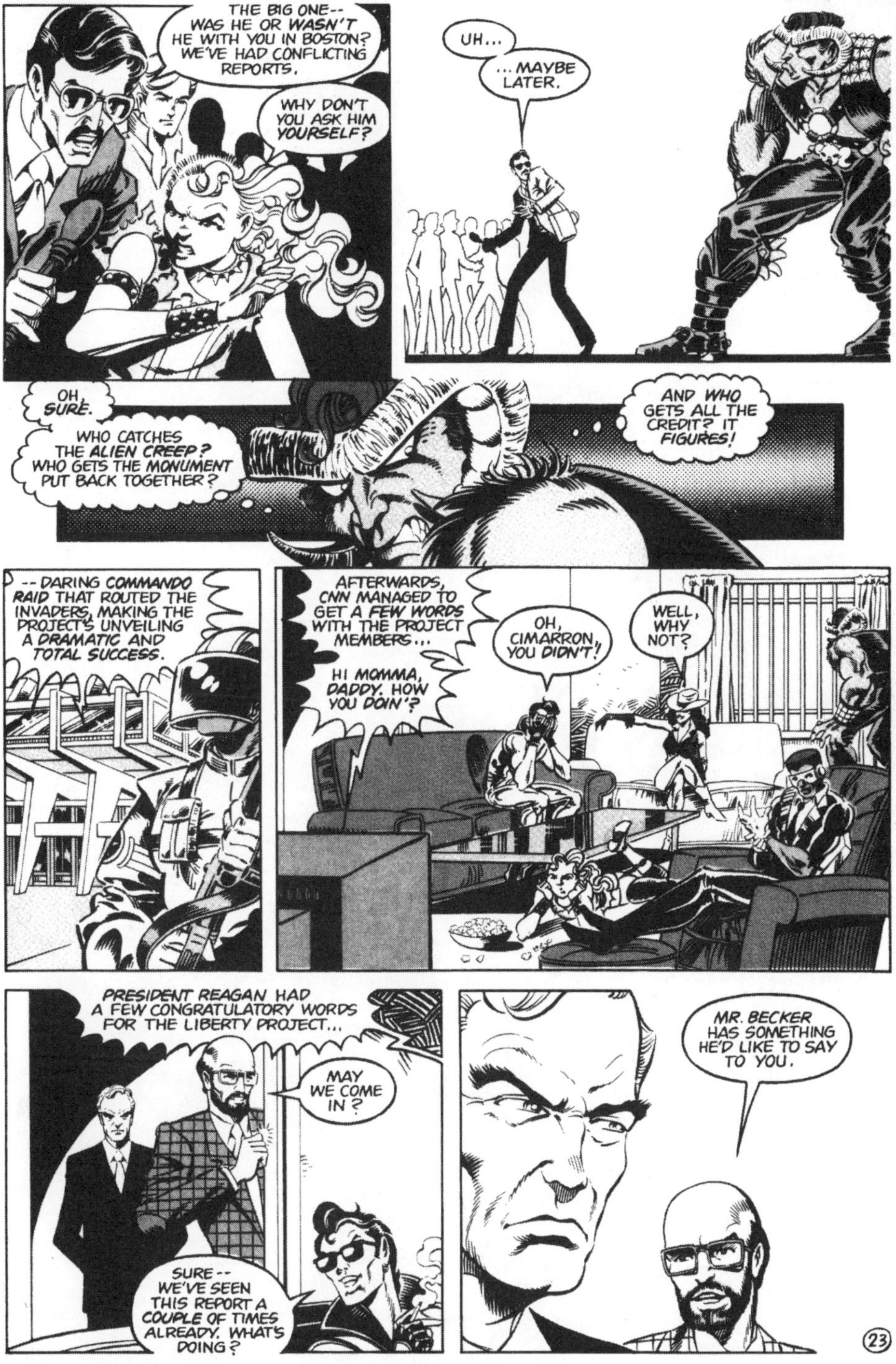
THE BIG ONE-- WAS HE OR WASN'T HE WITH YOU IN BOSTON? WE'VE HAD CONFLICTING REPORTS.
WHY DON'T YOU ASK HIM YOURSELF?
UH...
...MAYBE LATER.
OH, SURE.
WHO CATCHES THE ALIEN CREEP? WHO GETS THE MONUMENT PUT BACK TOGETHER?
AND WHO GETS ALL THE CREDIT? IT FIGURES!
-- DARING COMMANDO RAID THAT ROUTED THE INVADERS, MAKING THE PROJECT'S UNVEILING A DRAMATIC AND TOTAL SUCCESS.
AFTERWARDS, CNN MANAGED TO GET A FEW WORDS WITH THE PROJECT MEMBERS...
HI MOMMA, DADDY. HOW YOU DOIN'?
OH, CIMARRON, YOU DIDN'T!
WELL, WHY NOT?
PRESIDENT REAGAN HAD A FEW CONGRATULATORY WORDS FOR THE LIBERTY PROJECT...
MAY WE COME IN?
SURE-- WE'VE SEEN THIS REPORT A COUPLE OF TIMES ALREADY. WHAT'S DOING?
MR. BECKER HAS SOMETHING HE'D LIKE TO SAY TO YOU.
23

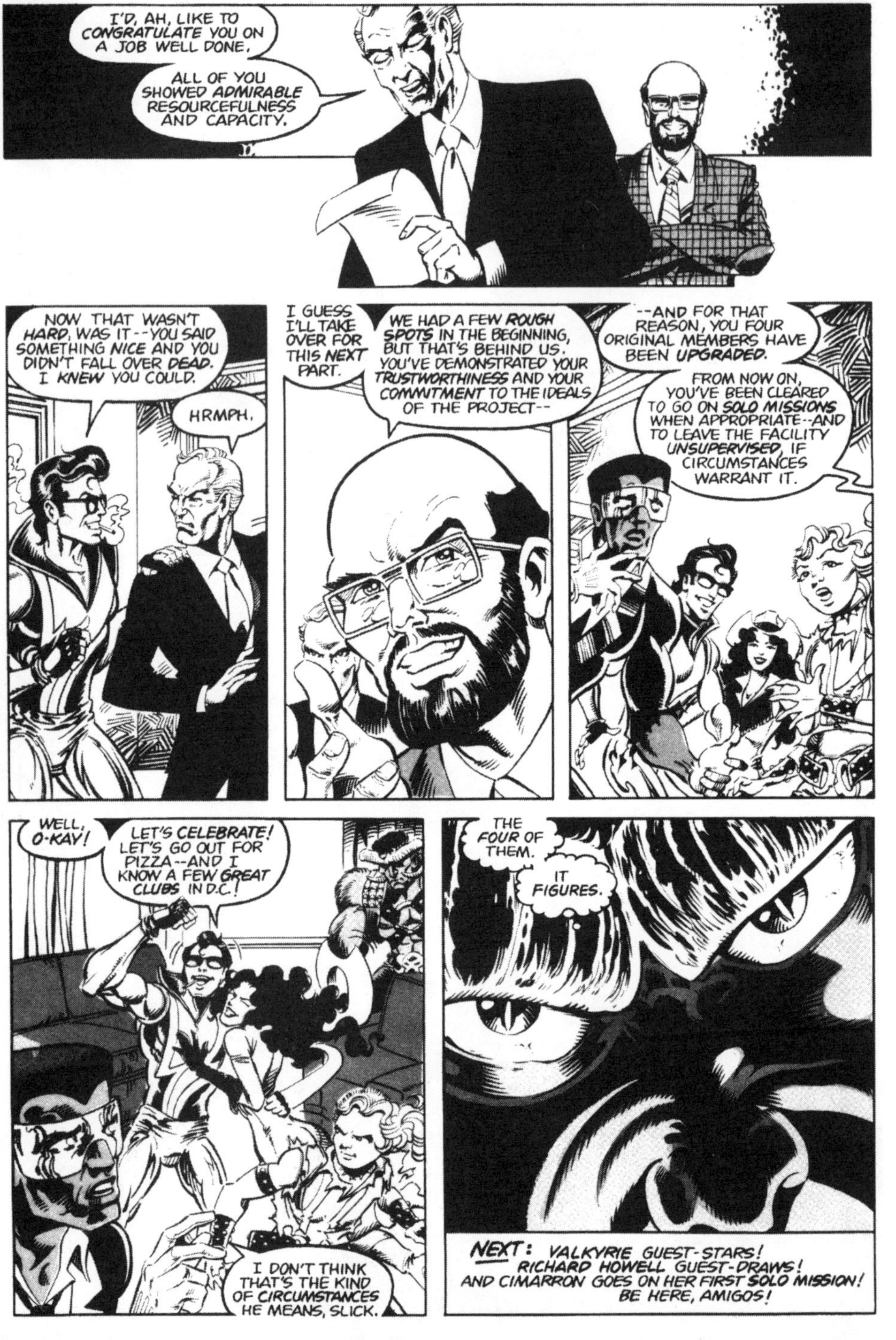
I'D, AH, LIKE TO CONGRATULATE YOU ON A JOB WELL DONE.
ALL OF YOU SHOWED ADMIRABLE RESOURCEFULNESS AND CAPACITY.
NOW THAT WASN'T HARD, WAS IT--YOU SAID SOMETHING NICE AND YOU DIDN'T FALL OVER DEAD. I KNEW YOU COULD.
HRMPH.
I GUESS I'LL TAKE OVER FOR THIS NEXT PART.
WE HAD A FEW ROUGH SPOTS IN THE BEGINNING, BUT THAT'S BEHIND US. YOU'VE DEMONSTRATED YOUR TRUSTWORTHINESS AND YOUR COMMITMENT TO THE IDEALS OF THE PROJECT--
--AND FOR THAT REASON, YOU FOUR ORIGINAL MEMBERS HAVE BEEN UPGRADED.
FROM NOW ON, YOU'VE BEEN CLEARED TO GO ON SOLO MISSIONS WHEN APPROPRIATE--AND TO LEAVE THE FACILITY UNSUPERVISED, IF CIRCUMSTANCES WARRANT IT.
WELL, O-KAY!
LET'S CELEBRATE! LET'S GO OUT FOR PIZZA--AND I KNOW A FEW GREAT CLUBS IN D.C.!
I DON'T THINK THAT'S THE KIND OF CIRCUMSTANCES HE MEANS, SLICK.
THE FOUR OF THEM.
IT FIGURES.
NEXT: VALKYRIE GUEST-STARS! RICHARD HOWELL GUEST-DRAWS! AND CIMARRON GOES ON HER FIRST SOLO MISSION! BE HERE, AMIGOS!

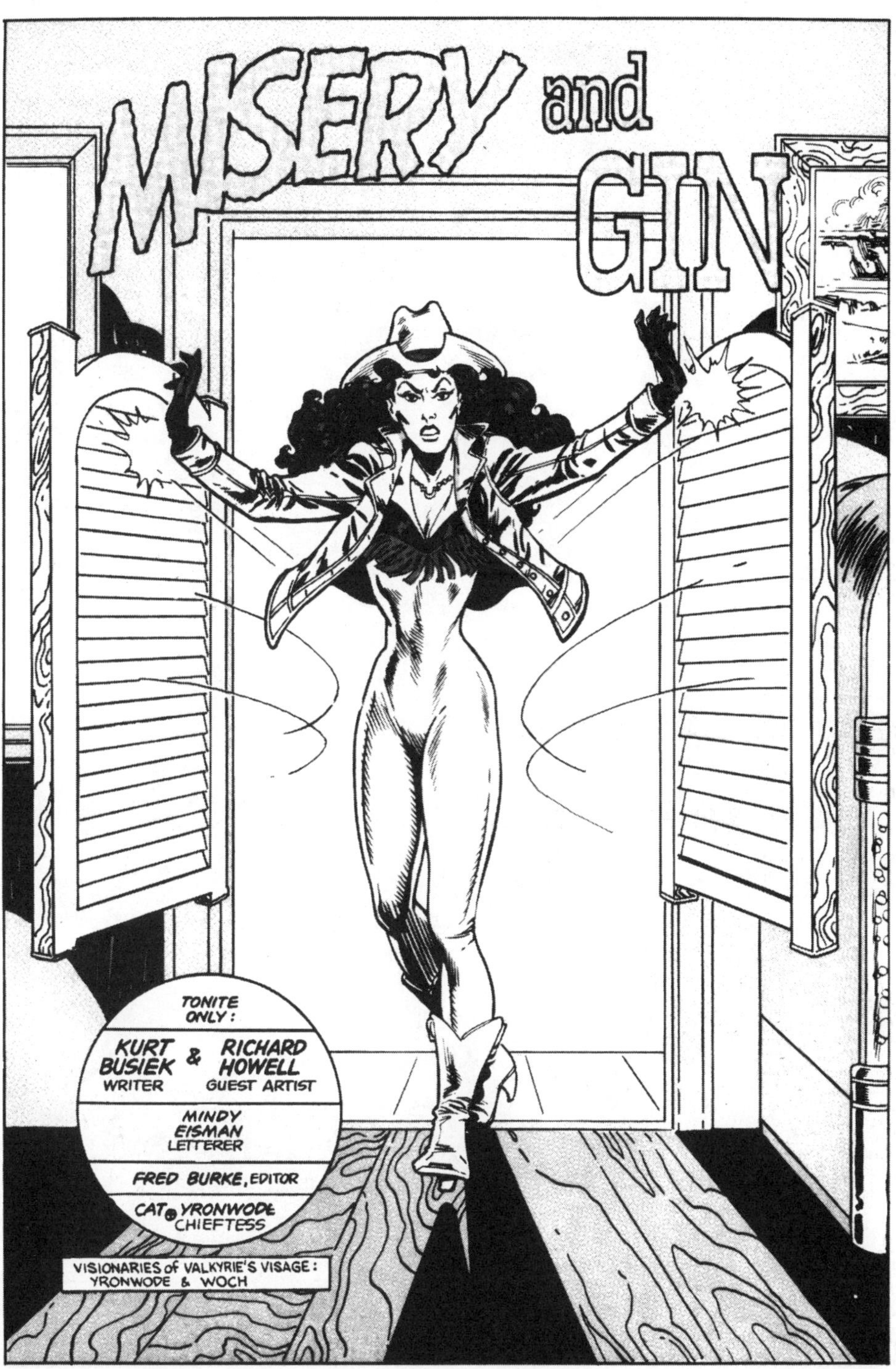
MISERY and GIN
TONITE ONLY:
KURT BUSIEK WRITER & RICHARD HOWELL GUEST ARTIST
MINDY EISMAN LETTERER
FRED BURKE, EDITOR
CAT YRONWODE CHIEFTESS
VISIONARIES of VALKYRIE'S VISAGE: YRONWODE & WOCH

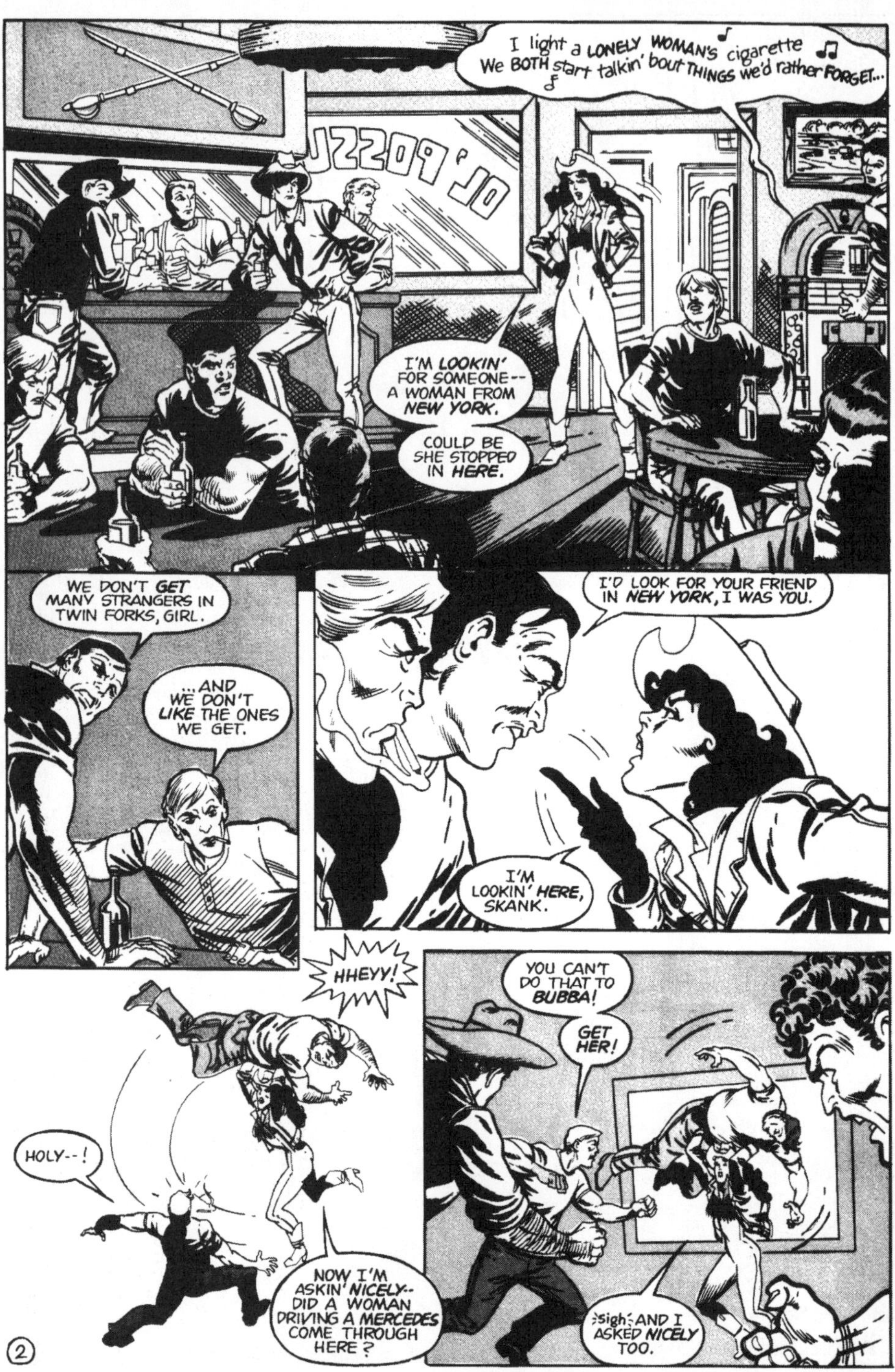

I light a LONELY WOMAN'S cigarette
We BOTH start talkin' bout THINGS we'd rather FORGET...
OL' POSSUM
I'M LOOKIN' FOR SOMEONE-- A WOMAN FROM NEW YORK.
COULD BE SHE STOPPED IN HERE.
WE DON'T GET MANY STRANGERS IN TWIN FORKS, GIRL.
...AND WE DON'T LIKE THE ONES WE GET.
I'D LOOK FOR YOUR FRIEND IN NEW YORK, I WAS YOU.
I'M LOOKIN' HERE, SKANK.
HHEYY!
HOLY--!
NOW I'M ASKIN' NICELY-- DID A WOMAN DRIVING A MERCEDES COME THROUGH HERE?
YOU CAN'T DO THAT TO BUBBA!
GET HER!
sigh AND I ASKED NICELY TOO.
2

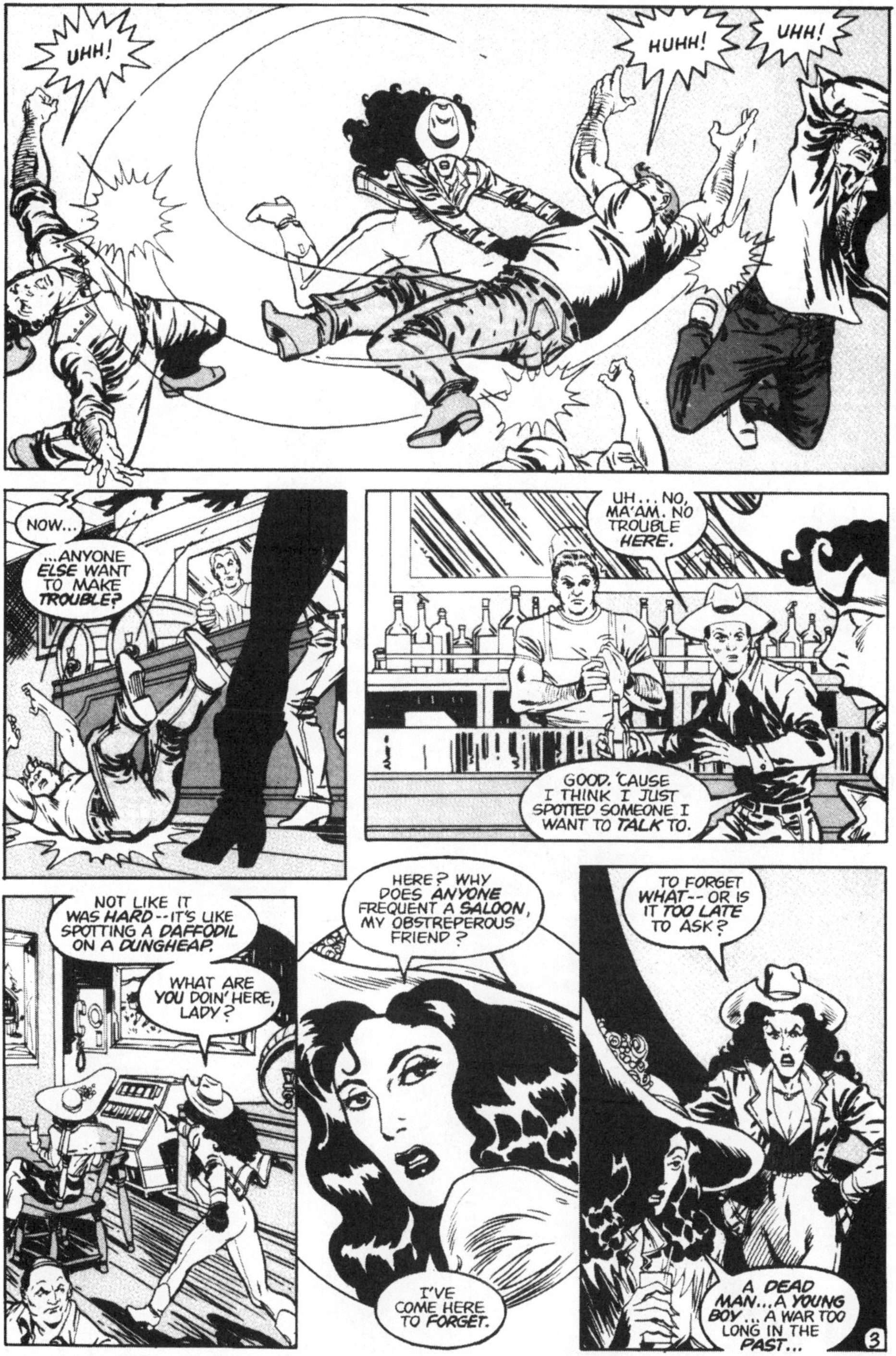
UHH!
HUHH!
UHH!
NOW...
...ANYONE ELSE WANT TO MAKE TROUBLE?
UH... NO, MA'AM. NO TROUBLE HERE.
GOOD. 'CAUSE I THINK I JUST SPOTTED SOMEONE I WANT TO TALK TO.
NOT LIKE IT WAS HARD--IT'S LIKE SPOTTING A DAFFODIL ON A DUNGHEAP.
WHAT ARE YOU DOIN' HERE, LADY?
HERE? WHY DOES ANYONE FREQUENT A SALOON, MY OBSTREPEROUS FRIEND?
I'VE COME HERE TO FORGET.
TO FORGET WHAT-- OR IS IT TOO LATE TO ASK?
A DEAD MAN... A YOUNG BOY... A WAR TOO LONG IN THE PAST...
3

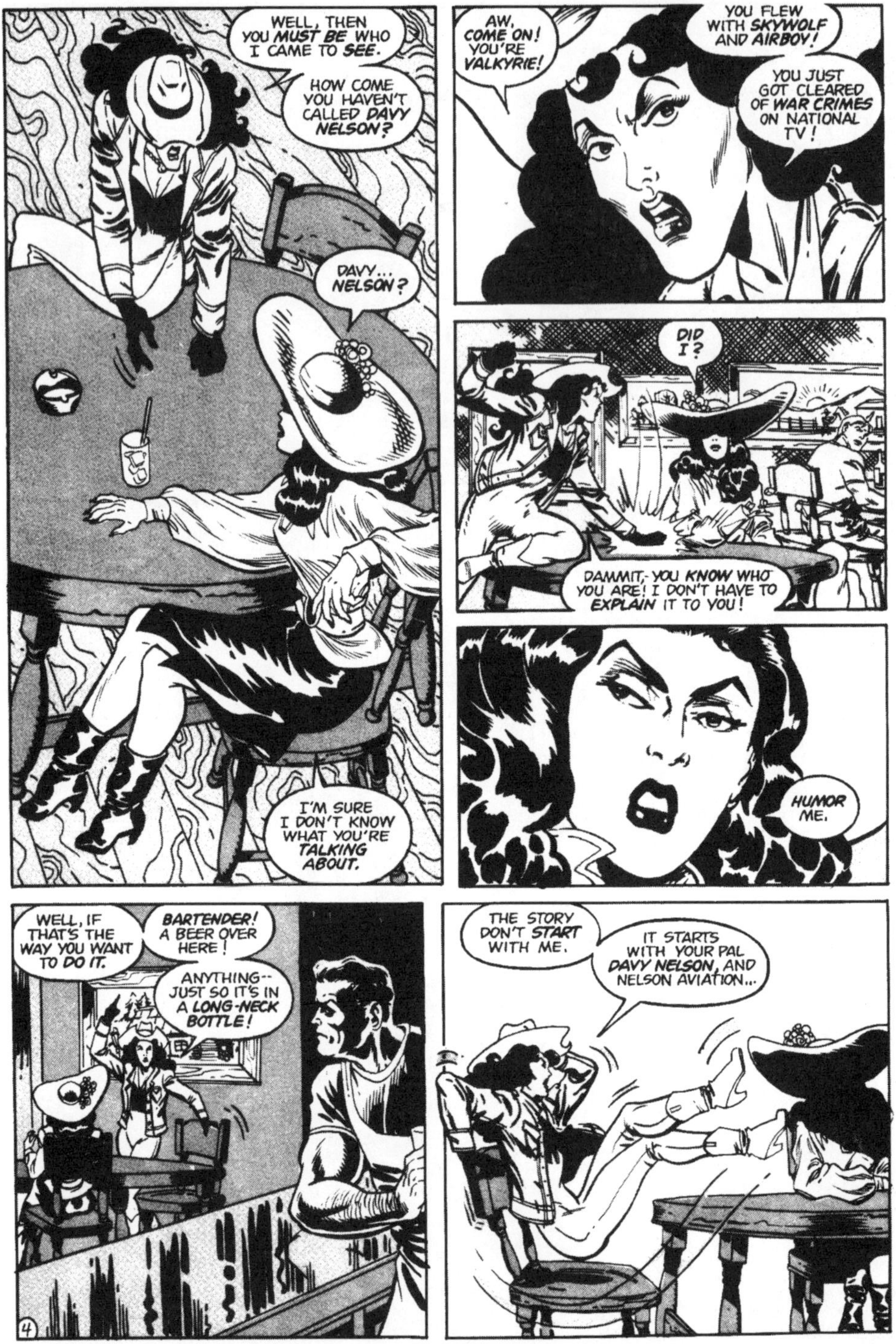
WELL, THEN YOU MUST BE WHO I CAME TO SEE.
HOW COME YOU HAVEN'T CALLED DAVY NELSON?
DAVY... NELSON?
I'M SURE I DON'T KNOW WHAT YOU'RE TALKING ABOUT.
AW, COME ON! YOU'RE VALKYRIE!
YOU FLEW WITH SKYWOLF AND AIRBOY!
YOU JUST GOT CLEARED OF WAR CRIMES ON NATIONAL TV!
DID I?
DAMMIT,- YOU KNOW WHO YOU ARE! I DON'T HAVE TO EXPLAIN IT TO YOU!
HUMOR ME.
WELL, IF THAT'S THE WAY YOU WANT TO DO IT.
BARTENDER! A BEER OVER HERE!
ANYTHING-- JUST SO IT'S IN A LONG-NECK BOTTLE!
4
THE STORY DON'T START WITH ME.
IT STARTS WITH YOUR PAL DAVY NELSON, AND NELSON AVIATION...

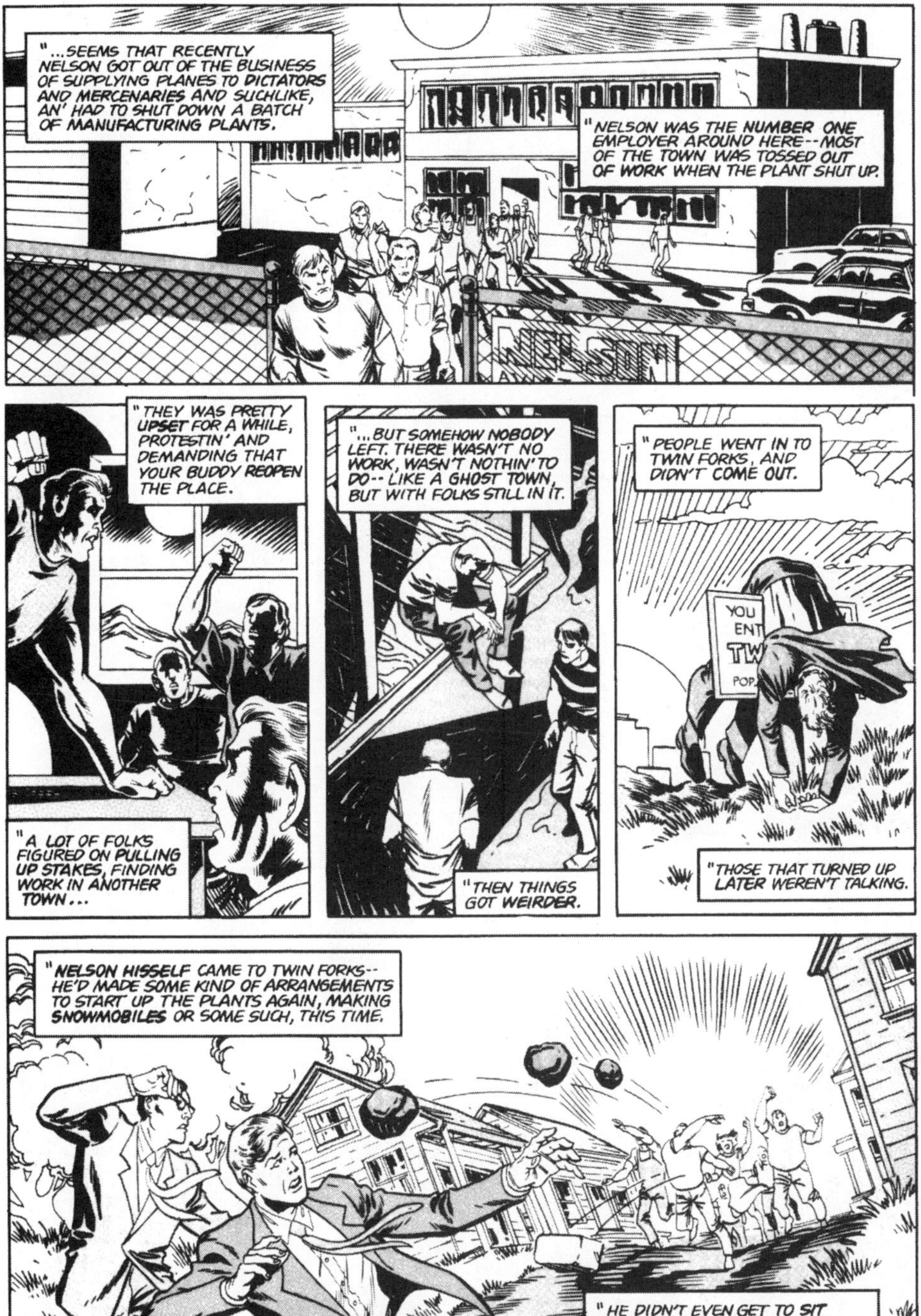
"...SEEMS THAT RECENTLY NELSON GOT OUT OF THE BUSINESS OF SUPPLYING PLANES TO DICTATORS AND MERCENARIES AND SUCHLIKE, AN' HAD TO SHUT DOWN A BATCH OF MANUFACTURING PLANTS.
"NELSON WAS THE NUMBER ONE EMPLOYER AROUND HERE--MOST OF THE TOWN WAS TOSSED OUT OF WORK WHEN THE PLANT SHUT UP.
"THEY WAS PRETTY UPSET FOR A WHILE, PROTESTIN' AND DEMANDING THAT YOUR BUDDY REOPEN THE PLACE.
"A LOT OF FOLKS FIGURED ON PULLING UP STAKES, FINDING WORK IN ANOTHER TOWN...
"...BUT SOMEHOW NOBODY LEFT. THERE WASN'T NO WORK, WASN'T NOTHIN' TO DO-- LIKE A GHOST TOWN, BUT WITH FOLKS STILL IN IT.
"THEN THINGS GOT WEIRDER.
"PEOPLE WENT IN TO TWIN FORKS, AND DIDN'T COME OUT.
"THOSE THAT TURNED UP LATER WEREN'T TALKING.
"NELSON HISSELF CAME TO TWIN FORKS-- HE'D MADE SOME KIND OF ARRANGEMENTS TO START UP THE PLANTS AGAIN, MAKING SNOWMOBILES OR SOME SUCH, THIS TIME.
"HE DIDN'T EVEN GET TO SIT DOWN-- THEY PRACTICALLY TRIED TO STRING HIM UP, SO HE JUST HAD TO UP AND LEAVE.
5

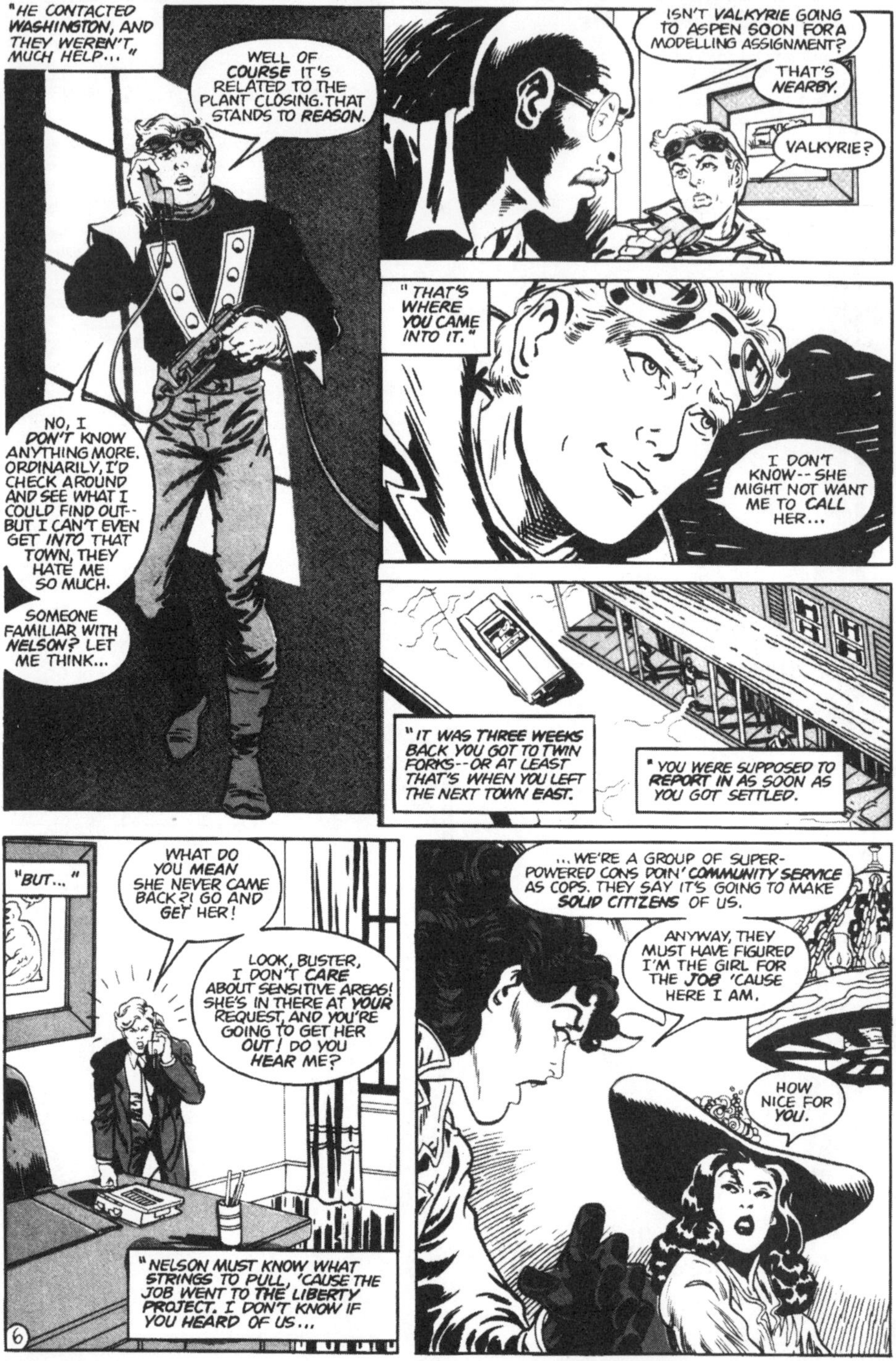
"HE CONTACTED WASHINGTON, AND THEY WEREN'T MUCH HELP..."
WELL OF COURSE IT'S RELATED TO THE PLANT CLOSING. THAT STANDS TO REASON.
NO, I DON'T KNOW ANYTHING MORE. ORDINARILY, I'D CHECK AROUND AND SEE WHAT I COULD FIND OUT-- BUT I CAN'T EVEN GET INTO THAT TOWN, THEY HATE ME SO MUCH.
SOMEONE FAMILIAR WITH NELSON? LET ME THINK...
ISN'T VALKYRIE GOING TO ASPEN SOON FOR A MODELLING ASSIGNMENT?
THAT'S NEARBY.
VALKYRIE?
"THAT'S WHERE YOU CAME INTO IT."
I DON'T KNOW-- SHE MIGHT NOT WANT ME TO CALL HER...
"IT WAS THREE WEEKS BACK YOU GOT TO TWIN FORKS--OR AT LEAST THAT'S WHEN YOU LEFT THE NEXT TOWN EAST.
"YOU WERE SUPPOSED TO REPORT IN AS SOON AS YOU GOT SETTLED.
"BUT..."
WHAT DO YOU MEAN SHE NEVER CAME BACK?! GO AND GET HER!
LOOK, BUSTER, I DON'T CARE ABOUT SENSITIVE AREAS! SHE'S IN THERE AT YOUR REQUEST, AND YOU'RE GOING TO GET HER OUT! DO YOU HEAR ME?
"NELSON MUST KNOW WHAT STRINGS TO PULL, 'CAUSE THE JOB WENT TO THE LIBERTY PROJECT. I DON'T KNOW IF YOU HEARD OF US...
6
...WE'RE A GROUP OF SUPER-POWERED CONS DOIN' COMMUNITY SERVICE AS COPS. THEY SAY IT'S GOING TO MAKE SOLID CITIZENS OF US.
ANYWAY, THEY MUST HAVE FIGURED I'M THE GIRL FOR THE JOB 'CAUSE HERE I AM.
HOW NICE FOR YOU.

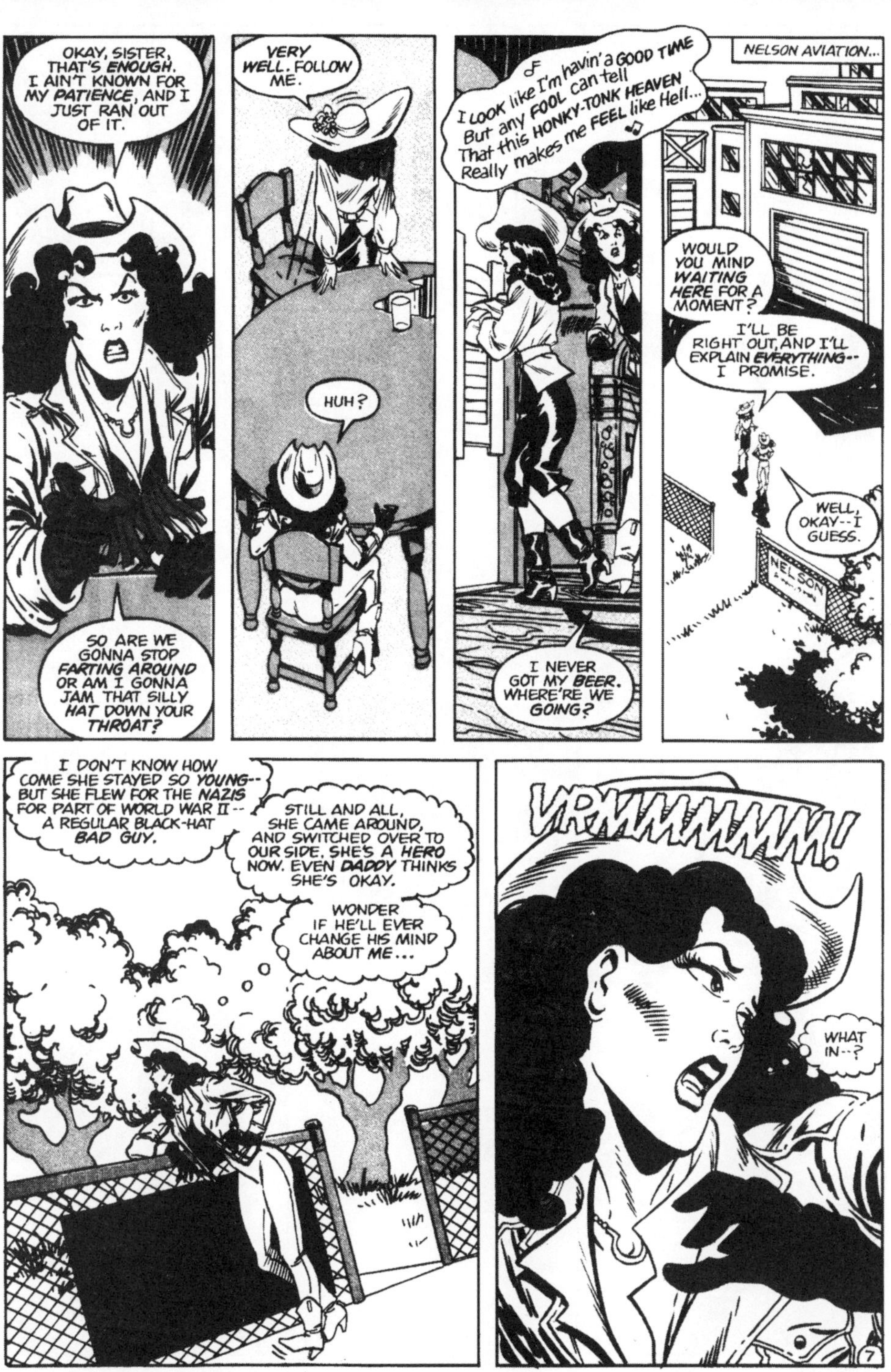
OKAY, SISTER, THAT'S ENOUGH. I AIN'T KNOWN FOR MY PATIENCE, AND I JUST RAN OUT OF IT.
SO ARE WE GONNA STOP FARTING AROUND OR AM I GONNA JAM THAT SILLY HAT DOWN YOUR THROAT?
VERY WELL. FOLLOW ME.
HUH?
I LOOK like I'm havin' a GOOD TIME But any FOOL can tell That this HONKY-TONK HEAVEN Really makes me FEEL like Hell...
I NEVER GOT MY BEER. WHERE'RE WE GOING?
NELSON AVIATION...
WOULD YOU MIND WAITING HERE FOR A MOMENT?
I'LL BE RIGHT OUT, AND I'LL EXPLAIN EVERYTHING-- I PROMISE.
WELL, OKAY--I GUESS.
NELSON
I DON'T KNOW HOW COME SHE STAYED SO YOUNG-- BUT SHE FLEW FOR THE NAZIS FOR PART OF WORLD WAR II-- A REGULAR BLACK-HAT BAD GUY.
STILL AND ALL, SHE CAME AROUND, AND SWITCHED OVER TO OUR SIDE. SHE'S A HERO NOW. EVEN DADDY THINKS SHE'S OKAY.
WONDER IF HE'LL EVER CHANGE HIS MIND ABOUT ME...
VRMMMMMMM!
WHAT IN--?
7

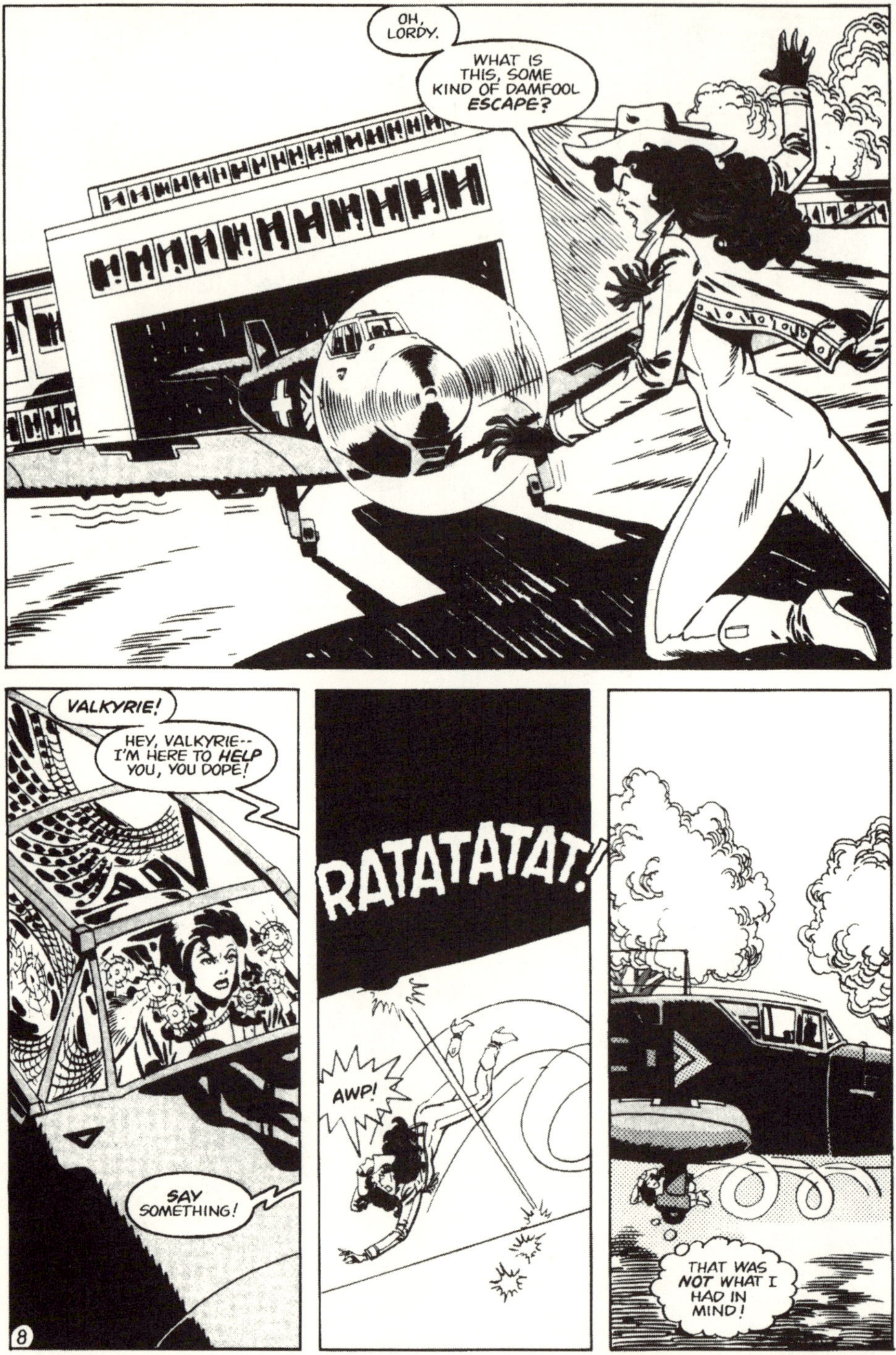
OH, LORDY.
WHAT IS THIS, SOME KIND OF DAMFOOL ESCAPE?
VALKYRIE!
HEY, VALKYRIE-- I'M HERE TO HELP YOU, YOU DOPE!
SAY SOMETHING!
8
RATATATAT!
AWP!
THAT WAS NOT WHAT I HAD IN MIND!

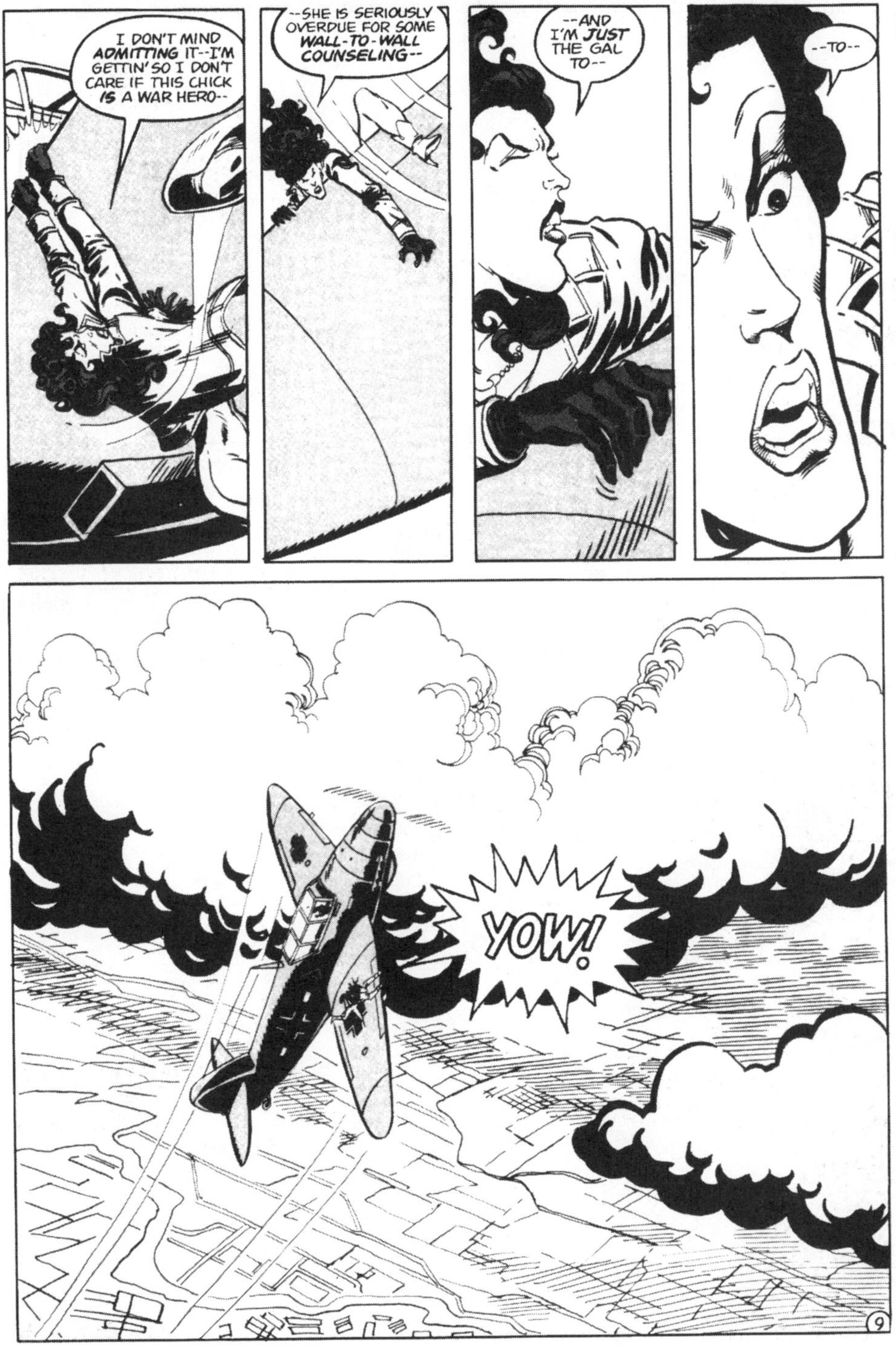
I DON'T MIND ADMITTING IT--I'M GETTIN' SO I DON'T CARE IF THIS CHICK IS A WAR HERO--
--SHE IS SERIOUSLY OVERDUE FOR SOME WALL-TO-WALL COUNSELING--
--AND I'M JUST THE GAL TO--
--TO--
YOW!
9

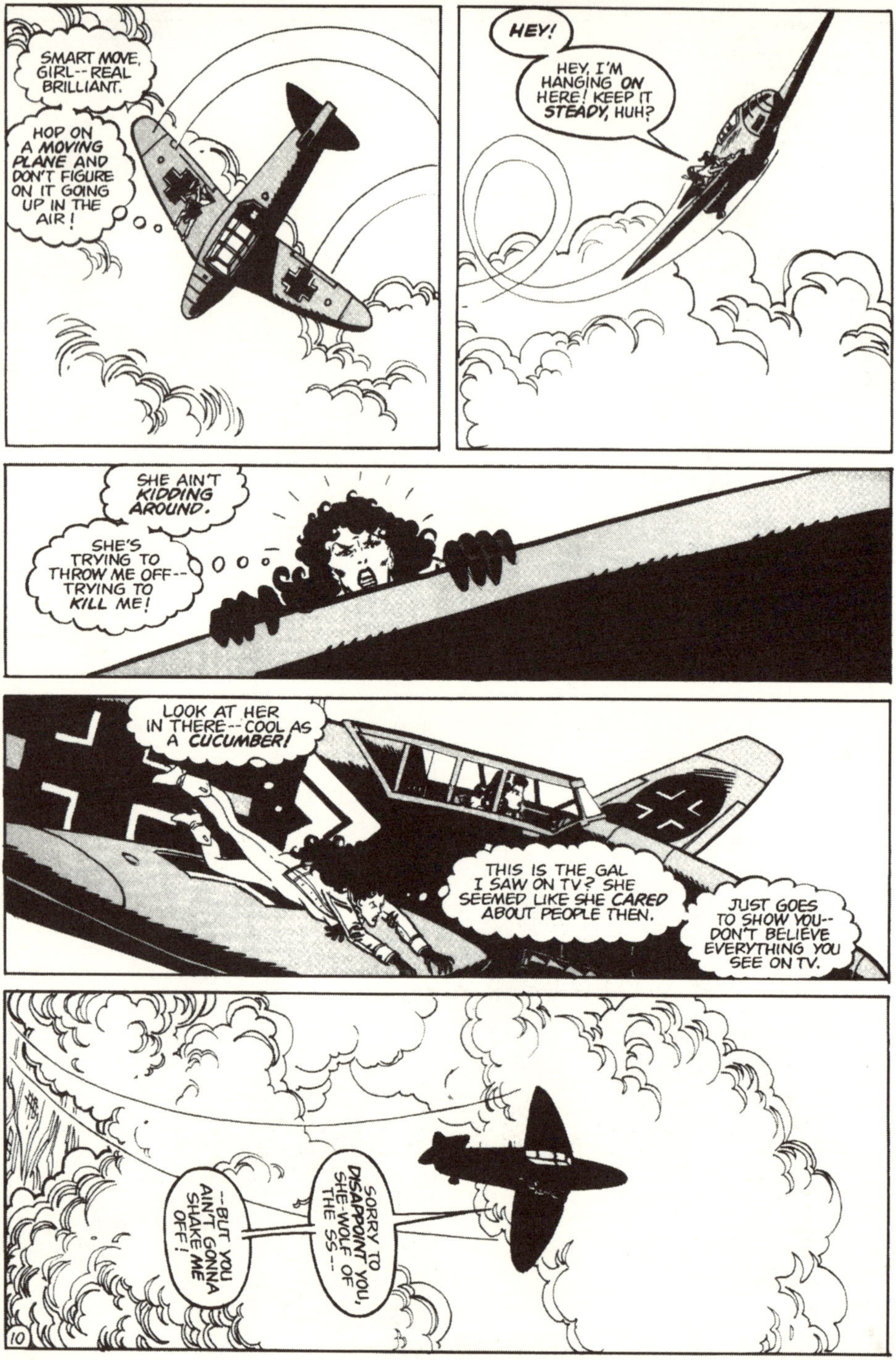
SMART MOVE, GIRL--REAL BRILLIANT.
HOP ON A MOVING PLANE AND DON'T FIGURE ON IT GOING UP IN THE AIR!
HEY!
HEY, I'M HANGING ON HERE! KEEP IT STEADY, HUH?
SHE AIN'T KIDDING AROUND.
SHE'S TRYING TO THROW ME OFF--TRYING TO KILL ME!
LOOK AT HER IN THERE--COOL AS A CUCUMBER!
THIS IS THE GAL I SAW ON TV? SHE SEEMED LIKE SHE CARED ABOUT PEOPLE THEN.
JUST GOES TO SHOW YOU--DON'T BELIEVE EVERYTHING YOU SEE ON TV.
SORRY TO DISAPPOINT YOU, SHE-WOLF OF THE SS...
--BUT YOU AIN'T GONNA SHAKE ME OFF!
10

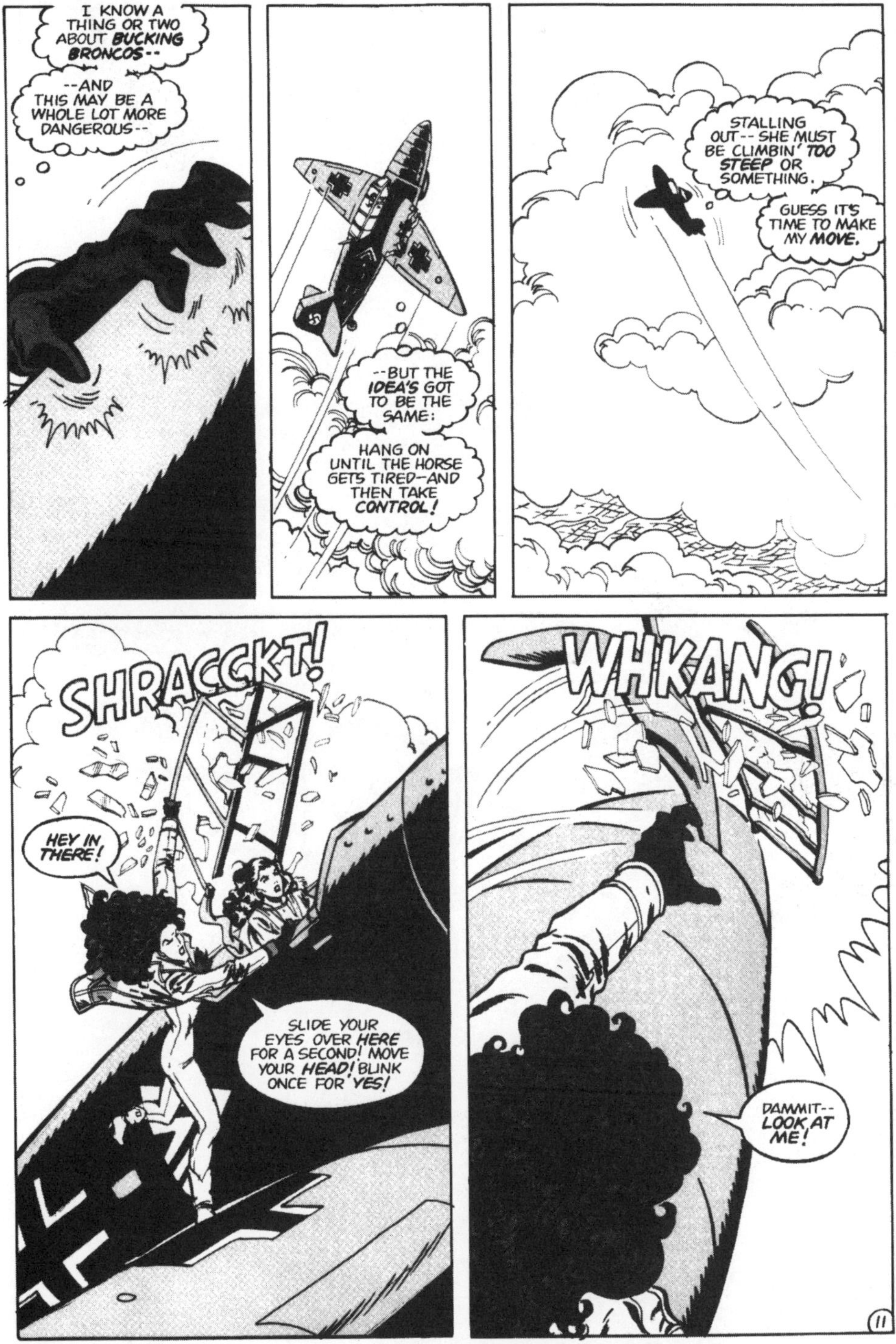
I KNOW A THING OR TWO ABOUT BUCKING BRONCOS--
--AND THIS MAY BE A WHOLE LOT MORE DANGEROUS--
--BUT THE IDEA'S GOT TO BE THE SAME:
HANG ON UNTIL THE HORSE GETS TIRED--AND THEN TAKE CONTROL!
STALLING OUT-- SHE MUST BE CLIMBIN' TOO STEEP OR SOMETHING.
GUESS IT'S TIME TO MAKE MY MOVE.
SHRACCKT!
HEY IN THERE!
SLIDE YOUR EYES OVER HERE FOR A SECOND! MOVE YOUR HEAD! BLINK ONCE FOR YES!
WHKANG!
DAMMIT-- LOOK AT ME!
11

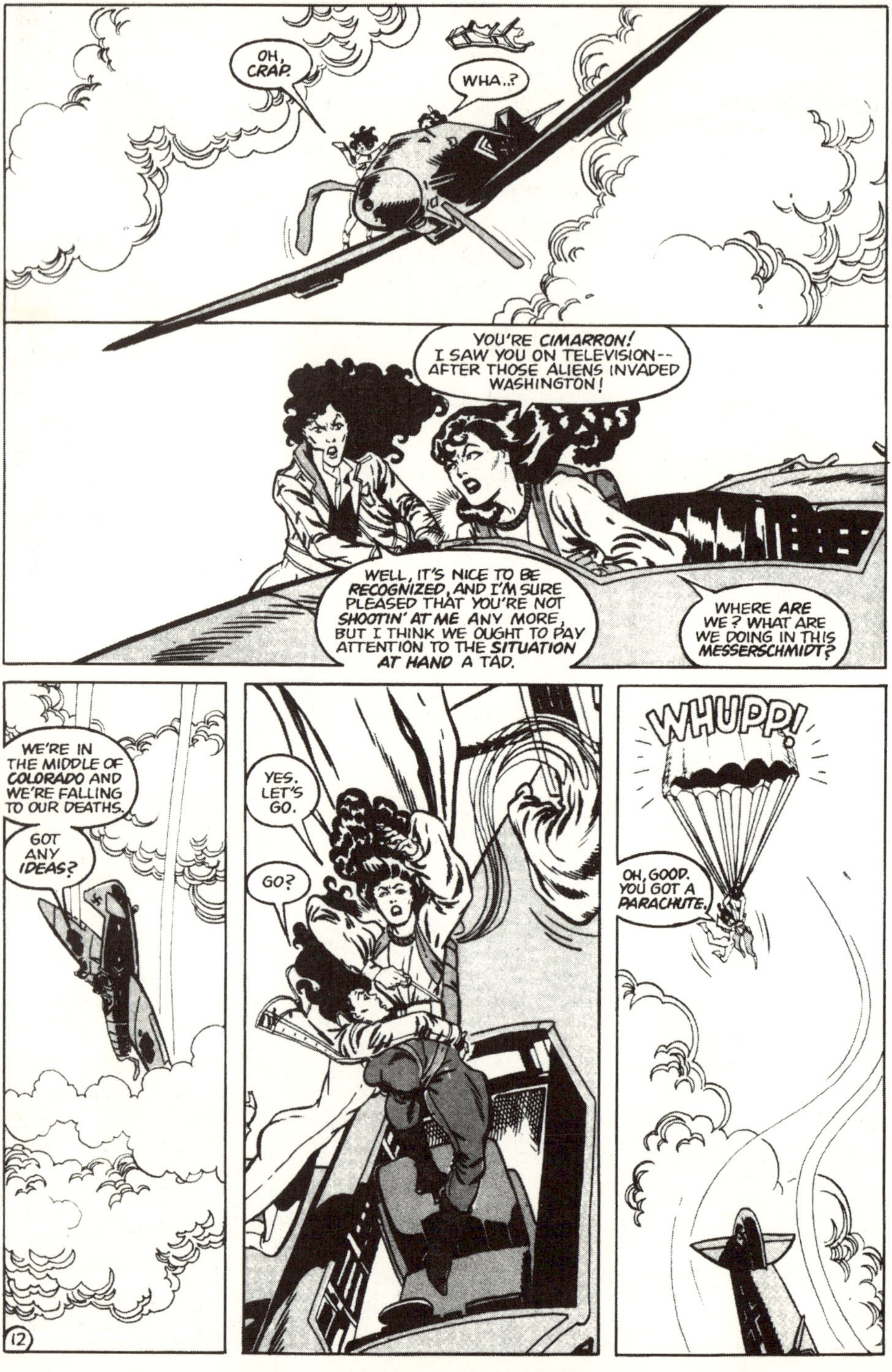
OH, CRAP.
WHA..?
YOU'RE CIMARRON! I SAW YOU ON TELEVISION-- AFTER THOSE ALIENS INVADED WASHINGTON!
WELL, IT'S NICE TO BE RECOGNIZED, AND I'M SURE PLEASED THAT YOU'RE NOT SHOOTIN' AT ME ANY MORE, BUT I THINK WE OUGHT TO PAY ATTENTION TO THE SITUATION AT HAND A TAD.
WHERE ARE WE? WHAT ARE WE DOING IN THIS MESSERSCHMIDT?
WE'RE IN THE MIDDLE OF COLORADO AND WE'RE FALLING TO OUR DEATHS.
GOT ANY IDEAS?
YES. LET'S GO.
GO?
WHUPP!
OH, GOOD. YOU GOT A PARACHUTE.
12

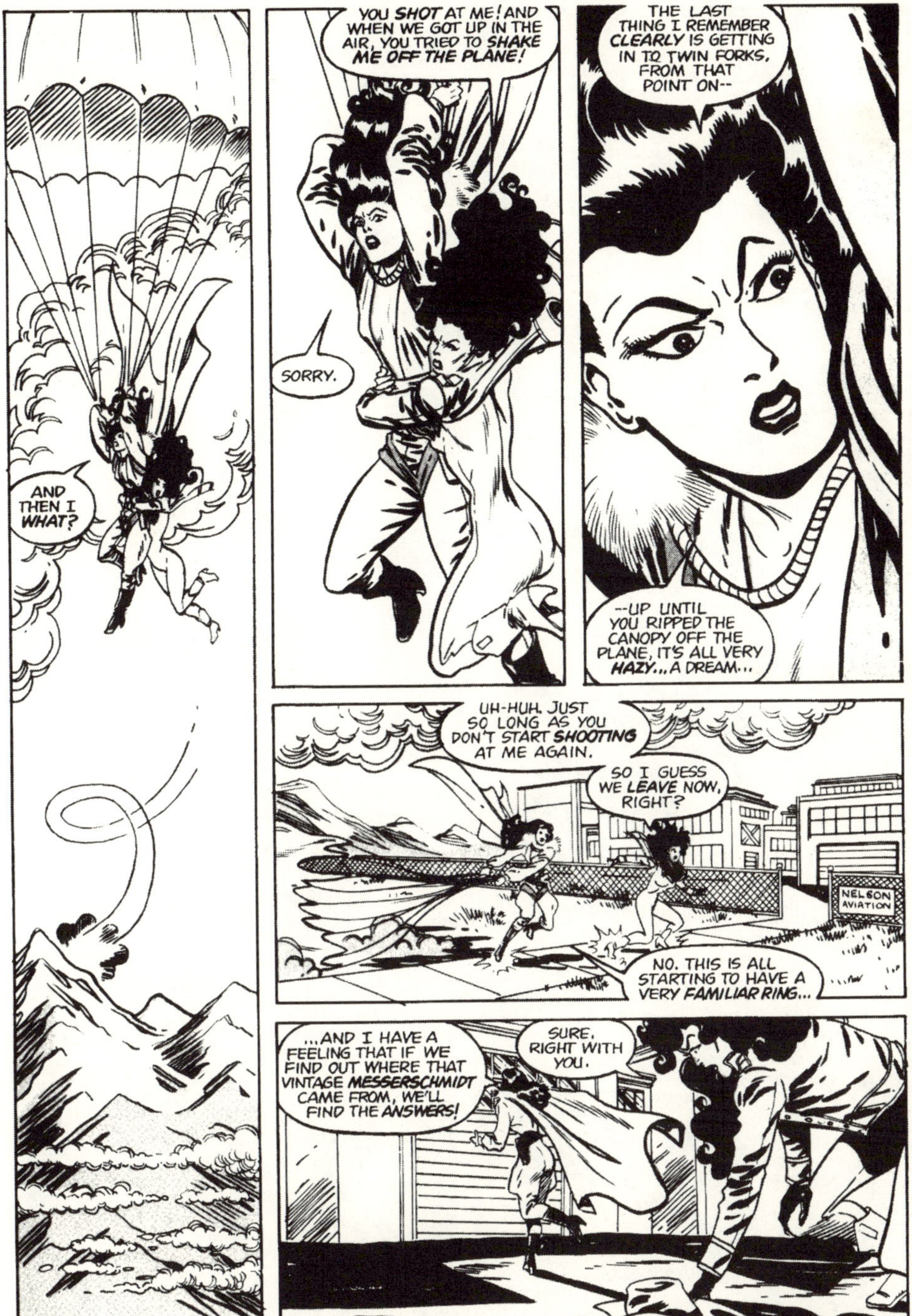
AND THEN I WHAT?
YOU SHOT AT ME! AND WHEN WE GOT UP IN THE AIR, YOU TRIED TO SHAKE ME OFF THE PLANE!
SORRY.
THE LAST THING I REMEMBER CLEARLY IS GETTING IN TO TWIN FORKS, FROM THAT POINT ON--
--UP UNTIL YOU RIPPED THE CANOPY OFF THE PLANE, IT'S ALL VERY HAZY... A DREAM...
UH-HUH. JUST SO LONG AS YOU DON'T START SHOOTING AT ME AGAIN.
SO I GUESS WE LEAVE NOW, RIGHT?
NELSON AVIATION
NO. THIS IS ALL STARTING TO HAVE A VERY FAMILIAR RING...
...AND I HAVE A FEELING THAT IF WE FIND OUT WHERE THAT VINTAGE MESSERSCHMIDT CAME FROM, WE'LL FIND THE ANSWERS!
SURE. RIGHT WITH YOU.
13

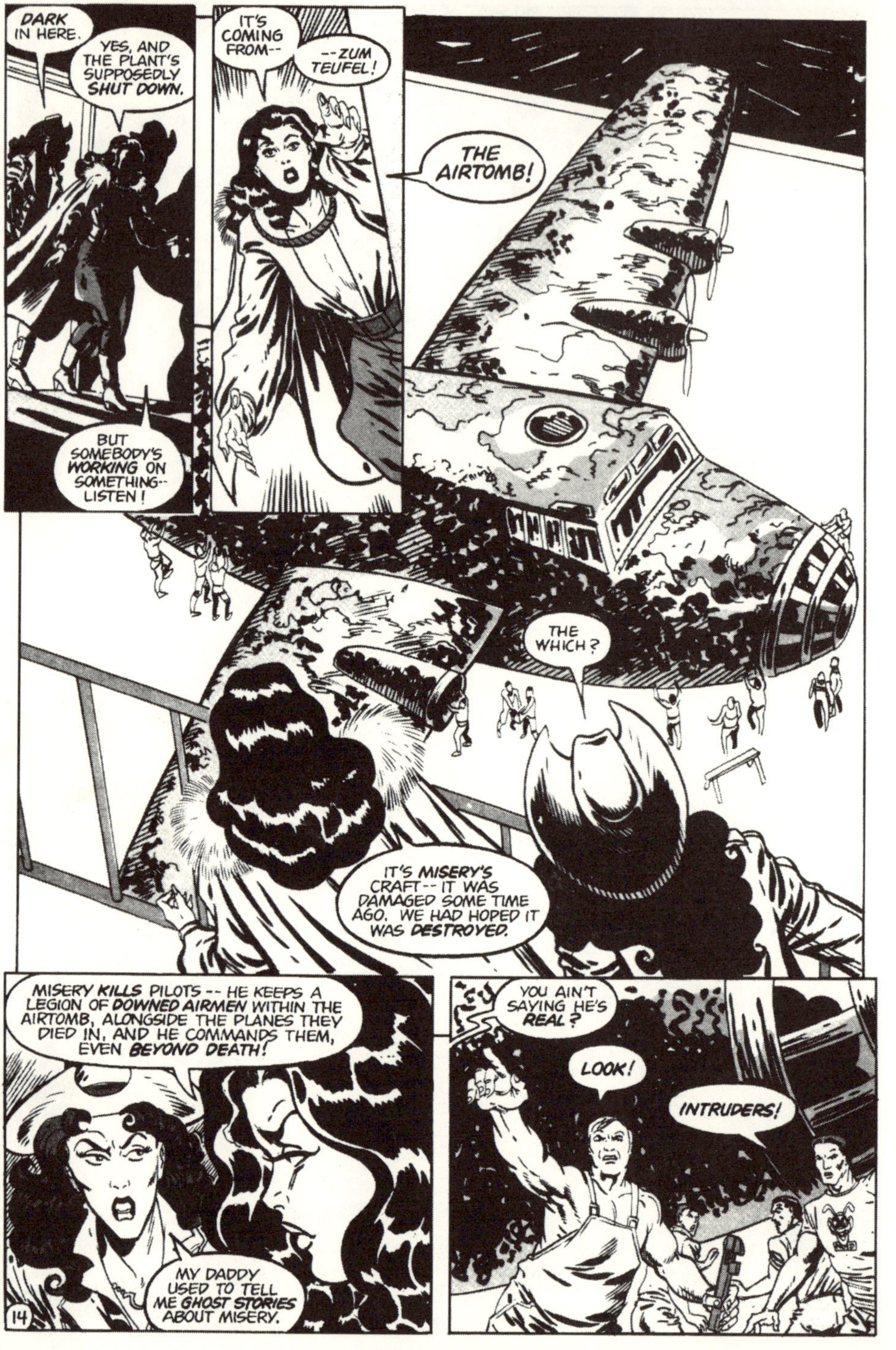
DARK IN HERE.
YES, AND THE PLANT'S SUPPOSEDLY SHUT DOWN.
BUT SOMEBODY'S WORKING ON SOMETHING-- LISTEN!
IT'S COMING FROM--
--ZUM TEUFEL!
THE AIRTOMB!
THE WHICH?
IT'S MISERY'S CRAFT-- IT WAS DAMAGED SOME TIME AGO. WE HAD HOPED IT WAS DESTROYED.
MISERY KILLS PILOTS -- HE KEEPS A LEGION OF DOWNED AIRMEN WITHIN THE AIRTOMB, ALONGSIDE THE PLANES THEY DIED IN, AND HE COMMANDS THEM, EVEN BEYOND DEATH!
MY DADDY USED TO TELL ME GHOST STORIES ABOUT MISERY.
14
YOU AIN'T SAYING HE'S REAL?
LOOK!
INTRUDERS!

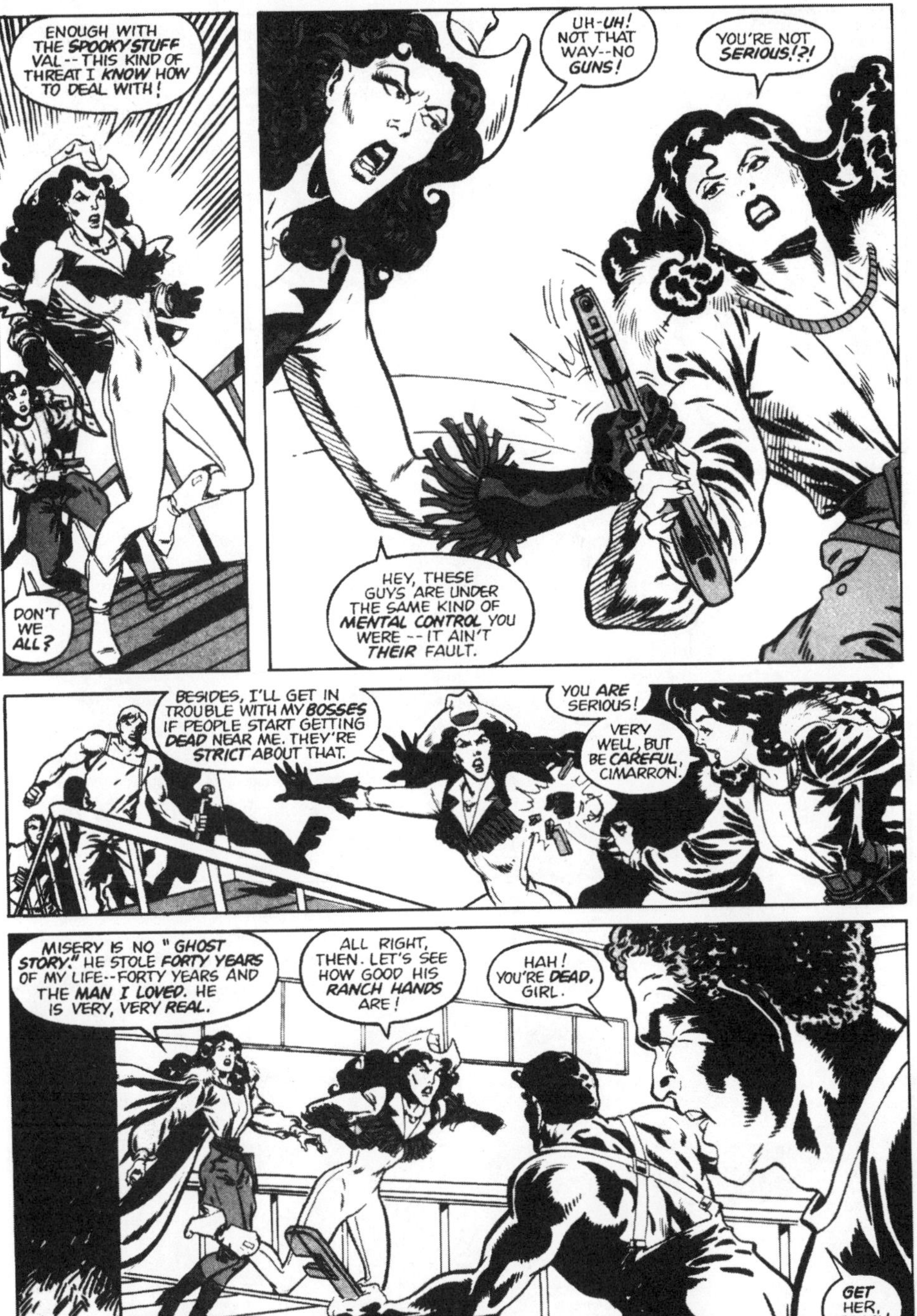
ENOUGH WITH THE SPOOKY STUFF VAL--THIS KIND OF THREAT I KNOW HOW TO DEAL WITH!
DON'T WE ALL?
UH-UH! NOT THAT WAY--NO GUNS!
YOU'RE NOT SERIOUS!?!
HEY, THESE GUYS ARE UNDER THE SAME KIND OF MENTAL CONTROL YOU WERE--IT AIN'T THEIR FAULT.
BESIDES, I'LL GET IN TROUBLE WITH MY BOSSES IF PEOPLE START GETTING DEAD NEAR ME. THEY'RE STRICT ABOUT THAT.
YOU ARE SERIOUS!
VERY WELL, BUT BE CAREFUL, CIMARRON.
MISERY IS NO "GHOST STORY." HE STOLE FORTY YEARS OF MY LIFE--FORTY YEARS AND THE MAN I LOVED. HE IS VERY, VERY REAL.
ALL RIGHT, THEN. LET'S SEE HOW GOOD HIS RANCH HANDS ARE!
HAH! YOU'RE DEAD, GIRL.
GET HER, SPIKE!
15

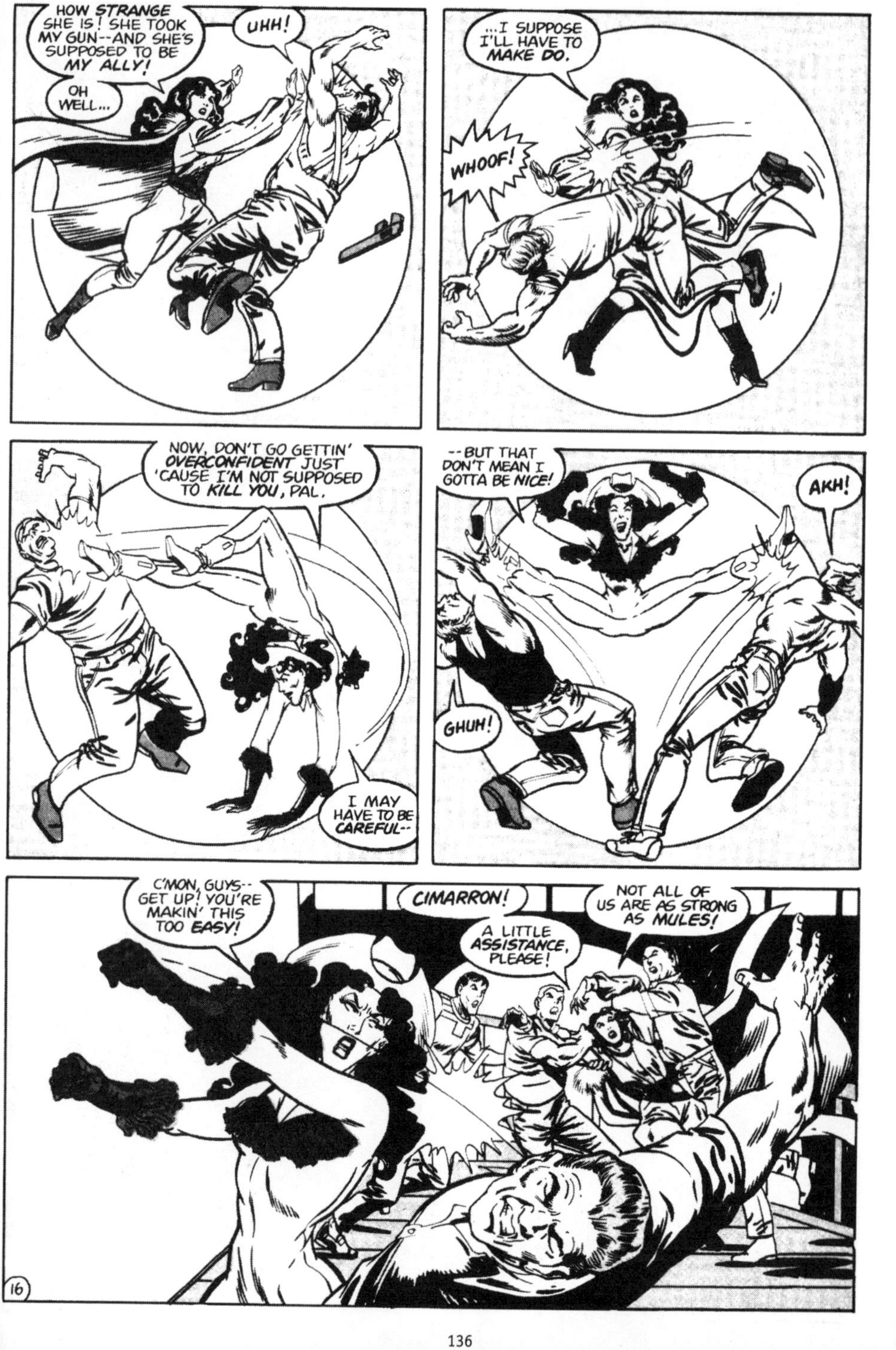
HOW STRANGE SHE IS! SHE TOOK MY GUN--AND SHE'S SUPPOSED TO BE MY ALLY!
OH WELL...
UHH!
...I SUPPOSE I'LL HAVE TO MAKE DO.
WHOOF!
NOW, DON'T GO GETTIN' OVERCONFIDENT JUST 'CAUSE I'M NOT SUPPOSED TO KILL YOU, PAL.
I MAY HAVE TO BE CAREFUL--
--BUT THAT DON'T MEAN I GOTTA BE NICE!
AKH!
GHUH!
C'MON, GUYS-- GET UP! YOU'RE MAKIN' THIS TOO EASY!
CIMARRON!
A LITTLE ASSISTANCE, PLEASE!
NOT ALL OF US ARE AS STRONG AS MULES!
16

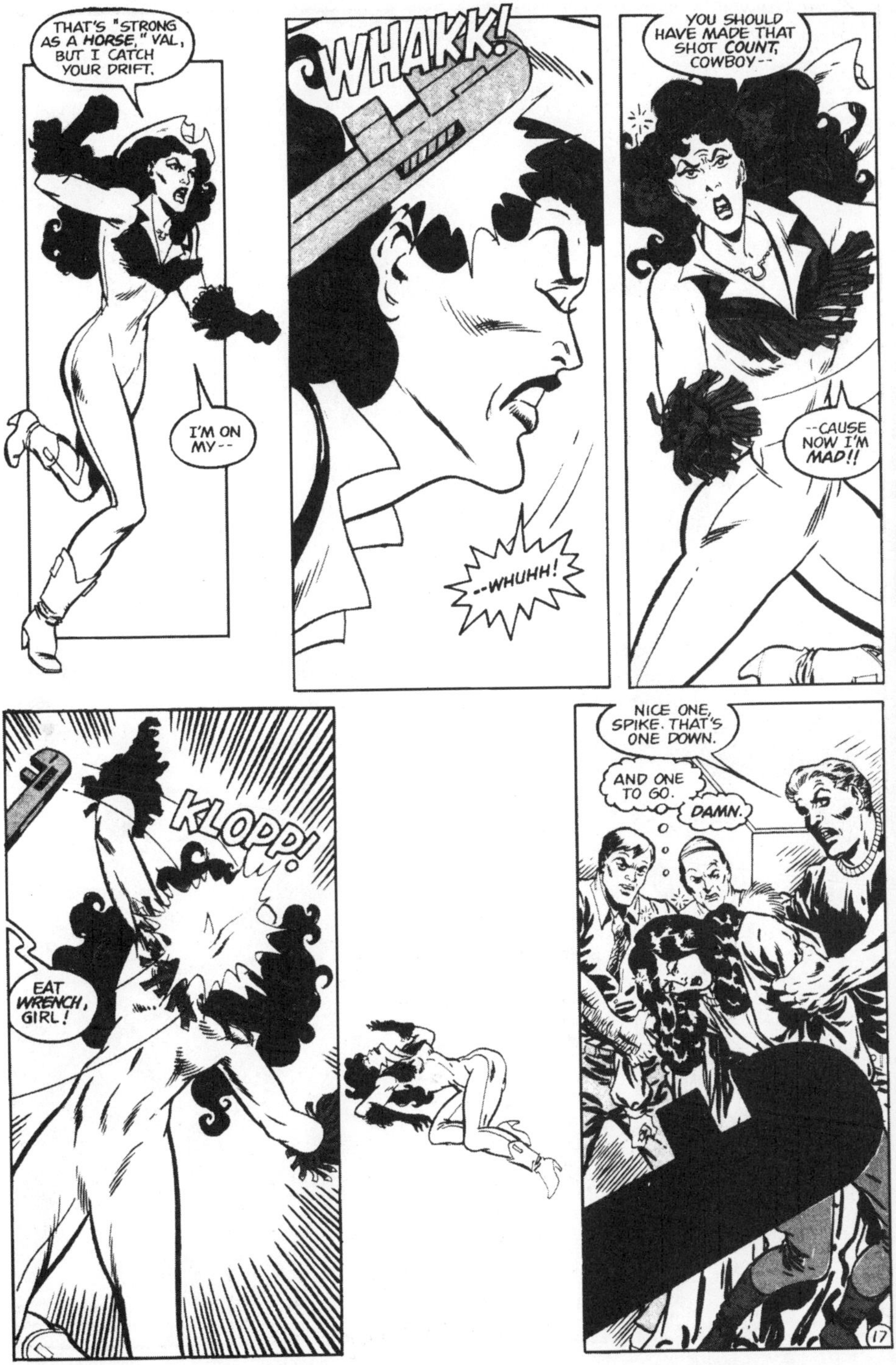
THAT'S "STRONG AS A HORSE," VAL, BUT I CATCH YOUR DRIFT.
I'M ON MY--
WHAKK!
--WHUHH!
YOU SHOULD HAVE MADE THAT SHOT COUNT, COWBOY--
--CAUSE NOW I'M MAD!!
KLOPP!
EAT WRENCH, GIRL!
NICE ONE, SPIKE. THAT'S ONE DOWN.
AND ONE TO GO.
DAMN.
17

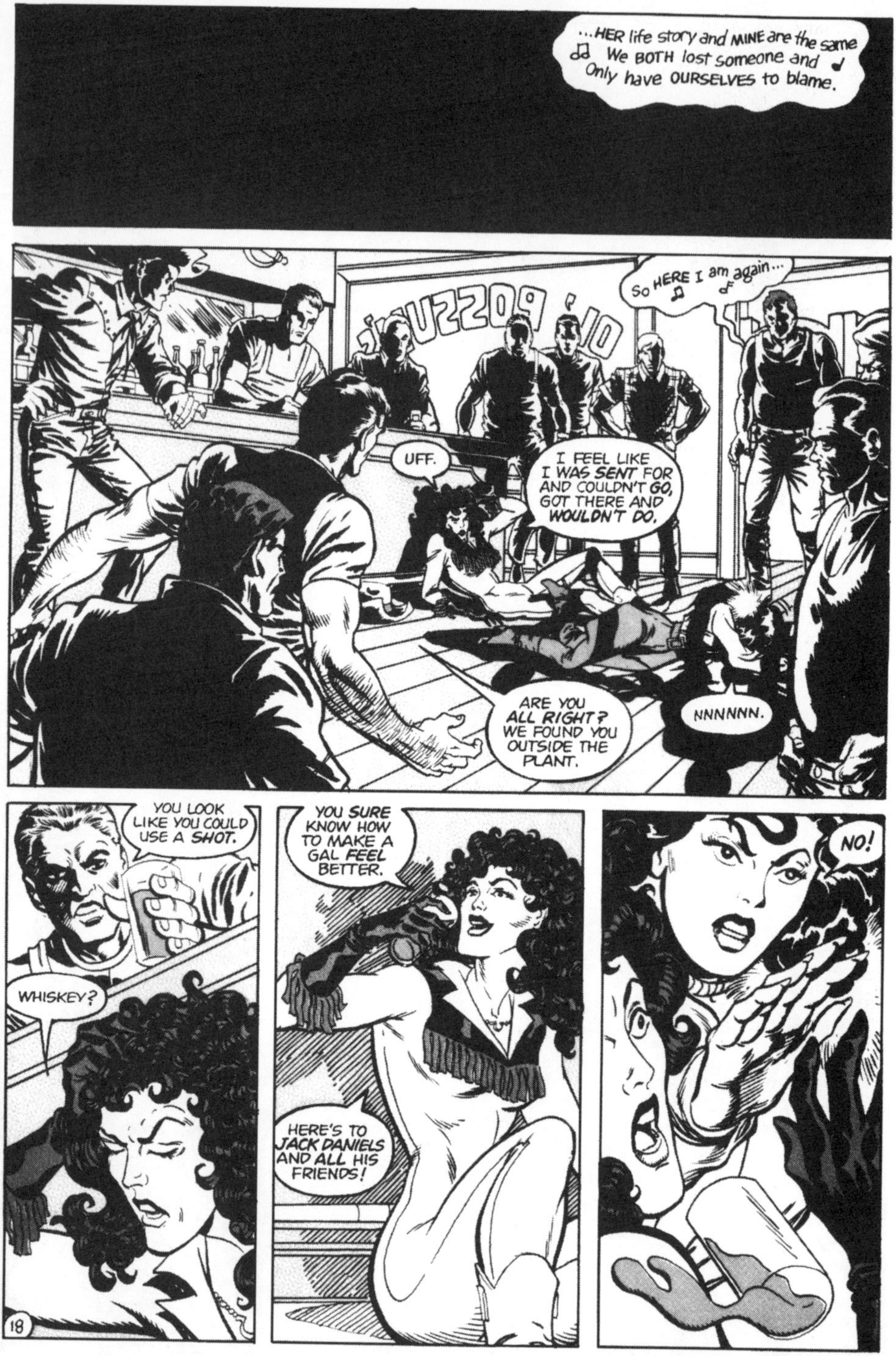
...HER life story and MINE are the same We BOTH lost someone and Only have OURSELVES to blame.
So HERE I am again...
OL' POSSUM'S
UFF.
I FEEL LIKE I WAS SENT FOR AND COULDN'T GO, GOT THERE AND WOULDN'T DO.
ARE YOU ALL RIGHT? WE FOUND YOU OUTSIDE THE PLANT.
NNNNNN.
YOU LOOK LIKE YOU COULD USE A SHOT.
WHISKEY?
YOU SURE KNOW HOW TO MAKE A GAL FEEL BETTER.
HERE'S TO JACK DANIELS AND ALL HIS FRIENDS!
NO!
18

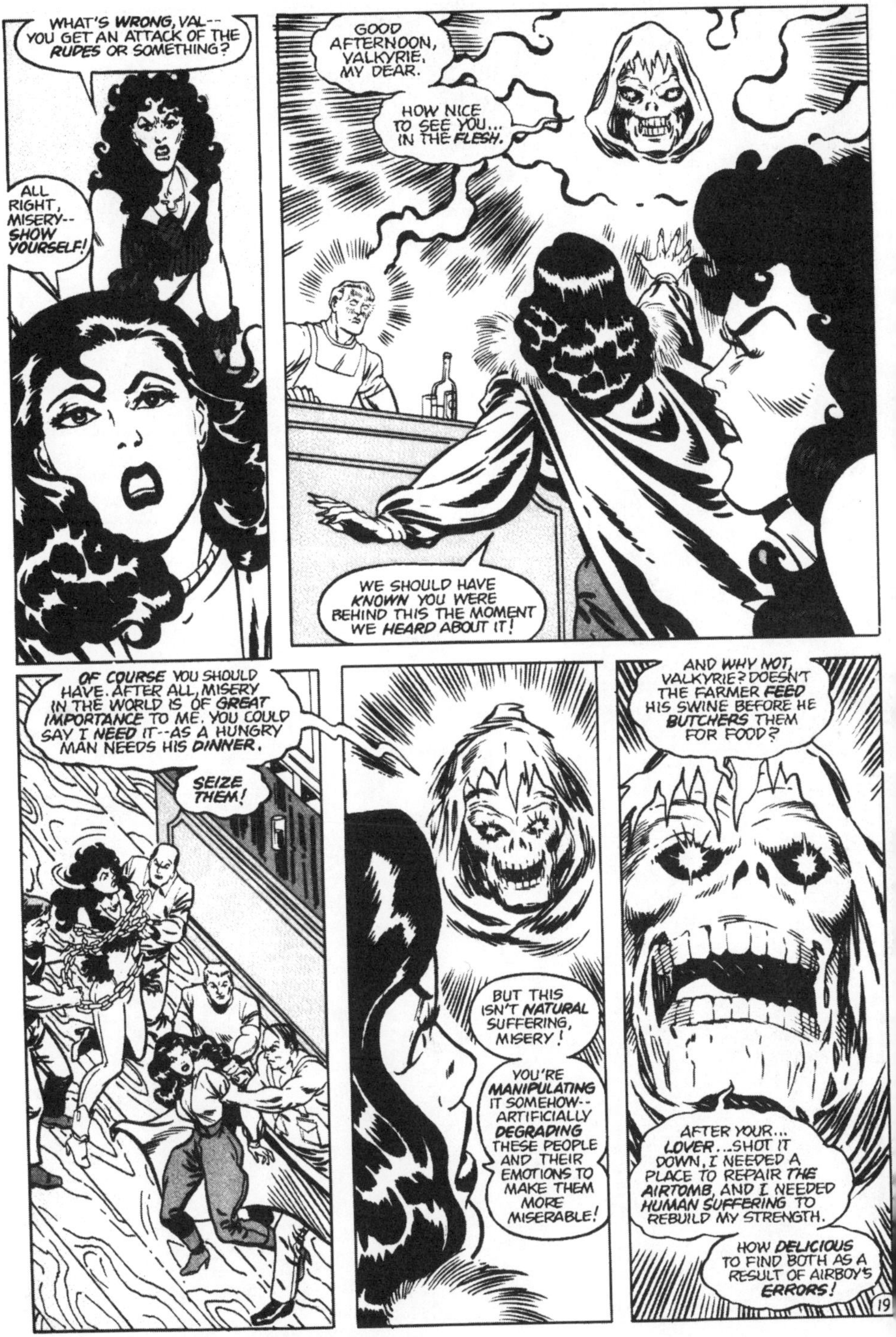
WHAT'S WRONG, VAL-- YOU GET AN ATTACK OF THE RUDES OR SOMETHING?
ALL RIGHT, MISERY-- SHOW YOURSELF!
GOOD AFTERNOON, VALKYRIE, MY DEAR.
HOW NICE TO SEE YOU... IN THE FLESH.
WE SHOULD HAVE KNOWN YOU WERE BEHIND THIS THE MOMENT WE HEARD ABOUT IT!
OF COURSE YOU SHOULD HAVE. AFTER ALL, MISERY IN THE WORLD IS OF GREAT IMPORTANCE TO ME. YOU COULD SAY I NEED IT--AS A HUNGRY MAN NEEDS HIS DINNER.
SEIZE THEM!
BUT THIS ISN'T NATURAL SUFFERING, MISERY!
YOU'RE MANIPULATING IT SOMEHOW-- ARTIFICIALLY DEGRADING THESE PEOPLE AND THEIR EMOTIONS TO MAKE THEM MORE MISERABLE!
AND WHY NOT, VALKYRIE? DOESN'T THE FARMER FEED HIS SWINE BEFORE HE BUTCHERS THEM FOR FOOD?
AFTER YOUR... LOVER...SHOT IT DOWN, I NEEDED A PLACE TO REPAIR THE AIRTOMB, AND I NEEDED HUMAN SUFFERING TO REBUILD MY STRENGTH.
HOW DELICIOUS TO FIND BOTH AS A RESULT OF AIRBOY'S ERRORS!
19

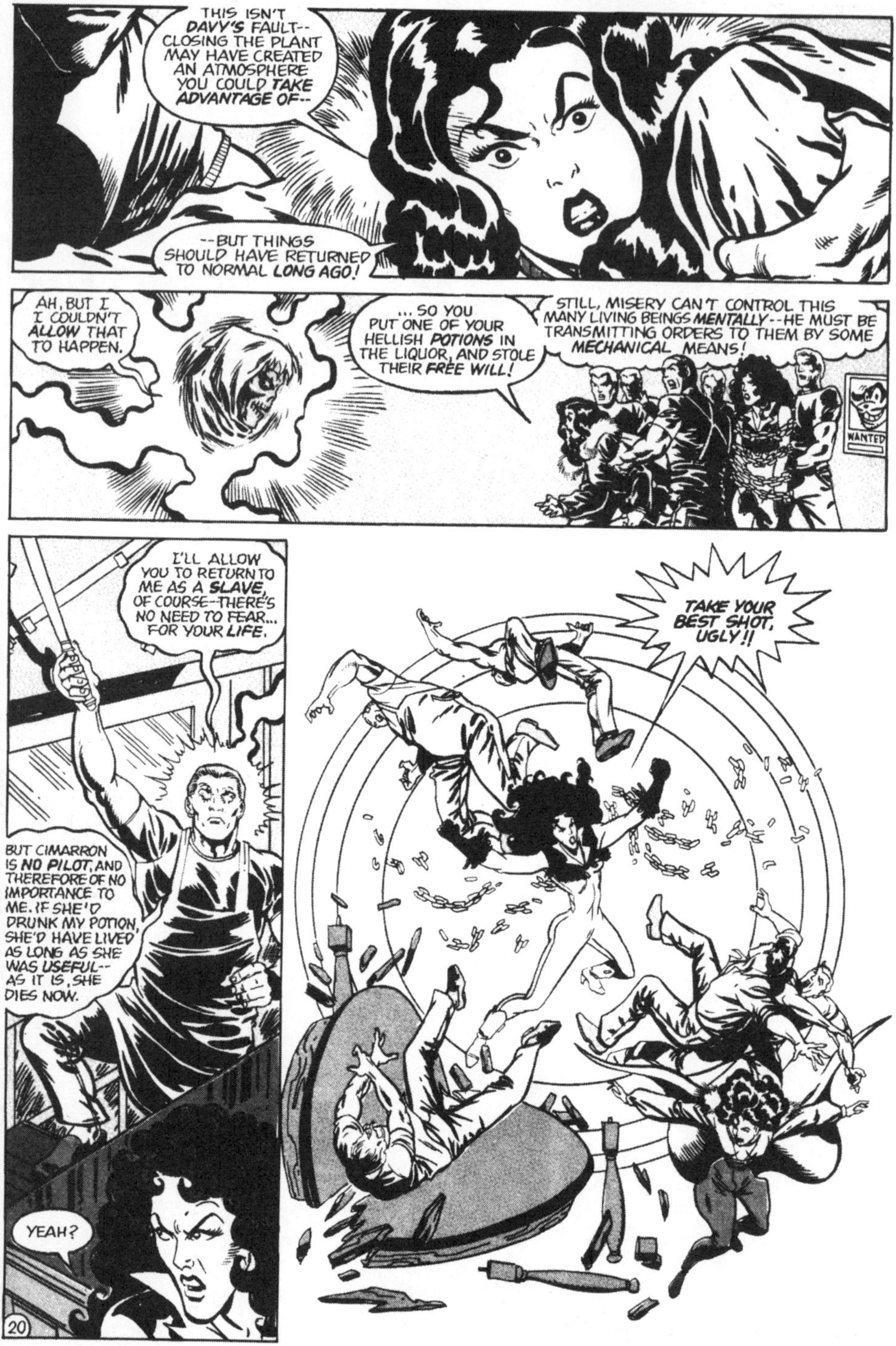

THIS ISN'T DAVY'S FAULT--CLOSING THE PLANT MAY HAVE CREATED AN ATMOSPHERE YOU COULD TAKE ADVANTAGE OF--
--BUT THINGS SHOULD HAVE RETURNED TO NORMAL LONG AGO!
AH, BUT I I COULDN'T ALLOW THAT TO HAPPEN.
...SO YOU PUT ONE OF YOUR HELLISH POTIONS IN THE LIQUOR, AND STOLE THEIR FREE WILL!
STILL, MISERY CAN'T CONTROL THIS MANY LIVING BEINGS MENTALLY--HE MUST BE TRANSMITTING ORDERS TO THEM BY SOME MECHANICAL MEANS!
WANTED
I'LL ALLOW YOU TO RETURN TO ME AS A SLAVE, OF COURSE--THERE'S NO NEED TO FEAR... FOR YOUR LIFE.
BUT CIMARRON IS NO PILOT, AND THEREFORE OF NO IMPORTANCE TO ME. IF SHE'D DRUNK MY POTION, SHE'D HAVE LIVED AS LONG AS SHE WAS USEFUL--AS IT IS, SHE DIES NOW.
YEAH?
TAKE YOUR BEST SHOT, UGLY!!
20

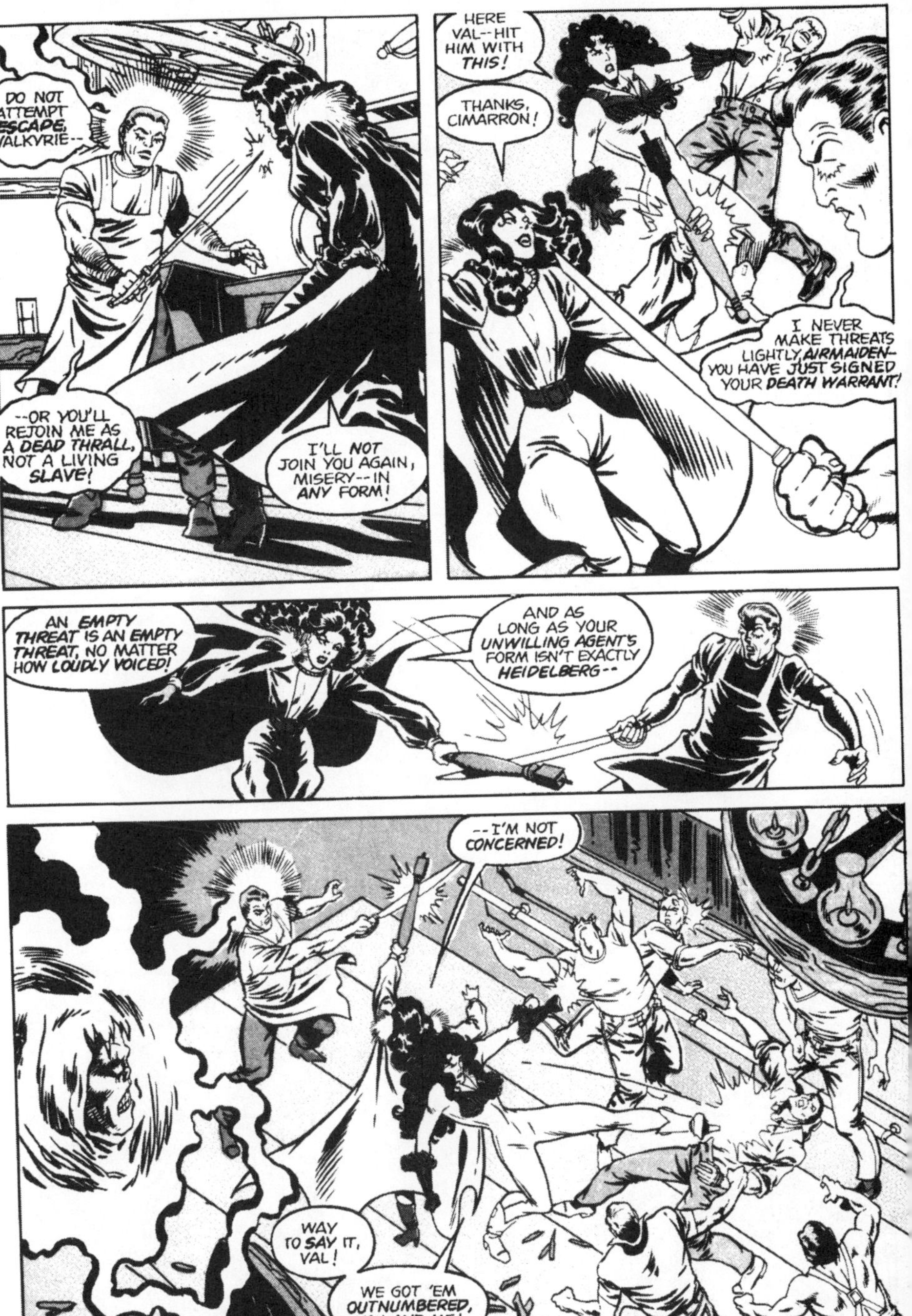
DO NOT ATTEMPT ESCAPE, VALKYRIE--
--OR YOU'LL REJOIN ME AS A DEAD THRALL, NOT A LIVING SLAVE!
I'LL NOT JOIN YOU AGAIN, MISERY--IN ANY FORM!
HERE VAL--HIT HIM WITH THIS!
THANKS, CIMARRON!
I NEVER MAKE THREATS LIGHTLY, AIRMAIDEN--YOU HAVE JUST SIGNED YOUR DEATH WARRANT!
AN EMPTY THREAT IS AN EMPTY THREAT, NO MATTER HOW LOUDLY VOICED!
AND AS LONG AS YOUR UNWILLING AGENT'S FORM ISN'T EXACTLY HEIDELBERG--
--I'M NOT CONCERNED!
WAY TO SAY IT, VAL!
WE GOT 'EM OUTNUMBERED, YOU AND ME!
2

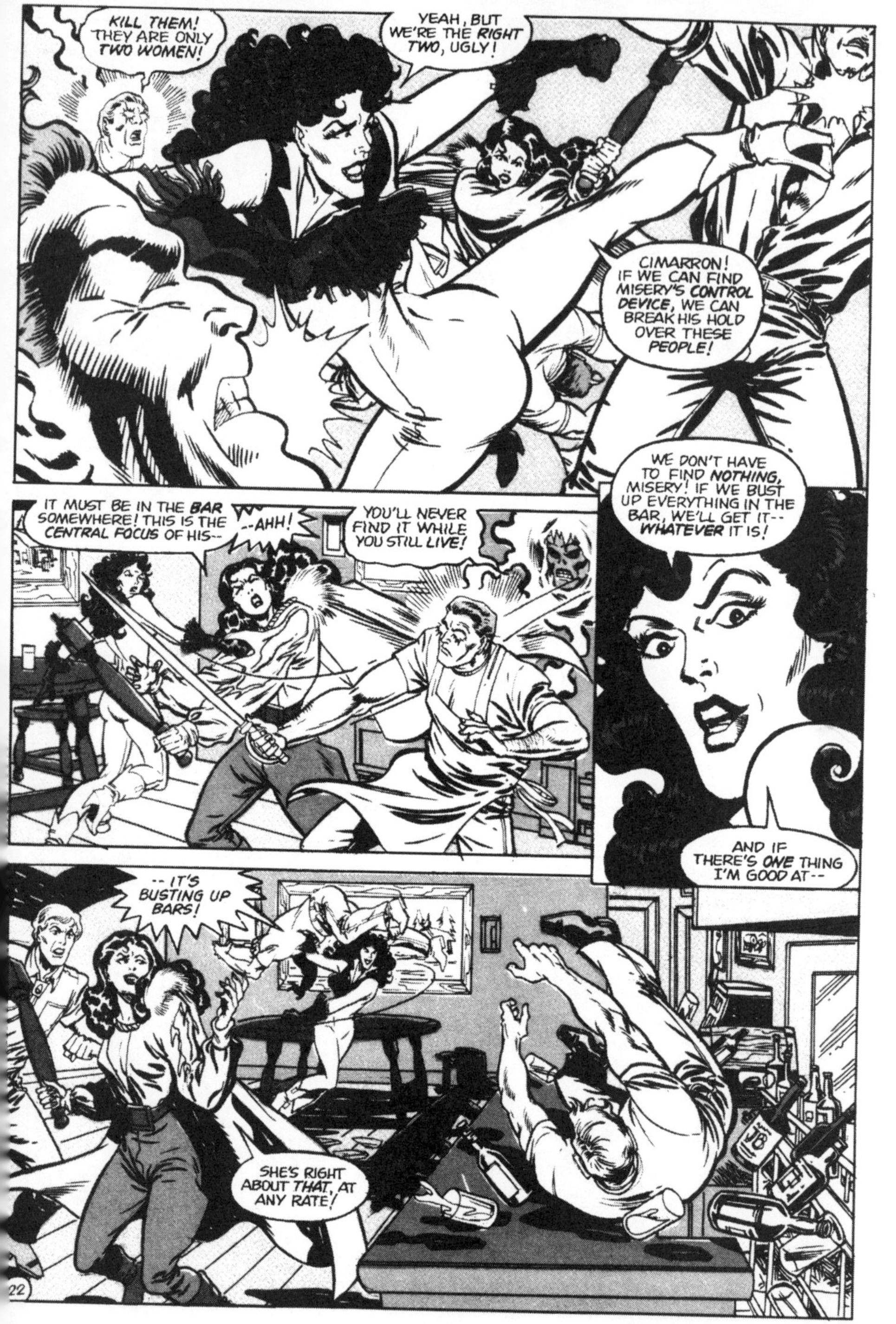
KILL THEM! THEY ARE ONLY TWO WOMEN!
YEAH, BUT WE'RE THE RIGHT TWO, UGLY!
CIMARRON! IF WE CAN FIND MISERY'S CONTROL DEVICE, WE CAN BREAK HIS HOLD OVER THESE PEOPLE!
IT MUST BE IN THE BAR SOMEWHERE! THIS IS THE CENTRAL FOCUS OF HIS--
--AHH!
YOU'LL NEVER FIND IT WHILE YOU STILL LIVE!
WE DON'T HAVE TO FIND NOTHING, MISERY! IF WE BUST UP EVERYTHING IN THE BAR, WE'LL GET IT-- WHATEVER IT IS!
AND IF THERE'S ONE THING I'M GOOD AT--
-- IT'S BUSTING UP BARS!
SHE'S RIGHT ABOUT THAT, AT ANY RATE!
22

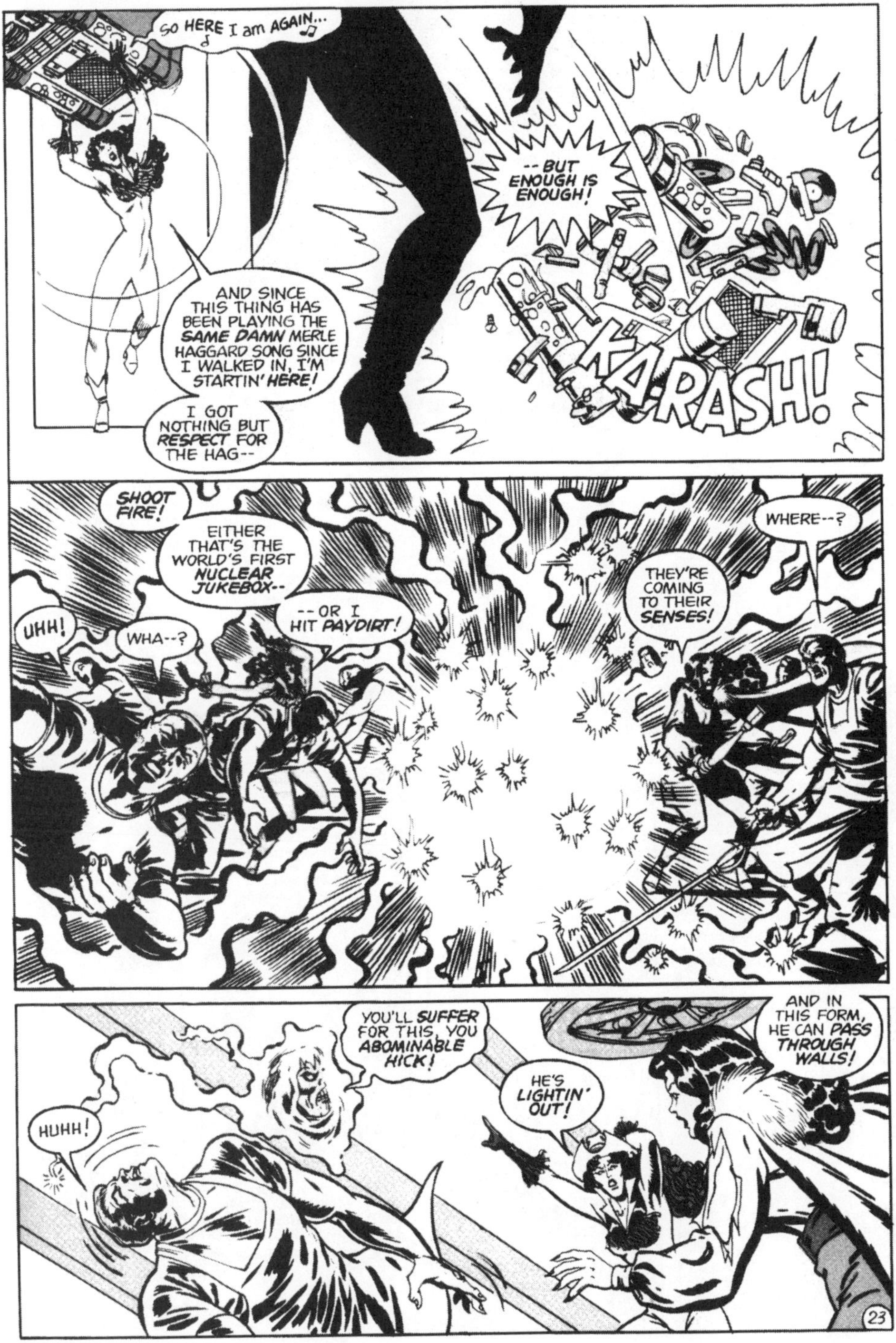
So HERE I am AGAIN...
-- BUT ENOUGH IS ENOUGH!
AND SINCE THIS THING HAS BEEN PLAYING THE SAME DAMN MERLE HAGGARD SONG SINCE I WALKED IN, I'M STARTIN' HERE!
I GOT NOTHING BUT RESPECT FOR THE HAG--
KA-RASH!
SHOOT FIRE!
EITHER THAT'S THE WORLD'S FIRST NUCLEAR JUKEBOX--
--OR I HIT PAYDIRT!
UHH!
WHA--?
WHERE--?
THEY'RE COMING TO THEIR SENSES!
HUHH!
YOU'LL SUFFER FOR THIS, YOU ABOMINABLE HICK!
HE'S LIGHTIN' OUT!
AND IN THIS FORM, HE CAN PASS THROUGH WALLS!
23

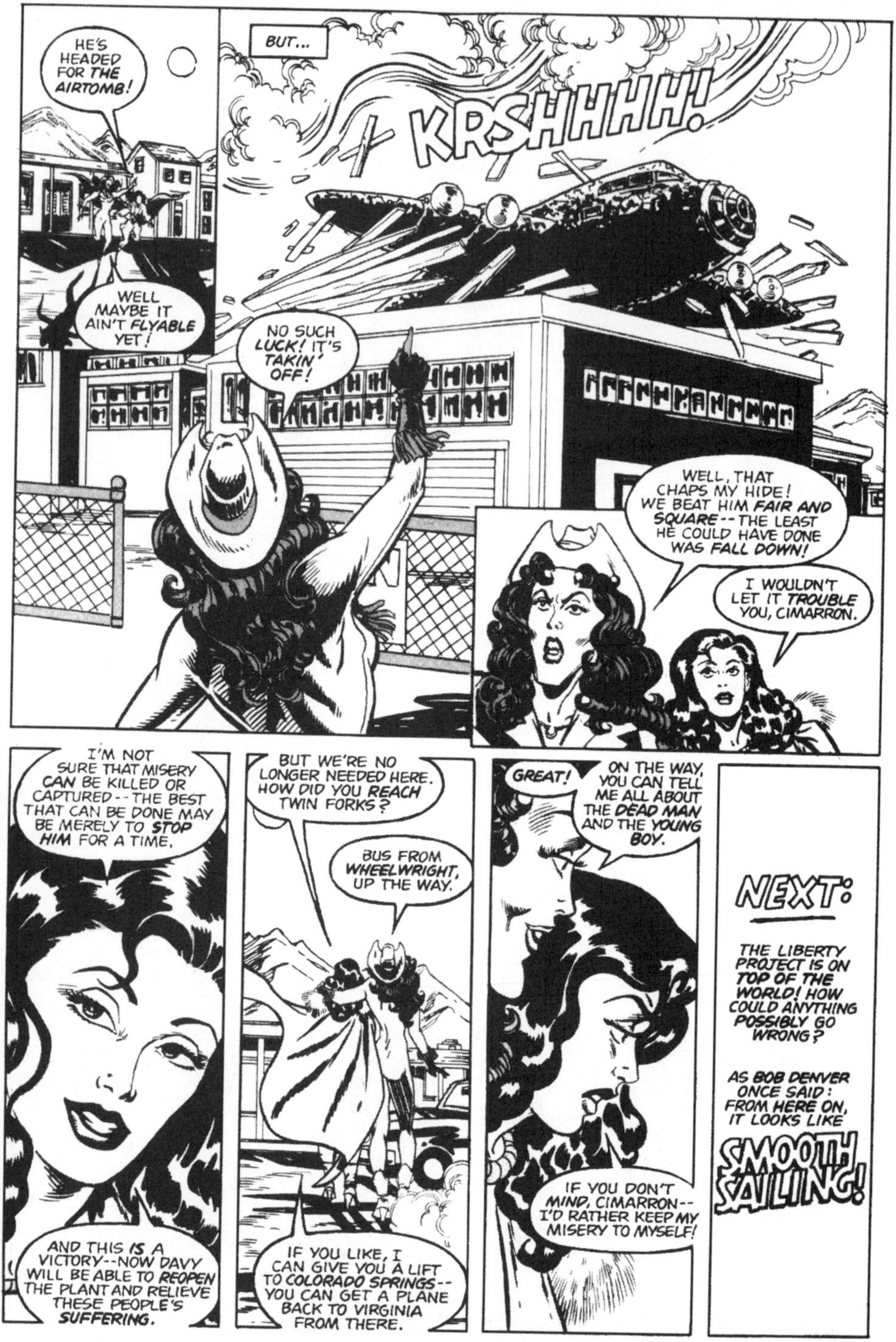
HE'S HEADED FOR THE AIRTOMB!
WELL MAYBE IT AIN'T FLYABLE YET!
BUT...
KRSHHHH!
NO SUCH LUCK! IT'S TAKIN' OFF!
WELL, THAT CHAPS MY HIDE! WE BEAT HIM FAIR AND SQUARE--THE LEAST HE COULD HAVE DONE WAS FALL DOWN!
I WOULDN'T LET IT TROUBLE YOU, CIMARRON.
I'M NOT SURE THAT MISERY CAN BE KILLED OR CAPTURED--THE BEST THAT CAN BE DONE MAY BE MERELY TO STOP HIM FOR A TIME.
AND THIS IS A VICTORY--NOW DAVY WILL BE ABLE TO REOPEN THE PLANT AND RELIEVE THESE PEOPLE'S SUFFERING.
BUT WE'RE NO LONGER NEEDED HERE. HOW DID YOU REACH TWIN FORKS?
BUS FROM WHEELWRIGHT, UP THE WAY.
IF YOU LIKE, I CAN GIVE YOU A LIFT TO COLORADO SPRINGS--YOU CAN GET A PLANE BACK TO VIRGINIA FROM THERE.
GREAT!
ON THE WAY, YOU CAN TELL ME ALL ABOUT THE DEAD MAN AND THE YOUNG BOY.
IF YOU DON'T MIND, CIMARRON--I'D RATHER KEEP MY MISERY TO MYSELF!
NEXT:
THE LIBERTY PROJECT IS ON TOP OF THE WORLD! HOW COULD ANYTHING POSSIBLY GO WRONG?
AS BOB DENVER ONCE SAID: FROM HERE ON, IT LOOKS LIKE
SMOOTH SAILING!

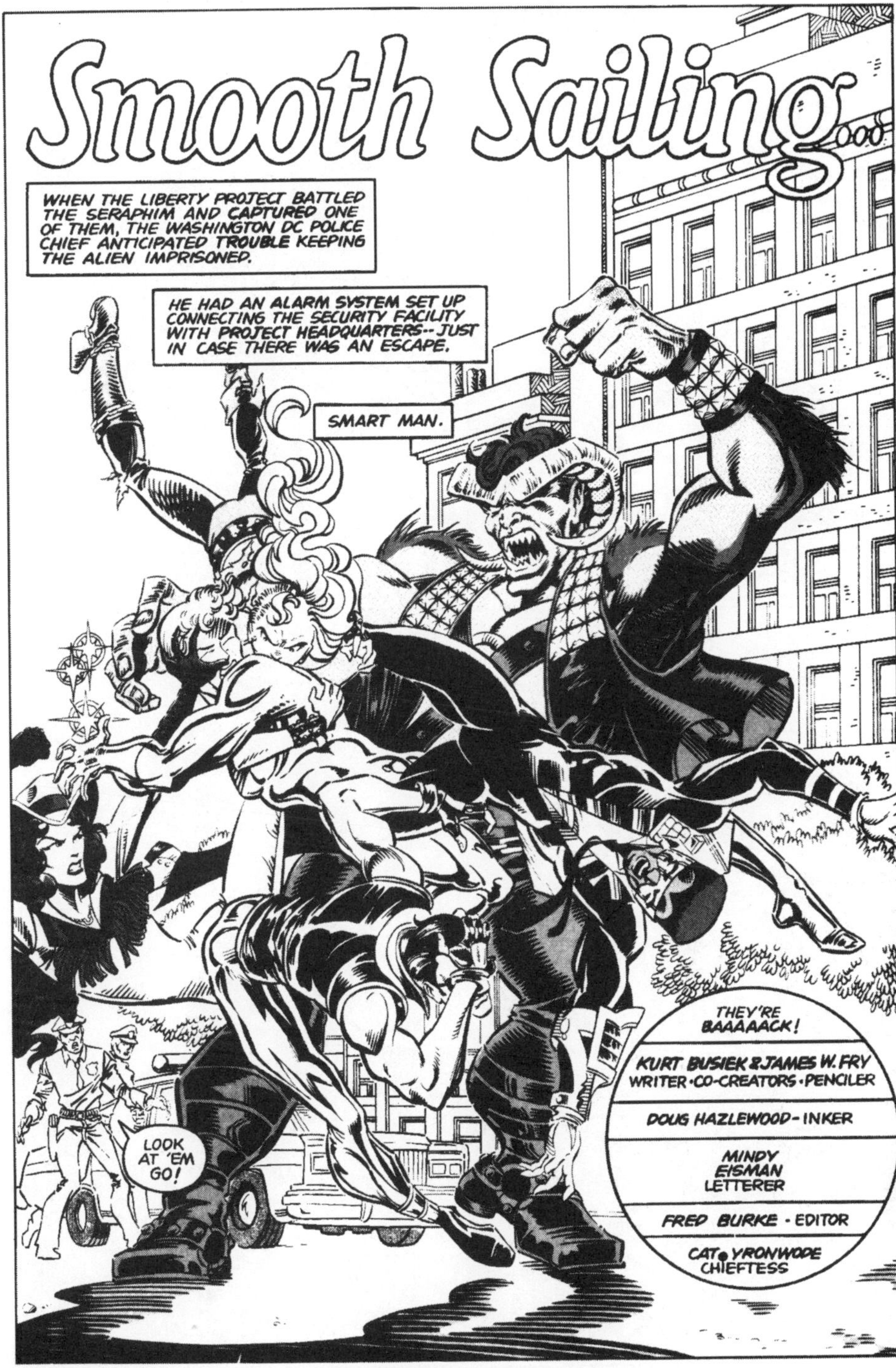
Smooth Sailing...
WHEN THE LIBERTY PROJECT BATTLED THE SERAPHIM AND CAPTURED ONE OF THEM, THE WASHINGTON DC POLICE CHIEF ANTICIPATED TROUBLE KEEPING THE ALIEN IMPRISONED.
HE HAD AN ALARM SYSTEM SET UP CONNECTING THE SECURITY FACILITY WITH PROJECT HEADQUARTERS-- JUST IN CASE THERE WAS AN ESCAPE.
SMART MAN.
LOOK AT 'EM GO!
THEY'RE BAAAAACK!
KURT BUSIEK & JAMES W. FRY
WRITER • CO-CREATORS • PENCILER
DOUG HAZLEWOOD - INKER
MINDY EISMAN
LETTERER
FRED BURKE - EDITOR
CAT YRONWODE
CHIEFTESS

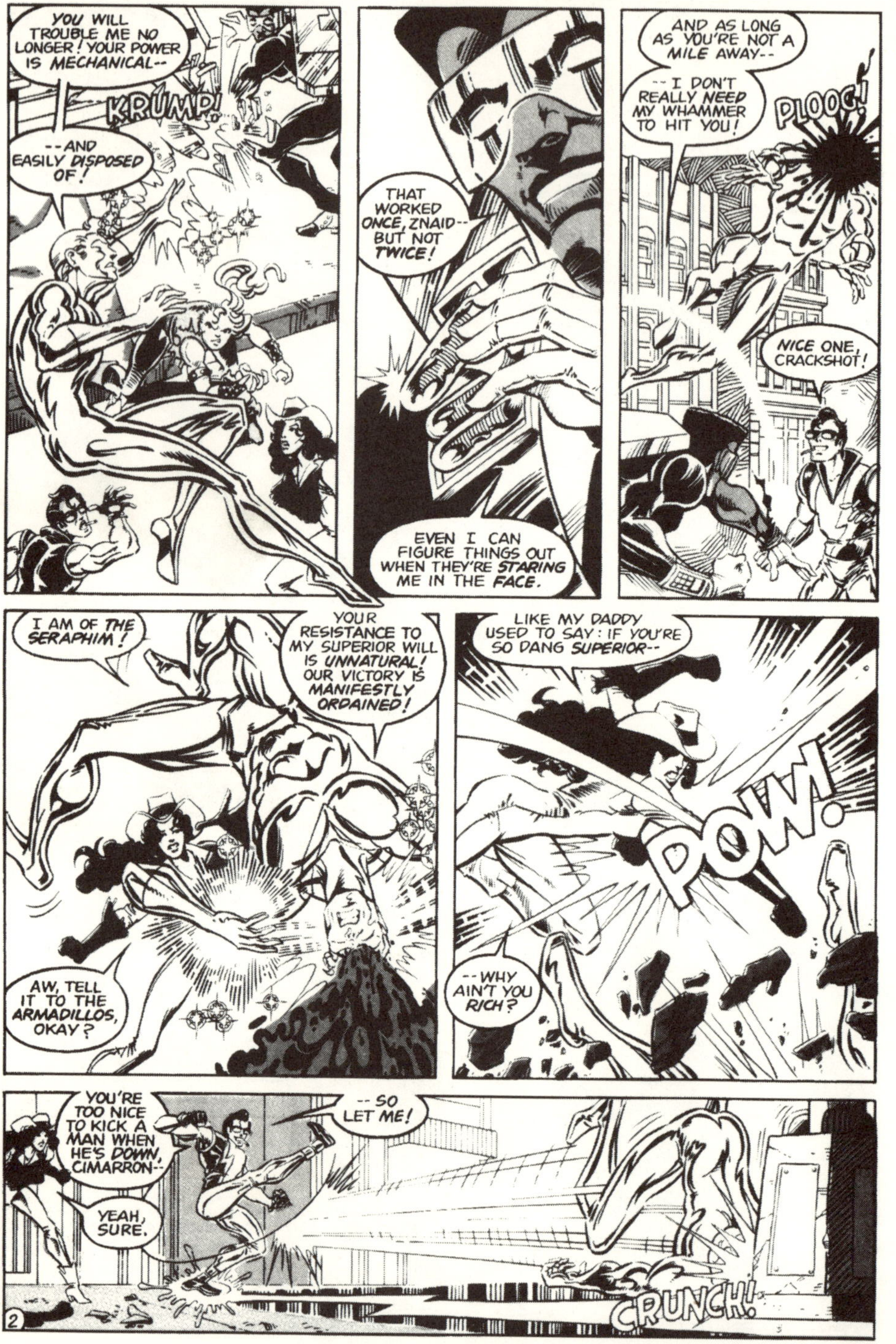
YOU WILL TROUBLE ME NO LONGER! YOUR POWER IS MECHANICAL--
KRUMP!
--AND EASILY DISPOSED OF!
THAT WORKED ONCE, ZNAID-- BUT NOT TWICE!
EVEN I CAN FIGURE THINGS OUT WHEN THEY'RE STARING ME IN THE FACE.
AND AS LONG AS YOU'RE NOT A MILE AWAY--
--I DON'T REALLY NEED MY WHAMMER TO HIT YOU!
PLOOC!
NICE ONE, CRACKSHOT!
I AM OF THE SERAPHIM!
YOUR RESISTANCE TO MY SUPERIOR WILL IS UNNATURAL! OUR VICTORY IS MANIFESTLY ORDAINED!
AW, TELL IT TO THE ARMADILLOS, OKAY?
LIKE MY DADDY USED TO SAY: IF YOU'RE SO DANG SUPERIOR--
POW!
--WHY AIN'T YOU RICH?
YOU'RE TOO NICE TO KICK A MAN WHEN HE'S DOWN, CIMARRON--
--SO LET ME!
YEAH, SURE.
CRUNCH!
2

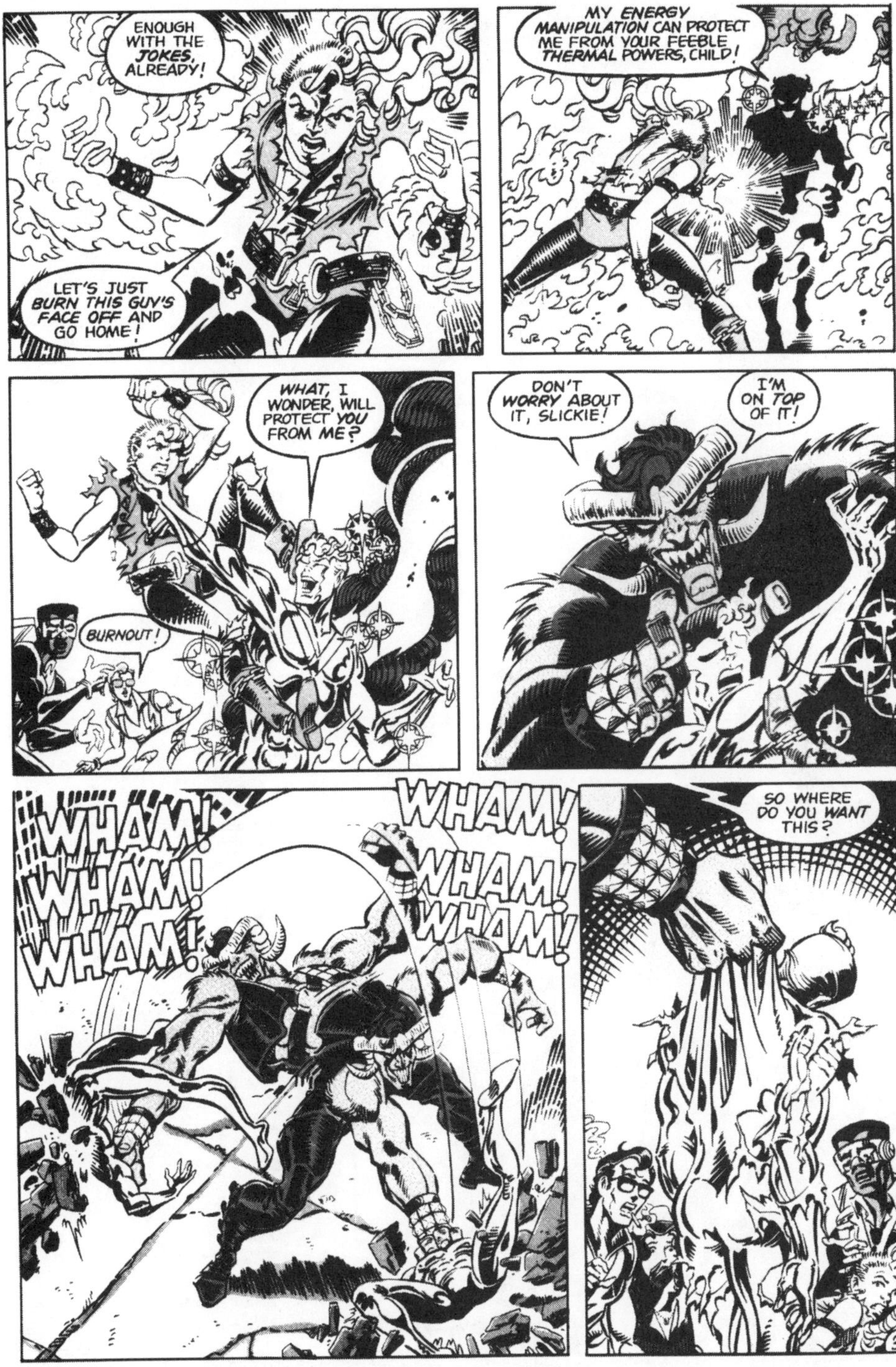
ENOUGH WITH THE JOKES, ALREADY!
LET'S JUST BURN THIS GUY'S FACE OFF AND GO HOME!
MY ENERGY MANIPULATION CAN PROTECT ME FROM YOUR FEEBLE THERMAL POWERS, CHILD!
WHAT, I WONDER, WILL PROTECT YOU FROM ME?
BURNOUT!
DON'T WORRY ABOUT IT, SLICKIE!
I'M ON TOP OF IT!
WHAM! WHAM! WHAM!
WHAM! WHAM! WHAM!
SO WHERE DO YOU WANT THIS?
3

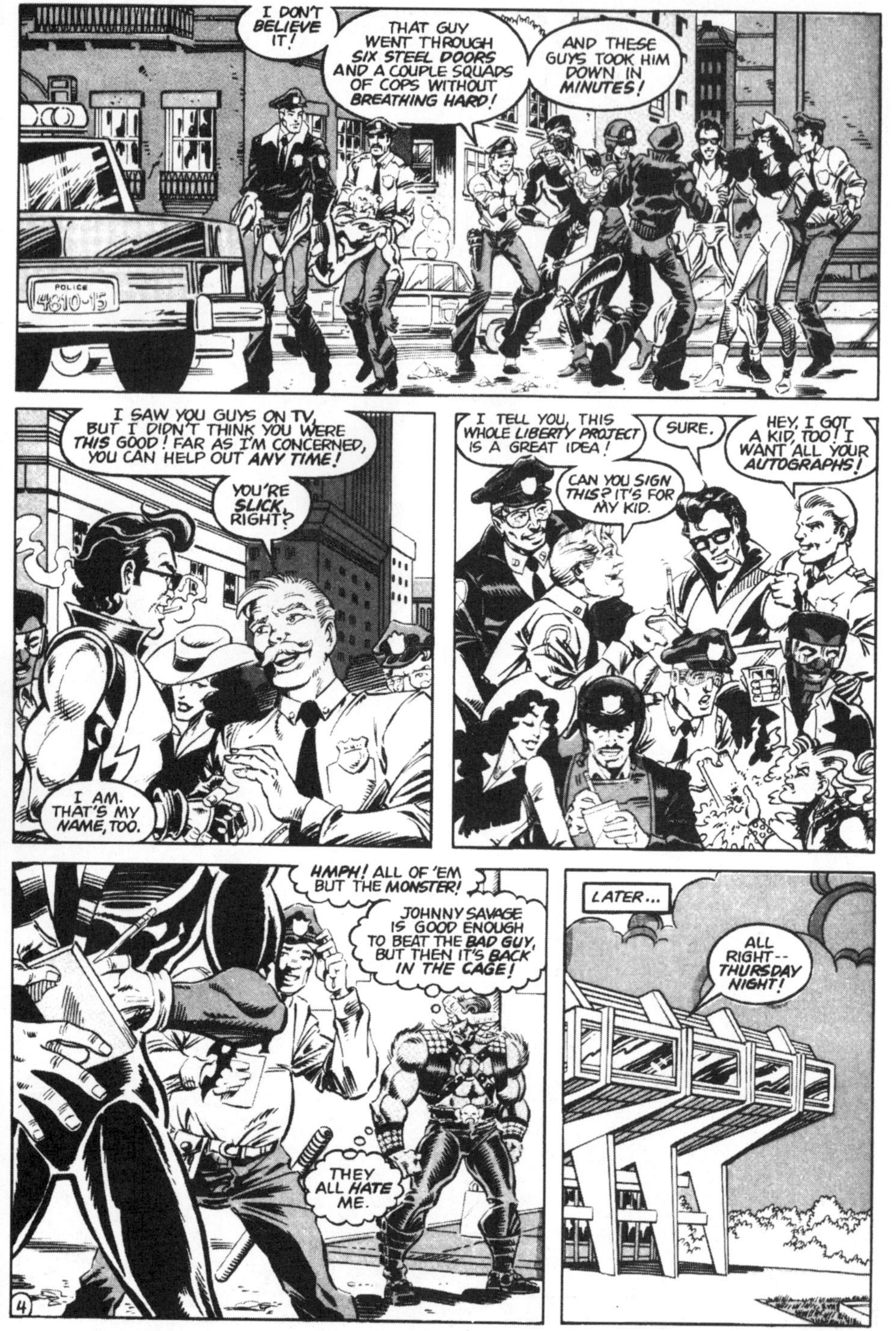
I DON'T BELIEVE IT!
THAT GUY WENT THROUGH SIX STEEL DOORS AND A COUPLE SQUADS OF COPS WITHOUT BREATHING HARD!
AND THESE GUYS TOOK HIM DOWN IN MINUTES!
I SAW YOU GUYS ON TV, BUT I DIDN'T THINK YOU WERE THIS GOOD! FAR AS I'M CONCERNED, YOU CAN HELP OUT ANY TIME!
YOU'RE SLICK, RIGHT?
I AM. THAT'S MY NAME, TOO.
I TELL YOU, THIS WHOLE LIBERTY PROJECT IS A GREAT IDEA!
SURE.
CAN YOU SIGN THIS? IT'S FOR MY KID.
HEY, I GOT A KID, TOO! I WANT ALL YOUR AUTOGRAPHS!
HMPH! ALL OF 'EM BUT THE MONSTER!
JOHNNY SAVAGE IS GOOD ENOUGH TO BEAT THE BAD GUY, BUT THEN IT'S BACK IN THE CAGE!
THEY ALL HATE ME.
4
LATER...
ALL RIGHT-- THURSDAY NIGHT!

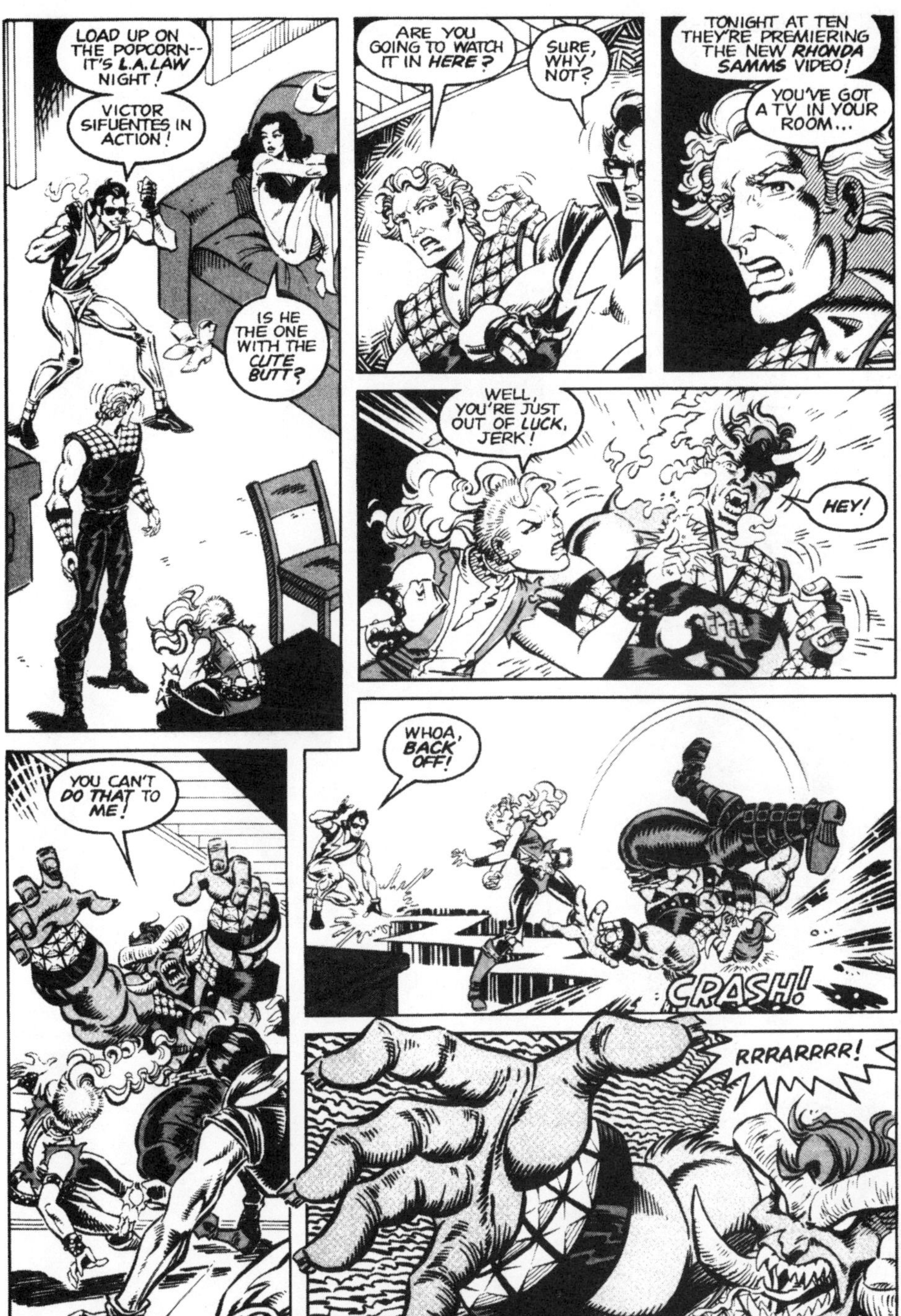
LOAD UP ON THE POPCORN-- IT'S L.A. LAW NIGHT!
VICTOR SIFUENTES IN ACTION!
IS HE THE ONE WITH THE CUTE BUTT?
ARE YOU GOING TO WATCH IT IN HERE?
SURE, WHY NOT?
TONIGHT AT TEN THEY'RE PREMIERING THE NEW RHONDA SAMMS VIDEO!
YOU'VE GOT A TV IN YOUR ROOM...
WELL, YOU'RE JUST OUT OF LUCK, JERK!
HEY!
YOU CAN'T DO THAT TO ME!
WHOA, BACK OFF!
CRASH!
RRRARRRR!
5

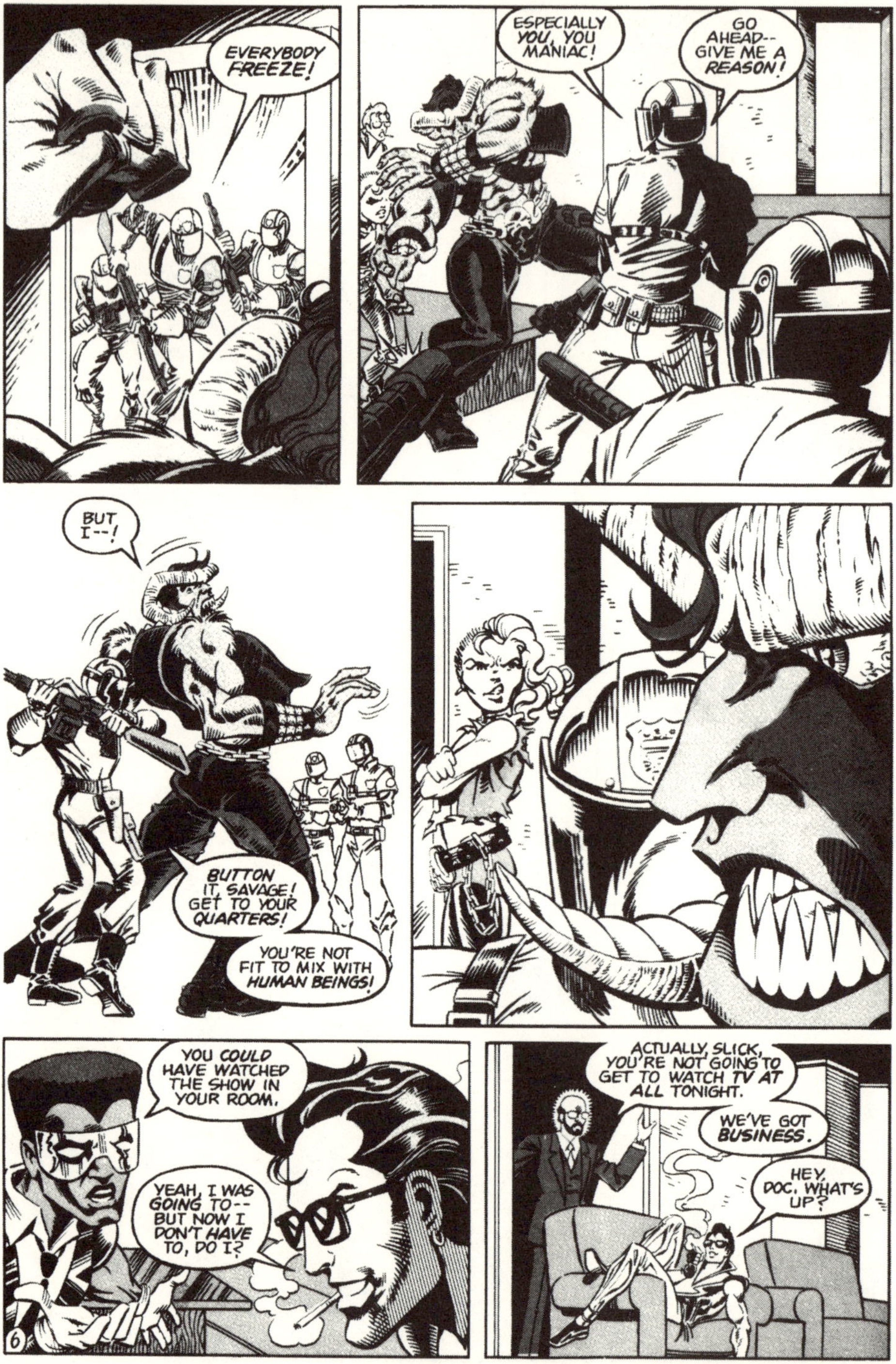
EVERYBODY FREEZE!
ESPECIALLY YOU, YOU MANIAC!
GO AHEAD-- GIVE ME A REASON!
BUT I--!
BUTTON IT, SAVAGE! GET TO YOUR QUARTERS!
YOU'RE NOT FIT TO MIX WITH HUMAN BEINGS!
YOU COULD HAVE WATCHED THE SHOW IN YOUR ROOM.
YEAH, I WAS GOING TO-- BUT NOW I DON'T HAVE TO, DO I?
6
ACTUALLY, SLICK, YOU'RE NOT GOING TO GET TO WATCH TV AT ALL TONIGHT.
WE'VE GOT BUSINESS.
HEY, DOC, WHAT'S UP?

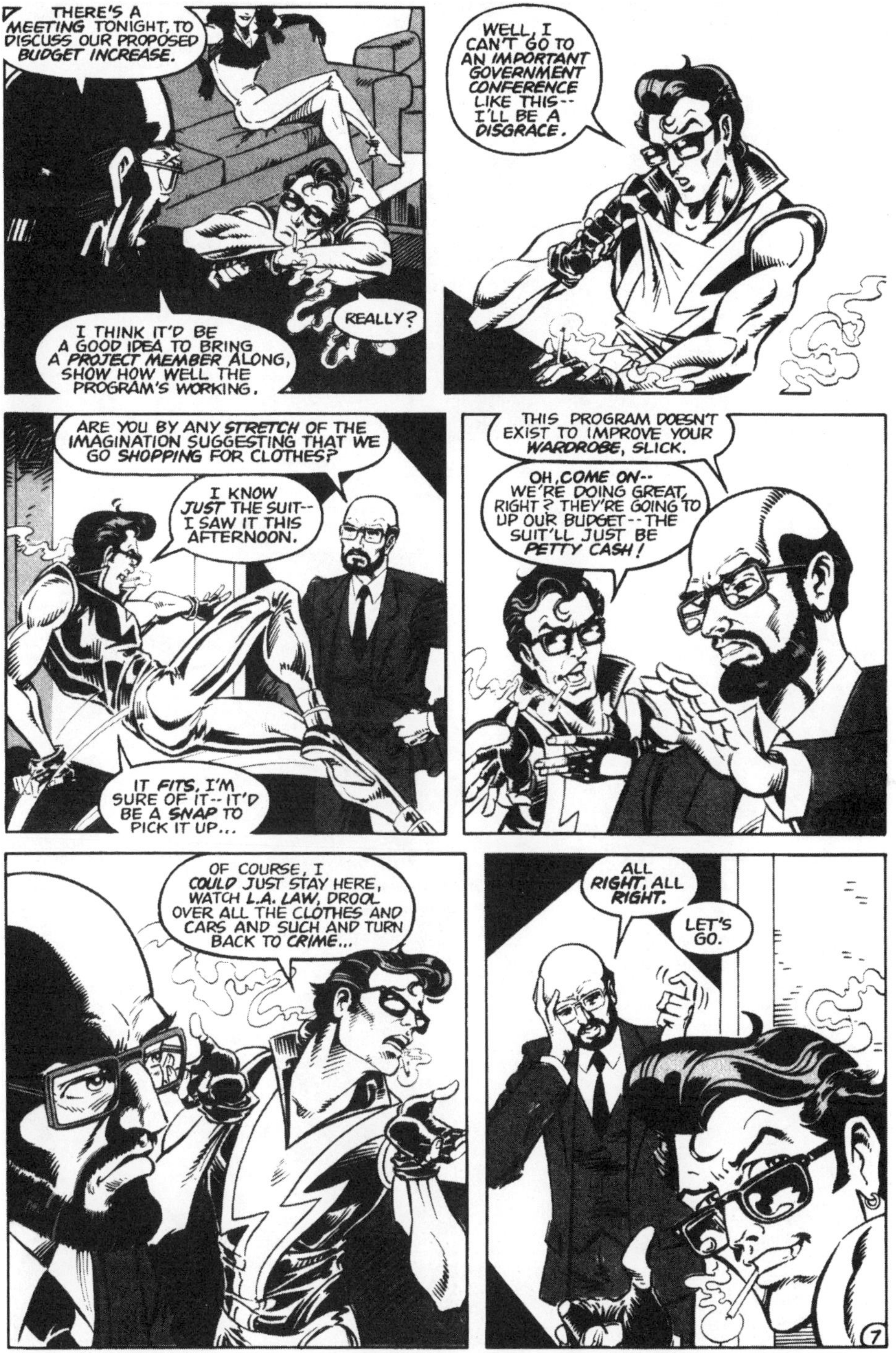
THERE'S A MEETING TONIGHT, TO DISCUSS OUR PROPOSED BUDGET INCREASE.
I THINK IT'D BE A GOOD IDEA TO BRING A PROJECT MEMBER ALONG, SHOW HOW WELL THE PROGRAM'S WORKING.
REALLY?
WELL, I CAN'T GO TO AN IMPORTANT GOVERNMENT CONFERENCE LIKE THIS-- I'LL BE A DISGRACE.
ARE YOU BY ANY STRETCH OF THE IMAGINATION SUGGESTING THAT WE GO SHOPPING FOR CLOTHES?
I KNOW JUST THE SUIT-- I SAW IT THIS AFTERNOON.
IT FITS, I'M SURE OF IT-- IT'D BE A SNAP TO PICK IT UP...
THIS PROGRAM DOESN'T EXIST TO IMPROVE YOUR WARDROBE, SLICK.
OH, COME ON-- WE'RE DOING GREAT, RIGHT? THEY'RE GOING TO UP OUR BUDGET--THE SUIT'LL JUST BE PETTY CASH!
OF COURSE, I COULD JUST STAY HERE, WATCH L.A. LAW, DROOL OVER ALL THE CLOTHES AND CARS AND SUCH AND TURN BACK TO CRIME...
ALL RIGHT, ALL RIGHT.
LET'S GO.
7

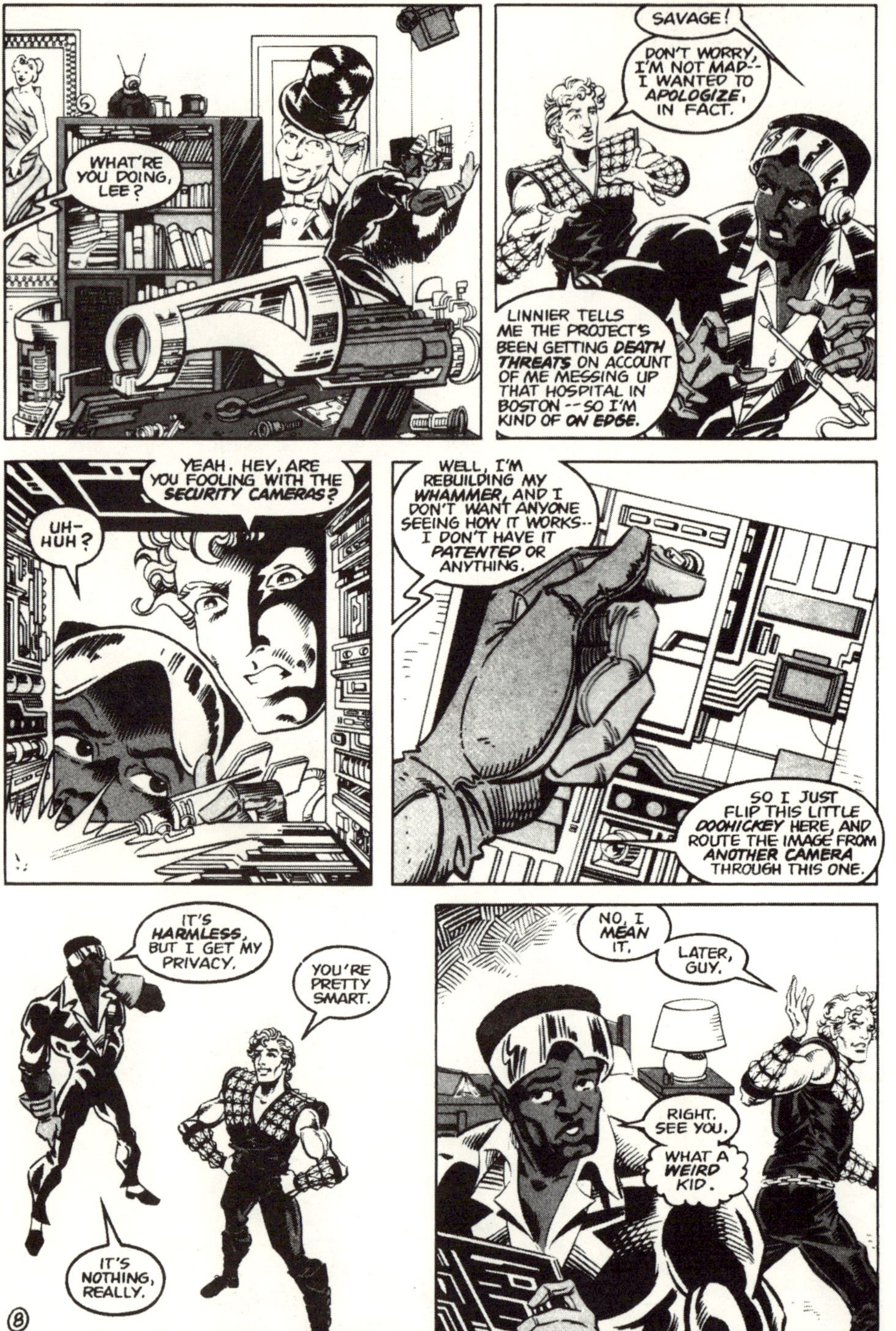
WHAT'RE YOU DOING, LEE?
SAVAGE!
DON'T WORRY, I'M NOT MAD-- I WANTED TO APOLOGIZE, IN FACT.
LINNIER TELLS ME THE PROJECT'S BEEN GETTING DEATH THREATS ON ACCOUNT OF ME MESSING UP THAT HOSPITAL IN BOSTON -- SO I'M KIND OF ON EDGE.
YEAH. HEY, ARE YOU FOOLING WITH THE SECURITY CAMERAS?
UH-HUH?
WELL, I'M REBUILDING MY WHAMMER, AND I DON'T WANT ANYONE SEEING HOW IT WORKS-- I DON'T HAVE IT PATENTED OR ANYTHING.
SO I JUST FLIP THIS LITTLE DOOHICKEY HERE, AND ROUTE THE IMAGE FROM ANOTHER CAMERA THROUGH THIS ONE.
IT'S HARMLESS, BUT I GET MY PRIVACY.
YOU'RE PRETTY SMART.
IT'S NOTHING, REALLY.
NO, I MEAN IT.
LATER, GUY.
RIGHT. SEE YOU.
WHAT A WEIRD KID.
8

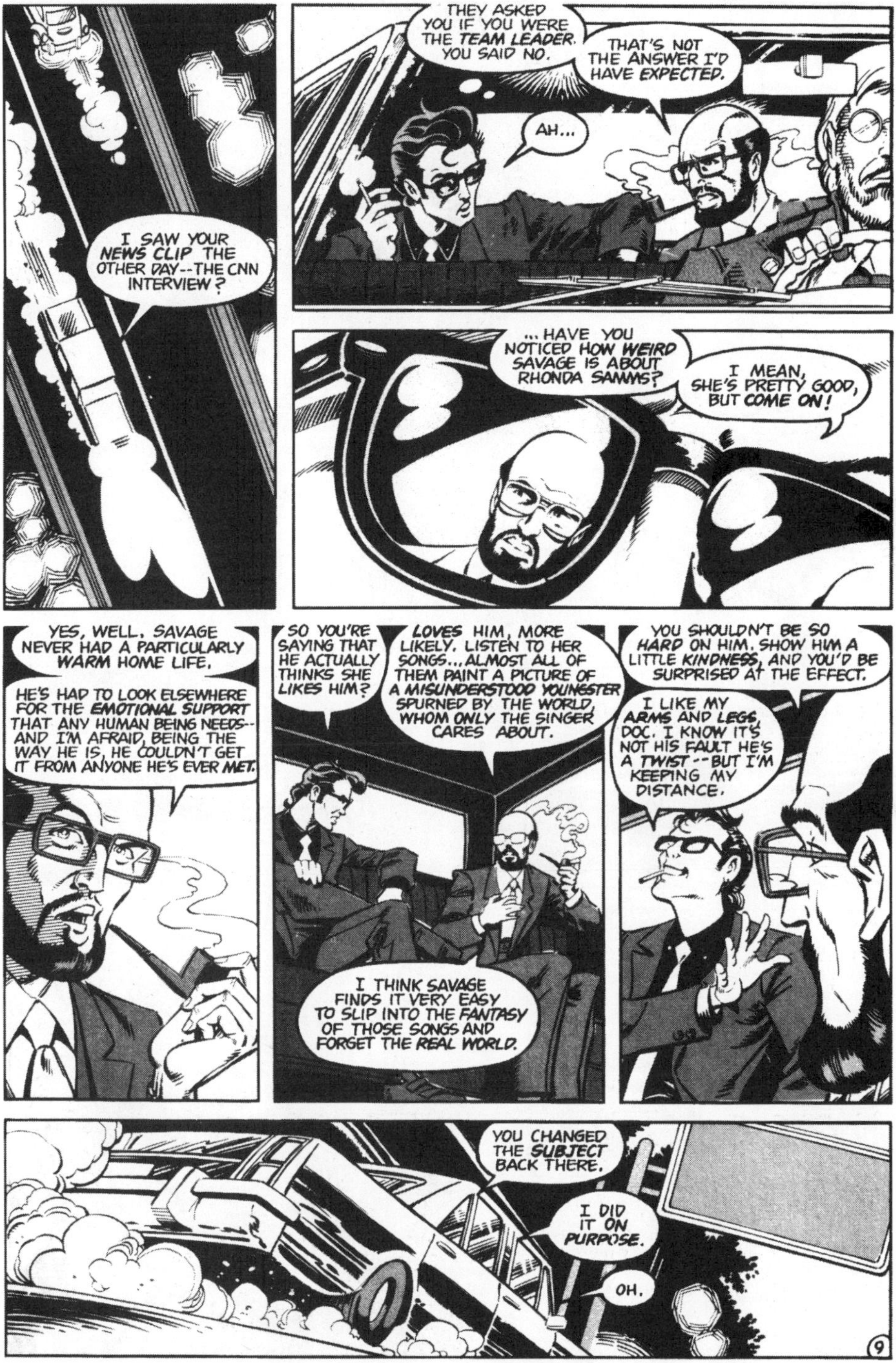
I SAW YOUR NEWS CLIP THE OTHER DAY--THE CNN INTERVIEW?
THEY ASKED YOU IF YOU WERE THE TEAM LEADER. YOU SAID NO.
THAT'S NOT THE ANSWER I'D HAVE EXPECTED.
AH...
...HAVE YOU NOTICED HOW WEIRD SAVAGE IS ABOUT RHONDA SAMMS?
I MEAN, SHE'S PRETTY GOOD, BUT COME ON!
YES, WELL. SAVAGE NEVER HAD A PARTICULARLY WARM HOME LIFE.
HE'S HAD TO LOOK ELSEWHERE FOR THE EMOTIONAL SUPPORT THAT ANY HUMAN BEING NEEDS--AND I'M AFRAID, BEING THE WAY HE IS, HE COULDN'T GET IT FROM ANYONE HE'S EVER MET.
SO YOU'RE SAYING THAT HE ACTUALLY THINKS SHE LIKES HIM?
LOVES HIM, MORE LIKELY. LISTEN TO HER SONGS... ALMOST ALL OF THEM PAINT A PICTURE OF A MISUNDERSTOOD YOUNGSTER SPURNED BY THE WORLD, WHOM ONLY THE SINGER CARES ABOUT.
I THINK SAVAGE FINDS IT VERY EASY TO SLIP INTO THE FANTASY OF THOSE SONGS AND FORGET THE REAL WORLD.
YOU SHOULDN'T BE SO HARD ON HIM. SHOW HIM A LITTLE KINDNESS, AND YOU'D BE SURPRISED AT THE EFFECT.
I LIKE MY ARMS AND LEGS, DOC. I KNOW IT'S NOT HIS FAULT HE'S A TWIST--BUT I'M KEEPING MY DISTANCE.
YOU CHANGED THE SUBJECT BACK THERE.
I DID IT ON PURPOSE.
OH.
9

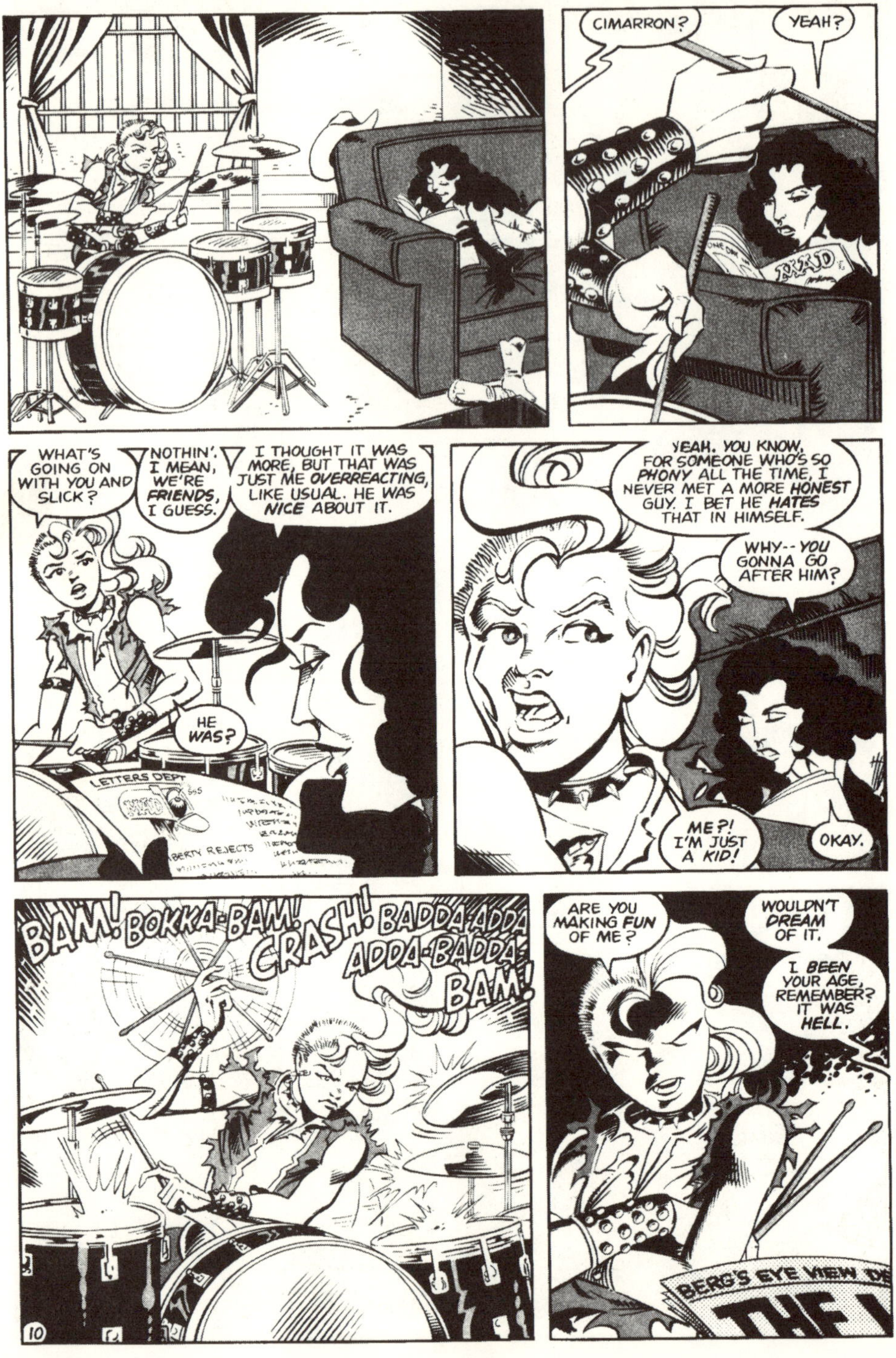
CIMARRON?
YEAH?
WHAT'S GOING ON WITH YOU AND SLICK?
NOTHIN'. I MEAN, WE'RE FRIENDS, I GUESS.
I THOUGHT IT WAS MORE, BUT THAT WAS JUST ME OVERREACTING, LIKE USUAL. HE WAS NICE ABOUT IT.
HE WAS?
LETTERS DEPT
YEAH. YOU KNOW, FOR SOMEONE WHO'S SO PHONY ALL THE TIME, I NEVER MET A MORE HONEST GUY. I BET HE HATES THAT IN HIMSELF.
WHY-- YOU GONNA GO AFTER HIM?
ME?! I'M JUST A KID!
OKAY.
BAM! BOKKA-BAM! CRASH! BADDA-ADDA ADDA-BADDA-BAM!
10
ARE YOU MAKING FUN OF ME?
WOULDN'T DREAM OF IT.
I BEEN YOUR AGE, REMEMBER? IT WAS HELL.
BERG'S EYE VIEW

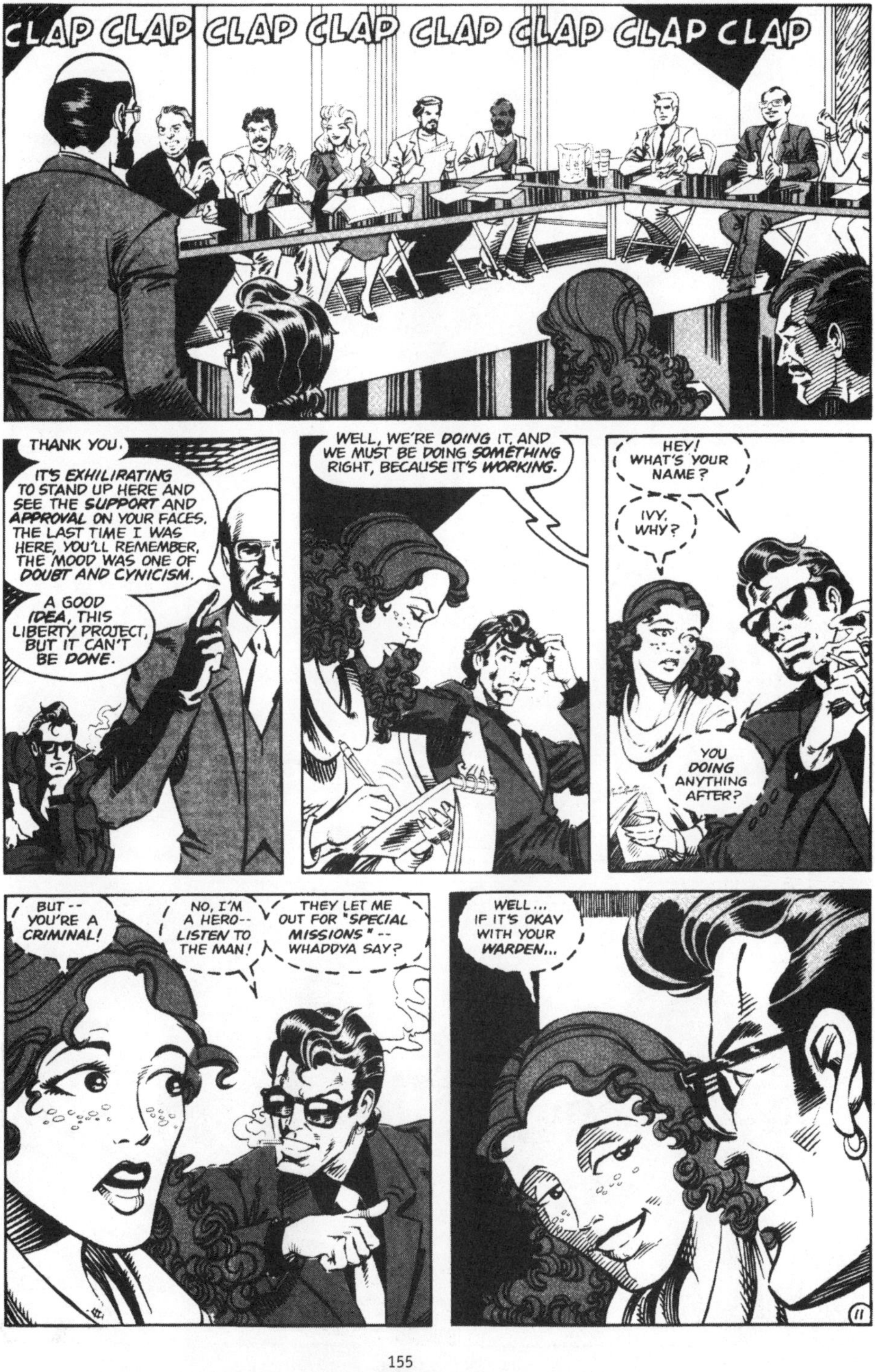
CLAP CLAP CLAP CLAP CLAP CLAP CLAP CLAP
THANK YOU.
IT'S EXHILIRATING TO STAND UP HERE AND SEE THE SUPPORT AND APPROVAL ON YOUR FACES. THE LAST TIME I WAS HERE, YOU'LL REMEMBER, THE MOOD WAS ONE OF DOUBT AND CYNICISM.
A GOOD IDEA, THIS LIBERTY PROJECT, BUT IT CAN'T BE DONE.
WELL, WE'RE DOING IT, AND WE MUST BE DOING SOMETHING RIGHT, BECAUSE IT'S WORKING.
HEY! WHAT'S YOUR NAME?
IVY. WHY?
YOU DOING ANYTHING AFTER?
BUT -- YOU'RE A CRIMINAL!
NO, I'M A HERO-- LISTEN TO THE MAN!
THEY LET ME OUT FOR "SPECIAL MISSIONS" -- WHADDYA SAY?
WELL... IF IT'S OKAY WITH YOUR WARDEN...
11

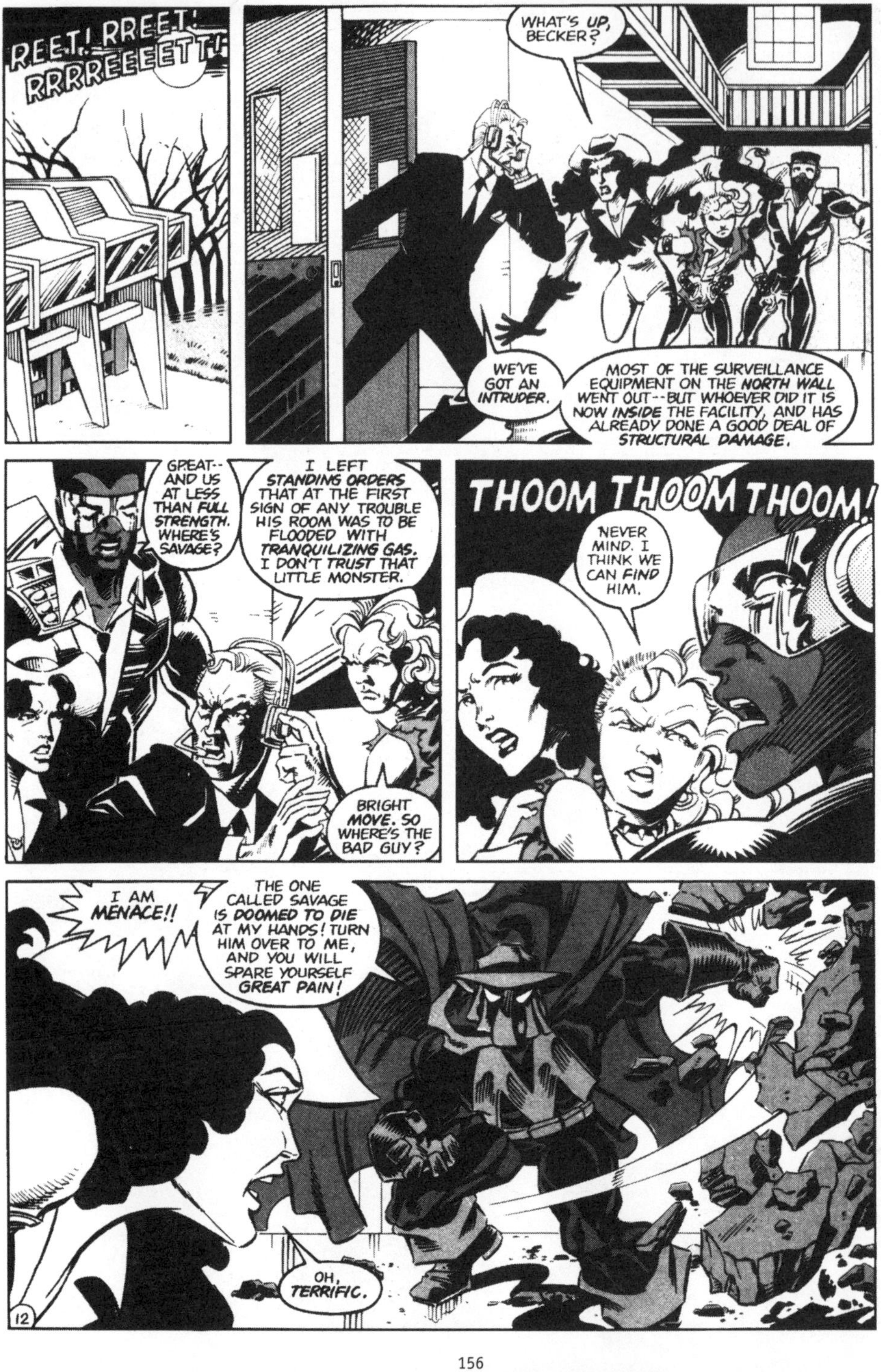
REET! RREET! RRRREEEEETT!
WHAT'S UP, BECKER?
WE'VE GOT AN INTRUDER.
MOST OF THE SURVEILLANCE EQUIPMENT ON THE NORTH WALL WENT OUT--BUT WHOEVER DID IT IS NOW INSIDE THE FACILITY, AND HAS ALREADY DONE A GOOD DEAL OF STRUCTURAL DAMAGE.
GREAT--AND US AT LESS THAN FULL STRENGTH. WHERE'S SAVAGE?
I LEFT STANDING ORDERS THAT AT THE FIRST SIGN OF ANY TROUBLE HIS ROOM WAS TO BE FLOODED WITH TRANQUILIZING GAS. I DON'T TRUST THAT LITTLE MONSTER.
BRIGHT MOVE. SO WHERE'S THE BAD GUY?
THOOM THOOM THOOM!
NEVER MIND. I THINK WE CAN FIND HIM.
I AM MENACE!!
THE ONE CALLED SAVAGE IS DOOMED TO DIE AT MY HANDS! TURN HIM OVER TO ME, AND YOU WILL SPARE YOURSELF GREAT PAIN!
OH, TERRIFIC.
12

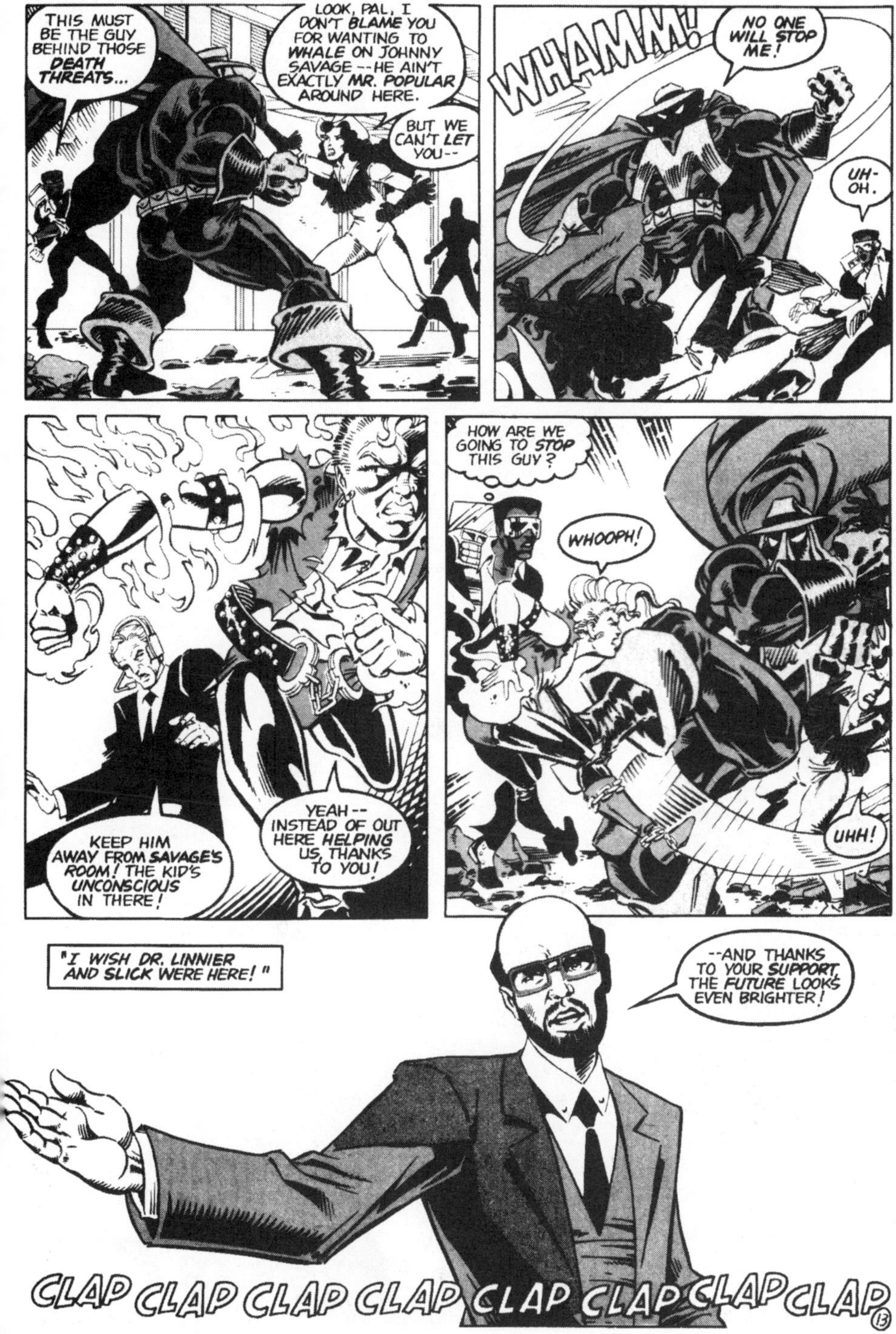

THIS MUST BE THE GUY BEHIND THOSE DEATH THREATS...
LOOK, PAL, I DON'T BLAME YOU FOR WANTING TO WHALE ON JOHNNY SAVAGE --HE AIN'T EXACTLY MR. POPULAR AROUND HERE.
BUT WE CAN'T LET YOU--
WHAMM!
NO ONE WILL STOP ME!
UH-OH.
KEEP HIM AWAY FROM SAVAGE'S ROOM! THE KID'S UNCONSCIOUS IN THERE!
YEAH -- INSTEAD OF OUT HERE HELPING US, THANKS TO YOU!
HOW ARE WE GOING TO STOP THIS GUY?
WHOOPH!
UHH!
"I WISH DR. LINNIER AND SLICK WERE HERE!"
--AND THANKS TO YOUR SUPPORT, THE FUTURE LOOKS EVEN BRIGHTER!
CLAP CLAP CLAP CLAP CLAP CLAP CLAP CLAP
13

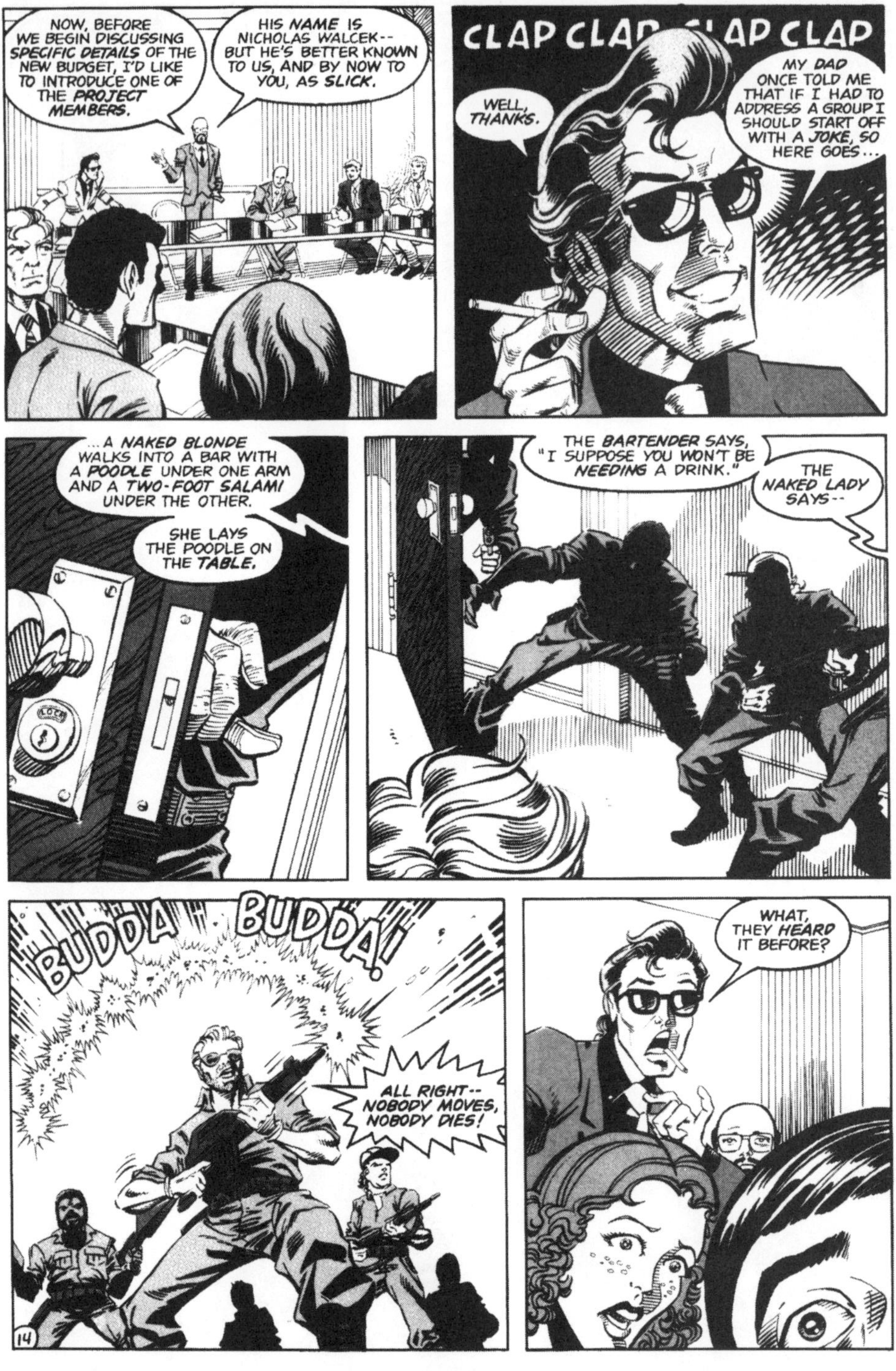
NOW, BEFORE WE BEGIN DISCUSSING SPECIFIC DETAILS OF THE NEW BUDGET, I'D LIKE TO INTRODUCE ONE OF THE PROJECT MEMBERS.
HIS NAME IS NICHOLAS WALCEK-- BUT HE'S BETTER KNOWN TO US, AND BY NOW TO YOU, AS SLICK.
CLAP CLAP CLAP CLAP
WELL, THANKS.
MY DAD ONCE TOLD ME THAT IF I HAD TO ADDRESS A GROUP I SHOULD START OFF WITH A JOKE, SO HERE GOES...
...A NAKED BLONDE WALKS INTO A BAR WITH A POODLE UNDER ONE ARM AND A TWO-FOOT SALAMI UNDER THE OTHER.
SHE LAYS THE POODLE ON THE TABLE.
THE BARTENDER SAYS, "I SUPPOSE YOU WON'T BE NEEDING A DRINK."
THE NAKED LADY SAYS--
BUDDA BUDDA!
ALL RIGHT-- NOBODY MOVES, NOBODY DIES!
14
WHAT, THEY HEARD IT BEFORE?

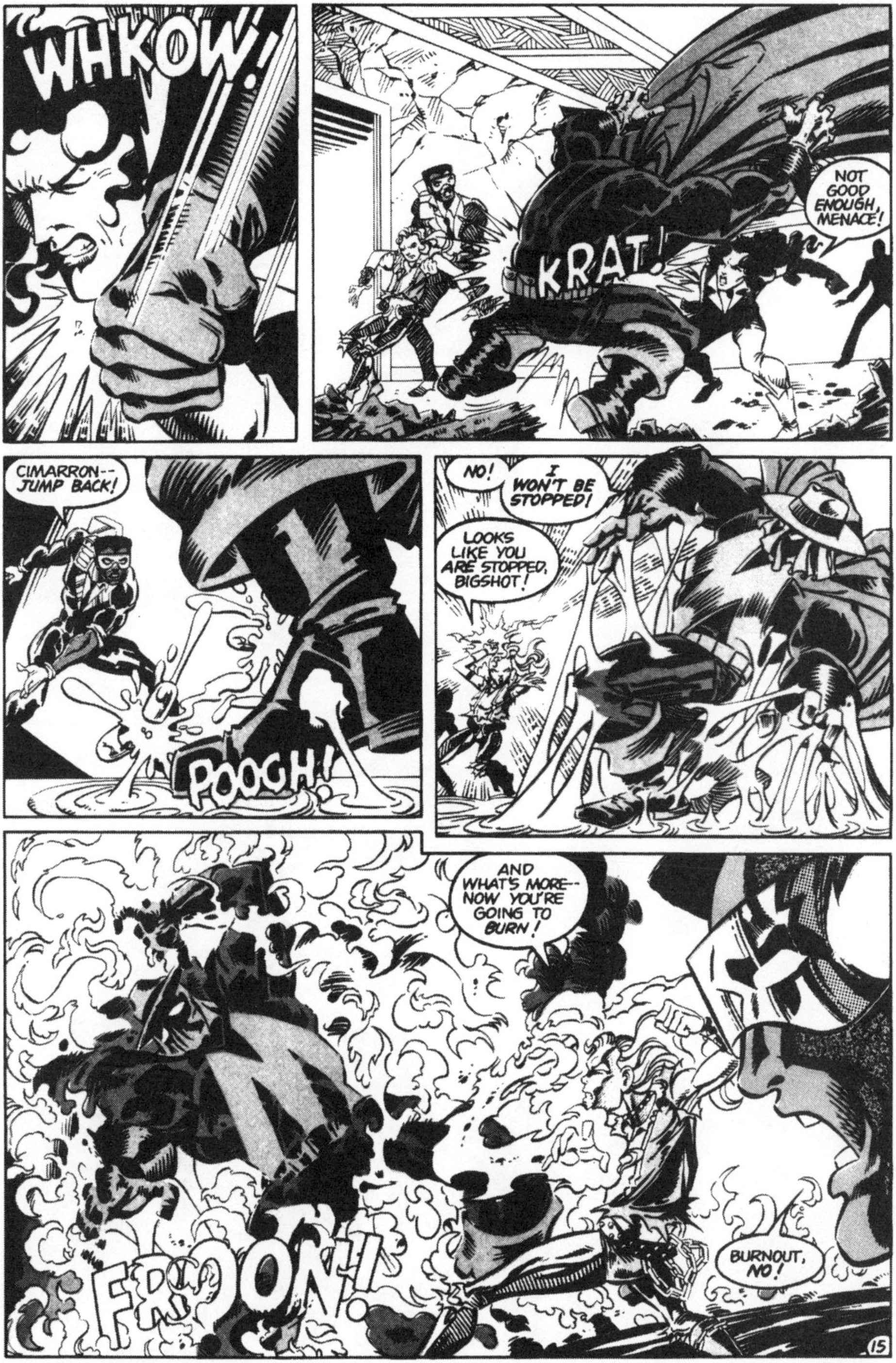
WHKOW!
NOT GOOD ENOUGH, MENACE!
KRAT!
CIMARRON-- JUMP BACK!
POOGH!
NO!
I WON'T BE STOPPED!
LOOKS LIKE YOU ARE STOPPED, BIGSHOT!
AND WHAT'S MORE-- NOW YOU'RE GOING TO BURN!
FROOM!
BURNOUT, NO!
15

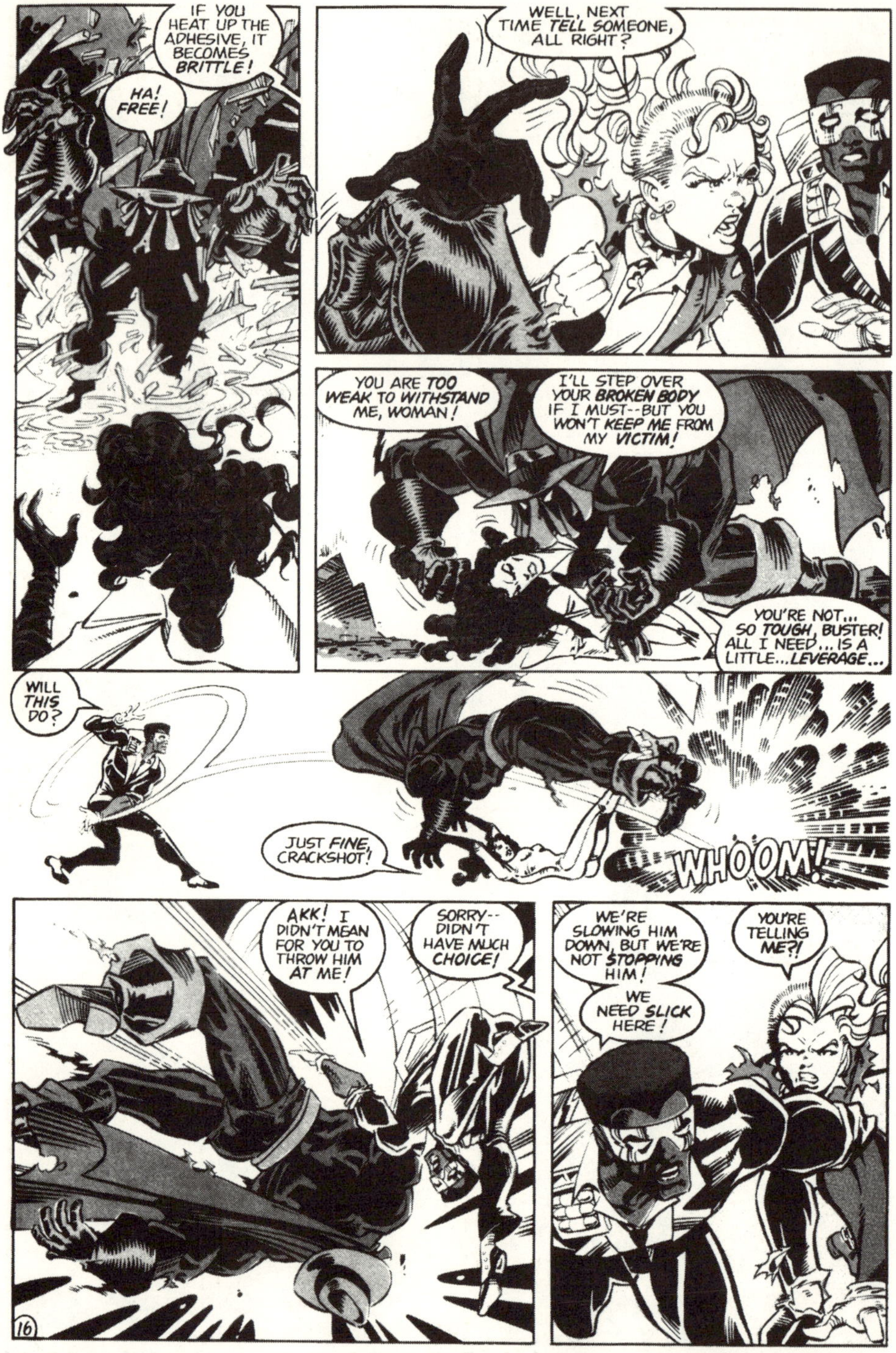
IF YOU HEAT UP THE ADHESIVE, IT BECOMES BRITTLE!
HA! FREE!
WELL, NEXT TIME TELL SOMEONE, ALL RIGHT?
YOU ARE TOO WEAK TO WITHSTAND ME, WOMAN!
I'LL STEP OVER YOUR BROKEN BODY IF I MUST--BUT YOU WON'T KEEP ME FROM MY VICTIM!
YOU'RE NOT... SO TOUGH, BUSTER! ALL I NEED... IS A LITTLE... LEVERAGE...
WILL THIS DO?
JUST FINE, CRACKSHOT!
WHOOM!
AKK! I DIDN'T MEAN FOR YOU TO THROW HIM AT ME!
SORRY-- DIDN'T HAVE MUCH CHOICE!
WE'RE SLOWING HIM DOWN, BUT WE'RE NOT STOPPING HIM!
WE NEED SLICK HERE!
YOU'RE TELLING ME?!
16

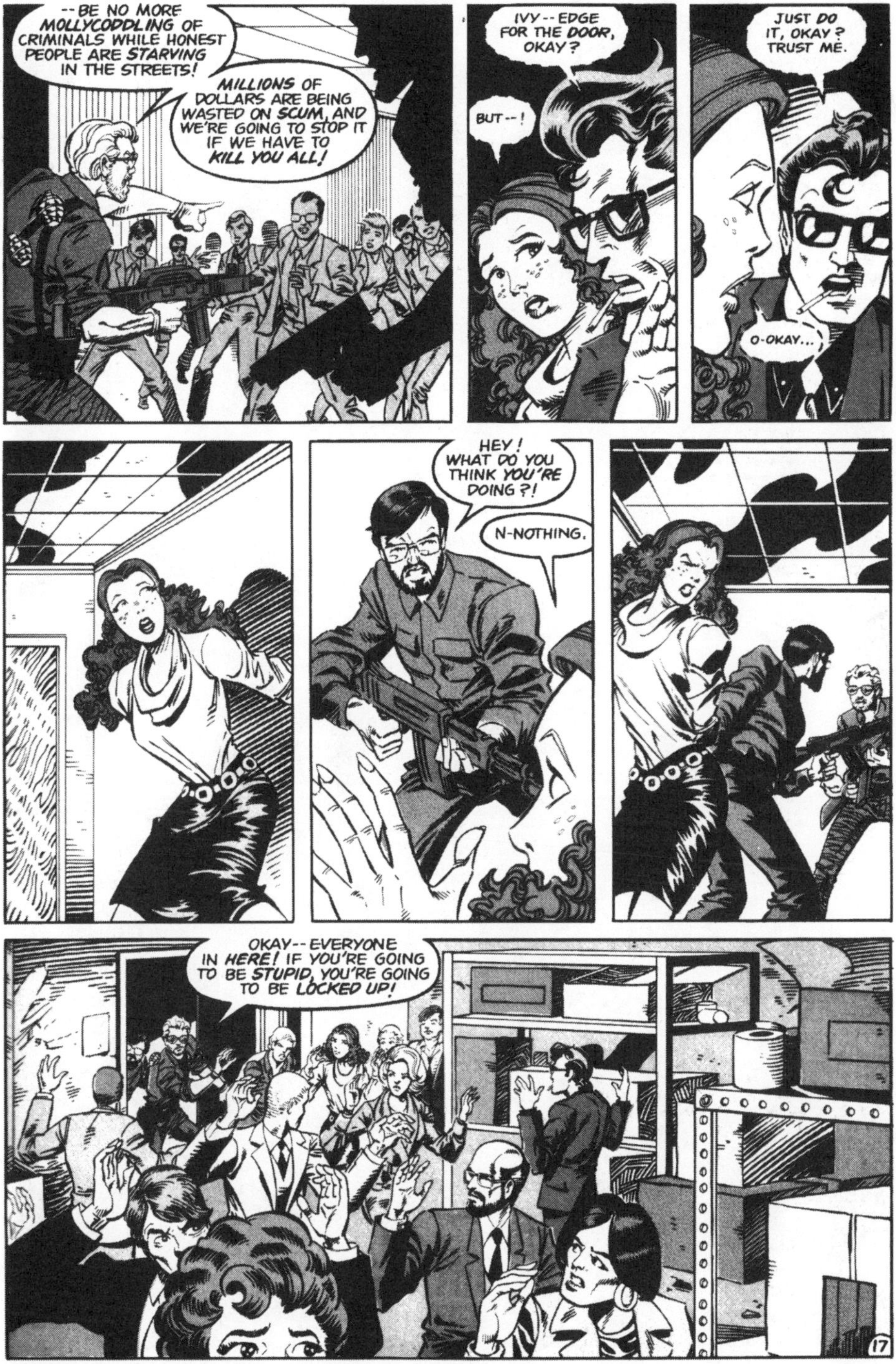
--BE NO MORE MOLLYCODDLING OF CRIMINALS WHILE HONEST PEOPLE ARE STARVING IN THE STREETS!
MILLIONS OF DOLLARS ARE BEING WASTED ON SCUM, AND WE'RE GOING TO STOP IT IF WE HAVE TO KILL YOU ALL!
IVY--EDGE FOR THE DOOR, OKAY?
BUT--!
JUST DO IT, OKAY? TRUST ME.
O-OKAY...
HEY! WHAT DO YOU THINK YOU'RE DOING?!
N-NOTHING.
OKAY--EVERYONE IN HERE! IF YOU'RE GOING TO BE STUPID, YOU'RE GOING TO BE LOCKED UP!
17

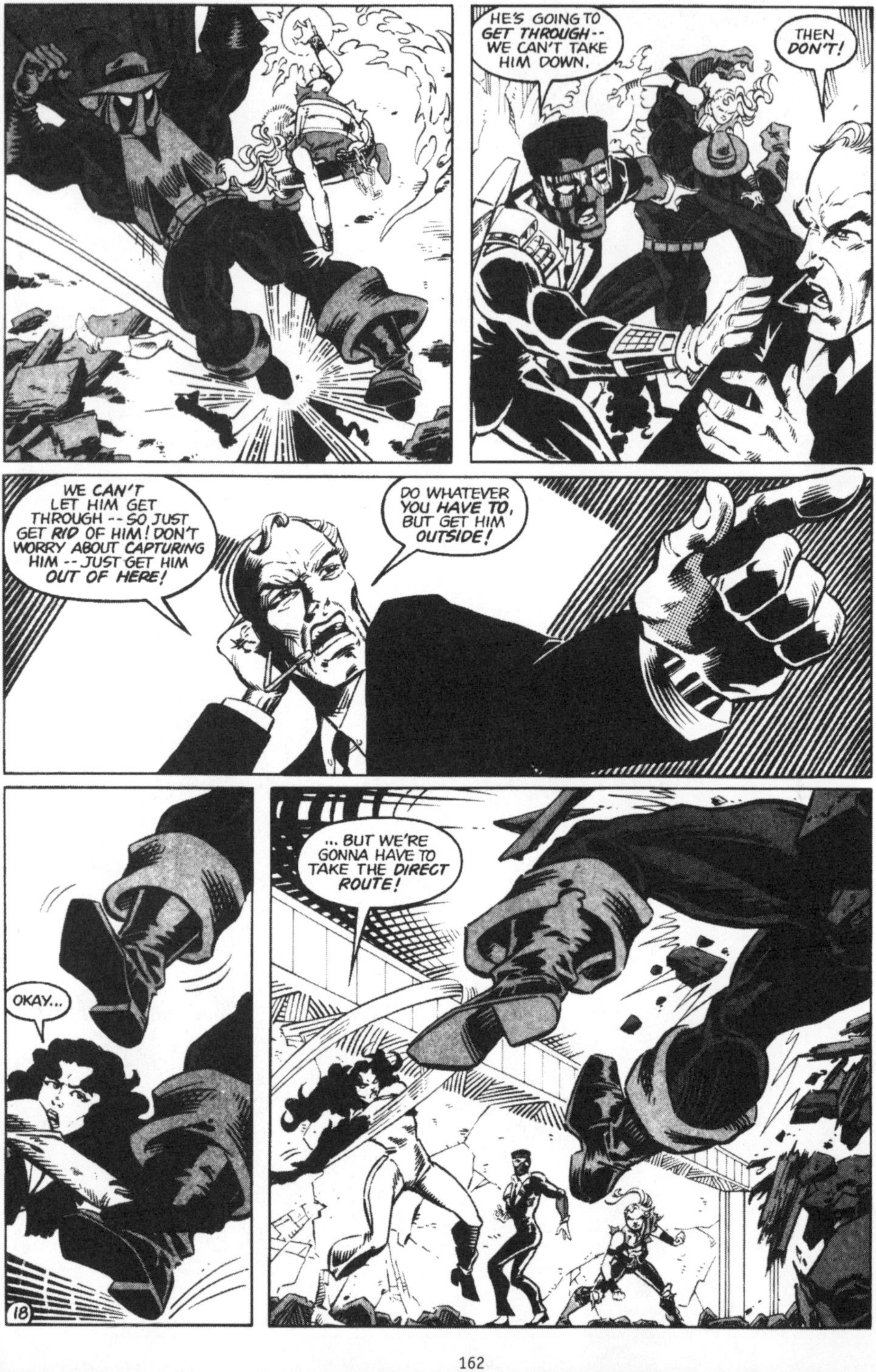
HE'S GOING TO GET THROUGH -- WE CAN'T TAKE HIM DOWN.
THEN DON'T!
WE CAN'T LET HIM GET THROUGH -- SO JUST GET RID OF HIM! DON'T WORRY ABOUT CAPTURING HIM -- JUST GET HIM OUT OF HERE!
DO WHATEVER YOU HAVE TO, BUT GET HIM OUTSIDE!
OKAY...
... BUT WE'RE GONNA HAVE TO TAKE THE DIRECT ROUTE!
18

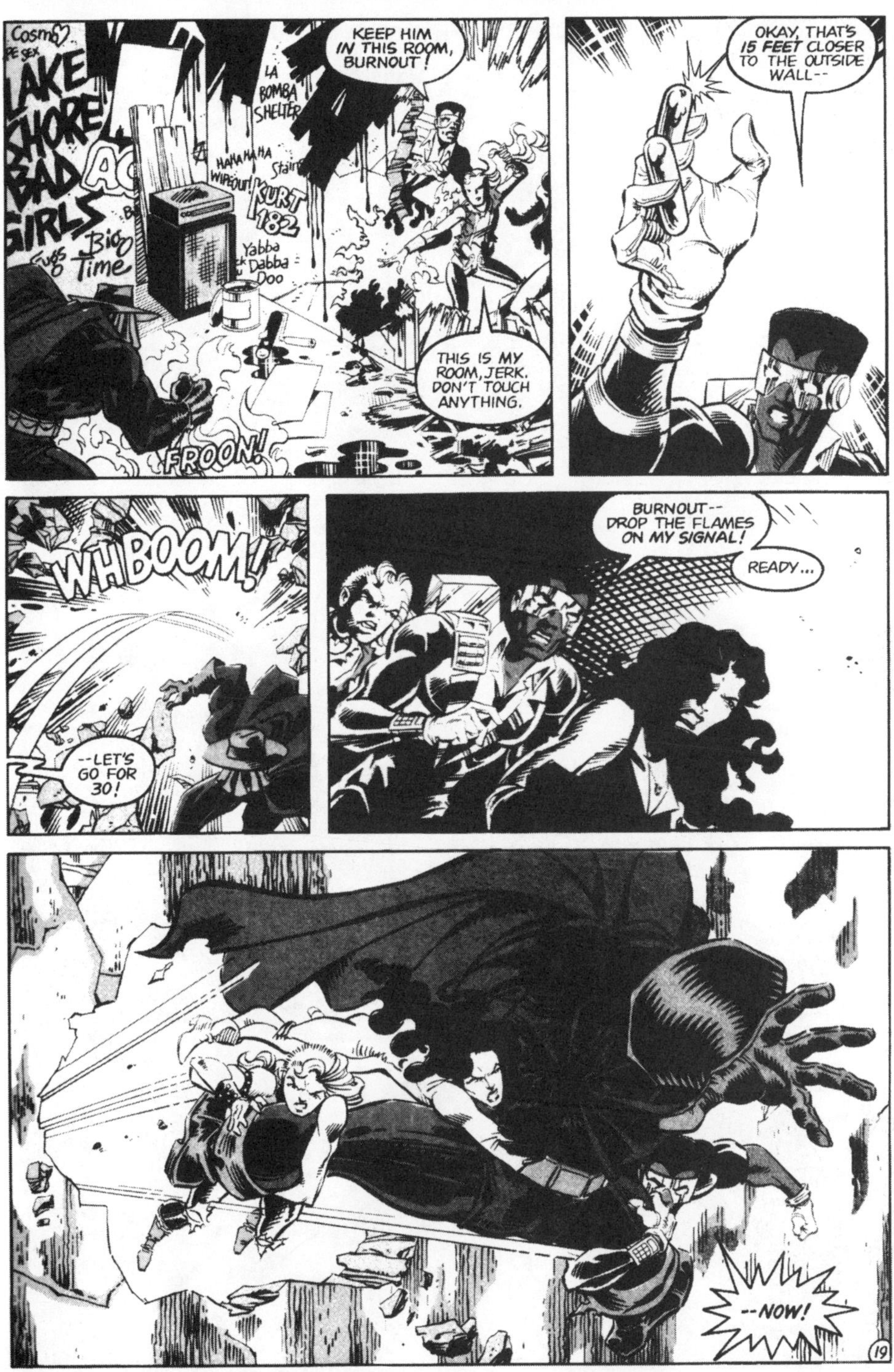
KEEP HIM IN THIS ROOM, BURNOUT!
THIS IS MY ROOM, JERK. DON'T TOUCH ANYTHING.
FROON!
OKAY, THAT'S 15 FEET CLOSER TO THE OUTSIDE WALL--
WHBOOM!
--LET'S GO FOR 30!
BURNOUT-- DROP THE FLAMES ON MY SIGNAL!
READY...
--NOW!
19

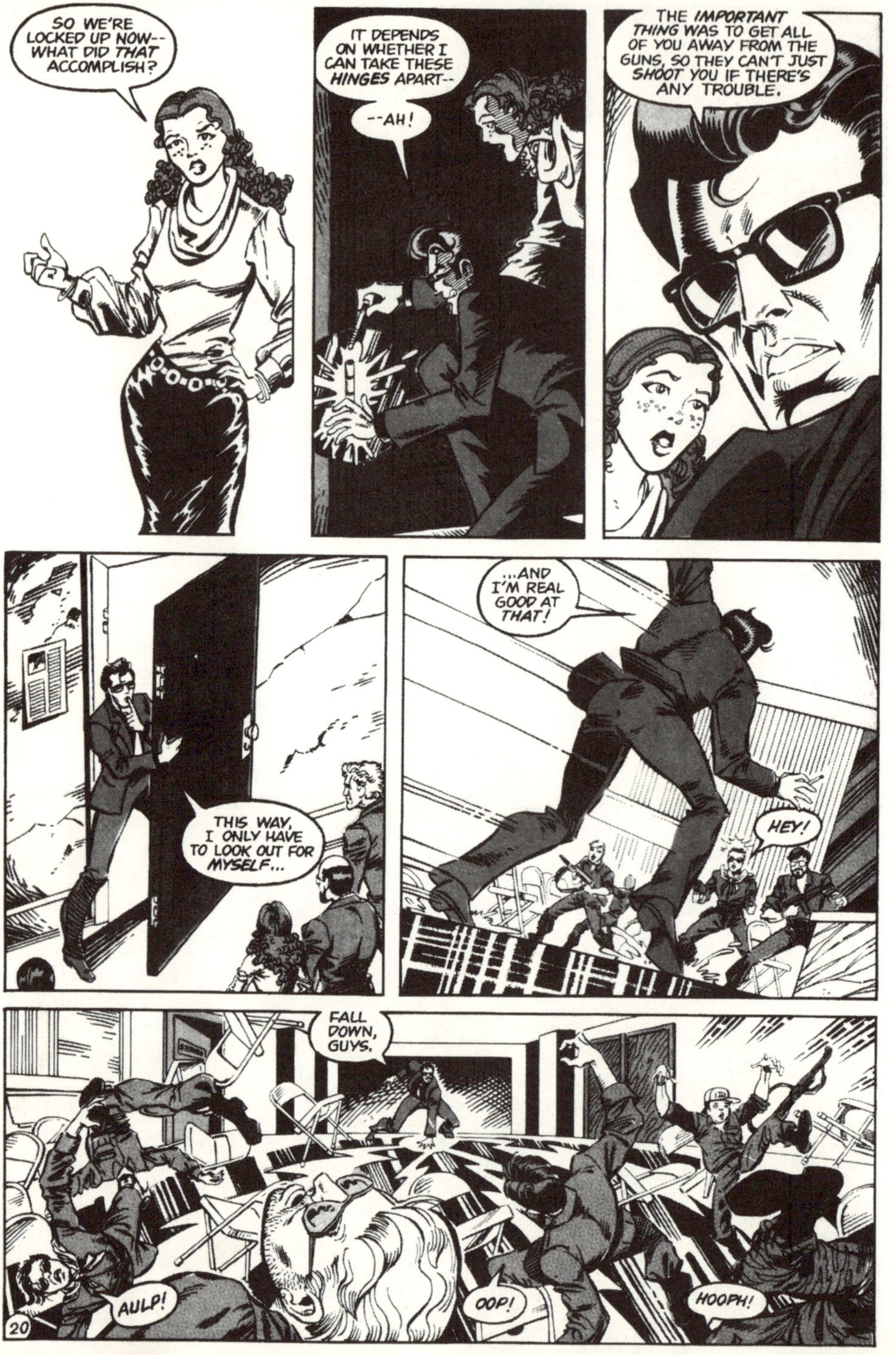
SO WE'RE LOCKED UP NOW-- WHAT DID THAT ACCOMPLISH?
IT DEPENDS ON WHETHER I CAN TAKE THESE HINGES APART--
--AH!
THE IMPORTANT THING WAS TO GET ALL OF YOU AWAY FROM THE GUNS, SO THEY CAN'T JUST SHOOT YOU IF THERE'S ANY TROUBLE.
THIS WAY, I ONLY HAVE TO LOOK OUT FOR MYSELF...
...AND I'M REAL GOOD AT THAT!
HEY!
FALL DOWN, GUYS.
AULP!
OOP!
HOOPH!
20

KILL HIM! KILL HIM!
OH, SHUT UP.
KRASH!
ZWIPPP
WHERE'D HE GO?
WHRACK!
ONLY ONE MORE...
COSMO
AKH!
BLAM!
HE'S... GETTING AWAY!
21

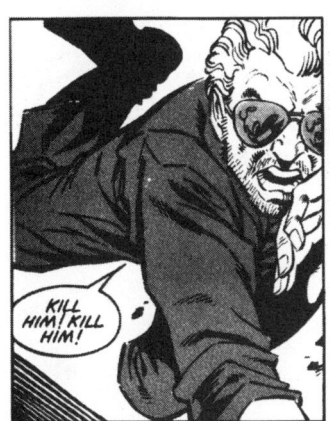

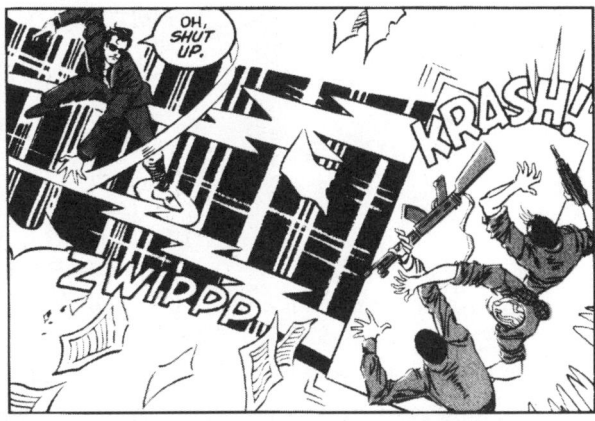

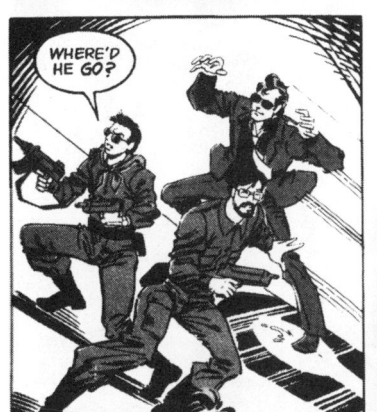

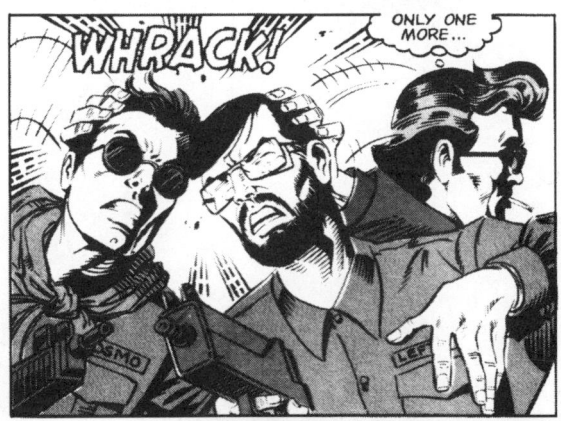

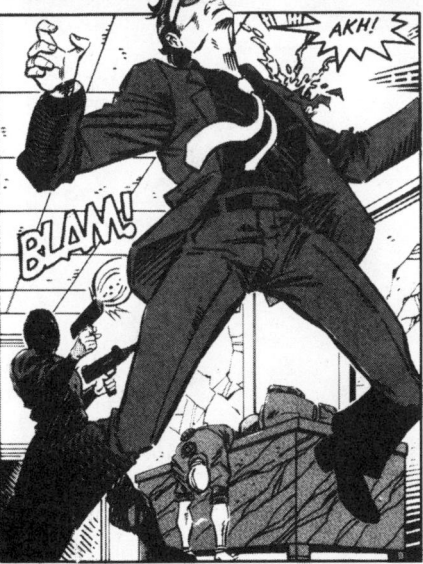

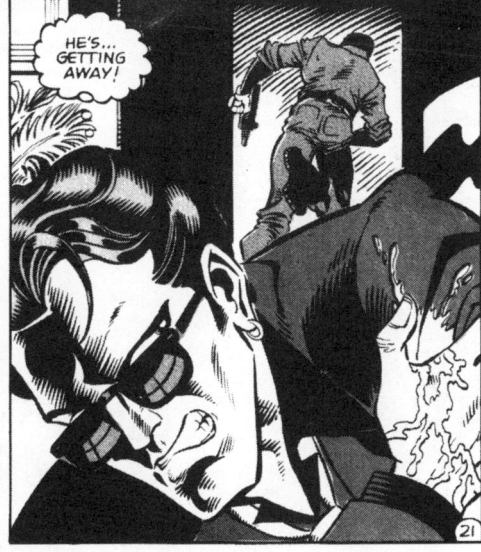

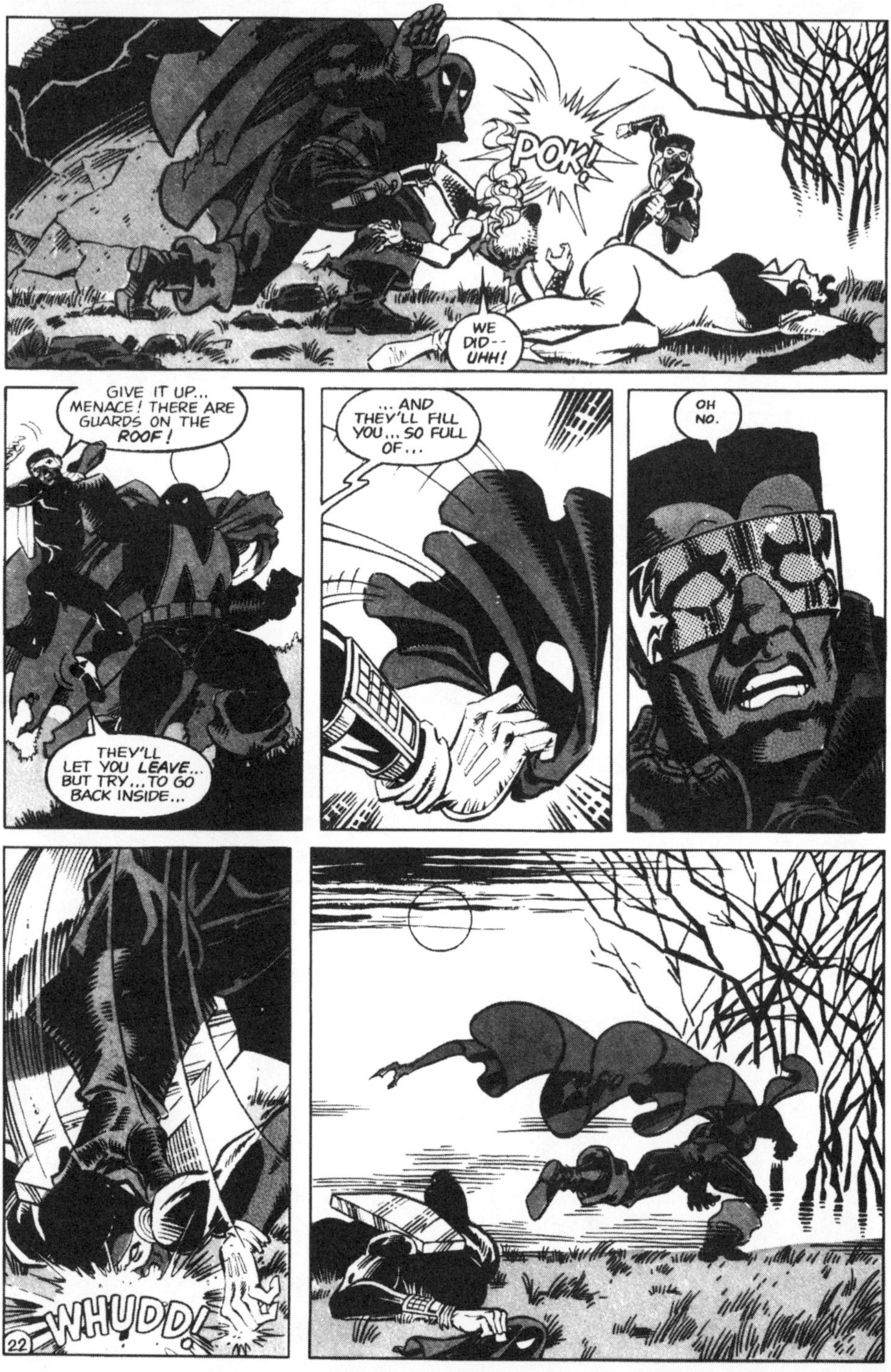
POK!
WE DID-- UHH!
GIVE IT UP... MENACE! THERE ARE GUARDS ON THE ROOF!
THEY'LL LET YOU LEAVE... BUT TRY... TO GO BACK INSIDE...
... AND THEY'LL FILL YOU... SO FULL OF...
OH NO.
WHUDD!
22

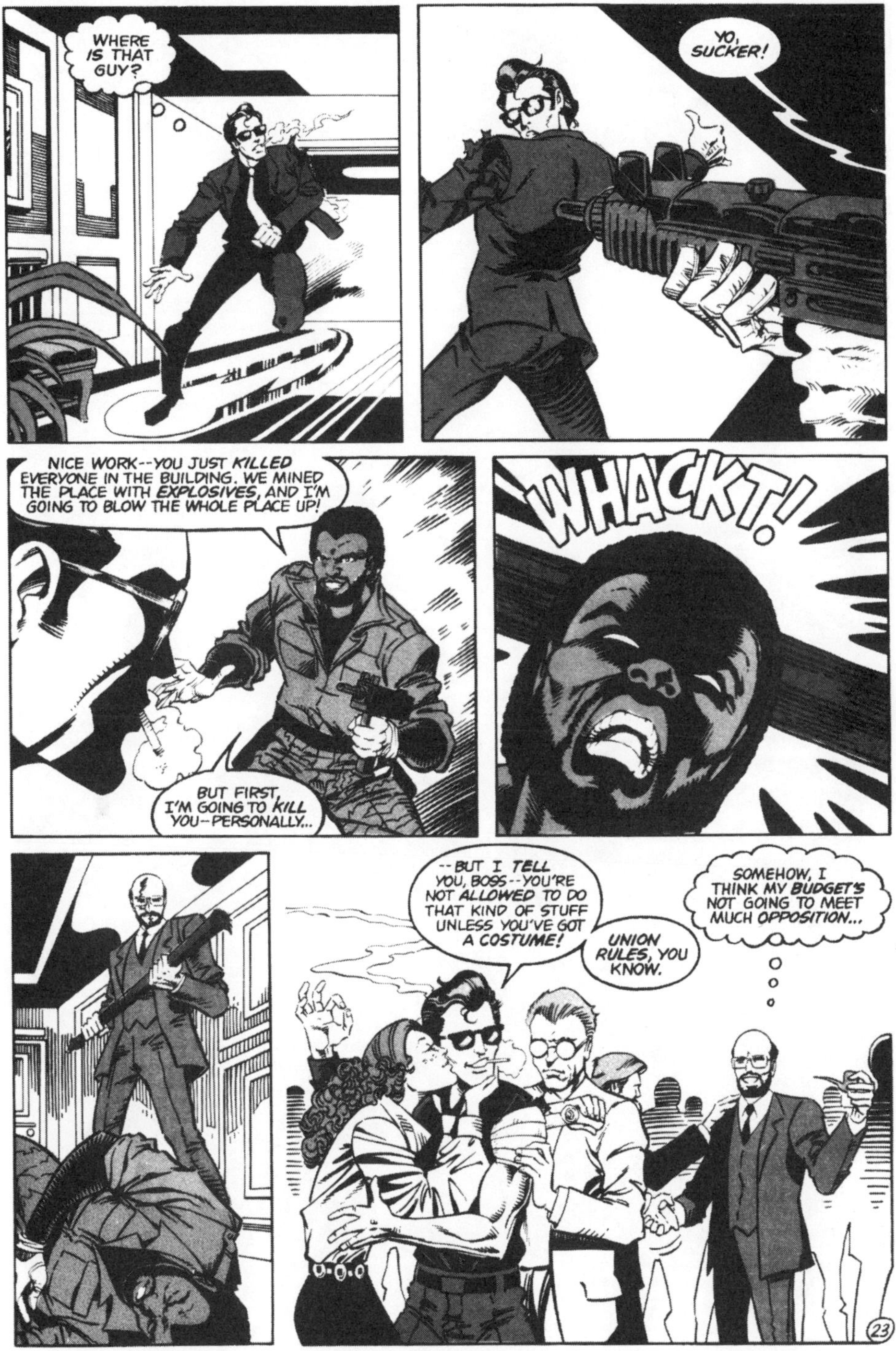
WHERE IS THAT GUY?
YO, SUCKER!
NICE WORK--YOU JUST KILLED EVERYONE IN THE BUILDING. WE MINED THE PLACE WITH EXPLOSIVES, AND I'M GOING TO BLOW THE WHOLE PLACE UP!
BUT FIRST, I'M GOING TO KILL YOU--PERSONALLY...
WHACKT!
--BUT I TELL YOU, BOSS--YOU'RE NOT ALLOWED TO DO THAT KIND OF STUFF UNLESS YOU'VE GOT A COSTUME!
UNION RULES, YOU KNOW.
SOMEHOW, I THINK MY BUDGET'S NOT GOING TO MEET MUCH OPPOSITION...
23

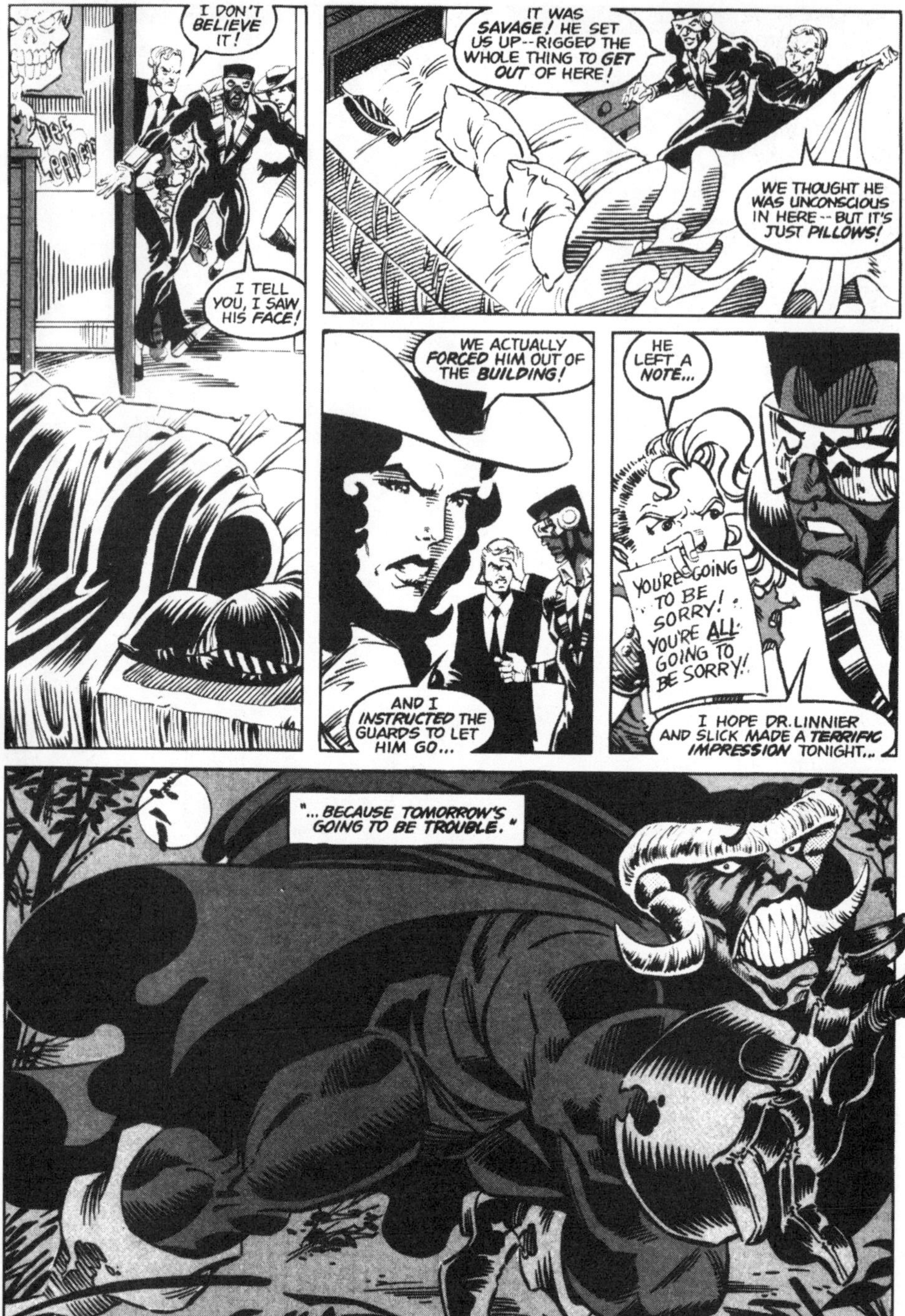
I DON'T BELIEVE IT!
I TELL YOU, I SAW HIS FACE!
IT WAS SAVAGE! HE SET US UP--RIGGED THE WHOLE THING TO GET OUT OF HERE!
WE THOUGHT HE WAS UNCONSCIOUS IN HERE -- BUT IT'S JUST PILLOWS!
WE ACTUALLY FORCED HIM OUT OF THE BUILDING!
AND I INSTRUCTED THE GUARDS TO LET HIM GO...
HE LEFT A NOTE...
YOU'RE GOING TO BE SORRY! YOU'RE ALL GOING TO BE SORRY!
I HOPE DR. LINNIER AND SLICK MADE A TERRIFIC IMPRESSION TONIGHT...
"...BECAUSE TOMORROW'S GOING TO BE TROUBLE."
END

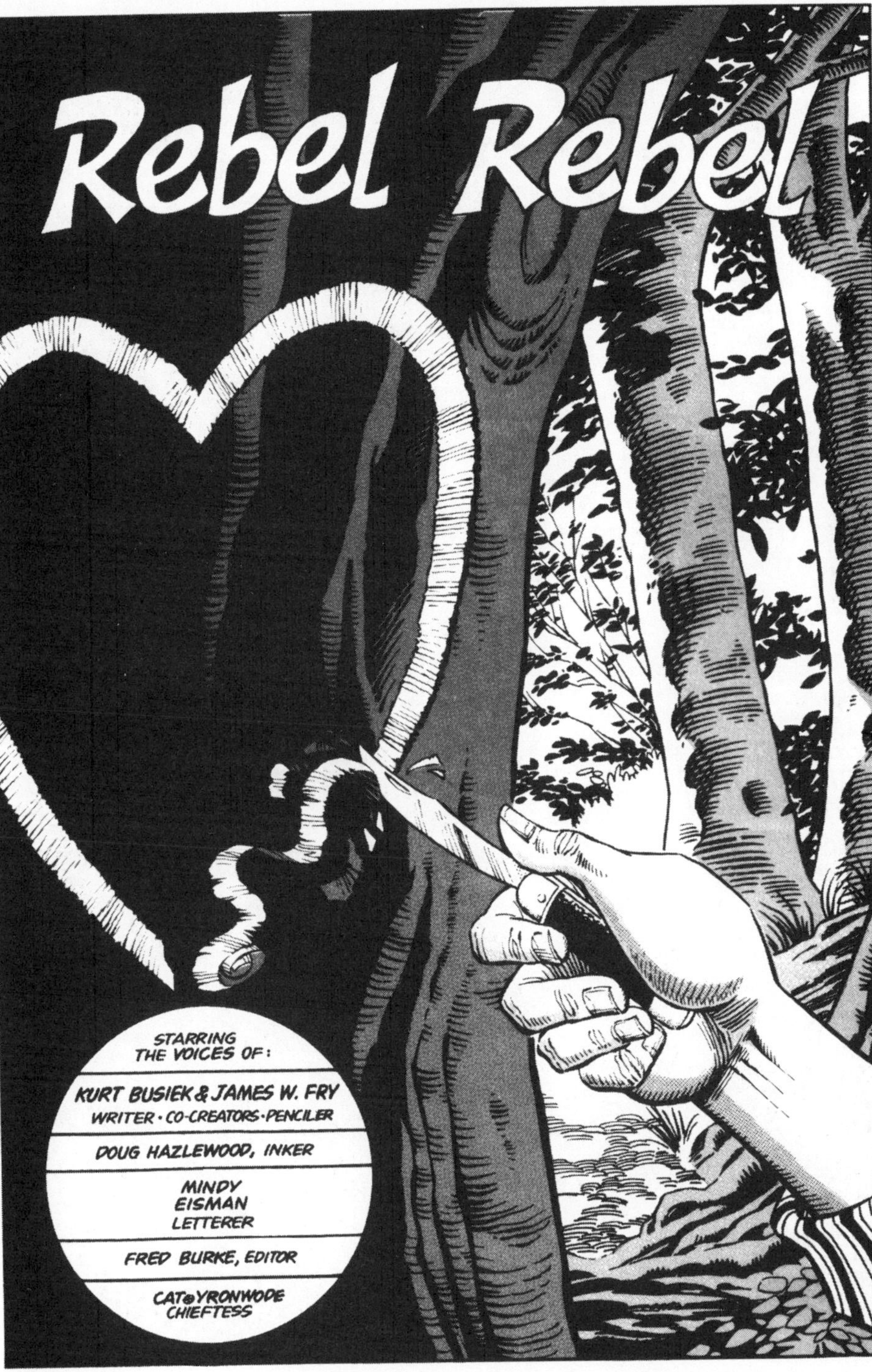
Rebel Rebel
STARRING THE VOICES OF:
KURT BUSIEK & JAMES W. FRY
WRITER · CO-CREATORS · PENCILER
DOUG HAZLEWOOD, INKER
MINDY EISMAN LETTERER
FRED BURKE, EDITOR
CAT YRONWODE CHIEFTESS

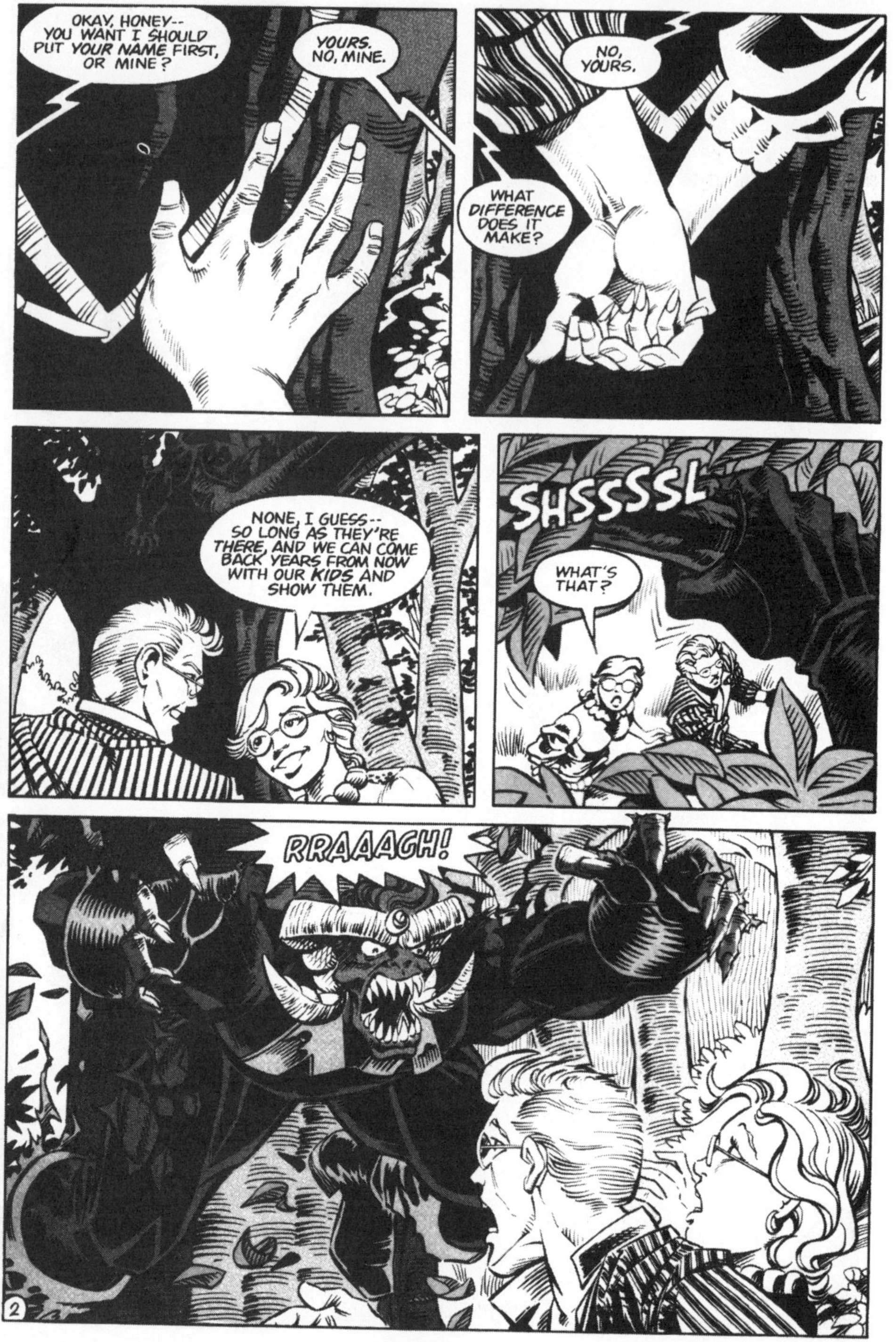

OKAY, HONEY-- YOU WANT I SHOULD PUT YOUR NAME FIRST, OR MINE?
YOURS. NO, MINE.
NO, YOURS.
WHAT DIFFERENCE DOES IT MAKE?
NONE, I GUESS-- SO LONG AS THEY'RE THERE, AND WE CAN COME BACK YEARS FROM NOW WITH OUR KIDS AND SHOW THEM.
SHSSSSL
WHAT'S THAT?
RRAAAGH!
2

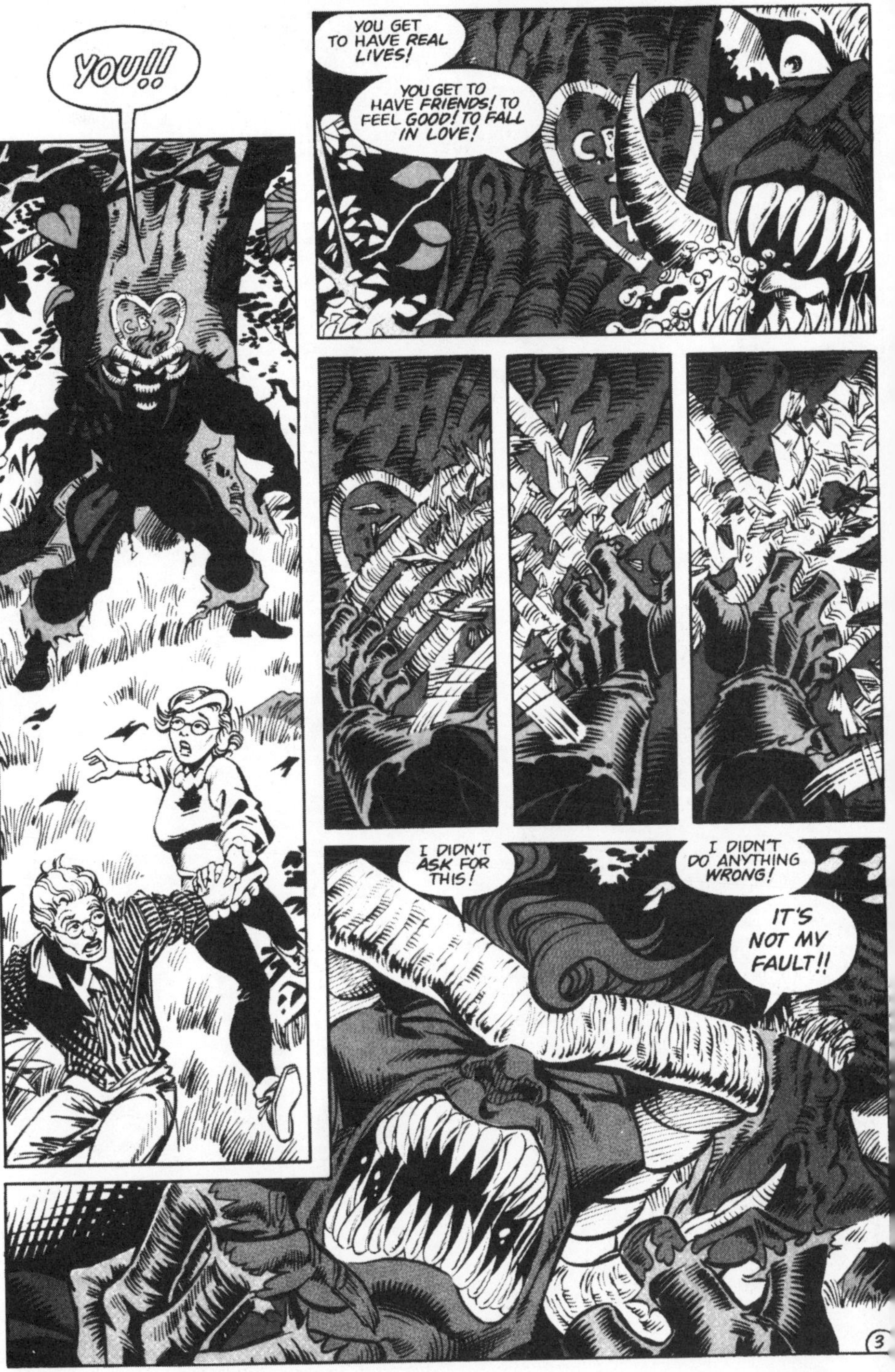
YOU!!
YOU GET TO HAVE REAL LIVES!
YOU GET TO HAVE FRIENDS! TO FEEL GOOD! TO FALL IN LOVE!
I DIDN'T ASK FOR THIS!
I DIDN'T DO ANYTHING WRONG!
IT'S NOT MY FAULT!!
3

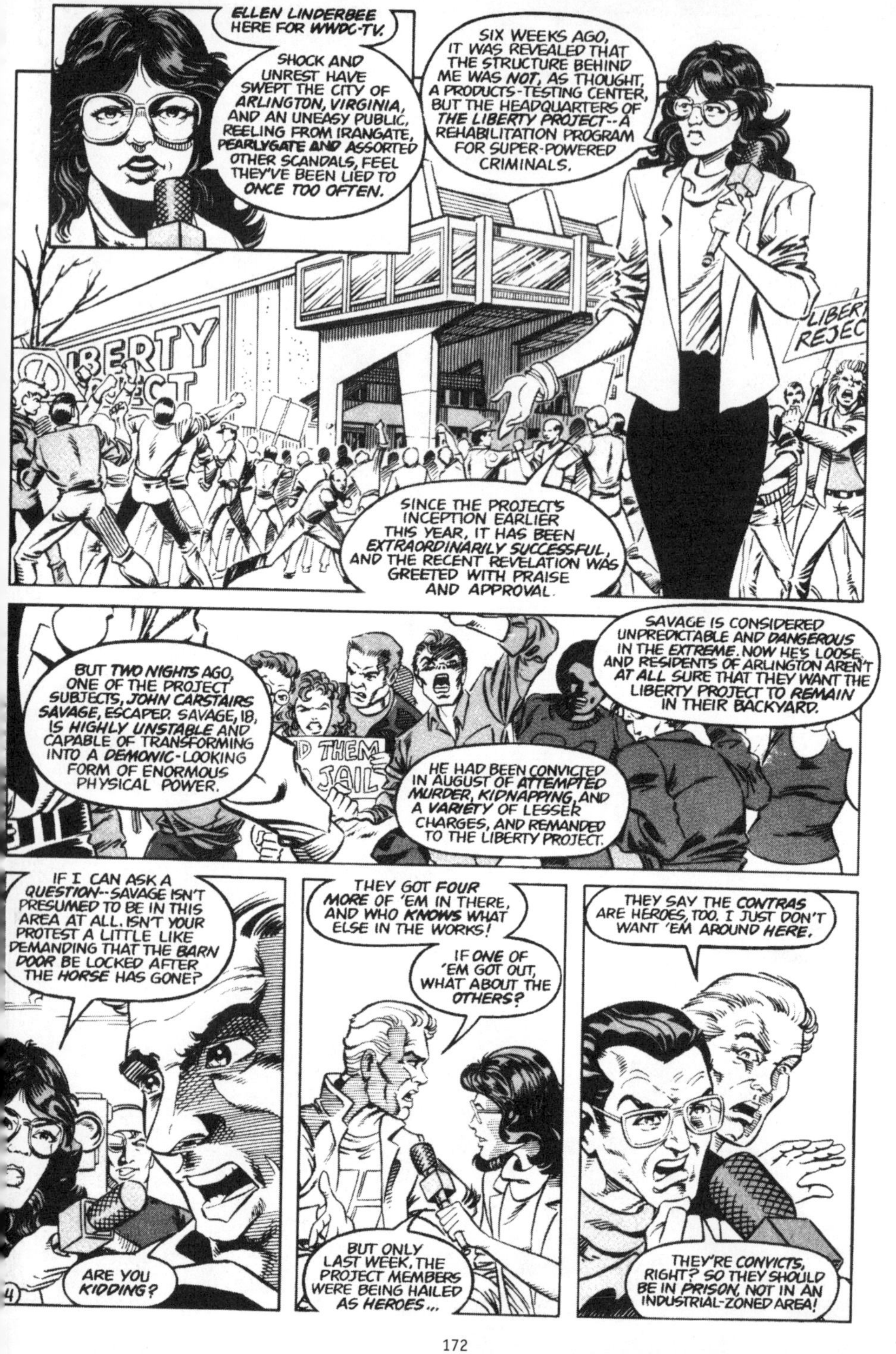
ELLEN LINDERBEE HERE FOR WWDC-TV.
SHOCK AND UNREST HAVE SWEPT THE CITY OF ARLINGTON, VIRGINIA, AND AN UNEASY PUBLIC, REELING FROM IRANGATE, PEARLYGATE AND ASSORTED OTHER SCANDALS, FEEL THEY'VE BEEN LIED TO ONCE TOO OFTEN.
SIX WEEKS AGO, IT WAS REVEALED THAT THE STRUCTURE BEHIND ME WAS NOT, AS THOUGHT, A PRODUCTS-TESTING CENTER, BUT THE HEADQUARTERS OF THE LIBERTY PROJECT--A REHABILITATION PROGRAM FOR SUPER-POWERED CRIMINALS.
LIBERTY PROJECT
SINCE THE PROJECT'S INCEPTION EARLIER THIS YEAR, IT HAS BEEN EXTRAORDINARILY SUCCESSFUL, AND THE RECENT REVELATION WAS GREETED WITH PRAISE AND APPROVAL.
BUT TWO NIGHTS AGO, ONE OF THE PROJECT SUBJECTS, JOHN CARSTAIRS SAVAGE, ESCAPED. SAVAGE, 18, IS HIGHLY UNSTABLE AND CAPABLE OF TRANSFORMING INTO A DEMONIC-LOOKING FORM OF ENORMOUS PHYSICAL POWER.
SAVAGE IS CONSIDERED UNPREDICTABLE AND DANGEROUS IN THE EXTREME. NOW HE'S LOOSE, AND RESIDENTS OF ARLINGTON AREN'T AT ALL SURE THAT THEY WANT THE LIBERTY PROJECT TO REMAIN IN THEIR BACKYARD.
HE HAD BEEN CONVICTED IN AUGUST OF ATTEMPTED MURDER, KIDNAPPING, AND A VARIETY OF LESSER CHARGES, AND REMANDED TO THE LIBERTY PROJECT.
IF I CAN ASK A QUESTION--SAVAGE ISN'T PRESUMED TO BE IN THIS AREA AT ALL. ISN'T YOUR PROTEST A LITTLE LIKE DEMANDING THAT THE BARN DOOR BE LOCKED AFTER THE HORSE HAS GONE?
ARE YOU KIDDING?
THEY GOT FOUR MORE OF 'EM IN THERE, AND WHO KNOWS WHAT ELSE IN THE WORKS!
IF ONE OF 'EM GOT OUT, WHAT ABOUT THE OTHERS?
BUT ONLY LAST WEEK, THE PROJECT MEMBERS WERE BEING HAILED AS HEROES...
THEY SAY THE CONTRAS ARE HEROES, TOO. I JUST DON'T WANT 'EM AROUND HERE.
THEY'RE CONVICTS, RIGHT? SO THEY SHOULD BE IN PRISON, NOT IN AN INDUSTRIAL-ZONED AREA!
4

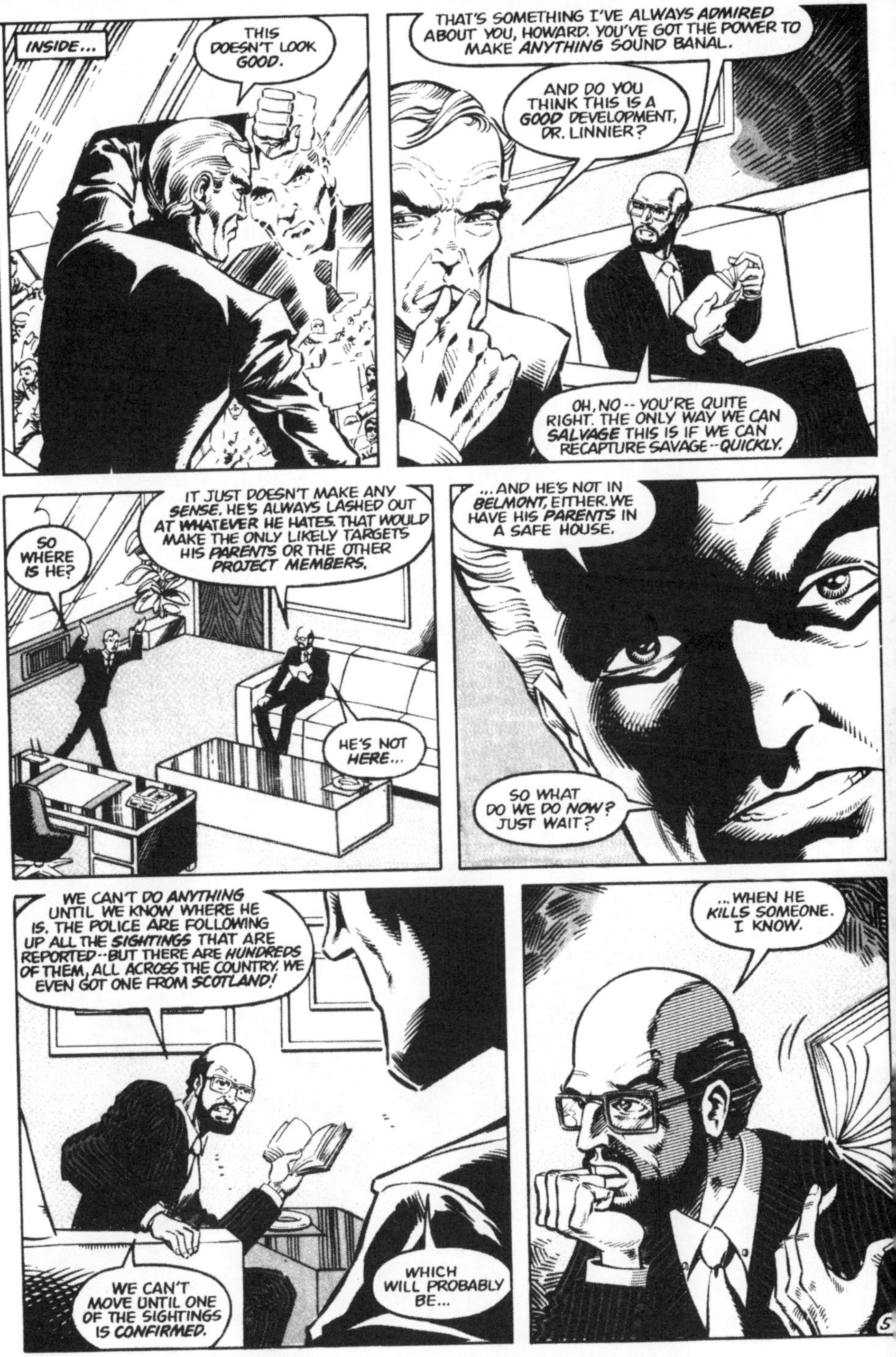
INSIDE...
THIS DOESN'T LOOK GOOD.
THAT'S SOMETHING I'VE ALWAYS ADMIRED ABOUT YOU, HOWARD. YOU'VE GOT THE POWER TO MAKE ANYTHING SOUND BANAL.
AND DO YOU THINK THIS IS A GOOD DEVELOPMENT, DR. LINNIER?
OH, NO -- YOU'RE QUITE RIGHT. THE ONLY WAY WE CAN SALVAGE THIS IS IF WE CAN RECAPTURE SAVAGE -- QUICKLY.
SO WHERE IS HE?
IT JUST DOESN'T MAKE ANY SENSE. HE'S ALWAYS LASHED OUT AT WHATEVER HE HATES. THAT WOULD MAKE THE ONLY LIKELY TARGETS HIS PARENTS OR THE OTHER PROJECT MEMBERS.
HE'S NOT HERE...
...AND HE'S NOT IN BELMONT, EITHER. WE HAVE HIS PARENTS IN A SAFE HOUSE.
SO WHAT DO WE DO NOW? JUST WAIT?
WE CAN'T DO ANYTHING UNTIL WE KNOW WHERE HE IS. THE POLICE ARE FOLLOWING UP ALL THE SIGHTINGS THAT ARE REPORTED -- BUT THERE ARE HUNDREDS OF THEM, ALL ACROSS THE COUNTRY. WE EVEN GOT ONE FROM SCOTLAND!
WE CAN'T MOVE UNTIL ONE OF THE SIGHTINGS IS CONFIRMED.
WHICH WILL PROBABLY BE...
...WHEN HE KILLS SOMEONE. I KNOW.
5

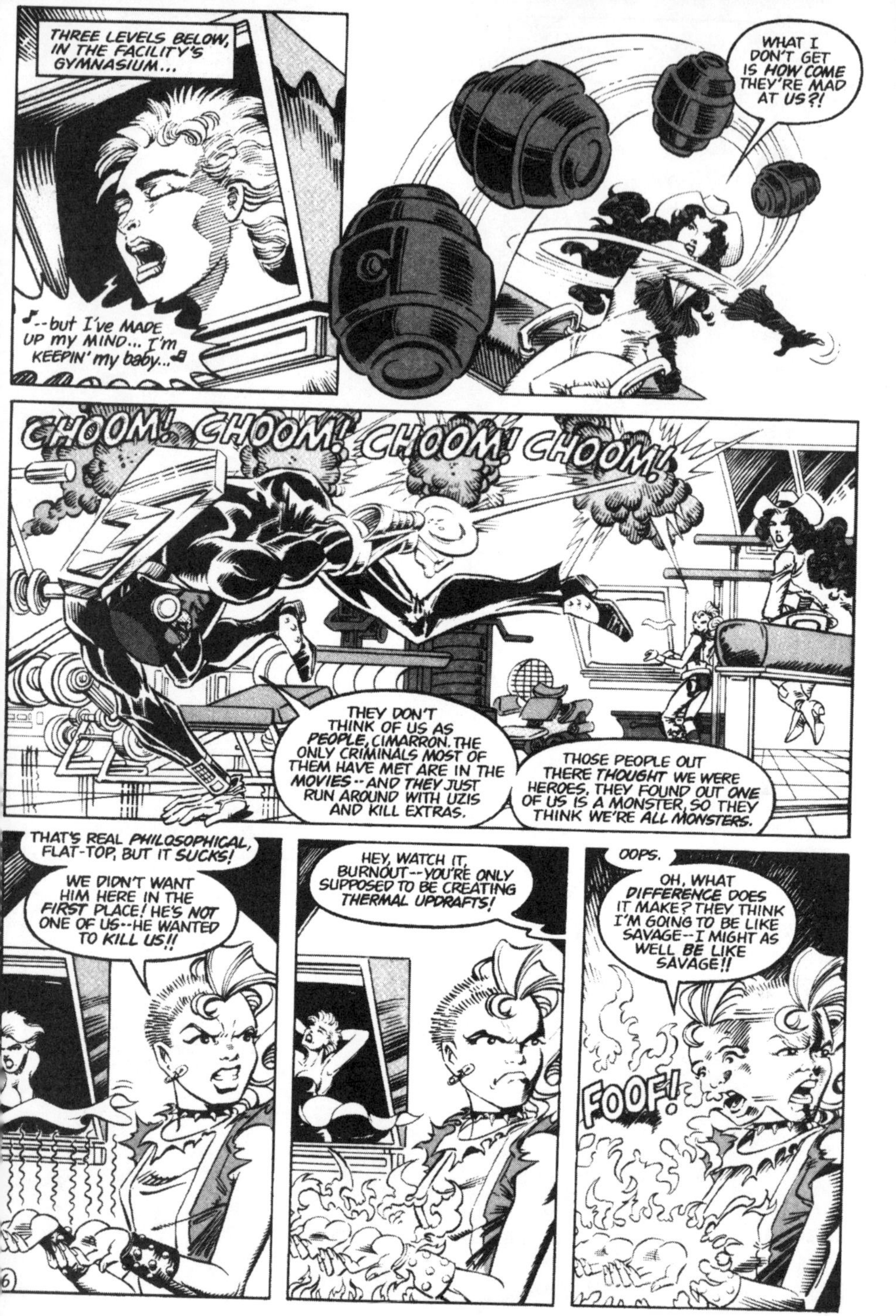
THREE LEVELS BELOW, IN THE FACILITY'S GYMNASIUM...
WHAT I DON'T GET IS HOW COME THEY'RE MAD AT US?!
♪--but I've MADE UP my MIND... I'm KEEPIN' my baby...♫
CHOOM! CHOOM! CHOOM! CHOOM!
THEY DON'T THINK OF US AS PEOPLE, CIMARRON. THE ONLY CRIMINALS MOST OF THEM HAVE MET ARE IN THE MOVIES--AND THEY JUST RUN AROUND WITH UZIS AND KILL EXTRAS.
THOSE PEOPLE OUT THERE THOUGHT WE WERE HEROES. THEY FOUND OUT ONE OF US IS A MONSTER, SO THEY THINK WE'RE ALL MONSTERS.
THAT'S REAL PHILOSOPHICAL, FLAT-TOP, BUT IT SUCKS!
WE DIDN'T WANT HIM HERE IN THE FIRST PLACE! HE'S NOT ONE OF US--HE WANTED TO KILL US!!
HEY, WATCH IT, BURNOUT--YOU'RE ONLY SUPPOSED TO BE CREATING THERMAL UPDRAFTS!
OOPS.
OH, WHAT DIFFERENCE DOES IT MAKE? THEY THINK I'M GOING TO BE LIKE SAVAGE--I MIGHT AS WELL BE LIKE SAVAGE!!
FOOF!
6

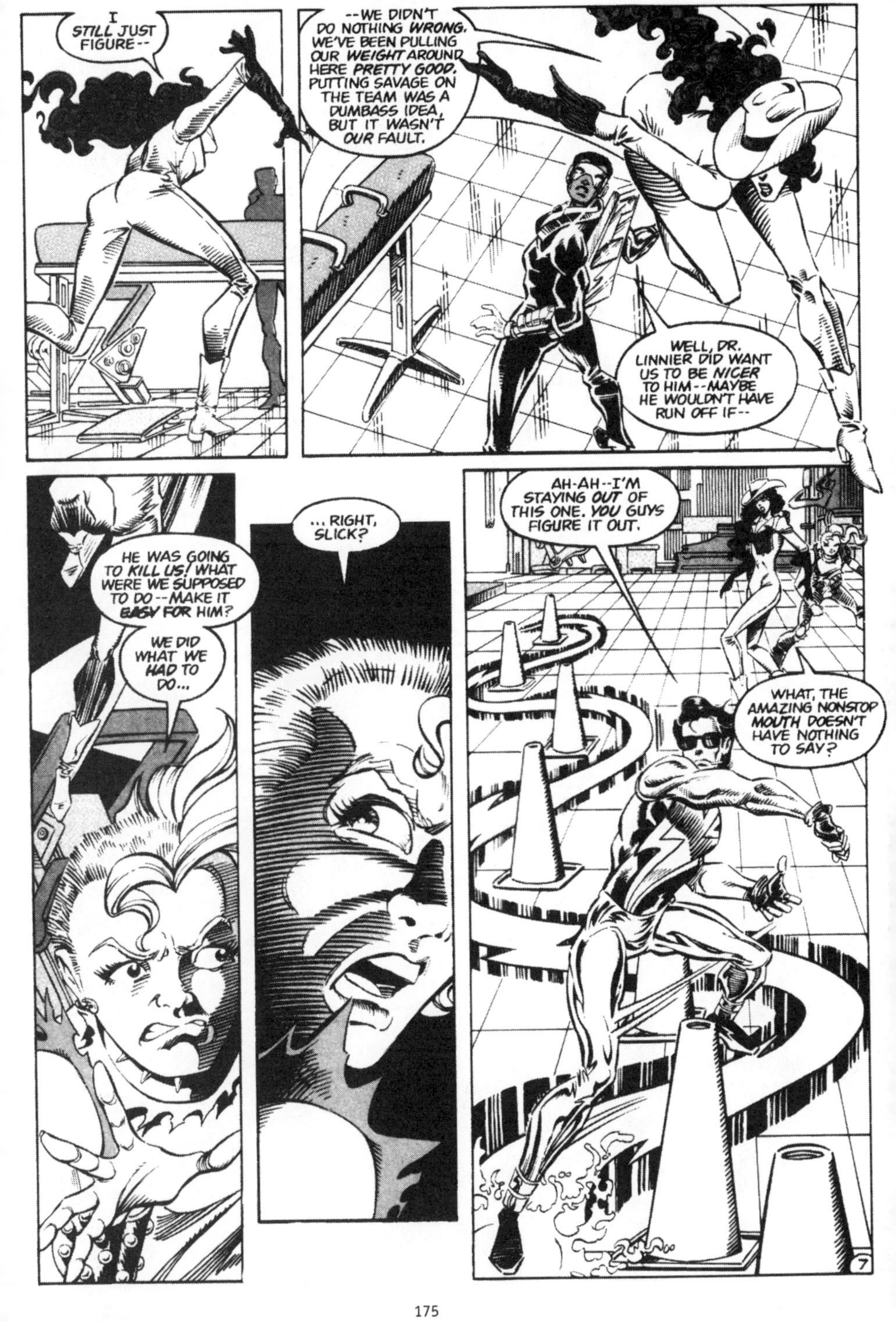
I STILL JUST FIGURE--
--WE DIDN'T DO NOTHING WRONG. WE'VE BEEN PULLING OUR WEIGHT AROUND HERE PRETTY GOOD. PUTTING SAVAGE ON THE TEAM WAS A DUMBASS IDEA, BUT IT WASN'T OUR FAULT.
WELL, DR. LINNIER DID WANT US TO BE NICER TO HIM--MAYBE HE WOULDN'T HAVE RUN OFF IF--
HE WAS GOING TO KILL US! WHAT WERE WE SUPPOSED TO DO--MAKE IT EASY FOR HIM?
WE DID WHAT WE HAD TO DO...
...RIGHT, SLICK?
AH-AH--I'M STAYING OUT OF THIS ONE. YOU GUYS FIGURE IT OUT.
WHAT, THE AMAZING NONSTOP MOUTH DOESN'T HAVE NOTHING TO SAY?
7

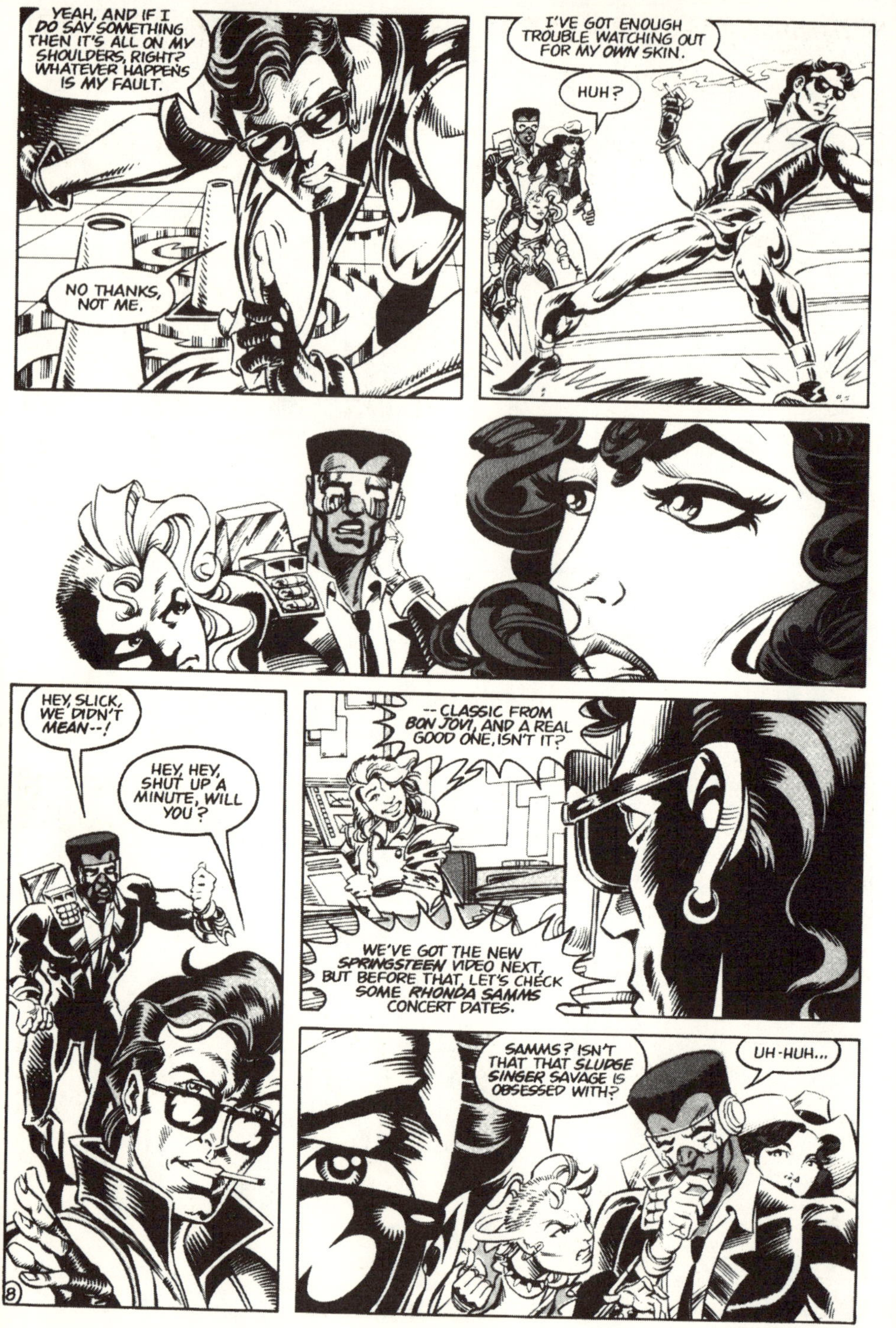

YEAH, AND IF I DO SAY SOMETHING THEN IT'S ALL ON MY SHOULDERS, RIGHT? WHATEVER HAPPENS IS MY FAULT.
NO THANKS, NOT ME.
I'VE GOT ENOUGH TROUBLE WATCHING OUT FOR MY OWN SKIN.
HUH?
HEY, SLICK, WE DIDN'T MEAN--!
HEY, HEY, SHUT UP A MINUTE, WILL YOU?
--CLASSIC FROM BON JOVI, AND A REAL GOOD ONE, ISN'T IT?
WE'VE GOT THE NEW SPRINGSTEEN VIDEO NEXT, BUT BEFORE THAT, LET'S CHECK SOME RHONDA SAMMS CONCERT DATES.
SAMMS? ISN'T THAT THAT SLUDGE SINGER SAVAGE IS OBSESSED WITH?
UH-HUH...
8

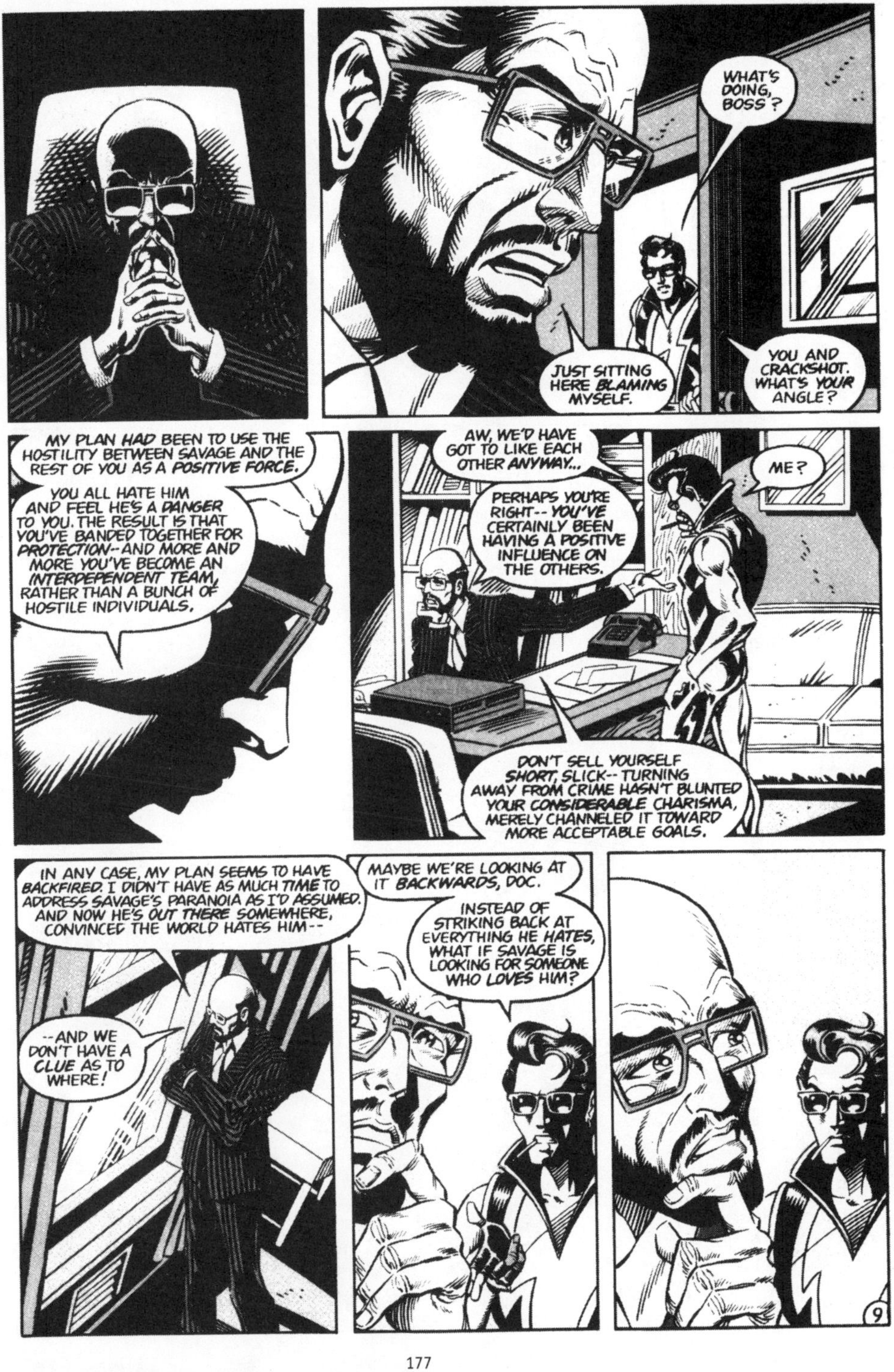

WHAT'S DOING, BOSS?
JUST SITTING HERE BLAMING MYSELF.
YOU AND CRACKSHOT. WHAT'S YOUR ANGLE?
MY PLAN HAD BEEN TO USE THE HOSTILITY BETWEEN SAVAGE AND THE REST OF YOU AS A POSITIVE FORCE.
YOU ALL HATE HIM AND FEEL HE'S A DANGER TO YOU. THE RESULT IS THAT YOU'VE BANDED TOGETHER FOR PROTECTION--AND MORE AND MORE YOU'VE BECOME AN INTERDEPENDENT TEAM, RATHER THAN A BUNCH OF HOSTILE INDIVIDUALS.
AW, WE'D HAVE GOT TO LIKE EACH OTHER ANYWAY...
PERHAPS YOU'RE RIGHT-- YOU'VE CERTAINLY BEEN HAVING A POSITIVE INFLUENCE ON THE OTHERS.
ME?
DON'T SELL YOURSELF SHORT, SLICK-- TURNING AWAY FROM CRIME HASN'T BLUNTED YOUR CONSIDERABLE CHARISMA, MERELY CHANNELED IT TOWARD MORE ACCEPTABLE GOALS.
IN ANY CASE, MY PLAN SEEMS TO HAVE BACKFIRED. I DIDN'T HAVE AS MUCH TIME TO ADDRESS SAVAGE'S PARANOIA AS I'D ASSUMED. AND NOW HE'S OUT THERE SOMEWHERE, CONVINCED THE WORLD HATES HIM--
--AND WE DON'T HAVE A CLUE AS TO WHERE!
MAYBE WE'RE LOOKING AT IT BACKWARDS, DOC.
INSTEAD OF STRIKING BACK AT EVERYTHING HE HATES, WHAT IF SAVAGE IS LOOKING FOR SOMEONE WHO LOVES HIM?
9

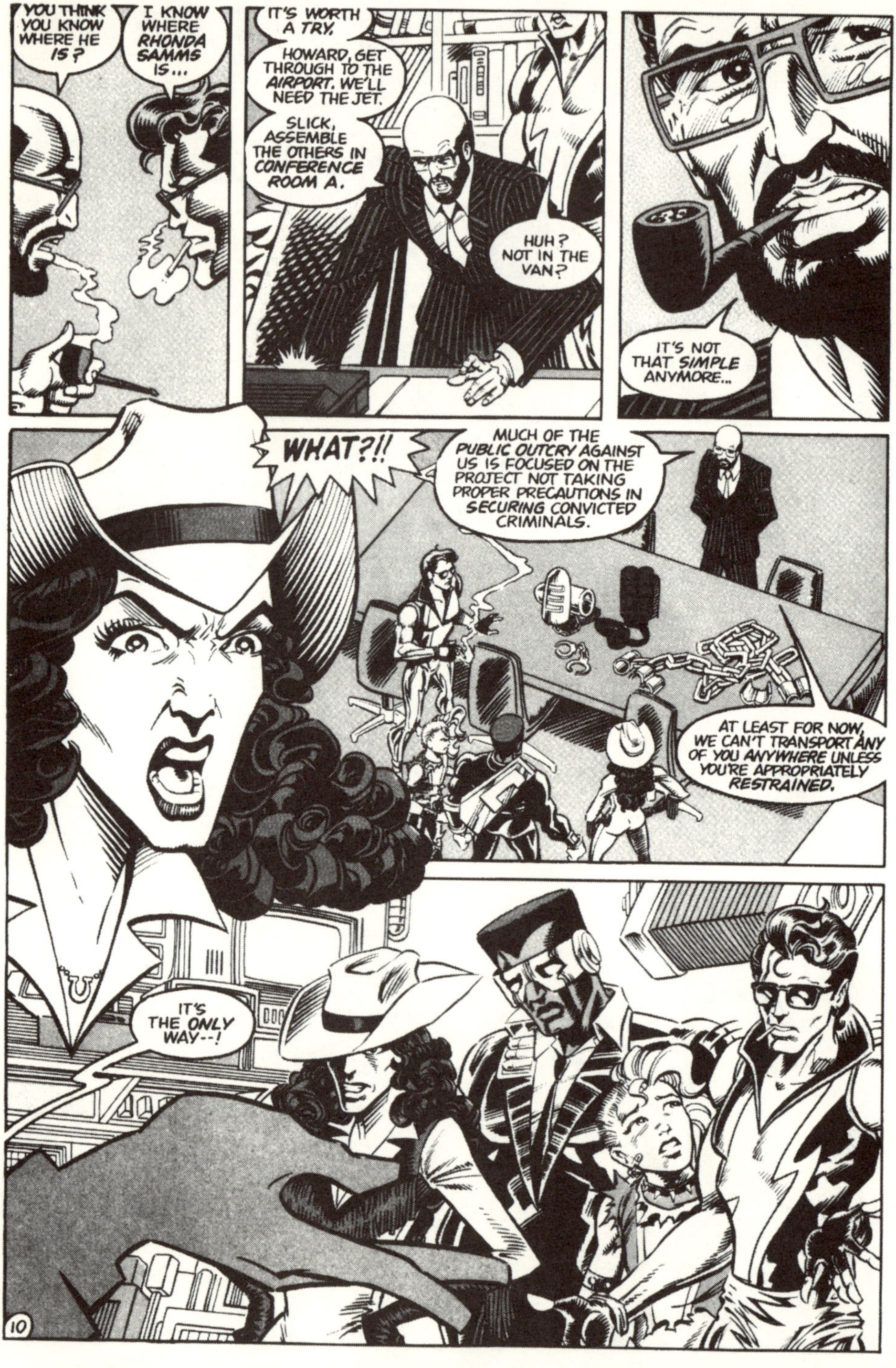
YOU THINK YOU KNOW WHERE HE IS?
I KNOW WHERE RHONDA SAMMS IS...
IT'S WORTH A TRY.
HOWARD, GET THROUGH TO THE AIRPORT. WE'LL NEED THE JET.
SLICK, ASSEMBLE THE OTHERS IN CONFERENCE ROOM A.
HUH? NOT IN THE VAN?
IT'S NOT THAT SIMPLE ANYMORE...
WHAT?!!
MUCH OF THE PUBLIC OUTCRY AGAINST US IS FOCUSED ON THE PROJECT NOT TAKING PROPER PRECAUTIONS IN SECURING CONVICTED CRIMINALS.
AT LEAST FOR NOW, WE CAN'T TRANSPORT ANY OF YOU ANYWHERE UNLESS YOU'RE APPROPRIATELY RESTRAINED.
IT'S THE ONLY WAY--!
10

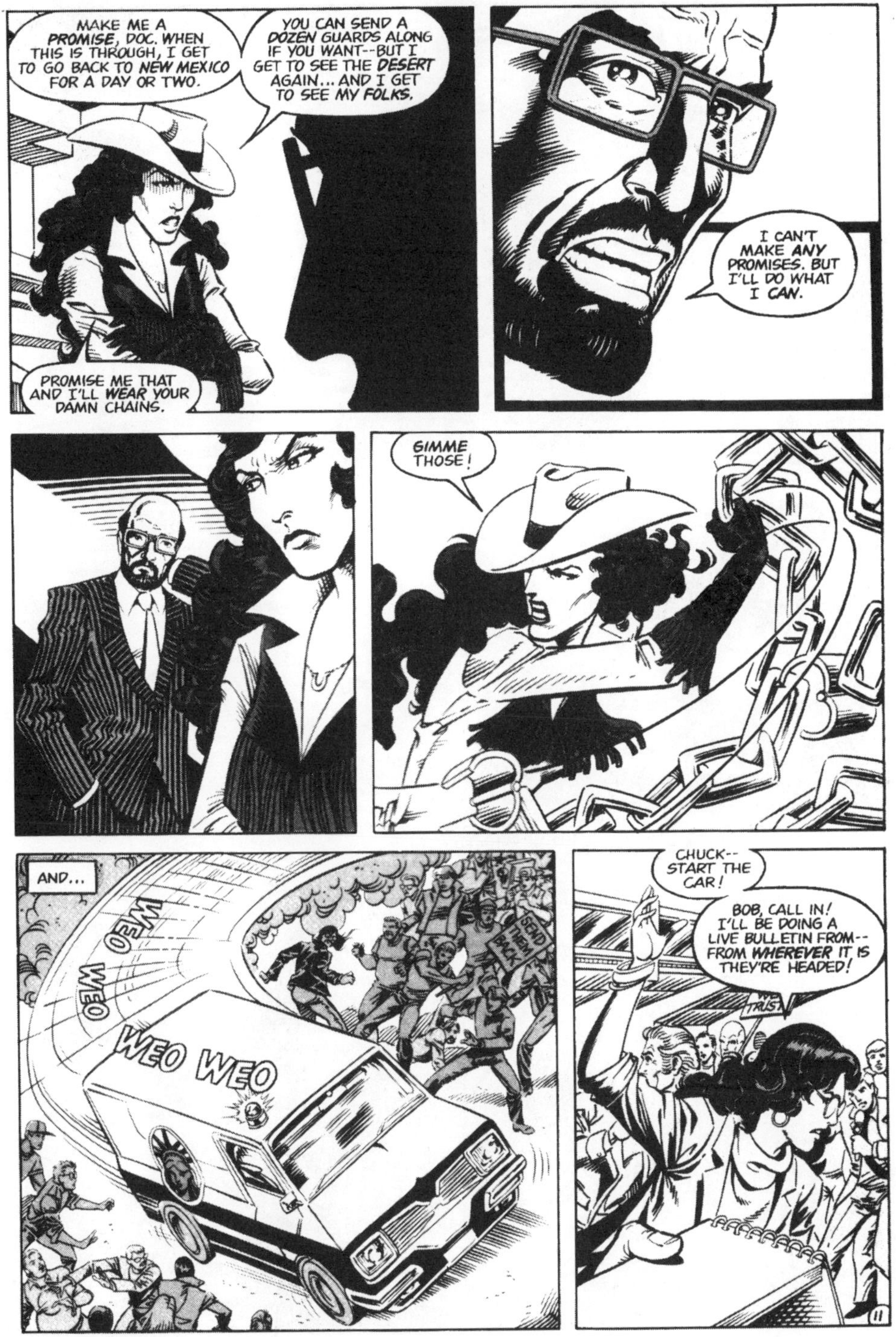
MAKE ME A PROMISE, DOC. WHEN THIS IS THROUGH, I GET TO GO BACK TO NEW MEXICO FOR A DAY OR TWO.
YOU CAN SEND A DOZEN GUARDS ALONG IF YOU WANT--BUT I GET TO SEE THE DESERT AGAIN... AND I GET TO SEE MY FOLKS.
PROMISE ME THAT AND I'LL WEAR YOUR DAMN CHAINS.
I CAN'T MAKE ANY PROMISES. BUT I'LL DO WHAT I CAN.
GIMME THOSE!
AND...
WEO WEO
WEO WEO
CHUCK-- START THE CAR!
BOB, CALL IN! I'LL BE DOING A LIVE BULLETIN FROM-- FROM WHEREVER IT IS THEY'RE HEADED!

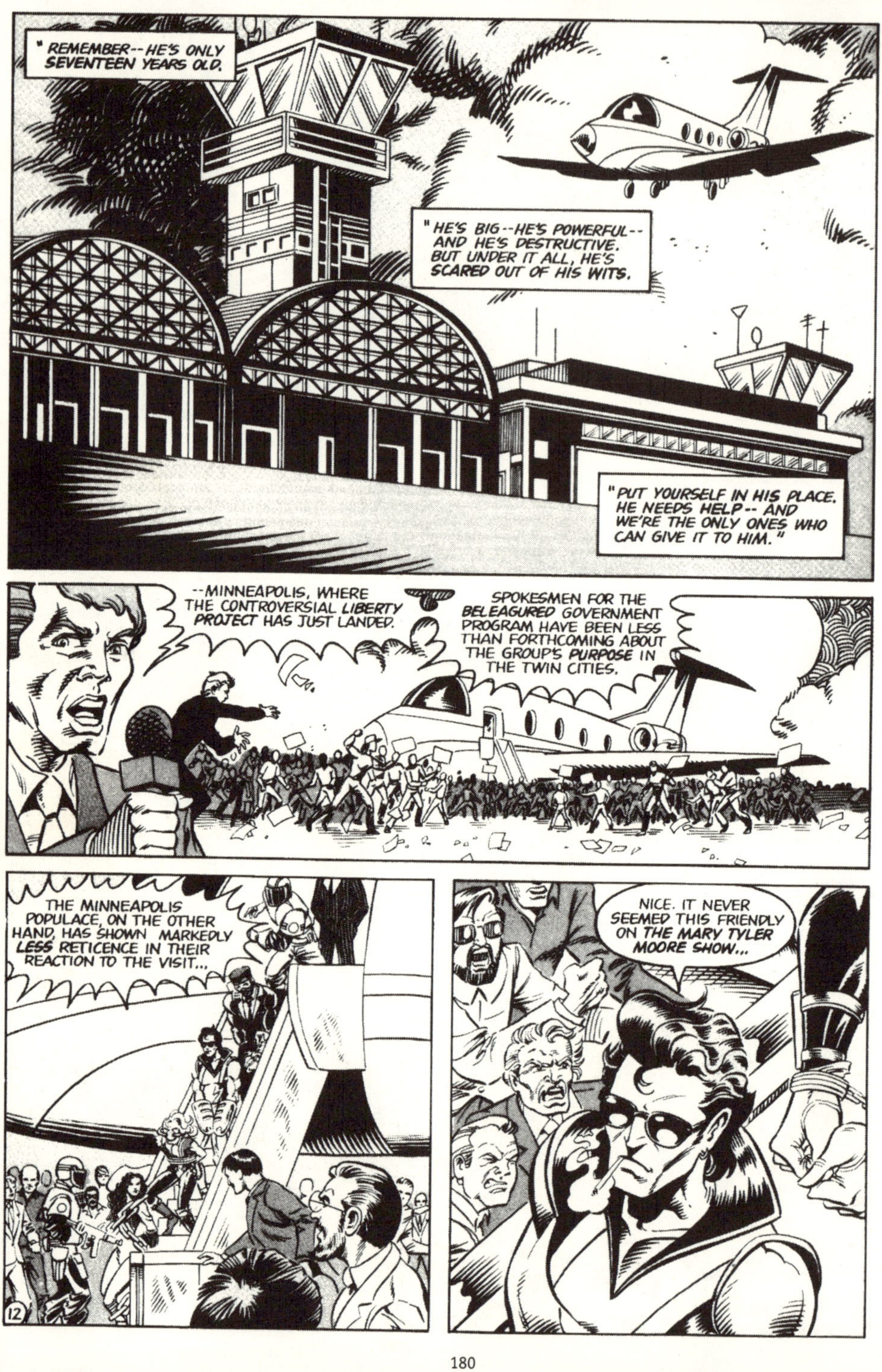
"REMEMBER--HE'S ONLY SEVENTEEN YEARS OLD.
"HE'S BIG--HE'S POWERFUL--AND HE'S DESTRUCTIVE. BUT UNDER IT ALL, HE'S SCARED OUT OF HIS WITS.
"PUT YOURSELF IN HIS PLACE. HE NEEDS HELP-- AND WE'RE THE ONLY ONES WHO CAN GIVE IT TO HIM."
--MINNEAPOLIS, WHERE THE CONTROVERSIAL LIBERTY PROJECT HAS JUST LANDED.
SPOKESMEN FOR THE BELEAGURED GOVERNMENT PROGRAM HAVE BEEN LESS THAN FORTHCOMING ABOUT THE GROUP'S PURPOSE IN THE TWIN CITIES.
THE MINNEAPOLIS POPULACE, ON THE OTHER HAND, HAS SHOWN MARKEDLY LESS RETICENCE IN THEIR REACTION TO THE VISIT...
12
NICE. IT NEVER SEEMED THIS FRIENDLY ON THE MARY TYLER MOORE SHOW...

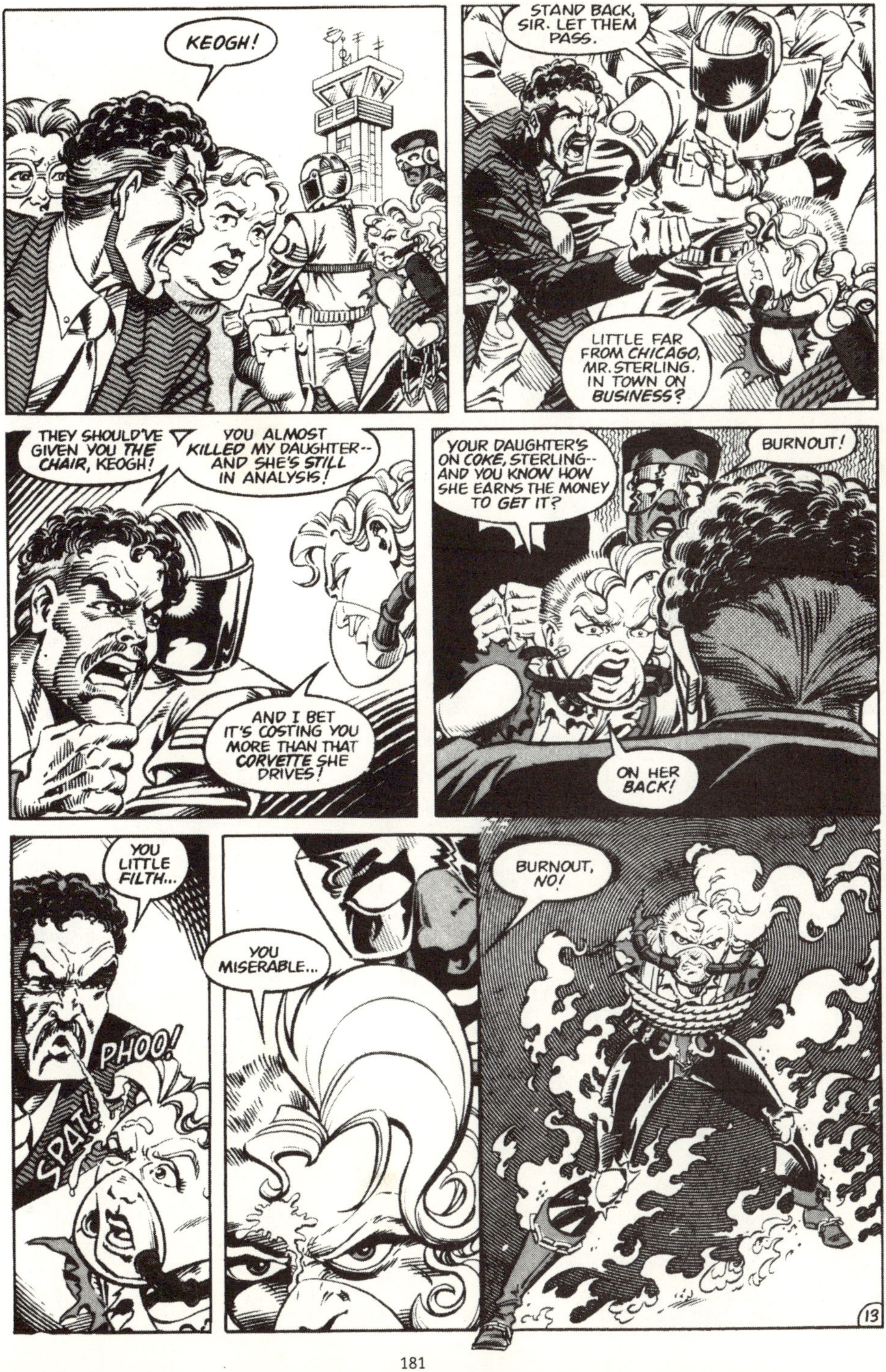
KEOGH!
STAND BACK, SIR. LET THEM PASS.
LITTLE FAR FROM CHICAGO, MR. STERLING. IN TOWN ON BUSINESS?
THEY SHOULD'VE GIVEN YOU THE CHAIR, KEOGH!
YOU ALMOST KILLED MY DAUGHTER-- AND SHE'S STILL IN ANALYSIS!
AND I BET IT'S COSTING YOU MORE THAN THAT CORVETTE SHE DRIVES!
YOUR DAUGHTER'S ON COKE, STERLING-- AND YOU KNOW HOW SHE EARNS THE MONEY TO GET IT?
BURNOUT!
ON HER BACK!
YOU LITTLE FILTH...
PHOO!
SPAT!
YOU MISERABLE...
BURNOUT, NO!
13

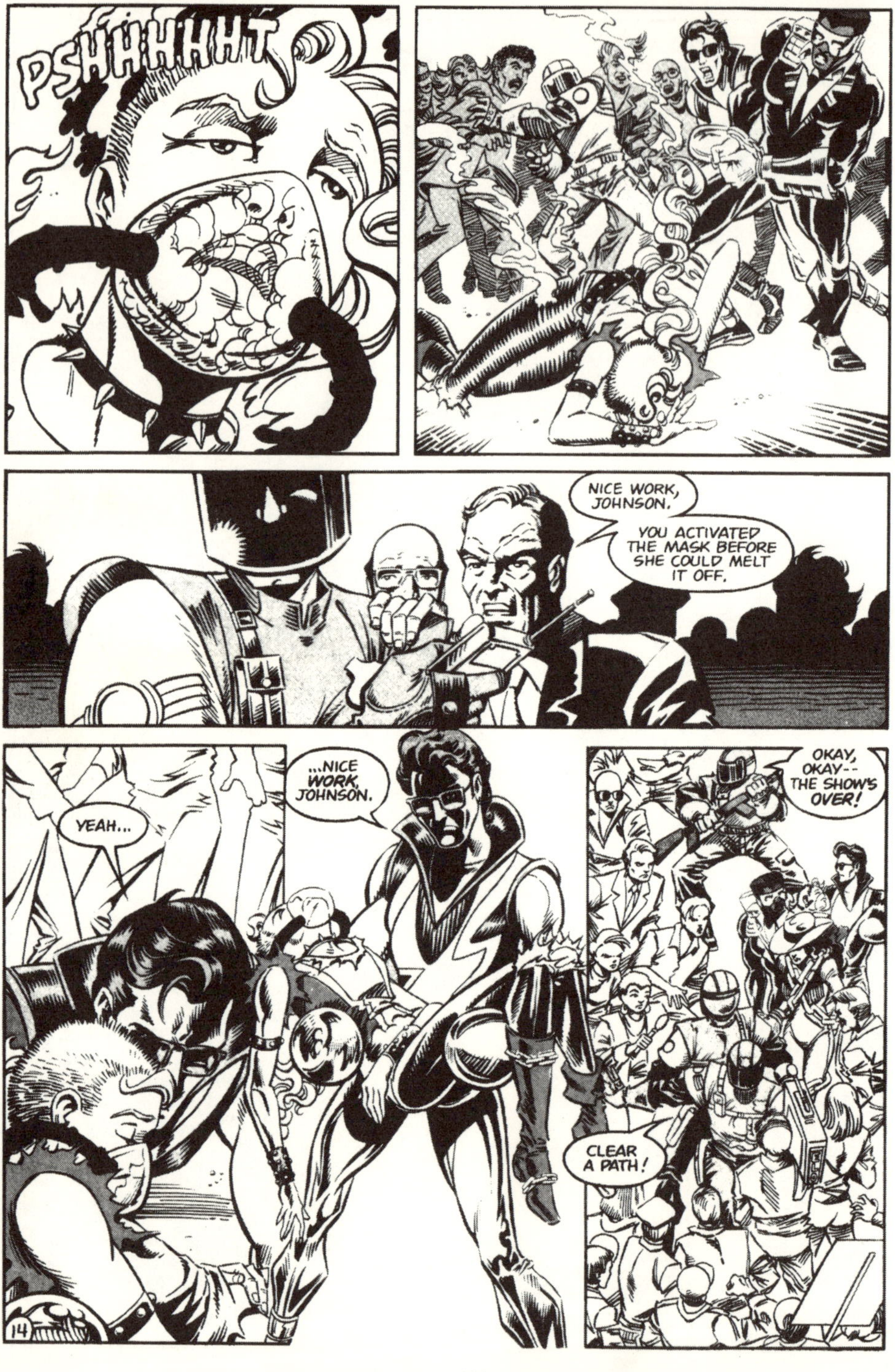
PSHHHHHT
NICE WORK, JOHNSON.
YOU ACTIVATED THE MASK BEFORE SHE COULD MELT IT OFF.
YEAH...
...NICE WORK, JOHNSON.
OKAY, OKAY-- THE SHOW'S OVER!
CLEAR A PATH!
14

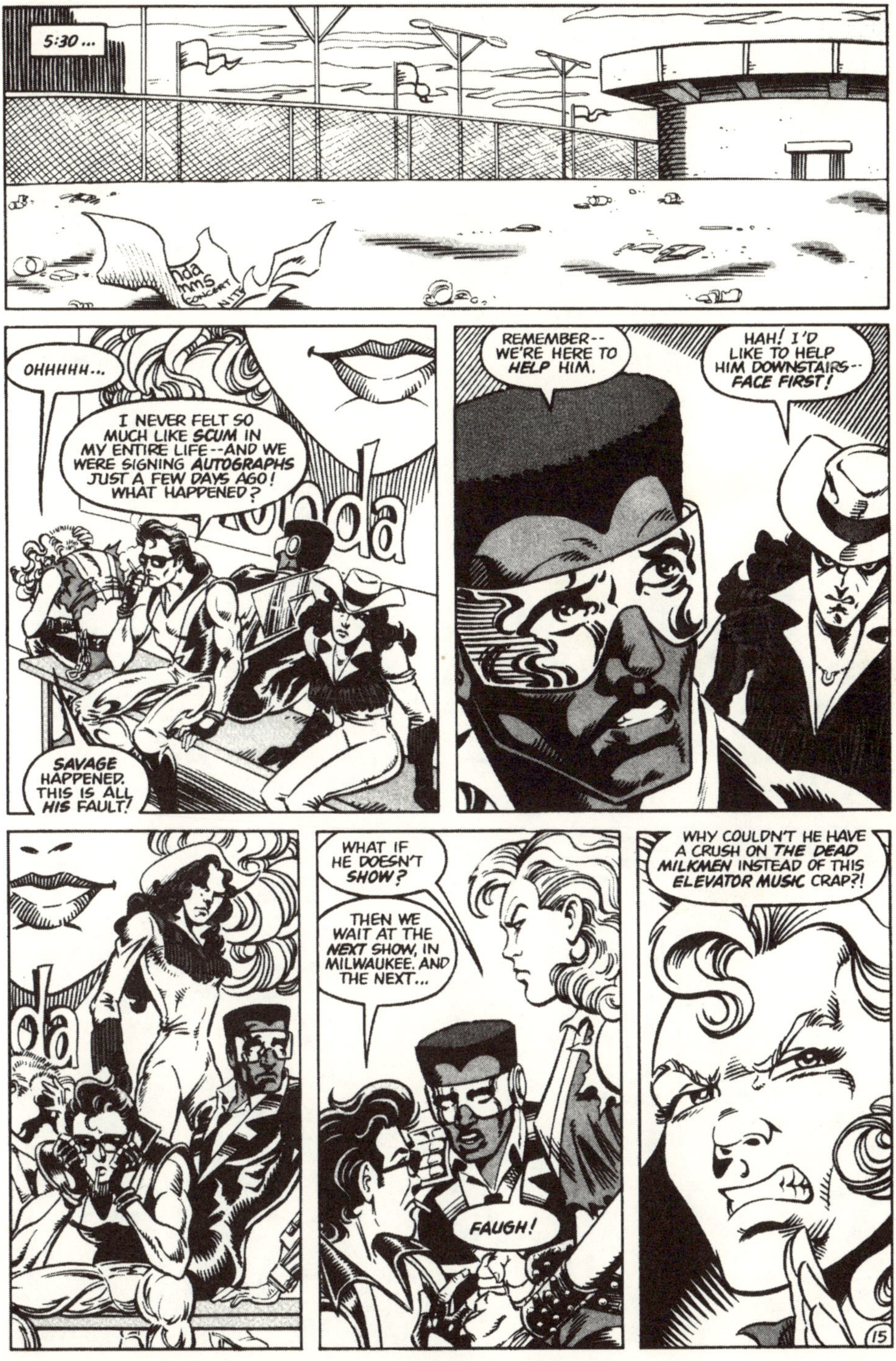
5:30...
nda
nms
CONCERT
NITE
OHHHHH...
I NEVER FELT SO MUCH LIKE SCUM IN MY ENTIRE LIFE--AND WE WERE SIGNING AUTOGRAPHS JUST A FEW DAYS AGO! WHAT HAPPENED?
SAVAGE HAPPENED. THIS IS ALL HIS FAULT!
REMEMBER--WE'RE HERE TO HELP HIM.
HAH! I'D LIKE TO HELP HIM DOWNSTAIRS--FACE FIRST!
WHAT IF HE DOESN'T SHOW?
THEN WE WAIT AT THE NEXT SHOW, IN MILWAUKEE. AND THE NEXT...
FAUGH!
WHY COULDN'T HE HAVE A CRUSH ON THE DEAD MILKMEN INSTEAD OF THIS ELEVATOR MUSIC CRAP?!
15

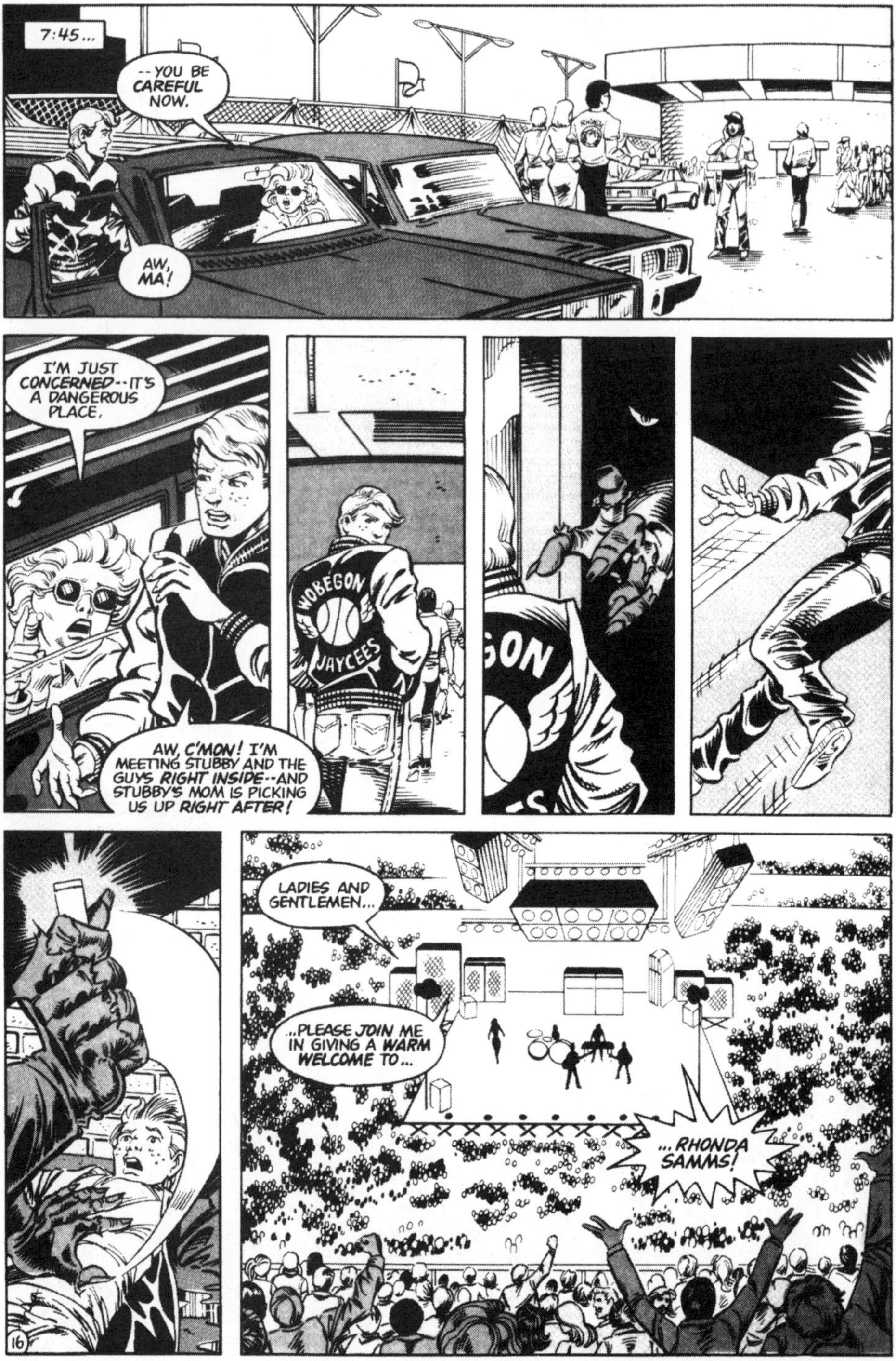
7:45...
--YOU BE CAREFUL NOW.
AW, MA!
I'M JUST CONCERNED--IT'S A DANGEROUS PLACE.
AW, C'MON! I'M MEETING STUBBY AND THE GUYS RIGHT INSIDE--AND STUBBY'S MOM IS PICKING US UP RIGHT AFTER!
WOBEGON JAYCEES
GON
16
LADIES AND GENTLEMEN...
...PLEASE JOIN ME IN GIVING A WARM WELCOME TO...
...RHONDA SAMMS!

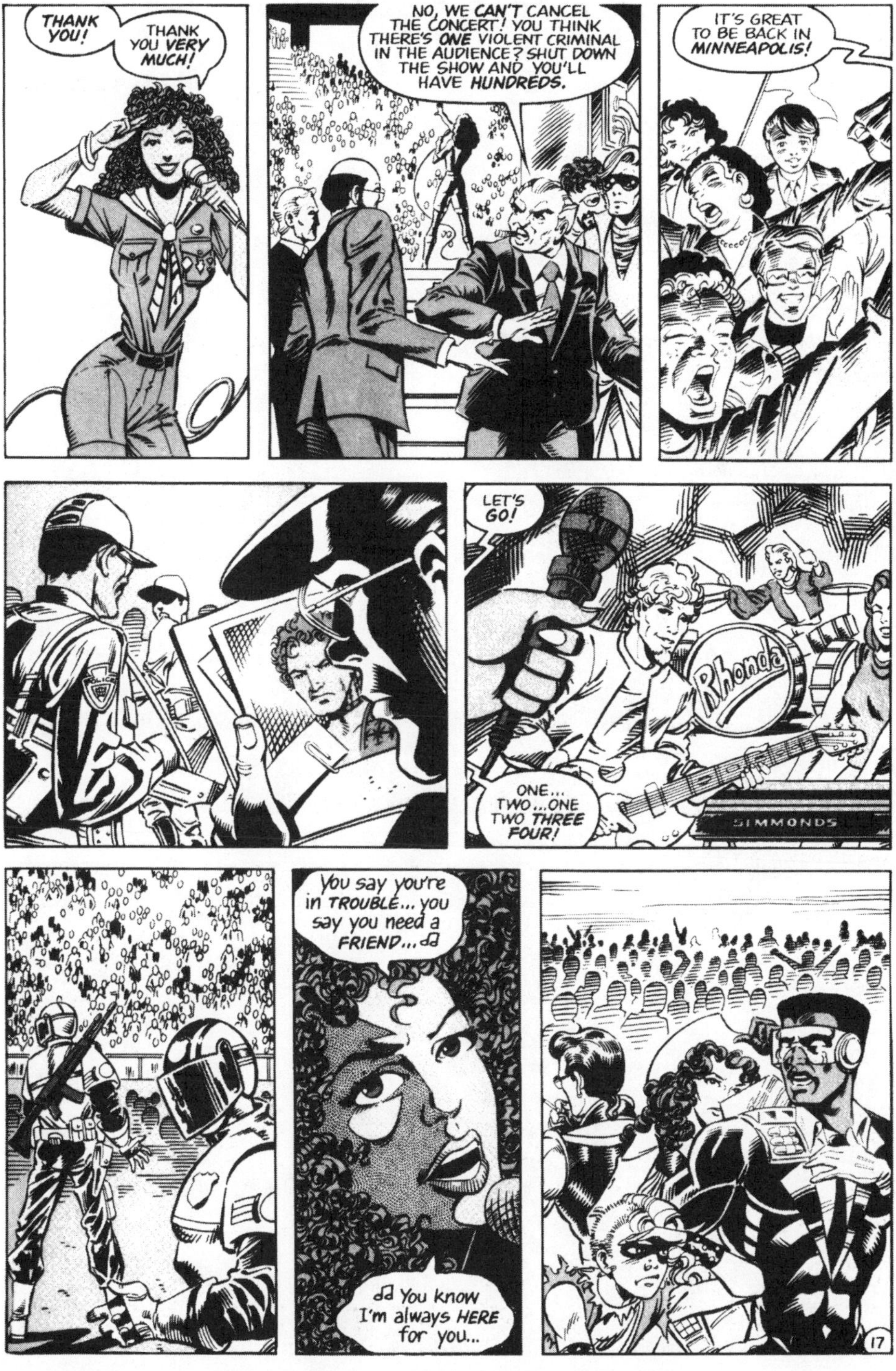
THANK YOU!
THANK YOU VERY MUCH!
NO, WE CAN'T CANCEL THE CONCERT! YOU THINK THERE'S ONE VIOLENT CRIMINAL IN THE AUDIENCE? SHUT DOWN THE SHOW AND YOU'LL HAVE HUNDREDS.
IT'S GREAT TO BE BACK IN MINNEAPOLIS!
LET'S GO!
Rhonda
ONE... TWO...ONE TWO THREE FOUR!
SIMMONDS
You say you're in TROUBLE... you say you need a FRIEND...
You know I'm always HERE for you...
17

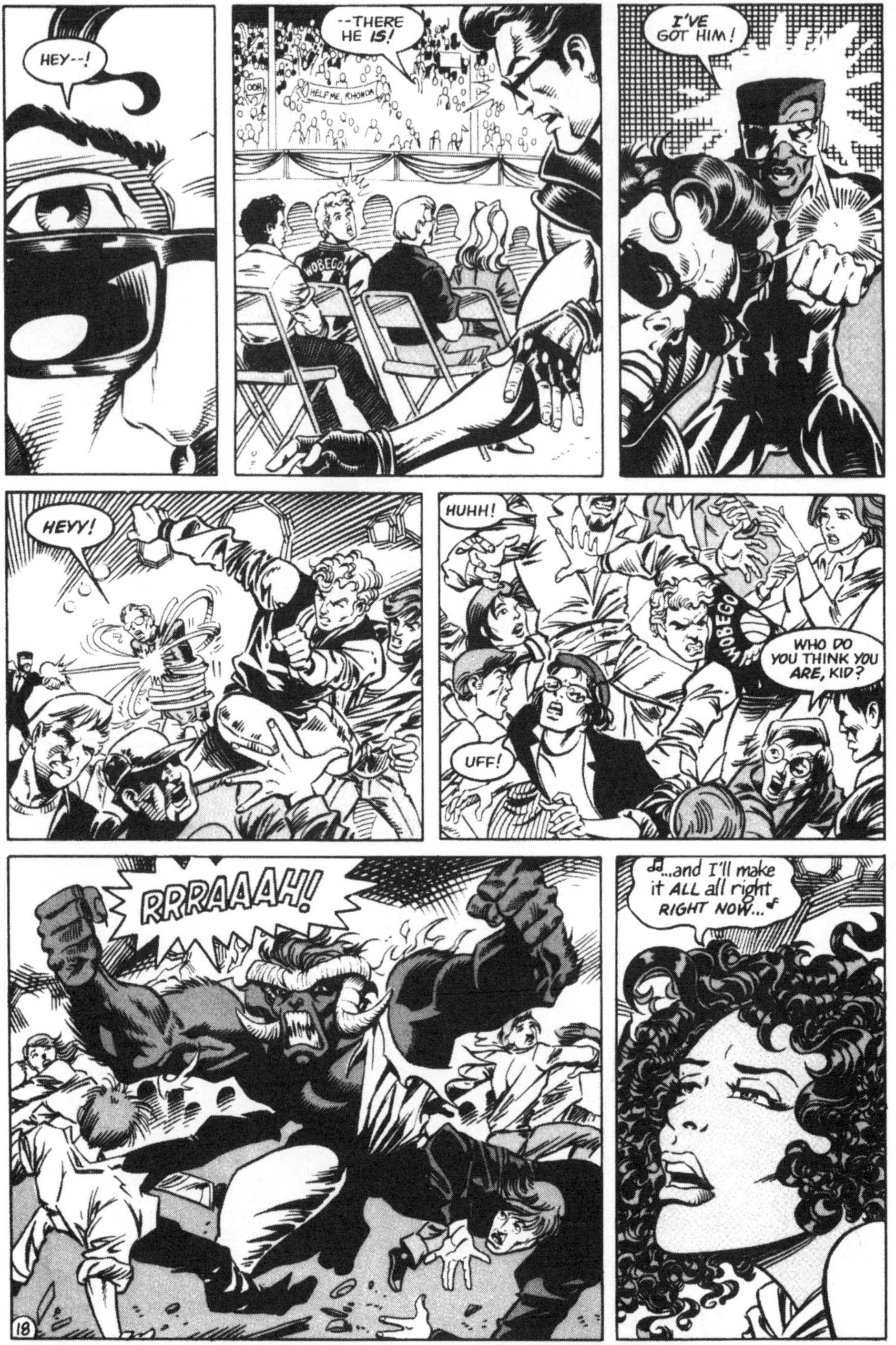
HEY--!
--THERE HE IS!
OOH
HELP ME, RHONDA
WOBEGON
I'VE GOT HIM!
HEYY!
HUHH!
WOBEGO
WHO DO YOU THINK YOU ARE, KID?
UFF!
RRRAAAH!
...and I'll make it ALL all right RIGHT NOW...
18

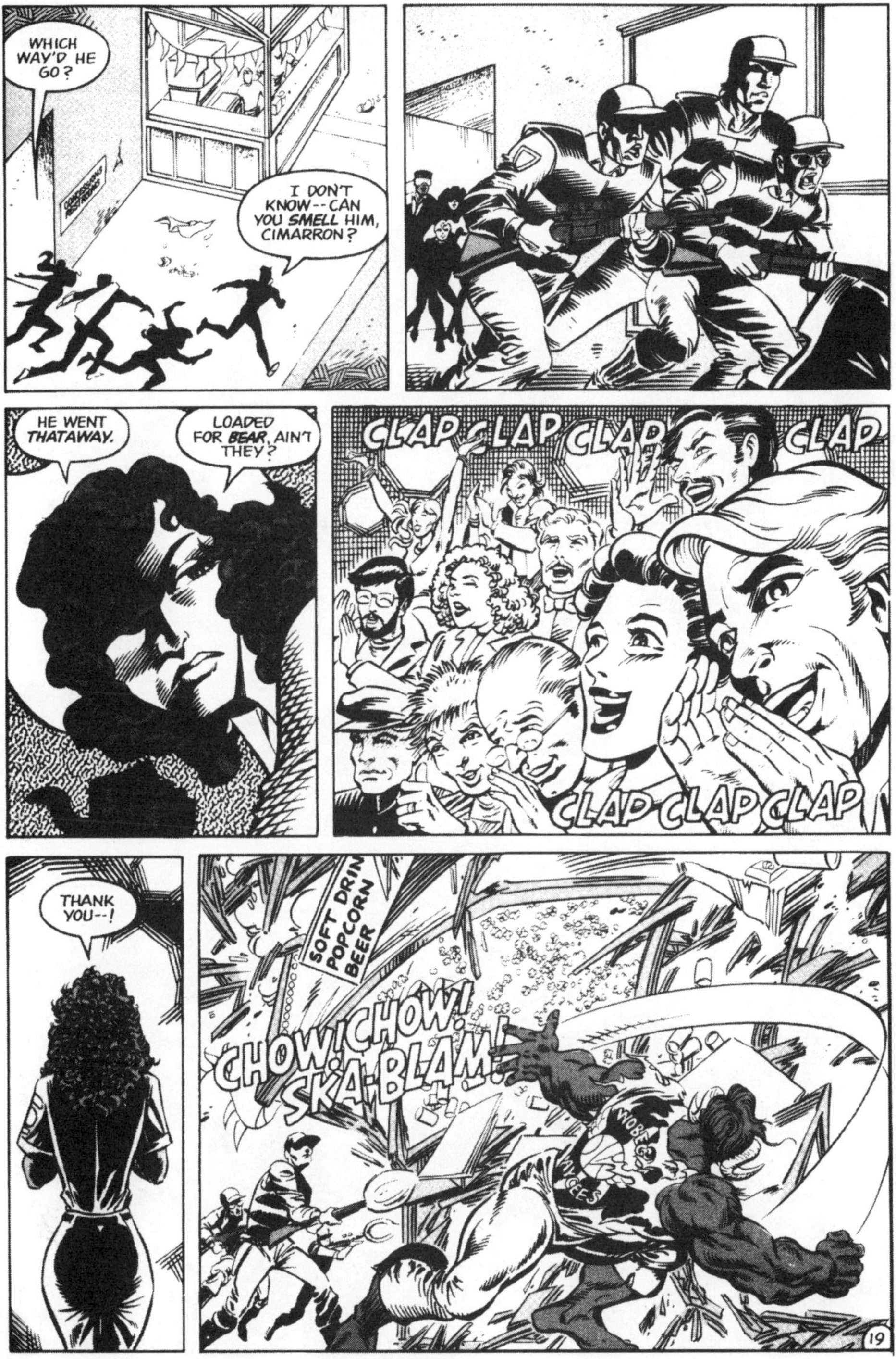
WHICH WAY'D HE GO?
I DON'T KNOW--CAN YOU SMELL HIM, CIMARRON?
HE WENT THATAWAY.
LOADED FOR BEAR, AIN'T THEY?
CLAP CLAP CLAP CLAP
CLAP CLAP CLAP
THANK YOU--!
SOFT DRIN
POPCORN
BEER
CHOW! CHOW! SKA-BLAM!
19

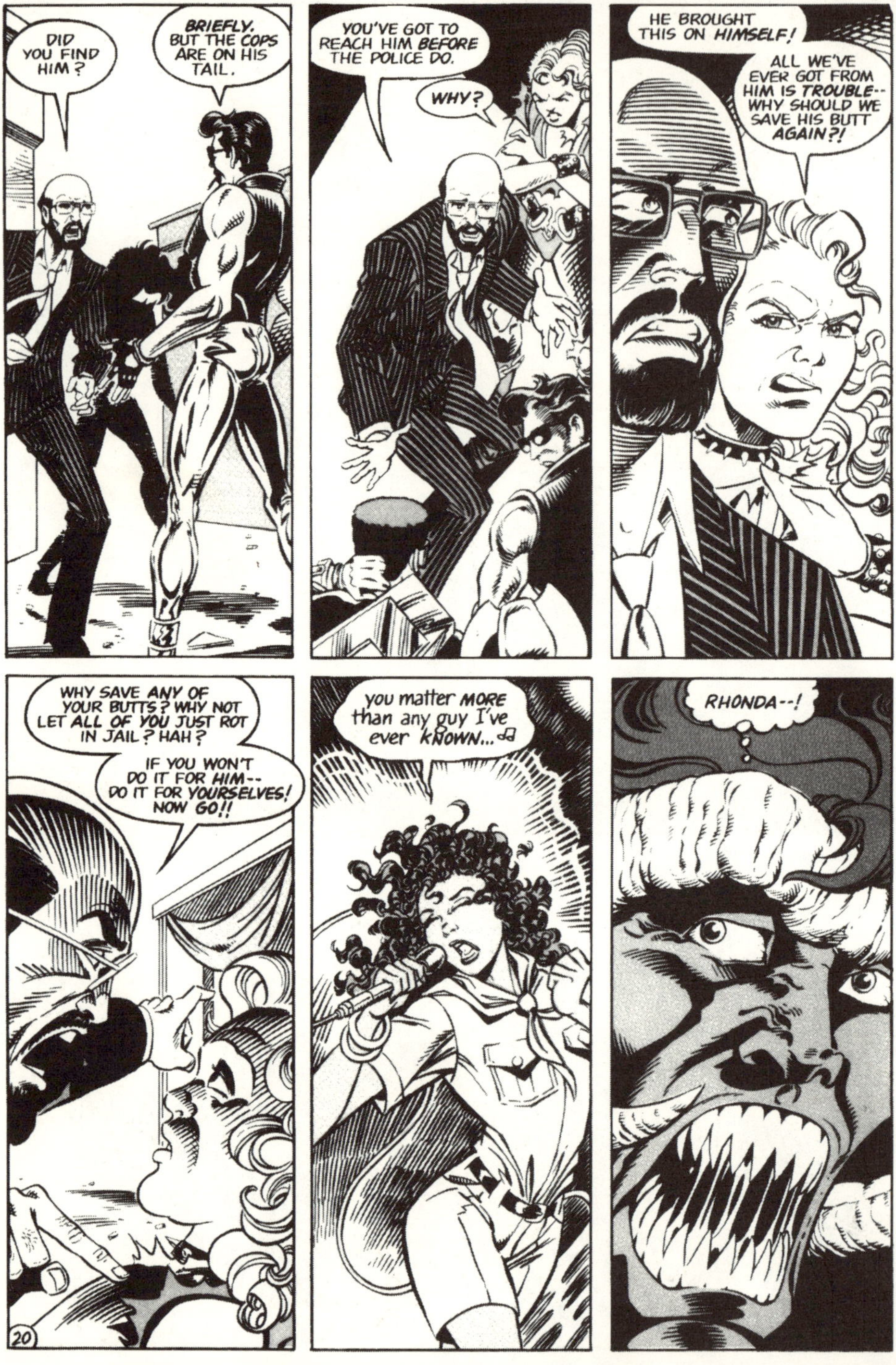
DID YOU FIND HIM?
BRIEFLY. BUT THE COPS ARE ON HIS TAIL.
YOU'VE GOT TO REACH HIM BEFORE THE POLICE DO.
WHY?
HE BROUGHT THIS ON HIMSELF!
ALL WE'VE EVER GOT FROM HIM IS TROUBLE-- WHY SHOULD WE SAVE HIS BUTT AGAIN?!
WHY SAVE ANY OF YOUR BUTTS? WHY NOT LET ALL OF YOU JUST ROT IN JAIL? HAH?
IF YOU WON'T DO IT FOR HIM-- DO IT FOR YOURSELVES! NOW GO!!
20
you matter MORE than any guy I've ever KNOWN...
RHONDA--!

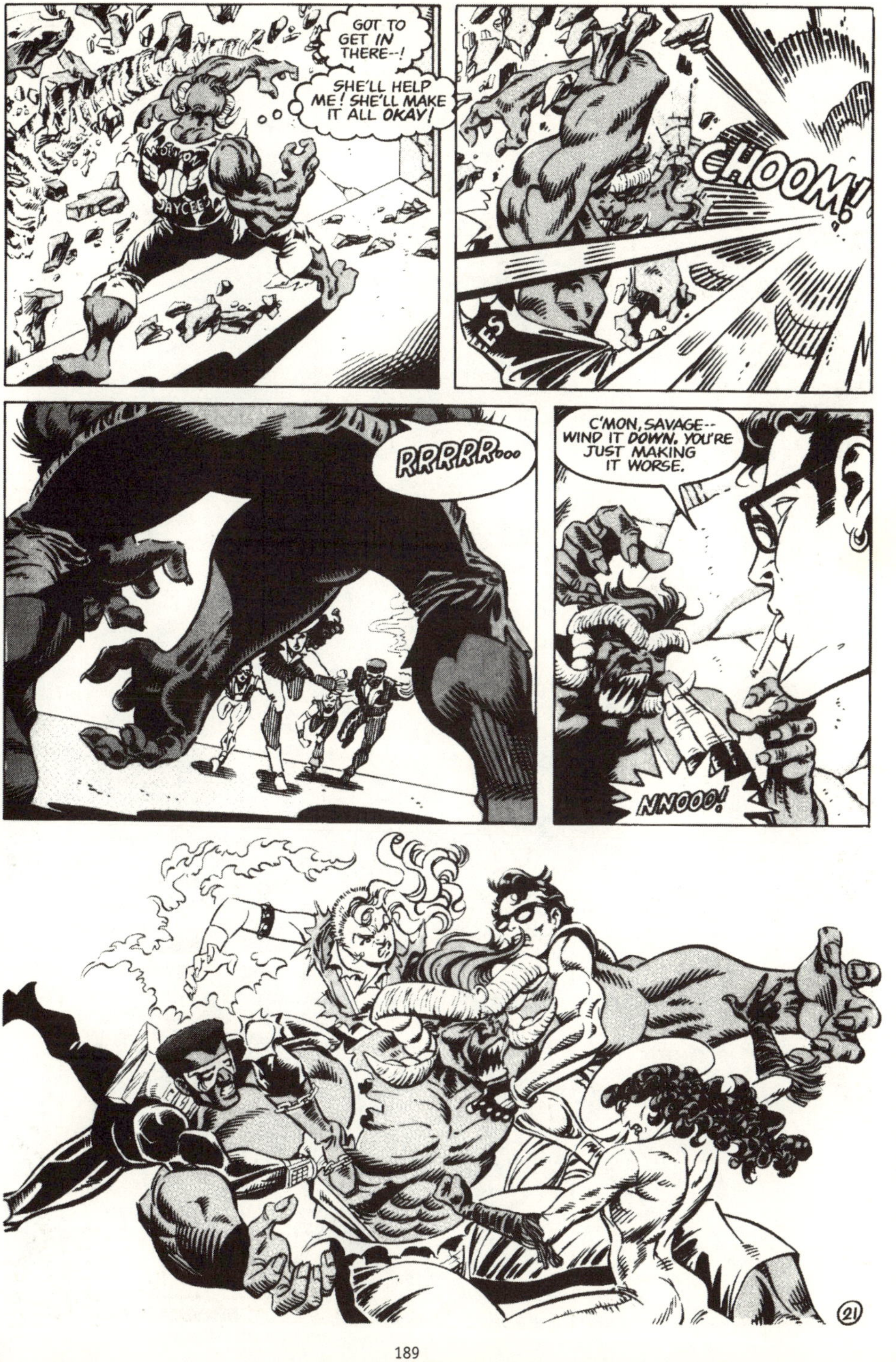
GOT TO GET IN THERE--!
SHE'LL HELP ME! SHE'LL MAKE IT ALL OKAY!
CHOOM!
RRRRR...
C'MON, SAVAGE-- WIND IT DOWN. YOU'RE JUST MAKING IT WORSE.
NNOOO!
21

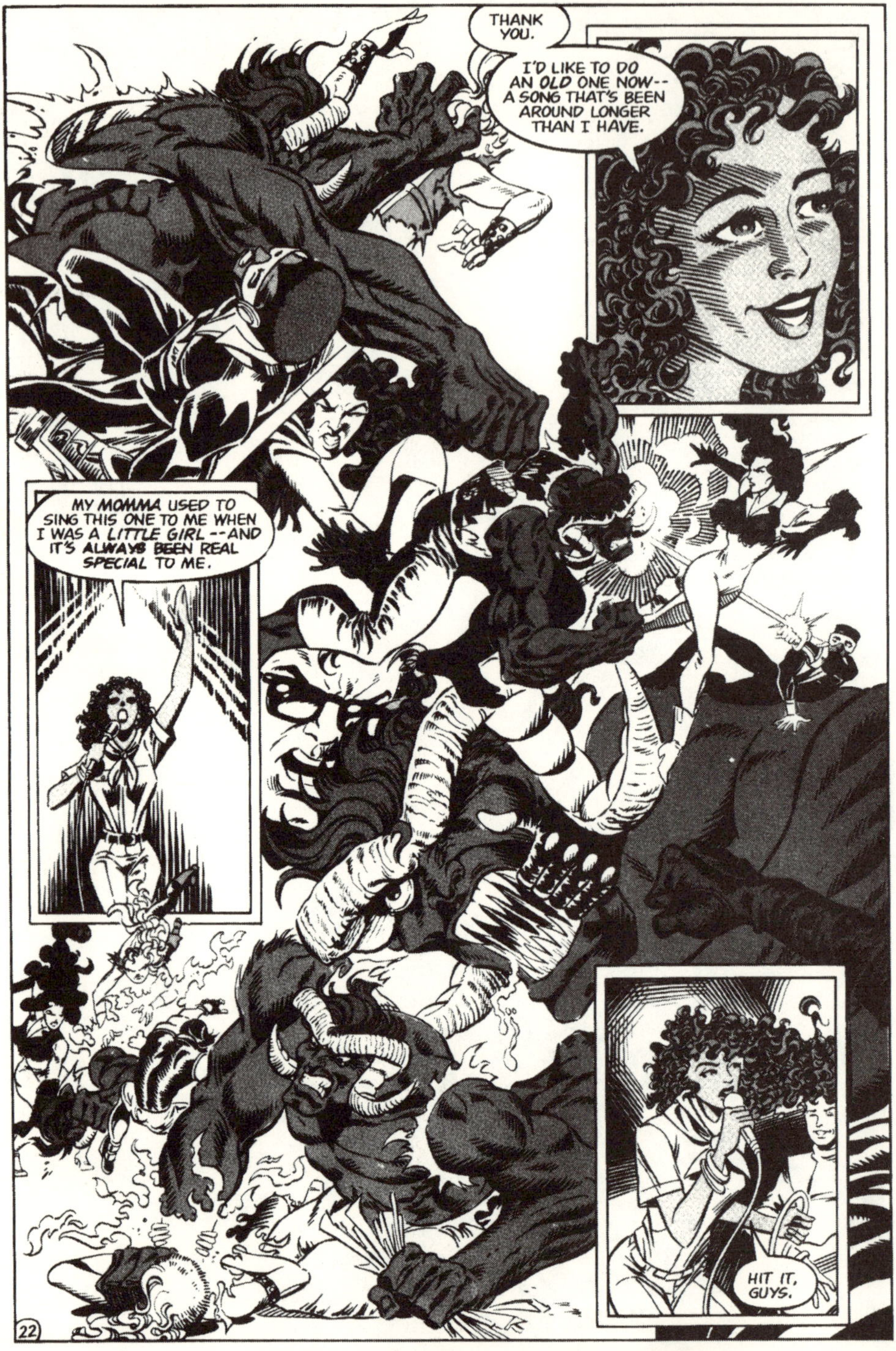
THANK YOU.
I'D LIKE TO DO AN OLD ONE NOW-- A SONG THAT'S BEEN AROUND LONGER THAN I HAVE.
MY MOMMA USED TO SING THIS ONE TO ME WHEN I WAS A LITTLE GIRL--AND IT'S ALWAYS BEEN REAL SPECIAL TO ME.
HIT IT, GUYS.
22

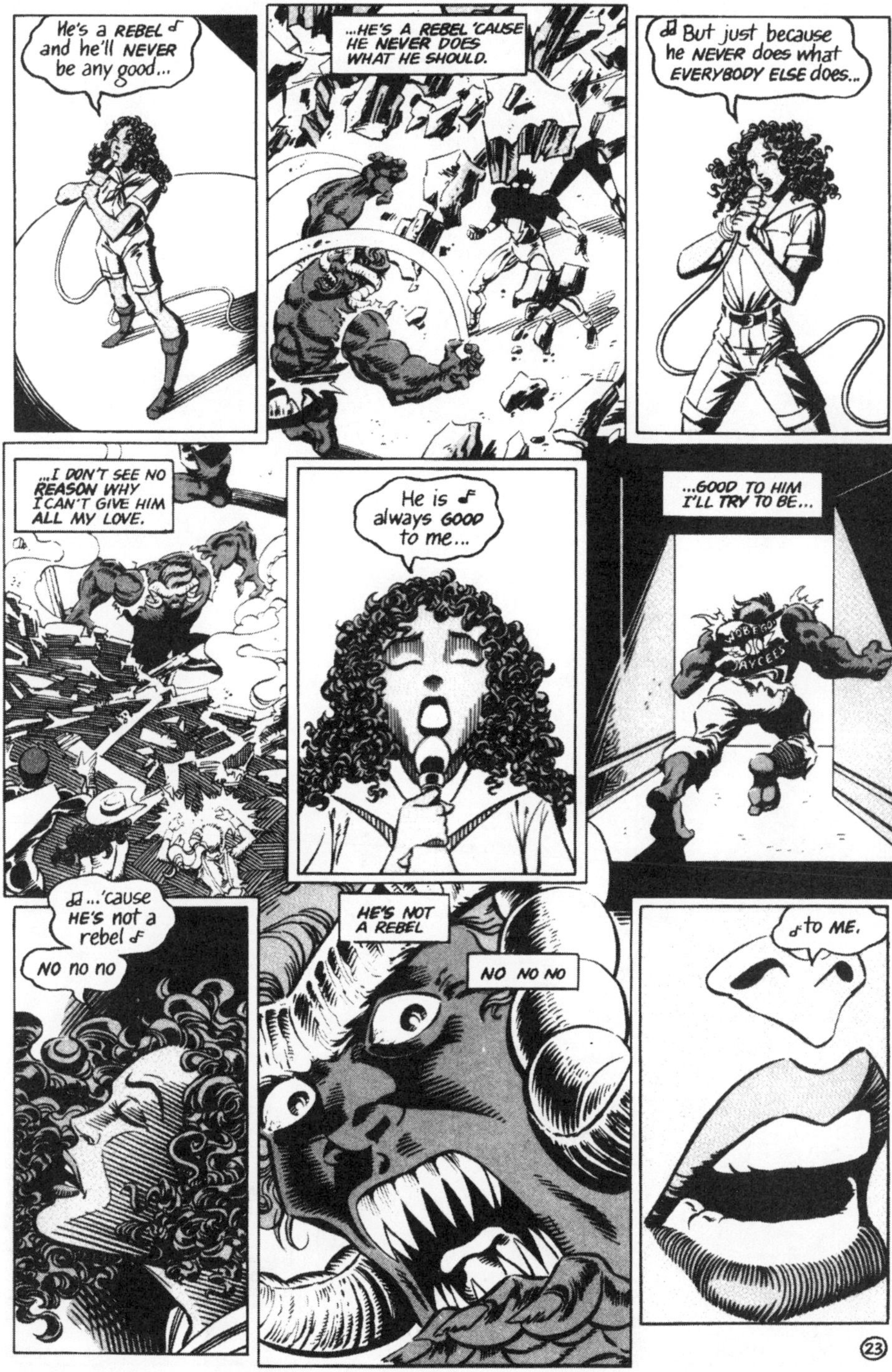
He's a REBEL and he'll NEVER be any good...
...HE'S A REBEL 'CAUSE HE NEVER DOES WHAT HE SHOULD.
But just because he NEVER does what EVERYBODY ELSE does...
...I DON'T SEE NO REASON WHY I CAN'T GIVE HIM ALL MY LOVE.
He is always GOOD to me...
...GOOD TO HIM I'LL TRY TO BE...
...'cause HE'S not a rebel
NO no no
HE'S NOT A REBEL
NO NO NO
to ME.
23

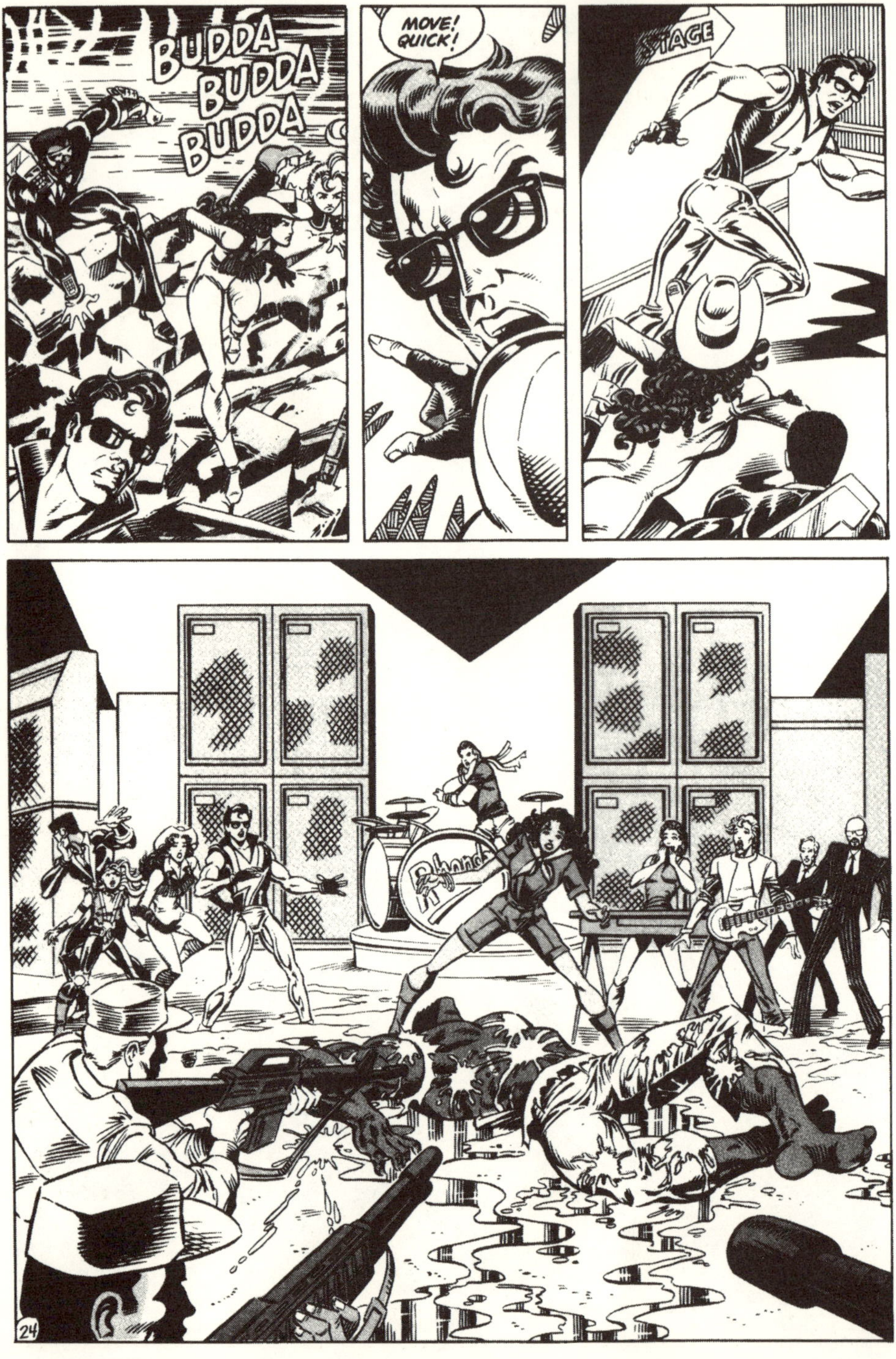
BUDDA
BUDDA
BUDDA
MOVE! QUICK!
STAGE
24

EPILOGUE

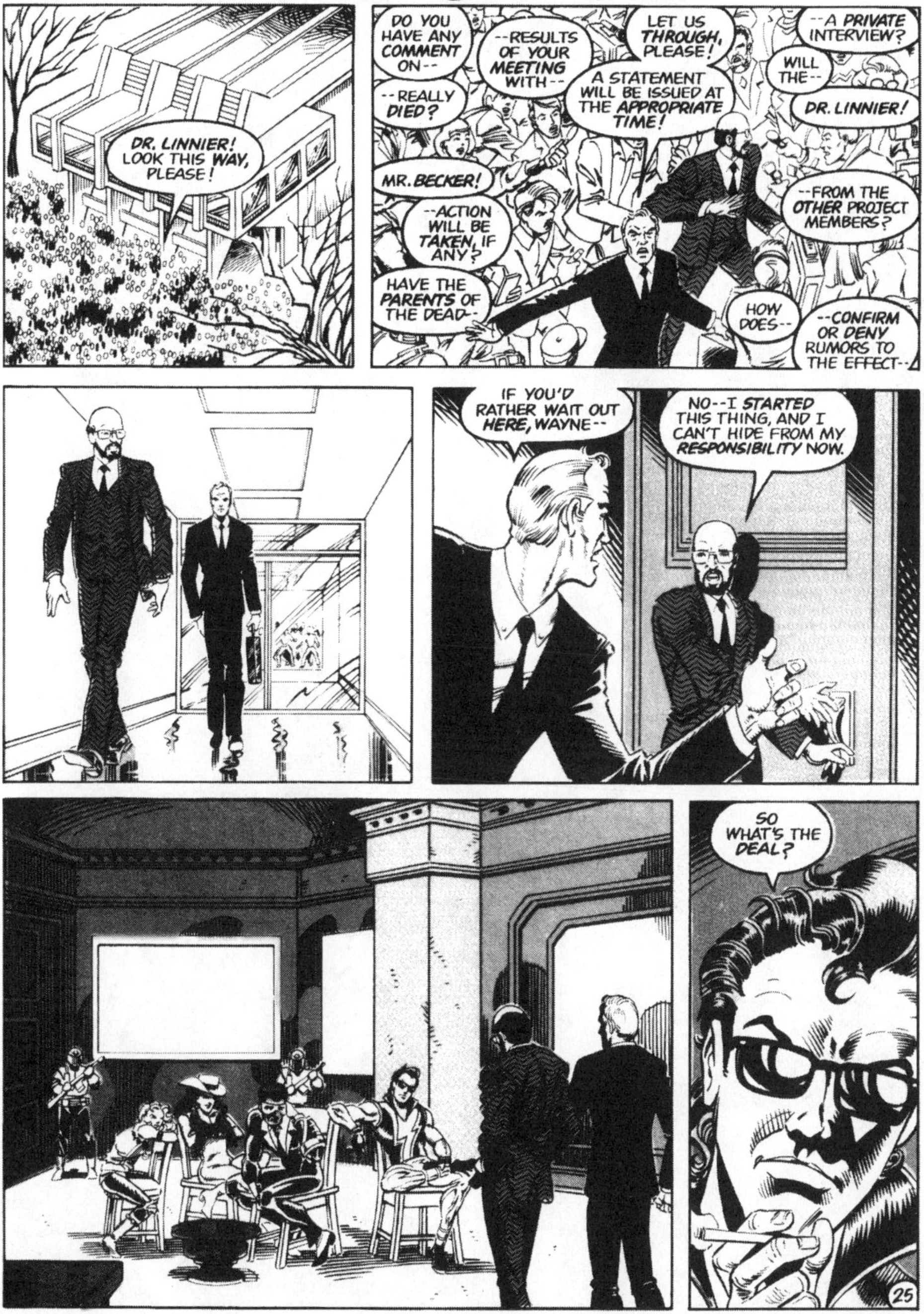
DR. LINNIER! LOOK THIS WAY, PLEASE!
DO YOU HAVE ANY COMMENT ON--
--RESULTS OF YOUR MEETING WITH--
LET US THROUGH, PLEASE!
A STATEMENT WILL BE ISSUED AT THE APPROPRIATE TIME!
--A PRIVATE INTERVIEW?
WILL THE--
DR. LINNIER!
--REALLY DIED?
MR. BECKER!
--ACTION WILL BE TAKEN, IF ANY?
HAVE THE PARENTS OF THE DEAD--
--FROM THE OTHER PROJECT MEMBERS?
HOW DOES--
--CONFIRM OR DENY RUMORS TO THE EFFECT--
IF YOU'D RATHER WAIT OUT HERE, WAYNE--
NO--I STARTED THIS THING, AND I CAN'T HIDE FROM MY RESPONSIBILITY NOW.
SO WHAT'S THE DEAL?
25

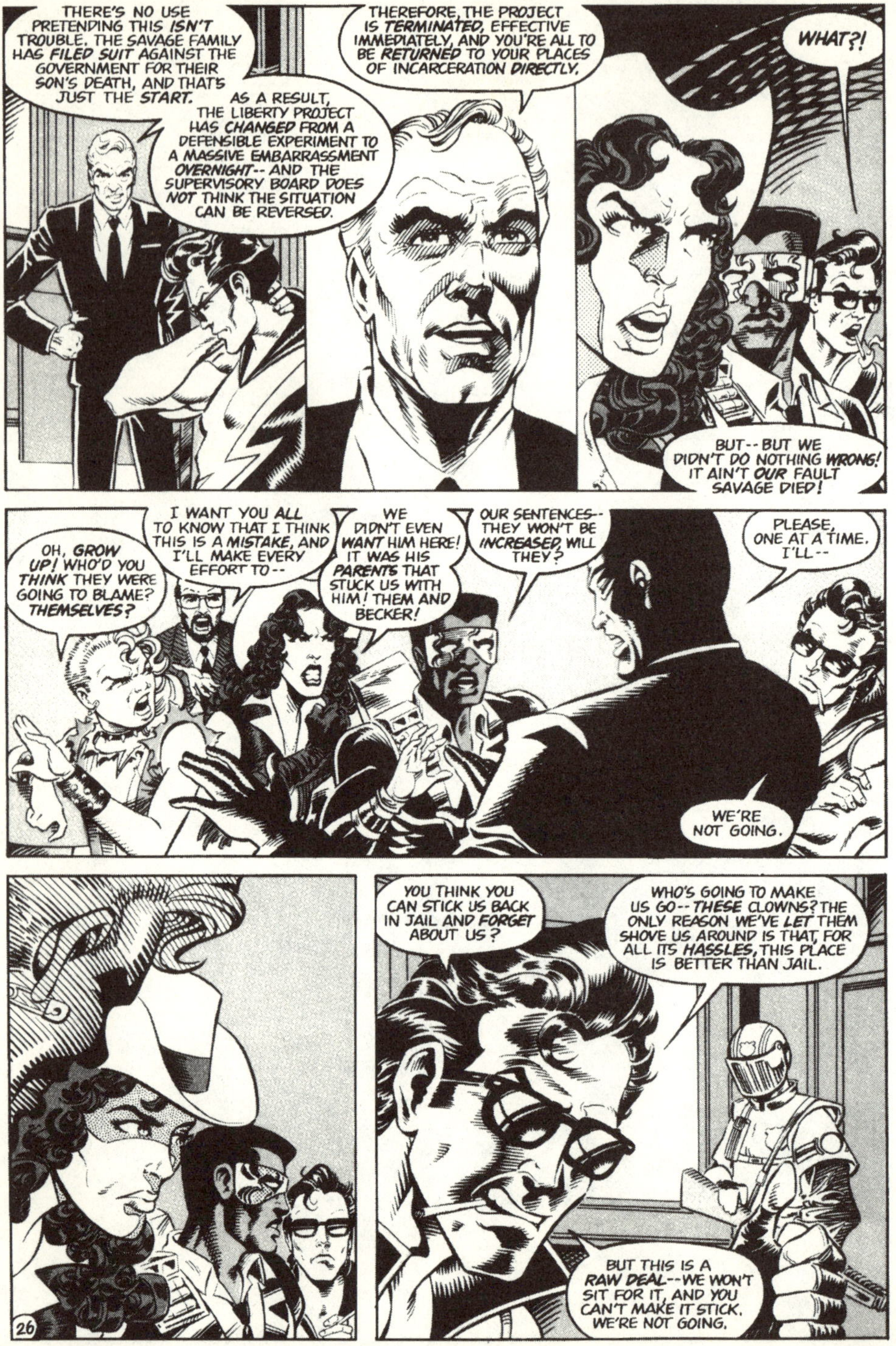
THERE'S NO USE PRETENDING THIS ISN'T TROUBLE. THE SAVAGE FAMILY HAS FILED SUIT AGAINST THE GOVERNMENT FOR THEIR SON'S DEATH, AND THAT'S JUST THE START.
AS A RESULT, THE LIBERTY PROJECT HAS CHANGED FROM A DEFENSIBLE EXPERIMENT TO A MASSIVE EMBARRASSMENT OVERNIGHT-- AND THE SUPERVISORY BOARD DOES NOT THINK THE SITUATION CAN BE REVERSED.
THEREFORE, THE PROJECT IS TERMINATED, EFFECTIVE IMMEDIATELY, AND YOU'RE ALL TO BE RETURNED TO YOUR PLACES OF INCARCERATION DIRECTLY.
WHAT?!
BUT-- BUT WE DIDN'T DO NOTHING WRONG! IT AIN'T OUR FAULT SAVAGE DIED!
OH, GROW UP! WHO'D YOU THINK THEY WERE GOING TO BLAME? THEMSELVES?
I WANT YOU ALL TO KNOW THAT I THINK THIS IS A MISTAKE, AND I'LL MAKE EVERY EFFORT TO--
WE DIDN'T EVEN WANT HIM HERE! IT WAS HIS PARENTS THAT STUCK US WITH HIM! THEM AND BECKER!
OUR SENTENCES-- THEY WON'T BE INCREASED, WILL THEY?
PLEASE, ONE AT A TIME. I'LL--
WE'RE NOT GOING.
YOU THINK YOU CAN STICK US BACK IN JAIL AND FORGET ABOUT US?
WHO'S GOING TO MAKE US GO-- THESE CLOWNS? THE ONLY REASON WE'VE LET THEM SHOVE US AROUND IS THAT, FOR ALL ITS HASSLES, THIS PLACE IS BETTER THAN JAIL.
BUT THIS IS A RAW DEAL-- WE WON'T SIT FOR IT, AND YOU CAN'T MAKE IT STICK. WE'RE NOT GOING.
26

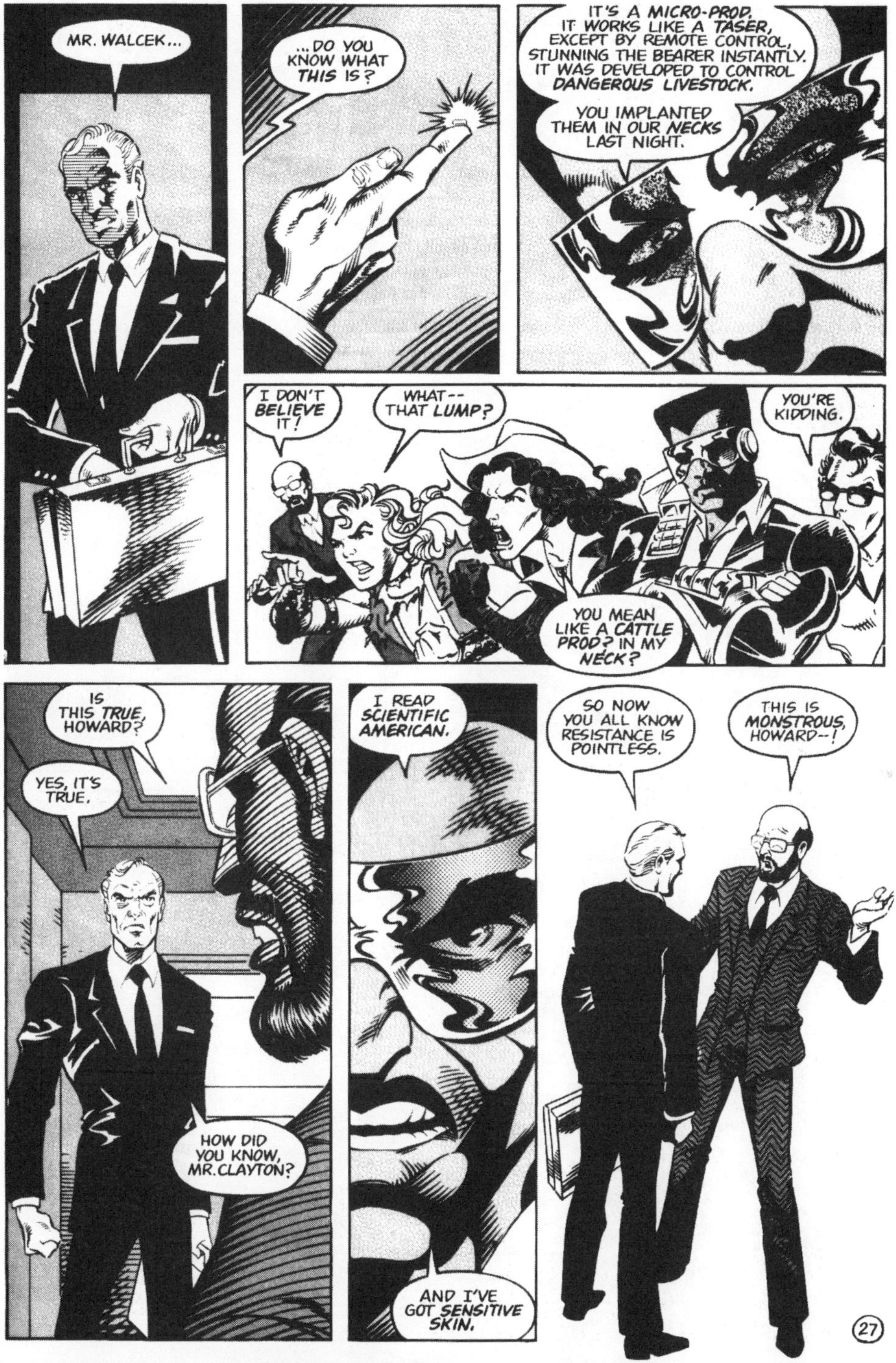
MR. WALCEK...
...DO YOU KNOW WHAT THIS IS?
IT'S A MICRO-PROD. IT WORKS LIKE A TASER, EXCEPT BY REMOTE CONTROL, STUNNING THE BEARER INSTANTLY. IT WAS DEVELOPED TO CONTROL DANGEROUS LIVESTOCK.
YOU IMPLANTED THEM IN OUR NECKS LAST NIGHT.
I DON'T BELIEVE IT!
WHAT-- THAT LUMP?
YOU'RE KIDDING.
YOU MEAN LIKE A CATTLE PROD? IN MY NECK?
IS THIS TRUE, HOWARD?
YES, IT'S TRUE.
HOW DID YOU KNOW, MR. CLAYTON?
I READ SCIENTIFIC AMERICAN.
AND I'VE GOT SENSITIVE SKIN.
SO NOW YOU ALL KNOW RESISTANCE IS POINTLESS.
THIS IS MONSTROUS, HOWARD--!
27

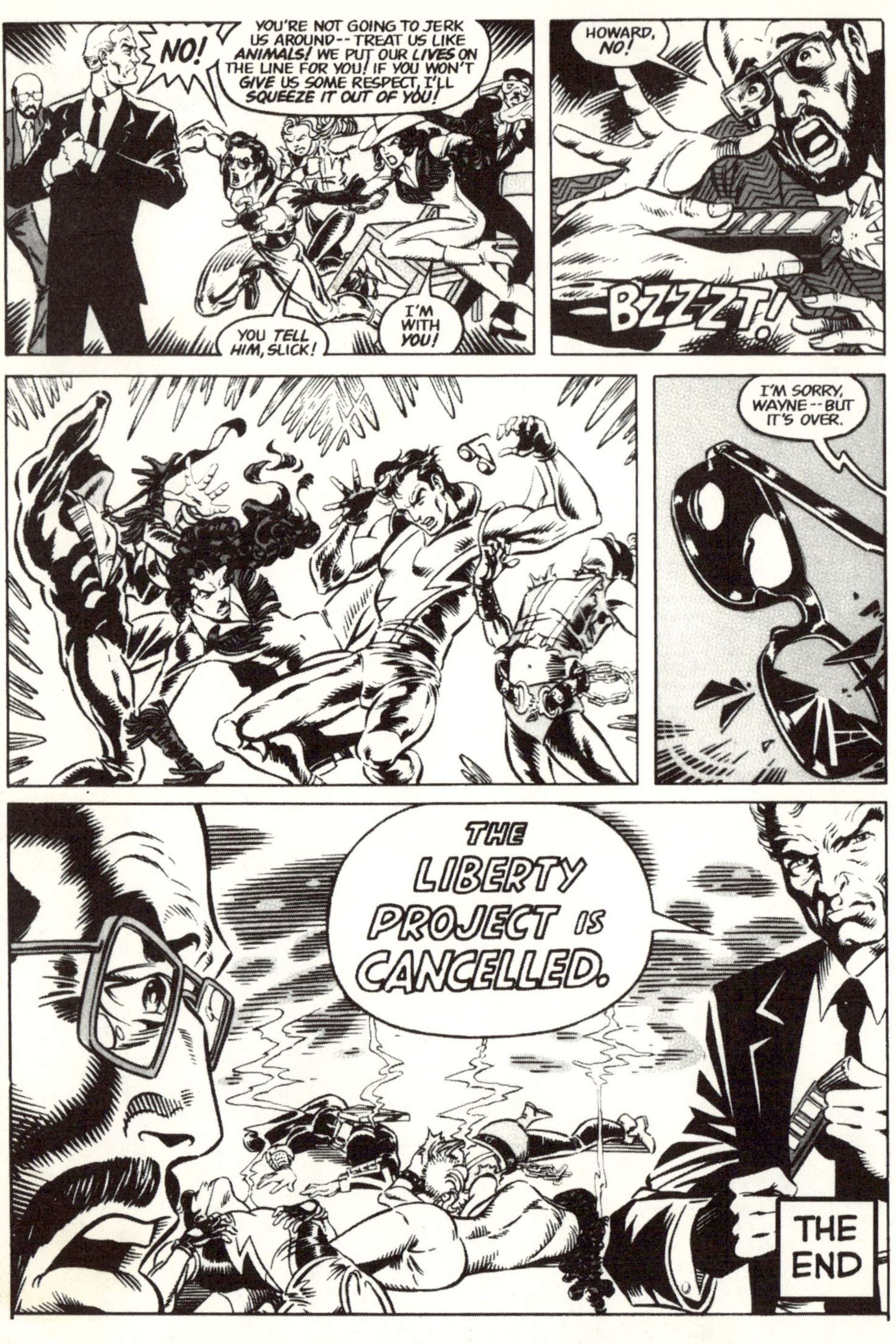
NO!
YOU'RE NOT GOING TO JERK US AROUND--TREAT US LIKE ANIMALS! WE PUT OUR LIVES ON THE LINE FOR YOU! IF YOU WON'T GIVE US SOME RESPECT, I'LL SQUEEZE IT OUT OF YOU!
YOU TELL HIM, SLICK!
I'M WITH YOU!
HOWARD, NO!
BZZZT!
I'M SORRY, WAYNE--BUT IT'S OVER.
THE LIBERTY PROJECT IS CANCELLED.
THE END

THE SERAPHIM OBJECTIVE

And Now A Pause For...

TOTAL ECLIPSE: A SERAPHIM DIGRESSION

Our next chapter is "The Seraphim Objective," but since it was part of a larger story, perhaps a few words of introduction are in order.

The larger story, *Total Eclipse*, was a big crossover event, featuring dozens of heroes – Airboy, Valkyrie and plenty of others, ranging from the British hero Miracleman to characters from Larry Marder's oddball fable, *Beanworld*, in a cosmic conflict involving multiple universes, control of time, and more. As of the start of *The Seraphim Objective*, here's what had happened:

Zzed, a millennia-old immortal with a death wish, sought to end his eternal life by destroying the universe. Guided by a mysterious voice, he was bringing about a universe-wide celestial alignment, which would release enough energy to kill him. To stop him, Airboy and other heroes formed a reluctant alliance with Misery — the mystic villain you saw earlier in this book — who wasn't all that keen on having the universe destroyed either.

As part of his plan, Zzed recruited the Seraphim to capture an ancient, powerful gemstone. Airboy in turn recruited the Liberty Project, springing them from jail for this one mission.

And Misery arranged for some assistance, sending the man-monster known as the Heap to assist the Liberty Project...

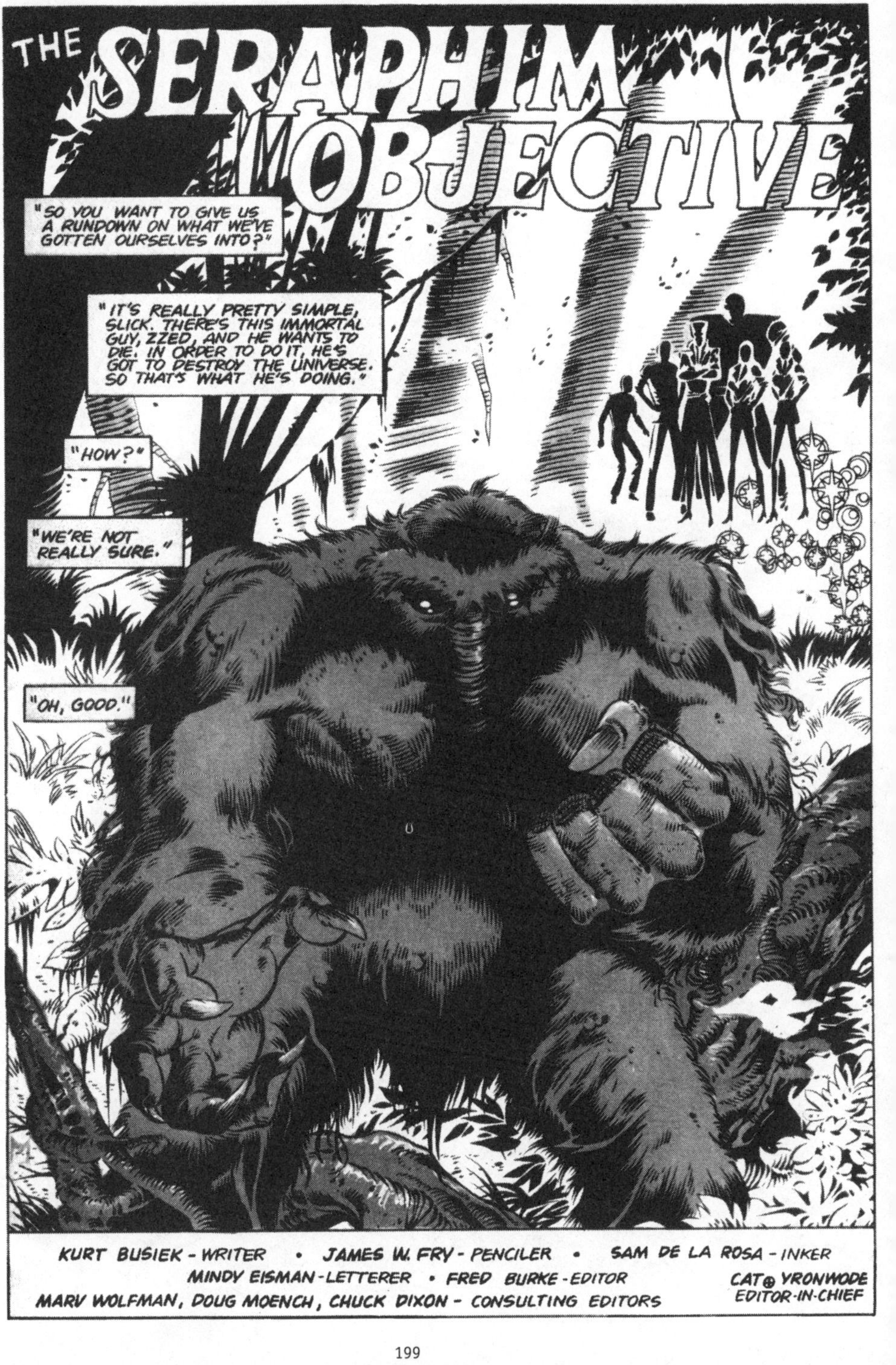
THE SERAPHIM OBJECTIVE
"SO YOU WANT TO GIVE US A RUNDOWN ON WHAT WE'VE GOTTEN OURSELVES INTO?"
"IT'S REALLY PRETTY SIMPLE, SLICK. THERE'S THIS IMMORTAL GUY, ZZED, AND HE WANTS TO DIE. IN ORDER TO DO IT, HE'S GOT TO DESTROY THE UNIVERSE. SO THAT'S WHAT HE'S DOING."
"HOW?"
"WE'RE NOT REALLY SURE."
"OH, GOOD."

KURT BUSIEK - WRITER • JAMES W. FRY - PENCILER • SAM DE LA ROSA - INKER
MINDY EISMAN - LETTERER • FRED BURKE - EDITOR
MARV WOLFMAN, DOUG MOENCH, CHUCK DIXON - CONSULTING EDITORS
CAT YRONWODE EDITOR-IN-CHIEF

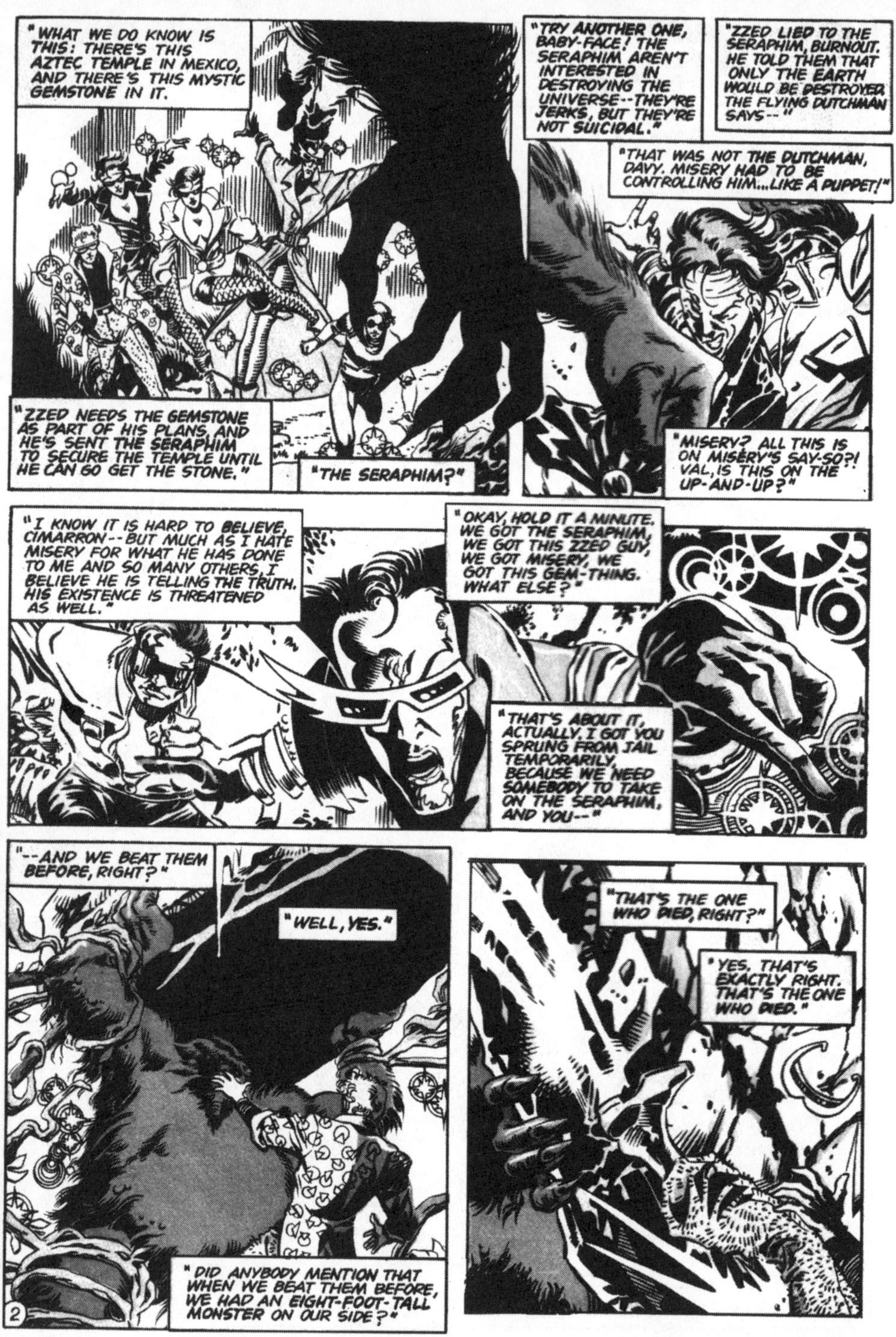
"WHAT WE DO KNOW IS THIS: THERE'S THIS AZTEC TEMPLE IN MEXICO, AND THERE'S THIS MYSTIC GEMSTONE IN IT.
"ZZED NEEDS THE GEMSTONE AS PART OF HIS PLANS, AND HE'S SENT THE SERAPHIM TO SECURE THE TEMPLE UNTIL HE CAN GO GET THE STONE."
"THE SERAPHIM?"
"TRY ANOTHER ONE, BABY-FACE! THE SERAPHIM AREN'T INTERESTED IN DESTROYING THE UNIVERSE--THEY'RE JERKS, BUT THEY'RE NOT SUICIDAL."
"ZZED LIED TO THE SERAPHIM, BURNOUT. HE TOLD THEM THAT ONLY THE EARTH WOULD BE DESTROYED. THE FLYING DUTCHMAN SAYS--"
"THAT WAS NOT THE DUTCHMAN, DAVY. MISERY HAD TO BE CONTROLLING HIM...LIKE A PUPPET!"
"MISERY? ALL THIS IS ON MISERY'S SAY-SO?! VAL, IS THIS ON THE UP-AND-UP?"
"I KNOW IT IS HARD TO BELIEVE, CIMARRON--BUT MUCH AS I HATE MISERY FOR WHAT HE HAS DONE TO ME AND SO MANY OTHERS, I BELIEVE HE IS TELLING THE TRUTH. HIS EXISTENCE IS THREATENED AS WELL."
"OKAY, HOLD IT A MINUTE. WE GOT THE SERAPHIM, WE GOT THIS ZZED GUY, WE GOT MISERY, WE GOT THIS GEM-THING. WHAT ELSE?"
"THAT'S ABOUT IT, ACTUALLY. I GOT YOU SPRUNG FROM JAIL TEMPORARILY, BECAUSE WE NEED SOMEBODY TO TAKE ON THE SERAPHIM, AND YOU--"
"--AND WE BEAT THEM BEFORE, RIGHT?"
"WELL, YES."
"DID ANYBODY MENTION THAT WHEN WE BEAT THEM BEFORE, WE HAD AN EIGHT-FOOT-TALL MONSTER ON OUR SIDE?"
2
"THAT'S THE ONE WHO DIED, RIGHT?"
"YES, THAT'S EXACTLY RIGHT. THAT'S THE ONE WHO DIED."

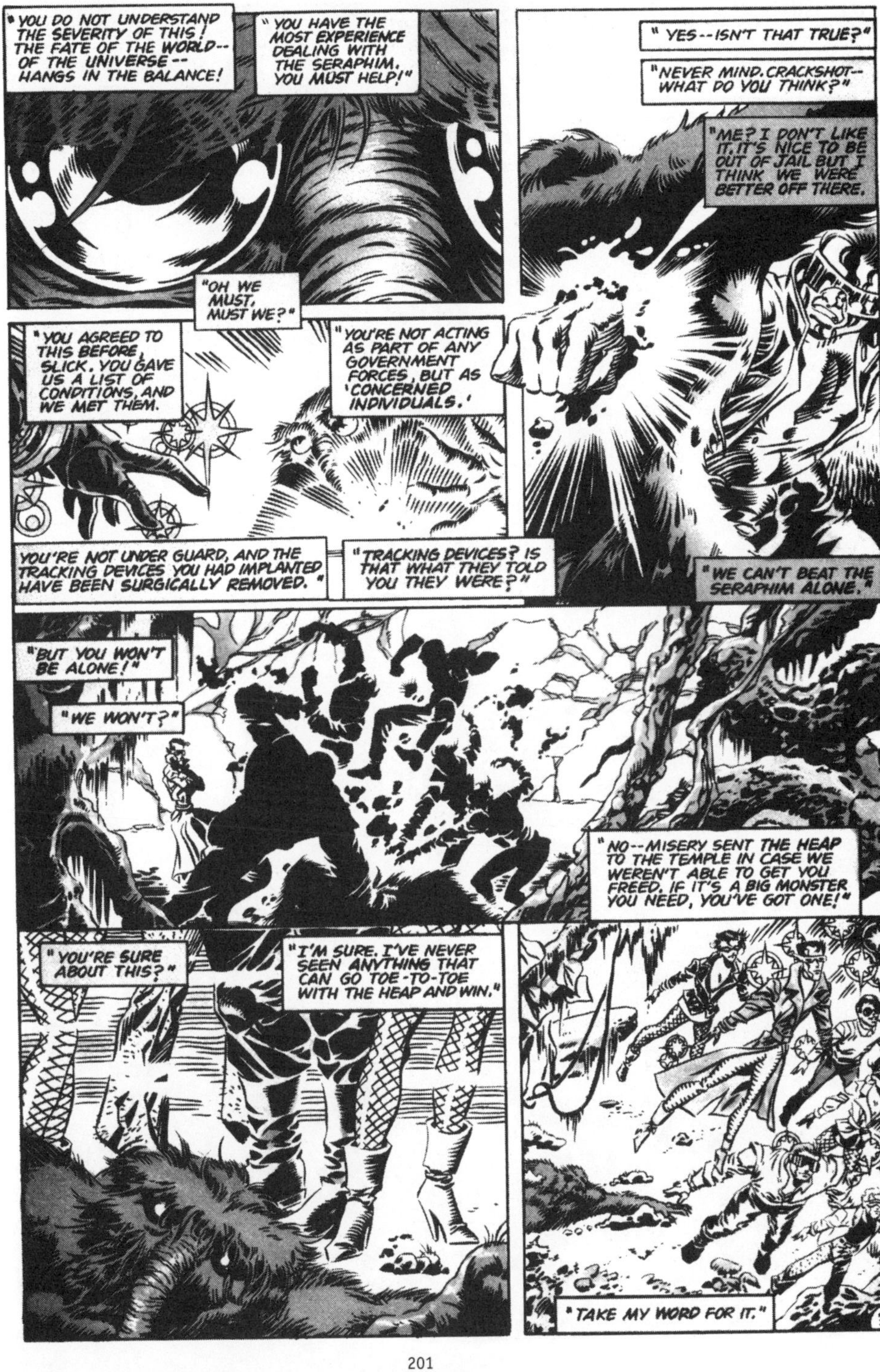
"YOU DO NOT UNDERSTAND THE SEVERITY OF THIS! THE FATE OF THE WORLD-- OF THE UNIVERSE-- HANGS IN THE BALANCE!
"YOU HAVE THE MOST EXPERIENCE DEALING WITH THE SERAPHIM. YOU MUST HELP!"
"OH WE MUST, MUST WE?"
"YOU AGREED TO THIS BEFORE, SLICK. YOU GAVE US A LIST OF CONDITIONS, AND WE MET THEM.
"YOU'RE NOT ACTING AS PART OF ANY GOVERNMENT FORCES, BUT AS 'CONCERNED INDIVIDUALS.'
YOU'RE NOT UNDER GUARD, AND THE TRACKING DEVICES YOU HAD IMPLANTED HAVE BEEN SURGICALLY REMOVED."
"TRACKING DEVICES? IS THAT WHAT THEY TOLD YOU THEY WERE?"
"YES--ISN'T THAT TRUE?"
"NEVER MIND. CRACKSHOT-- WHAT DO YOU THINK?"
"ME? I DON'T LIKE IT. IT'S NICE TO BE OUT OF JAIL BUT I THINK WE WERE BETTER OFF THERE.
"WE CAN'T BEAT THE SERAPHIM ALONE."
"BUT YOU WON'T BE ALONE!"
"WE WON'T?"
"NO--MISERY SENT THE HEAP TO THE TEMPLE IN CASE WE WEREN'T ABLE TO GET YOU FREED. IF IT'S A BIG MONSTER YOU NEED, YOU'VE GOT ONE!"
"YOU'RE SURE ABOUT THIS?"
"I'M SURE. I'VE NEVER SEEN ANYTHING THAT CAN GO TOE-TO-TOE WITH THE HEAP AND WIN."
"TAKE MY WORD FOR IT."
3

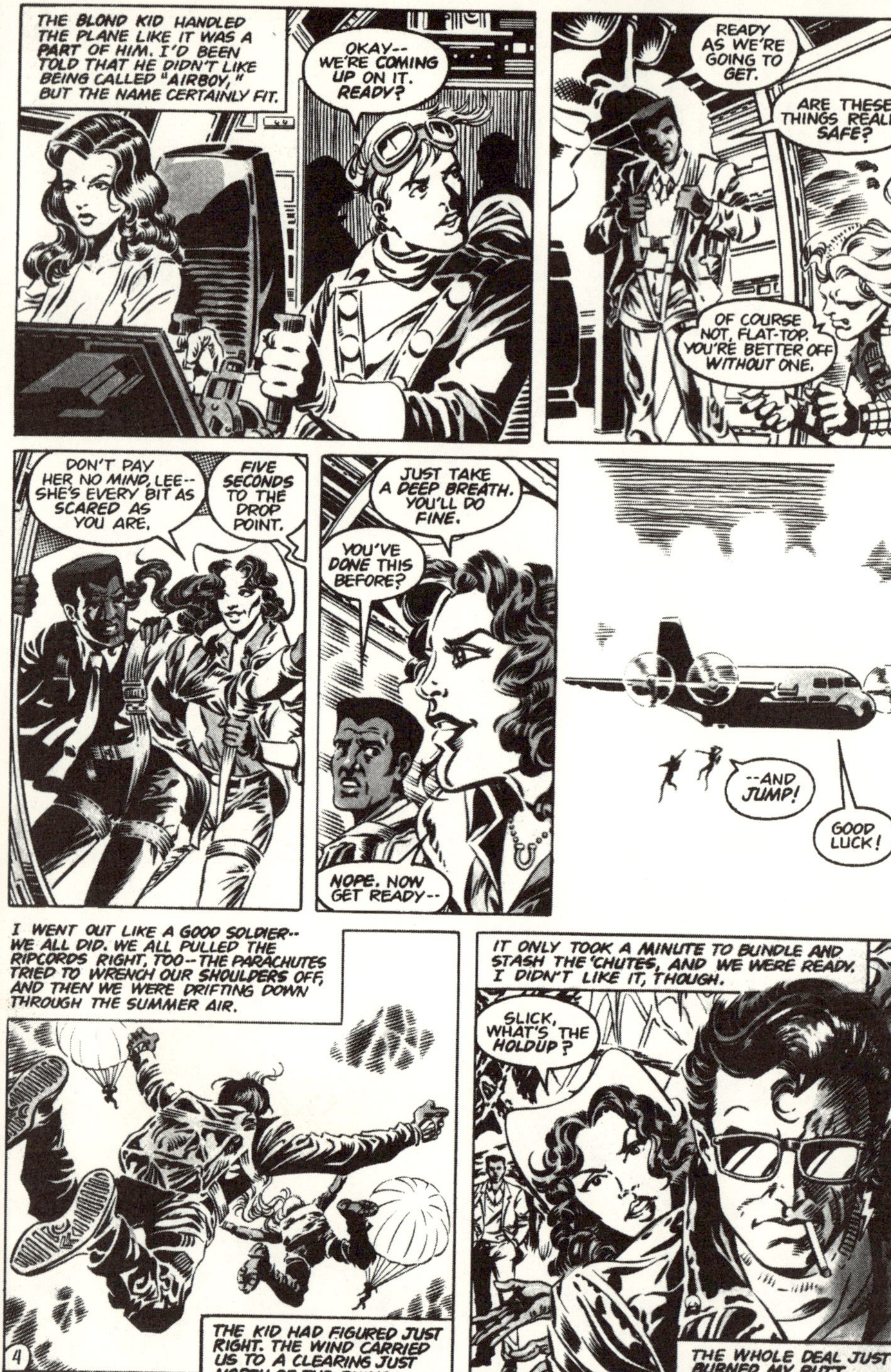
THE BLOND KID HANDLED THE PLANE LIKE IT WAS A PART OF HIM. I'D BEEN TOLD THAT HE DIDN'T LIKE BEING CALLED "AIRBOY," BUT THE NAME CERTAINLY FIT.
OKAY-- WE'RE COMING UP ON IT. READY?
READY AS WE'RE GOING TO GET.
ARE THESE THINGS REALLY SAFE?
OF COURSE NOT, FLAT-TOP. YOU'RE BETTER OFF WITHOUT ONE.
DON'T PAY HER NO MIND, LEE-- SHE'S EVERY BIT AS SCARED AS YOU ARE.
FIVE SECONDS TO THE DROP POINT.
JUST TAKE A DEEP BREATH. YOU'LL DO FINE.
YOU'VE DONE THIS BEFORE?
NOPE. NOW GET READY--
--AND JUMP!
GOOD LUCK!
I WENT OUT LIKE A GOOD SOLDIER-- WE ALL DID. WE ALL PULLED THE RIPCORDS RIGHT, TOO--THE PARACHUTES TRIED TO WRENCH OUR SHOULDERS OFF, AND THEN WE WERE DRIFTING DOWN THROUGH THE SUMMER AIR.
4
THE KID HAD FIGURED JUST RIGHT. THE WIND CARRIED US TO A CLEARING JUST NORTH OF THE RUINS.
IT ONLY TOOK A MINUTE TO BUNDLE AND STASH THE 'CHUTES, AND WE WERE READY. I DIDN'T LIKE IT, THOUGH.
SLICK, WHAT'S THE HOLDUP?
THE WHOLE DEAL JUST BURNED MY BUTT.

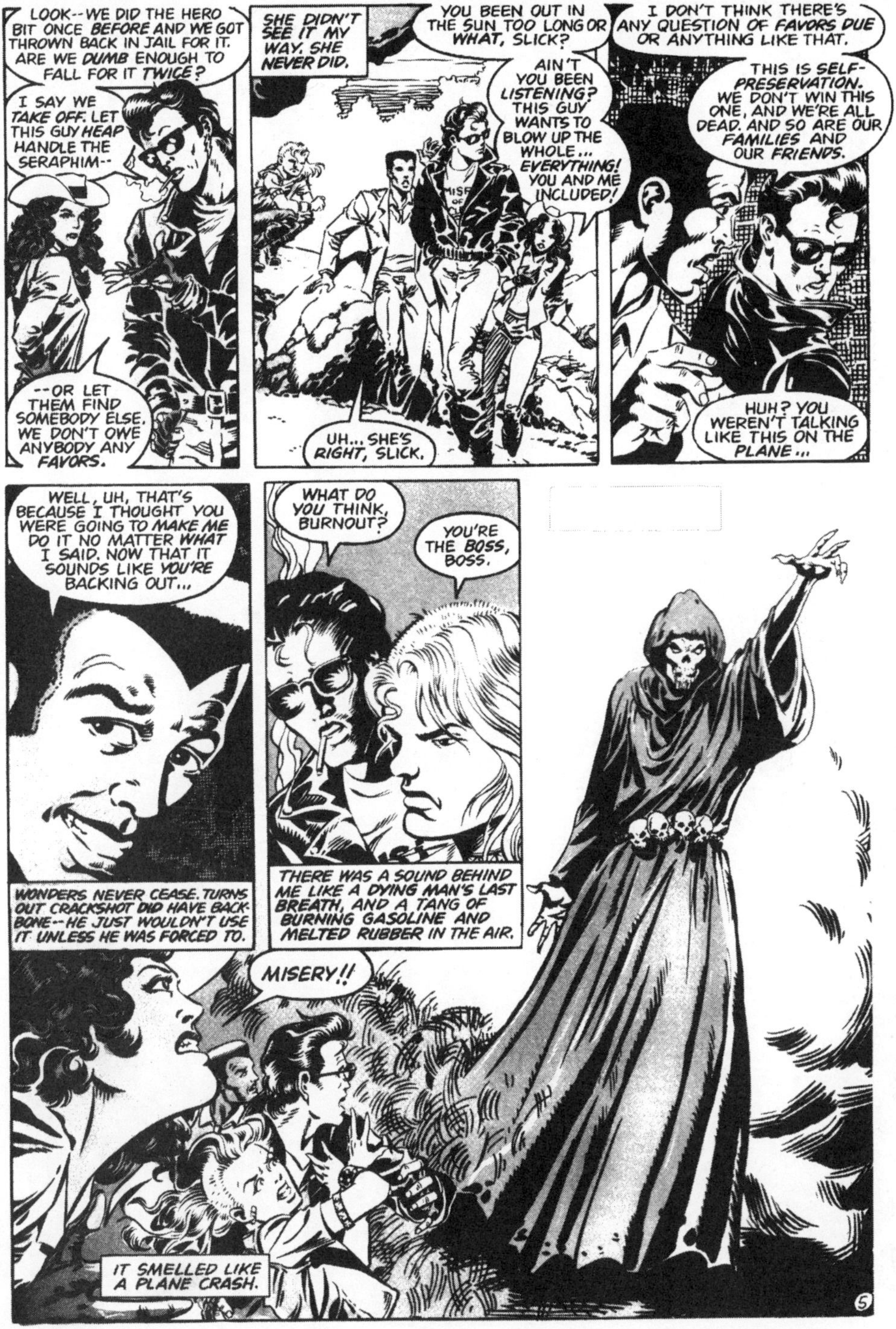
LOOK--WE DID THE HERO BIT ONCE BEFORE AND WE GOT THROWN BACK IN JAIL FOR IT. ARE WE DUMB ENOUGH TO FALL FOR IT TWICE?
I SAY WE TAKE OFF. LET THIS GUY HEAP HANDLE THE SERAPHIM--
--OR LET THEM FIND SOMEBODY ELSE. WE DON'T OWE ANYBODY ANY FAVORS.
SHE DIDN'T SEE IT MY WAY. SHE NEVER DID.
YOU BEEN OUT IN THE SUN TOO LONG OR WHAT, SLICK?
AIN'T YOU BEEN LISTENING? THIS GUY WANTS TO BLOW UP THE WHOLE... EVERYTHING! YOU AND ME INCLUDED!
UH... SHE'S RIGHT, SLICK.
I DON'T THINK THERE'S ANY QUESTION OF FAVORS DUE OR ANYTHING LIKE THAT.
THIS IS SELF-PRESERVATION. WE DON'T WIN THIS ONE, AND WE'RE ALL DEAD. AND SO ARE OUR FAMILIES AND OUR FRIENDS.
HUH? YOU WEREN'T TALKING LIKE THIS ON THE PLANE...
WELL, UH, THAT'S BECAUSE I THOUGHT YOU WERE GOING TO MAKE ME DO IT NO MATTER WHAT I SAID. NOW THAT IT SOUNDS LIKE YOU'RE BACKING OUT...
WONDERS NEVER CEASE. TURNS OUT CRACKSHOT DID HAVE BACKBONE--HE JUST WOULDN'T USE IT UNLESS HE WAS FORCED TO.
WHAT DO YOU THINK, BURNOUT?
YOU'RE THE BOSS, BOSS.
THERE WAS A SOUND BEHIND ME LIKE A DYING MAN'S LAST BREATH, AND A TANG OF BURNING GASOLINE AND MELTED RUBBER IN THE AIR.
MISERY!!
IT SMELLED LIKE A PLANE CRASH.
5

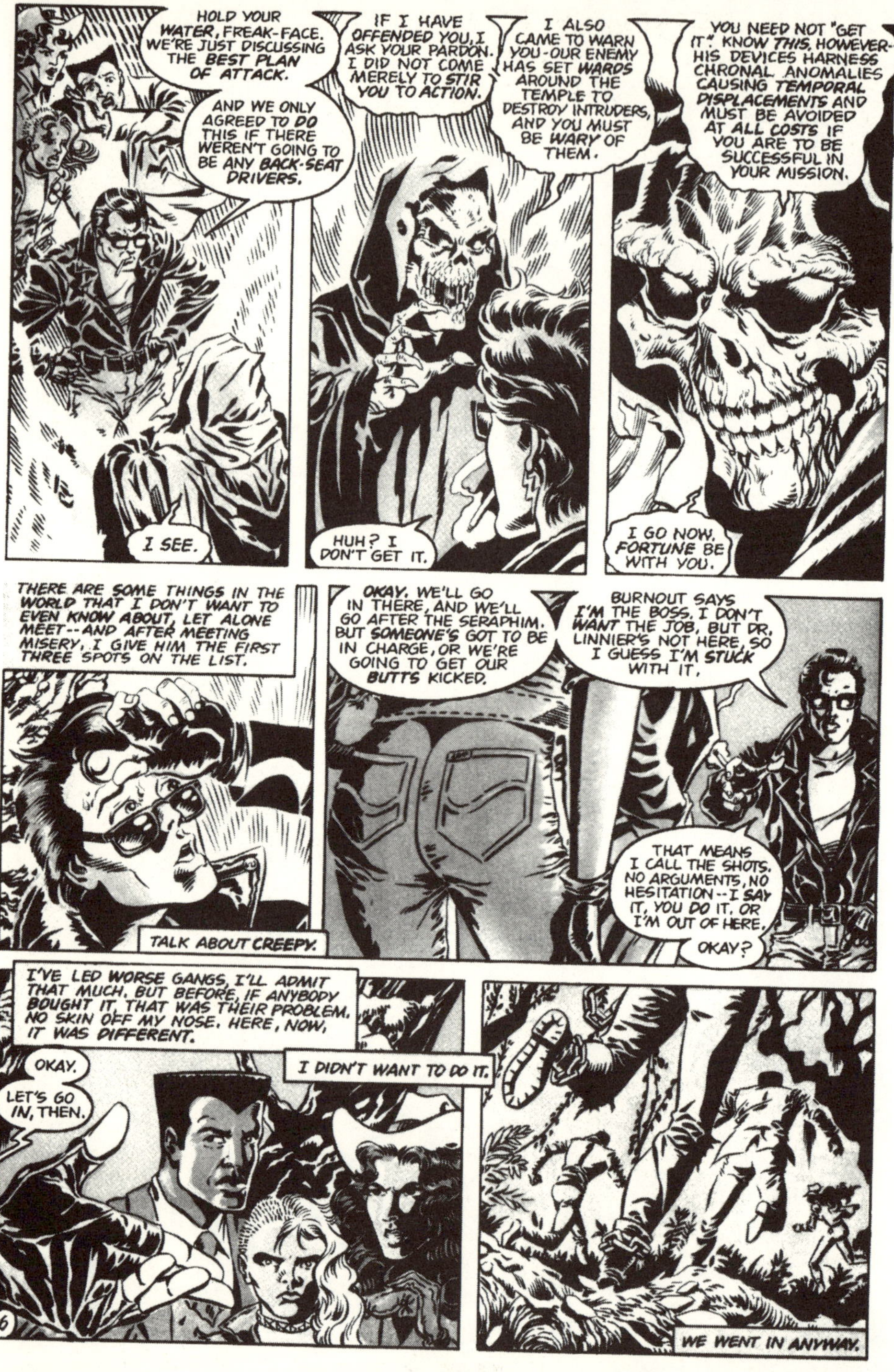
HOLD YOUR WATER, FREAK-FACE. WE'RE JUST DISCUSSING THE BEST PLAN OF ATTACK.
AND WE ONLY AGREED TO DO THIS IF THERE WEREN'T GOING TO BE ANY BACK-SEAT DRIVERS.
I SEE.
IF I HAVE OFFENDED YOU, I ASK YOUR PARDON. I DID NOT COME MERELY TO STIR YOU TO ACTION.
I ALSO CAME TO WARN YOU - OUR ENEMY HAS SET WARDS AROUND THE TEMPLE TO DESTROY INTRUDERS, AND YOU MUST BE WARY OF THEM.
HUH? I DON'T GET IT.
YOU NEED NOT "GET IT". KNOW THIS, HOWEVER-- HIS DEVICES HARNESS CHRONAL ANOMALIES CAUSING TEMPORAL DISPLACEMENTS AND MUST BE AVOIDED AT ALL COSTS IF YOU ARE TO BE SUCCESSFUL IN YOUR MISSION.
I GO NOW. FORTUNE BE WITH YOU.
THERE ARE SOME THINGS IN THE WORLD THAT I DON'T WANT TO EVEN KNOW ABOUT, LET ALONE MEET--AND AFTER MEETING MISERY, I GIVE HIM THE FIRST THREE SPOTS ON THE LIST.
TALK ABOUT CREEPY.
OKAY. WE'LL GO IN THERE, AND WE'LL GO AFTER THE SERAPHIM. BUT SOMEONE'S GOT TO BE IN CHARGE, OR WE'RE GOING TO GET OUR BUTTS KICKED.
BURNOUT SAYS I'M THE BOSS. I DON'T WANT THE JOB, BUT DR. LINNIER'S NOT HERE, SO I GUESS I'M STUCK WITH IT.
THAT MEANS I CALL THE SHOTS. NO ARGUMENTS, NO HESITATION--I SAY IT, YOU DO IT. OR I'M OUT OF HERE.
OKAY?
I'VE LED WORSE GANGS, I'LL ADMIT THAT MUCH. BUT BEFORE, IF ANYBODY BOUGHT IT, THAT WAS THEIR PROBLEM. NO SKIN OFF MY NOSE. HERE, NOW, IT WAS DIFFERENT.
I DIDN'T WANT TO DO IT.
OKAY.
LET'S GO IN, THEN.
6
WE WENT IN ANYWAY.

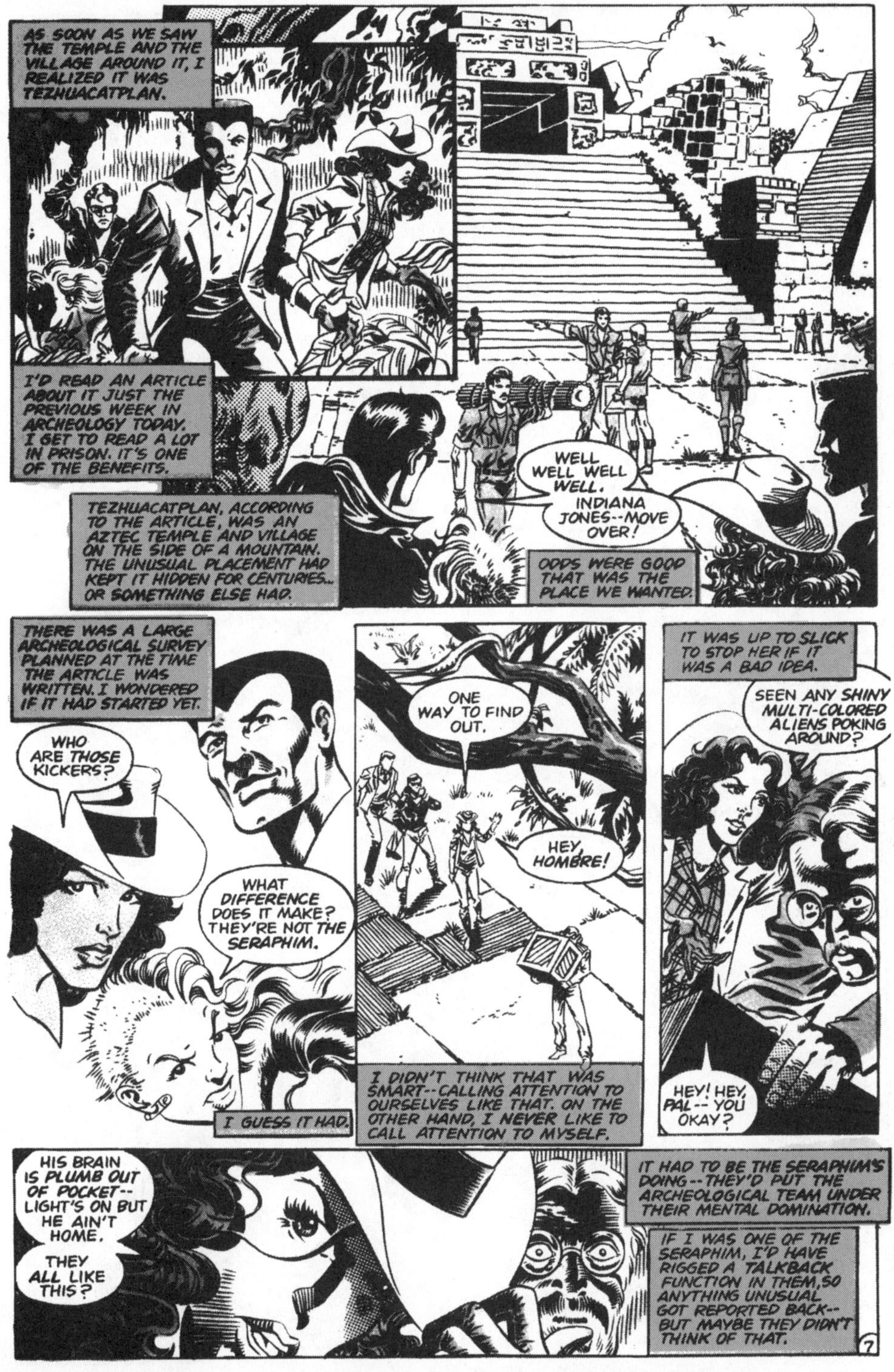
AS SOON AS WE SAW THE TEMPLE AND THE VILLAGE AROUND IT, I REALIZED IT WAS TEZHUACATPLAN.
I'D READ AN ARTICLE ABOUT IT JUST THE PREVIOUS WEEK IN ARCHEOLOGY TODAY. I GET TO READ A LOT IN PRISON. IT'S ONE OF THE BENEFITS.
TEZHUACATPLAN, ACCORDING TO THE ARTICLE, WAS AN AZTEC TEMPLE AND VILLAGE ON THE SIDE OF A MOUNTAIN. THE UNUSUAL PLACEMENT HAD KEPT IT HIDDEN FOR CENTURIES... OR SOMETHING ELSE HAD.
WELL WELL WELL WELL. INDIANA JONES--MOVE OVER!
ODDS WERE GOOD THAT WAS THE PLACE WE WANTED.
THERE WAS A LARGE ARCHEOLOGICAL SURVEY PLANNED AT THE TIME THE ARTICLE WAS WRITTEN. I WONDERED IF IT HAD STARTED YET.
WHO ARE THOSE KICKERS?
WHAT DIFFERENCE DOES IT MAKE? THEY'RE NOT THE SERAPHIM.
I GUESS IT HAD.
ONE WAY TO FIND OUT.
HEY, HOMBRE!
I DIDN'T THINK THAT WAS SMART--CALLING ATTENTION TO OURSELVES LIKE THAT. ON THE OTHER HAND, I NEVER LIKE TO CALL ATTENTION TO MYSELF.
IT WAS UP TO SLICK TO STOP HER IF IT WAS A BAD IDEA.
SEEN ANY SHINY MULTI-COLORED ALIENS POKING AROUND?
HEY! HEY, PAL-- YOU OKAY?
HIS BRAIN IS PLUMB OUT OF POCKET-- LIGHT'S ON BUT HE AIN'T HOME.
THEY ALL LIKE THIS?
IT HAD TO BE THE SERAPHIM'S DOING--THEY'D PUT THE ARCHEOLOGICAL TEAM UNDER THEIR MENTAL DOMINATION.
IF I WAS ONE OF THE SERAPHIM, I'D HAVE RIGGED A TALKBACK FUNCTION IN THEM, SO ANYTHING UNUSUAL GOT REPORTED BACK-- BUT MAYBE THEY DIDN'T THINK OF THAT.
7

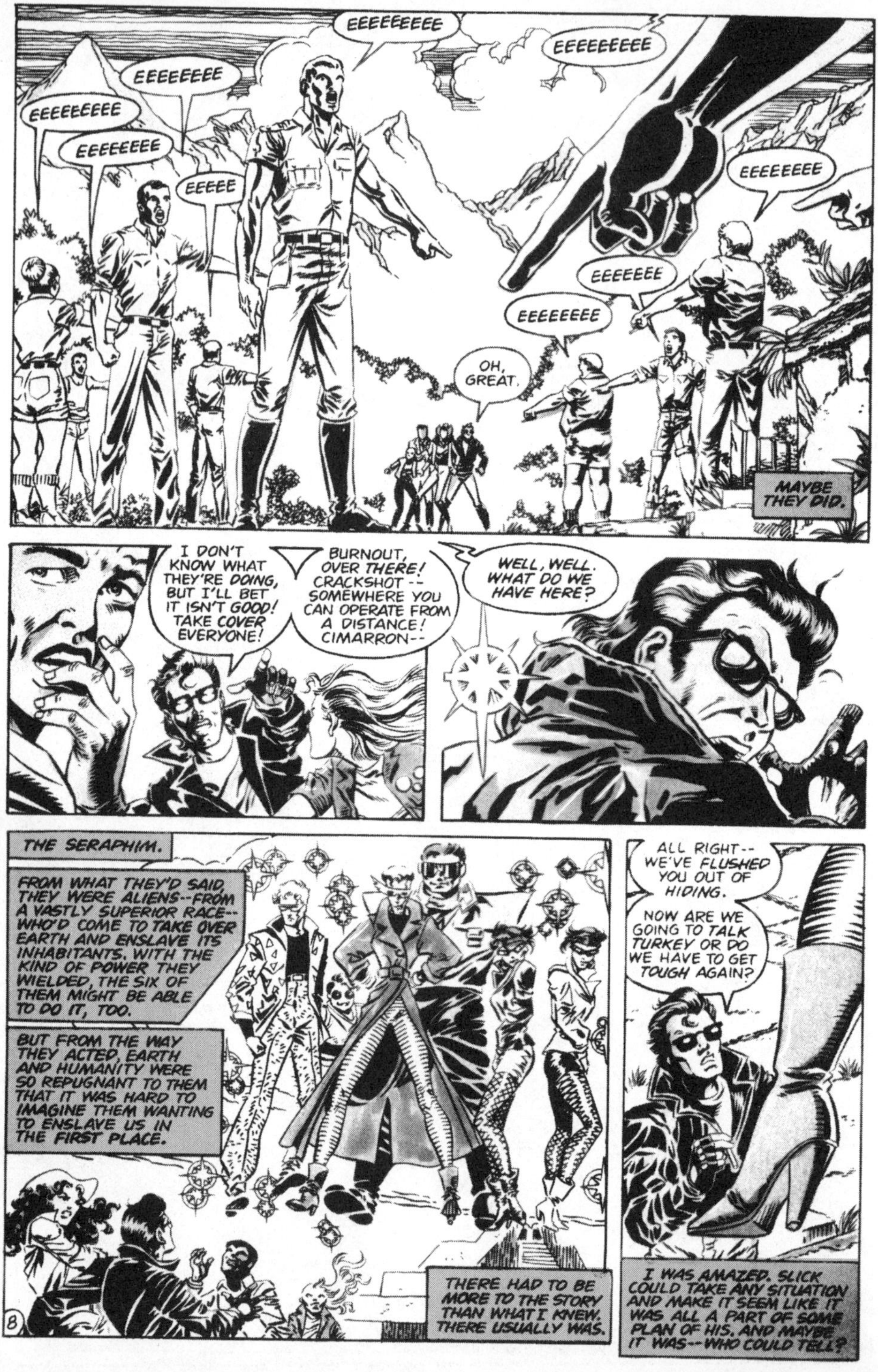
EEEEEEEEE
EEEEEEEE
EEEEEEEEE
EEEEEEEE
EEEEE
EEEEEEEEE
EEEEEEEE
EEEEEEE
EEEEEEEE
OH, GREAT.
MAYBE THEY DID.
I DON'T KNOW WHAT THEY'RE DOING, BUT I'LL BET IT ISN'T GOOD! TAKE COVER EVERYONE!
BURNOUT, OVER THERE! CRACKSHOT -- SOMEWHERE YOU CAN OPERATE FROM A DISTANCE! CIMARRON--
WELL, WELL. WHAT DO WE HAVE HERE?
THE SERAPHIM.
FROM WHAT THEY'D SAID, THEY WERE ALIENS--FROM A VASTLY SUPERIOR RACE--WHO'D COME TO TAKE OVER EARTH AND ENSLAVE ITS INHABITANTS. WITH THE KIND OF POWER THEY WIELDED, THE SIX OF THEM MIGHT BE ABLE TO DO IT, TOO.
BUT FROM THE WAY THEY ACTED, EARTH AND HUMANITY WERE SO REPUGNANT TO THEM THAT IT WAS HARD TO IMAGINE THEM WANTING TO ENSLAVE US IN THE FIRST PLACE.
THERE HAD TO BE MORE TO THE STORY THAN WHAT I KNEW. THERE USUALLY WAS.
ALL RIGHT-- WE'VE FLUSHED YOU OUT OF HIDING.
NOW ARE WE GOING TO TALK TURKEY OR DO WE HAVE TO GET TOUGH AGAIN?
I WAS AMAZED. SLICK COULD TAKE ANY SITUATION AND MAKE IT SEEM LIKE IT WAS ALL A PART OF SOME PLAN OF HIS. AND MAYBE IT WAS--WHO COULD TELL?
8

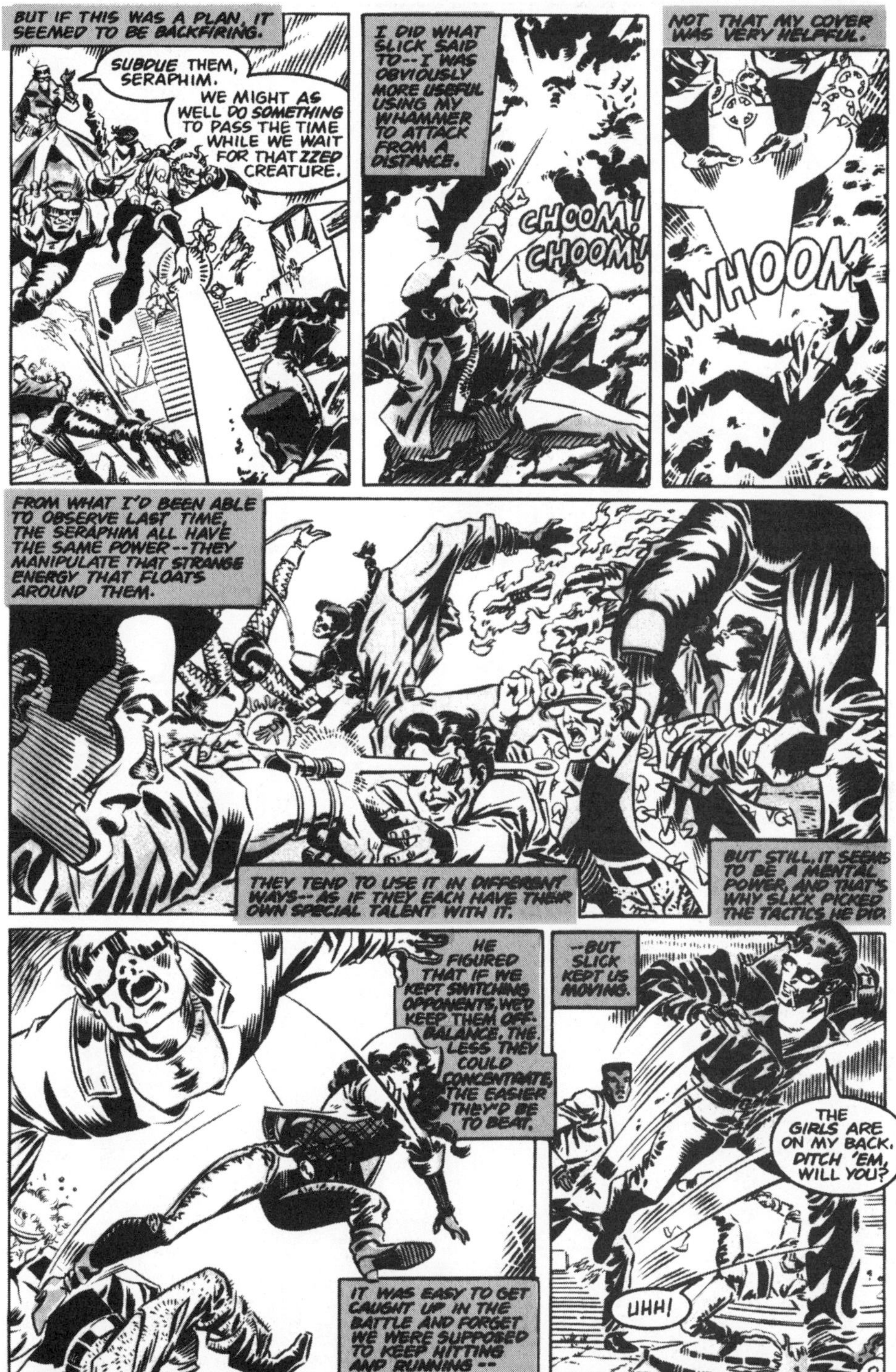
BUT IF THIS WAS A PLAN, IT SEEMED TO BE BACKFIRING.
SUBDUE THEM, SERAPHIM.
WE MIGHT AS WELL DO SOMETHING TO PASS THE TIME WHILE WE WAIT FOR THAT ZZED CREATURE.
I DID WHAT SLICK SAID TO-- I WAS OBVIOUSLY MORE USEFUL USING MY WHAMMER TO ATTACK FROM A DISTANCE.
CHOOM! CHOOM!
NOT THAT MY COVER WAS VERY HELPFUL.
WHOOM
FROM WHAT I'D BEEN ABLE TO OBSERVE LAST TIME, THE SERAPHIM ALL HAVE THE SAME POWER--THEY MANIPULATE THAT STRANGE ENERGY THAT FLOATS AROUND THEM.
THEY TEND TO USE IT IN DIFFERENT WAYS-- AS IF THEY EACH HAVE THEIR OWN SPECIAL TALENT WITH IT.
BUT STILL, IT SEEMS TO BE A MENTAL POWER, AND THAT'S WHY SLICK PICKED THE TACTICS HE DID.
HE FIGURED THAT IF WE KEPT SWITCHING OPPONENTS, WE'D KEEP THEM OFF-BALANCE. THE LESS THEY COULD CONCENTRATE, THE EASIER THEY'D BE TO BEAT.
IT WAS EASY TO GET CAUGHT UP IN THE BATTLE AND FORGET WE WERE SUPPOSED TO KEEP HITTING AND RUNNING--
--BUT SLICK KEPT US MOVING.
THE GIRLS ARE ON MY BACK. DITCH 'EM, WILL YOU?
UHH!

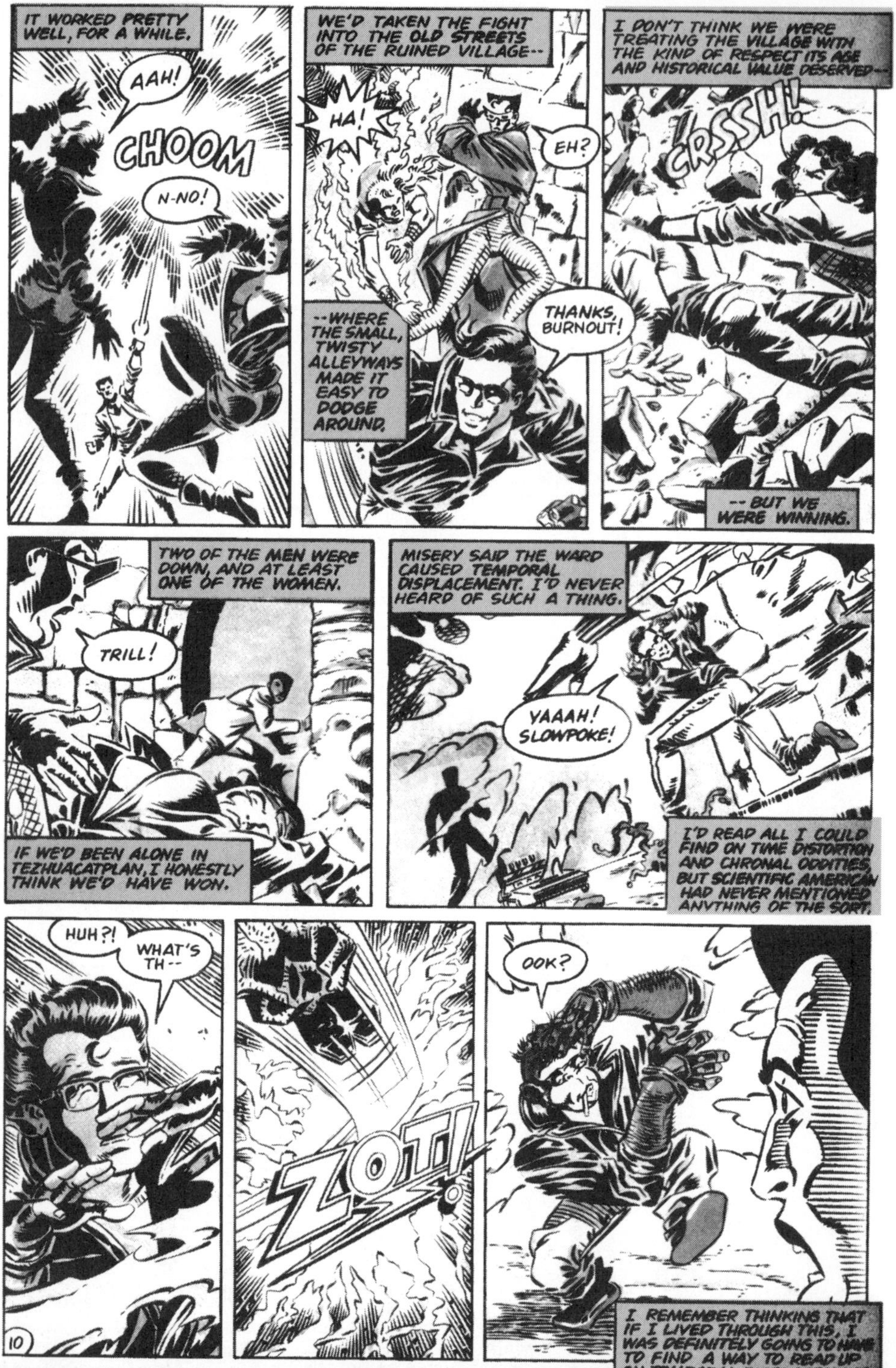
IT WORKED PRETTY WELL, FOR A WHILE.
AAH!
CHOOM
N-NO!
WE'D TAKEN THE FIGHT INTO THE OLD STREETS OF THE RUINED VILLAGE--
HA!
EH?
--WHERE THE SMALL, TWISTY ALLEYWAYS MADE IT EASY TO DODGE AROUND.
THANKS, BURNOUT!
I DON'T THINK WE WERE TREATING THE VILLAGE WITH THE KIND OF RESPECT ITS AGE AND HISTORICAL VALUE DESERVED--
CRSSSH!
--BUT WE WERE WINNING.
TWO OF THE MEN WERE DOWN, AND AT LEAST ONE OF THE WOMEN.
TRILL!
IF WE'D BEEN ALONE IN TEZHUACATPLAN, I HONESTLY THINK WE'D HAVE WON.
MISERY SAID THE WARD CAUSED TEMPORAL DISPLACEMENT. I'D NEVER HEARD OF SUCH A THING.
YAAAH! SLOWPOKE!
I'D READ ALL I COULD FIND ON TIME DISTORTION AND CHRONAL ODDITIES, BUT SCIENTIFIC AMERICAN HAD NEVER MENTIONED ANYTHING OF THE SORT.
HUH?!
WHAT'S TH--
ZOT!
OOK?
I REMEMBER THINKING THAT IF I LIVED THROUGH THIS, I WAS DEFINITELY GOING TO HAVE TO FIND A WAY TO READ UP ON TEMPORAL DISPLACEMENT.
10

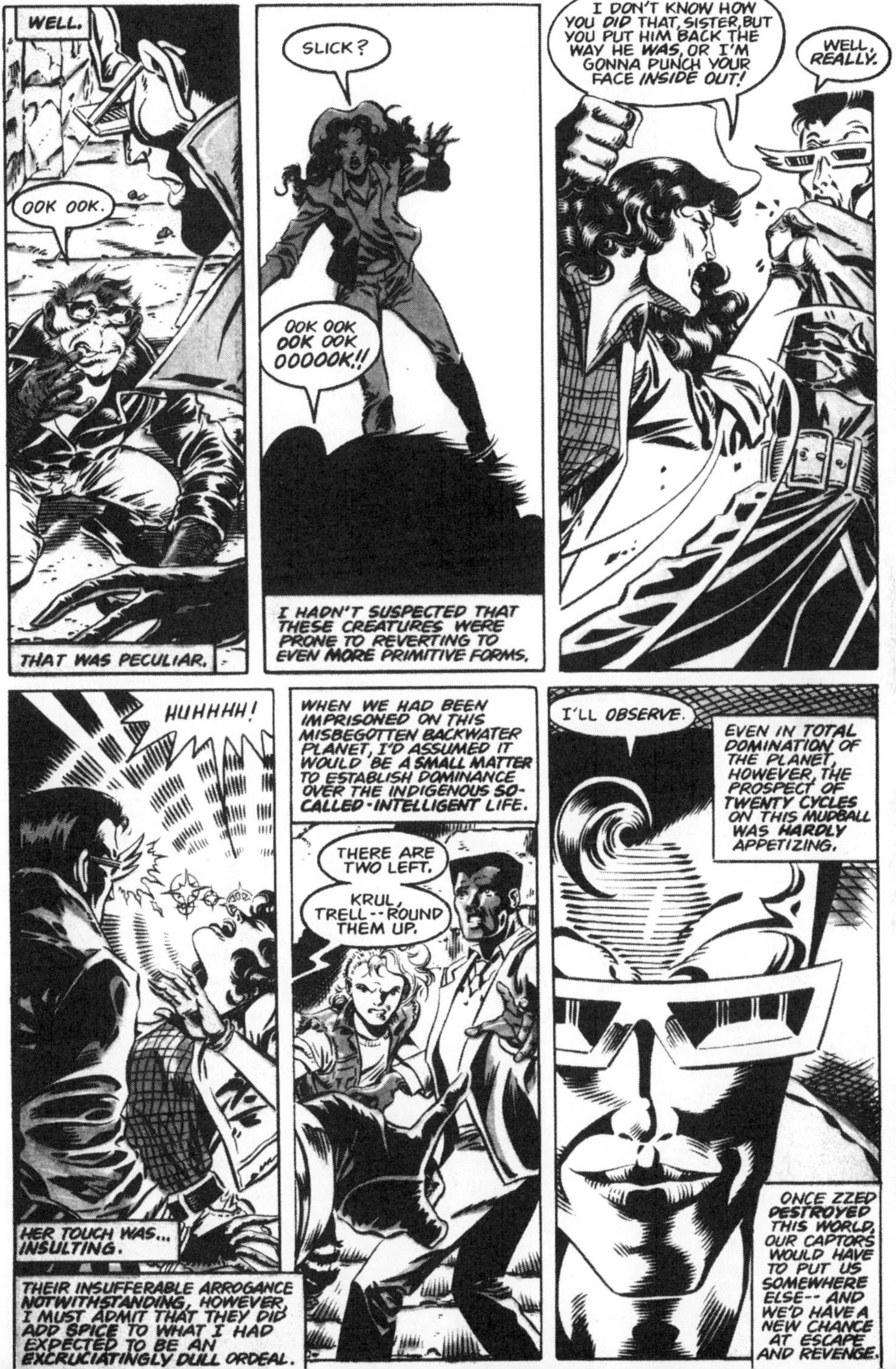
WELL.
OOK OOK.
THAT WAS PECULIAR.
SLICK?
OOK OOK OOK OOK OOOOOK!!
I HADN'T SUSPECTED THAT THESE CREATURES WERE PRONE TO REVERTING TO EVEN MORE PRIMITIVE FORMS.
I DON'T KNOW HOW YOU DID THAT, SISTER, BUT YOU PUT HIM BACK THE WAY HE WAS, OR I'M GONNA PUNCH YOUR FACE INSIDE OUT!
WELL, REALLY.
HUHHHH!
HER TOUCH WAS... INSULTING.
THEIR INSUFFERABLE ARROGANCE NOTWITHSTANDING, HOWEVER, I MUST ADMIT THAT THEY DID ADD SPICE TO WHAT I HAD EXPECTED TO BE AN EXCRUCIATINGLY DULL ORDEAL.
WHEN WE HAD BEEN IMPRISONED ON THIS MISBEGOTTEN BACKWATER PLANET, I'D ASSUMED IT WOULD BE A SMALL MATTER TO ESTABLISH DOMINANCE OVER THE INDIGENOUS SO-CALLED-INTELLIGENT LIFE.
THERE ARE TWO LEFT.
KRUL, TRELL--ROUND THEM UP.
I'LL OBSERVE.
EVEN IN TOTAL DOMINATION OF THE PLANET, HOWEVER, THE PROSPECT OF TWENTY CYCLES ON THIS MUDBALL WAS HARDLY APPETIZING.
ONCE ZZED DESTROYED THIS WORLD, OUR CAPTORS WOULD HAVE TO PUT US SOMEWHERE ELSE-- AND WE'D HAVE A NEW CHANCE AT ESCAPE AND REVENGE.

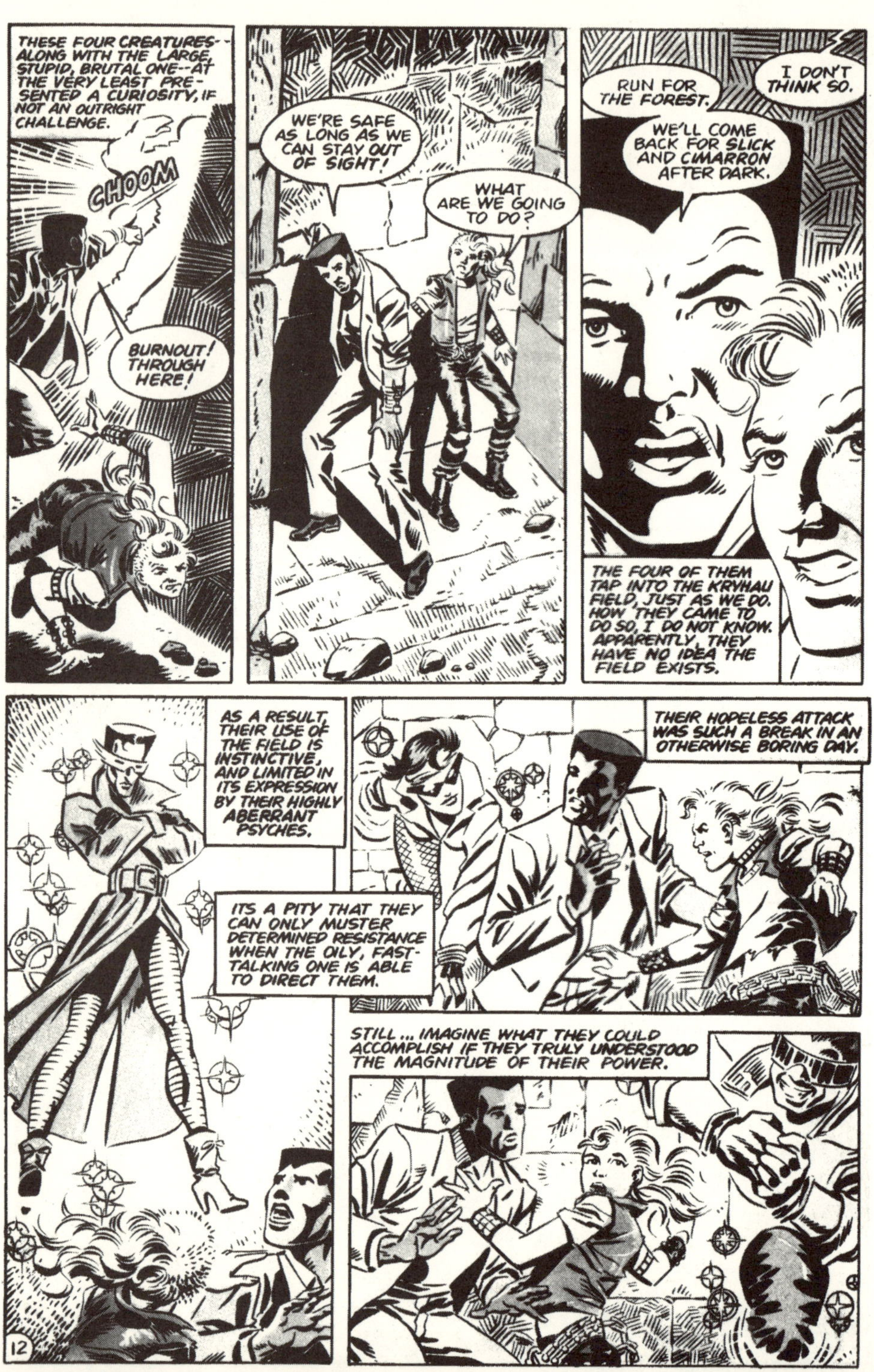
THESE FOUR CREATURES--ALONG WITH THE LARGE, STUPID, BRUTAL ONE--AT THE VERY LEAST PRESENTED A CURIOSITY, IF NOT AN OUTRIGHT CHALLENGE.
CHOOM
BURNOUT! THROUGH HERE!
WE'RE SAFE AS LONG AS WE CAN STAY OUT OF SIGHT!
WHAT ARE WE GOING TO DO?
RUN FOR THE FOREST.
I DON'T THINK SO.
WE'LL COME BACK FOR SLICK AND CIMARRON AFTER DARK.
THE FOUR OF THEM TAP INTO THE KRYHAU FIELD, JUST AS WE DO. HOW THEY CAME TO DO SO, I DO NOT KNOW. APPARENTLY, THEY HAVE NO IDEA THE FIELD EXISTS.
AS A RESULT, THEIR USE OF THE FIELD IS INSTINCTIVE, AND LIMITED IN ITS EXPRESSION BY THEIR HIGHLY ABERRANT PSYCHES.
ITS A PITY THAT THEY CAN ONLY MUSTER DETERMINED RESISTANCE WHEN THE OILY, FAST-TALKING ONE IS ABLE TO DIRECT THEM.
THEIR HOPELESS ATTACK WAS SUCH A BREAK IN AN OTHERWISE BORING DAY.
STILL ... IMAGINE WHAT THEY COULD ACCOMPLISH IF THEY TRULY UNDERSTOOD THE MAGNITUDE OF THEIR POWER.
12

YOU AIN'T GETTIN' AWAY WITH THIS!
WE'LL FIND A WAY TO BUST FREE-- AND THEN WE'LL BE ON YOUR BUTTS LIKE CREAM ON STRAWBERRIES!
SHE WAS VERY LIKELY RIGHT. WHATEVER SHE MEANT.
THAT WAS, OF COURSE, ASSUMING THAT WE WOULD ALLOW THEM TO RETAIN THEIR FREE WILL, WHICH WAS OUT OF THE QUESTION.
ZNAID-- IF YOU WILL?
OF COURSE.
ZNAID'S BRAND OF PSIONIC SUBJUGATION IS BOTH EFFICIENT AND EFFECTIVE. IT'S A PITY WE CAN'T USE IT TO TAKE OVER THE ENTIRE PLANET--
--BUT WHILE IT'S QUITE USEFUL IN CONTROLLING INDIVIDUALS, IT DOES HAVE TO BE DONE INDIVIDUALLY. THERE ARE BILLIONS OF THESE "HUMANS" ON THIS PLANET--
--WERE WE TO TRY TO SUBJUGATE THEM ALL, WE'D STILL BE AT IT WHEN OUR SENTENCES OF IMPRISONMENT WERE UP.
POP!
UHH!
WHAT--WHAT HAPPENED?
INTERESTING. THE EFFECT WAS TEMPORARY.
ZORCH!
NO MATTER. ZNAID COULD DO FOUR AS EASILY AS THREE.
THE SMALL ONE WAS TERRIFIED. RAGE AND FEAR HAD COMPLETELY OVERWHELMED HER THOUGHTS.
ZORCH!
NOT THAT HER CHAOTIC AND TROUBLED MIND WAS EVER PARTICULARLY USEFUL TO HER.
SHE SHOULD REALLY HAVE THANKED ZNAID.
ZORCH!
HE WAS SOLVING ALL OF HER EMOTIONAL PROBLEMS.

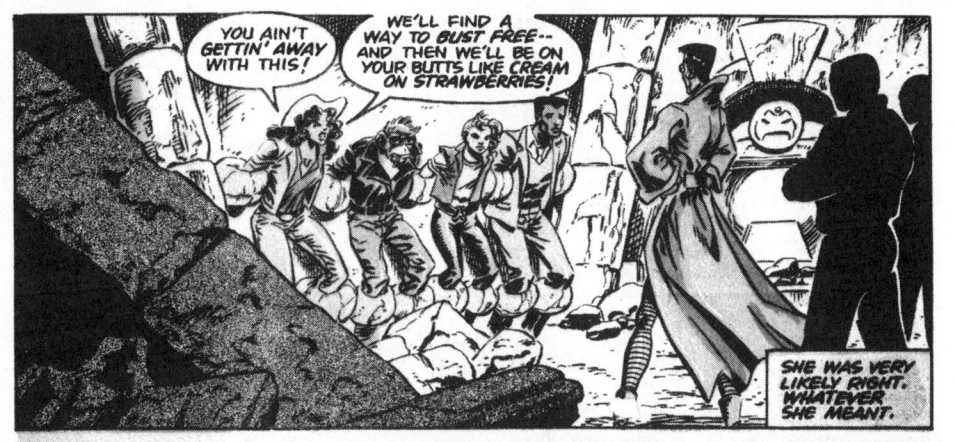

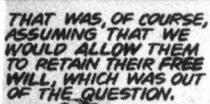

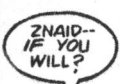

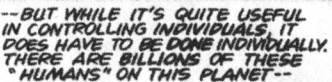

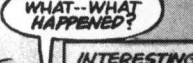

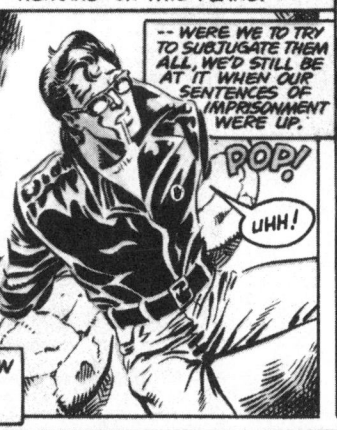

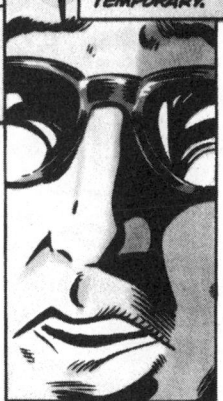

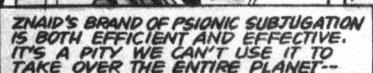

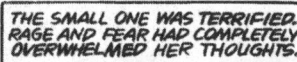

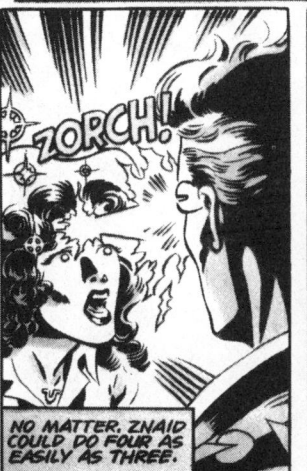

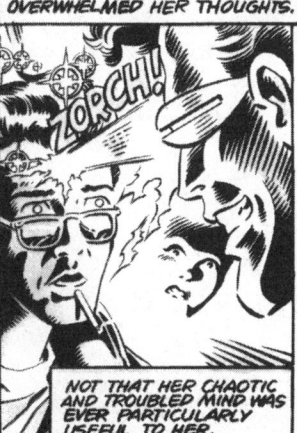

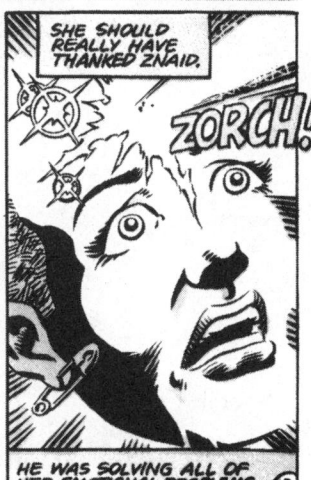

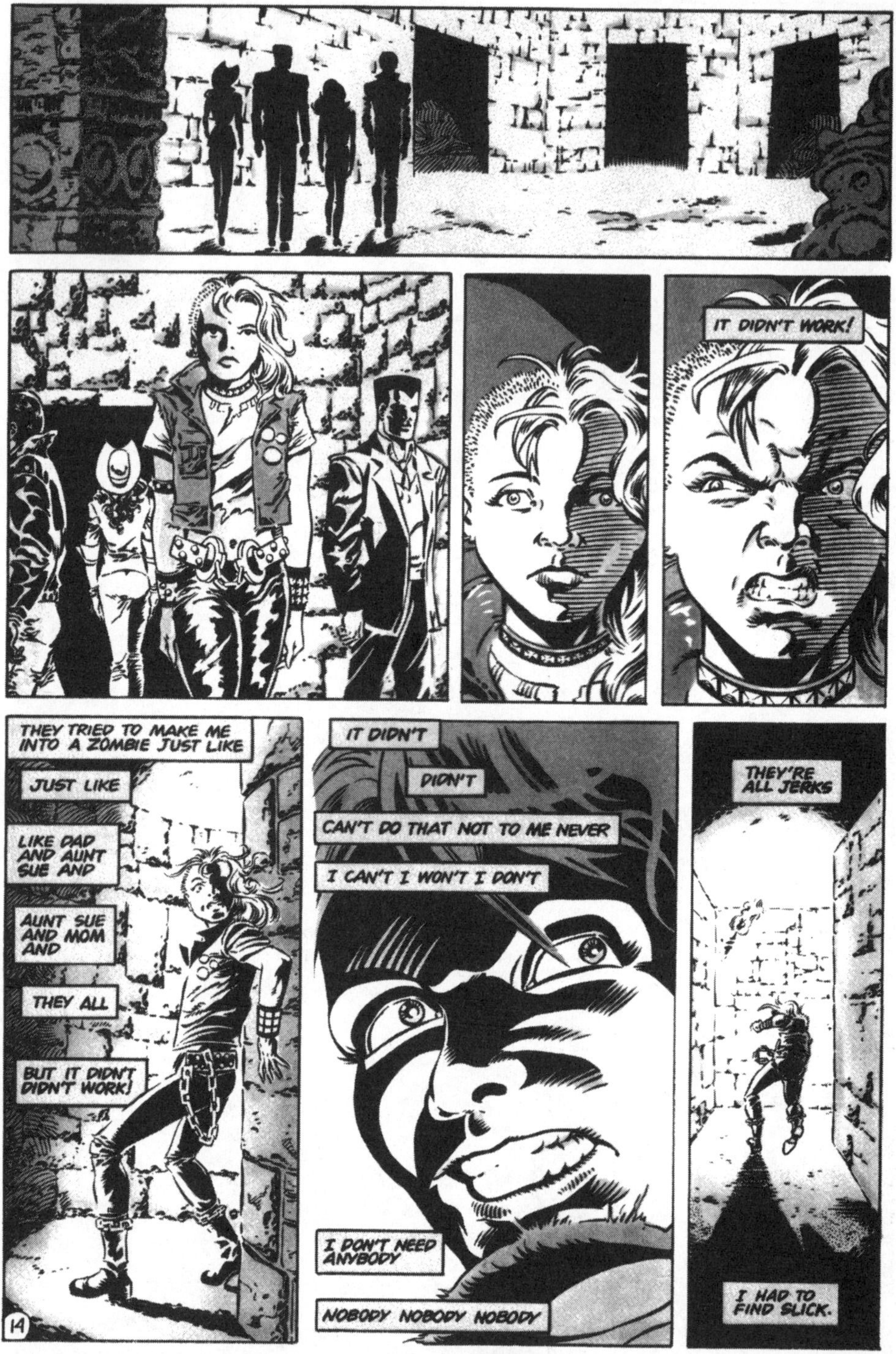
IT DIDN'T WORK!
THEY TRIED TO MAKE ME INTO A ZOMBIE JUST LIKE
JUST LIKE
LIKE DAD AND AUNT SUE AND
AUNT SUE AND MOM AND
THEY ALL
BUT IT DIDN'T DIDN'T WORK!
14
IT DIDN'T
DIDN'T
CAN'T DO THAT NOT TO ME NEVER
I CAN'T I WON'T I DON'T
I DON'T NEED ANYBODY
NOBODY NOBODY NOBODY
THEY'RE ALL JERKS
I HAD TO FIND SLICK.

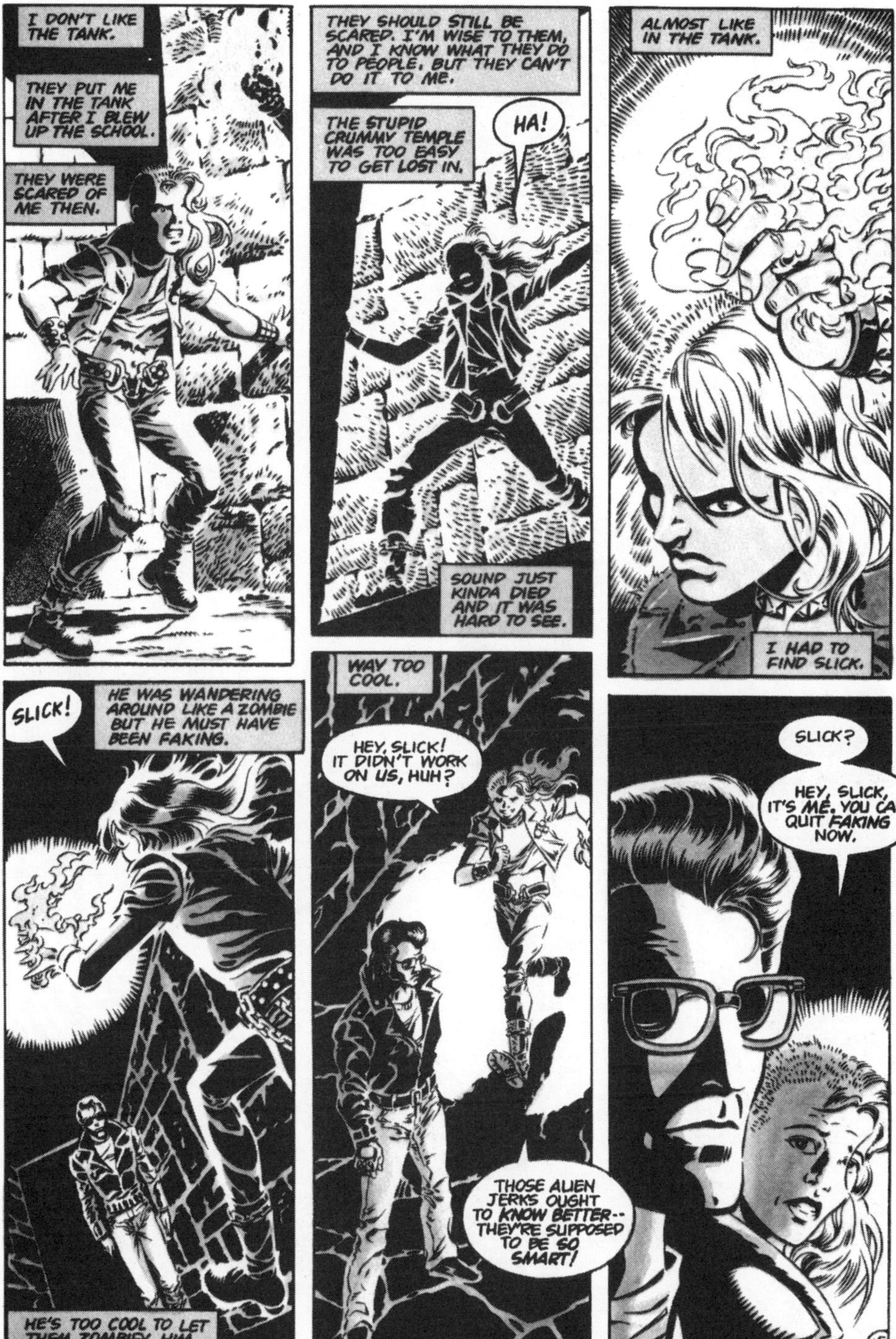
I DON'T LIKE THE TANK.
THEY PUT ME IN THE TANK AFTER I BLEW UP THE SCHOOL.
THEY WERE SCARED OF ME THEN.
THEY SHOULD STILL BE SCARED. I'M WISE TO THEM, AND I KNOW WHAT THEY DO TO PEOPLE. BUT THEY CAN'T DO IT TO ME.
THE STUPID CRUMMY TEMPLE WAS TOO EASY TO GET LOST IN.
HA!
SOUND JUST KINDA DIED AND IT WAS HARD TO SEE.
ALMOST LIKE IN THE TANK.
I HAD TO FIND SLICK.
SLICK!
HE WAS WANDERING AROUND LIKE A ZOMBIE BUT HE MUST HAVE BEEN FAKING.
HE'S TOO COOL TO LET THEM ZOMBIFY HIM.
WAY TOO COOL.
HEY, SLICK! IT DIDN'T WORK ON US, HUH?
THOSE ALIEN JERKS OUGHT TO KNOW BETTER-- THEY'RE SUPPOSED TO BE SO SMART!
SLICK?
HEY, SLICK, IT'S ME. YOU CAN QUIT FAKING NOW.
15

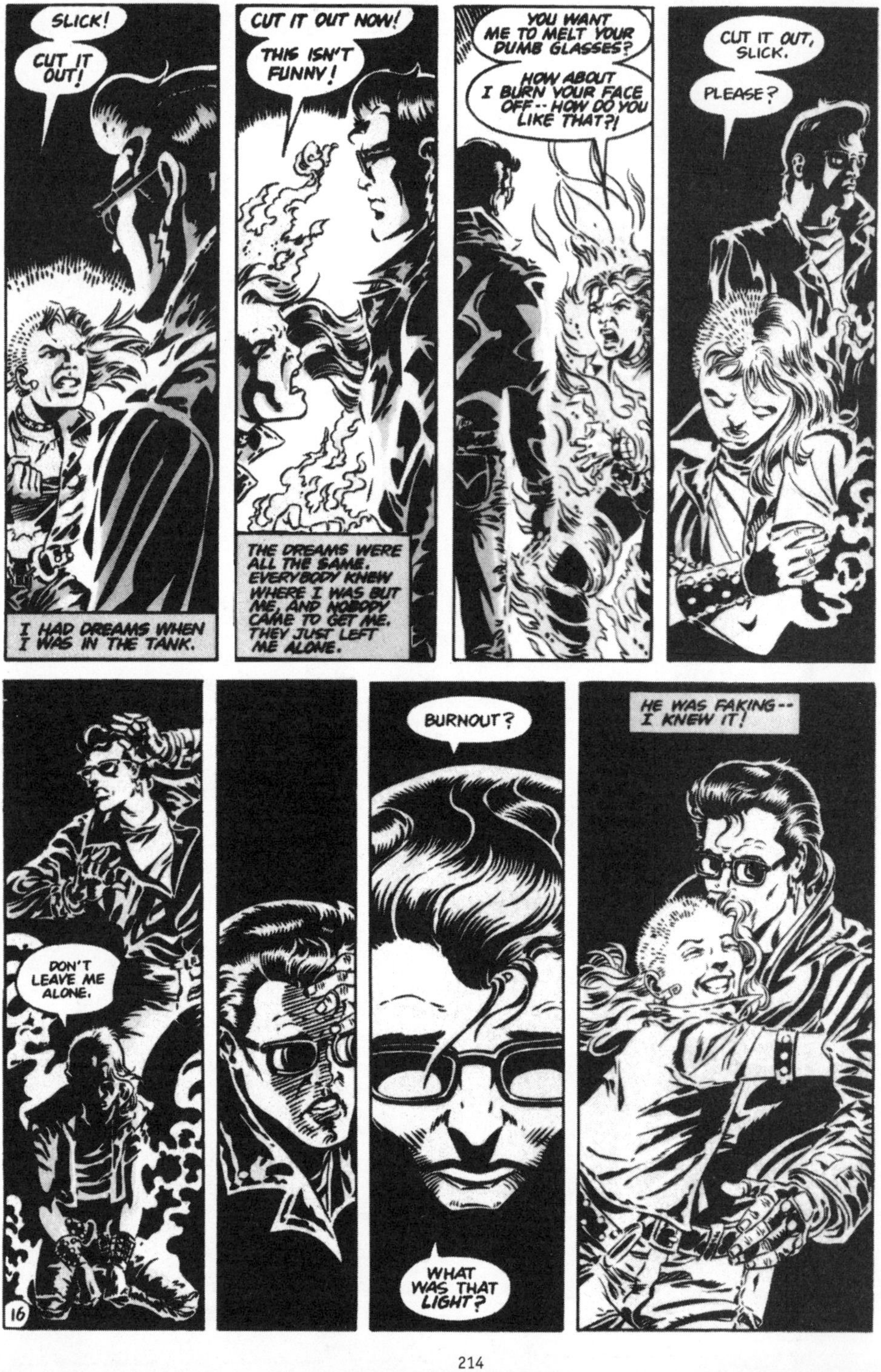
SLICK!
CUT IT OUT!
I HAD DREAMS WHEN I WAS IN THE TANK.
CUT IT OUT NOW!
THIS ISN'T FUNNY!
THE DREAMS WERE ALL THE SAME. EVERYBODY KNEW WHERE I WAS BUT ME, AND NOBODY CAME TO GET ME. THEY JUST LEFT ME ALONE.
YOU WANT ME TO MELT YOUR DUMB GLASSES?
HOW ABOUT I BURN YOUR FACE OFF -- HOW DO YOU LIKE THAT?!
CUT IT OUT, SLICK.
PLEASE?
DON'T LEAVE ME ALONE.
16
BURNOUT?
WHAT WAS THAT LIGHT?
HE WAS FAKING -- I KNEW IT!

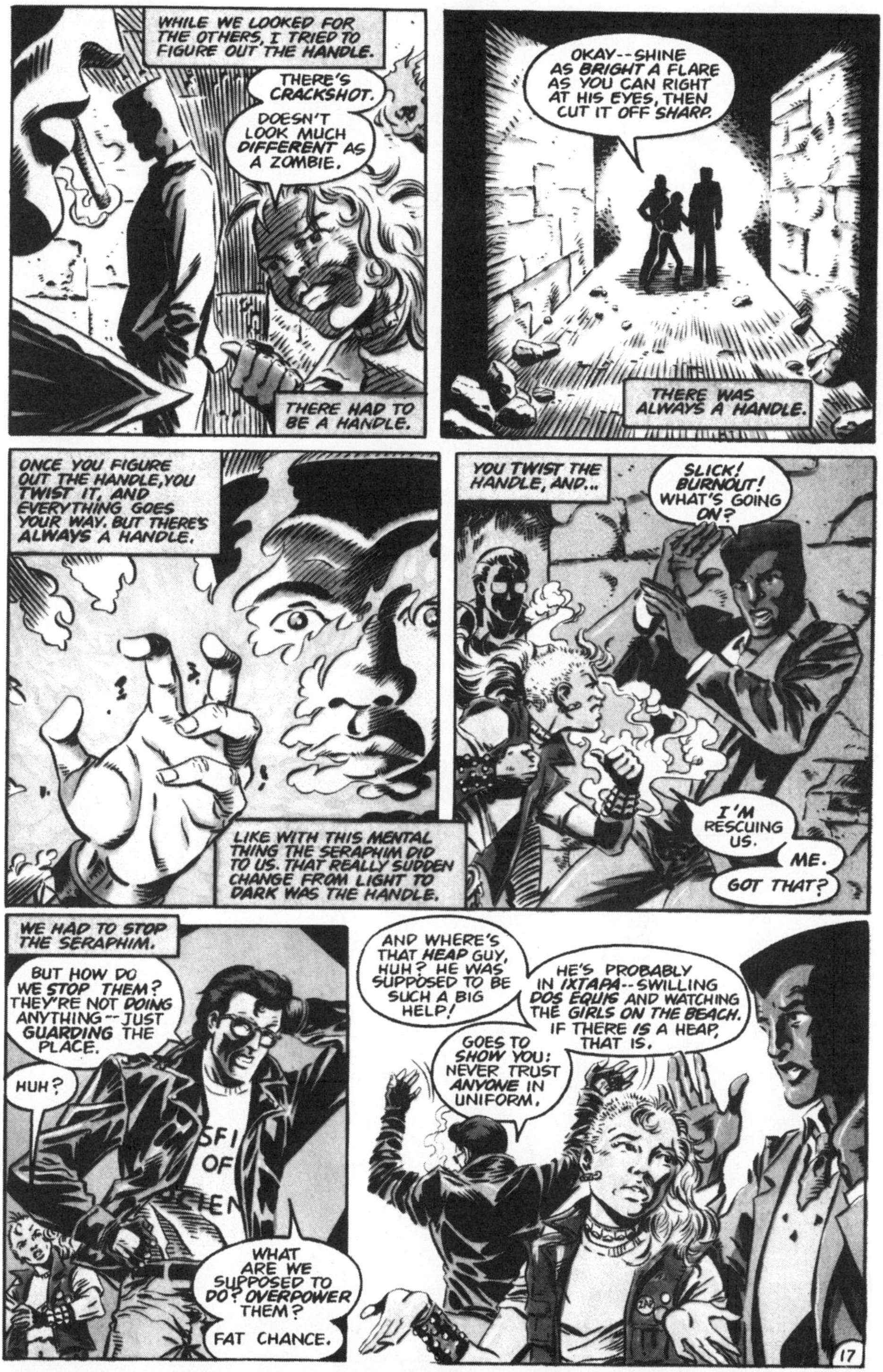
WHILE WE LOOKED FOR THE OTHERS, I TRIED TO FIGURE OUT THE HANDLE.
THERE'S CRACKSHOT.
DOESN'T LOOK MUCH DIFFERENT AS A ZOMBIE.
THERE HAD TO BE A HANDLE.
OKAY--SHINE AS BRIGHT A FLARE AS YOU CAN RIGHT AT HIS EYES, THEN CUT IT OFF SHARP.
THERE WAS ALWAYS A HANDLE.
ONCE YOU FIGURE OUT THE HANDLE, YOU TWIST IT, AND EVERYTHING GOES YOUR WAY. BUT THERE'S ALWAYS A HANDLE.
LIKE WITH THIS MENTAL THING THE SERAPHIM DID TO US. THAT REALLY SUDDEN CHANGE FROM LIGHT TO DARK WAS THE HANDLE.
YOU TWIST THE HANDLE, AND...
SLICK! BURNOUT! WHAT'S GOING ON?
I'M RESCUING US.
ME.
GOT THAT?
WE HAD TO STOP THE SERAPHIM.
BUT HOW DO WE STOP THEM? THEY'RE NOT DOING ANYTHING--JUST GUARDING THE PLACE.
HUH?
WHAT ARE WE SUPPOSED TO DO? OVERPOWER THEM?
FAT CHANCE.
AND WHERE'S THAT HEAP GUY, HUH? HE WAS SUPPOSED TO BE SUCH A BIG HELP!
HE'S PROBABLY IN IXTAPA--SWILLING DOS EQUIS AND WATCHING THE GIRLS ON THE BEACH. IF THERE IS A HEAP, THAT IS.
GOES TO SHOW YOU: NEVER TRUST ANYONE IN UNIFORM.

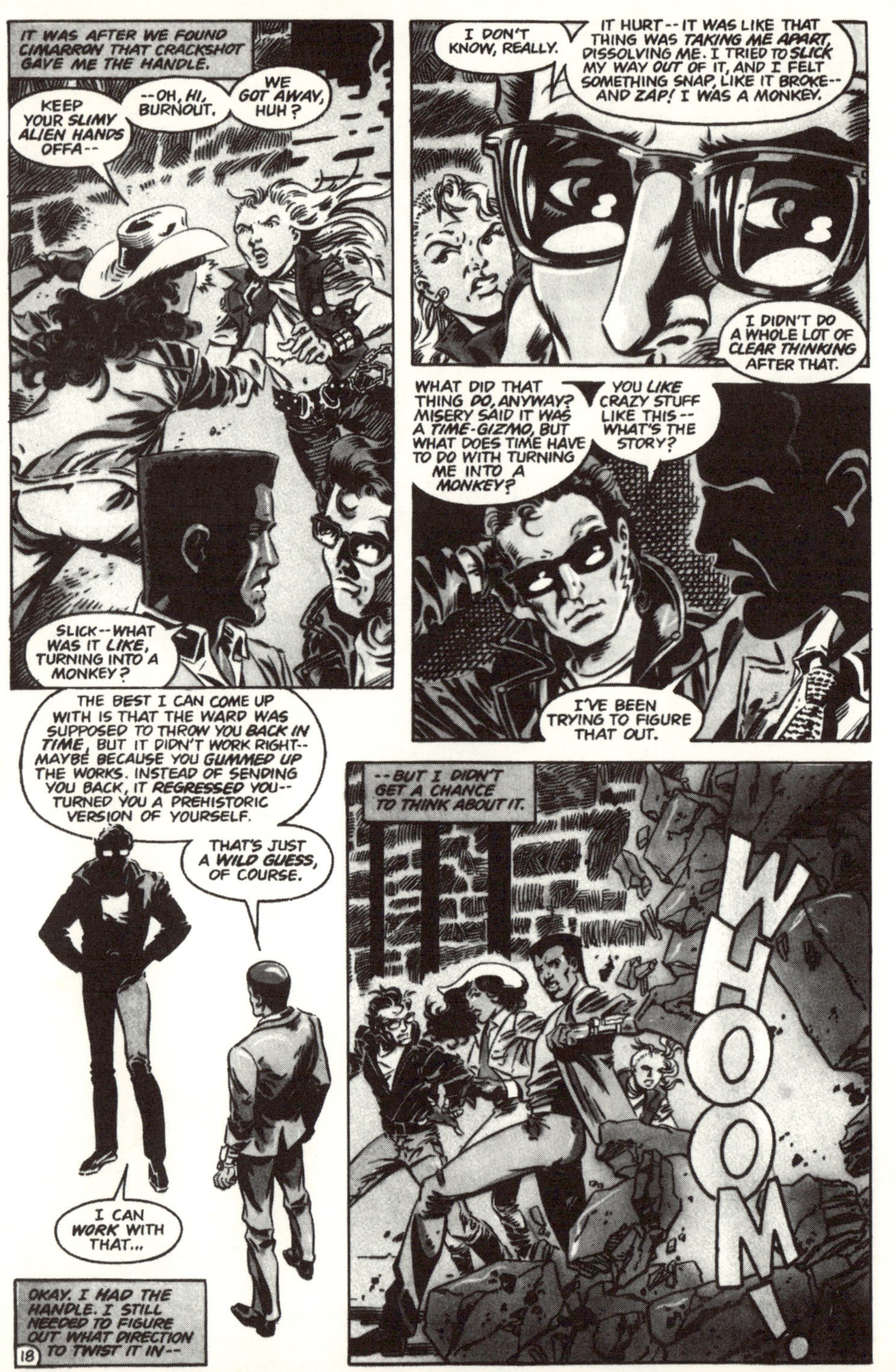
IT WAS AFTER WE FOUND CIMARRON THAT CRACKSHOT GAVE ME THE HANDLE.
KEEP YOUR SLIMY ALIEN HANDS OFFA--
--OH, HI, BURNOUT.
WE GOT AWAY, HUH?
SLICK--WHAT WAS IT LIKE, TURNING INTO A MONKEY?
I DON'T KNOW, REALLY.
IT HURT--IT WAS LIKE THAT THING WAS TAKING ME APART, DISSOLVING ME. I TRIED TO SLICK MY WAY OUT OF IT, AND I FELT SOMETHING SNAP, LIKE IT BROKE--AND ZAP! I WAS A MONKEY.
I DIDN'T DO A WHOLE LOT OF CLEAR THINKING AFTER THAT.
WHAT DID THAT THING DO, ANYWAY? MISERY SAID IT WAS A TIME-GIZMO, BUT WHAT DOES TIME HAVE TO DO WITH TURNING ME INTO A MONKEY?
YOU LIKE CRAZY STUFF LIKE THIS--WHAT'S THE STORY?
I'VE BEEN TRYING TO FIGURE THAT OUT.
THE BEST I CAN COME UP WITH IS THAT THE WARD WAS SUPPOSED TO THROW YOU BACK IN TIME, BUT IT DIDN'T WORK RIGHT--MAYBE BECAUSE YOU GUMMED UP THE WORKS. INSTEAD OF SENDING YOU BACK, IT REGRESSED YOU--TURNED YOU A PREHISTORIC VERSION OF YOURSELF.
THAT'S JUST A WILD GUESS, OF COURSE.
I CAN WORK WITH THAT...
OKAY. I HAD THE HANDLE. I STILL NEEDED TO FIGURE OUT WHAT DIRECTION TO TWIST IT IN--
--BUT I DIDN'T GET A CHANCE TO THINK ABOUT IT.
WHOOM!

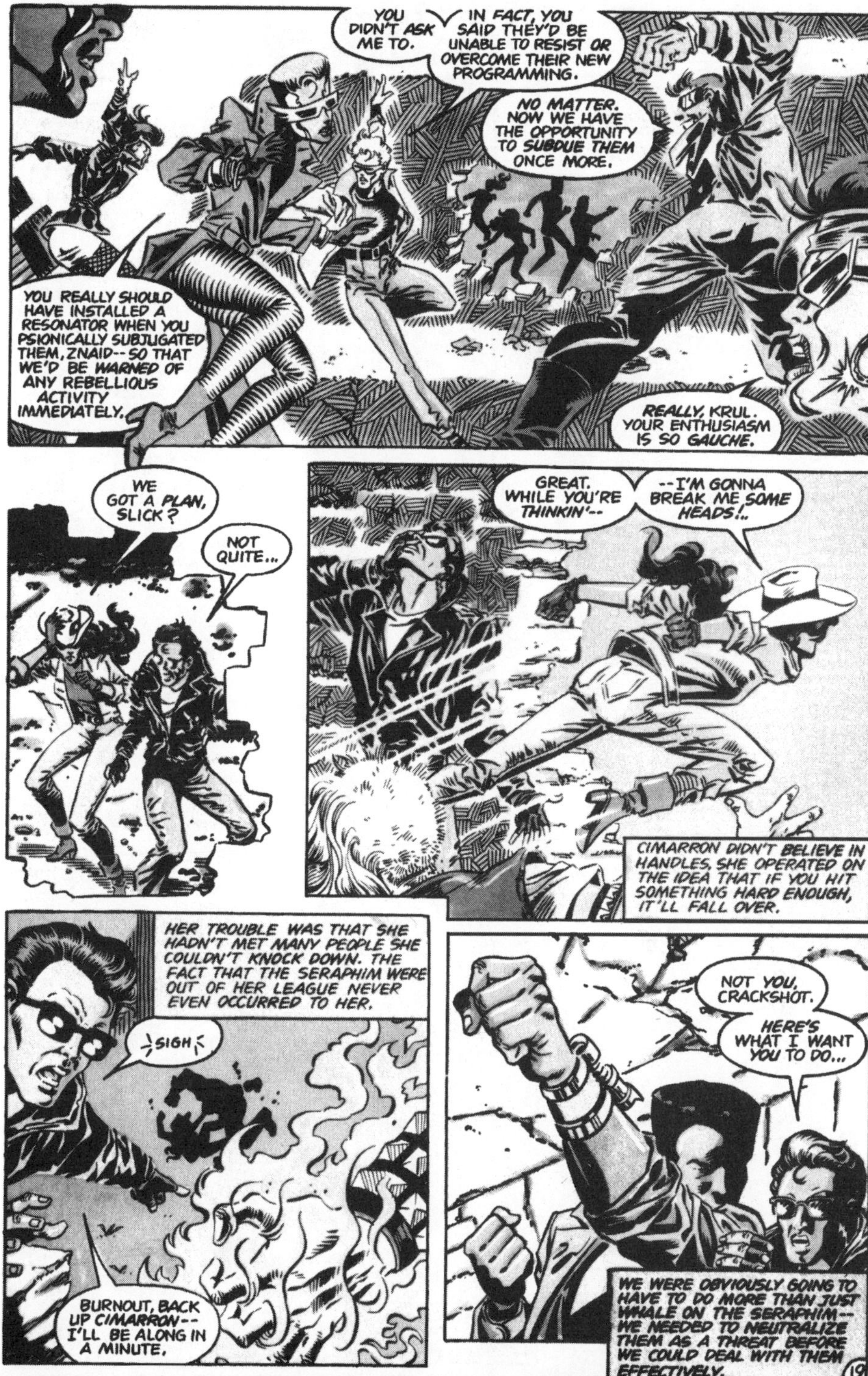

YOU DIDN'T ASK ME TO.
IN FACT, YOU SAID THEY'D BE UNABLE TO RESIST OR OVERCOME THEIR NEW PROGRAMMING.
NO MATTER. NOW WE HAVE THE OPPORTUNITY TO SUBDUE THEM ONCE MORE.
YOU REALLY SHOULD HAVE INSTALLED A RESONATOR WHEN YOU PSIONICALLY SUBJUGATED THEM, ZNAID-- SO THAT WE'D BE WARNED OF ANY REBELLIOUS ACTIVITY IMMEDIATELY.
REALLY, KRUL. YOUR ENTHUSIASM IS SO GAUCHE.
WE GOT A PLAN, SLICK?
NOT QUITE...
GREAT. WHILE YOU'RE THINKIN'--
--I'M GONNA BREAK ME SOME HEADS!..
CIMARRON DIDN'T BELIEVE IN HANDLES, SHE OPERATED ON THE IDEA THAT IF YOU HIT SOMETHING HARD ENOUGH, IT'LL FALL OVER.
HER TROUBLE WAS THAT SHE HADN'T MET MANY PEOPLE SHE COULDN'T KNOCK DOWN. THE FACT THAT THE SERAPHIM WERE OUT OF HER LEAGUE NEVER EVEN OCCURRED TO HER.
SIGH
BURNOUT, BACK UP CIMARRON-- I'LL BE ALONG IN A MINUTE.
NOT YOU, CRACKSHOT.
HERE'S WHAT I WANT YOU TO DO...
WE WERE OBVIOUSLY GOING TO HAVE TO DO MORE THAN JUST WHALE ON THE SERAPHIM-- WE NEEDED TO NEUTRALIZE THEM AS A THREAT BEFORE WE COULD DEAL WITH THEM EFFECTIVELY.

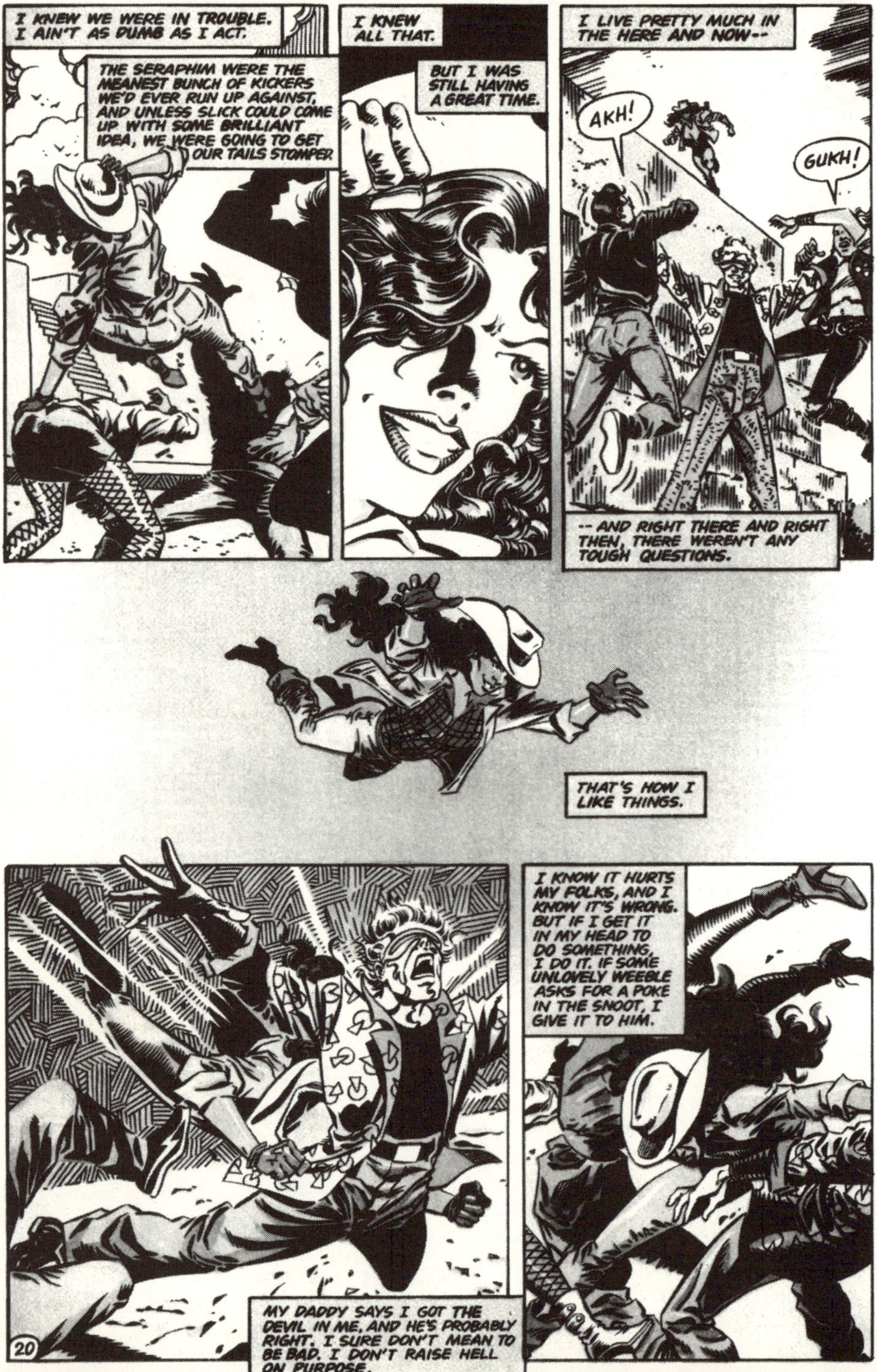
I KNEW WE WERE IN TROUBLE. I AIN'T AS DUMB AS I ACT.
THE SERAPHIM WERE THE MEANEST BUNCH OF KICKERS WE'D EVER RUN UP AGAINST, AND UNLESS SLICK COULD COME UP WITH SOME BRILLIANT IDEA, WE WERE GOING TO GET OUR TAILS STOMPED.
I KNEW ALL THAT.
BUT I WAS STILL HAVING A GREAT TIME.
I LIVE PRETTY MUCH IN THE HERE AND NOW--
AKH!
GUKH!
--AND RIGHT THERE AND RIGHT THEN, THERE WEREN'T ANY TOUGH QUESTIONS.
THAT'S HOW I LIKE THINGS.
MY DADDY SAYS I GOT THE DEVIL IN ME, AND HE'S PROBABLY RIGHT. I SURE DON'T MEAN TO BE BAD. I DON'T RAISE HELL ON PURPOSE.
I KNOW IT HURTS MY FOLKS, AND I KNOW IT'S WRONG. BUT IF I GET IT IN MY HEAD TO DO SOMETHING, I DO IT. IF SOME UNLOVELY WEEBLE ASKS FOR A POKE IN THE SNOOT, I GIVE IT TO HIM.

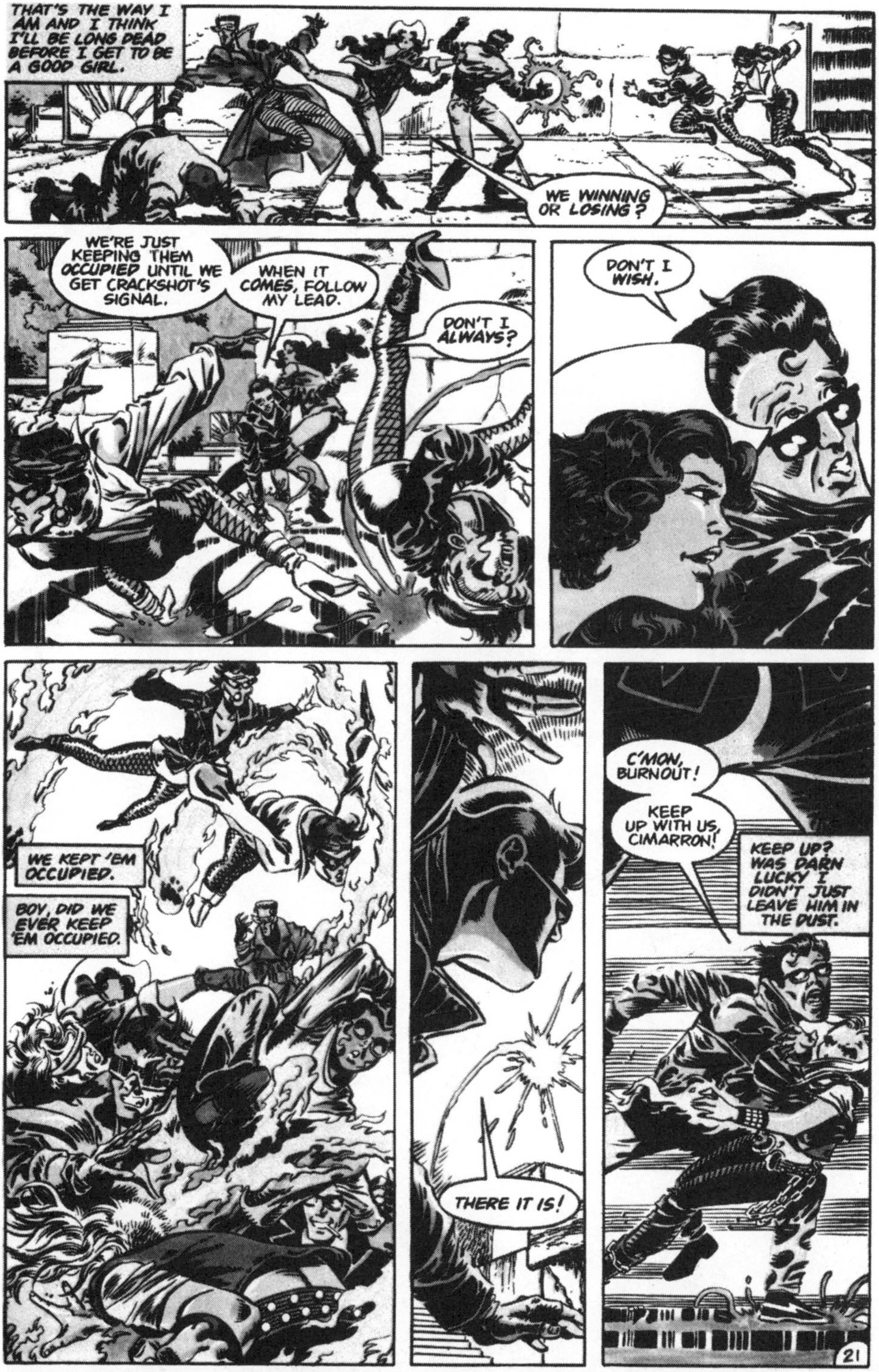

THAT'S THE WAY I AM AND I THINK I'LL BE LONG DEAD BEFORE I GET TO BE A GOOD GIRL.
WE WINNING OR LOSING?
WE'RE JUST KEEPING THEM OCCUPIED UNTIL WE GET CRACKSHOT'S SIGNAL.
WHEN IT COMES, FOLLOW MY LEAD.
DON'T I ALWAYS?
DON'T I WISH.
WE KEPT 'EM OCCUPIED.
BOY, DID WE EVER KEEP 'EM OCCUPIED.
THERE IT IS!
C'MON, BURNOUT!
KEEP UP WITH US, CIMARRON!
KEEP UP? WAS DARN LUCKY I DIDN'T JUST LEAVE HIM IN THE DUST.

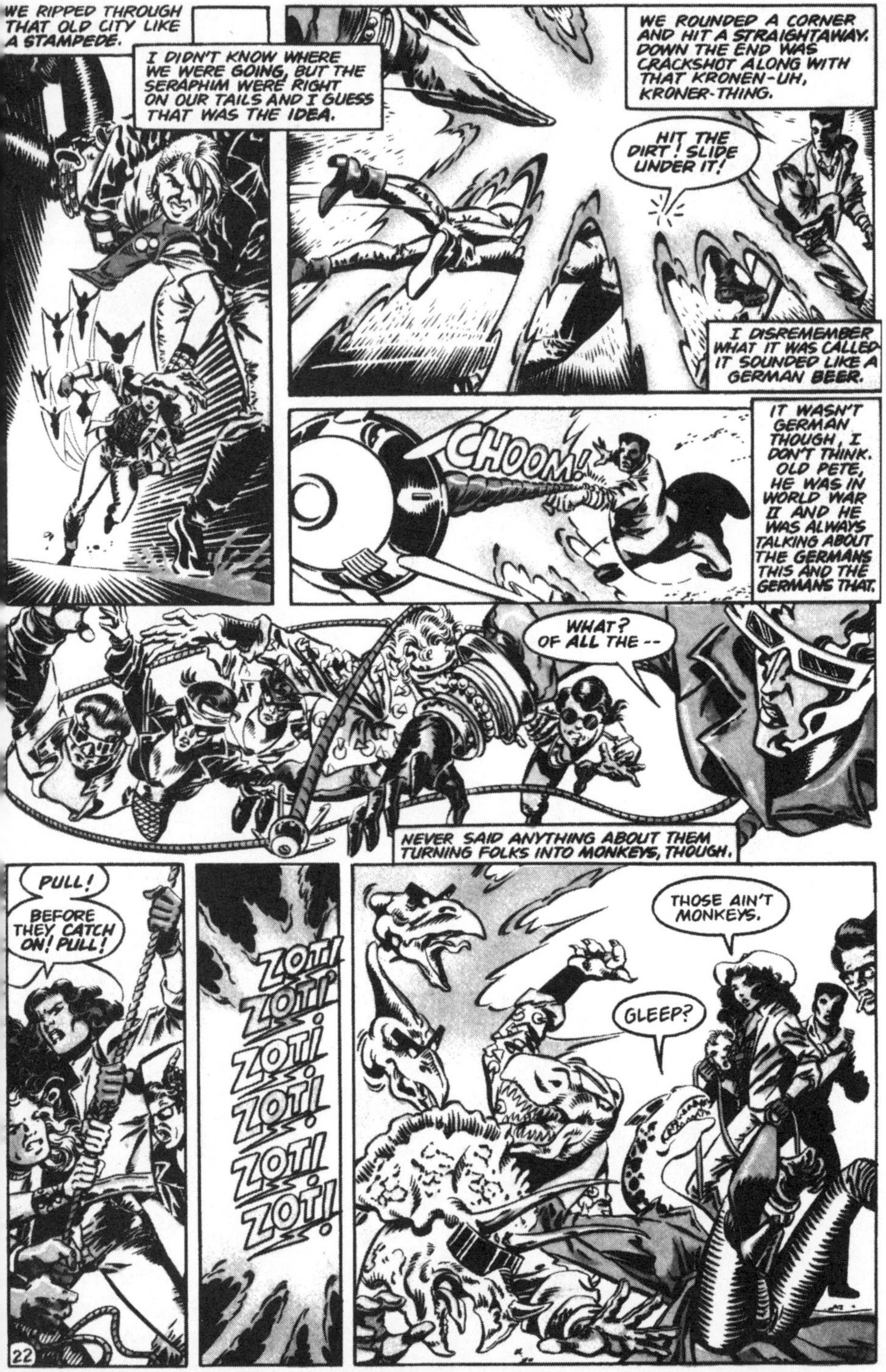

WE RIPPED THROUGH THAT OLD CITY LIKE A STAMPEDE.
I DIDN'T KNOW WHERE WE WERE GOING, BUT THE SERAPHIM WERE RIGHT ON OUR TAILS AND I GUESS THAT WAS THE IDEA.
WE ROUNDED A CORNER AND HIT A STRAIGHTAWAY. DOWN THE END WAS CRACKSHOT ALONG WITH THAT KRONEN-UH, KRONER-THING.
HIT THE DIRT! SLIDE UNDER IT!
I DISREMEMBER WHAT IT WAS CALLED. IT SOUNDED LIKE A GERMAN BEER.
CHOOM!
IT WASN'T GERMAN THOUGH, I DON'T THINK. OLD PETE, HE WAS IN WORLD WAR II AND HE WAS ALWAYS TALKING ABOUT THE GERMANS THIS AND THE GERMANS THAT.
WHAT? OF ALL THE --
NEVER SAID ANYTHING ABOUT THEM TURNING FOLKS INTO MONKEYS, THOUGH.
PULL!
BEFORE THEY CATCH ON! PULL!
ZOT! ZOT! ZOT! ZOT! ZOT! ZOT!
THOSE AIN'T MONKEYS.
GLEEP?

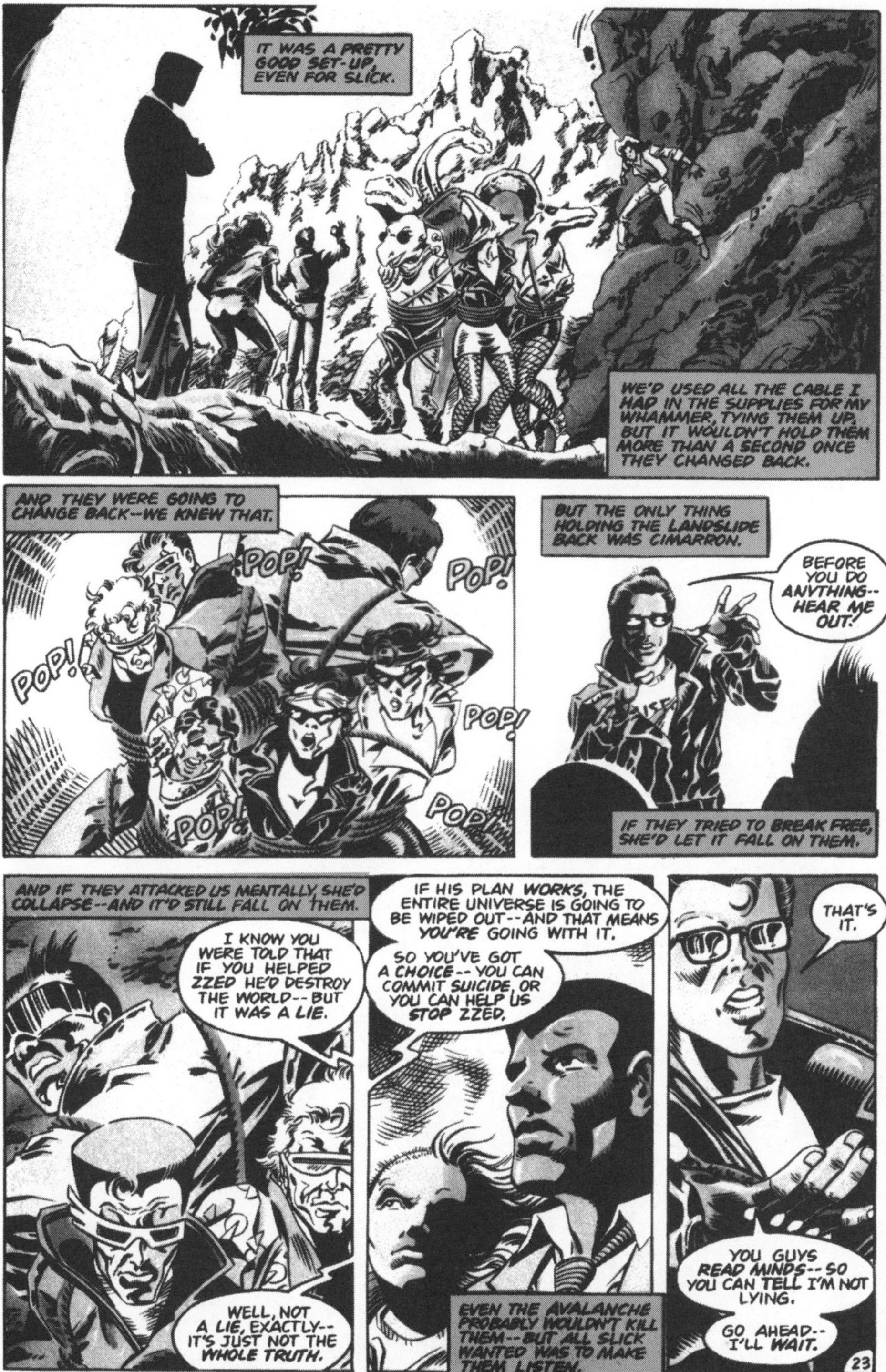
IT WAS A PRETTY GOOD SET-UP, EVEN FOR SLICK.
WE'D USED ALL THE CABLE I HAD IN THE SUPPLIES FOR MY WHAMMER, TYING THEM UP, BUT IT WOULDN'T HOLD THEM MORE THAN A SECOND ONCE THEY CHANGED BACK.
AND THEY WERE GOING TO CHANGE BACK--WE KNEW THAT.
POP!
POP!
POP!
POP!
POP!
POP!
BUT THE ONLY THING HOLDING THE LANDSLIDE BACK WAS CIMARRON.
BEFORE YOU DO ANYTHING--HEAR ME OUT!
IF THEY TRIED TO BREAK FREE, SHE'D LET IT FALL ON THEM.
AND IF THEY ATTACKED US MENTALLY, SHE'D COLLAPSE--AND IT'D STILL FALL ON THEM.
I KNOW YOU WERE TOLD THAT IF YOU HELPED ZZED HE'D DESTROY THE WORLD--BUT IT WAS A LIE.
WELL, NOT A LIE, EXACTLY--IT'S JUST NOT THE WHOLE TRUTH.
IF HIS PLAN WORKS, THE ENTIRE UNIVERSE IS GOING TO BE WIPED OUT--AND THAT MEANS YOU'RE GOING WITH IT.
SO YOU'VE GOT A CHOICE--YOU CAN COMMIT SUICIDE, OR YOU CAN HELP US STOP ZZED.
EVEN THE AVALANCHE PROBABLY WOULDN'T KILL THEM--BUT ALL SLICK WANTED WAS TO MAKE THEM LISTEN.
THAT'S IT.
YOU GUYS READ MINDS--SO YOU CAN TELL I'M NOT LYING.
GO AHEAD--I'LL WAIT.

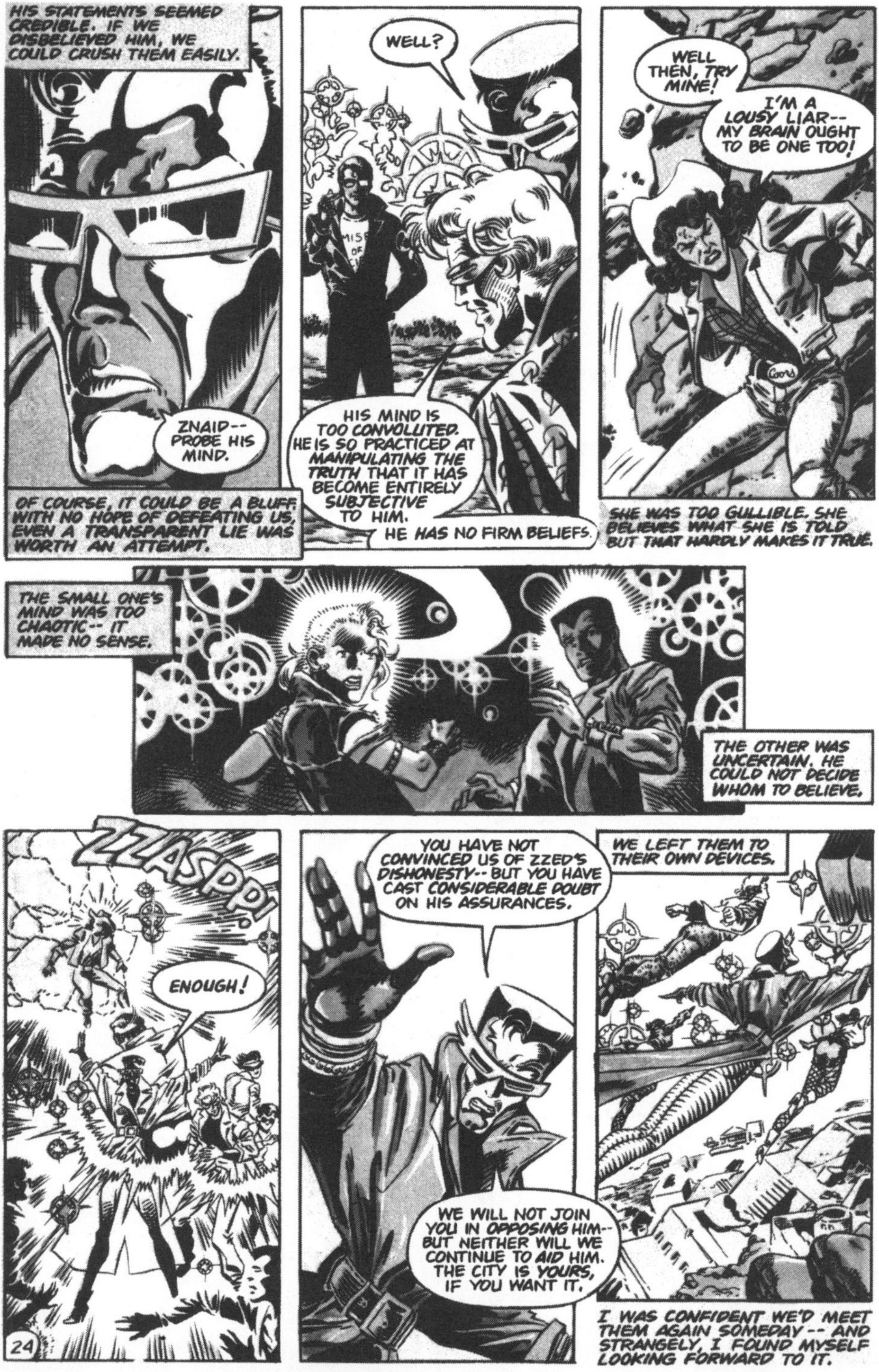
HIS STATEMENTS SEEMED CREDIBLE. IF WE DISBELIEVED HIM, WE COULD CRUSH THEM EASILY.
ZNAID-- PROBE HIS MIND.
OF COURSE, IT COULD BE A BLUFF. WITH NO HOPE OF DEFEATING US, EVEN A TRANSPARENT LIE WAS WORTH AN ATTEMPT.
WELL?
HIS MIND IS TOO CONVOLUTED. HE IS SO PRACTICED AT MANIPULATING THE TRUTH THAT IT HAS BECOME ENTIRELY SUBJECTIVE TO HIM.
HE HAS NO FIRM BELIEFS.
WELL THEN, TRY MINE!
I'M A LOUSY LIAR-- MY BRAIN OUGHT TO BE ONE TOO!
Coors
SHE WAS TOO GULLIBLE. SHE BELIEVES WHAT SHE IS TOLD BUT THAT HARDLY MAKES IT TRUE.
THE SMALL ONE'S MIND WAS TOO CHAOTIC-- IT MADE NO SENSE.
THE OTHER WAS UNCERTAIN. HE COULD NOT DECIDE WHOM TO BELIEVE.
ZZZASPP!
ENOUGH!
YOU HAVE NOT CONVINCED US OF ZZED'S DISHONESTY-- BUT YOU HAVE CAST CONSIDERABLE DOUBT ON HIS ASSURANCES.
WE WILL NOT JOIN YOU IN OPPOSING HIM-- BUT NEITHER WILL WE CONTINUE TO AID HIM. THE CITY IS YOURS, IF YOU WANT IT.
WE LEFT THEM TO THEIR OWN DEVICES.
I WAS CONFIDENT WE'D MEET THEM AGAIN SOMEDAY-- AND STRANGELY, I FOUND MYSELF LOOKING FORWARD TO IT.

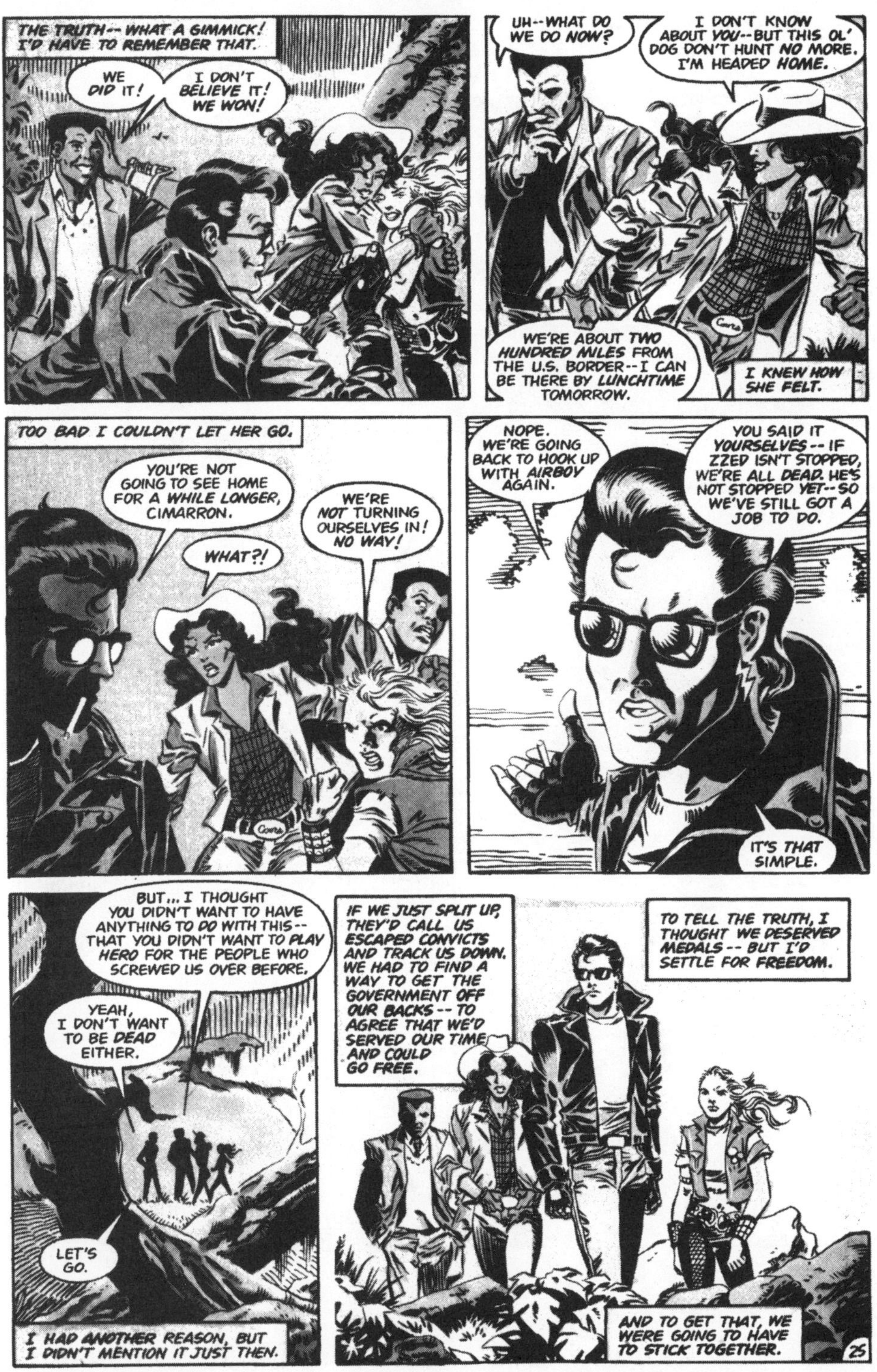

THE TRUTH-- WHAT A GIMMICK! I'D HAVE TO REMEMBER THAT.
WE DID IT!
I DON'T BELIEVE IT! WE WON!
UH--WHAT DO WE DO NOW?
I DON'T KNOW ABOUT YOU--BUT THIS OL' DOG DON'T HUNT NO MORE. I'M HEADED HOME.
WE'RE ABOUT TWO HUNDRED MILES FROM THE U.S. BORDER--I CAN BE THERE BY LUNCHTIME TOMORROW.
I KNEW HOW SHE FELT.
TOO BAD I COULDN'T LET HER GO.
YOU'RE NOT GOING TO SEE HOME FOR A WHILE LONGER, CIMARRON.
WHAT?!
WE'RE NOT TURNING OURSELVES IN! NO WAY!
NOPE. WE'RE GOING BACK TO HOOK UP WITH AIRBOY AGAIN.
YOU SAID IT YOURSELVES-- IF ZZED ISN'T STOPPED, WE'RE ALL DEAD. HE'S NOT STOPPED YET--SO WE'VE STILL GOT A JOB TO DO.
IT'S THAT SIMPLE.
BUT... I THOUGHT YOU DIDN'T WANT TO HAVE ANYTHING TO DO WITH THIS-- THAT YOU DIDN'T WANT TO PLAY HERO FOR THE PEOPLE WHO SCREWED US OVER BEFORE.
YEAH, I DON'T WANT TO BE DEAD EITHER.
LET'S GO.
I HAD ANOTHER REASON, BUT I DIDN'T MENTION IT JUST THEN.
IF WE JUST SPLIT UP, THEY'D CALL US ESCAPED CONVICTS AND TRACK US DOWN. WE HAD TO FIND A WAY TO GET THE GOVERNMENT OFF OUR BACKS-- TO AGREE THAT WE'D SERVED OUR TIME AND COULD GO FREE.
TO TELL THE TRUTH, I THOUGHT WE DESERVED MEDALS -- BUT I'D SETTLE FOR FREEDOM.
AND TO GET THAT, WE WERE GOING TO HAVE TO STICK TOGETHER.

EPILOGUE

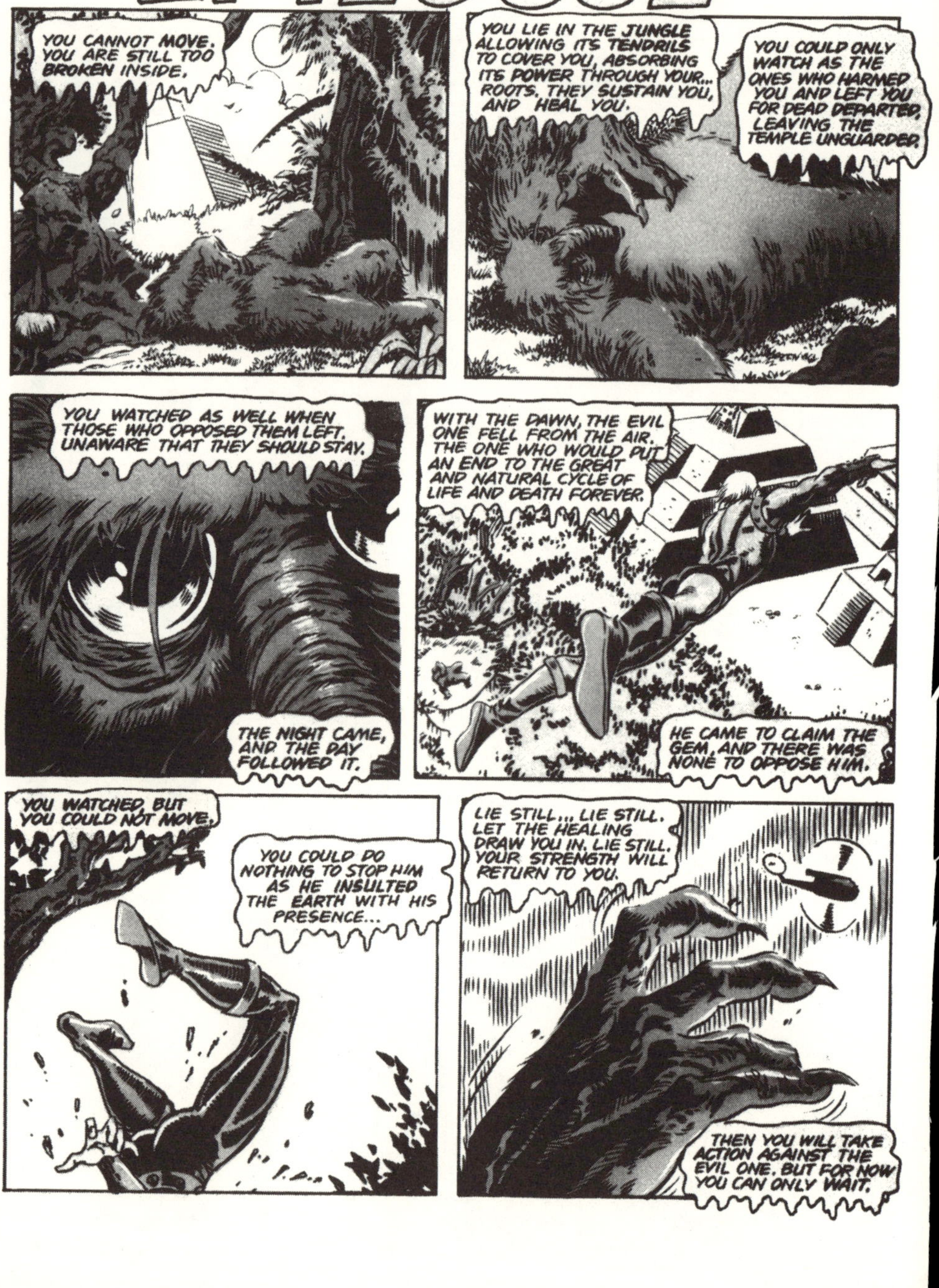

YOU CANNOT MOVE. YOU ARE STILL TOO BROKEN INSIDE.
YOU LIE IN THE JUNGLE ALLOWING ITS TENDRILS TO COVER YOU, ABSORBING ITS POWER THROUGH YOUR... ROOTS. THEY SUSTAIN YOU, AND HEAL YOU.
YOU COULD ONLY WATCH AS THE ONES WHO HARMED YOU AND LEFT YOU FOR DEAD DEPARTED, LEAVING THE TEMPLE UNGUARDED.
YOU WATCHED AS WELL WHEN THOSE WHO OPPOSED THEM LEFT. UNAWARE THAT THEY SHOULD STAY.
THE NIGHT CAME, AND THE DAY FOLLOWED IT.
WITH THE DAWN, THE EVIL ONE FELL FROM THE AIR. THE ONE WHO WOULD PUT AN END TO THE GREAT AND NATURAL CYCLE OF LIFE AND DEATH FOREVER.
HE CAME TO CLAIM THE GEM, AND THERE WAS NONE TO OPPOSE HIM.
YOU WATCHED BUT YOU COULD NOT MOVE.
YOU COULD DO NOTHING TO STOP HIM AS HE INSULTED THE EARTH WITH HIS PRESENCE...
LIE STILL... LIE STILL. LET THE HEALING DRAW YOU IN. LIE STILL. YOUR STRENGTH WILL RETURN TO YOU.
THEN YOU WILL TAKE ACTION AGAINST THE EVIL ONE. BUT FOR NOW YOU CAN ONLY WAIT.

And In Case You Want to Know How It All Worked Out...

The celestial alignment happened. Zzed got transformed into a hero. His mysterious adviser turned out to be a time-manipulator named Nine-Crocodile, the true villain behind it all. Misery betrayed the heroes to Nine-Crocodile. The heroes fought back against hopeless odds. Misery betrayed Nine-Crocodile, too (well, what did you expect? He's a villain!). The heroes eked out a narrow victory. And the universe was saved. Phew!

The Liberty Project took part in it all, fighting sarcastically but well, and when it was over, went on the lam rather than return to jail. And that was the last anyone saw of them for years.

You'd think saving the universe would count for something. But no...

Afterword: **Memories of Liberty**

There you go. That was *The Liberty Project*. Hope you liked it.

Or, if you're the type of reader who reads afterwords first — here, this is *The Liberty Project*. Go, read, enjoy. Hope you like it.

I have to admit, I'm happy out of all proportion to have this material collected into a book. Yeah, About Comics is a small publisher — albeit one whose previous projects put us in some very good company — and none of us are expecting this to be a sales blockbuster. And sure, it's not going to challenge *Marvels* or *Astro City* or whatever might come next as the work of my career, though I was proud of it at the time, and still am. So why so absurdly delighted? Because this was a first for me, a project very close to my heart, and I'd thought it was more than likely gone forever.

Liberty Project was the first ongoing title I ever co-created — or more accurately, the first one that ever made it to print. And there's something about breaking that barrier, about creating, building and developing a world, even for the short time we managed it here, that can never quite be duplicated. *Liberty Project* will always mean to me a certain heady rush of possibility, late nights talking with James (at the office, or at America, a Manhattan restaurant where a lot of the Proj came to life), working out who "Rude Girl" was and what role she'd play in the team, planning long term twists and developments, turning dumb jokes into story concepts, putting the building blocks in place as the structure took shape, and watching as our first ambitious creation actually came to life, to succeed or fail in front of an audience. It's a feeling of power, of freedom, of invention — the sense an inventor must have when he flips the switch and the whatever-it-is chugs to life and actually *works*.

There's still a sense of accomplishment, of satisfaction, in creation, even after you've been doing it for twenty years — at least there is for me, and I hope there is for everyone else — but that first breakthrough is accompanied by a sense of discovery, a joy in proving to yourself that you actually can *do* this thing, that's at the very least different, muted, when you've already done it once.

To you, the reader, it's a comic book, and you'll judge it as a good comic or not as you read it. It doesn't make a whole lot of difference whether the creators are newbies or old hands, as long as they deliver the goods. But to James and me, this was a watershed event. And it will always feel that way.

So I'm happy to have it back.

•

I met James Fry, my co-conspirator on this book, at Marvel Comics, where I was working as a freelance assistant editor and he was working in the art corrections department. We were both young, eager, full of ideas and energy, and looking for chances to do more comics than we'd had so far. More importantly, we got along — we loved a lot of the same comics, the same kind of dumb humor, and had naturally fallen together in the offices, talking until late hours after work about movies, music, comics, what we liked, what we didn't, what we hoped to do. James is knowledgeable, mercurial and passionate

— and a conversation with him can be like a ride in a hurricane, as digressions, new subjects, jokes, pop-culture references and spleen-venting pile up in a kind of verbal traffic jam that I've always found engaging, challenging and rewarding. What with distance, work, family and more, I don't talk with James these days nearly as much as I used to, and I regret it immensely.

But it was during one of those marathon, multi-focus conversations that the idea for *The Liberty Project* was born, first as a pitch for a *Captain America* series and then, when an editor told us that if this idea about Cap as the mentor to a group of young super-villains reforming and redeeming themselves didn't need Cap, and might be a better idea on its own, as the proposal that we showed around to Marvel, DC and Eclipse, where my pal Scott McCloud was doing his ground-breaking *Zot!* series.

[As a side note, the editor who gave us that suggestion was Tom DeFalco, who also, years later, suggested that maybe this *Marvels* series idea would work better if it was built around actual major events in Marvel history rather than newly-created continuity-implant stories. It strikes me that I owe Tom more than he may realize.]

And Eclipse won us over, both with their enthusiasm and with the deal they offered. Marvel and DC had both been interested, but the wheels of progress ground exceedingly slowly there, while at Eclipse, Cat Yronwode and Dean Mullaney were both responsive and encouraging, commenting in detail on what they thought the strengths of the concept were, and making it clear they wanted the book at Eclipse. And while the money they could pay was, shall we say, not the major inducement, there was a real attraction in the fact that at Eclipse, we could own the book ourselves, while at Marvel or DC, the company would have owned it.

We had the help of a lot of talented people — Kyle Baker, who inked the proposal illustration that became our first cover; Doug Hazlewood, fresh from winning the Marvel Try-Out Book inking contest; Adam Philips, then my roommate, who had been doing some coloring for DC; Mindy Eisman, the daughter of cartoonist Hy Eisman and a fine letterer; editor Fred Burke, and more.

We were ready to go, full of enthusiasm and excitement. We were off to the races at last, and in 1987, we made our grand debut.

•

And, well, as you can tell from the thickness of this book, which contains the whole run of the series *plus* an extra-length special, we did not come back covered in garlands and bearing a trophy.

We lasted eight issues.

We could do a post-mortem on whether it was a good idea to do what was at heart a very mainstream superhero series at a smaller publisher during a time most superhero fans didn't glance beyond the boundaries of Marvel and DC — today's domination of the market by the Big Two is practically a level playing field by comparison — or whether we were ready to compete in an industry that was in the full flush of post-*Watchmen*, post-*Crisis*, post-*Dark Knight* innovation, or whatever, but it doesn't really matter, not at this late date. What matters to me is that that heady feeling of wonder, of creative energy and possibility, lasted the whole time we were working on the series. We had a blast. And those readers we did attract seem to have had a blast along with us. We got good reviews, we got good mail, we got positive feedback at conventions — even today, it's a rare convention that someone doesn't bring up a set of the series to be signed, or ask if we'll ever be bringing it back.

To that extent, at least — creating something that resonated in the minds of readers and lasts in memory today — we succeeded. On the other hand, so did the creators of *Jet Dream and Her Stuntgirl Counterspies* (well, except for the good reviews), so go figure.

•

When it became clear that *The Liberty Project's* days were numbered, Eclipse was as supportive as they'd been all along. We got extra pages in the final issue to wrap up the series (#8 would have originally ended on p. 24; a fine issue break, but an unsatisfying series ending, I think you'll agree), and plans were made to relaunch the series, first through the *Total Eclipse* crossover that was in the works at that time, and then in a new black-and-white series.

But, well, *Total Eclipse* didn't create the influx of readers that had been hoped for, and the new series didn't materialize, and that was that, at least for a while.

•

And had we been a company-owned series, that would likely have been it forever, aside from the odd, out-of-our-hands cameo here and there, or the gratuitous killing-off of the team for shock value in some other series.

The Proj, however, has made one more appearance to date – in a series called *Jack Kirby's Teenagents*, which I wrote for Topps Comics in 1994. The editor there, Jim Salicrup, had been one of the editors at Marvel interested in the series, and suggested I bring them back for a guest appearance. So after years in Limbo, the Liberty Project were seen again in *Teenagents* #3-4, drawn by Neil Vokes — but even so, they weren't quite the same. There were two new members, Crackshot had "graduated" and gone on to life as a free man ... it had obviously been some years, with some developments on the way, between then and now. Thanks to owning the characters, we were able to do that ... and thanks to owning them, we may someday get to tell you the story of what happened in between.

There've been a few other plans to bring members of the Proj back here and there, plans that didn't come about for one reason or another, but who knows what might come in the future? And the idea of doing a book collection of the series came up now and then, but until now, it was an impossibility.

When Eclipse was going out of business, I was offered the printer's film on the series for the price of shipping it to me. Sure, I said. Just let me know how much, and I'll pay it. But it never happened, and when the company when bankrupt, the film was lost or destroyed. The color seps were long gone, the original art scattered to the winds of collectordom ... there was nothing to reproduce the series from, except the printed issues. And while the occasional comic's been reprinted that way, I've never been happy with the quality of the reproduction. Briefly, it looked like we might be able to find the film from the Spanish printing of the Proj series ... but alas, no luck there either.

So I figured that was it. *The Liberty Project* would have to live on, if it did, in back-issue bins.

•

And that's where Nat Gertler and About Comics enter the picture.

Nat showed me samples of black-and-white art produced by working with high-quality scans of the printed comics. Not as crisp as they would be from film, perhaps, but better than I'd have thought possible. Better than a lot of books that do get published these days. So here we are ... fifteen years after the book was cancelled, and at